150

GIOVANNI BOCCACCIO was born in 1313 in Florence, Italy, and died in the same city in 1375. His life thus coincided with the flowering of the early Renaissance, and, indeed, his closest friend was Petrarch, the other towering literary figure of the period. During his lifetime, Boccaccio was a diplomat, businessman, and international traveler as well as the creator of numerous works of prose and poetry. Of his achievements, *The Decameron*, completed sometime between 1350 and 1352, remains his lasting contribution—immensely popular from its original appearance to the present day—to world literature.

MARK MUSA and PETER BONDANELLA are professors at the Center for Italian Studies at Indiana University. Mark Musa, a former Fulbright and Guggenheim Fellow, is the author of a highly acclaimed translation of Dante's *Divine Comedy*. Peter Bondanella, a former Younger Humanist and Senior Fellow of the National Endowment for the Humanities, has published, among other works, *Machiavelli and the Art of Renaissance History* and *Federico Fellini: Essays in Criticism*. He is co-editor of *The Dictionary of Italian Literature* and *The Portable Machiavelli*.

Classic Italian Literature in MENTOR Editions

THE
DECAMERON

Giovanni Boccaccio

Translated by Mark Musa and Peter Bondanella
With an Introduction by Thomas G. Bergin

A MENTOR BOOK
NEW AMERICAN LIBRARY
NEW YORK AND SCARBOROUGH, ONTARIO

Library of Congress Catalog Card Number: 82-81667

First Printing, October, 1982

2 3 4 5 6 7 8 9 10

PRINTED IN THE UNITED STATES OF AMERICA

Dedication

AL LETTORE MALEVOLO

[Contents]

❖

children to her, honors her, and has others honor her, as the
Marchioness. **672**

[Introduction: Presenting Giovanni Boccaccio]

❖

GIOVANNI BOCCACCIO was born in 1313, the illegitimate son of an Italian merchant known as Boccaccino di Chelo, originally of Certaldo but living in Florence, and a woman as yet unidentified. The date is certified by a passage in a letter of Petrarch in which he reveals that he is nine years older than his disciple. Since it is known that Petrarch was born on July 30, 1304, it is tempting to put Boccaccio's birthdate at the same time nine years later; however, Petrarch's wording does not suggest any such precision. In the "Vision of Love" Boccaccio refers gratefully to his father's acknowledgment of paternity, but we have no firm evidence of any kind with regard to the place of birth or the identity of his mother. Boccaccino had frequent occasion to visit Paris on his business affairs, and Boccaccio in certain veiled "autobiographical" allusions in his early romances stated that he was born in Paris, the child of a French woman (in one case he speaks of her as of high degree). These allusions are full of inconsistencies and therefore suspect; the view of contemporary scholars is that the French mother is made of dream-stuff, shaped by the young storyteller to lend a romantic color to his early years; it is now generally believed that the woman or girl who gave birth to Boccaccino's love-child was probably from Florence, perhaps from Certaldo, and that the historical *accouchement* took place in one of those centers—if not strictly on the banks of the Arno, yet a long way from the shores of the Seine.

Though born out of wedlock, Giovanni was not an unwelcome child. His father not only legitimized him (apparently some time before 1320) but took him into his house (in due course providing him with a stepmother and a half-brother) and gave him a good practical education. In his old age Boccaccio complained of the utilitarian nature of his early studies, regretting that he had not had better preparation for the practice of poetry (that is, study of rhetoric and the classical authors), but he might well have been grateful for the groundwork in "arismetica" which made it worth Boccaccino's while to take the lad with him when, in 1327, he left Florence and set up his office, under the aegis of the great banking house of the Bardi, in Naples, the busy and colorful capital of the Kingdom of the Two Sicilies.

Although banking was not to the taste of the youth (he later persuaded his father to let him enroll in the University of Naples as a student of canon law), it is clear that the Neapolitan years were both exciting and fruitful for the observant and responsive Boccaccio; they were probably the happiest years of his life. Naples was a truly cosmopolitan center in the time of the good king Robert, with sailors, merchants, and diplomats streaming in from all corners of the earth. It was a Court city too, thronging with an affluent nobility which delighted in pageantry, parades, and parties. Boccaccio's function in the service of his bank was, it would seem, of sufficient dignity to give him entrée to aristocratic circles; he had a useful mentor in the person of his fellow Florentine Niccolò d'Acciaiuoli, only slightly older than Boccaccio himself and destined, through his own talents and the benevolence of Catherine de Courtenay, Queen of Jerusalem and sister-in-law to King Robert, to play a major role in the affairs of the Kingdom.

Such connections no doubt gave our embryonic poet the run of the Royal Library, already famous for the richness of its holdings in both classical and vernacular letters. In the library he came to know and venerate such scholars as Paolo da Perugia and Andalò del Negro. In the university he studied at the feet of Dante's friend Cino da Pistoia, a contact that must have reinforced Boccaccio's all but congenital devotion to the author of the *Comedy*. In like manner his acquaintance with the Augustinian friend of Petrarch, Dionigi da Borgo San Sepolcro, probably confirmed, if it did not initially inspire, the admiration Boccaccio had for the sage of Vaucluse. Among other figures significant for the young poet's future trajectory, the Calabrian monk Barlaam, "learned in things Greek," must be mentioned. He was responsible for Boccaccio's enthusiasm for Greek letters, which later led him to learn the language and may explain the fanciful titles of such works as the *Filocolo* and the *Filostrato*.

It was in Naples, too, probably at about the time he enrolled in the university, that Boccaccio encountered the great love of his life. Even as on Good Friday of 1327 the vision of Laura had first captivated Petrarch, so in suspiciously similar fashion on Easter Saturday (the year is uncertain—perhaps as early as 1331 or as late as 1336) the sight of the glamorous Fiammetta (in the Church of San Lorenzo) won forever the heart of young Giovanni. So he tells us, very circumstantially, in the first book of his first major work, the *Filocolo*. However, on close scrutiny, "Fiammetta" seems to be made of the same synthetic substance as the poet's French mother. Boccaccio would have her the illegitimate daughter of Robert of Naples and a lady of the house of Aquino—impressive connections indeed, but history seems to know nothing of her. The seductive princess is in all likelihood yet another creation of Boccaccio's mood, no more "real" than Criseida, which is not to say that the young man's heart may not have been stirred and his pen inspired by the sight of a "real live girl" (and not impossibly seen in San Lorenzo on an Easter Saturday), later given appropriate fictional adornment by her devoted swain. Certainly, real or synthetic, "Fiammetta" will linger long in Boccaccio's heart. She is the *primum mobile* of the *Filocolo*, and she reappears in successive works of the canon: the *Teseida*, the *Vision of Love*, the *Comedy of the Florentine Nymphs*. She tells her own sad tale in the *Elegy of Madonna Fiammetta;* she is one of the storytellers in *The Decameron*, and the poet will give her permanent residence in the third heaven in the last sonnet he ever wrote.

Boccaccio's first work, aside from a few sonnets of Petrarchan-Dantean inspiration, was an allegorical narrative in *terza rima* called *Diana's Hunt*. Both in outline and in many details of the work, the inspiration of Dante is clearly visible; the conclusion, however, gives us a moral essentially glorifying sensual love. The *Hunt* was soon followed by the Fiammetta-inspired *Filocolo*. to which we have alluded; it is a long, sometimes tedious account of the travails of the lovers Florio and Biancofiore. With all its faults the *Filocolo* is a landmark in European letters: Thomas C. Chubb rightly called it "our first prose romance." The *Filostrato*, a poem with considerable resonance in literary annals, exploited in turn by Chaucer and Shakespeare, tells (in *ottava rima*) of the betrayal of the Trojan prince Troilus by the faithless Criseida. Since Fiammetta is not specifically mentioned in this work, some critics suspect that it may have preceded the *Filocolo*. The chronology of Boccaccio's earlier works is very uncertain; all we can say for sure is that all of the aforementioned items were begun and probably finished between 1331 and 1341, the year the poet left Naples. It seems likely too that the *Teseida* (intended to be an epic but turning out to be a chival-

rous romance against a classical backdrop), written in *ottava
rima,* was likewise begun in Naples but probably finished after
the author's return to Tuscany—a return occasioned in all prob-
ability by his father's business reverses. (These were not happy
times for Florentine bankers.) Sometime before the end of 1341
Boccacino left Naples, accompanied, no doubt reluctantly, by his
son.

Readjustment to life in Florence was difficult, both psychologi-
cally and on the practical level; Boccaccio seems to have lived
at times on the brink of poverty. He never did solve, as Petrarch
did so gracefully, the economic problem inherent in the pursuit
of a literary career in the days before Gutenburg. He never at-
tracted such generous patrons as the Colonna or the Visconti;
for that matter he never had the support of such noble benefac-
tors as Can Grande della Scala or Guido da Polenta, who pro-
vided so solicitously for Dante. He enjoyed briefly, in the
mid-forties, the patronage of the Lords of Forlì and Ravenna,
but neither connection endured. Gradually, as we shall see, the
Commune of Florence came to recognize his talents and entrust-
ed him with various commissions; yet even so, to the end of his
life financial security eluded him.

The return to Tuscany was not without its effect on Boccac-
cio's Muse. After the *Teseida* the poet turned from chivalrous
romance (material suited to an aristocratic court but not to the
intellectual currents of Florentine society) to the kind of didac-
tic allegory which Dante (and other poets) had brought into the
Tuscan tradition. The first of these, *The Comedy of the Floren-
tine Nymphs,* is an elaborate allegory of the Virtues, narrated,
like Dante's *Vita nuova,* in prose with periodic interpolations of
verse passages. More complicated is the somewhat enigmatic
Vision of Love, also told in *terza rima,* with numerous recogniz-
able links to Dante's poem but with an ambiguous and dis-
concerting conclusion that makes the work a subversive parody
of the *Comedy.* More appealing to readers of today are the two
other works composed in the late forties: the prose first-person
Elegy of Fiammetta, a very "modern" account of a hopeless ob-
session, and the tender and touching *Nymph of Fiesole,* an idyll
in *ottava rima* of true classical artistry.

The year 1348, in which Boccaccio attained to that midpoint
of life's journey of which Dante speaks, was also the year the
Black Death came to Florence, and it is probable that Boccaccio
witnessed its ravages at firsthand. It carried off about a third of
the city's inhabitants, including Boccaccio's stepmother. The
death of his father, less than a year later, left him in charge of

his half-brother; Boccaccio discharged this responsibility faithfully and even solicitously. The plague is exploited as the background for *The Decameron;* one may see in it as well a kind of aesthetic-moral basis for the action and color of the world portrayed in that masterpiece.

Critics believe that the writing of *The Decameron* was begun in 1348 and that the work was finished perhaps as early as 1350 and no later than 1352. It is tempting to think of it as being finished, at least in a first draft, before the memorable first meeting with Petrarch in 1350—more crucial for the direction of Boccaccio's intellectual life than the encounter with Fiammetta in Naples. Taking advantage of Petrarch's visit to Rome for the jubilee celebration of 1350, Boccaccio persuaded his hero to stop off at Florence on the way. The meeting was a joyous one for both writers. It was the beginning of a firm and enduring friendship, characterized by unflagging admiration on Boccaccio's part and sincere if occasionally somewhat patronizing affection on the part of the older scholar. For the years that remained to them, both men would cultivate this friendship, corresponding frequently, meeting as often as the hazardous circumstances of their times permitted.

For better or for worse the meeting with Petrarch marked a change in Boccaccio's literary development. He had always admired the sage of Vaucluse not merely for the serene and Christian tenor of his life but as a quintessential poet. By poetry he did not so much mean the vernacular sonnets for Laura as the great Latin epic on which Petrarch was engaged and which, later, Boccaccio claimed he had seen. For both men of letters "poetry" was not mere rhyme-making, nor even imaginative creation, but rather moral indoctrination, under a "veil" of fiction, set forth with cunning rhetoric and saturated with classical erudition. What Boccaccio admired in his older friend was really the scholar and the humanist. In dutiful emulation he would henceforth abandon his creative romances (and with them the use of the vernacular) and turn to Latin compilations such as *The Fates of Illustrious Men* and *Concerning Famous Women* (overtly following Petrarch's example), or the pseudo-pastoral eclogues that make up the *Bucolicum Carmen* (modeled after those of the master), or the great encyclopedia of the *Genealogies of the Pagan Gods.* After *The Decameron,* with the exception of the atrabilious and one might say *ad hoc* item of the *Corbaccio,* we have no truly creative work from Boccaccio's pen, and save for that same *Corbaccio* and the works of Dante criticism, no further exercise in the vernacular. The poet yields to the

scholar, erudition supplants fancy. A new piousness comes to re-
place the carefree spirit of youthful days; at some time in the
late fifties Boccaccio took orders and his account of his terrified
response to the dire warnings of a holy man who in 1362 bade
him give up letters and think only of things eternal is evidence
of his new spiritual orientation. Fortunately Petrarch reassured
his disciple and persuaded him not to abandon his studies.

In the two decades that followed the meeting with Petrarch,
Boccaccio's time was divided between service to the Commune
of Florence and intense literary or scholarly activity. During
these years he served his city as ambassador on a number of im-
portant missions—to Ludwig of Bavaria in the Trentino (1351),
to the Papal Court at Avignon (in 1354 and 1365), and to Pope
Urban V, temporarily resident in Rome (1366). He also served
at various times on the *condotta,* a department of the commune
charged with disbursement of expenses for military operations.

In addition to his official missions he found time for a number
of journeys for his own purposes. He visited Petrarch in Milan
(1359), in Venice (1363), and in Padua (1367). He took three
trips to Naples: in 1355 (it is not certain that he actually
reached the city, but he spent a profitable time in the library of
the abbey of Montecassino, guest of his school friend Zanobi da
Strada), again in 1362, and finally in 1370. The visit to Petrarch
in 1359 is of some significance in cultural history; it was on that
occasion that Boccaccio made the acquaintance of the "wild
man" Leontius Pilatus, from whom both he and Petrarch hoped
to learn Greek. Boccaccio did—and furthermore persuaded the
Commune of Florence to appoint Leontius to the chair of Greek
in the university, the first such appointment since classical days
and a milestone in the history of humanism. The journey to
Naples in 1362 is noteworthy too: Boccaccio went on the invita-
tion of Niccolò Acciaiuoli, Grand Seneschal of the Realm; he
hoped to be named court "literatus," enjoying prestige and sub-
sidies similar to those the Visconti had bestowed on Petrarch.
Something went wrong: Acciaiuoli treated his guest shabbily and
Boccaccio came back in a huff, permanently estranged from the
friend of his youth. On his final visit to the city (1370) Boccac-
cio was well received; Queen Joan invited him to take up
residence at the court, but the invitation came too late; the old
scholar, ill and weary, chose to spend his last days in his native
Certaldo.

Throughout these busy years the service of letters was not
neglected. Most critics assign the date of 1355 to the composi-
tion of Boccaccio's last creative work, the misogynistic *Corbac-*

cio. In the fifties he drafted early versions of the *Life of Dante*
(the definitive one is probably of 1363) and toiled manfully on
the Latin works. *The Fates of Illustrious Men* was written at
some time between 1355 and 1360; *Concerning Famous Women*
was finished in 1361; compilation of the *Genealogies* went on
probably from 1350 to 1363, followed with revisions up to the
scholar's last years. The *Bucolicum Carmen* was released with a
covering letter in 1372. *The Decameron* was recopied and re-
touched in 1372 (in spite of the author's public repudiation of
the work).

In the spring of 1371 Boccaccio returned from Naples to Cer-
taldo. During the summer of 1372 he suffered a severe illness;
nevertheless, in the fall of that year he began his series of public
lectures on Dante's *Comedy* under the sponsorship of the Com-
mune of Florence. The sessions continued until the spring of
1374, a year of great sadness for Boccaccio since that summer
marked the death of his revered "preceptor" and dearest friend.
A letter to Petrarch's son-in-law, dated November 3, 1374, is
moving evidence of the depth of the writer's grief. Boccaccio's
finest sonnet, "Now art thou risen, cherished lord of mine," en-
visions Laura and her lover united at last in the third heaven of
Paradise. The disciple did not linger long after his master's de-
parture; Boccaccio died on December 21, 1375.

The importance of Giovanni Boccaccio's contributions to the
world of letters cannot be overestimated. The so-called "minor
works" in the vernacular were almost without exception original
and seminal; without the pioneering examples of such works as
the *Filocolo*, the *Filostrato*, the *Teseida*, and *The Comedy of the
Florentine Nymphs*, the shape of Italian literature (which had a
powerful influence on other national literatures) would have been
different; it is hard to think what course it might have taken.
The learned Latin studies, particularly the *Genealogies*, were in-
valuable in the development and direction of the new humanism
which would give shape and substance to the High Renais-
sance. Critics today, however, while readily recognizing the
historical importance of both the early romances and the er-
udite *compendia*, exalt Boccaccio primarily as the author of *The
Decameron*, a work which is neither romance nor scholarship but
a joyous naturalistic creation, eloquent of its time and for all
times. Appreciation of the masterpiece was late in coming,
though its popularity was evidenced even in its own day by the
numerous imitations that followed its dissemination. Yet for cen-
turies literary historians dismissed *The Decameron* with patron-

izing comment on its frivolous nature and reproach for the scandalous tone of some of the tales. At long last, in the tolerant climate of the nineteenth century, the Italian critic Francesco De Sanctis recognized *The Decameron* for what it truly is: in historical terms a token of the emancipation of western culture from the dogmatic rigidities of the Middle Ages; a proclamation of man's dignity and worth, *qua* man; and *sub specie aeternitatis*, a great Human Comedy, of scope and depth worthy to stand beside the *Divine Comedy* of Boccaccio's idol. Studies of *The Decameron* since the time of De Sanctis have reinforced his conclusions and sharpened our awareness of the magnitude of Boccaccio's achievement.

The comparison with the *Divine Comedy* is helpful. Both Dante and Boccaccio worked on large canvases; *The Decameron* portrays a world of vast dimensions; if we do not go to the depths of Hell or to the lofty Empyrean we yet survey all the known world from the Orient to the British Isles.

The cast of characters includes, to quote E. H. Wilkins, "kings, princes, princesses, ministers of state, knights, squires, abbots, abbesses, monks, nuns, priests, soldiers, doctors, lawyers, philosophers, pedants, students, painters, bankers, wine merchants, innkeepers, millers, bakers, coopers, usurers, troubadours, minstrels, peasants, servants, simpletons, pilgrims, misers, spendthrifts, sharpers, bullies, thieves, pirates, parasites, gluttons, drunkards, gamblers, police—and lovers of all sorts and kinds." If a work of relatively small compass (*The Decameron* is not an outsize book) can contain such a variety of human specimens, it is because Boccaccio knows the great secret of tactical selectivity. He does not elaborate on incidentals such as background; he is not one to linger on local color or poetic descriptions of town or country. Nor did he spend much time on psychological analysis of his characters. He sets them before us, lets them talk and act; personality is revealed by action: above all the story is the thing. This strategy, I think, makes *The Decameron* the most readable of all recognized masterpieces that come readily to mind. The better stories—which is to say, the majority—have the irresistible appeal of a thriller; the narrative moves on at a fast pace and carries the reader with it.

If *The Decameron* ushers a new democracy into the world of letters (as Wilkins's catalogue suggests), it is no less notable for its current of almost revolutionary feminism. Neither angel nor temptress (as she had hitherto been compelled to be) the woman of *The Decameron* is as human as the man, no less aware of what she wants (and how to get it) than her male counterpart, ready to speak and act for herself—a *person*, in short, in her own right. In his Preface Boccaccio states that he is telling his stories with an audience of women in mind, particularly those who may be in need of some distraction from the pains of love. There is no good reason not to take him at his word, and it is apparent from the distribution of the storytellers or "frame characters" (seven women and three men) that the fair sex is going to have its say in the course of the house party. A census of the characters in the tales themselves shows, to be sure, that men are in the majority (it is still a man's world) but the female protagonists of many of the better stories collectively make a stronger impact than the male leads. We would not anticipate readers' discoveries in this area; we shall merely suggest that they ponder such case histories as those of Madam Beritola (II, 6), Ghismunda (IV, 2), Lisabetta (IV, 5) and—if they want to hear a true spokeswoman of "women's lib" *avant la lettre,* let them attend to saucy Filippa of Pisa (VI, 7). If there are in the Decameronian republic passive women like Alatiel and silly ones like Elena—well, they are outnumbered by the gullible and ineffectual males among their fellow citizens.

The actors on the Decameronian stage are not concerned much with eternal, transcendent values. In the sense that Dante or Milton can be called "inspirational," Boccaccio assuredly cannot. Yet the savor of his book is wholesome and *au fond* not without its own kind of inspiration. Having no didactic axe to grind—"Boccaccio doesn't want to teach anybody anything," to quote Umberto Bosco—the author reports serenely on what he sees. His engaging depiction of a world full of pitfalls for a fallible humanity at the mercy of its own fragility and the caprices of fortune, yet withal a world where with good use of one's wits, common decency, and a sense of proportion a good life is quite possible, is somehow bracing and reassuring. Never mind about Heaven; this world, properly appreciated and if necessary manipulated, is not to be scorned. Indeed it can be vastly entertaining. *The Decameron,* to quote Wilkins again, is primarily "a book of laughter"—but neither frivolous nor (in spite of its reputation in more censorious times) bawdy laughter. For centuries readers, highly diverted and sometimes titillated by the inventive vivacity of the stories, have admired *The Decameron;* today, perhaps more than ever, we can appreciate its perceptions and its wise tolerance. *The Decameron* is a very modern book.

The new translation of Mark Musa and Peter Bondanella is

remarkably faithful to the original in both letter and spirit. The
collaborators are both scholars of Italian literature and experi-
enced translators, at home in the literary idiom of fourteenth-
century Italian and therefore well equipped to deal with the
vocabulary and, what is more challenging, the stylistic nuances
of Boccaccio's masterpiece. Their experience and their perceptive
sensitivity enable them to present the reader with an English
version which is smooth, graceful, and eminently readable. The
manner, no less than the matter, of Boccaccio's swift-paced and
buoyant narrative is very effectively conveyed. No doubt all
great books are best read in the original, but the reader of this
translation may be assured that he is, though in another tongue,
truly reading *The Decameron.*

> *Thomas G. Bergin*
> Sterling professor of Romance Languages Emeritus,
> Yale University

[Translators' Preface]

❖

PERHAPS most important to the translation of a medieval classic is the problem of proper diction. This involves several problems: first, to render into English approximately the same thing Boccaccio means to say in Italian (something which is by no means always crystal clear); second and even more important, to retain in the translation those qualities of the original text which made the work what it was in the fourteenth century. Any conscious attempt to introduce into Boccaccio's prose an archaic or anachronistic tone is the greatest mistake a translator of this century can make. *The Decameron* is no more like Victorian pseudo-medieval English than Dante is like Milton or Virgil. Thous, thees, and hasts will never supply a medieval "flavor" to Boccaccio, because the authentic medieval flavor of *The Decameron* lies somewhere else—in precisely the contemporary and completely fresh tone of its language. This does not imply that a good English translation should lack eloquence or formal precision, but it does require a sensitivity to the many levels of style reflected in Boccaccio's prose.

Boccaccio's modern critics have demonstrated quite clearly the debt of *The Decameron* to the Ciceronian prose models of the rhetoricians. When Boccaccio feels the need for a more patterned or more eloquent level of discourse than is typical of normal conversation, he will turn to these complicated Latinate periods where subordinate clauses abound and a conscious effort is made to exploit the entire range of rhetorical devices for artistic effects. Some translators feel the need to break Boccaccio's lengthy and complicated period into as many as four shorter sentences, thus transforming this unique style into something terser and more conversational. While shorter sentences may be more appealing to the general reader, we feel that great works of liter-

ature have earned the right to make certain demands upon their
audience. One of the demands Boccaccio makes upon his reader
and his translator arises precisely from his sometimes extremely
complex sentence structure. But patterned prose and an elevated,
solemn diction do not exhaust Boccaccio's range of styles, for his
prose contains an infinite variety: colloquial expressions; famil-
iar, conversational passages; puns on words (often obscene);
patterns that connote clear or implied social or regional distinc-
tions of speech. For the careful translator of *The Decameron*,
such passages are always the most demanding, containing as
they often do much of Boccaccio's matchless humor, wordplay,
and linguistic innovation. The stories which are the easiest to un-
derstand are thus paradoxically the most difficult to translate
into English. But the translator must also resist the temptation
to tidy up Boccaccio's prose. When loose ends, apparently con-
fusing *non sequiturs*, and puzzling passages are to be found in
the original, these must be respected, and rendered in an appro-
priate manner in the translation, or—if absolutely necessary—
explained in a footnote.

Up to this point, we have emphasized the translator's obliga-
tion to the author—capturing the essence of his linguistic inno-
vation and retaining what is most peculiar of his personal style
or to his audience, avoiding outmoded archaisms or translator's
language which bears no relationship to contemporary American
English. But we also have an obligation to the scholarly image of
Boccaccio and his *Decameron* as it is reflected in the best of
contemporary research. In many instances, scholarship resolves
the vexing dilemmas the text poses to the translator and may il-
luminate his way. But even more crucial than individual points
of erudition is the more general image of Boccaccio in today's
critical literature: a good contemporary version of *The De-
cameron* in English must make of Boccaccio's classic work not
merely a naughty collection of risqué tales or even only a mer-
cantile epic, for *The Decameron* is an open-ended, multifaceted,
highly challenging, and ambivalent book, composed by a master
narrator who is in constant control of all the marvelous narra-
tive plots, games, characters, and storytellers he weaves together.
We have aimed to provide the reader of today with a *De-
cameron* that speaks in American English and in as elevated or
low a style as the original demands, one at ease both with put-
ting Rustico's devil in Hell or sticking Father Gianni's tail on his
magic mare and in the eloquent world of Ghismunda or the exas-
perating and slightly unreal universe of patient Griselda.

The present translation can fairly claim to be the first English version of *The Decameron* to be based upon an authoritative and reliably edited Italian text—that done by Vittore Branca in 1975 for the Accademia della Crusca and reprinted by Mondadori of Milan in the same year, as well as in subsequent editions. Readers should bear several consequences of our reliance on the Branca text in mind. First of all, the headings which have been printed within brackets are not in the original manuscript; they are provided here, as in most modern editions and translations, to enable the reader to locate the individual stories within a single day's storytelling with ease. Secondly, following the original Italian, we have respected the spellings of most Italian proper names or place names, including slight spelling variations of the same name within individual stories. In most cases, the variations cause the reader no real difficulty, and since the author left them in the autograph manuscript he transcribed during the last part of his life (the Hamiltonian 90, the basis of Branca's edition), we see no good reason why an English translation should not respect them. Thirdly, time in Boccaccio's day was commonly told not by specific hours but rather by the seven canonical hours which prescribed special forms of prayers at specified times of the day. We have respected this practice, and we list them here for the reader's convenience, since they appear too frequently in the text to define them in individual footnotes: matins (dawn); prime (about 6:00 A.M.); tierce (the third hour after sunrise, about 9:00 A.M.); sext (noon); nones (the ninth hour after sunrise, about 3:00 P.M.); vespers (late afternoon); and compline (in the evening just before retiring). The text includes a number of explanatory or historical footnotes which may assist the reader. However, we have reserved the bulk of our critical and aesthetic commentary for a reader's guide and critical companion to *The Decameron* destined for future publication.

THE STRUCTURE OE THE DECAMERON

Author's Preface and Introduction: The narrator addresses his reader directly, explains the origins of his *novelle,* introduces his ten storytellers (Pampinea, Filomena, Neifile, Filostrato, Fiammetta, Elissa, Dioneo, Lauretta, Emilia, and Panfilo), and describes the Black Plague of 1348 in Florence. Each of the storytellers will tell a story on each of ten days of storytelling, and each storyteller (except Dioneo) must tell a story which follows a topic determined by the King or Queen of the previous day. The entire collection contains 100 *novelle.*

Day I: Subjects freely chosen (the reign of Pampinea).

Day II: Stories about those who attain a state of unexpected happiness after a period of misfortune (the reign of Filomena).

Day III: Stories about people who have attained difficult goals or who have recovered something previously lost (the reign of Neifile).

Day IV, Introduction: The narrator defends himself from the criticism that greeted the stories of the first three days of storytelling.

Day IV: Love stories with unhappy endings (the reign of Filostrato).

Day V: Love stories which end happily after a period of misfortune (the reign of Fiammetta).

Day VI: Stories about how intelligence helps to avoid danger, ridicule, or discomfort (the reign of Elissa).

Day VII: Stories about tricks played by wives on their husbands (the reign of Dioneo).

Day VIII: Stories about tricks played by both men and women on each other (the reign of Lauretta).

Day IX: Subjects freely chosen (the reign of Emilia).

Day X: Stories about those who have performed generous deeds and who have acquired fame in so doing (the reign of Panfilo).

Author's Conclusion: The narrator defends the tone of his work against those critics who view it as obscene or others who claim the stories are sometimes too long, as well as against those who accuse him of slandering churchmen or betraying his scholarly inclinations by composing such a frivolous work as *The Decameron.*

SUGGESTIONS FOR AN ABRIDGED READING

WE hope that the reader will want to read all of this magnificent book from cover to cover. However, we are well aware that this translation may be employed as one of many texts in university courses, and our suggestions for an abridged reading of *The Decameron* may prove useful to students and instructors. Therefore, we suggest that any initial examination of the book include a selection from the following: the Author's Preface and Introduction: Day I, Stories 1–3; Day II, Stories 4–7, 10; Day III, Stories 1, 2, 9, 10; Author's Prologue to Day IV; Day IV, Stories 1, 2, 5, 9; Day V, Stories 1, 4, 8–10; Day VI, Stories 1, 4, 5, 7, 10; Day VII, Stories 2, 9, 10; Day VIII, Stories 3, 5–10; Day IX, Stories 2, 3, 5, 6, 10; Day X, Stories 3, 4, 8–10; Author's Conclusion.

Mark Musa
Peter Bondanella
Center for Italian Studies
Indiana University

THE
DECAMERON

[Preface]

❧

Here begins the book called The Decameron,* *also known as* Prince Galeotto,† *in which one hundred tales are contained, told in ten days by seven ladies and three young men.*

To have compassion for those who suffer is a human quality which everyone should possess, especially those who have required comfort themselves in the past and have managed to find it in others. Now, if any man ever had need of compassion and appreciated it or derived comfort from it, I am that person; for from my earliest youth until the present time I have been aflame beyond all measure with a most exalted and noble love, perhaps too much so for my lowly station, if I were to tell about it. And even though those judicious people who knew about my love praised me and held me in high regard because of it, it was, nevertheless, still extremely difficult to bear: certainly not because of the cruelty of the lady I loved but rather because of the overwhelming passion kindled in my mind by my unrestrained desire, which, since it would not allow me to rest content with any acceptable goal, often caused me to suffer more pain than was necessary. In my suffering, the pleasant conversation

---

*This title of Greek derivation means "ten days" and refers to the total number of days spent telling stories; it is modeled on that of a work by Saint Ambrose, *Hexameron,* as well as on medieval treatises on the six days of the world's creation.

†According to Arthurian legend and medieval literary tradition, Galeotto acted as a go-between in the love affair of Lancelot and Queen Guinevere; here Boccaccio refers specifically to a line in Dante's *Inferno* (V, 137), where a book described as the instigator of the fatal love affair between Paolo and Francesca is compared to Galeotto's role in bringing Lancelot and Guinevere together.

and the admirable consolation of a friend on a number of occasions gave me much relief, and I am firmly convinced I should now be dead if it had not been for that. But since He who is infinite had been pleased to decree by immutable law that all earthly things should come to an end, my love, more fervent than any other, a love which no resolution, counsel, public shame, or danger that might result from it could break or bend, diminished by itself in the course of time, and at present it has left in my mind only that pleasure which it usually retains for those who do not venture too far out on its deep, dark waters; and thus where there once used to be a source of suffering, now that all torment has been removed, there remains only a sense of delight.

But while the pain has ceased, I have not lost the memory of favors already received from those who were touched by my heavy burdens; nor, I believe, will this memory ever pass, except with my death. And because it is my feeling that gratitude is the most praiseworthy of all qualities, and that its opposite the most worthy of reproach, in order not to appear ungrateful, I have promised myself to use my limited talents in doing whatever possible (now that I am able to say I am free of love) in exchange for what I have received—if not to repay with consolation those who helped me (since their intelligence and their good fortune will perhaps make this unnecessary), then, at least, to assist those who may be in need of it. And however slight my support or, if you prefer, comfort may be to those in need, nevertheless I believe it should still be available where the need is greatest, for there it will be the most useful and the most appreciated.

And who will deny that such comfort, no matter how insufficient, is more fittingly bestowed on charming ladies than on men? For they, in fear and shame, conceal the hidden flames of love within their delicate breasts, a love far stronger than one which is openly expressed, as those who have felt and suffered this know; and furthermore, restricted by the wishes, whims, and commands of fathers, mothers, brothers, and husbands, they remain most of the time limited to the narrow confines of their bedrooms, where they sit in apparent idleness, now wishing one thing and now wishing another, turning over in their minds a number of thoughts which cannot always be pleasant ones. And because of these thoughts, if there should arise within their minds a sense of melancholy brought on by burning desire, these ladies will be forced to suffer this terrible pain unless it is replaced by new interests. Furthermore, they are less able than men to bear these discomforts; this does not happen to a man who is in love, as we can plainly see. If men are afflicted by melancholy or ponderous thoughts, they have many ways of alleviating or forgetting them: if they wish, they can take a walk and listen to or look at many different things; they can go hawking, hunting, or fishing; they can ride, gamble, or attend to business. Each of these pursuits has the power, either completely or in part, to occupy a man's mind and to remove from it a painful thought, even if only for a brief moment; and so, in one way or another, either consolation follows or the pain becomes less. Therefore, I wish to make up in part for the wrong done by Fortune, who is less generous with her support where there is less strength, as we witness in the case of our delicate ladies. As support and diversion for those ladies in love (to those others who are not I leave the needle, spindle, and wool winder), I intend to tell one hundred stories, or fables, or parables, or histories, or whatever you wish to call them, as they were told in ten days (as will become quite evident) by a worthy group of seven ladies and three young men who came together during the time of the plague (which just recently took so many lives), and I shall also include several songs sung for their delight by these same ladies. These stories will contain a number of different cases of love, both bitter and sweet, as well as other exciting adventures taken from modern and ancient times. And in reading them, the ladies just mentioned will, perhaps, derive from the delightful things that happen in these tales both pleasure and useful counsel, inasmuch as they will recognize what should be avoided and what should be sought after. This, I believe, can only result in putting an end to their melancholy. And should this happen (and may God grant that it does), let them thank Love for it, who, in freeing me from his bonds, has given me the power to attend to their pleasure.

[Introduction]

✤

Here begins the first day of The Decameron, *in which, after the author has explained why certain people (soon to be introduced) have gathered together to tell stories, they speak, under the direction of Pampinea, on any subject that pleases them most.*

WHENEVER, most gracious ladies, I consider how compassionate you are by nature, I realize that in your judgment the present work will seem to have had a serious and painful beginning, for it recalls in its opening the unhappy memory of the deadly plague just passed, dreadful and pitiful to all those who saw or heard about it. But I do not wish to frighten you away from reading any further, by giving you the impression that all you are going to do is spend your time sighing and weeping while you read. This horrible beginning will be like the ascent of a steep and rough mountainside, beyond which there lies a most beautiful and delightful plain, and the degree of pleasure derived by the climbers will be in proportion to the difficulty of the climb and the descent. And just as pain is the extreme limit of pleasure, so, then, misery ends with unanticipated happiness. This brief pain (I say brief since it contains few words) will be quickly followed by the sweetness and the delight which I promised you before, and which, had I not promised, might not be expected from such a beginning. To tell the truth, if I could have conveniently led you by any other way than this, which I know is a bitter one, I would have gladly done so; but since it is otherwise impossible to demonstrate how the stories you are about to read came to be told, I am obliged, as it were, by necessity to write about it this way.

5

Let me say, then, that thirteen hundred and forty-eight years* had already passed after the fruitful Incarnation of the Son of God when into the distinguished city of Florence, more noble than any other Italian city, there came a deadly pestilence. Either because of the influence of heavenly bodies or because of God's just wrath as a punishment to mortals for our wicked deeds, the pestilence, originating some years earlier in the East, killed an infinite number of people as it spread relentlessly from one place to another until finally it had stretched its miserable length all over the West. And against this pestilence no human wisdom or foresight was of any avail; quantities of filth were removed from the city by officials charged with the task; the entry of any sick person into the city was prohibited; and many directives were issued concerning the maintenance of good health. Nor were the humble supplications rendered not once but many times by the pious to God, through public processions or by other means, in any way efficacious; for almost at the beginning of springtime of the year in question the plague began to show its sorrowful effects in an extraordinary manner. It did not assume the form it had in the East, where bleeding from the nose was a manifest sign of inevitable death, but rather it showed its first signs in men and women alike by means of swellings either in the groin or under the armpits, some of which grew to the size of an ordinary apple and others to the size of an egg (more or less), and the people called them *gavoccioli*.† And from the two parts of the body already mentioned, in very little time, the said deadly *gavoccioli* began to spread indiscriminately over every part of the body; then, after this, the symptoms of the illness changed to black or livid spots appearing on the arms and thighs, and on every part of the body—sometimes there were large ones and other times a number of little ones scattered all around. And just as the *gavoccioli* were originally, and still are, a very definite indication of impending death, in like manner these spots came to mean the same thing for whoever contracted them. Neither a doctor's advice nor the strength of medicine could do anything to cure this illness; on the contrary, either the nature of the illness was such that it afforded no cure, or else the doctors were so ignorant that they did not recognize its cause

*In Boccaccio's day, Florentines began the first of each year not with the first of January, as is done today, but rather with the traditional date of the Annunciation (March 25).

†*Gavoccioli*—or *bubboni*, in modern Italian—are called "buboes" in modern English, the source of the phrase "bubonic plague." The plague of 1348 is often known as the Black Plague or Black Death because of the black spots Boccaccio describes.

and, as a result, could not prescribe the proper remedy (in fact, the number of doctors, other than the well-trained, was increased by a large number of men and women who had never had any medical training); at any rate, few of the sick were ever cured, and almost all died after the third day of the appearance of the previously described symptoms (some sooner, others later), and most of them died without fever or any other side effects.

This pestilence was so powerful that it was transmitted to the healthy by contact with the sick, the way a fire close to dry or oily things will set them aflame. And the evil of the plague went even further: not only did talking to or being around the sick bring infection and a common death, but also touching the clothes of the sick or anything touched or used by them seemed to communicate this very disease to the person involved. What I am about to say is incredible to hear, and if I and others had not witnessed it with our own eyes, I should not dare believe it (let alone write about it), no matter how trustworthy a person I might have heard it from. Let me say, then, that the plague described here was of such virulence in spreading from one person to another that not only did it pass from one man to the next, but, what's more, it was often transmitted from the garments of a sick or dead man to animals that not only became contaminated by the disease but also died within a brief period of time. My own eyes, as I said earlier, were witness to such a thing one day: when the rags of a poor man who died of this disease were thrown into the public street, two pigs came upon them, and, as they are wont to do, first with their snouts and then with their teeth they took the rags and shook them around; and within a short time, after a number of convulsions, both pigs fell dead upon the ill-fated rags, as if they had been poisoned. From these and many similar or worse occurrences there came about such fear and such fantastic notions among those who remained alive that almost all of them took a very cruel attitude in the matter; that is, they completely avoided the sick and their possessions, and in so doing, each one believed that he was protecting his own good health.

There were some people who thought that living moderately and avoiding any excess might help a great deal in resisting this disease, and so they gathered in small groups and lived entirely apart from everyone else. They shut themselves up in those houses where there were no sick people and where one could live well by eating the most delicate of foods and drinking the finest of wines (doing so always in moderation), allowing no one to speak about or listen to anything said about the sick and the dead outside; these people lived, entertaining themselves with music and other pleasures that they could arrange. Others thought the opposite: they believed that drinking excessively, enjoying life, going about singing and celebrating, satisfying in every way the appetites as best one could, laughing, and making light of everything that happened was the best medicine for such a disease; so they practiced to the fullest what they believed by going from one tavern to another all day and night, drinking to excess; and they would often make merry in private homes, doing everything that pleased or amused them the most. This they were able to do easily, for everyone felt he was doomed to die and, as a result, abandoned his property, so that most of the houses had become common property, and any stranger who came upon them used them as if he were their rightful owner. In addition to this bestial behavior, they always managed to avoid the sick as best they could. And in this great affliction and misery of our city the revered authority of the laws, both divine and human, had fallen and almost completely disappeared, for, like other men, the ministers and executors of the laws were either dead or sick or so short of help that it was impossible for them to fulfill their duties; as a result, everybody was free to do as he pleased.

Many others adopted a middle course between the two attitudes just described: neither did they restrict their food or drink so much as the first group nor did they fall into such dissoluteness and drunkenness as the second; rather, they satisfied their appetites to a moderate degree. They did not shut themselves up, but went around carrying in their hands flowers, or sweet-smelling herbs, or various kinds of spices; and they would often put these things to their noses, believing that such smells were a wonderful means of purifying the brain, for all the air seemed infected with the stench of dead bodies, sickness, and medicines.

Others were of a crueler opinion (though it was, perhaps, a safer one): they maintained that there was no better medicine against the plague than to flee from it; convinced of this reasoning and caring only about themselves, men and women in great numbers abandoned their city, their houses, their farms, their relatives, and their possessions and sought other places, going at least as far away as the Florentine countryside—as if the wrath of God could not pursue them with this pestilence wherever they went but would only strike those it found within the walls of the city! Or perhaps they thought that Florence's last hour had come and that no one in the city would remain alive.

And not all those who adopted these diverse opinions died, nor did they all escape with their lives; on the contrary, many of those who thought this way were falling sick everywhere, and since they had given, when they were healthy, the bad example of avoiding the sick, they in turn were abandoned and left to languish away without any care. The fact was that one citizen avoided another, that almost no one cared for his neighbor, and that relatives rarely or hardly ever visited each other—they stayed far apart. This disaster had struck such fear into the hearts of men and women that brother abandoned brother, uncle abandoned nephew, sister left brother, and very often wife abandoned husband, and—even worse, almost unbelievable—fathers and mothers neglected to tend and care for their children as if they were not their own.

Thus, for the countless multitude of men and women who fell sick, there remained no support except the charity of their friends (and these were few) or the greed of servants, who worked for inflated salaries without regard to the service they performed and who, in spite of this, were few and far between; and those few were men or women of little wit (most of them not trained for such service) who did little else but hand different things to the sick when requested to do so or watch over them while they died, and in this service, they very often lost their own lives and their profits. And since the sick were abandoned by their neighbors, their parents, and their friends and there was a scarcity of servants, a practice that was previously almost unheard of spread through the city: when a woman fell sick, no matter how attractive or beautiful or noble she might be, she did not mind having a manservant (whoever he might be, no matter how young or old he was), and she had no shame whatsoever in revealing any part of her body to him—the way she would have done to a woman—when necessity of her sickness required her to do so. This practice was, perhaps, in the days that followed the pestilence, the cause of looser morals in the women who survived the plague. And so, many people died who, by chance, might have survived if they had been attended to. Between the lack of competent attendants that the sick were unable to obtain and the violence of the pestilence itself, so many, many people died in the city both day and night that it was incredible just to hear this described, not to mention seeing it! Therefore, out of sheer necessity, there arose among those who remained alive customs which were contrary to the established practices of the time.

It was the custom, as it is again today, for the women relatives and neighbors to gather together in the house of a dead person and there to mourn with the women who had been dearest to him; on the other hand, in front of the deceased's home, his male relatives would gather together with his male neighbors and other citizens, and the clergy also came, many of them or sometimes just a few, depending upon the social class of the dead man. Then, upon the shoulders of his equals, he was carried to the church chosen by him before death with the funeral pomp of candles and chants. With the fury of the pestilence increasing, this custom, for the most part, died out and other practices took its place. And so not only did people die without having a number of women around them, but there were many who passed away without having even a single witness present, and very few were granted the piteous laments and bitter tears of their relatives; on the contrary, most relatives were somewhere else, laughing, joking, and amusing themselves; even the women learned this practice too well, having put aside, for the most part, their womanly compassion for their own safety. Very few were the dead whose bodies were accompanied to the church by more than ten or twelve of their neighbors, and these dead bodies were not even carried on the shoulders of honored and reputable citizens but rather by gravediggers from the lower classes that were called *becchini*. Working for pay, they would pick up the bier and hurry it off, not to the church the dead man had chosen before his death but, in most cases, to the church closest by, accompanied by four or six churchmen with just a few candles, and often none at all. With the help of these *becchini*, the churchmen would place the body as fast as they could in whatever unoccupied grave they could find without going to the trouble of saying long or solemn burial services.

The plight of the lower class and, perhaps, a large part of the middle class was even more pathetic: most of them stayed in their homes or neighborhoods either because of their poverty or because of their hopes for remaining safe, and every day they fell sick by the thousands; and not having servants or attendants of any kind, they almost always died. Many ended their lives in the public streets, during the day or at night, while many others who died in their homes were discovered dead by their neighbors only by the smell of their decomposing bodies. The city was full of corpses. The dead were usually given the same treatment by their neighbors, who were moved more by the fear that the decomposing corpses would contaminate them than by any charity they might have felt toward the deceased: either by themselves or with the assistance of porters (when they were available), they would drag the corpse out of the home and place it in front of the doorstep, where, usually in the morning, quantities of dead bodies could be seen by any passerby; then they were laid out on biers, or for lack of biers, on a plank. Nor did a bier carry only one corpse; sometimes it was used for two or three at a time. More than once, a single bier would serve for a wife and husband, two or three brothers, a father or son, or other relatives, all at the same time. And very often it happened that two priests, each with a cross, would be on their way to bury someone, when porters carrying three or four biers would just follow along behind them; and whereas these priests thought they had just one dead man to bury, they had, in fact, six or eight and sometimes more. Moreover, the dead were honored with no tears or candles or funeral mourners; in fact, things had reached such a point that the people who died were cared for as we care for goats today. Thus it became quite obvious that the very thing which in normal times wise men had not been able to resign themselves to, even though then it struck seldom and less harshly, became as a result of this colossal misfortune a matter of indifference to even the most simpleminded people.

So many corpses would arrive in front of a church every day and at every hour that the amount of holy ground for burials was certainly insufficient for the ancient custom of giving each body its individual place; when all the graves were full, huge trenches were dug in all of the cemeteries of the churches and into them the new arrivals were dumped by the hundreds; and they were packed in there with dirt, one on top of another, like a ship's cargo, until the trench was filled.

But instead of going over every detail of the past miseries which befell our city, let me say that the hostile winds blowing there did not, however, spare the surrounding countryside any evil; there, not to speak of the towns which, on a smaller scale, were like the city, in the scattered villages and in the fields the poor, miserable peasants and their families, without any medical assistance or aid of servants, died on the roads and in their fields and in their homes, as many by day as by night, and they died not like men but more like animals. Because of this they, like the city dwellers, became careless in their ways and did not look after their possessions or their businesses; furthermore, when they saw that death was upon them, completely neglecting the future fruits of their past labors, their livestock, their property, they did their best to consume what they already had at hand. So it came about that oxen, donkeys, sheep, pigs, chickens, and even dogs, man's most faithful companion, were driven from their homes into the fields, where the wheat was left not only unharvested but also unreaped, and they were allowed to roam where they wished; and many of these animals, almost as if they were rational beings, returned at night to their homes without any guidance from a shepherd, full after a good day's meal.

Leaving the countryside and returning to the city, what more can one say except that so great was the cruelty of Heaven, and, perhaps, also that of man, that from March to July of the same year, between the fury of the pestiferous sickness and the fact that many of the sick were badly treated or abandoned in need because of the fear that the healthy had, more than one hundred thousand human beings are believed to have lost their lives for certain inside the walls of the city of Florence—whereas before the deadly plague, one would not even have estimated there were actually that many people dwelling in the city.

Oh, how many great palaces, beautiful homes, and noble dwellings, once filled with families, gentlemen, and ladies, were now emptied, down to the last servant! How many notable families, vast domains, and famous fortunes remained without legitimate heir! How many valiant men, beautiful women, and charming young boys, who might have been pronounced very healthy by Galen, Hippocrates, and Aesculapius (not to mention lesser physicians), ate breakfast in the morning with their relatives, companions, and friends and then in the evening dined with their ancestors in the other world!

Reflecting upon so many miseries makes me very sad; therefore, since I wish to pass over as many as I can, let me say that as our city was in this condition, almost emptied of inhabitants, it happened (as I heard it later from a person worthy of trust) that one Tuesday morning in the venerable church of Santa Maria Novella there was hardly anyone there to hear the holy services except seven young ladies, all dressed in garments of mourning as the times demanded, each of whom was a friend, a neighbor, or relative of the other, and none of whom had passed her twenty-eighth year, nor was any of them younger than eighteen; all were intelligent and of noble birth and beautiful to look at, well-mannered and gracefully modest. I would tell you their real names, if I did not have a good reason for not doing so, which is this: I do not wish any of them to be embarrassed in the future because of what they said and what they listened to—all of which I shall later recount. Today the laws relating to pleasure are rather strict, more so than at that time, when they were very lax (for the reasons mentioned above), not only for ladies of their age but even for older women; nor would I wish to give an opportunity to the envious, who are always ready to attack every praiseworthy life, to diminish in any way with their indecent talk the dignity of these worthy ladies. But so that you may understand clearly what each of them had to say, I intend to give them names which are either completely or in part appropriate to their personalities. We shall call the first and the oldest Pampinea and the second Fiammetta, the third Filomena, and the fourth Emilia, and we shall name the fifth Lauretta and the sixth Neifile, and the last, not without reason, we shall call Elissa.* Not by any previous agreement, but purely by chance, they gathered together in one part of the church and were seated almost in a circle, saying their prayers; after many sighs, they began to discuss among themselves various matters concerning the nature of the times, and after a while, when the others were silent, Pampinea began to speak in this manner:

"My dear ladies, you have often heard, as I have, how proper use of reason can do harm to no one. It is only natural for everyone born on this earth to sustain, preserve, and defend his own life to the best of his ability; this is a right so taken for granted that it has, at times, permitted men to kill each other without blame in order to defend their own lives. And if the laws dealing with the welfare of every human being permit such a thing, how wrong or offensive could it be for us, or anyone else, to take all possible precautions to preserve our own lives? When I consider what we have been doing this morning and in the past days and what we have spoken about, I understand, and you must understand too, that each one of us is afraid for her life; nor does this surprise me in the least—rather I am greatly amazed that since each of us has the natural feelings of a woman, we do not find some remedy for ourselves to cure what each one of us dreads. We live in the city, in my opinion, for no other reason than to bear witness to the number of dead bodies that are carried to burial, or to hear whether or not the friars (whose number has been reduced to almost nothing) chant their offices at the prescribed hours, or to demonstrate to anyone who comes here the quality and the quantity of our miseries by the clothes we wear. And if we leave the church, either we see dead or sick bodies being carried all about, or we see those who were once condemned to exile for their crimes by the authority of the

---

*There is no general agreement on the meaning of the names Boccaccio gives his storytellers: some critics suggest they are allegories, representations of the seven virtues, or symbols of other moral qualities; it has also been suggested that the names reflect, in a general manner, Boccaccio's literary background.

public laws making sport of these laws, running about wildly through the city, because they know that those who enforce these laws are either dead or dying; or we see the scum of our city, excited with the scent of our blood, who call themselves *becchini* and who ride all over the place on horseback, mocking everything, and with their disgusting songs adding insult to our injuries. Nor do we hear anything but 'So-and-so is dead,' and 'So-and-so is dying'; and if there were anyone left to mourn, we should hear nothing but piteous laments everywhere. I do not know if what happens to me also happens to you in your homes, but when I go home I find no one there except my maid, and I become so afraid that my hair stands on end, and wherever I go or sit in my house, I seem to see the shadows of those who have passed away, not with the faces that I remember, but with horrible expressions that terrify me. For these reasons, I am uncomfortable here in church, outside, and in my home, and the more so since it appears that no one like ourselves, who has the financial means and some other place to go, has remained here except us. And if there are any who remain, according to what I hear and see, they do whatever their hearts desire, making no distinction between what is proper and what is not, whether they are alone or with others, by day or by night; and not only laymen but also those who are cloistered in convents have broken their vows of obedience and have given themselves over to pleasures of the flesh, for they have made themselves believe that these things are permissible for them and are improper for others, and thinking that they will escape with their lives in this fashion, they have become wanton and dissolute.

"If this is the case, and plainly it is, what are we doing here? What are we waiting for? What are we dreaming about? Why are we slower to protect our health than all the rest of the citizens? Do we hold ourselves less dear than all the others do? Or do we believe that our own lives are tied to our bodies with stronger chains than others have and, therefore, that we need not worry about anything which might have the power to harm them? We are mistaken and deceived, and we are mad if we believe this. To have clear proof of this we need only call to mind how many young men and ladies have been struck down by this cruel pestilence. I do not know if you agree with me, but I believe that in order not to fall prey, out of reluctance or indifference, to what we could well avoid, it might be a good idea for all of us to leave this city, just as many others before us have done and are still doing. Let us avoid like death itself the ugly example of others, and go to live in a more dignified fashion in our country houses (of which we all have several), and there let us take what enjoyment, what happiness, and what pleasure we can, without in any way going beyond the bounds of reason. There we can hear the birds sing, and we can see the hills and the pastures turning green, the wheat fields moving like the sea, and a thousand kinds of trees; and we shall be able to see the heavens more clearly, the heavens which, though they still may be cruel, nonetheless will not deny to us their eternal beauties and which are much more pleasing to look at than the deserted walls of our city. Besides all this, in the country the air is much fresher, and the necessities for living in such times as these are plentiful, and there are just fewer troubles in general; though the peasants are dying there even as the townspeople here, the displeasure is the less in that there are fewer houses and inhabitants than in the city. Here, on the other hand, if I judge correctly, we would not be abandoning anyone; on the contrary, we can honestly say it is we ourselves that have been abandoned, for our loved ones are either dead or have fled and have left us on our own in the midst of such affliction as though we were no part of them. No reproach, therefore, can come to us if we follow this course of action, whereas sorrow, worry, and perhaps even death can come if we do not follow such a course. So, whenever you please, I think we would do well to take our servants, have everything we need sent after us, and go from one place one day to another the next, enjoying what happiness and merriment these times permit; let us live in this manner (unless we are overtaken first by death) until we see what end Heaven has in store for these horrible times. And remember that it is no less proper for us to leave blamelessly than it is for most other women to remain here dishonorably."

When they had listened to what Pampinea had said, the other ladies not only praised her advice but were so anxious to follow it that they had already begun discussing among themselves the details, as if they were going to leave that very instant. But Filomena, who was most discerning, said:

"Ladies, regardless of how convincing Pampinea's arguments are, that is no reason to rush into things, as you seem to wish to do. Remember that we are all women, and any young girl can tell you that women do not know how to reason in a group when they are without the guidance of some man who knows how to control them. We are fickle, quarrelsome, suspicious, timid, and fearful, because of which I suspect that this company will soon break up without honor to any of us if we do not take a guide other than ourselves. We would do well to resolve this matter before we depart."

Then Elissa said:

"Men are truly the leaders of women, and without their guidance, our actions rarely end successfully. But how are we to find these men? We all know that the majority of our relatives are dead and those who remain alive are scattered here and there in various groups and have no idea of where we are (they, too, are fleeing precisely what we seek to avoid), and since taking up with strangers would be unbecoming to us, we must, if we wish to leave for the sake of our health, find a means of arranging it so that while going for our own pleasure and repose, no trouble or scandal follow us."

While the ladies were discussing this, three young men came into the church, none of whom was less than twenty-five years of age. Neither the perversity of the times nor the loss of friends or parents nor fear for their own lives had been able to cool, much less extinguish, the love they bore in their hearts. One of them was called Panfilo, another Filostrato, and the last Dioneo,* each one very charming and well-bred; and in those turbulent times they sought their greatest consolation in the sight of the ladies they loved, all three of whom happened to be among the seven ladies previously mentioned, while the others were close relatives of one or the other of the three men. No sooner had they sighted the ladies than they were seen by them, whereupon Pampinea smiled and said:

"See how Fortune favors our plans and has provided us with these judicious and virtuous young men, who would gladly be our guides and servants if we do not hesitate to accept them for such service."

Then Neifile blushed out of embarrassment, for she was one of those who was loved by one of the young men, and she said:

"Pampinea, for the love of God, be careful what you say! I realize very well that nothing but good can be said of any of them, and I believe that they are capable of doing much more than that task and, likewise, that their good and worthy company would be fitting not only for us but for ladies much more beautiful and attractive than we are, but it is quite obvious that some of them are in love with some of us who are here present, and I fear that if we take them with us, disgrace and disapproval will follow, through no fault of ours or of theirs."

*Unlike the women's names, the names of the three men are usually explained etymologically: "completely in love" (Panfilo); "overcome by love" (Filostrato); and "lustful" (Dioneo).

Then Filomena said:

"That does not matter at all; as long as I live with dignity and have no remorse of conscience about anything, let anyone who wishes say what he likes to the contrary: God and Truth will take up arms in my defense. Now, if they were only willing to come with us, as Pampinea says, we could truly say that Fortune was favorable to our departure."

When the others heard her speak in such a manner, the argument was ended, and they all agreed that the young men should be called over, told about their intentions, and asked if they would be so kind as to accompany the ladies on such a journey. Without further discussion, then, Pampinea, who was related to one of the men, rose to her feet and made her way to where they stood gazing at the ladies, and she greeted them with a cheerful expression, outlined their plan to them, and begged them, in everyone's name, to keep them company in the spirit of pure and brotherly affection.

At first the young men thought they were being mocked, but when they saw that the lady was speaking seriously, they gladly consented; and in order to start without delay and put the plan into action, before leaving the church they agreed upon what preparations had to be made for their departure. And when everything had been arranged and word had been sent on to the place they intended to go, the following morning (that is, Wednesday) at the break of dawn, the ladies with some of their servants and the three young men with three of their servants left the city and set out on their way; they had traveled no further than two short miles when they arrived at the first stop they had agreed upon.

The place was somewhere on a little mountain, at some distance from the road, full of different kinds of shrubs and plants with rich, green foliage—most pleasant to look at; at the top of this hill there was a country mansion with a beautiful large inner courtyard containing loggias, halls, and bedrooms, all of them beautifully proportioned and decorated with gay and interesting paintings; it was surrounded by meadows and marvelous gardens, with wells of cool water and cellars full of the most precious wines, the likes of which were more suitable for expert drinkers than for dignified and respectable ladies. And the group discovered, to their no little delight, that the entire palace had been cleaned, all the beds had been made, fresh flowers were everywhere, and the floors had been strewn with rushes. Soon after they arrived and were resting, Dioneo, who was more attractive and wittier than either of the other young men, said:

"Ladies, more than our preparations, it was your intelligence that guided us here. I do not know what you intend to do with your troubled thoughts, but I left mine inside the city walls when I passed through them in your company a little while ago; and so you must either make up your minds to enjoy yourselves and laugh and sing with me (as much, let me say, as your dignity permits), or you must give me leave to return to my worries and to remain in our troubled city."

To this Pampinea, who had driven away her sad thoughts in the same way, replied happily:

"Dioneo, what you say is very true: let us live happily, for after all it was unhappiness that made us flee the city. But when things lack order they cannot long endure, and since it was I who began the discussions which brought this fine company together, and since I desire the continuation of our happiness, I think we should choose a leader from among us, whom we shall honor and obey as our superior and whose only thought shall be to keep us happily entertained. And in order that each one of us may feel the burden of this responsibility together with the pleasure of its authority, so that no one of us who has not experienced it can envy the others, let me say that both the burden and the honor should be granted to each one of us in turn for a day; the first will be elected by all of us; then, as the hour of vespers approaches, it will be the duty of the one who rules for that day to choose his or her successor; this ruler, as long as his reign endures, will prescribe the place and the manner in which we shall spend our time."

These words greatly pleased everyone, and they unanimously elected Pampinea Queen for the first day; Filomena quickly ran to a laurel bush, whose leaves she had always heard were worthy of praise and bestowed great honor upon those crowned with them; she plucked several branches from it and wove them into a handsome garland of honor, which whenever it was placed upon the head of any of them was to be to all in the group a definite symbol of royal rule and authority over the rest of them for as long as their company stayed together.

After she had been chosen Queen, Pampinea ordered everyone to refrain from talking; then she sent for the four servants of the ladies and for those of the three young men, and as they stood before her in silence, she said:

"So that I may set the first example for all of you which may be bettered and thus allow our company to live an orderly and pleasurable existence without any shame for as long as we wish, I first appoint Parmeno, Dioneo's servant, as my steward, and I commit to his care and management all our household and everything which pertains to the services of the dining hall. I want Sirisco, Panfilo's servant, to act as our buyer and treasurer and to follow Parmeno's orders. Tindaro, who is in the service of Filostrato, shall wait on Filostrato and Dioneo and Panfilo in their bedchambers when the other two are occupied with their other duties and cannot do so. Misia, my servant, and Licisca, Filomena's, will be occupied in the kitchen and will prepare those dishes which are ordered by Parmeno. Chimera, Lauretta's servant, and Stratilia, Fiammetta's servant, will take care of the bedchambers of the ladies and the cleaning of those places we use. And in general, we desire and command each of you, if you value our favor and good graces, to be sure—no matter where you go or come from, no matter what you hear or see—to bring us back nothing but good news."

And once these orders, announced so summarily and praised by all present, were delivered, Pampinea rose happily to her feet and said:

"Here there are gardens and meadows and many other delightful places, which all of us can wander about in and enjoy as we like; but at the hour of tierce let everyone be here so that we can eat in the cool of the morning."

After the merry group had been given the new Queen's permission, the young men, together with the beautiful ladies, set off slowly through a garden, discussing pleasant matters, weaving themselves lovely garlands of various leaves and singing love songs. After the time granted them by the Queen had elapsed, they returned home and found Parmeno busy carrying out the duties of his task; for as they entered a hall on the ground floor, they saw the tables set with the whitest of linens and with glasses that shone like silver and everything decorated with broom blossom; then they washed their hands and, at the Queen's command, they all sat down in the places assigned them by Parmeno. The delicately cooked foods were brought in and fine wines were ready to be poured; then, without a word, the three servants began to serve the tables. Everyone was delighted to see everything so beautiful and well arranged, and the meal was accompanied by merriment and pleasant conversation. Since all the ladies and young men knew how to dance (and some of them even knew how to play music and sing very well), when the tables had been cleared, the Queen ordered that instruments be brought, and on her command, Dioneo picked up a lute and Fiammetta a viola, and they began softly playing a dance tune. After the Queen had sent the servants off to eat, she began to dance a *carola** with the other ladies and two of the young men; and when that was over, they all began to sing gay and carefree songs. In this manner they continued until the Queen felt that it was time to retire; therefore, at the Queen's request, the three young men went off to their chambers (which were separate from those of the ladies), where they found their beds prepared and the rooms as full of flowers as the halls; the ladies, too, discovered their chambers decorated in like fashion. Then they all undressed and lay down to rest.

Not long after the hour of nones, the Queen arose and had the other ladies and young men awakened, stating that too much sleep in the daytime was harmful; then they went out into a meadow whose tall, green grass was protected from the sun; and there, with a gentle breeze caressing them, they all sat in a circle upon the green grass, as was the wish of their Queen. She then spoke to them in this manner:

"As you see, the sun is high, the heat is great, and nothing can be heard except the cicadas in the olive groves; therefore, to wander about at this hour would indeed be foolish. Here it is cool and fresh, and, as you can see, there are games and chessboards with which all of you can amuse yourselves to your liking. But if you take my advice in this matter, I suggest we spend this hot part of the day not playing games (a pastime which of necessity disturbs the player who loses without providing much pleasure either for his opponents or for those who watch) but rather telling stories, for this way one person, by telling a story, can provide amusement for the entire company. In the time it takes for the sun to set and the heat to become less oppressive, you will each have told a little story, and then we can go wherever we like to amuse ourselves; so, if what I say pleases you (and in this I am willing to follow your pleasure), then, let us do it; if not, then let everyone do as he or she pleases until the hour of vespers."

The entire group of young men and young ladies liked the idea of telling stories.

"Then," said the Queen, "if this is your wish, for this first day I wish for each of you to be free to tell a story treating any subject which most pleases you."

And turning to Panfilo, who sat on her right, she ordered him in a gracious manner to begin with one of his stories; whereupon, hearing her command, Panfilo, with everyone listening, began at once as follows:

---

*A popular round dance, usually accompanied by music and song.

[First Day, First Story]

❋

Ser Cepparello tricks a holy friar with a false confession and dies; although he was a very evil man during his lifetime, he is after death reputed to be a saint and is called Saint Ciappelletto.

DEAREST ladies, it is fitting that everything done by man should begin with the marvelous and holy name of Him who was the Creator of all things; therefore, since I am to be the first to begin our storytelling, I intend to start with one of His marvelous deeds, so that when we have heard about it, our faith in Him will remain as firm as ever and His name be ever praised by us.

It is clear that since earthly things are all transitory and mortal, they are in themselves full of worries, anguish, and toil, and are subject to countless dangers which we, who live with them and are part of them, could neither endure nor defend ourselves from if strength and foresight were not granted to us through God's special grace. Nor should we believe that such special grace descends upon us and within us through any merit of our own, but rather it is sent by His own kindness and by the prayers of those who, like ourselves, were mortal and who have now become eternal and blessed with Him, for they followed His will while they were alive. To these saints, as to advocates who from experience are aware of our weakness, we ourselves offer our prayers concerning those matters we deem desirable, because we are not brave enough to offer them to so great a judge directly. And yet in Him we discern His generous mercy toward us, and since the human eye cannot penetrate the secrets of the divine mind in any way, it sometimes happens that, deceived by popular opinion, we choose as an advocate before His majesty one

21

who is sentenced by Him to eternal exile; nevertheless He, to whom nothing is hidden, pays more attention to the purity of the one who prays than to his ignorance or the damnation of his intercessor and answers those who pray to Him just as if these advocates were blessed in His presence. All this will become most evident in the tale I am about to tell: I say evident, in accordance with the judgment of men and not that of God.

Now, there was a very rich man named Musciatto Franzesi who was a famous merchant in France and had become a knight; he was obliged to come to Tuscany with Lord Charles Landless, the brother of the King of France, who had been sent for and encouraged to come by Pope Boniface.* Musciatto found that his affairs, like those of most merchants, were so entangled in every which way that he could not easily or quickly liquidate them, so he decided to entrust them to a number of different people, and he found a means of disposing of everything—only one difficult thing remained to be done, to find a person capable of recovering certain loans made to several people in Burgundy. The reason for his hesitation was that he had been told the Burgundians were a quarrelsome lot, of evil disposition, and disloyal; and he could not think of an equally evil man (in whom he could place his trust) who might be able to match their wickedness with his own. After thinking about this matter for a long time, he remembered a certain Ser† Cepparello from Prato, who had often been a guest in his home in Paris. This person was short and he dressed with an affected kind of elegance; and the French, who did not know the meaning of the word "Cepparello" (believing it meant *cappello*, in their tongue "garland"), used to call him not Ciappello but Ciappelletto, since he was short; and as Ciappelletto he was known to everyone, and few knew him as Ser Cepparello.

Ciappelletto was, by profession, a notary; he was very much ashamed when any of his legal documents (of which he drew up many) was discovered to be anything but fraudulent. He would have drawn up, free of charge, as many false ones as were requested of him, and more willingly than another man might have

---

*Charles (1270–1325), Count of Valois, Maine, and Anjou, and third son of Philip III, King of France. Upon the request of Pope Boniface VIII (Benedetto Caetani, 1235?–1303), Charles crossed the Alps in 1301 to assist Guelph forces in Italy.

†Ser, the shortened form of Messer(e) is the equivalent of Sir, Mister, or Master. A similar expression commonly used to address women of a certain position is Madonna, meaning "my lady," also found in the shortened forms Mona or Monna.

done for a large sum of money. He gave false testimony with
the greatest of pleasure, whether he was asked to give it or not;
and since in those days in France great faith was placed on
sworn oaths, and since he did not object to taking a false oath,
he won a great many lawsuits through his wickedness every time
he was called on to swear upon his faith to tell the truth. He
took special pleasure and went to a great deal of trouble to stir
up scandal, mischief, and enmities between friends, relatives,
and anyone else, and the more evil that resulted from it, the
happier he was. If he was asked to be a witness at a murder or
at any other criminal affair, he would attend very willingly,
never refusing, and he frequently found himself happily wound-
ing or killing men with his very own hands. He was a great
blasphemer of God and the saints, losing his temper at the
slightest pretext, as if he were the most irascible man alive. He
never went to church, and he made fun of all the church's
sacraments, using abominable language to revile them; on the
other hand, he frequented taverns and other dens of iniquity
with great pleasure. He was as fond of women as dogs are of a
beating with a stick; he was, in fact, more fond of men, more so
than any other degenerate. He could rob and steal with a con-
science as clean as a holy man making an offering. He was such
a great glutton and big drinker that he often suffered the filthy
price of his overindulgence; he was a gambler who frequently
used loaded dice. But why am I wasting so many words on him?
He was probably the worst man that ever lived! His cunning,
for a long time, had served the wealth and the authority of
Messer Musciatto, on whose behalf he was many times spared
both by private individuals, whom he often abused, and by the
courts, which he always abused.

When this Ser Cepparello came to the mind of Messer Musci-
atto, who was well acquainted with his way of life, he decided
that this was just the man to deal with the evil nature of the
Burgundians; and summoning him, he spoke as follows:

"Ser Ciappelletto, as you know, I am about to leave here for
good, and since, among others, I have to deal with these tricky
Burgundians, I know of no one more qualified than yourself to
recover my money from them; and since you are doing nothing
else at the moment, if you look after this matter for me, I shall
gain the favor of the court for you and I shall give you a just
portion of what you manage to recover."

Ser Ciappelletto, then unemployed and in short supply of
worldly goods, saw refuge and support about to depart, and
without further delay, constrained, as it were, by necessity, made

up his mind and announced that he would be happy to go. After they had made their agreement, and Ser Ciappelletto had received the power of attorney and necessary letters of recommendation from the King, Messer Musciatto departed and Ciappelletto went to Burgundy, where hardly a soul knew him: and there, in a kind and gentle manner, unlike his nature, he began to collect the debts and to do what he had been sent to do—it was almost as though he were saving all his anger for the conclusion of his visit. And while he was doing this, he was lodged in the home of two Florentine brothers who lent money at usurious rates and who showed him great respect (out of their love for Messer Musciatto); during this time he fell ill. The two brothers had doctors and nurses brought in immediately to care for him, and they provided everything necessary to restore his health. But all help was useless, for the good man (according to what the doctors said) was already old and had lived a disordered life, and every day his condition went from bad to worse, like someone with a fatal illness. The brothers were most concerned about this, and one day, standing rather close to the bedchamber where Ser Ciappelletto lay ill, they began talking to each other:

"What are we going to do with him?" said one to the other. "We're in a fine fix on his account! Throwing him out of our house, as sick as he is, would surely earn us reproaches and would obviously make little sense, since people have seen how we received him at first, and then how we had him cared for and treated so well; and now what will they say if they see him, at the point of death, being thrown out of our house all of a sudden without having done anything to displease us? On the other hand, he has been such a wicked man that he does not wish to confess himself or to receive any of the church's sacraments; and if he dies without confession, no church will wish to receive his body, and he will be thrown into a ditch just like a dead dog. And suppose he does confess? His sins are so many and so horrible that the same thing will happen, since neither friar nor priest will be willing or able to absolve him, and so, without absolution, he will be thrown into a ditch just the same. And if this happens, the people of this city, who already speak badly of us because of our profession (which they consider iniquitous) and who wish to rob us, will rise up in a mob when they see this and cry out: 'These Lombard dogs are not accepted by the church; we won't put up with them any longer!' They will run to our house and rob us not only of our property but of our lives as well. In any case, we are in trouble if he dies."

Ser Ciappelletto, who as we said was lying near the place where they were talking, had sharp ears, as is often the case with the sick, and he heard what they said about him. He had them summoned and told them:

"I don't want you to worry on my account or be afraid that you will suffer because of me; I heard what you said about me, and I am very sure that things would, indeed, happen as you say they would if everything went as you think it might; but things will turn out differently. Since I have committed so many offenses against God during my lifetime, committing one more against Him now will make no difference. So find me the most holy and worthy priest that you can (if such a one exists), and leave everything to me, for I guarantee you that I shall set both your affairs and mine in order in a way that will satisfy you."

Although the two brothers did not feel very hopeful about this, they went, nevertheless, to a monastery of friars and asked for some holy and wise priest to hear the confession of a Lombard who had fallen ill in their home; and they were given an old friar who was a good and holy man, an expert in the Scriptures, and a most venerable man, for whom all the citizens had a very great and special devotion; and they took him with them. When the friar reached the bedchamber where Ser Ciappelletto was lying, he sat down at his side; first, he began to comfort him kindly, and then he asked him how long it had been since his last confession. To this question, Ser Ciappelletto, who had never in his life made a confession, replied:

"Father, I usually confess myself at least once a week, but there were many weeks that I confessed more often; and the truth is that since I have been ill—almost eight days now—I have not been to confession, so grave has been my illness."

Then the friar said:

"My son, you have done well, and you must continue to do so; but I see that since you have confessed so often, there will be little for me to ask or listen to."

Ser Ciappelletto replied:

"Father, don't say that; I have never confessed so many times or so often that I have not always wished to confess again all the sins I can remember from the day of my birth to the moment I am confessing; therefore, I beg you, my good father, that you ask me point by point about everything, as if I had never confessed before, and do not let my illness stand in your way, for I prefer to mortify this flesh of mine rather than, in treating it gently, do something which might lead to the perdition of my soul, which our Savior has redeemed with His precious blood."

These words pleased the holy man very much, and they seemed to him to be the sign of a well-disposed mind; and after he had commended Ser Ciappelletto highly for his practice, he began by asking him if he had ever sinned in lust with any woman. To this Ser Ciappelletto replied with a sigh:

"Father, on this account I am ashamed to tell the truth for fear of sinning from pride."

To this the friar answered:

"Speak freely, for the truth was never a sin either in confession or elsewhere."

Then Ser Ciappelletto said:

"Since you assure me that this is the case, I shall tell you: I am as virgin today as when I came from my mother's womb."

"Oh, you are blessed by God!" said the friar. "How well you have done! And in so doing, you merit even more praise, for you have enjoyed more freedom to do the opposite than we and others who are bound by religious rules enjoy."

Then, he asked if he had displeased God through the sin of gluttony. To this, breathing a heavy sigh, Ser Ciappelletto replied that he had, and many times; for in addition to the periods of fasting which are observed during the year by the devout, he fasted every week for at least three days on bread and water, but he had drunk the water with the same delight and appetite as any great drinker of wine would—especially after he had worn himself out in prayer or in going on a pilgrimage; and he had often longed for one of those little salads made of wild herbs—the kind women make out in the country—and on occasion eating had seemed better to him than it should have seemed to someone like himself who fasted out of religious devotion. To this the friar replied:

"My son, these sins are natural ones and are very minor; therefore, I do not want you to burden your conscience with them more than necessary. No matter how very holy he may be, every man thinks that eating after a long fast and drinking after hard work is good."

"Oh, father," said Ser Ciappelletto, "don't say this just to console me; as you well know, things done in God's service should be done completely and without any hesitation; anyone who does otherwise sins."

The friar, who was most pleased to hear this, said:

"I am happy that you feel this way, and your pure and good conscience pleases me very much. But tell me, have you ever

committed the sin of avarice by coveting more than was proper
or by keeping what you should not have kept?"

To this Ser Ciappelletto answered:

"Father, do not suspect me of this because I am in the home
of these usurers. I have nothing whatsoever to do with their pro-
fession; on the contrary, I came here to admonish and chastise
them and to save them from this abominable kind of profit-tak-
ing, and I believe that I might have accomplished this if God
had not struck me down in this manner. But you should know
that my father left me a rich man, and when he died, I gave the
larger part of his possessions to charity; then, to sustain my life
and to enable me to aid Christ's poor, I carried on my little
business deals, and while in my work I did wish to make a
profit, I always divided these profits with God's poor, giving one
half to them and keeping the other half for my own needs; and
my Creator has aided me so well in this regard that my business
affairs have always prospered."

"Well done!" replied the friar. "But, now, how many times
have you lost your temper?"

"Oh," said Ser Ciappelletto, "I certainly have, and very often.
And who could keep himself from doing so, seeing all around me,
every day, men doing evil deeds, disobeying God's command-
ments, and not fearing His judgments? Many times there have
been days I would have rather been dead than live to see young
men chasing after the vanities of this world and to hear them
swear and perjure themselves, to see them going to taverns, not
going to church, and pursuing the ways of the world rather than
those of God."

Then the friar said:

"My son, this is righteous anger, and I can impose no penance
upon you for that. But, by any chance, did your wrath ever lead
you to commit murder or to abuse anyone or to do any other
kind of injury?"

To this Ser Ciappelletto answered:

"Alas, father! How could you say such things and be a man
of God? If I had even so much as thought about doing any of
those things you mentioned, do you believe that God would have
done so much for me? These things are for criminals and evil
men, and every time I met such a man, I always said: 'Begone!
And may God convert you!' "

Then the friar said:

"May God bless you, my son! Have you ever given false testi-
mony against anyone, or spoken ill of anyone, or taken their
property against their will?"

"Yes, indeed," answered Ser Ciappelletto, "I have spoken ill of others, for I once had a neighbor who did nothing but beat his wife unjustly, and one time I spoke badly about him to his wife's relatives, such was the pity I had for that poor creature; only God can tell you how he beat her every time he drank too much."

Then the friar said:

"Now then, you tell me you have been a merchant. Have you ever tricked anyone, as merchants are wont to do?"

"Of course," replied Ser Ciappelletto, "but I do not know who he was; all I know is that he was a man who brought me money which he owed me for some cloth I sold him, and I put it in my strongbox without counting it; a month later I discovered that he had given me four pieces more than he owed me, and since I saved the money for more than a year in order to return it to him but did not see him again, I finally donated it to charity."

"That was a small matter," said the friar, "and you did well in doing what you did with it."

And besides this, the holy friar asked him about many other matters, always receiving from him similar replies. And as he was about to give him absolution, Ser Ciappelletto said:

"Father, there is another sin which I have not mentioned."

The friar asked him what it was, and he answered:

"I recall that one Saturday after the hour of nones, I had my servant sweep the house and did, therefore, not show the proper reverence for the Holy Sabbath."

"Oh," said the friar, "that is a minor matter, my son."

"No," replied Ser Ciappelletto, "don't call it a minor matter. Sunday can never be honored too much, for on that day our Savior rose from the dead."

Then the friar asked:

"What else have you done?"

"Father," replied Ser Ciappelletto, "one time without thinking I spat in the house of God."

The friar began to smile and said:

"My son, that is nothing to worry about; we priests, who are religious men, spit there all day long."

Then Ser Ciappelletto said:

"Then you do great harm, for no place should be kept as clean as a holy temple in which we give sacrifice to God."

And, in brief, he told the friar many things of this sort; and finally he began to sigh and then to weep loudly, which he was very good at doing whenever he wished. The holy friar asked:

"My son, what's the matter?"

Ser Ciappelletto replied:

"Alas, father, there is one remaining sin which I shall never confess, such is the shame I have of mentioning it, and every time it comes to mind, I cry as you see me doing now, and I feel sure that God will never have mercy on me because of such a sin."

Then the holy man said:

"There now, my son, what's this you're saying? If all the sins which were ever committed by all men, or which will ever be committed as long as the world lasts, were all in one man, and he was as penitent and contrite as I see you are, the kindness and mercy of God is so great that if he were to confess, God would freely forgive him of all those sins. Therefore, speak without fear."

Still crying loudly, Ser Ciappelletto said:

"Alas, father, mine is too great a sin, and I can hardly believe that God will forgive me unless your prayers are forthcoming."

To this the friar replied:

"Speak freely, for I promise to pray to God for you."

But Ser Ciappelletto kept on crying without speaking, while the friar continued urging him to speak. But after Ser Ciappelletto had kept the friar in suspense with his prolonged weeping, he heaved a great sigh and said:

"Father, since you promise to pray to God on my behalf, I shall tell you: when I was just a little boy, I cursed my mother one time."

And having said this, he began crying loudly again. The friar answered:

"Now there, my son, does this seem like such a great sin to you? Oh! Men curse God all day, and He gladly forgives those who repent for having blasphemed against Him; do you not believe that He will forgive you as well? Do not cry; take comfort, for He will surely forgive you with the contrition I see in you—even if you were one of those who placed Him upon the cross."

Then Ser Ciappelletto said:

"Alas, father! What are you saying? My sweet mother, who carried me in her womb nine months, day and night, and who took me in her arms more than a hundred times! Cursing her was too evil, and the sin was too great; and if you do not pray to God on my behalf, He will not forgive me."

When the friar saw that Ser Ciappelletto had nothing more to say, he absolved him and gave him his blessing, thinking him to be a most holy man, just as he fully believed everything Ser Ciappelletto had told him. And who would not have believed it, seeing a man at the point of death confess in such a way? And then, after all this, he said to him:

"Ser Ciappelletto, with the help of God you will soon be well; but if it happens that God calls your blessed and well-disposed soul to Himself, would you like to have your body buried in our monastery?"

To this Ser Ciappelletto answered:

"Yes, sir, I would. Nor would I want to be anywhere else, since you have promised to pray to God for me; moreover, I have always been especially devoted to your order. Therefore, when you return to your monastery, I beg you to send me that most true body of Christ which you consecrate each morning upon the altar—although I am not worthy of it—so that I may, with your permission, partake of it, and afterward may I receive Holy Extreme Unction, for if I have lived as a sinner, at least I shall die as a Christian."

The holy man said that he would be pleased to do this and that he had spoken well and that he would arrange it so that the Sacrament should be brought to him immediately, which it was. The two brothers, who had strongly suspected that Ser Ciappelletto would trick them, had placed themselves near a partition which divided the bedchamber where Ser Ciappelletto was lying from another room, and as they listened, they could easily overhear and understand everything Ser Ciappelletto said to the friar; and at times they had such a desire to break out laughing that they would from time to time say to each other:

"What kind of man is this? Neither old age nor illness, nor fear of death (which is so close), nor fear of God (before whose judgment he must soon stand), has been able to turn him from his wickedness, or make him wish to die differently from the manner in which he has lived!"

But when they heard it announced that he would be received for burial in the church, they did not worry about anything else. Shortly afterward, Ser Ciappelletto took Communion, and growing worse, without remedy, he received Extreme Unction; and just after vespers on the same day during which he had made his good confession, he died. Whereupon the two brothers, using his own money, took all the necessary measures to bury him honorably, and they sent word to the friars' monastery for them to watch over the body during the evening, according to custom, and to come for it in the morning. The holy friar that had confessed him, hearing that he had passed away, went with the Prior of the monastery and had the assembly bell rung, and

to the assembled friars he described what a holy man Ser Ciap-
pelletto had been, according to what he had been able to learn
from his confession; and hoping that God might perform many
miracles through him, he convinced his brothers that they ought
to receive his body with the greatest reverence and devotion.
The Prior and other friars—all of them gullible—agreed to this,
and in the evening, when they went to where the body of Ser Ci-
appelletto was lying, they held a great and solemn vigil over it,
and the following morning, chanting and all dressed in their vest-
ments with their prayer books in hand, and preceded by their
crosses, they went to get his body, and with the greatest ceremo-
ny and solemnity they carried it to their church, followed by al-
most every person in the city, men and women alike; once the
body had been placed in the church, the holy friar who had
confessed him mounted the pulpit and began to preach mar-
velous things about him and his life, his fastings, his virginity,
his simplicity, innocence, and holiness, recounting, among other
things, what Ser Ciappelletto had tearfully confessed to him as
his greatest sin, and describing to them how he was scarcely able
to convince him God might forgive him for it; from this he
turned to reprove the people who were listening, and he said:

"And you, God's wretched sinners, blaspheme against Him,
His Mother, and all the saints in Paradise when a little blade of
straw is caught under your feet!"

And besides this, he said a good deal more about his loyalty
and his purity; in short, with his words, which were taken by the
people of the countryside as absolute truth, he fixed Ser Ciappel-
letto so firmly in the minds and the devotions of all those who
were present there that after the service was over, everyone
pressed forward to kiss the hands and feet of the deceased, and
all his garments were torn off his corpse, since anyone who could
get hold of a piece of them considered himself blessed. And it
was necessary to keep his body there the entire day, so that all
those who wanted to were able to look upon him. Then, the fol-
lowing night, he was honorably buried in a chapel within a
marble tomb, and immediately the next morning, people began
going there to light candles and to worship him and to make
vows to him and to hang wax images as *ex votos*. And mean-
while, the fame of his sanctity and the devotion in which he was
held grew so much that no other saint received as many vows as
he did from every poor person who found himself in difficulty;
and they called him and still continue to call him Saint Ciappel-
letto, and they claim that God has performed many miracles

through him and continues to perform them to this day for any-
one who seeks his intercession.

It was in this manner, then, that Ser Cepparello of Prato lived
and died and became a saint, just as you have heard; nor do I
wish to deny that it might be possible for him to be in the
blessed presence of God, since although his life was evil and sin-
ful, he could have become so truly sorry at his last breath that
God might well have had pity on him and received him into His
kingdom; this is hidden from us, but from what is clear to us, I
believe that he is, instead, in the hands of the Devil in Hell
rather than in Paradise. And if this is the case, we can recognize
the greatness of God's mercy toward us, which pays more atten-
tion to the purity of our faith than to our errors by granting our
prayers in spite of the fact that we choose His enemy as our in-
tercessor—fulfilling our requests to Him just as if we had chosen
a true saint as intermediary for His grace. And so, that we may
be kept healthy and safe through the present adversity and in
this joyful company by His grace, praising the name of Him
who began our storytelling, let us hold Him in reverence and
commend ourselves to Him when we are in need, being most cer-
tain that we shall be heard.

And here Panfilo fell silent.

[First Day, Second Story]

❦

*A Jew named Abraham, encouraged by Giannotto di Civignì,
goes to the court of Rome, and after observing the wickedness of
the clergy, he returns to Paris and becomes a Christian.*

PANFILO'S story was praised in its entirety by the ladies, and
parts of it moved them to laughter; after all had listened care-
fully and it had come to an end, the Queen ordered Neifile, who
was sitting next to Panfilo, to continue with a story of her own
the order of the entertainment thus begun. Neifile, who was en-
dowed no less with courtly manners than with beauty, answered
that she would gladly do so, and she began in this manner:

Panfilo has shown us in his storytelling that God's mercy over-
looks our errors when they result from matters that we cannot

fathom; in my own tale, I intend to show you how this same
mercy patiently endures the faults of those who with their words
and deeds ought to bear witness to this mercy and yet do the
contrary; I shall show how it makes these things an argument of
His infallible truth so that with firmer conviction we may prac-
tice what we believe.

I have heard it told, gracious ladies, that in Paris there once
lived a great merchant and a good man by the name of Gian-
notto di Civignì, a most honest and upright man, who had a
flourishing business in cloth; and he had a very close friend who
was a rich Jew named Abraham, also a merchant and a straight-
forward, trustworthy person. Giannotto, recognizing his friend's
honesty and upright qualities, began to feel deep regret that the
soul of such a valiant, wise, and good man through lack of faith
would have to be lost to Hell. Because of this he began to plead
with him in a friendly fashion to abandon the errors of the
Jewish faith and to turn to the Christian truth, which, as he
said, his friend could see prospering and increasing continuously,
for it was holy and good, while in contrast, he could observe his
own Judaism growing weak and coming to nothing. The Jew re-
plied that he believed no faith was holy or good except the
Jewish faith and that since he had been born into it, he intended
to live and die within it; nor could anything cause him to turn
away from it. Giannotto did not, however, abstain on this ac-
count from addressing similar words to him some days later and
from indicating to him in a clumsy way, as most merchants are
wont to do, the reasons why our faith is better than the Jewish
one. Although the Jew was a great master of Jewish Law he
nonetheless, moved by the great friendship he had for Giannotto,
or perhaps by the words which the Holy Spirit sometimes places
in the mouth of an ignorant man, began to find Giannotto's argu-
ments very entertaining; but he still remained fixed in his own
beliefs and would not let himself be converted. And the more
stubborn he remained, the more Giannotto continued to entreat
him, until the Jew, won over by such continuous insistence, de-
clared:

"Now see here, Giannotto, you want me to become a Chris-
tian. Well, I am willing to do so on one condition: first I want to
go to Rome to observe the man you say is God's vicar on earth;
I want to observe his ways and customs and also those of his
brother cardinals; and if they seem to me to be such men that,
between your words and their actions, I am able to comprehend
that your faith is better than my own, just as you have worked

to demonstrate it to me, I shall do what I told you; but if this is not the case, I shall remain the Jew that I am now."

When Giannotto heard this, he was extremely sad and he said to himself:

"I have wasted my time which I thought I had employed so well, believing that I might convert him, but if he goes to the court of Rome and sees the wicked and filthy lives of the clergy, not only will he not change from a Jew to a Christian, but if he had already become a Christian before, he would, without a doubt, return to being a Jew."

So, turning to Abraham, he said:

"Listen, my friend, why do you want to go to all that trouble and expense traveling from here to Rome? Not to mention the fact that for a rich man like yourself the trip is full of dangers both by land and by sea. Don't you think you can find someone to baptize you right here? And should you have any doubts concerning the faith that I have explained to you, where would you find better teachers and wiser men capable of clarifying anything you want to know than right here? For these reasons, in my opinion, your journey is unnecessary. Remember that the priests there are just like those we have here, except for the fact that they are better insofar as they are nearer to the Head of the Flock; therefore, you can save this journey for another time, for a pilgrimage to forgive your sins, and I may, perhaps, accompany you."

To this the Jew replied:

"I am convinced, Giannotto, that things are the way you say they are, but to be brief about it, if you want me to do what you have begged me so often to do, I am determined to go there—otherwise I shall do nothing about the matter."

When Giannotto saw his friend's determination he said: "Go, then, with my blessing!"—and he thought to himself that he would never become a Christian once he saw the Court of Rome; but since it would make little difference one way or the other, he stopped insisting. The Jew got on his horse and set out as quickly as he could for the court of Rome, and upon his arrival, he was received with honor by his Jewish friends. While he was living there, without telling anyone why he had come, the Jew began carefully to observe the behavior of the Pope, the cardinals, and the other prelates and courtiers; and from what he heard and saw for himself—he was a very perceptive man—from the highest to the lowest of them, they all shamelessly participated in the sin of lust, not only the natural kind of lust but also the sodomitic variety, without the least bit of remorse or shame. And this they did to the extent that the influence of whores and young boys was of no little importance in obtaining great favors. Besides this, he observed that all of them were open gluttons, drinkers, and sots, and that after their lechery, just like animals, they were more servants of their bellies than of anything else; the more closely he observed them, the more he saw that they were all avaricious and greedy for money and that they were just as likely to buy and sell human (even Christian) blood as they were to sell religious objects pertaining to the sacraments or connected to benefices, and in these commercial ventures they carried on more trade and had more brokers than there were engaged in the textile or any other business in Paris; they called their blatant simony "mediation" and their gluttony "maintenance," as if God did not know the intention of these wicked minds (not to mention the meaning of their words) and might allow Himself to be fooled like men by the mere names of things. These, along with many other matters best left unmentioned, so displeased the Jew (for he was a sober and upright man) that he felt he had seen enough and decided to return to Paris—and so he did. When Giannotto learned that he had returned, the last thing he thought about was his conversion, and he went to his friend and together they celebrated his return; then, when he had rested for a few days, Giannotto asked his friend what he thought of the Holy Father and the cardinals and the other courtiers. To his question the Jew promptly replied:

"I don't like them a bit, and may God condemn them all; and I tell you this because as far as I was able to determine, I saw there no holiness, no devotion, no good work or exemplary life, or anything else among the clergy; instead, lust, avarice, gluttony, fraud, envy, pride, and the like and even worse (if worse than this is possible) were so completely in charge there that I believe that city is more of a forge for the Devil's work than for God's: in my opinion, that Shepherd of yours and, as a result, all of the others as well are trying as quickly as possible and with all the talent and skill they have to reduce the Christian religion to nothing and to drive it from the face of the earth when they really should act as its support and foundation. And since I have observed that in spite of all this, they do not succeed but, on the contrary, that your religion continuously grows and becomes brighter and more illustrious, I am justly of the opinion that it has the Holy Spirit as its foundation and support, and that it is truer and holier than any other religion; therefore, although I once was adamant and unheeding to your pleas and did not want to become a Christian, now I tell you most frankly that I would allow nothing to prevent me from becoming a Christian. So, let us go to church, and there, according to the custom of your holy faith, I shall be baptized."

Giannotto, who had expected his friend to say exactly the opposite, was the happiest man there ever was when he heard the Jew speak as he did; so he accompanied him to Notre Dame, and asked the priests there to baptize Abraham. At his request, they did so immediately, and Giannotto raised him from the baptismal font and renamed him Giovanni, and immediately afterward he had him thoroughly instructed in our faith by the most distinguished teachers. He learned quickly and became a good and worthy man who lived a holy life.

[First Day, Third Story]

*

Melchisedech, a Jew, by means of a short story about three rings, escapes from a trap set for him by Saladin.

NEIFILE'S tale was praised by all, and when she had finished talking, Filomena, at the Queen's command, began to speak in this fashion:

The tale that Neifile told brings back to my memory a dangerous incident that once happened to a Jew; and since God and the truth of our faith have already been well dealt with by us, from now on nothing should prevent us from descending to the acts of men. Now, I shall tell you this story, and when you have heard it, perhaps you will become more cautious when you reply to questions put to you.

You should know, my dear companions, that just as stupidity can often remove one from a state of happiness and place him in the greatest misery, so, too, intelligence can rescue the wise man from the gravest of dangers and restore him to his secure state. The fact that stupidity leads one from a state of happiness to one of misery is shown by many examples which, at present, I do not intend to relate, since thousands of clear illustrations of this appear every day; but, as I promised, I shall demonstrate briefly with a little story how intelligence may be the cause of some consolation.

Saladin,* whose worth was such that from humble beginnings he became Sultan of Babylon and won many victories over Christian and Saracen kings, one day discovered on an occasion in which he needed a large amount of money that he had consumed all his wealth fighting many wars and displaying his grandiose magnificence. Not being able to envision a means of obtaining what he needed in a short time, he happened to recall a rich Jew, whose name was Melchisedech, who loaned money at usurious rates in Alexandria, and he thought that this man might be able to assist him, if only he would agree to do so. But this Jew was so avaricious that he would not agree of his own free will, and the Sultan did not wish to have recourse to force; therefore, as his need was pressing, he thought of nothing but finding a means of getting the Jew to help him, and he decided to use some colorful pretext to accomplish this. He had him summoned, and after welcoming him in a friendly manner, he had him sit beside him and said to him:

"Worthy man, I have heard from many people that you are very wise and most versed in the affairs of God; because of this, I would like you to tell me which of the three Laws you believe to be the true one: the Jewish, the Saracen, or the Christian."

The Jew, who really was a wise man, realized all too well that Saladin was trying to trap him with his words in order to pick an argument with him, and so he understood he could not praise any of the three Laws more than the other without Saladin's achieving his goal; therefore, like one who seems to be searching for an answer in order not to be entrapped, he sharpened his wits, knowing full well already what he had to say, and declared:

"My lord, the question which you have put to me is a good one, and in order to give you an answer, I shall have to tell you a little story which you shall now hear. If I am not mistaken, I remember having heard many times that there once was a great and wealthy man who had a most beautiful and precious ring among the many fine jewels in his treasury. Because of its worth and its beauty, he wanted to honor it by bequeathing it to his descendants forever, and he ordered that whichever of his sons would be found in possession of this ring, which he would have left him, should be honored and revered as his true heir and head of the family by all the others. The man to whom he left

*This ruler (1137-93) enjoyed a legendary reputation for courtesy and magnanimity throughout medieval Europe, in spite of the fact that he reconquered Jerusalem (1187) and opposed the Crusaders.

the ring did the same as his predecessor had, having left behind the same instructions to his descendants; in short, this ring went from hand to hand through many generations, and finally it came into the possession of a man who had three handsome and virtuous sons, all of whom were obedient to their father, and for this reason, all three were equally loved by him. Since the father was growing old and they knew about the tradition of the ring, each of the three men was anxious to be the most honored among his sons, and each one, as best he knew how, begged the father to leave the ring to him when he died. The worthy man, who loved them all equally, did not know himself to which of the three he would choose to leave the ring, and since he had promised it to each of them, he decided to try to satisfy all three: he had a good jeweler secretly make two more rings which were so much like the first one that he himself, who had had them made, could hardly tell which was the real one. When the father was dying, he gave a ring to each of his sons in secret, and after he died each son claimed the inheritance and position, and one son denied the claims of the other, each bringing forth his ring to prove his case, and when they discovered the rings were so much alike that they could not recognize the true one, they put aside the question of who the true heir was and left it undecided, as it is to this day.

"And let me say the same thing to you, my lord, concerning the three Laws given to three peoples by God our Father which are the subject of the question you put to me: each believes itself to be the true heir, to possess the true Law, and to follow the true commandments, but whoever is right, just as in the case of the rings, is still undecided."

Saladin realized how the man had most cleverly avoided the trap which he had set to snare him, and for that reason he decided to make his needs known openly to him and to see if he might wish to help him; and he did so, revealing to him what he had had in mind to do if the Jew had not replied to his question as discreetly as he had. The Jew willingly gave Saladin as much money as he desired, and Saladin later repaid him in full; in fact, he more than repaid him: he gave him great gifts and always esteemed him as his friend and kept him near him at court in a grand and honorable fashion.

[First Day, Fourth Story]

✦

A monk, having committed a sin deserving of the most severe punishment, saves himself by accusing his Abbot of the same sin and escapes punishment.

HAVING completed her story, Filomena fell silent and Dioneo, who was sitting close to her, without awaiting any further order from the Queen (for he realized by the order already begun that he was the next to speak), started speaking in the following manner:

Lovely ladies, if I have understood your intention correctly, we are here in order to amuse ourselves by telling stories, and therefore, as long as we do nothing contrary to this, I think that each one of us ought to be permitted (and just a moment ago our Queen said that we might) to tell whatever story he thinks is likely to be the most amusing. Therefore, having heard how the good advice of Giannotto di Civigni saved Abraham's soul and how Melchisedech defended his riches against the schemes of Saladin, I am going to tell you briefly, without fear of disapproval, how cleverly a monk saved his body from a most severe punishment.

In Lunigiana, a town not too far from here, there was a monastery (once more saintly and full of monks than it now is), in which there lived a young monk whose virility and youth could not be diminished by fasts or by vigils. One day around noon while the other monks were sleeping, he happened to be taking a solitary walk around the church—which was somewhat isolated—when he spotted a very beautiful young girl (perhaps the daughter of one of the local workers) who was going through the fields gathering various kinds of herbs. The moment he saw her, he was passionately attacked by carnal desire.

He went up to her and began a conversation. One subject led to another, and finally, they came to an understanding; he took the girl to his cell without anyone's noticing them. His excessive desire got the better of him while he was playing with the girl, and it happened that the Abbot, who had just got up from his nap, was passing quietly by the monk's cell when he heard the commotion the pair was making. So that he might better recognize the voices, he silently edged up to the entrance of the cell to listen, and it was clear to him that there was a woman inside. At first he was tempted to have them open the door, but then he thought of using a different tactic; so he returned to his room and waited for the monk to come out.

Although the monk was, to his great pleasure and delight, quite occupied with this young lady, he nevertheless suspected something, for he thought he had heard some footsteps in the corridor. In fact, he had peeked out a small opening and had clearly seen the Abbot standing there and listening: he was well aware the Abbot must have realized that the young girl was in his cell, and knowing that he would be severely punished, he was very worried; but without revealing his anxiety to the girl, he immediately began to think of a number of alternative plans, in an attempt to come up with one which might save him. But then he thought of an original scheme which would achieve the exact end he had in mind, and pretending that he felt they had stayed together long enough, he said to the girl:

"I have to go and find a way for you to leave without being seen, so stay here until I come back."

Having left his cell and locked it with his key, he went immediately to the Abbot's room (as every monk must do before leaving the monastery) and with a straight face he said:

"Sir, this morning I could not bring in all of the firewood that was cut for me; with your permission, I should like to go to the forest to have it carried in."

The Abbot, thinking that the monk did not know he had been observed by him, was happy at this turn of events, and since this offered him the opportunity to get more firsthand information on the sin committed by the monk, he gladly took the monk's key and gave him permission to leave. And when he saw him go off, he began to plan what he would do first: either to open the monk's cell in the presence of all the monks in order to have them see what the sin was—and in doing so prevent any grumbling when he punished the monk—or to hear first from the girl how the affair had started. But then thinking that she might very well be the wife or the daughter of some person of importance and not wanting to shame such a person in front of all his monks, he decided first to see who the girl was and then to make his decision. And so he quietly went to the cell, opened it, entered the room, and closed the door.

When the young girl saw the Abbot come in, she became frightened and began to cry out of shame. Master Abbot gave her a quick look and found her to be beautiful and fresh, and although he was old, he immediately felt the warm desires of the flesh, which were no less demanding than those the young monk had felt, and he thought to himself:

"Well, now! Why shouldn't I have a little fun when I can get it? Troubles and worries I can get every day! This is a pretty young girl, and no one knows she's here. If I can persuade her to serve my pleasure, I don't see any reason why I shouldn't! Who will be the wiser? No one will ever know, and a sin that's hidden is half forgiven! This opportunity may never present itself again. I believe it is a sign of great wisdom for a man to profit from what God sends others."

Having thought all this and having completely changed the purpose of his visit, he drew nearer to the girl and gently began to comfort her, begging her not to cry; and, as one thing will lead to another, he eventually explained to her what he wanted.

The young girl, who was by no means as hard as iron or diamond, most willingly agreed to the Abbot's wishes. He took her in his arms and kissed her many times, then lay down on the monk's bed. And perhaps out of concern for the heavy weight of his dignified person and the tender age of the young girl (or perhaps just because he was afraid to lay too much weight on her) he did not lie on top of her but rather placed her on top of him, and there he amused himself with her for a quite a while.

Meanwhile, pretending to have gone into the woods, the monk had concealed himself in the dormitory; when he saw the Abbot enter his cell alone, he was reassured that his plan would be successful. And when he saw the Abbot lock himself inside, he knew it for certain. Leaving his hiding place, he quietly crept up to an opening through which he could see and hear everything the Abbot did and said.

When the Abbot decided that he had stayed long enough with the girl, he locked her in the cell and returned to his own room. And after a while, having heard the monk return and believing that he had come back from the woods, he decided that it was time to give him a sound talking to—he would have him locked up in prison in order to enjoy by himself the spoils they had both gained. He had him summoned, and he reprimanded him very severely, and with a stern face he ordered that he be put into prison.

The monk promptly replied:

"But sir, I have not been a member of the Order of Saint Benedict long enough to have had the opportunity to learn every detail of the order's rules. And up until just a moment ago, you never showed me how monks were supposed to support the

weight of women as well as fasts and vigils. But now that you
have shown me how, I promise you that if you forgive me this
time, I shall sin no more in this respect; on the contrary, I shall
always behave as I have seen you behave."

The Abbot, who was a clever man, realized immediately that
the monk had outsmarted him: he had been witness to what he
had done; because of this, and feeling remorse for his own sin,
he was ashamed of inflicting upon the monk the same punish-
ment that he himself deserved. And so he pardoned him and
made him promise never to reveal what he had seen. They
quickly got the young girl out of the monastery, and as one
might well imagine, they often had her brought back in again.

[First Day, Fifth Story]

❧

*By means of a banquet of chicken and some witty words, the
Marchioness of Montferrato squelches the foolish love of the
King of France.*

At first, the story told by Dioneo pricked the hearts of the
ladies who were listening with a bit of embarrassment, which
was made evident by the modest blushes on their faces; but
then, as they looked at each other, they could hardly keep from
laughing, and they smiled as they listened. As soon as the story
came to an end, they reprimanded Dioneo with a few gentle re-
marks in order to show him that such tales were not to be told
among ladies; afterward the Queen turned to Fiammetta, who
was seated on the grass near him, and commanded her to take
her turn. With a cheerful expression, she gracefully began:

It pleases me that with our stories we have begun to show
how powerful the force of witty and ready retorts may be, and
also how it is a sign of great intelligence in men always to seek
the love of a woman from a better family than their own, and
how in women, too, it is a mark of greatest discernment to know
how to protect themselves from the loving attention of a man of
greater station—so, lovely ladies, I have in mind to show you, in
the story that it is my turn to tell, how a noble woman with her
actions and words protected herself from such a man and sent
him packing.

The Marquis of Montferrato was a most worthy man, a Standardbearer of the Church, who had gone overseas on a crusade with a Christian army. And when there was talk of his merits at the court of King Philip the One-Eyed,* who was making ready to depart on the same crusade, one knight remarked that there existed under all the stars in the world no couple equal to the Marquis and his lady; for inasmuch as he was renowned among knights for every virtue, his lady was likewise considered most beautiful and worthy among all the women of the world. These words took root in the heart of the King of France so deeply that without ever having seen her, he immediately and passionately began to love her, and he decided not to put to sea for the crusade from any port but Genoa so that by traveling overland, he might have a plausible reason for visiting the Marchioness; and with her husband away he thought he could consummate his desires. He proceeded to carry out his scheme: after sending his troops ahead, he set out with a small escort and some noblemen, and when he neared the lands of the Marquis, he sent one of them ahead to the lady to tell her she should expect him to dine with her the next day.

The lady, who was prudent and wise, cheerfully replied that she considered this a great honor and that he would be most welcome. But then she began to wonder what all this meant—the fact that a king would come to visit her when her husband was away; nor was she deceived when she concluded that he was drawn there by the renown of her beauty. Nevertheless, since she was a worthy lady she prepared to honor him, and she gathered together all the eminent gentlemen still remaining at her court in order to make all the appropriate arrangements with their advice. She alone, however, would see to the banquet and the food. Without delay she collected as many chickens as there were in the countryside and ordered her cooks to use only these chickens in the various dishes for the royal banquet.

The King then arrived on the appointed day and was received by the lady with great festivity and honor. When he saw her, she seemed more beautiful, virtuous, and courtly than he had been given to believe from the knight's description, and he was greatly amazed and praised her profusely, discovering that his passion had become even more ardent upon learning that the lady was even more beautiful than he had imagined. And after he had rested for a time in bedchambers decorated suitably for the reception of a great king, it was time for the banquet. The King

*One of the leaders of the Third Crusade (1165–1223).

and the Marchioness were seated together, and the others, according to their station, were honored at other tables.

The King was most pleased, for he was served with many courses accompanied by the finest and most precious wines, and, moreover, from time to time he would gaze at the beautiful Marchioness with delight. But as one dish followed another, he began to wonder, for at his table, no matter how many different dishes were served, all of them had been prepared with chicken.

The King was familiar with the surrounding countryside and knew that it must be full of different game, and since he had announced his arrival to the lady, he felt he had given her ample time to plan a hunt. All this amazed him so much that he would have her talk of nothing but her chickens; and so he turned to her cheerfully, saying:

"Madam, are there only hens and no cocks born in this part of the country?"

The Marchioness, who understood his question very well indeed, and believed that God, according to her wishes, had provided a most opportune moment for clarifying her intentions, turned boldly toward him and answered:

"No, my lord, but though they may differ in dress and rank, the women here are the same as they are elsewhere."

When the King heard this remark, he understood very well the motive behind the banquet of chicken as well as the virtue concealed beneath her words, and he realized that his words of persuasion would be in vain with such a woman and that force was out of the question; and since he had unwisely become enamored with her, he now thought, for his honor's sake, to wisely extinguish the dishonestly conceived flames of his passion. So he continued to dine with no hope of success and with no further attempts at jesting, for he feared her retorts; and immediately after dinner, in order to cover up a dishonest arrival with a hasty departure, he thanked her for the honor she had done him, commended her to God, and left for Genoa.

[First Day, Sixth Story]

✤

With a witty remark a worthy man confounds the wicked hypocrisy of the clergy.

Once all the ladies had commended the courage and the clever reproach the Marchioness had given to the King of France, Emilia, who was sitting near Fiammetta, at the request of her Queen boldly began to speak:

I remember another stinging reproach, this one made by an honest layman to a greedy clergyman by means of a remark no less amusing than commendable.

Not long ago, my dear young ladies, there lived in our city a minor friar, an official inquirer into all kinds of depraved heresies, who was no less a skillful investigator of those who possessed a full purse than of those who were empty of religious faith—although as all clergymen do, he tried very much to appear a saintly and tender admirer of the Christian faith.

Because of his diligence he came by chance upon a good man, more endowed with means than with intelligence, who, not through any lack of faith but merely because his conversation was warmed by a bit of wine or by too much merrymaking, came to remark to his companions one day that he had a wine of such a vintage that Christ himself would drink it.

When this was reported to the inquisitor, who had heard the man's estates were large and his purse was fat, he descended *cum gladiis et fustibus** impetuously upon the man bringing a most serious accusation against him, thinking not so much to reform his faith in the inquisition as to fill his own pockets with the man's florins, which he actually did.

He had him summoned and asked if what had been said against him was true. The good man replied that it was and explained how it happened. To this the most holy inquisitor, a devotee of Saint John Golden-Beard, answered:

"So you made Christ into a drinker and a lover of fine wines, as if he were Cinciglione or one of your sots, drunkards, or pub-crawlers. And now you speak humbly and want to pass the

*"with swords and staves" (Matthew 26:47).

matter off as of little importance, but it's not as simple as you think. You deserve to be burned at the stake when we take action against you, as we must."

With these and many other words and with a threatening look on his face, the friar spoke to the poor man as if he had been Epicurus denying the immortality of the soul. In short, he frightened him so much that the good man by means of certain go-betweens greased his palms with a fair amount of the ointment of Saint John Golden-Mouth* (a most efficacious remedy for the plaguelike greed that afflicts the clergy, and especially the minor friars, who do not dare to touch money), so that the friar might treat him more mercifully.

In spite of the fact that this ointment is most powerful, Galen does not mention it in any part of his treatise on medicine; but the man applied it so well and so copiously that the flames which once menaced him were miraculously commuted to the wearing of a cross on his clothing; it was as if the friar had given him a banner to take on crusade, and to make it more beautiful, it was to be worn yellow on a black background. And even after the priest had received his money, he kept the man under guard for several days and ordered him to attend Mass in Santa Croce every morning and to present himself before him at breakfast, after which he could do what he pleased for the rest of the day.

All this was carried out to the last detail. Then it happened one morning at Mass during the singing of the Gospel that the man heard the words: "For every one you shall receive a hundredfold, and shall inherit everlasting life." These words stuck in his mind; and, at breakfast time, following his orders as usual, he went to the inquisitor and found him eating. The inquisitor asked him if he had heard Mass that morning.

To this question the man promptly replied: "Yes, Monsignor."

Then the inquisitor said: "Did you hear anything during the Mass which raised some doubts in you, or anything you have questions about?"

"I certainly have no doubts about anything I heard; on the contrary, everything I heard I take to be completely true. But one thing I heard made me and still makes me feel the greatest compassion for you and your fellow friars when I think about the sorry state in which you will be in the afterlife."

---

*Saint John the Baptist, patron saint of Florence, whose image was stamped upon the gold florin, the currency avidly sought by the greedy cleric in this story.

Then the inquisitor remarked:

"And what was the passage which moved you to have such pity for us?"

The worthy man replied:

"It was, Monsignor, the part of the Gospel which says: 'For every one you shall receive a hundredfold.' "

The inquisitor said: "That is accurate: but why did this passage move you so?"

"Monsignor," replied the good man, "I will tell you. Since I have been coming here, I have observed every day that a crowd of poor people outside has been given one or two huge caldrons of broth which contain your own leftovers and those of the friars of this convent; so if in the next world you receive a hundredfold for every one you give here, you're going to have so much soup there that you'll all drown in it!"

Everyone at the inquisitor's table laughed, but the inquisitor was enraged at hearing this stab taken at their soupy hypocrisy; had he not already been criticized for what he had previously done to the man, he would have brought additional charges against him for the witty retort which had stung both him and the other lazy rascals like him. And so, in a rage, he told the man to mind his own business and not to show his face around there ever again.

[First Day, Seventh Story]

*

With a story about Primasso and the Abbot of Cluny, Bergamino properly rebukes an unusual fit of avarice on the part of Messer Can della Scala.

EMILIA'S story and the pleasing way she told it made the Queen and all the others laugh and praise this new witticism of the "crusader." But when the laughter died down and all were silent again, Filostrato, whose turn it now was to tell a story, began to speak in this manner:

Worthy ladies, it is one thing to strike a target that does not move, but it is quite another thing, something marvelous, when the unexpected suddenly appears and is quickly brought down by the archer.

The vicious and disgusting life the clerics lead provides an easy and wicked target for anyone who so desires to speak against it, attack it, or reproach it. While I approve of the worthy man who struck at the inquisitor through the hypocritical charity of the friars, who donate to the poor what should better be given to a pig or thrown away, I find even more praiseworthy the man about whom I shall now tell you, and whom I was reminded of by the last tale. This man by means of an amusing tale demonstrates through his characters what he wished to say about himself and his magnificent lord, Messer Cane della Scala,* who all of a sudden was caught in an unusual fit of avarice. And the story goes as follows.

As almost the entire world knows through his great fame, Messer Can della Scala, whom Fortune had favored in many ways, was one of the most noble and most magnificent lords that Italy had known since the reign of Emperor Frederick the Second.† Now, he arranged to give a wonderful and splendid festival in Verona, and to this festival he invited many people from various places, especially courtly entertainers of every kind. But suddenly, for some reason, he changed his mind, and giving them a partial compensation for coming, he told them to leave.

Only one person, a man named Bergamino, whose manner of speaking was polished beyond the imagination of anyone who had not actually heard it, remained there with no compensation or permission to leave, and in so doing he hoped it would be to his future advantage. But Messer Cane had the notion that anything he gave to Bergamino would be as wasted as tossing it into the fire, so he said nothing to him about this, nor did he have anyone else say so.

Several days passed, and Bergamino saw that he was not summoned or required for any services and, moreover, that his horses and his servants and he himself were consuming all his money at his inn, and he began to grow melancholy; but still he waited, thinking it not a good idea to leave. He had brought with him three handsome, rich-looking suits of clothes which had been given to him by other lords so that he might look respectable at their festivities. When the innkeeper asked to be paid, he first gave him one of these and then, as he stayed on longer, he was obliged to give him the second if he wished to remain with his host; and finally he began to live off the pledge of the third suit,

*Cangrande della Scala (1291–1329), lord of Verona.
†Frederick II (1194–1250), ruler of the Holy Roman Empire and patron of the so-called Sicilian School of early Italian poetry.

disposed as he was to remain as long as that one lasted and then to depart.

Now, while he was living off his third suit of clothes, he happened one day to find himself with a gloomy expression on his face in the presence of Messer Cane, who was having dinner, and Messer Can, noticing him, more with the idea of mocking Bergamino than taking delight in anything he might say, asked:

"Bergamino, what's the matter? You look so gloomy. Say something to us."

Spontaneously, but with the skill of one who had prepared his speech long in advance, Bergamino quickly came up with a story relating to his own predicament which goes as follows:

"My Lord, let me begin by telling you that Primasso was a very great grammarian who composed better verse with more facility than any other writer; these qualities made him so famous and respected that even though he was not known to everyone by sight, there was almost no one who did not know who Primasso was by name or by reputation.

"Now it happened that one time when he found himself in Paris without much money (a state in which he lived most of the time, since those with means enough to help him placed little value on his ability), he heard people speak of a certain Abbot of Cluny, who was thought, because of the revenues he received from his estates, to be the richest prelate there was, richer than any churchman besides the Pope. He heard wonderful and magnificent things said about this Abbot; for example, how he always held court and how no one who ever went there was ever denied food or drink, provided he requested it while the Abbot was dining.

"When Primasso heard all this, as a man who delighted in meeting worthy men and lords, he decided to go there to see for himself the magnificence of this Abbot. He asked how far away the man lived from Paris and was told that the Abbot lived in one of his residences about six miles away; Primasso decided that if he left early enough in the morning, he could arrive there by mealtime. He found out which road to take, but not finding anyone who was going in the same direction, Primasso feared that by some misfortune he might lose his way and reach some place where a meal might be harder to find; this being the case, in order not to suffer discomfort from lack of food, he decided to take with him three loaves of bread, believing that he would always be able to find some water to drink, no matter how little he liked water. Putting the loaves inside his tunic, he started on his way and made such good time that he reached the Abbot's residence before mealtime. He entered the place, and looking around at everything, and noticing the great number of tables set and the other things made ready for the meal, he said to himself: 'This man is truly as magnificent as people claim.' And while he was standing there gazing at all this, dinnertime came and the Abbot's steward ordered water to be brought in for all to wash their hands. Once this was done, he seated everyone at the table. And by chance it happened that Primasso was seated just opposite the door of the chamber from which the Abbot was to pass in order to enter the dining room. It was the custom of the court that neither wine nor bread nor anything else to eat or drink be placed on the table until the Abbot had entered the room and sat down at the table; so when the steward had arranged the tables, he sent word to the Abbot that the meal was ready whenever it pleased him. The Abbot had the doors opened for his entrance into the hall, and as he entered and looked around him, the first person he happened to notice was Primasso, who was dressed rather shabbily and was not known to him by sight. As soon as he saw him, a mean thought crossed his mind—one which had never occurred to him before, and he said to himself: 'Just look at the kind of person I'm feeding!'

"So he turned around, ordering that the door to his chamber be closed, and asked those with him if anyone knew the uncouth person sitting in front of the door of his chambers. Everyone answered that he did not.

"Primasso was starving and not in the habit of fasting, so after waiting for some time and not seeing the Abbot make his appearance, he took from his tunic one of the three loaves of bread which he had brought with him, and began to eat. Meanwhile, having waited for a while, the Abbot sent one of his servants to see if this Primasso fellow had left yet. The servant replied: 'No, sir; on the contrary, he seems to be eating some bread which he must have brought with him.' Then the Abbot said: 'Then let him eat his own bread, if he has any, for today he shall not eat any of ours!'

"The Abbot would have preferred for Primasso to leave on his own accord, for he felt that it would be discourteous to send him away. When Primasso had eaten the first loaf and the Abbot still had not arrived, he began to eat the second, and this fact was also reported to the Abbot by someone he sent to see if Primasso had left yet.

"Finally, with the Abbot still not having arrived and Primasso having finished the second loaf, he started on the third: this was also reported to the Abbot, who began to ponder the matter, saying to himself:

"'What has come over me today, why have I become so miserly? Why do I show such contempt, and for whom? For many years now I have given my food to anyone who wished to eat it, without asking if he was a gentleman or peasant, rich or poor, merchant or swindler; with my own eyes I have seen countless scoundrels devouring my food, and never until this man came along had such a thought as this entered my mind. Certainly no man of little importance could afflict me with such avarice; the man who appears a scoundrel to me must indeed be an important person, since I have denied him my hospitality.'

"Having said this to himself, the Abbot was anxious to know who the man was; and when he discovered that he was Primasso and that he had come there to see if the tales he had heard about his magnificence were true, he was very much ashamed, for he was also aware of Primasso's reputation as a worthy man. Eager to make amends to him, he set about to honor him in every way. After dining him in a manner befitting Primasso's merits, he had him nobly dressed, gave him money and a horse, and offered him the run of the household. Very pleased by all this, Primasso heartily thanked the Abbot and returned to Paris on horseback, from whence he had departed on foot."

Messer Cane, who was an intelligent lord, understood very well what Bergamino meant to say without further explanation, and smiling at him he announced:

"Bergamino, you have very clearly outlined the wrongs you have suffered, as well as your own worth and my avarice, and what you desire of me; and to tell the truth, I was never attacked by avarice except now in your case, but I shall drive it away with this stick that you yourself have furnished for me."

His host saw to it that Bergamino's innkeeper was paid, then he had Bergamino dressed most elegantly in one of his own suits of clothes, gave him money and a horse, and offered him the freedom of the household during his visit.

[First Day, Eighth Story]

❦

With a witty saying Guiglielmo Borsiere rebukes the avarice of Messer Ermino de' Grimaldi.

SITTING next to Filostrato was Lauretta, who, having listened to the praise of Bergamino's cleverness, realized that it was her turn to speak, and without waiting for the command she began to speak charmingly as follows:

Dear companions, the previous tale moves me to tell you how a worthy courtier, in like fashion and not without results, attacked the covetous ways of a very rich merchant; and although the gist of this story is similar to the last, I would not have you find it less pleasing, since good eventually resulted from it.

Now, some time ago there lived in Genoa a nobleman named Messer Ermino de' Grimaldi, whose rich estates and enormous wealth far surpassed that of every other rich citizen then known in Italy. And just as he outdid every other Italian in his wealth, so did he surpass beyond all measure in avarice and stinginess every miser or greedy person in all the world, for not only in entertaining others did he keep his purse strings tight, but even in those matters pertaining to his own person (contrary to the general custom of the Genoese, who are used to dressing elegantly) he would deprive himself, and he did the same with food and drink. Because of this, and rightly so, he lost the surname Grimaldi and everyone called him simply Messer Ermino Miser.

Now, while he was increasing his wealth by not spending a thing, it happened that at that time a worthy, cultivated, and witty courtier named Guiglielmo Borsiere came to Genoa, a man completely unlike those courtiers of today who shamefully wish to be called and reputed gentlemen and lords in spite of their corrupt and disgraceful habits, when they should, instead, be called asses, bred as they are on the dungheap of the wickedness of the most vile of men rather than at the courts. In the past, their task involved, and all their energy was consumed in, making peace where quarrels or disputes had arisen between gentlemen, or in arranging marriages, alliances or friendships, or in refreshing the minds of the weary and in amusing the courts with pleasant and clever words, or in rebuking, as fathers do, the defects of the wicked with harsh reproaches—and all this with very little reward; today, however, they dedicate themselves to wasting time speaking badly of each other, to sowing discord, to saying wicked and wretched things and, what is worse, actually doing such things in the presence of others; they accuse each other of true or false wrongdoings, shameful and wretched deeds; and they tempt gentlemen with their flattery and lead them into vile and wicked actions. And the man who is today held most dear and most honored and is most richly rewarded by those ignoble and lewd lords is the man who speaks the most abominable words or performs the most abominable deeds: a great shame and accusation against the modern world and clear proof that the virtues have departed from us and have abandoned the unhappy living to the dregs of vice.

But to return to my story—from which this righteous indignation of mine has led me further astray than I had intended—let me say that the aforementioned Guiglielmo was honored and eagerly received by all the gentlemen of Genoa; and after he had been in the city for a few days, he heard so much about the miserliness and the greed of Messer Ermino that he wished to meet him. Messer Ermino had heard that this Guiglielmo Borsiere was a worthy man, and since, despite his stinginess, he still retained some glimmer of gentility, he received Guiglielmo cheerfully and with words of friendship; and while discussing a number of different matters, he took him and other Genoese gentlemen who were present to one of his new homes, which he had had constructed in a most handsome manner.

After he had shown them all around, he said:

"Well, Messer Guiglielmo, since you have seen and heard a great many things in your day, might you be able to tell me about something never before seen that I could have painted in the main hall of this house of mine?"

To these boorish words of his Guiglielmo replied:

"Sir, I do not believe that I could suggest a topic that has never been observed before, unless it be a fit of sneezing or something similar; but if you wish, I could certainly tell you about something which it seems to me you yourself have never seen."

Messer Ermino said:

"Well, then, I beg you to tell me what it is," never expecting Guiglielmo to answer in the way he did.

To which Guiglielmo then immediately replied: "Have 'Generosity' painted there."

When Messer Ermino heard this, he was so overcome with

shame by the power of that word that his character completely changed from what it had been until that moment, and he announced:

"Messer Guiglielmo, I shall have it painted there in such a way that neither you nor anyone else will ever have occasion to accuse me of not ever observing or knowing it again."

So powerful was the word pronounced by Guiglielmo that from that day on he became the most generous and affable of gentlemen, a man who entertained more splendidly both foreign visitors and fellow citizens than any other in Genoa during his lifetime.

[First Day, Ninth Story]

*

Rebuked by a lady of Gascony, the King of Cyprus is transformed from a faint-hearted man into a courageous ruler.

THE Queen's last orders were reserved for Elissa, who began most joyously without waiting to receive them:

Young ladies, it often happens that a remark uttered more by accident than *ex proposito** has succeeded where various reproaches and much pain have proved to be ineffectual. And this appears to be quite clear from the story told by Lauretta, and I intend to demonstrate this to you again with another much shorter tale: for good stories may always prove to be useful and should always be pondered, no matter who the storyteller may be.

Let me say, then, that during the reign of the first King of Cyprus after the conquest of the Holy Land by Godfrey of Bouillon,† it happened that a noble woman from Gascony went on a pilgrimage to the Sepulcher, and on her return home she was villainously attacked by some wicked men in Cyprus. Having complained without receiving any consolation whatsoever, she decided to seek redress before the King; but she was informed by someone that this would be a waste of time, since the King was so meek and of so little account that not only would he permit the wrongs done to others to go unpunished but he would with

*"On purpose."
†Jerusalem fell to the Crusaders in 1099.

shameful cowardice suffer countless insults to himself—in fact, if
anyone was angry enough, he would vent his anger by shaming
or insulting the King.

When the lady learned this, she lost all hope of revenge, but
as some small consolation for her troubles she decided she would
go to the King and rebuke him for his worthlessness. Appearing
before him in tears, she said:

"My lord, I come before you not in expectation of any ven-
geance for the wrongs which have been done to me, but to gain
some compensation for my injury, and I beg you to teach me
how you yourself endure all those which I have been told are in-
flicted upon you; in this way I may learn from you how to bear
my own wrongs more patiently; and God knows I would gladly
give mine to you if I could, since you bear them so well."

The King, who until that moment had been lazy and passive,
seemed to awaken from a dream; first he harshly avenged the
injury inflicted upon this woman, and then from that time on he
became a most severe persecutor of anyone who committed an
act against the honor of his crown.

[First Day, Tenth Story]

❦

*Master Alberto of Bologna properly shames a lady who had in
turn tried to make him feel ashamed for being in love with her.*

ELISSA was silent, and now the last task of storytelling fell to
the Queen, who began with womanly charm to speak as follows:

Worthy young ladies, just as the stars decorate the heavens on
cloudless nights and the green meadows are bedecked with flow-
ers in springtime, so, too, are good manners and pleasing conver-
sations embellished by witty sayings; moreover, since they are
brief, they are much more suitable to ladies than to men, and
speaking at length, especially if it can be avoided, is more unbe-
coming to ladies than to gentlemen; but these days few if any
women understand a single witty remark or, if they do under-
stand, know how to reply to one—a source of universal shame
for us all and for every woman alive today. That which used to
reside in the minds of women of the past has now been trans-
formed by modern women into decorations for the body; and the
woman who dresses herself with the loudest colors and stripes

and with ornaments embellishing her clothes believes that she should be more highly regarded and honored than all other women, forgetting the fact that if anyone were to dress up an ass in such garments or merely put them on the animal's back, that ass could wear far more than any woman could—nor would this fact make us treat it as anything more than an ass! I am ashamed to say this, since I cannot speak against others without speaking against myself, but these overdressed, painted, gaudy women either stand around like mute and insensitive marble statues or, if they reply when spoken to, it would be much better for them to remain silent; and they deceive themselves in believing that their inability to converse with ladies and with worthy gentlemen comes from their purity of soul, calling their stupidity modesty, as if the only modest women were those who speak only to their maid, their washerwoman, or their cook—if this had been Nature's intent, as they would have us believe, she would have found some other means to limit their chattering.

It is true that in this as well as in other matters, it is necessary to bear in mind the time and the place and with whom one is speaking, for it sometimes happens that when a lady or a man tries to make another person blush with some clever little remark, having misjudged the other person's powers she finds that the blush which was intended to be put on the other person has been turned back and put on herself. And so that you may learn to defend yourselves and, moreover, prevent people from verifying the proverb which is heard everywhere, namely that women always choose the worst in everything, I wish to instruct you about such matters by means of this last of today's tales, which it is now my turn to tell, and in this manner just as you are set apart from other women by your nobility of mind, you will also show yourselves to be superior through your excellence of manners.

Not many years ago there lived in Bologna a most distinguished physician, famous all over the world, who is perhaps still alive today, whose name was Master Alberto. Although he was almost seventy years old, his nobility of soul was so great that even though almost every spark of natural warmth had left his body, that body did not reject the flames of love. While attending a feast one day he saw a most beautiful widow called, according to some, Madonna Malgherida dei Ghisolieri; she was most pleasing to him, and as if he were a young man, the flames of love flared up in his elderly bosom—so much so that he was not able to sleep well at night unless he had seen the pleasing and delicate face of the beautiful lady during the day; and for this reason he began to frequent the street in front of this woman's home, either on foot or on horseback, whenever the opportunity arose. This lady and many other ladies knew why he would walk by, and they often joked among themselves to see a man so old in years and rich in wisdom fall in love, as if they thought that the extremely delightful passion of love should dwell only in the foolish minds of the young and nowhere else.

Master Alberto continued to pass in front of her house, and on a certain holiday, this lady happened to be sitting with many other ladies at her doorway, and when they saw Master Alberto coming toward them from a distance, all of them decided that they would receive him and entertain him, and then, afterward, make fun of him for being in love, and they did just that. They all stood up and invited him inside, leading him into a cool courtyard where exquisite wines and sweets were served; finally as politely and graciously as possible they asked him how he could have fallen in love with this beautiful lady when he knew that she was courted by a number of handsome, noble, and clever young men.

Hearing himself mocked in so courteous a fashion, the doctor with a cheerful face replied:

"My lady, that I am in love should not surprise a wise person, and especially one that I am in love with, for you are so deserving of this love, and while older men are by nature deficient in the strength which is required in amorous undertaking, this does not imply that they have lost their goodwill nor their understanding of who should be loved; on the contrary, since they have more experiences, they naturally have better judgment than young men. The hope which moves me, as an older man, to love you, who are loved by many younger men, is this: I have often been in places where I have observed ladies eating a light meal of lentils and leeks; and while no part of the leek is truly good, its root part happens to be less distasteful and more pleasing to the palate, but you ladies, moved by some perverse appetite, usually hold the bulb part in your hand and eat the leaves, instead, which are not only good for nothing but have an unpleasant taste. And how am I to know, my lady, if in choosing your lovers you will not make the same mistake? If you do, then I shall be your chosen lover, and the others will be thrown away."

The noble lady, as well as the others present, felt very ashamed, and she replied:

"Doctor, you have indeed most courteously corrected us for our presumptuousness, yet your love is dear to me, for it is the love of a wise and worthy man; therefore, feel free to ask me for anything you will, save for my honor, and it shall be yours!"

The doctor, rising from the company of the ladies, thanked the lady, and took his leave of her amidst laughter and merrymaking, and then departed. And so the lady, who had underestimated the one she chose to tease, instead of emerging victorious was herself defeated; and if you are wise, you will be very careful not to make the same mistake.

[First Day, Conclusion]

❦

THE SUN was already sinking toward evening and the heat of the day was diminishing by the time the young ladies and the three young men had finished telling their stories. And so their Queen happily announced:

"AND now, my dear companions, nothing remains for me to do during today's reign except to provide you with a new Queen, who will decide, according to her own judgment, how she and we shall spend our time tomorrow in seemly pleasures. My reign should last until nightfall, but those who do not set aside time beforehand cannot prepare for things to come. I believe that this is the most suitable time for beginning all of the following days, since the new Queen can make any preparations she wishes for the next day. And thus, with reverence for Him in whose name all things live and for your own amusement, let Filomena, a most discerning young lady, be the Queen who shall govern our realm on this second day."

And when she had spoken these words, Pampinea rose to her feet, removed her laurel garland, and reverently placed it upon Filomena's head; then she herself, followed by all the other ladies and young men, hailed her as their Queen and pledged themselves cheerfully to her rule.

Filomena, realizing that she had been crowned Queen, blushed a little out of modesty, but then, recalling the words just spoken by Pampinea and not wishing to appear foolish, she renewed her courage. First of all she confirmed all of the orders given by Pampinea, and then made arrangements for whatever had to be done for the following morning as well as for that evening's supper, taking into account the place in which they were staying. Then she began to speak:

"Dearest companions, although Pampinea has made me your Queen, more out of her own kindness than my own merits, I do not intend to follow merely my own personal judgment in organizing our life together here, but yours as well; and so that you may know what I have in mind to do and thus be at liberty to make any alterations that please you, I shall explain it to you briefly.

"Unless I am mistaken, the formalities observed by Pampinea today are both praiseworthy and enjoyable; therefore, until such time as they become tedious by repetition or for some other reason, I believe they should not be modified.

"Now that we have provided an order for the activities we have embarked upon, let us get up from here and go off to amuse ourselves; when the sun is about to set, we shall have supper in the open air, and then after a few songs and some other entertainment, we would do well to retire for the night. Tomorrow morning, we shall arise early while it is still cool, and once again we shall go off to amuse ourselves somewhere in whatever way we please, and as we have done today, at the appointed hour we shall return to dine and dance; and when we have risen from our afternoon nap, we shall do as we have done today, and return here to our storytelling, which seems to me to provide us with a great deal of pleasure and an equal degree of profit. And I wish to begin a practice which Pampinea, because she was elected late as our Queen, was unable to institute: that is, to restrict the subject matter of our storytelling to some limits and to announce that subject to you in advance so that each of us will have sufficient time to think of a good story on the theme prescribed. Ever since the world began, men have been subject to the various turns of Fortune, and they will be so subject to the end of time, so let each one of us, then, if you will agree, take as our theme those who having gone through a series of misfortunes come to an unexpected happy end."

This arrangement was praised as much by the young ladies as the young men, and all agreed to follow it; but when all the others fell silent, Dioneo remarked:

"My lady, as all the others have said, I, too, say that the order given by you is laudable and most pleasing. But I beg that you confer on me a special grace for as long as this company of ours shall last, and it is this: that I shall not be bound to follow the rule of telling a story on the proposed topic but shall remain free whenever I like to tell whatever tale I please. And so that

no one will claim that I ask for this privilege because I am a
man who does not have stories at the tip of my tongue, from
now on I shall be happy always to be the last one to speak."

The Queen, knowing Dioneo to be an entertaining and jovial
person and clearly realizing that the only reason he requested
this privilege was that he might cheer up the company with a
lively tale should they become weary of telling stories on the
same topic, happily granted him the favor, having first acquired
the consent of the others. Then they stood up and wandered
slowly toward a stream that was crystal clear and lined with
smooth stones and verdant, tender grass, which flowed down a
small hill into a valley thickly shaded with trees. Reaching the
stream barefoot and with naked arms, they waded into the water
and began to amuse each other with different games. But when
the time for supper drew near, they made their way back to the
house, and there they ate with delight. After the meal, instru-
ments were brought and the Queen ordered that a dance begin
which Lauretta was to lead, while Emilia sang a song accompa-
nied by Dioneo on the lute. In obedience to this command
Lauretta promptly began to dance, leading all the others, while
Emilia sang the following song in amorous tones:

> So struck am I by my own beauty
> that never could I heed
> another love nor find delight therein.
>
> I see within that beauty in my mirror,
> that good which satisfies the intellect;
> and no new circumstance or ancient thought
> can ever cheat me of such dear delight.
> What other charming thing, then, could I hope
> to ever gaze upon
> that would stir new delight within my heart?
>
> This good of mine never fades away, for I
> can always gaze upon it in my solace;
> this beauty, to my pleasure, is so fine
> that no words can be found
> to celebrate its meaning,
> and there is no man who can understand
> unless he, too, burns with the same delight.
>
> The more I keep my eyes fixed in this joy,
> the brighter burns my flame,

I give my whole self to it, I surrender
totally, enjoying now what it has promised me,
and even greater joy I hope to have,
the kind of happiness
no one has ever felt before this time.

Even though this song caused some to ponder the meaning of
its words, everyone happily joined in the singing, and after they
had spent part of the night dancing, it pleased the Queen to bring
the first day to a close. She called for torches to be lit and or-
dered everyone to retire until the following morning, and all
went to their bedrooms, as they were told.

[Second Day, Title Page]

✤

Here ends the first day of The Decameron, *and the second begins, wherein under the rule of Filomena, stories are told about people who after a series of misfortunes attain a state of unexpected happiness.*

[Second Day, Introduction]

✤

THE sun with its light had already issued in the new day and the birds singing their pleasant verses on the green boughs were announcing its arrival to the ear when all the young ladies and the three young men arose and went into the gardens; and there they amused themselves by wandering about from one part to another, tredding upon the dew-covered grass and amusing themselves for a long time weaving beautiful garlands. And as they had done on the previous day, so they did on this one. Having eaten outside in the cool open air, they danced for a while and then went to rest, and around the hour of nones rising from their slumber, as their Queen commanded, they went to a cool meadow and sat in a circle around her. She, crowned with her garland of laurel leaves and looking very beautiful with her lovely face, waited for a brief moment, gazing upon all of her company, and then ordered Neifile to begin the day's storytelling with one of her tales. Without any further ado, Neifile cheerfully began to speak.

[Second Day, First Story]

♣

Pretending to be paralyzed, Martellino makes it appear that he has been cured by being placed upon the body of Saint Arrigo; and when his ruse is discovered, he is beaten and then arrested; after very nearly being hanged by the neck, he finally escapes.

DEAREST ladies, it happens many times that someone who attempts to fool others, especially in those matters worthy of reverence, is himself tricked, often to his own harm. Hence, in deference to the Queen's command and in order to begin the proposed theme of the day, I shall begin our storytelling with a tale which tells what happened to a fellow citizen of ours who was at first most unlucky but then, contrary to all his expectations, things changed for the better.

Not long ago there lived at Treviso a German named Arrigo, who was just a poor fellow who hired himself out as a porter to anyone who would take him on but who, nonetheless, was reputed by everyone to be a most holy and good man. Whether this was true or not, the people of Treviso claimed that when he died, at the hour of his death all the bells of the largest church in Treviso began to ring without anyone pulling them. Taking this to be a miracle, everyone proclaimed Arrigo to be a saint; and the whole town ran to his house where his body lay and carried it off to their cathedral as if it were the body of a saint, and they brought along with them the lame, the crippled, the blind, and anyone with any kind of infirmity or deformity with the belief that all of them would be cured by touching this body.

In the midst of all this turmoil and the going and coming of the populace, there happened to arrive in Treviso three of our fellow citizens whose names were Stecchi, Martellino, and Marchese, all men who frequented the courts of various lords, entertaining their audiences by putting on disguises and making strange gestures by means of which they could impersonate anyone they wished. They had never been to Treviso before and they were amazed to see everyone running about this way, and when they learned the reason for this they became most anxious to go to see what was happening for themselves.

They left their belongings at an inn, and Marchese said:

"We want to go to see this saint, but I don't know how we

can manage to get there, for I am told that the square is full of Germans and other armed troops which the lord of this city has stationed there to prevent riots; and besides this, from what I hear, the church is so crammed full of people that hardly one more soul could fit inside."

Then Martellino, who was anxious to see this spectacle, said: "Don't let that bother you; I'll find a good way of getting to the saint's holy body."

"How?" asked Marchese.

"I'll tell you," Martellino answered: "I will disguise myself as a cripple with you on one side of me and Stecchi on the other, and as if I couldn't walk on my own, the two of you will go along holding me up, pretending to take me to be cured by this saint, and there won't be a soul who will not make room and let us pass when he sees us."

Marchese and Stecchi liked this solution, and without further delay, they left the inn, and when all three had come to a deserted spot Martellino contorted his hands, his fingers, his arms, his legs, as well as his mouth, his eyes, and his entire face to the point that he became so frightful a sight to behold that anyone who saw him would have truly believed that he was a completely hopeless and paralytic case. And disguised this way, he was led in the direction of the church by Marchese and Stecchi, whose faces were full of piety as they asked humbly and for the love of God that those in front of them make way. This they easily accomplished, and before long, with everyone paying attention to them and almost everyone in the crowd yelling "Make way! Make way!" they reached the spot where the body of Saint Arrigo was laid; and Martellino was immediately lifted up by some gentlemen standing nearby and was placed upon the corpse of the saint so that he might acquire the benefit of its holiness.

Martellino lay still for a while as all the people stared at him to see what would happen; then, like the clever impersonator he was, he slowly began to pretend to straighten out first one of his fingers, then his hand, and then his arm, until he had unwound himself completely. When the people saw all this, they roared with such praise for Saint Arrigo that a crash of thunder would have gone unheard at that moment.

By chance there was a Florentine nearby who knew Martellino very well, but since he was so well disguised while being led into the cathedral, he had not recognized him at once and immediately began to laugh and to exclaim:

"God damn that fellow! Who would not have believed he was really crippled when they saw him come in that way?"

Some of the Trevisans overheard this remark and quickly asked him:

"What? You mean he's not a cripple?"

To this the Florentine replied:

"God forbid! He has always stood as straight as any of us here, but as you have been able to observe, he is better than anyone at disguising himself in whatever manner he chooses."

Once they heard this, there was no need to say more; they pushed their way up to the front of the crowd and began to shout:

"Seize this traitor, that mocker of God and the saints who came here disguised as a cripple with the intention of mocking us and our saint!"

And as they said this, they grabbed him and dragged him away from the place where he lay, took him by the hair, tore the clothes from his back, and began to punch and kick him. To Martellino it seemed that there wasn't a man in the crowd who didn't rush up to take a whack at him as he cried "For God's sake, have mercy!" and he defended himself as best he could, but it was of no use: the mob grew thicker as it piled up on him.

When Stecchi and Marchese saw this, they began to think that things weren't going as well as they should, but fearing for themselves, they did not dare to help him, so they screamed "Kill him!" as loud as the others did, while at the same time they were trying to figure out a way to rescue him from the hands of the mob; and certainly he would have been killed if it had not been for a plan which suddenly occurred to Marchese. The entire force of the city's guards was stationed outside the cathedral, and, as quickly as he could, Marchese rushed up to the head officer of the *podestà** and said:

"For God's sake! Inside there's a crook who stole my purse with at least a hundred gold florins in it! I beg you to arrest him so I can get my money back."

Hearing this, at least a dozen guards ran to where poor Martellino was being soundly beaten,† and with the greatest of difficulty they broke through the mob and grabbed the bruised and

---

*The highest office in a city-state's government between the late twelfth and early fourteenth century, usually granted to a noble foreigner for a period of six months.

†The original text (*senza pettine carminato*) literally means "being carded without a wool-comb," a colloquial expression, probably current among the woolen workers of Boccaccio's day, for suffering a beating.

beaten man from their hands and led him off to the palace, and a number of people who felt they had been taken in by Martellino followed them there, and as soon as they heard that he had been arrested as a pickpocket, they realized that this was as good a way as any to make things difficult for him, and all of them started to claim that he had snatched their purses. When the judge, who was a rough customer himself, heard all this, he quickly took Martellino aside and began to question him about the incident. But Martellino started answering him with smart remarks, as if he gave little importance to the fact that he had been arrested, and this angered the judge, who had him tied to the rack and given several good turns to make him confess to whatever the others accused him of before he was hanged by the neck.

Once his feet were back on the ground, the judge asked him if what everyone accused him of was true, and since denying it would have been useless, Martellino answered:

"My lord, I am ready to confess the truth to you, but you must have each man who accuses me tell when and where I took his purse, and then I shall tell you if I did or did not take it."

The judge replied, "That's fine with me," and he had some of the people brought forward. One claimed that his purse had been stolen eight days ago, another six days before, a third just four days before, and some even said that he had snatched theirs that very same day.

When Martellino heard this, he exclaimed:

"My lord, all these people are lying through their teeth! And I can give you proof that I am telling the truth, for I have never set foot in these parts until a short time ago when I had the bad fortune of going to see the holy body, and there I was beaten up as you can well see for yourself; and that I am telling you the truth can be verified by the customs officer at the city's gates, by his checking his register book, and by asking my innkeeper as well. And if you discover that I am telling the truth, I beg you not to have me tortured and executed at the instigation of these evil men."

While things were in this state, word had reached Marchese and Stecchi that the judge was giving Martellino a rough time and had already put him on the rack. Very much afraid for their friend, they said to each other:

"We have handled this very badly: we've pulled him out of the frying pan and dropped him straight into the fire."

Turning all their attention to this problem, they tracked down their innkeeper and told him what had happened. After a good

laugh about it, the innkeeper took them to a certain Sandro Ago-
lanti, who lived in Treviso and had a great deal of influence with
the governor of the town and to whom he told the whole story,
and joined by the two men, he begged him to intervene on Mar-
tellino's behalf.

After much laughter, Sandro went off to see the governor and
implored him to send for Martellino, and this was done. The
men who were sent to fetch him found him still standing before
the judge dressed only in his shirt, completely bewildered and
very much afraid, for the judge refused to hear anything said in
his defense; on the contrary, as he happened to hold some sort
of grudge against Florentines, he was fully determined to see
Martellino hanged by the neck, and by no means would he turn
him over to the governor, not until, finally, he was forced to do
so against his will. When Martellino stood before the governor,
he told him everything that had happened, and he begged as a
special favor that he should be allowed to leave the city, for un-
til he reached Florence again he would always feel the rope's
noose around his neck. The governor broke into a fit of laughter
at hearing the whole affair, and he ordered that each man be
given a new suit of clothes. Thus, all three escaped from this
great danger better than they ever expected and returned safe
and sound to their homes.

[Second Day, Second Story]

✤

*Rinaldo d'Asti is robbed, arrives at Castel Guiglielmo, and is of-
fered lodging by a widow; after he has recovered his possessions,
he returns to his home safe and sound.*

THE ladies laughed heartily at Neifile's account of Martellino's
misadventures, and among the young men Filostrato was the
most amused; since he was sitting next to Neifile, the Queen or-
dered him to tell the next story. Without the slighest hesitation,
he began:

Beautiful ladies, the story that attracts my interest most con-
tains a mixture of piety, misfortune, and love, and perhaps it
serves no other purpose than its usefulness, but the story will be
especially helpful to those who journey along the uncertain roads

of love where those who do not regularly say the Our Father of St. Julian may very often find a good bed but a bad lodging.

During the reign of the Marquis Azzo da Ferrara, there was a merchant named Rinaldo d'Asti who had come to Bologna on business; he was on his way home after completing his business when on the road from Ferrara to Verona he happened to fall in with some men who looked like merchants but who were actually thieves of a disreputable sort with whom he incautiously conversed as they rode along. When these men saw that he was a merchant and guessed that he might be carrying money, they decided to rob him at the first opportunity, and to this end, so that he might in no way suspect their plans, they assumed an air of modesty and respectability as they rode along with him, speaking only of honesty and fair dealings, thus making themselves appear to him as humble and harmless as they could. Consequently, Rinaldo considered himself quite lucky to have met them, for he was traveling by himself on horseback with only one servant.

As they traveled along, with the conversation, as it usually does, passing from one thing to another, they came to the topic of prayers that men offer to God, and one of the bandits, of which there were three, asked Rinaldo:

"What about you, sir? What kind of prayer do you normally say when you are traveling?"

To this question, Rinaldo replied:

"To tell the truth, I am a rather simple and down-to-earth sort in these matters; I'm the old-fashioned kind of guy who calls them as he sees them,* and I know very few prayers; nevertheless, it is my usual practice when traveling never to leave an inn in the morning without saying one Our Father and one Hail Mary for the souls of St. Julian's mother and father, after which I pray to God and to St. Julian to grant me a suitable lodging for the coming night. And in my journeys I have often found myself in grave danger, from which I have nonetheless managed to escape and find myself in a safe place with good lodgings that same evening; so I firmly believe that St. Julian, in whose honor I say my prayers, has obtained this favor for me through his intercession with God, and if I had not recited my

---

*The original text (*e lascio correr due soldi per ventiquattro denari*) employs coinage of the period and literally means: "and I would take two *soldi* for twenty-four *denari*" (two *soldi* were the equivalent of twenty-four *denari*).

prayer that morning, I don't think I could manage to travel safely during the day or arrive safely by nightfall."

"Did you say your prayers this morning?" wondered the man who had asked the question.

"Yes, of course," replied Rinaldo.

Then the man, who already knew how this affair was going to turn out, said to himself:

"You're really going to need it, for if all goes as planned, I think you're going to lodge rather badly tonight"; and then he said to Rinaldo:

"I have traveled a lot myself, but I myself have never said that particular prayer, although I have heard it recommended by many, and yet I have found nothing but good lodging; and perhaps this very evening you will discover which of the two of us finds the better lodging, you who have said this prayer or I who have not said it. But I do, in place of this prayer, you can be sure, recite the *Dirupisti* or the *Intemerata* or the *De profundi,** all of which, according to what my grandmother used to say, are quite effective."

And so they all went along their way talking, with the three men biding their time and waiting for a suitable place to carry out their wicked plan. Then it happened that late in the day, they all came to a river crossing on the road to Castel Guiglielmo, and the three men, seeing that the hour was late and the place deserted and concealed, attacked and robbed Rinaldo of everything he had, leaving him afoot without his horse and wearing nothing but his shirt. And as they left, they cried:

"Now go and see if your St. Julian gives you as good a lodging tonight as our saint will provide for us." Then they crossed the river and rode off.

When Rinaldo's servant saw him attacked, like a coward he did nothing to rescue him but instead turned his horse around and rode without stopping until he reached Castel Guiglielmo, since it was late. When he entered the town, without giving the matter another thought, he found himself lodgings for the night.

Barefoot and wearing only a shirt, Rinaldo did not know what to do, for it was very cold and was snowing hard and steadily; it was getting darker, his teeth were chattering, and he was afraid as he began to look around him for some shelter where he might spend the night and not die from the cold, but he found no shelter, for there had recently been a war in the surrounding coun-

*These are the opening words of three Latin prayers commonly invoked during the period.

tryside during which everything had been burned to the ground, so driven on by the cold he set off at a quick pace in the direction of Castel Guiglielmo, not knowing if his servant had fled there or elsewhere but hoping that if he could enter the town, God would send him some help. But when the darkness of the night fell he was still more than a mile from the castle, and when he finally arrived there it was so late that the gates to the fortress were already barred and the drawbridges were up, and he was unable to enter the town. He felt miserable and was in tears as he looked around for some place where he might at least be protected from the snow, and by chance, he caught sight of a house that jutted out a bit from the castle walls, so he decided to go and take refuge there under its eaves until the break of day. When he reached the spot, he discovered that the door under the eaves was locked, so in front of it he put together some straw that he found nearby and lay down there, all unhappy and miserable, complaining at frequent intervals to St. Julian, declaring that this was a situation not worthy of the faith he had placed in him. But St. Julian, who still kept an eye on him, was preparing to provide him good lodging in not too long a time.

Now in this town there lived a widow who was the most beautiful woman in the whole world and whom the Marquis Azzo loved as much as life itself and whom he kept there for his pleasure; and this lady lived in the very house under whose eaves Rinaldo had taken shelter. At it happened, during the day the Marquis had come to the lady's house with the intention of sleeping with her that night and had secretly arranged for a magnificent supper to be prepared and a bath to be drawn for him beforehand. Everything was ready (and the lady's mind set exclusively on the arrival of the Marquis) when it happened that a servant arrived at the gate with a message for the Marquis calling him to depart at once, so he left word for the lady not to wait for him and rode off. The lady was somewhat displeased, and not knowing what to do with herself, she decided to take the bath drawn for the Marquis herself and then to eat and go to bed. And so, into the bath she stepped.

This bath was near the doorway on the other side of which the miserable Rinaldo had taken shelter, and while the lady was in the bath, she could hear Rinaldo moaning and a chattering of teeth which sounded like a stork; so she called her maidservant and said: "Go upstairs and look down outside the wall by this door and find out who is there and what he is doing."

The maid went up and in the clear night air she saw, just as we described earlier, a barefoot man in his shirtsleeves sitting there shivering all over, and she asked him who he was. Rinaldo, chattering so much that he could hardly form his words, told her as briefly as possible who he was and how and why he was there; then he began piteously to implore her to do whatever she could not to leave him there to die in the cold during the night. The maid, who felt sorry for him, returned to her lady and recounted the whole affair to her. She also felt pity for Rinaldo, and remembering that she had the key to the door, which was sometimes used for the clandestine comings and goings of the Marquis, she said:

"Go and let him in quietly; there's a supper here without anyone to eat it, and there's plenty of room to put him up."

The maid commended her lady for her kindness, then went to let him in, and when he was inside, seeing that he was almost frozen, the lady said: "Quickly, my good man, step into this bath, which is still warm."

Without waiting for any further invitation, Rinaldo did so most gladly, and with the heat from the bath reviving his body, he felt as if he had been completely returned from the dead to the living. The lady had some clothes brought to him which belonged to her husband, who had recently passed away, and when he put them on, they fit him perfectly. As he awaited further instructions from the lady, he began to thank God and St. Julian for saving him from the cruel night which he had been expecting and leading him to what appeared to be such good lodgings. The lady, who in the meantime had been resting for a while, had a big fire lit in one of her rooms, to which she came, asking what had happened to the gentleman.

To this question, her maid replied:

"My lady, he is dressed and he is a handsome man who appears to be quite proper and well mannered."

"Go then and ask him to come," said the lady, "and tell him to have some supper here by the fire, for I know he has not eaten."

Entering the room, Rinaldo, judging from the lady's appearance that she was a person of quality, greeted her respectfully, thanking her as best he knew how for the kindness she had shown him. The lady observed Rinaldo, and as she listened to him speak, she agreed that he was all that her maid had reported him to be, and she gladly received him, bidding him to sit near her by the fire and asking him about the misfortune which had brought him there, whereupon Rinaldo responded in great detail to all her questions. The lady had heard something of the incident after the arrival of Rinaldo's servant at the castle, and so she believed everything that he told her; then she told him what she knew of his servant and how he could easily find him again in the morning. But by now the table was set and Rinaldo, after washing his hands, sat down to eat with the lady at her request.

Rinaldo was a tall, fine, good-looking man in the prime of manhood with impeccable and gracious manners; the lady had more than once cast a glance in his direction and praised him, and her carnal instincts were all aroused, since her mind was filled with the thought of the Marquis, who was to have lain with her that night. After supper she left the table to consult her maid as to whether or not, since the Marquis had stood her up, she should take advantage of this gift which Fortune had bestowed upon her.

The maid, who was aware of her lady's desire, urged her to follow her instinct for all it was worth, and so, returning to the fireplace where she had left Rinaldo by himself, the lady began to gaze at him amorously and say:

"Now, Rinaldo, why are you so unhappy? Don't you think you can make up in some way for the loss of a horse and some clothes? Console yourself, be happy, make yourself at home here! In fact, there is something else I have been meaning to tell you: seeing you there wearing those clothes which belonged to my late husband, you remind me so much of him that all evening I have had the impulse to kiss and embrace you more than a hundred times, and had I not been afraid that this might have displeased you, I certainly would have done so."

When he heard these words and saw the gleam in the lady's eyes, Rinaldo, who was no fool, moved toward her with open arms and said:

"My lady, I owe my life to you, and considering the situation from which you have rescued me, it would be most discourteous on my part if I did not try to please you in every way; so, fulfill your desire to embrace and kiss me as much as you like, for I shall be more than willing to kiss and embrace you in return."

After this no more words were necessary. The lady, who was all aflame with amorous desire, instantly threw herself into his arms, and embracing him passionately, she kissed him more than a thousand times as he kissed her back; then they retired to her bedroom, and wasting no time getting into bed, before the day dawned they satisfied their desires to the fullest, and many times over. They arose at the break of day as was the lady's wish, for she did not want anyone to suspect anything, and after giving Rinaldo some rather old clothes and filling his purse with money, she then explained which road he should take to find his servant in the fortress, and letting him out by the same door he had entered, she begged him to keep their encounter a secret.

As soon as it was broad day and the city gates were open, pretending to arrive from far away, he entered the town and found his servant; after changing into some of his own clothes which were in his saddlebags, he was about to mount his servant's horse when, as if by divine decree, it happened that the three thieves who had robbed him the previous evening were being led into the fortress, having been arrested for another crime they had just committed. They had made a voluntary confession, and Rinaldo's horse, his clothes, and his money were returned to him, and all he lost was a pair of garters which the thieves could no longer remember where they had placed. Thus Rinaldo, giving thanks to God and St. Julian, mounted his horse and rode back home safe and sound, and the three thieves on the following day found themselves dangling their heels in the north wind.*

[Second Day, Third Story]

Three young men squander their possessions and become impoverished; while returning home in despair, a nephew of theirs meets an Abbot whom he discovers to be the daughter of the King of England; she takes him for her husband, and he restores his uncles' losses, thus returning them all to a comfortable state.

THE young ladies and men listened in amazement to the adventures of Rinaldo d'Asti, praising his devotion and giving thanks both to God and to St. Julian for rescuing him in the moment of his greatest need; nor did anyone think that the lady had acted foolishly—at least no one openly said she did—in taking advantage of the blessing that God bestowed on her home. And while they talked and giggled over the pleasant night the lady had enjoyed, Pampinea, finding herself sitting next to Filostrato and realizing that soon it would be her turn to speak, collected her thoughts and began to think about what she would

*That is to say, they were hanged.

say; and after receiving the Queen's command, in a manner as confident as it was lively, she began to speak:

Worthy ladies, if we examine closely the ways of Fortune, we will see that the more said about her ways, the more there remains to be said, and no one should be surprised at this fact, if he or she bears in mind that all those affairs which we foolishly call our own are in her hands, and as a result it is she who, according to her own secret judgment, endlessly moves and rearranges things from one place to another and then back again without any discernible plan whatsoever. And while the truth of this can be clearly discerned in the course of a day's events as well as in some of the previous stories, nevertheless, as it pleases our Queen to speak on this topic, I shall now add to those already told one of my own tales, which I believe will be pleasing and perhaps even useful to those who hear it.

There once lived in our city a nobleman whose name was Messer Tebaldo, who, according to some people, belonged to the Lamberti family, while others claimed he was one of the Agolanti, their decision, perhaps, being influenced by the fact that his sons later on pursued a trade which the Agolanti had always followed and still do follow to this day. But setting aside the question to which of the two families he belonged, let me say that in his day he was one of the most wealthy nobles, and he had three sons: the first was named Lamberto, the second Tedaldo, and the third Agolante—all handsome and fashionable young men, even though the eldest had not yet reached the age of eighteen by the time the very rich Messer Tebaldo met his death, leaving all his goods and personal property to them as his legitimate heirs.

When they found that they were very wealthy both in cash and in possessions, they began to spend recklessly, without restraint, allowing pleasure to be their only guide; they kept a large household of servants and many fine horses, dogs, and birds, and they constantly entertained, gave gifts, and sponsored tournaments—they did not only what noblemen were expected to do, but also whatever appealed to their youthful appetites. They had not been living this sort of life for very long before the riches left them by their father began to dwindle; and as their income became insufficient to meet their normal commitments, they began to borrow money and to sell their remaining possessions, and by selling one thing today and another the next, they were hardly aware of being reduced to nothing until finally poverty opened their eyes just as wealth had closed them.

Because of this, one day Lamberto called his two brothers to-

gether and pointed out to them the contrast between their fa-
ther's magnificence and their own condition and how through
reckless spending their wealth had been reduced to poverty, and
as best he knew how, he urged them to join with him in selling
what little remained and going away before their misery be-
came even more apparent. They agreed to do so, and without
making a fuss over their departure, they left Florence and did
not stop traveling until they reached England, where they took a
small house in London, spending as little as possible to live, and
there they began lending money avidly at harsh rates of interest,
and Fortune was so good to them in this that in a few years
they accumulated a great quantity of money.

As a result, with this money, one by one, they were able to re-
turn to Florence, where they bought back a great part of their
possessions and much else besides, and they all took wives. Since
they continued to lend out money in England, they sent a young
nephew of theirs named Alessandro to attend to their affairs;
and while the three of them remained in Florence, they forgot
the desperate straits to which their reckless spending had once
brought them, and though all of them were raising families, they
began spending their money more foolishly than ever before and
were granted immediate credit by every merchant and for any
amount they desired. For a few years they managed to sustain
their expenditures with the money Alessandro sent them, for he
had begun to loan money to barons on the security of their
castles and other revenues, which brought him in a handsome
profit.

Meanwhile, the three brothers went on spending wastefully
and borrowing when they needed money, relying as always on
England, when, quite contrary to everyone's expectations, a war
broke out in England between the King and one of his sons
which divided the entire island, some taking one side and others
supporting the other. Because of this war Alessandro lost all of
the barons' castles and now he received no other income from
anything at all, but since Alessandro hoped that from one day to
the next peace would be made between the King and his son
and, as a result, everything would be restored to him, both the
capital and the interest, he did not leave the island; on the other
hand, the three brothers in Florence went on spending exces-
sively, borrowing more and more money every day. But then as
the years passed, they realized that their hopes were without
foundation, and the three brothers not only lost their credit but
since those to whom they owed money now wanted to be paid,
and since their personal belongings proved insufficient to cover

payment, they were quickly thrown in prison, where they would have to remain until their debts were paid off, leaving their wives and small children behind, one taking to the country, one wandering here, another there, all in a very sorry state with the expectation of only a life of misery.

Alessandro, who had waited for a number of years for peace to come in England, realizing that it was not about to come, now felt it was not only futile but even dangerous to remain there any longer, and he decided to return to Italy. Setting out all alone, while he was leaving Bruges, he happened to see an Abbot dressed in white who was also leaving the city, preceding many monks, a large retinue of servants, and a great baggage train, while directly behind him there rode two elderly knights, relatives of the King, with whom Alessandro was acquainted. And so he greeted them and was readily received into their company.

As Alessandro rode along with them, he asked politely who the monks riding ahead with so many servants were and where they were going. To this question, one of the knights replied:

"The person riding ahead of us is one of our young relatives who has just been elected Abbot of one of the largest abbeys in England, but since he is too young to be inducted legally into such a high office, we are going with him to Rome to ask the Holy Father to grant him a dispensation and to confirm him in this high position in spite of his age; no one, however, is to know about this."

As the new Abbot rode along, sometimes ahead of his retinue and sometimes behind, as has always been the custom of gentlemen when on the road, he happened to see near him Alessandro, who was still young, most handsome and well built, and also as well-mannered, pleasant, and polite as a person could be. At first glance he pleased the Abbot more than anything else had ever pleased him before, and calling him to his side he began to speak to him in a friendly fashion, asking him who he was, from where he had come, and where he was going. Alessandro satisfied his questions, explaining his situation quite openly to the Abbot and offering his services to him in any capacity, no matter how slight they might be. Hearing his charming and well-ordered manner of speaking and observing his ways in more detail, the Abbot judged Alessandro to be a gentleman in spite of his servile occupation, and he was more pleased with him than ever; and already full of compassion for his misfortunes, he tried most affectionately to console him, telling him not to lose hope, for he was a worthy man and God would restore him to the position from which Fortune had cast him down, and perhaps even to a

higher one, and since Alessandro and he were going in the same
direction toward Tuscany, the Abbot asked him to remain in his
company. Alessandro thanked him for the consolation and de-
clared that he was ready to obey his every command.

So the Abbot rode along, fascinated by the sight of Alessan-
dro, which filled him with unusual feelings, until after a number
of days it happened that they reached a town which was not
very well furnished with inns. Since it was the Abbot's wish to
stop there, Alessandro had him dismount at the home of an inn-
keeper who had once been his servant, and saw to it that he was
given the least uncomfortable room in the house. Alessandro,
who was an experienced traveler and had by now become the
Abbot's majordomo, arranged as best he could for quarters for
the Abbot's entire company, lodging some in one place and some
in another. The Abbot had dined, a good part of the night had
already passed, and everyone had gone to bed when Alessandro
asked the innkeeper where he could sleep.

To this question, the innkeeper replied:

"To tell the truth, I don't know. As you can see, everything is
occupied, and my family and I are sleeping on benches, but
there are some grain chests in the Abbot's room, and if you like
I can show you where they are and have some sort of bed fixed
up for you in there where you can sleep as best you can for
tonight."

To this Alessandro answered:

"How can I fit in the Abbot's room? It's so small that none of
his monks could even lie down there in that narrow space. If
only I had known about this before the curtains of the Abbot's
bed were drawn, I could have made his monks sleep on the
chests, and I could have slept where the monks are sleeping!"

Then the innkeeper said:

"That's how things stand; if you like, you can be quite com-
fortable there. The Abbot is sleeping and his curtains are drawn;
I can quietly put a mattress there for you and you can go to
sleep."

When he realized that he could do this without bothering the
Abbot, Alessandro agreed, and they arranged matters there as
quietly as they could. But the Abbot was not sleeping; rather, he
was meditating intensely on his newly aroused desires, and he
overheard what the innkeeper and Alessandro were saying as
well as where Alessandro was going to be sleeping. With great
delight he began saying to himself:

"God has given me the opportunity, and if I do not take advantage of it, the chance may not come my way again for a long time."

Determined to take advantage of it, the Abbot waited until all was completely quiet in the inn and then in a low voice he called Alessandro and told him to lie down beside him. After many a polite refusal, Alessandro undressed and did so. The Abbot placed his hand on Alessandro's breast and began to caress him the way young girls do their lovers, and Alessandro, who was amazed at this, feared that the Abbot had been seized by some unnatural passion or else he would not have grabbed him in this manner. But either by intuition or from some movement on Alessandro's part, the Abbot immediately sensed Alessandro's suspicion and smiled, then, quickly opening his own shirt, he took Alessandro's hand and placed it upon his breast, saying:

"Alessandro, get rid of that foolish idea; put your hand here and find out what I am hiding."

Alessandro placed his hand upon the Abbot's chest and discovered two nicely shaped little breasts, as firm and as delicate as if they had been carved out of ivory. When he discovered them and realized instantly that the Abbot was a woman, awaiting no further invitation, he quickly embraced her and wanted to kiss her, when she declared:

"Before you come any closer, listen to what I have to tell you. As you can see for yourself, I am a woman and not a man; I left my home a virgin, and I was going to the Pope to be married, and through your good fortune or my own misfortune, whatever the case may be, I fell so much in love with you when I saw you the other day that no woman ever burned with more love for another man. For this reason I have decided to take you as my husband over all other men; so if you do not wish to take me as your wife, leave here immediately and return to where you were."

Although Alessandro knew nothing about her, he judged from the company she kept that she must be noble and wealthy, and he could see for himself that she was very beautiful; so, without giving the matter another thought, he replied that if the arrangement pleased her, it was certainly most pleasing to him. Then she sat up in bed, and in front of a small table where an image of Our Lord stood, she placed a ring on his finger and made him promise to marry her; afterward they embraced and kissed and to the great pleasure of both parties, they enjoyed each other for the rest of the night. After agreeing to certain arrangements and deciding exactly what to do, at daybreak Alessandro got out of bed and left the room as silently as he had entered it, without anyone knowing where he had spent the night; then, content beyond all measure, he set out once more with the Abbot and her company, and after many days they reached Rome.

After they had been there for several days, the Abbot, accompanied only by the two knights and Alessandro, went to visit the Pope, and after paying him their respects in the customary manner, the Abbot began to speak in this fashion:

"Holy Father, as you know better than all others, anyone who wishes to live a good and honest life must avoid, insofar as he is able, everything which might lead him to do the opposite; to this end, I myself, being a person who wishes to lead a totally honest life, set out dressed in the clothes you see on me now to seek the blessing of your holiness for my marriage, but I have fled in secret, taking with me a large part of the treasures belonging to my father, the King of England, who planned to have me marry the King of Scotland, who is an extremely old man, whereas I, as you can see, am so young. What caused me to flee was not so much the old age of the King of Scotland but rather the fear that if I were married to him, because of the fragility of my youth, I might commit some act contrary to divine law and against the honor of the royal blood of my father. In this frame of mind I was on my way here when God, Who alone knows what is best for all of us, moved, as I believe, by His compassion, set before my eyes the man whom He chose to be my husband, and that person is the very man," she said as she pointed to Alessandro, "whom you see standing by my side, whose manners and valor are worthy of any great lady, even if his blood is perhaps not as obviously noble as that of a person of royal birth. Therefore, I have taken him and it is he I desire, nor will I ever accept any other man no matter what my father or others might think; thus, the main reason for my journey has been removed, but I should like to make my journey complete by visiting the holy and sacred sites of which this city abounds and by meeting your holiness so that through you, the marriage contract made between Alessandro and me, in the presence of God alone, may be made public in your presence and in the presence of all men. I humbly beseech you, then, that what was found pleasing to God and to myself may also find favor with you and that you give us your blessing, so that with more certainty of pleasing Him whose vicar you are on earth, we may, to the glory of God and yourself, live together until death do us part."

When Alessandro heard that his wife was the daughter of the King of England, he was both astonished and filled with a wonderful secret joy, but the two knights were even more amazed and were so upset that if they had been anywhere else other than in the presence of the Pope, they would have harmed Alessandro and perhaps even the lady as well. The Pope, too, was amazed both by the manner in which the lady was dressed and by her choice of husbands, but realizing that there was no turning back now, he decided to grant her request. He was aware that the knights were angry, so first he mollified them; then, having reconciled them with the lady and Alessandro, he arranged for what was to be done. On the appointed day, before all his cardinals and a large number of distinguished noblemen who were invited to the magnificent celebration arranged by the Pope, he summoned the lady, who came forth regally dressed, so beautiful and charming that she was praised by all present; and then Alessandro, in like manner, came forward so splendidly attired and honorably accompanied by two knights that his appearance and manners made him seem more like a man of royal blood than one who loaned money as a profession; then the Pope solemnly celebrated the nuptials from the beginning, and following a sumptuous wedding feast, he dismissed them with his blessing.

On leaving Rome, it was the wish of Alessandro and the lady to go to Florence, where the news of their marriage had already arrived, and where they were received with the highest honors by her citizens. The lady had the three brothers released from prison, after seeing to it that all of their creditors were paid, and then had them and their wives restored to their possessions, and with the good wishes of all concerned, Alessandro and his lady, taking Agolante with them, left Florence and came to Paris, where they were honorably received by the King.

From there the two knights went to England and worked on the King to the extent that he pardoned his daughter and received her and his son-in-law with a magnificent celebration, not long after which with great pomp and ceremony he knighted his son-in-law and made him the Earl of Cornwall. Alessandro was clever and skillful enough to reconcile the King with his son, which was most beneficial to the entire island, and in so doing he won the love and the favor of all its inhabitants; Agolante, in the meantime, recovered everything that was owed him, and rich beyond all measure he returned to Florence, having been knighted by Lord Alessandro. As for the Earl, he lived most gloriously with his lady, and some people even claim that with his intelligence and valor, and the assistance of his father-in-law, he later conquered Scotland and was crowned its King.

[Second Day, Fourth Story]

❦

Landolfo Rufolo is impoverished, becomes a pirate, and is ship-wrecked after being captured by the Genoese, but he escapes on a chest filled with very precious jewels; after he is rescued by a woman on Corfu, he returns home a rich man.

WHEN Lauretta, who was sitting next to Pampinea, saw that she had brought her tale to its glorious conclusion, without further delay she began to speak in this manner:

Most gracious ladies, in my opinion there can be no greater act of Fortune than to see someone raised from the depths of poverty to a royal estate, as Pampinea's story demonstrated to us in the case of what happened to Alessandro. And since no one telling a story on the proposed topic can possibly exceed the limits she has established, I shall not be ashamed to tell you a tale which, while it may yet contain greater misfortunes, nevertheless does not end in such a splendid fashion. I am very well aware that when the previous story is kept in mind, my own will be listened to less attentively, but I trust you will forgive me, since it is the best I can do.

The coast between Reggio and Gaeta is considered to be probably the most delightful part of Italy; in this region close to Salerno there is a stretch of land overlooking the sea which the inhabitants call the Amalfi coast, and it is full of small towns, gardens, and fountains, and also full of as rich and successful merchants as you can find anywhere. Among those small towns there is one called Ravello in which, while there is many a wealthy man living there today, there was one in those days who was very rich indeed named Landolfo Rufolo; but unsatisfied with his wealth and wishing to double it, he very nearly lost it all and his life as well.

This man, then, having made the sort of calculations that merchants are accustomed to do, purchased a very large ship, loaded it down with various goods bought at his own expense, and sailed with it all to Cyprus. There he found that other ships had docked carrying the very same kinds of merchandise he had brought over, and because of this, not only was he forced to sell his cargo at a lower price than he had paid for it, but he was practically obliged to give his merchandise away for nothing, thus being brought to the verge of ruin. Very much upset by this affair, not knowing what to do, and seeing himself who once had been a very wealthy man now become in a brief time almost impoverished, he decided that he would either kill himself or make up his losses by stealing, in this way not having to return home poor after having been rich. He found a buyer for his large ship, and with that money together with what he had made from selling his cargo, he bought a smaller, lighter ship, suited to a pirate, and armed and fitted it out splendidly for such an enterprise, and set out to make other men's property his own, especially that belonging to the Turks.

In this enterprise, Fortune was much more favorable to him than she had been to his trading business. Within the space of about a year, he had plundered and seized so many Turkish ships that he found he had not only regained what he had lost as a merchant, but had by now more than doubled his wealth. Made wary by the pain of his first loss, he determined not to risk a second mistake and persuaded himself that what he had was quite sufficient, and so he decided to return home with the loot. Still, fearful of any commercial, business ventures, he did not bother to invest his money elsewhere, and oars at full speed, he set out for home in the small ship which had earned him his money. When he reached the Archipelago, one evening a sirocco wind began blowing head-on, making the sea very rough and unmanageable for his small boat, and so he took shelter in an inlet on the leeward side of a little island, where he decided to wait for a better wind. Not long afterward, two large Genoese merchant ships, which had set sail from Constantinople, with difficulty reached the same inlet to escape the same bad weather from which Landolfo had taken shelter. These ships were blocking Landolfo's escape route, and when the crew aboard them recognized his ship, knowing who he was and how rich he had become, being by nature greedy and rapacious men, they decided to seize his ship. They sent part of their well-armed party ashore with crossbows and placed them in such a position that no one could disembark from Landolfo's ship without being shot down with their arrows; the rest of their crew launched rowboats and, aided by the current, drew near to Landolfo's smaller vessel and captured it and its entire crew with very little trouble and in little time without losing a single man in the struggle. They removed Landolfo and put him on one of their ships dressed only in an old jacket; then they removed all the cargo from the ship and sank it.

The following day the wind changed, and the two ships set sail on a westerly course, and everything went well that day; but toward evening a gale began to blow, causing high seas, and the two ships were separated. And with the force of this wind, it happened that the ship which carried the miserable and destitute Landolfo struck a sandbank off the island of Cephalonia with a tremendous crash, splitting apart, breaking up into small pieces like a glass smashed against a wall. As is usually the case in such accidents, the sea was now strewn with floating cargo, chests, and planks, and although the night was pitch-black and there was a heavy swell, the unfortunate wretches who had been on the ship and knew how to swim began to cling to any object that happened to float by.

Poor Landolfo was among them, and while the day before he had called upon Death to take him, preferring to die rather than return home impoverished as he was now, seeing Death close at hand, he was afraid, and like the others he, too, clung to the first plank that came within reach in the hope that perhaps if he delayed his drowning, God might come to his rescue; he lay straddled on the plank as best he could, and tossed back and forth by the sea and the wind, he held on until daybreak. When he saw the light of day, he looked around him and found nothing but clouds and sea and a chest which floated on the waves, and from time to time, to his great terror, it would drift toward him, for he was afraid that it might hit him and drown him; and every time it got too close to him, as best he could, with his hand and with the little strength he had left, he would push it away. But as luck would have it, suddenly the sea was struck by a strong gust of wind that drove the chest against the plank to which Landolfo was clinging, turning it over and causing Landolfo to lose his grip and sink beneath the waves; thanks more to his fear than his strength, he came up swimming only to see that his plank had floated far off, and so, fearing that he might not be able to reach it, he swam toward the chest, which was closer, and he draped himself over its lid, as best he could, keeping it upright with his arms. And in this fashion, tossed about this way and that by the sea, without a thing to eat and far more to drink than he might have wished, not knowing where he was and seeing nothing but ocean, he floated all that day and the following night.

The next day Landolfo, who had almost turned into a sponge, was gripping tightly with both hands the edges of the chest the way a man about to drown will grab onto anything that will save him, when either through God's will or the wind's force, he reached the coast of the island of Corfu, where he was spotted by a poor woman who happened to be scouring her pots in the sand and seawater. She could not make out what the shapeless form of Landolfo was as it approached, and afraid, she ran off screaming. Landolfo could not speak and could see very little, so he said nothing to her, but as the current brought him closer to the shore, the woman recognized the shape of a chest and gradually, as she looked closer, she could make out first his arms hanging over the chest, then, catching a glimpse of his face, she realized what it was. And moved by compassion, she waded out into the ocean, which was by now calm, took Landolfo by the hair, and dragged him and the chest onto the land, and there, with some difficulty, she loosened Landolfo's hands from the chest and placed it on the head of her young daughter who was with her, while she picked up Landolfo the way you would a small child and carried him to the village, where she put him in a warm bath and scrubbed him down and washed him off with warm water until some of the warmth and strength which he had lost returned. And when she thought the time was right, she took him out of the water and nourished him with some good wine and confections,* and after she had nursed him for several days as best she could, he recovered his strength and began to realize where he was. Then the good woman thought it was time for her to give him back his chest, which she had salvaged for him, and to tell him that it was time for him to leave and fend for himself; and this she did.

Landolfo had forgotten about the chest, but he took it when the good woman presented it to him, thinking that even if it was of little value, he might yet make several days' living expenses out of it; but when he discovered that it was very light, his hopes began to diminish considerably. Nevertheless, when the good woman was out of the house, he pried it open to see what was inside, and inside he discovered many precious stones, some in settings and others loose; Landolfo, who knew something about such stones, realized the moment he saw them that they were of great value, and he thanked God that He had not decided to abandon him yet, and he was considerably cheered up by this. But as a man who had been fiercely buffeted two times by Fortune in a short space of time and was wary of a third, he thought that this time a great deal of caution would be necessary

---

*Whenever Boccaccio uses the term *confetto* or *confetti*, we usually translate it as "confections," meaning a sweet and nourishing preparation, often meant to accompany wine.

in order to bring those jewels safely home; therefore, he wrapped them, as carefully as he could, in some old rags, and told the good woman that he no longer needed the chest but that if she liked she could keep it in exchange for a sack.

The good woman did so most willingly, and after Landolfo had thanked her as best he knew how for all the good she had done him, he threw his sack over his shoulder and left her; first he embarked on a ship going to Brindisi and then, traveling along the coastline, he went up to Trani, where he ran into some of his own townspeople who were cloth merchants. Without making mention of the chest he recounted all his adventures to them, and they, for the love of God, gave him new clothes, loaned him a horse, and found him an escort that would take him as far as Ravello, where he wished to return at all costs.

Finding himself safe at home, he thanked God for guiding him there and opened his sack, and after examining every jewel with more care than he had previously done, he realized that he had so many stones and that they were of such quality that even by selling them at a reasonable price, or even less, he would be twice as rich as when he had set out. When he found a way of selling the stones, all the way to Corfu as a reward for her services he sent a large sum of money to the good woman who had pulled him out of the sea, and he did likewise to those who had given him new clothes in Trani. The rest he kept and without ever again wishing to practice the trade of a merchant, he lived splendidly the rest of his life.

[Second Day, Fifth Story]

❖

Andreuccio from Perugia goes to Naples to buy horses, is caught up in three unfortunate adventures in one night, escapes from them all, and returns home with a ruby.

THE precious stones found by Landolfo—said Fiammetta, whose turn it was to tell the next tale—remind me of a story no less full of dangers than the one recounted by Lauretta, but it differs from hers in that these dangers all occur within the space of a single night, as you are about to hear, whereas in her story they happened over a period of several years.

There once lived in Perugia, according to what I have been

told, a young man whose name was Andreuccio di Pietro, a dealer in horses who, when he heard that in Naples horses were being sold at a low price, put five hundred gold florins in his purse and, though he had never been outside of his own town before, set out for Naples with some other merchants and arrived there on Sunday evening around vespers, and at the advice of his landlord the following morning he went to the marketplace, where he saw many horses, a good number of which he liked, but he was not able to strike a bargain no matter how hard he tried; in fact, to show that he was really ready to do business, being the crass and incautious fool that he was, more than once he pulled out his purse full of florins in front of everyone who passed by. While he was in the midst of these dealings, with his purse on full display, a young and very beautiful Sicilian lady— one who, for a small price, would be happy to please any man—passed close to him, and without being seen by him, she caught a glimpse of his purse and immediately said to herself:

"Who would be better off than I if that money were mine?"—and she walked past.

With this young lady there was an old woman, also Sicilian, who, when she saw Andreuccio, let her young companion walk ahead while she ran up to him and embraced him affectionately; when the young girl saw this, she said nothing, and waited nearby for her companion. Andreuccio turned around, recognized the old woman, and greeted her with a great deal of pleasure, and after she promised to visit him at his inn, they said no more and parted company, and Andreuccio returned to his bargaining; but he bought nothing that morning.

The young woman who had first seen Andreuccio's purse as well as his familiarity with her older companion cautiously began to ask who that man was and where he came from and what he was doing there and how her friend knew him, in order to see if she could find a way of getting that money of his—if not all of it, at least a part. The old woman told her everything about Andreuccio almost as well as he himself might have told it, for she had lived a long time in Sicily and then in Perugia with Andreuccio's father; she also told her where he was staying and why he had come. Once the young woman felt herself well enough informed about his relatives and their names, she devised a cunning trick, based on what she had learned, to satisfy her desires. As soon as she returned home, she sent the old woman on errands for the entire day so that she would not be able to return to Andreuccio; then, around vespers, she sent one of her young servant girls, whom she had well trained for such missions, to the inn where Andreuccio was staying. Arriving there, the servant girl found Andreuccio by chance alone at the door, and she asked him where Andreuccio was. When he told her he was standing right before her, drawing him aside, she said:

"Sir, a genteel lady who lives in this city would like to speak to you at your leisure."

When Andreuccio heard this, he immediately assumed, for he considered himself a handsome young man, that such a woman as that must be in love with him (as if there were no man in all of Naples as handsome as he), and he immediately replied that he was ready and asked her where and when this lady wished to speak to him. To this, the young servant girl answered:

"Sir, whenever you wish to come, she awaits you at her home."

Quickly, and without mentioning anything to anyone at the inn, Andreuccio replied:

"Let's go, then, you lead the way; I'll follow you."

Whereupon the servant girl led him to her house, which was in a district called the Malpertugio, which was as respectable a district as its very name implies.* But Andreuccio knew or suspected nothing, believing he was going to a most respectable place and to the house of a respectable lady, and so he calmly followed the servant girl into the house. Climbing up the stairs, the servant girl called to her mistress: "Here's Andreuccio!" and he saw her appear at the head of the stairs to greet him.

She was still very young, tall, with a very beautiful face, and elegantly dressed and adorned. Andreuccio started toward her, and she descended three steps to greet him with open arms, and throwing her arms around his neck, she remained in that position for a while without saying a word—as if some overpowering emotion had stolen her words—then she started crying and kissing his forehead, and in a broken voice she said:

"Oh my Andreuccio, how happy I am to see you!"

Andreuccio, amazed at such tender greetings, and completely astonished, replied:

"My lady, the pleasure is mine!"

Then she took his hand and led him through her sitting room, and from there, without saying a word, into her bedroom, which was all scented with roses, orange blossoms, and other fragrances; there he saw a very beautiful curtained bed, and many dresses hanging on pegs (as was the custom there), and

*This ill-famed district of Naples actually existed in Boccaccio's day, and its name might best be rendered into English as "Evilhole."

other very beautiful and expensive things. And since all those lovely things were new to him, Andreuccio was convinced that she had to be nothing less than a great lady. They sat together on a chest at the foot of her bed, and she began speaking to him:

"Andreuccio, I am quite sure that you are amazed at my tears and caresses, for perhaps you do not know me or do not remember hearing of me; but you are about to hear something that will amaze you even more: I am your sister! And now that God has granted me the favor of seeing one of my brothers before I die (oh, how I wish I could see them all!), I assure you I shall pass away content. Since you know nothing about this, I shall tell you. Pietro, your father and mine, as I think you probably know, resided for a long time in Palermo, and because of his kindness and friendliness, he was dearly loved and still is loved by those who knew him; but among those who loved him very much, my mother, who was a lady of noble birth and then a widow, was the one who loved him the most, so much so that she put aside the fear of her father and brothers and her own honor and lived with him in so intimate a way that I was born, and here I am right here before your eyes. Then when Pietro had to leave Palermo and return to Perugia, he left me, a tiny child, with my mother, and as far as I know, he never thought of me or my mother again. If he were not my father, I would criticize him severely for his ingratitude toward my mother (to say nothing of the love he owed me, his daughter, not born from any servant girl or from some woman of low birth), who had put herself as well as her possessions into his hands, moved by a true love for a man she did not really know.

"But what does it matter? Things done badly in the past are more easily criticized than amended—that's how it all ended. He abandoned me as a little girl in Palermo, where, grown up almost as much as I am now, my mother, who was a rich lady, gave me as a wife to a rich man of noble birth from Agrigento who, out of his love for me and my mother, came to live in Palermo; and there, as he was an avid supporter of the Guelfs,* he began to carry on some kind of intrigue with our King Charles. But King Frederick discovered the plot before it could be put into effect, and this was the cause of our fleeing from

---

*The Guelfs, supporters of the Papacy, were opposed by the Ghibellines, the imperial party in medieval Italy. The names are derived from "Waiblingen" and "Welf," the names of two twelfth-century families heading rival parties in the Holy Roman Empire.

Sicily—and just when I was about to become the greatest lady that island ever knew. Taking with us those few things we could (I say "few" as compared to the many things we owned), we abandoned our lands and palaces and took refuge in this land, where we found King Charles so grateful to us that he restored in part the losses which we had suffered on his account, and he gave us property and houses; and he continues to provide my husband, your brother-in-law, with a good salary, as you can see for yourself; and so, my sweet brother, here I am, and with no thanks to you but rather through the mercy of God I have come to meet you."

And having said all this, she embraced him once more, and continuing to weep tenderly, she kissed his forehead. Hearing this fable so carefully and skillfully told by the young lady, who never hesitated over a word or fumbled in any way, Andreuccio recalled it was indeed true that his father had been in Palermo, and since he himself knew the ways of young men who easily fall in love when they are young and since he had just witnessed the piteous tears, the embraces, and the pure kisses of this young lady, he took everything she said to be the absolute truth; and when she had finished speaking, he said:

"My lady, it should not surprise you to see me amazed, for to tell the truth, either my father never spoke of you and your mother, or, if he did, I never heard a word about it, for I had no more knowledge of you than if you never existed; but I am all the more delighted to have found a sister, for I am completely alone here, and I never hoped for such a thing and, truly, I don't know of any man of whatever rank or station to whom you would not be very dear, not to mention an insignificant merchant like me. But I beg you to clarify one thing for me: how did you know I was here?"

To this she answered:

"I was told about it this morning by a poor woman whom I often see, and according to her story, she was with our father for a long time both in Palermo and in Perugia; and if it were not for the fact that it seemed to me more proper for you to come to my house than for me to visit you in a stranger's house, I would have come to see you much sooner."

Then she began to ask about all his relatives individually by name, and Andreuccio replied to all her questions about them, and her questions made him believe even more of what he should not have believed at all. They talked for a long time, and since it was so hot that day, she had Greek wine and confections served to Andreuccio; then it was suppertime, and Andreuccio got up to leave, but the lady would not hear of this, and pretending to get angry, she said as she embraced him:

"Alas, poor me! How clearly I see that you care very little for me! How is it possible? Here you are with a sister of yours that you have never seen before, and she is in her own house, where you ought to be staying, and you want to leave her, to eat at some inn? You shall certainly dine with me, and though my husband is not here (a fact which displeases me a great deal) I shall honor you as best a woman can."

Not knowing what to say to this, Andreuccio replied:

"I hold you as dear as one can hold a sister, but if I don't leave, they'll wait all evening for me to come to supper, and I'll make a bad impression."

And she said:

"God be praised! As if I did not have anyone to send to tell them not to wait for you! But you would do me an even greater courtesy by inviting all of your companions to have supper here and then, if you still wished to leave, you could all leave together."

Andreuccio replied that he did not want to be with his companions that evening, and that he would stay as she wished. Then she pretended to send someone to notify the inn that he should not be expected for supper; and, after much conversation, they finally sat down and were served a number of splendid courses, and she cleverly prolonged the supper until night came; then, when they got up from the table and Andreuccio decided it was time to leave, she said that under no circumstances would she permit it, for Naples was not the kind of town in which to wander around at night, especially if you were a stranger, and furthermore, she said that when she had sent the message telling them not to expect him for supper, she had also told them not to expect him back that night. Since he believed everything she said and enjoyed being with her, because of his false belief, he decided to stay with her. After supper, and not without her reasons, she kept him engaged in a lengthy conversation; and when a good part of the night had passed, she left Andreuccio in her bedroom in the company of a young boy who would assist him if he wanted anything, and she withdrew into another bedroom with her chambermaids.

The heat of the night was intense, and because of this and since he was alone, Andreuccio quickly stripped to his waist and took off his pants, placing them at the head of the bed; and then the natural need of having to deposit the superfluous load in his stomach beckoned him, so he asked the boy servant where he should do it, and the boy pointed to a place in one corner of the bedroom and said: "Go in there."

Andreuccio innocently entered the place and as he did, by chance he happened to step on a plank which was not nailed to the beam it rested on; this overturned the plank, and he with the plank plunged down through the floor. But by the love of God he was spared from hurting himself in the fall, in spite of the height from which he fell; he was, however, completely covered by the filth that filled the place. In order for you to understand better just what took place and what was going to take place, I shall now describe to you the kind of place it was. Andreuccio was in a narrow alley like the kind we often see between two houses; some planks had been nailed on two beams placed between one house and the other, and there was a place to sit down; and the plank which plunged with him to the bottom was precisely one of these two supporting planks.

Andreuccio, finding himself down there in the alley, to his great discomfort, began calling the boy, but as soon as the boy heard Andreuccio fall, he ran to tell the lady, and she rushed to Andreuccio's bedroom and quickly checked to see if his clothes were still there. She found his clothes and in them his money, which he stupidly always carried with him, for he did not trust anyone; and when this woman of Palermo, pretending to be the sister of a Perugian, had gotten what she had set her trap for, she quickly locked the exit he had gone through when he fell, and she no longer was concerned about him.

When the boy did not answer, Andreuccio began to call him more loudly, but that did not help either; then he became suspicious, and began to realize (only too late) that he had been tricked. He climbed over a small wall which closed that alley from the street and ran to the door of the house, which he recognized all too well, and there he shouted and shook and pounded on the door for a long time, but all in vain. Then, as one who sees clearly his misfortune, he began to sob, saying:

"Alas, poor me! I have lost five hundred florins and a sister, and in so short a time!"

And after many such laments, he began all over again to beat on the door and to scream; and he kept this up for so long that many of the neighbors were awakened and forced out of bed by the disturbance; one of the lady's servants, pretending to be sleepy, came to the window and said in a complaining tone of voice: "Who's that knocking down there?"

"Oh," said Andreuccio, "don't you recognize me? I am Andreuccio, brother to Madam Fiordaliso."

To this the servant replied:

"My good man, if you've drunk too much, go sleep it off and come back in the morning; I don't know what Andreuccio you are talking about or any other nonsense. Off with you, and let us sleep, if you please!"

"What," said Andreuccio, "you don't know what I'm talking about? You've got to know; but if this is what it is like to be related in Sicily—that you forget your ties so quickly—then at least give me back the clothes I left up there, and in God's name I'll gladly be off!"

To this, in a laughing voice the woman replied:

"You must be dreaming, my good man!"

No sooner had she said this than she shut the window. Andreuccio, now most certain of his loss, was so vexed that his anger was turning to rage, and he decided to get back by force what he could not get back with words: he picked up a large stone and began all over again—but with harder blows this time—to beat furiously at the door, and many of the neighbors who had been aroused from their beds not long before thought that he was some sort of pest who had invented all this to bother that good lady, and so they took offense at the racket he was making. They appeared at their windows, and began to shout in a way not unlike all the dogs in a neighborhood who bark at a stray:

"It's an outrage to come at this hour to a decent lady's house and shout such foul things. In God's name leave, good man; let us sleep, if you don't mind; if you have any business with her, come back tomorrow and don't bother us anymore tonight."

The good woman's pimp, who was inside the house and whom Andreuccio had neither seen nor heard, taking courage from his neighbors' words, exclaimed in a horrible, ferocious, roaring voice:

"Who's down there?"

Andreuccio raised his head at the sound of that voice and saw someone who, as far as he could tell, looked like some sort of big shot; he had a thick black beard and was yawning and rubbing his eyes as if he had just been awakened from a sound sleep. Andreuccio, not without fear, replied:

"I am the brother of the lady who lives here . . ."

But the man did not wait for Andreuccio to finish what he had to say; with a voice more menacing than the first time, he howled:

"I don't know what's keeping me from coming down there and

beating the shit out of you, you dumb ass, you drunken sot—you're not going to let anybody get any sleep tonight, are you?"

He turned inside and banged the window shut. Some of the neighbors, who knew this man for what he was, said to Andreuccio in a kindly way:

"For God's sake, man, get out of here quick before you witness your own murder tonight! For your own good, leave!"

Frightened by the voice and face of the man at the window and persuaded by the advice of the neighbors, who seemed kindly disposed toward him, Andreuccio, as sorrowful as anyone ever could be and despairing over the loss of his money, and not knowing which way to go, started moving in the direction that the servant girl had led him that day, as he tried to find his way back to the inn. Even *he* found the stench he was giving off disgusting; so, turning to the left, he took a street called Catalan Street and headed for the sea in order to wash himself off; but he was heading toward the upper part of town, and in so doing, he happened to see two men with lanterns in their hands coming in his direction, and fearing that they might be the police or other men who could do him harm, he cautiously took shelter in a hut he saw nearby. But the two men were headed for the very same spot and they, too, entered the hut; once inside, one of them put down the iron tools he was carrying and began examining them and discussing them with the other. All of a sudden, one of them remarked:

"What's going on here? That's the worst stink I've ever smelled!"

As he said this, he tilted his lantern up a bit and saw Andreuccio, the poor devil. Amazed, he asked:

"Who's there?"

Andreuccio did not utter a word; the two men drew closer with the light, and one of them asked him how he had gotten so filthy; Andreuccio told them everything that had happened to him. Having guessed where all this must have taken place, they said to each other:

"This guy really knows the head of the Mafia—he's been to Spitfire's place!"*

Turning to Andreuccio, one of them said:

"My good man, you might have lost your money, but you still have God to thank for not going back into the house after you

---

*Spitfire (*Buttafuoco*) is called a *scarabone* by the two men in the original Italian, meaning an important figure in the local criminal underworld—what is known today as the Camorra, a Neapolitan equivalent of the Sicilian Mafia.

fell; if you had not fallen, you can be sure that before you fell
asleep, you would have been murdered and, along with your
money, you would have lost your life. You have as much chance
of getting a penny of your money back as you do of plucking a
star from the sky! You could even get killed if that guy finds
out you ever said a word about it!"

After telling him this, he consulted with his companion for a
while, then said:

"Look, we've taken pity on you, so if you want to come with
us and do what we plan to do, we're sure that your share of
what we all get will be more than what you've lost."

Andreuccio was so desperate that he said he was willing to go
along. That day an Archbishop of Naples named Messer Filippo
Minutolo had been buried, and with him the richest of vestments
and a ruby on his finger which was worth more than five
hundred gold florins; this is what they were out to get, and they
let Andreuccio in on their plan. More avaricious than wise, he
set off with them, and as they made their way toward the cathe-
dral, Andreuccio stank so badly that one of them said:

"Can't we find some way for this guy to wash up a little, so
that he doesn't stink so bad?"

The other answered:

"All right. We're near a well that should have a pulley and a
large bucket; let's go give him a quick washing up."

When they reached the well, they discovered that the rope
was there but the bucket had been removed, so they decided be-
tween themselves that they would tie Andreuccio to the rope and
lower him into the well, and he could wash himself down there;
then, when he was washed, he could tug on the rope and they
would pull him up. And this is what they did. It happened that
no sooner had they lowered him into the well than some police
watchmen, who had been chasing someone else and were thirsty
because of the heat, came to the well for a drink; when the two
men saw the police heading for the well, they quickly fled with-
out being seen.

Andreuccio, who had just cleaned himself up at the bottom of
the well, gave a pull on the rope. The thirsty night watchmen
had just laid down their shields, arms, and other gear and were
beginning to pull up the rope, thinking that a bucket full of
water was at the other end. When Andreuccio saw himself near-
ing the rim of the well, he dropped the rope and grabbed the
edge with his two hands; when the night watchmen saw him,
they were terrified, and dropping the rope without wasting a
word, they began to run away as fast as they could. Andreuccio

was very surprised at all this, and if he had not held on tightly, he would have fallen back to the bottom of the well and perhaps have hurt himself seriously or even killed himself; when he climbed out and discovered the weapons, which he knew his companions had not brought with them, he became even more puzzled. Afraid, not understanding a thing, and lamenting his misfortune, he decided to leave that spot without touching a thing; and off he went, not knowing where he was going.

But on his way, he ran into his two companions, who were on their way back to pull him out of the well, and when they saw him, they were amazed and asked him who had pulled him out of the well. Andreuccio replied that he did not know, and then he told them exactly what had happened and what he had discovered near the well. They then realized what had actually taken place and, laughing, they told him why they had run away and who the people were who had pulled him up. Without any further conversation (for it was already midnight), they went to the cathedral and managed to get in without any trouble at all; they went up to the tomb, which was very large and made of marble; with their iron bars, they raised up the heavy cover just as much as was necessary for a man to get inside, and then they propped it up. And when this was done, one of them said:

"Who'll go inside?"

To this, the other replied:

"Not me!"

"Not me either," answered the other. "You go, Andreuccio."

"Not me," said Andreuccio.

Both of them turned toward Andreuccio and said:

"What do you mean, you won't go in? By God, if you don't, we'll beat your head in with one of these iron bars till you drop dead!"

This frightened Andreuccio, so he climbed in, and as he entered the tomb, he thought to himself:

"These guys are making me go into the tomb to cheat me: as soon as I give them everything that's inside and I am trying to get out of the tomb, they will take off with the goods and leave me with nothing!"

And so he thought about protecting his own share from the start: he remembered the two men had talked about an expensive ring, so as soon as he had climbed into the tomb, he took the ring from the Archbishop's finger and placed it on his own; then he handed out the Archbishop's staff, his miter, and his gloves, and stripping him down to his shirt, he handed over everything to them, announcing, finally, that there was nothing left, but they insisted that the ring must be there and told him to look all over for it; but Andreuccio answered that he could not find it, and he kept them waiting there for some time while he pretended to search for it. The other two, on the other hand, were just as tricky as Andreuccio was trying to be, and at the right moment they pulled away the prop that held up the cover and fled, leaving Andreuccio trapped inside the tomb.

When Andreuccio heard this, you can imagine how he felt. He tried time and again, with both his head and his shoulders, to raise the cover, but he labored in vain; overcome with despair, he fainted and fell upon the dead body of the Archbishop; and anyone seeing the two of them there together would have had a hard time telling which one of them was really dead: he or the Archbishop. Regaining consciousness, he began to sob bitterly, realizing that being where he was, without any doubt one of two kinds of death awaited him: either he would die in the tomb from hunger and from the stench of the maggots on the dead body (that is, if no one came to open the tomb); or, if someone came and found him in the tomb, he would be hanged as a thief.

With this terrible thought in his head, and filled with grief, he heard people walking and talking in the church; they were people, it seemed to him, who had come to do what he and his companions had already done—this terrified him all the more! As soon as these people raised the cover of the tomb and propped it up, they began arguing about who should go in, and no one wanted to do so; then, after a long discussion, a priest said:

"Why are you afraid? Do you think he is going to eat you? The dead don't eat the living! I'll go inside myself."

After saying this, he leaned his chest against the rim of the tomb, then swung around and put his legs inside, and he was about to climb down when Andreuccio saw him and rose to his feet, grabbing the priest by one of his legs and pretending to pull him down. When the priest felt this, he let out a terrible scream and instantly jumped out of the tomb. This terrified all the others, who, leaving the tomb open, began to flee as if a hundred thousand devils were chasing them.

Andreuccio, happy beyond his wildest dreams, jumped out of the tomb and left the church by the way he had come in. It was almost dawn, and he started wandering about with the ring on his finger until finally he reached the waterfront and stumbled upon his inn, where he found that the innkeeper and his companions had been up all night worried about him.

He told them the story of what had happened to him, and the

innkeeper advised him to leave Naples immediately; he did so at once and returned to Perugia, having invested his money in a ring when he had set out to buy horses.

[Second Day, Sixth Story]

❦

Madam Beritola, after losing her two sons, is found on an island with two roebucks and goes to Lunigiana; there one of her sons joins the service of its lord, sleeps with his daughter, and is put into prison; after Sicily rebels against King Charles and the son is recognized by his mother, he marries his lord's daughter, finds his brother, and everyone returns home to high-ranking positions.

THE young ladies and men all laughed heartily over Andreuccio's adventures as recounted by Fiammetta, and when Emilia saw that the story had come to an end, at the Queen's command she began as follows:

The vicissitudes of Fortune can be painful and irritating, but since whenever they are discussed, our minds, which are easily lulled to sleep by her promises, are as often rudely awakened, I nevertheless believe that no one, whether he be fortunate or unfortunate, should ever tire of hearing about them, since these accounts provide the fortunate with a warning and the unfortunate with consolation. Though a good deal has already been said on the subject, I intend to tell you a story no less true than moving, and while it may have a happy ending, the grief it entails was so great and lasted for so long a time that I can hardly believe it was sweetened by the happiness which followed.

Dear ladies, you should know that Manfred,* who was crowned King of Sicily, after the death of Frederick the Second, held no one at his court in higher esteem than a gentleman from Naples named Arrighetto Capece, who had a beautiful and noble wife, also from Naples, named Madam Beritola Caracciola. While Arrighetto was governing the island, he learned that King Charles had defeated and killed Manfred at Benevento and that the entire island had gone over to King Charles's side; placing

---

*Manfred (1232–66), a Ghibelline and ex-communicate, was killed at the battle of Benevento.

little reliance upon the faithfulness of the Sicilians and not wishing to become the subject of his master's enemy, Arrighetto prepared to flee. But when this was discovered by the Sicilians, he and many other friends and servants of King Manfred were immediately taken prisoner and given up to King Charles, along, shortly afterward, with possession of the whole island. In this sudden change of affairs, Madam Beritola, not knowing what had become of Arrighetto, frightened by what had occurred, and fearing for her honor, abandoned everything she owned, and, pregnant and impoverished, set sail on a small boat with her son of nearly eight years, named Giuffredi, and fled to Lipari, where she gave birth to another male child, whom she named the Outcast; after engaging a nurse, she embarked with them all on a ship to return to Naples and her parents.

But events proved contrary to her hopes, for a strong wind drove the ship, which was headed for Naples, to the island of Ponza, where they dropped anchor in a small bay and waited for weather more favorable to their course. Like all the others, Madam Beritola went ashore, and there she sought out a solitary and remote spot where she could mourn for her Arrighetto. She observed this practice of hers every day, until one day it happened that while she was alone and plunged in her grief, all of a sudden a pirate galley swooped down, capturing the sailors and all the others, who were taken by surprise, and then sailed off.

After completing her daily lament, Madam Beritola, as was her custom, returned to the shore to see her children again, but no one was to be found there; at first she was surprised, but then, suspecting what had happened, she looked out to sea and saw, not too far away, the galley towing the small boat behind it, and then she realized that now she had lost her sons just as she had lost her husband. Finding herself there impoverished, alone, and abandoned, and not knowing how she would ever find any of them again, calling out to her husband and children, she fell unconscious upon the shore. There was no one there to revive her weakened spirits with cold water or any other remedy, and therefore it was a good long time before she returned to her senses, but when finally her lost strength returned to her miserable body, amid tears and lamentations she called out to her sons as she wandered, looking for them at length in every cave she found. But when she realized that her efforts were in vain and that night was approaching, she began to think of her own needs, and hoping she knew not what, she left the shore and returned to the cave where she was accustomed to cry and lament.

She spent the night in great fear and anguish impossible to

describe; a new day dawned and it was already past the hour of tierce, and because she had not eaten since the previous evening she was compelled by hunger to feed on the grass. Feeding herself as best she could, she wept as she began brooding over what was to become of her. While she was lost in such thoughts, she noticed a doe which came toward her, entered a nearby cave, and then some time later emerged from it, running off into the woods; she got up and entered the cave the doe had left, and inside she discovered two roebucks, perhaps born on that very day, that seemed to her to be the sweetest and most charming sight in all the world. And as the milk from her own breast had not yet dried up after her recent childbirth, she picked them up tenderly and placed them to her breast. They did not refuse her kindness, and so she suckled them just as their own mother might have done, and from that moment on they made no distinction between her and their mother. Thus the gentle lady felt that she had found some company in that deserted place, and then having become as familiar with the doe as with her two offspring, she resolved to spend the rest of her life there feeding on the grass, drinking the water, and weeping whenever she recalled her husband, her children, and her past life.

As a result of living in this fashion, the gentle lady had become much like an animal herself when after a number of months it happened that a Pisan boat driven by a chance storm arrived in the same bay where she had landed and remained there for several days. On board that boat was a nobleman of the Malespini family named Currado who was returning home with his worthy and pious wife from a pilgrimage to all the holy places in the Kingdom of Puglia. In order to relieve some of the boredom of the delay, Currado with his lady and some of his servants and his dogs went ashore to explore the island, and not far away from the place where Madam Beritola was, Currado's dogs began to pursue the two roebucks, which had by now grown big and were grazing. Chased by the dogs, the two roebucks ran to no other spot than to the very cave in which Madam Beritola was staying. Seeing what was happening, she rose to her feet, and with a stick she had picked up she drove the dogs off. When Currado and his lady, who had been following the dogs, arrived and saw her there, so brown in color, so tan, thin, and shaggy, they were amazed, and she was even more amazed than they were. Once she had persuaded Currado to call off his dogs and after much coaxing on their part, they persuaded her to tell them who she was and what she was doing there, and she told them all about herself and all her misfortunes, ending with her firm decision to remain on the island.

When Currado heard this, as he had known Arrighetto Capece very well, he wept out of compassion, and he tried with many words to dissuade her from such a firm decision, offering to take her back home or to keep her with him in as honorable estate as his own sister, at least long enough that God might grant her a kinder fortune. When his proposals failed to persuade the lady, Currado decided to leave his wife with her, telling her to have food brought for the lady and, since she was all in rags, to arrange for some of her own clothes to be given her to wear and to do everything possible to bring her back with her. The noble lady, remaining alone with her, wept profusely over the misfortunes of Madam Beritola, and then she had clothing and food brought, which she had the greatest difficulty in the world convincing her to accept; finally, after many entreaties, and after the lady declared that she would never go to a place in which she was known, she convinced her to come with them to Lunigiana together with the two roebucks and the roe deer, which, in the meanwhile, had returned and to the amazement of Currado's wife greeted Madam Beritola most happily.

And so when good weather returned, Madam Beritola, Currado, and his lady, along with the roe deer and the two roebucks, went aboard ship, and as most of the people on board did not know her name, they referred to her as Cavriuola.* With a good wind they soon reached the mouth of the Magra River, where they disembarked and journeyed up to their castle. There, dressed in widow's weeds, Madam Beritola remained with Currado's wife, living as her modest, humble, and obedient lady-in-waiting, and continuing to love and care for her roebucks.

In the meantime the pirates, who had captured Madam Beritola's ship and who had unwittingly left her behind at Ponza, arrived at Genoa with all their captives. When the owners of the galley had divided their spoils, it happened by chance that along with the other goods Madam Beritola's nurse and the two boys with her were assigned to a certain Messer Guasparrino Doria, who sent the woman along with the children to his home, intending to use them as domestic servants. Sorrowful beyond measure over the loss of her lady and the wretched fortune into which she and the two children had fallen, the nurse wept for a long while. Though she was a woman of low station she was nevertheless sensible and prudent, and once she realized that her

*"Doe."

tears were of no avail in freeing herself and the children from
bondage, she did the best she could to comfort the children, and
considering where they were, she believed that if by chance the
two children were recognized, they could easily be harmed; fur-
thermore, she was hoping that sooner or later their fortune would
change and that if they were still alive they might be returned
to their former estate, so she decided not to reveal who they
were to anyone until the proper occasion presented itself, and in
the meantime to anyone who would question her about it, she
would reply that they were her own children, calling the older
one Giannotto di Procida rather than Giuffredi, and not bother-
ing to change the name of the younger. With the greatest of care
she explained to Giuffredi why she had changed his name and
what danger he might incur if he was recognized, and she re-
minded him of this not once but time and time again and with
such insistence that the young boy, who was intelligent, followed
the instructions of his wise nurse to the letter. And so the two
boys, poorly clothed and worse shod, lived there in Messer
Guasparrino's home with their nurse for many years, patiently
performing every sort of menial task.

But Giannotto, reaching sixteen years of age and possessing
more spirit than an ordinary servant, began to disdain the
lowness of his servile condition and left the service of Messer
Guasparrino to enlist aboard the galleys traveling between Alex-
andria and Genoa. However, even though he sailed far and wide,
he was unable to improve his condition. Finally, about three or
four years after he had left the service of Messer Guasparrino,
having by now become a tall and handsome young man, while he
was wandering about and despairing of his fortune, he heard that
his father, whom he had presumed to be dead, was still alive and
kept in a prison by King Charles. Coming to Lunigiana, Gian-
notto happened to enter the service of Currado Malaspina,
whom he served to Currado's great satisfaction. He rarely saw
his mother, who was always with Currado's wife, and when he
did, neither recognized the other, for age had changed both of
them since they had last seen each other.

While Giannotto was in Currado's service, it happened that
one of Currado's daughters, whose name was Spina, was left a
widow by a certain Niccolò da Grignano and returned to her fa-
ther's home. She was a very graceful and beautiful girl of little
more than sixteen when by chance she caught sight of Giannotto
and he saw her. They fell passionately in love. It was not long
before this love was consummated, and since many months
passed before anyone took note of it, they became too confident

and began to act in a manner less discreet than such affairs require. One day as the young lady was strolling with Giannotto through a beautiful, thickly wooded forest they walked ahead of their companions, finally leaving them all behind, and when they thought they were far enough ahead of the rest, they withdrew into a delightfully enclosed spot surrounded by trees and covered with grass and flowers, and there they began to make love. They lay together for a long time, but the pleasure they received made them lose all sense of time and soon they were caught there by surprise, first by the girl's mother and then by Currado. The latter, sorrowful beyond all measure upon witnessing the sight, without giving a word of explanation, had both of them bound and taken by three of his servants to one of his castles; then he walked off, seething with anger and rage, intent on having them both put to a shameful death.

The young girl's mother was upset and felt her daughter deserved every sort of cruel punishment for her transgression, but as soon as she understood from a few of Currado's remarks what his state of mind was toward the culprits, she could not bear the thought of it. She hurried to catch up with her enraged husband and implored him not to rush headlong into becoming the murderer of his own daughter in his old age or to soil his hands with the blood of one of his servants, and she advised him to find another means of satisfying his anger, such as having them put into prison, where they might languish and lament the sin they had committed. The saintly woman said these and many other things to her husband with such fervor that he changed his mind about killing them; instead, he ordered that they be imprisoned in separate places, that they be well guarded there, and that they receive little food and a good deal of discomfort until such time as he decided otherwise. And so this was done.

You can imagine for yourself what their life in captivity was like, weeping incessantly and fasting longer than they were accustomed to. When Giannotto and Spina had been living this sorrowful existence for a year and Currado had dismissed them from his mind, it happened that Peter, King of Aragon, with the aid of a plot led by Messer Gian di Procida, fomented a rebellion in Sicily and captured the island from King Charles, and Currado, being a Ghibelline, was overjoyed to hear the news.

When Giannotto heard about this from one of his jailers, he heaved a deep sigh and said:

"Alas! For fourteen years I have wandered around the world leading a wretched life hoping for nothing but this to happen, and now that it has finally happened, to prove the vanity of my hopes, I find myself here in prison without the slightest hope of leaving until the day I die!"

"What?" said the jailer. "How can what great kings do be any concern to you? What do you have to do with Sicily?"

To this question Giannotto replied: "It breaks my heart to remember what my father was once there: although I was still a small boy when I fled the island, I remember seeing him as the island's ruler when King Manfred was alive."

"And who was your father?" asked the jailer.

"My father's name," replied Giannotto, "can now be safely revealed, since I no longer have to fear the danger of disclosing it: he was called (and still is if he is alive) Arrighetto Capece, and my name is not Giannotto but Giuffredi; if I were released and returned to Sicily, I have not the slightest doubt that I could acquire a very important position."

Without further questioning, the worthy man at the first opportunity he had recounted all this to Currado. When Currado heard this, he pretended to the jailer that it was of little importance to him and then went straight to Madam Beritola and asked her kindly if she had ever borne a son to Arrighetto whose name was Giuffredi. Weeping, the lady replied that if the older of the two sons she had was alive, that would be his name and he would be twenty-two years old.

When Currado heard this, he felt that his prisoner must be the same person, and it occurred to him that if this was so, he was in a position to perform a great act of mercy and at the same time wipe out his own shame and that of his daughter by giving her in marriage to him; therefore, having Giannotto brought to him in secret, he interrogated him carefully about every aspect of his past life, and once he confirmed by every indication that he was truly Giuffredi, son of Arrighetto Capece, he said to him:

"Giannotto, you know the great wrong you have done me through the person of my daughter, whereas I always treated you as well as I would a friend; you, as a good servant, should have done everything to promote and defend my honor and that of my family. There are many who would have put you shamefully to death had you done to them what you have done to me, but mercy would not allow me to bring myself to do it. Now, since, as you say, you are the son of a nobleman and a noblewoman, I wish, if you so desire, to put an end to your anguish, to release you from the wretched captivity you now live in and at the same time restore your honor and my own to its proper place. As you know, Spina, with whom you formed an amorous attachment (though to do so was improper for you both), is a widow, and her dowry is indeed a substantial one; you are acquainted with her ways as well as those of her father and mother; of your present condition I need say nothing. Therefore, if you are willing, I am disposed to make her your chaste wife instead of your unchaste mistress, and allow you to live here with her and with me as if you were my own son and for as long as you wish."

Prison had wasted away Giannotto's body but it had in no way diminished his innate spirit of nobility, nor in any way had it lessened the perfect love which he bore for his lady. And although he fervently desired that which Currado offered him and knew that he was in his power, in no way with his reply did he debase the promptings of his noble spirit, and he answered:

"Currado, neither lust for power nor desire for wealth nor any other motive has ever made me a traitor to you or to your possessions. I loved your daughter, and I shall always love her, for I consider her worthy of my love; and if I acted with her in a manner which the ignorant consider to be dishonorable, I committed that sin which is always inseparable from youth, and should one wish to abolish that act, he must abolish youth as well, and if old men were to remember what they were when they were young and were they to measure the defects of others against their own and their own against others, it would not appear nearly so serious a sin as you and many others make it out to be—and I committed it as a friend, not as an enemy. That which you offer me now I have always desired, and had I thought you might agree to it, I would have asked it of you a long time ago, and such an offer is now even more gratifying to me, coming as it does at this moment when I had so little hope of it. But if your intentions do not reflect your words, do not feed me on vain hopes, but have me taken back to prison, and there have me tortured as much as you wish, for no matter what you do, I shall always love Spina and for her sake always love and respect you."

Currado, listening to this, was amazed, and considering him to be a man of great spirit, he judged his love to be true and held him in even higher esteem; and so, rising to his feet, he embraced and kissed him, and without further hesitation ordered that Spina be brought there in secret. She had become thin, pale, and weak in prison, and like Giannotto, she, too, seemed to be almost like another person; in Currado's presence by mutual consent they exchanged the marriage vows according to our custom.

Without anyone knowing what had occurred, a few days afterward, Currado, having provided the couple with everything they could ever need or desire, now felt that it was time to make the two mothers happy, so, summoning his lady and Cavriuola, he spoke to them in this manner:

"What would you say, my lady, if I were to return your oldest son to you as the husband of one of my daughters?"

To this Cavriuola replied:

"I could only say that if it were possible for me to be more obliged to you than I already am, then I would be even more obliged to you if you returned to me something I value more than my own life; and returning him to me in the manner which you describe, you would be restoring a part of my lost hope," and weeping, she fell silent.

Then Currado said to his own lady: "And what would you think, lady, if I were to give you such a son-in-law?"

To this the lady replied:

"If it would please you, I should be pleased even to receive a peasant into our family, not to mention a man of noble birth."

Then Currado said:

"Within a few days I hope to make you both happy women."

And once he saw the two young people restored to their former selves, Currado had them dressed honorably and asked Giuffredi:

"Would it not add to the happiness you now feel if you were to see your mother here?"

To this Giuffredi replied:

"I cannot believe that the sorrows of her unhappy misfortunes have left her alive; but if she is alive, I would be very happy to see her again, for with her advice I believe I could recover a large portion of my estates in Sicily."

Currado then had the two ladies brought before him. They both greeted the new bride with great rejoicing, although both were much amazed at what could have inspired Currado with such kindness to unite her in marriage with Giannotto. Madam Beritola, remembering Currado's earlier words, began staring at Giannotto, and then some secret force stirred within her, causing her to recall the boyish features of her son's face, and without further proof she threw her arms around his neck; nor did her great love and maternal joy permit her to utter even a single word but, on the contrary, they so overcame her every sense that she fell into the arms of her son as if she were dead. Giannotto was greatly surprised, for he could recall having seen her many times before in that same castle without ever recognizing her; nevertheless, now he instinctively recognized the maternal bond, and reproaching himself for his former insensitivity, in tears he received her into his arms, kissing her tenderly. Then, assisted lovingly by Currado's lady and by Spina, who applied cold water and other remedies of theirs, Madam Beritola regained her senses, and once again, with many tears and tender words, she embraced her son, and full of maternal affection, she kissed him a thousand times or more, while he, accepting all her tenderness, gazed at her in reverence.

And when this glad, ceremonious embrace had been repeated several times to the great approval and delight of the onlookers, and each had recounted to the other all of their misfortunes, Currado announced the new marriage to his friends (to their great pleasure) and then gave orders to prepare a beautiful and magnificent celebration, whereupon Giuffredi said to him:

"Currado, you have made me happy in many ways and have honored my mother for a long time; now, so that nothing within your power may rest undone, I beg you to gladden my mother, my wedding feast, and myself with the presence of my brother, who in the disguise of a servant is kept in the home of Messer Guasparrin Doria, who, as I told you earlier, captured both him and me on the high seas; I also beg you to send someone to Sicily who may fully inform himself as to the conditions there and to the state of the island and may set himself to learning whether Arrighetto, my father, is living or dead and, if he is alive, in what condition he is in, and that he may return to us after he has been thoroughly informed about everything."

Giuffredi's request pleased Currado, who without a moment's delay sent a number of prudent envoys to Genoa and to Sicily. The man who went to Genoa found Messer Guasparrino and begged him most diligently on Currado's behalf to send him the Outcast and his nurse, giving him a precise account of all that Currado had done for Giuffredi and his mother.

Messer Guasparrin was most amazed to hear this and said:

"It is true that I would do anything I could to please Currado, and for some fourteen years I have had the boy that you mention and his mother living in my home, and I shall gladly send him to Currado. But do tell him on my behalf to be cautious in believing any of the stories fabricated by Giannotto, who now calls himself Giuffredi, for he is more cunning than Currado may realize."

Having said this, he had the good man properly cared for and then in secret he called for the nurse and questioned her carefully on this matter. Since the nurse had already learned of the rebellion in Sicily and had heard that Arrighetto was alive, the fear that she had once felt was expelled, and she told him everything in detail, explaining, as well, her motives for behaving as she had. On finding that the story of the nurse corresponded perfectly to that of Currado's envoy, Messer Guasparrino began to believe in what she was saying, and since he was a most clever man, in one way and another he began to look into the matter more deeply, and doing so, he found more and more evidence which made him believe all the more in the story. Ashamed of how ignobly he had treated the boy, in order to make amends, he bestowed on the boy as his wife his own pretty little daughter, who was eleven years old, as well as a large dowry, for he realized who Arrighetto was and had been. Having celebrated this event with a great feast, he embarked on a well-armed galley along with the boy, his daughter, Currado's envoy, and the nurse, and sailed for Lerici; there he was received by Currado, and the entire company went to one of Currado's castles, not very far from there, where a great celebration had been prepared.

The joy of that celebration—whether it be the mother upon seeing her son again, or that of the two brothers, or that of their greeting Messer Guasparrino and his daughter and vice versa, or that of the entire group together with Currado and his wife, children and friends—cannot be described in words, and so, ladies, I shall leave it to your imagination. But to complete their joy, the good Lord, who is a most generous provider once He has begun, saw to it that the happy news reached them of the survival and good health of Arrighetto Capece.

For in the midst of this great celebration and while the guests, both men and women, were still at the table on the first course, the other envoy who had been sent to Sicily returned. Among many other things, he reported how Arrighetto had been held prisoner by King Charles and how when the rebellion against that king broke out, the people stormed the prison in anger, killing the guards and setting him free, and how since he was a sworn enemy of King Charles, they appointed him their leader and followed him in pursuing and killing the French. Because of this, he had come into the very good graces of King Peter, who had all his positions and titles restored to him, and so now he held a position of great estate; the envoy added that Arrighetto had received him with the highest honors and greeted the news about his wife and son with indescribable joy, as he had heard nothing whatsoever of them after his imprisonment and, moreover, that he was sending a brig for them manned by a number of his noblemen who were due to arrive soon. The messenger was received and listened to with great cheers and rejoicing, and Currado immediately went out with some of his friends to meet Arrighetto's noblemen who were coming to get Madam Beritola and Giuffredi, and receiving them warmly, he brought them back to his banquet, which was by now not yet half over.

Such was the delight of Beritola and Giuffredi, as well as all the others on seeing the new arrivals, that they welcomed them with cheers the likes of which had never been heard before; then before they sat down to eat, as best they knew and were able, they returned the greetings, and thanking Currado and his lady for the honor they had bestowed upon Arrighetto's wife and son, on Arrighetto's behalf they placed his every possession at their disposal. They then turned to Messer Guasparrin, whose kindness had been unexpected, and declared they were most certain that when Arrighetto learned what he had done for the Outcast, similar or even greater thanks would be rendered to him. Having done this, happily they returned to feasting the two new brides and their new bridegrooms.

Currado's celebration of his son-in-law and his other friends and relatives lasted not just that day alone but went on for many days more. Then, after the festivities had ended and Madam Beritola, Giuffredi and the others felt it was time to depart, with many tears, they took leave of Currado, his wife, and Messer Guasparrino and went aboard the brig, taking Spina along with them. And with favorable winds, they soon reached Sicily, and on their arrival at Palermo they were all, both sons and the ladies alike, received by Arrighetto with the kind of rejoicing that is impossible to describe. There it is believed they all lived happily and for a long time, grateful to the good Lord for all the benefits He bestowed upon them.

[Second Day, Seventh Story]

❦

The Sultan of Babylon sends one of his daughters as a wife for the King of Algarve; in a series of misadventures, she passes through the hands of nine men in different lands in the space of four years; finally, she is returned to her father, who believes

*she is still a virgin, and then continues on her way, as she had
before, to the King of Algarve to marry him.*

IF Emilia's tale had perhaps lasted a bit longer, the compassion
felt by the young ladies for Madam Beritola's misfortunes would
have caused them all to weep. But since it had come to an end,
it pleased the Queen that Panfilo continue with his own story; he
was most obedient and began as follows:

It is most difficult, fair ladies, for us to know what is in our
own best interests, for, as we have had the opportunity to observe
on numerous occasions, there are many people who believe they
could live a secure and carefree life if only they were wealthy,
and so they seek to acquire such wealth not only by praying to
God for it but also by eagerly sparing themselves no toil or dan-
ger whatsoever to acquire it, and no sooner have they succeeded
than they find themselves murdered by someone tempted by the
desire to possess such a substantial legacy as theirs, someone
who before they became rich was their friend. Others have
risen from a lowly estate to the heights of rulers, through a
thousand dangerous battles, shedding the blood of their brothers
and friends, believing they would attain for themselves the
greatest possible happiness, but instead, as they could have al-
ready seen and heard for themselves, they find their position full
of infinite cares and fears, and they come to discover at the cost
of their own lives that in the gold chalices of royal banquets,
poison may be drunk. There have been many people who had
ardently sought after physical strength and beauty or certain
other personal ornaments, only to learn that the things they so
unwisely desired were the very cause of their death or unhap-
piness. But in order not to let myself get involved in a detailed
discussion of human desires in general, let me state that no man
alive can choose any one desire as being wholly secure from the
accidents of chance, and so if we wish to live properly, we
should resign ourselves to accepting and possessing whatever is
given to us by Him who alone knows what we need and has the
power to provide it for us. But there are many ways in which
people sin through their desires, and you, gracious ladies, sin in a
most particular way: that is, in desiring to be beautiful—inas-
much as, finding the attractions bestowed upon you by Nature to
be insufficient, you go to astonishing lengths to improve upon
them; and therefore I would like to tell you a story about an
unfortunately beautiful young Saracen girl whose beauty caused
her, in about the space of four years, to marry no less than nine
times over.

Quite a long time ago, there was a Sultan of Babylon whose name was Beminedab, and during his reign he was fortunate in all he did. Among his many children, both male and female, this man had a daughter named Alatiel who was, according to everyone who saw her, the most beautiful woman ever seen in the world in those times. Now, the Sultan had been attacked by a great army of Arabs, but with the timely assistance of the King of Algarve,* he managed to rout them; in return, as a special favor to the King, who had asked for his daughter's hand, he promised her to him as his wife, and putting her on a well-armed and well-furnished vessel with an honorable escort of men and women together with many noble and precious gifts, he sent her on her way, commending her to God's protection.

The sailors saw that the weather was good, and setting their sails to the winds they left the port of Alexandria and sailed happily for many days. One day, once they had passed Sardinia and felt their voyage was nearing its end, there arose contrary winds which were so unusually strong that they buffeted the lady's ship and caused the crew on more than one occasion to give themselves up for lost. But, brave men that they were, they tried with all their strength and skill to withstand the beating of the heavy seas, and they did so for two days; the storm got progressively worse, and on the third night the tempest was at its peak; the sailors did not know where they were, and they could not determine their position by calculations or by sight, for the heavens were pitch-black from the clouds and the night itself, and they were drifting not far from the coast of Majorca when they realized their boat had sprung a leak.

Seeing no other means of escape and everyone thinking only of himself, the officers launched a lifeboat and got into it, deciding to trust it more than the foundering ship; although the men already in the lifeboat tried with knives to fight off the others and prevent them from joining them, every last sailor on board managed to jump into the lifeboat, and thinking in this way to avoid death, they all met it: in such weather the lifeboat could not support so many passengers; it went under and everyone in it perished. Even though the ship was leaking and nearly full of water, it was swept by a gust of wind and driven swiftly onto the shore of the island of Majorca—and on board the vessel there were, by this time, no other passengers except the King's daugh-

*Italians of Boccaccio's day called this region, which included the Moorish kingdom in North Africa opposite Spain as well as part of what is today modern Spain and Portugal, *Garbo.*

ter and her ladies-in-waiting, all of whom were half-dead from
fear and the tempest. The shock of the crash was so great that
the ship lodged itself tightly in the sand about a stone's throw
from the beach, and there it remained all night, battered by the
sea, but resistant to the force of the wind.

By daybreak the tempest had calmed down a good deal, and
the lady, half-dead and weak as she was, raised her head, and
began calling now to one of her servants, now to another, but to
no avail—they were all too far away. Receiving no reply and
seeing there was no one on board, she was greatly amazed, and
soon she began to feel frightened; she got to her feet as best she
could, and saw her maids of honor and a number of other ladies
lying all around her, and as she called to one and then another,
she soon realized that most of them had died from seasickness
and fear. This further increased the lady's terror. Finding herself
completely alone there and not knowing where she was, she felt
the need of advice, and so she started shaking those who were
still alive until she got them on their feet; and when she found
out that none of her ladies knew where the men had gone and
that the ship had struck land and was full of water, she began to
weep bitterly with them.

It was past the hour of nones before they saw anyone on the
beach or anywhere else who they might hope would help them.
Around that time, returning from his estates, a gentleman whose
name was Pericone da Visalgo happened to be passing by there
on horseback with some of his servants; he spotted the ship and,
immediately realizing what had occurred, ordered one of his ser-
vants to try to climb aboard as quickly as possible and to report
to him what he found there. The servant climbed aboard with
much difficulty and found the young lady hiding in fear under
the bowsprit with the few companions she had left. When they
saw the man, they broke into tears and begged for his mercy,
but when they realized that they could not understand each
other's language, they tried to explain their misadventures to him
with sign language.

The servant checked over everything on board as best he
could, and then told Pericone what he had found; Pericone im-
mediately had the women brought down, along with their most
precious belongings (those which were not waterlogged), and he
had them taken to one of his castles, where they were properly
provided with food and rest. From Alatiel's elegant clothes and
the honor paid her by the other women, he concluded that she
was of very noble birth. Although the lady was pale and dishev-
eled as a result of her harrowing experience at sea, she neverthe-

less seemed most beautiful to Pericone; and because of this he immediately decided to take her for his wife, if she had no husband, or to have her as his mistress, if he could not have her as his wife.

Pericone was a very robust, bold-looking man. He saw to it that the lady was served in the best of fashions, and after several days, when she was completely recovered, he saw that she was even more beautiful than he had imagined, and he was most unhappy that they could not understand each other's language, for he was unable to learn who she was. But he remained moved beyond measure by her beauty, and with gracious and amorous deeds he kept trying to induce her to fulfill his desires without resistance. But all this was to no avail: she rejected all of his advances, and in so doing she increased all the more Pericone's passion for her—and the lady perceived this. After a few days, she guessed by the clothing worn by those around her that she was among Christians and approximately where she was; she realized that identifying herself was of little value and that sooner or later she would have to give in to Pericone's desires either by force or love; therefore, proudly deciding to rise above the misery of her fortune, she ordered her three servants (for no more than three remained alive) never to tell anyone who they were unless they found themselves in a situation where revealing their identity offered a clear opportunity for obtaining their freedom; besides this, she advised them, above all else, to preserve their chastity, declaring that she herself had decided never to let anyone but her husband enjoy her. Her women commended her for this and said they would do all in their power to obey her.

Burning with desire day by day, and burning even more when he saw the thing he craved so close and yet denied him, Pericone realized that his flattery was of no avail and turned to cunning and deceit, reserving force as a last resort. He had noticed on several occasions that the lady liked wine—as happens with those who are not accustomed to drinking it because their religion prohibits it—so he decided that he might be able to possess her by using wine as an assistant to Venus; and pretending not to care that she rejected him, one evening for a festive occasion he gave a sumptuous dinner to which the lady came; and since the dinner provided many good things to eat, Pericone ordered the man serving her to give her various mixed wines to drink. He did this very skillfully; and since she was not on her guard and found herself rather attracted by the pleasure of drinking, she had more than her decorum might have required; forgetting

her past misfortunes, she became very merry, and seeing some
women doing Majorcan dances, she began to dance in the
Alexandrian style.

When Pericone saw this, he felt he was nearing his goal, and
he prolonged the supper for much of the night by providing an
abundance of food and drink. Finally, when the guests had left,
he went alone with the lady to her bedroom, where she, being
hotter with wine than tempered by virtue, took off all her clothes
without a moment's hesitation of shame at being in his presence,
as if Pericone were one of her maidservants, and got into bed.
Pericone was not long following her; he put out all the lights and
quickly lay down beside her, and taking her in his arms, with no
resistance from her, he began to enjoy her amorously. When she
felt what it was like, never before having felt the horn men use
to butt, she repented of having rejected Pericone's previous ad-
vances; and not waiting a second time to be beckoned to such
sweet nights again, she often invited herself—not with words,
since she did not know how to make herself understood, but with
actions.

While she and Pericone enjoyed each other, Fortune, not con-
tent to have made the wife of a king the mistress of a lord,
prepared an even crueler love for the lady. Pericone had a
brother named Marato who was twenty-five years old, hand-
some, and as fresh as a rose; when he saw the lady, he was im-
mensely attracted to her, and judging from the signs he got from
her, he saw that he was in her good graces. He decided that
nothing stood in his way except the strict watch Pericone kept
over her, and he devised a cruel plan whose evil effects followed
quickly upon its inception.

There was at that time, by chance, in the harbor of the city a
ship which was loaded with merchandise to be taken to Chi-
arenza in the Morea* and which was owned by two young men
from Genoa; it had already hoisted its sails in preparation to de-
part with the first favorable winds. Marato came to an agree-
ment with its owners, arranging for them to take him aboard
along with the lady the following night. When this was done, as
soon as night fell, he decided how he would proceed: he went
secretly to the home of Pericone, who was not at all suspicious
of his brother, and hid in the house according to the plan which
he had devised with some of his most trusted companions, to

---

*The original text reads *Romania*, a term which Italians of Boc-
caccio's day employed for the Morea or the Greek Peloponnesus, the
peninsula south of the Gulf of Corinth.

whom he had revealed what he intended to do. And in the middle of the night, he let his companions into the house and took them to where Pericone was sleeping with the lady; they went into the bedroom and murdered Pericone in his sleep, and the lady, awake and weeping, they threatened with death if she made any noise while they took her away. With a large part of Pericone's valuable possessions, they went quickly to the harbor unobserved, and there without delay Marato and the lady boarded the ship while his companions returned home. The sailors, with a strong, fresh wind, set sail on their journey.

The lady grieved bitterly over her second misfortune, as she had over her first, but with the assistance of the holy Stiff-in-Hand God gave to man, Marato began to console her in such a way that she soon settled down with him, forgetting about Pericone; but she no sooner felt happy than Fortune, as if not content with her past woes, was preparing a new unhappiness for her: the lady, as was mentioned more than once, was extremely beautiful and most gracious, and the young owners of the ship fell in love with her so passionately that they forgot every other problem on board and thought of nothing but how to serve and please her, always taking care that Marato would not notice anything.

Since each of them knew that the other was in love, they came to a secret agreement, deciding to share the lady's love between them—as if love could be shared like merchandise or money. The fact that she was well guarded by Marato created an obstacle to their plan. So one day, while the ship was sailing along at a good speed and Marato, unsuspecting, stood at the stern looking out to sea, the two men seized him quickly from behind and threw him into the water; and they sailed over a mile before anyone noticed that Marato had fallen overboard. When the lady heard about this and saw no way of saving him, she began to bewail her new grief on the ship. The two lovers immediately came to comfort her with sweet words and great promises—none of which she really understood—but she was crying far more over her own misfortune than over the loss of Marato. And after they had talked with her on several occasions and tried to console her, they began to argue about who would be the first to sleep with her. Each one wanted to be the first, but neither could come to an agreement with the other, and so they began to argue fiercely with strong words, and this grew into a rage, then finally they went at each other furiously with their knives in hand. Before the other men on board could separate them, they had given each other so many blows that one fell dead on the spot while the other, seriously wounded, remained alive. This displeased the lady very much, for she saw herself there alone without the aid or counsel of anyone, and she was very much afraid that the anger of the relatives and friends of the two shipowners might turn on her; but the pleas of the wounded man and their swift arrival at Chiarenza rescued her from the danger of death.

She got off the ship with the wounded man and went with him to an inn, and the reputation of her great beauty immediately spread throughout the city, finally reaching the ears of the Prince of Morea, who was at that time in Chiarenza; whereupon he wished to see her for himself, and when he did, he thought that her beauty was even greater than what he had heard, and right then and there, he fell so passionately in love with her that he could think of nothing else; and having heard about the circumstances of her arrival there, he thought that he ought to be able to have her.

When the relatives of the wounded man heard the Prince was looking for a way of possessing her, they quickly sent her to him; this pleased the Prince a great deal, as it also did the lady, since she felt that she had avoided one great danger. The Prince saw that besides her beauty she had royal manners, and he guessed that she must be of noble birth (even though he was not otherwise able to learn who she was), and his love for her increased and became so great that he treated her more like his own wife than his mistress. The lady thought over her past misfortunes and now she considered herself to be quite well off; as she was consoled she became cheerful again, and her beauty flowered to such an extent that all of the Peloponnesus seemed to be talking of nothing else. Because of this, the Duke of Athens—a handsome and brave young man, and a friend and relative of the Prince—desired to see her, and with the excuse that he had come to visit the Prince, as he was accustomed to do on occasion, he arrived at Chiarenza with a numerous and honorable retinue and was received nobly and most festively.

After a few days passed, the two men started discussing the charms of this lady, and the Duke asked if she was as marvelous as people claimed; to this the Prince replied:

"Far more so, but I want you to judge for yourself with your own eyes and not by my words."

On the Prince's invitation, the two men went to where the lady was staying; having been advised of their coming, the lady received them most politely and with a smile. She sat down between the two men, but they were not able to enjoy the pleasure of her conversation, for they understood little or nothing of her language; therefore, each of them stared at this marvelous creature—especially the Duke, who could hardly believe that she was a mortal; and as he gazed at her, not realizing that with his eyes he was drinking the poison of love, thinking that he was merely satisfying his curiosity by looking at her, he found himself totally ensnared by her charms, and he fell deeply in love with her. After leaving the lady with the Prince and having had time to think things over, he came to the conclusion that the Prince was happier than any other man, having such a beautiful lady at his pleasure; after many and various thoughts, with his burning love weighing upon him more than his sense of honor, he decided that no matter what, he had to deprive the Prince of this happiness and do what he could to make it his own.

Wishing to speed up matters, he put aside all reason and justice and turned his thoughts solely to treachery. One day, in accordance with the evil plan he devised, together with a most trusted servant of the Prince, whose name was Ciuriaci, he prepared all his horses and his belongings for departure, and that night, together with an armed accomplice, he was let quietly into the Prince's bedroom by the aforementioned Ciuriaci. It was a very hot night, and he found the lady asleep and the Prince standing naked at a window facing the sea, enjoying a breeze blowing from that direction; his accomplice, who had been told earlier what he was to do, quietly crossed the room toward the window and stabbed the Prince in the back with a knife that went right through him, then, quickly catching him before he fell, he threw him out the window.

The palace stood very high above the ocean, and the window where the Prince had been standing looked over a group of houses which had been destroyed by the sea, and so people rarely or never went there; therefore, just as the Duke had predicted earlier, no one heard the Prince's body fall. As soon as the Duke's accomplice saw that the deed was done successfully, he quickly drew out a rope which he had secretly carried with him and, pretending to embrace Ciuriaci, he threw it around his neck and pulled hard enough to keep him from making a sound, and when the Duke came in, they strangled Ciuriaci and threw his body down to join the Prince's. When this was done, certain that they had not been heard by either the lady or anyone else, the Duke took a light in his hand and carried it over to the bed, and, silently uncovering the lady, who was deep in sleep, he thoroughly examined her body, praising it most highly; as she had pleased him clothed, naked she pleased him beyond all measure. Burning now with even more desire and unconcerned with the crime he had just committed, with his hands still bloody, he lay down beside the lady, and made love to her while she, half-asleep, mistook him for the Prince.

After he had lain with her for some time, with the greatest of pleasure, he got up and had several of his attendants come in and take the lady quietly out through a secret door—the same one by which he had entered—and making as little noise as possible he had her put on horseback; then the Duke, with all his men, set out for Athens. But since he already had a wife, the grieving lady was not taken to Athens but rather to one of his very beautiful villas situated just outside the city above the sea, and there in secret he kept her and had her honorably served, satisfying her every need.

The following morning, the Prince's courtiers waited until the hour of nones for him to awaken, but hearing nothing, they opened the door of the bedroom (which was only half-closed), and finding no one inside, they thought that he had gone somewhere in secret to spend a few pleasureable days with that beautiful lady of his, and they worried about it no more. The following day a madman happened to be wandering through the ruins where the bodies of the Prince and Ciuriaci were lying, and he pulled Ciuriaci out by the rope around his neck, and went around dragging the dead man behind him. Many people recognized the body and were astonished; they managed to coax the madman into leading them back to where he had found the body, and there, to the very great sorrow of the entire city, they discovered the body of the Prince, which they then buried most honorably. In attempting to find out who might be responsible for such a heinous crime, they found the Duke of Athens was no longer there but had departed in secret, and they judged, and rightly so, that he must have committed this crime and taken the lady away with him. They immediately took as their new ruler the brother of the dead man, and they strongly urged him to take revenge. When more evidence was found establishing as true what they had guessed to be correct, the Prince called together his friends and relatives and vassals from various regions and without delay formed a very large and powerful army to wage war on the Duke of Athens.

When the Duke heard of this, he, too, made ready all his forces for his defense, and many noblemen came to his aid, among whom was the Emperor of Constantinople's son Constanzio and nephew Manovello, sent by the Emperor together with a large body of men. These men were most honorably received by the Duke and even more so by the Duchess, who was Constanzio's sister. As the day of war came closer and closer, the Duchess, at an appropriate moment, had both relatives brought to her bedroom, and there with many tears and words she told them the whole story, explaining to them the reasons for the war and how offended she was by the Duke, who thought she did not know that he was keeping that woman of his secretly; and complaining of all this most bitterly, she begged them, for the sake of the Duke's honor and for her own consolation, to make amends as best they could. The young men already knew all about the matter, and so, without asking too many questions, they comforted the Duchess to the best of their ability, and renewing her hope, they departed, having learned from her where the lady was staying. Having so often heard the marvelous beauty of the lady praised, they wished to see her for themselves and begged the Duke to show her to them; remembering very little of what had happened to the Prince for allowing him to see her, he promised to do so: he had a magnificent banquet prepared in a beautiful garden where the lady lived, and he took them and a few other companions there the following morning to dine with her.

Constanzio sat beside her, and looking at her in amazement, he told himself that he had never seen anything as beautiful as she and that one must certainly excuse the Duke, or anyone else, for using whatever treacherous means existed in order to possess such a beautiful creature; and as he looked at her over and over, praising her more each time, something not unlike what had happened to the Duke happened to him: he fell madly in love with her, and by the time he left her, he had completely abandoned all thought of war, giving himself over to thinking only about how he could take her from the Duke, and concealing with care his love from everyone.

But while he burned with his desire, the time came to march against the Prince, who was already nearing the Duke's territories; and so the Duke, Constanzio, and all the others marched from Athens, according to a previously established plan, to the border territories in order to prevent the Prince from advancing further. And all the time he was there, Constanzio's heart and thoughts were fixed upon that lady. Since the Duke was away, he thought he could easily convince her to fulfill his desire, so, in order to have the chance to return to Athens, he pretended to be very ill; with the permission of the Duke, he turned his command over to Manovello and returned to his sister in Athens. A few days after he had been there, he brought up the topic of the insult which she felt had been done her by the Duke in the person of the mistress he was keeping, and he told her that he would gladly assist her in this matter, if she wished, by taking Alatiel away.

Thinking that Constanzio was doing this out of love for her and not for that lady, the Duchess said that this would please her very much, if it could be done in such a way that the Duke would never know she had consented to it. Constanzio gave his promise, and the Duchess agreed that he should proceed in whatever way seemed best to him.

Constanzio secretly equipped a swift ship, and sent it one evening to a place near the garden where the lady was living. The sailors aboard were given their instructions, and the Duke with some friends went to the palace where the lady stayed, where he was cordially received by those in her service and then by the lady herself; then, accompanied by her servants and by the companions of Constanzio, they all, at her request, went into the garden. Then, pretending to wish to speak to the lady privately on the Duke's behalf, he walked with her alone toward a gate which opened out onto the sea; it had already been opened by one of his friends, and the ship signaled to come to that spot, when Constanzio quickly had the lady seized and taken aboard. Then, turning to her servants, he said:

"Let no one move or make a sound unless he wants to die! I am not stealing the Duke's mistress; I am removing the shame he has inflicted upon my sister!"

No one dared reply to this, and Constanzio boarded the ship with his companions and sat beside the lady, who was weeping; then he gave orders for the oars to be placed in the water and the ship to set sail, and those oars were more like wings, for they arrived at Aegina close to dawn the following day. There they left the ship to rest on land, and Constanzio consoled the lady, who wept over her unfortunate beauty; then they boarded the ship again and within a few days reached Chios. Fearing his father's reprimands and that the lady might be taken away from him, he decided to remain there in a safe place; the beautiful lady continued to weep over her misfortune for some days, but as soon as she received the same comfort from Constanzio as she had from the others before him, she began to enjoy what Fortune had prepared for her.

While things were going as they were, Osbech, who at that time was King of the Turks and constantly at war with the Emperor, came, by chance, to Smyrna; and when he heard how Constanzio was living such a lascivious life on Chios with some woman he had stolen and how he was taking no precautions to protect himself, he went there one night with some lightly armed ships and men; he quietly landed at Chios with his men, and took by surprise many of Constanzio's men, who were still in their beds and unaware that the enemy was upon them; the others, those who did awaken, ran for their weapons and were killed; the entire city was burned, plunder and prisoners were placed aboard the ships, and all returned to Smyrna.

Osbech, who was a young man, discovered the beautiful lady while examining his plunder, and when he understood that this was the one who had been taken while asleep in bed with Constanzio, he was most happy to see her; without further delay, he made her his wife, celebrated the wedding, and slept with her happily for a number of months.

Before these events took place, the Emperor had been negotiating with Basano, King of Cappadocia, for him to attack Osbech from one side with his forces while he with his men would attack him from the other, but they had not yet completely come to an agreement, for the Emperor did not wish to grant some of the demands which Basano was making, believing them to be somewhat excessive. But when he heard what had happened to his son, he was so grieved that without further delay, he granted what the King of Cappadocia had requested and asked him to attack Osbech as soon as he was able, while he was making ready to attack from the opposite side.

When Osbech heard about this, he assembled his army in order to avoid being trapped between these two powerful rulers, and he proceeded to attack the King of Cappadocia, leaving his beautiful lady guarded by one of his friends and faithful vassals; before long he met the King of Cappadocia in combat, but his army was defeated and scattered, and he himself was killed. Victorious, Basano began to advance toward Smyrna, meeting little opposition, and as he approached, everyone paid homage to him as the conqueror.

Antioco, Osbech's vassal, in whose care the lady had been left, saw how beautiful she was, and although he was an old man, he found himself unable to keep the trust he had pledged his friend and lord, and he fell in love with her. He knew her language (something which pleased her very much, for she had been forced to live many years almost like a deaf-mute, not understanding anyone and unable to make anyone understand her), and urged on by love, Antioco became so intimate with her in just a few days that not long afterward, forgetting about their lord who was away at war, they made their intimacy more passionate than friendly, enjoying each other most exquisitely between the sheets.

But when they heard that Osbech had been defeated and killed and that Basano was seizing everything in his path, they both decided not to await his arrival there; they gathered up the greatest part of Osbech's most valuable possessions, and together they went secretly to Rhodes, but they were there for only a short time before Antioco fell mortally ill. They had, by chance, gone to live with a Cypriot merchant who was a most beloved friend of Antioco, and when he felt that he was near death, he decided to leave all his belongings as well as his dear lady to his friend. About to die, he called them both to his side and said:

"There is no doubt I am coming to my end, and this grieves me, for living has never pleased me so much as it does now. There is one thing that, in truth, will allow me to die happy: if I must die, let me die in the arms of those two persons whom I love the most, more than any others in the world—in your arms, dear friend, and in those of this lady whom I have loved more than myself from the very day I met her. It truly grieves me to die and to leave her here, a foreigner without aid or counsel; it would be even more grievous if I did not know you were here, for I believe that out of affection for me, you will care for her just as you would care for me; therefore, should I die, I beg you with all my strength to take charge of my possessions and of her, and do with them whatever you feel will serve as a consolation to my soul. And you, dearest lady, I beg you not to forget me after my death, so that I may boast in the hereafter that I was loved by the most beautiful woman that was ever created by Nature. If you will reassure me on these two matters, I shall be able to pass away with no doubts and in peace."

Hearing these words, the merchant friend and the lady began to weep, and when Antioco finished speaking, they comforted him, giving him their word of honor to do what he had asked in the event of his death; not long afterward he passed away and was buried honorably by them. Then, a few days later, the Cypriot merchant, having concluded his business in Rhodes, decided to return to Cyprus on a Catalan merchant ship which was already in port, and he asked the beautiful lady what she wanted to do, since he had to go back to Cyprus. The lady replied that if he was willing, she would gladly go with him, and that she hoped she would be treated and regarded by him as a sister because of his love for Antioco. The merchant said that he would be happy to do anything she wished, and as a protection from any harm which might befall her before they reached Cyprus, he suggested that she pose as his wife.

They boarded the ship and were given a small cabin in the stern, and in order to keep up the pretense, the merchant and the lady slept together in a rather small bed; because of this, something happened which was not intended to happen by either one of them when they left Rhodes: the dark, the comfort, and the warmth of the bed (the power of which is by no means small) excited them, and they forgot about their friendship and love for the dead Antioco, and drawn together by mutual passion, they began to stimulate each other, and before they reached Paphos, where the Cypriot lived, they had begun sleeping together as if they were married; after their arrival at Paphos, she stayed for some time with the merchant.

One day it happened by chance that a nobleman named Antigono came to Paphos on business; he was old and very wise but rather poor, and although he had served the King of Cyprus in many matters, Fortune had been unkind to him. One day, after the Cypriot merchant had gone to Armenia on a business voyage, Antigono just happened to be passing the house where the lovely lady lived when he caught sight of her and then remembered that he had seen her on another occasion, but no matter how hard he tried he could not recall where.

The beautiful lady who for so long had been Fortune's toy now was about to see the end of her misfortunes approaching; when she saw Antigono, she remembered that he had held a position of no little importance among her father's servants in Alexandria; suddenly she was filled with the hope of returning to her royal position with his help; and since her merchant was not there, she sent for Antigono as soon as she could. He came, and timidly she asked if he might not be Antigono of Famagusta, as she believed he was. Antigono replied that he was, and then he said:

"My lady, I seem to recognize you, but I cannot remember where I saw you; I beg you, if you please, to recall to my memory who you are."

The lady knew from his words who he was, and breaking into tears, she embraced him—all of this amazed him—and then she asked him if he had ever seen her in Alexandria. When Antigono heard this question, he immediately recognized her as Alatiel, the daughter of the Sultan, whom he believed to have died at sea; he tried to pay her the customary respect, but she would not hear of it, and asked him to sit with her for a while. Antigono did so, and he respectfully asked her how and when and from where she had come there, for all of Egypt was convinced that she had drowned at sea some years ago. To this the lady replied:

"I would have preferred for my life to have ended that way rather than to have led the life I have lived, and I think my father would wish the same thing if he ever found out about it."

Saying this, she began once again to weep profusely, and Antigono said to her:

"My lady, do not give up hope before there is need to; if you will, tell me what happened to you and what your life has been like, and perhaps the matter can be treated in such a way that we can, with God's help, find a remedy."

"Antigono," said the beautiful lady, "seeing you here is like seeing my own father, and moved by that love and tenderness which I am obliged to bear for him, I revealed my identity to you, although I could have kept it hidden. There are very few people that would give me greater pleasure to see than yourself; therefore, I shall reveal to you, as if to my own father, all of my wretched misfortunes which I have always kept concealed from everyone. After you have heard them, if you see any means of restoring me to my rightful station, I beg you to employ them; if not, I beseech you never to tell a soul that you have seen me or have heard anything about me."

Having said this, continuing to weep, she told him what had happened to her from the day she was shipwrecked off the coast of Majorca to the present moment, and, out of pity, Antigono began to cry. After considering the matter for a while, he said:

"My lady, since you have always concealed your identity during your misfortunes, I am certain that I shall be able to restore you more beloved than ever to your father, and then see you become the wife of the King of Algarve."

When she asked him how, he explained in detail what she had to do; and to avoid any more delays, Antigono returned at once to Famagusta and presented himself to the King, saying:

"My lord, if it please you, you can do great honor to yourself and be of inestimable service to me (who have grown poor in your service) without great cost to yourself."

The King asked how this might be done, and Antigono answered:

"The beautiful young daughter of the Sultan has arrived at Paphos, the one who was long thought to have been drowned at sea, and in preserving her chastity, she has long suffered the greatest of hardships; now she is poverty-stricken and wishes to return to her father. If it would please you to send her back to him in my care, you would do great honor to yourself and be of great help to me, nor do I believe the Sultan would ever forget such a favor."

The King, moved by regal magnanimity, immediately agreed; he sent for the lady and had her brought to Famagusta, where he and the Queen received her with great festivity and honor. When she was questioned about her misadventures, she answered, telling all, according to the instructions given her by Antigono. At her own request a few days later, the King returned her to the Sultan in the handsome and honorable company of ladies and noblemen under the command of Antigono; no one need ask how well she or Antigono and the rest of her party were received. After she had rested awhile, the Sultan wished to know how she managed to be still alive and where she had lived for so long a time without ever sending word concerning her condition. The young lady, who had memorized Antigono's instructions very well, began to speak to her father in this fashion:

"Father, about the twentieth day after my departure from you, our ship foundered in a fierce storm one night and was driven onto some western shores not far from a place called Aiguesmortes,* and what happened to the sailors who were aboard the ship I could not tell you; I only remember that when it was day and I came to life, almost as if from the dead, the wrecked ship had already been spotted by peasants who ran to plunder it from all over the countryside. I went ashore with two of my women servants, who were immediately seized by young men and taken off in different directions—what ever became of them, I never knew; then two young men seized me and dragged me off by my hair, and while I was resisting and weeping bitterly, it happened that as the men dragging me were crossing a road to get to a great forest, four men on horseback were passing by there at that moment, and when my captors saw them, they quickly abandoned me and took to flight.

"When the four men, who seemed to be persons of authority, saw them flee, they galloped over to where I was and asked me many questions, and I answered, but they did not understand my language nor I theirs. After a long discussion, they put me on one of their horses and took me to a convent which was organized according to their religious laws, and there, because of whatever it was they said, I was most kindly received and honored by the nuns, and with great devotion I joined them in serv-

*An important medieval port in the French region of Provence, from which King Louis IX embarked for Egypt in 1248 and for Tunis in 1270 to begin the Seventh and Eighth Crusades.

ing St. Peter-the-Big-in-the-Valley, for whom the women of the country had great affection. After I had lived for some time with them and learned some of their language, they asked me who I was and where I came from, and since I knew where I was and feared, if I told the truth, that I might be driven away as an enemy of their religion, I replied that I was the daughter of a great nobleman from Cyprus who was sending me to Crete to be married when, unfortunately, we were driven ashore and shipwrecked.

"And many times in many ways, fearing the worst, I followed their customs; and when I was asked by the oldest of those women, whom they call 'Abbess,' if I wanted to return to Cyprus, I answered that I desired no other thing. But since she was concerned for my honor, she never wanted to entrust me to anyone who was going in the direction of Cyprus until about two months ago, when several French gentlemen arrived there with their ladies, among whom there was some relative of the Abbess. When she heard that they were going to Jerusalem to visit the sepulcher where the man they consider their God was buried after he was murdered by the Jews, she entrusted me to their care and begged them to take me to my father in Cyprus.

"It would be too long a story to tell just how much these noblemen honored me and how warmly I was received by their ladies. We boarded a ship, and after some days we arrived at Paphos; I did not know anyone there, nor did I know what I should say to the noblemen who wished to return me to my father according to the instructions that the worthy Abbess had given them; but God provided a way out for me, perhaps because He took pity on me, for just as we were disembarking at Paphos, Antigono was there on the shore; I called out to him at once, and so that I would not be understood by either the gentlemen or their ladies, I told him in our own language to welcome me as if I were his daughter. He understood me immediately, and once he had greeted me accordingly and thanked those gentlemen and those ladies as his poverty permitted, he took me with him to the King of Cyprus, who received me and sent me on to you with such honor that I could never describe it. If there is anything else left to tell, let Antigono tell you, for he has often heard me speak of my adventures."

Antigono then turned to the Sultan and said:

"My lord, all she has told you here, she has many times told me, and those ladies and noblemen with whom she came have told me the same thing; she has only left out one part of her story, which I think she has omitted because she feels it is not appropriate for her to mention: that these noblemen and ladies with whom she came spoke very highly about the virtuous life she led with the nuns and about her praiseworthy behavior, and both the ladies and the men shed many tears and expressed their regrets when they put her in my charge and had to leave her. Were I to tell you everything they said to me, not only the present day but the coming night would not be sufficient; let it suffice for me to say that according to their own words and what I was able to witness for myself, you certainly may boast of having the most beautiful, the most virtuous, and the most chaste daughter that any ruler who wears a crown today possesses."

The Sultan was extremely pleased to hear these things, and many times he prayed God to grant him the grace to be able to reward properly whoever had honored his daughter, and especially the King of Cyprus for having honorably returned her to him; and some days later, he presented Antigono with sumptuous gifts and gave him leave to return to Cyprus, bringing with him to the King by letter and by special ambassadors his deepest gratitude for the great kindness he had shown to his daughter. After this, he decided to carry out what he had originally planned to do, that is, to make his daughter the wife of the King of Algarve; so he wrote to him, telling him everything that had happened to her, and said that if he still wished to marry her, he should send for her. This pleased the King of Algarve very much, and he sent an honorable escort for her and received her most joyously. And she, who had lain with eight men perhaps ten thousand times, went to bed with the King as if she were a virgin, and she made him believe that she still was one. And from then on she lived happily with him as his Queen. This is why it is said: "A mouth that is kissed loses no flavor, but, like the moon, is renewed."

[Second Day, Eighth Story]

✺

The Count of Antwerp, being unjustly accused, goes into exile;
he leaves two of his children in different parts of England; he
returns to Scotland, unknown to them, and finds them in good
condition; then he joins the army of the King of France as a

*groom, and after he is proved innocent, he is restored to his
former position.*

THE ladies breathed many a sigh over the beautiful woman's
various adventures; but who knows what caused their sighs?
Perhaps some of them sighed no less because of their longing for
such frequent embraces than because of their compassion for
Alatiel. But setting this problem aside for the moment, after
they had all had a good laugh over Panfilo's last words, which
the Queen took to mean that his tale was completed, she turned
to Elissa and asked her to continue the proceedings with a tale
of her own. Happy to do so, Elissa began:

The field through which we are wandering about today is very
wide, and there is no one here who could not easily run not one
but ten courses, so generously has Fortune stocked it with her
wonders and afflictions; but since from among an infinite number
of these I must choose to tell only one, I shall do so.

When Roman power passed from the French to the Germans,
a most serious enmity as well as bitter and continuous warfare
broke out between the two nations, so to defend their own land
and to attack the other, the King of France and one of his sons,
employing every resource of their kingdom, together with as
many friends and relatives as they could gather, assembled a
very large army to march against the enemy. But before they
proceeded further and in order not to leave their kingdom with-
out a ruler, as they knew Gualtieri, Count of Antwerp, to be a
noble and wise man and a most faithful friend and servant of
theirs, in spite of the fact that he was very skilled in the arts of
warfare, they felt he was even more suited to delicate matters of
state, and they left him there in their place as the Vicar General
of the entire government of the Kingdom of France and went on
their way. Gualtieri, therefore, began the fulfillment of his office
with discernment and organization, always consulting with the
Queen and her daughter-in-law on every matter; and although
they were left under his care and jurisdiction, he nevertheless
chose to honor them as his lords and superiors. The aforemen-
tioned Gualtieri was a physically handsome man of about forty
years of age, and he was as pleasing and well-mannered as any
nobleman could possibly be; moreover, not only was he the most
elegantly dressed, but also the most gracious and most refined
knight known in those times.

Now it happened that while the King of France and his son
were fighting the aforementioned war, Gualtieri's wife died, leav-
ing him alone with two small children, a son and a daughter;

and while Gualtieri continued to hold court with the aforesaid ladies, consulting with them often about the needs of the kingdom, the wife of the King's son cast her eyes upon him, and greatly impressed by his person and manners, she secretly fell madly in love with him. Considering her own youthfulness and freshness as well as the fact that he had no wife, she believed she could easily obtain what she wanted and with no other hindrance than her shame, and so she decided to set that aside and to reveal her love openly to him. And so one day, finding herself alone and feeling that the time was right, she sent for Gualtieri under the pretext of discussing other matters with him.

The Count, whose thoughts were far removed from those of the lady, went to her at once; she was sitting all alone on a couch in her bedroom, and as she requested, he sat down beside her, and twice he asked her why she had summoned him; silent at first, but finally driven by her love, the lady blushed a deep crimson with shame and finally, driven by her love, on the verge of tears and trembling all over, she began to speak in a broken voice as follows:

"Most dear and sweet friend and my lord, as a wise man you can easily understand how weak both men and women are and the many different reasons why some are weaker than others; therefore, the same sin committed by different classes of people should not receive the same punishment from a fair judge. And who would deny that a poor man or a poor woman obliged to earn a living by manual labor should be more strongly reproached for following love's bidding than should a wealthy and idle woman who lacks nothing for the gratification of her desires? I certainly believe no one would deny this. So I think that a situation such as this ought to excuse in large measure such a woman, if she by chance allows herself to overstep her bounds by falling in love; and if the woman has chosen a wise and worthy lover, then she needs no further justification. Since both of these requirements, I believe, are present in my situation, and moreover since there are other inducements for loving, such as my youth and the absence of my husband, it is only fitting now that these serve to defend my ardent love in your presence, and if these reasons carry as much influence as they ought to among wise men, I beg you to offer me counsel and assistance in what I am about to ask you. The fact is that because of my husband's absence, I cannot resist the desires of the flesh nor the force of love, which are so powerful that even the strongest of men, not to mention a frail woman, have often succumbed to them in the past and will continue to do so. Living in the luxury and idleness in which you find me, I have allowed myself to dwell on the pleasures of love, and now I have fallen in love. I realize, however, that were this to become known it would be considered most improper, but if it remains hidden, I do not see anything wrong with it, especially since Love has so favored me by not depriving me of my good judgment in choosing a lover; on the contrary, Love has enlightened it by showing me that you are worthy of being loved by a woman of my station, and unless I am sadly deceived, you are the most handsome, the most charming, the most attractive and wisest knight to be found in all the Kingdom of France. Just as I can say that I am without a husband, so you, too, are without a wife. Because of this I implore you, in the name of the love I bear for you, not to deny me your love and to take pity on my youth, which is truly melting away for you, as ice does near fire."

Such an abundance of tears accompanied these words that while she had intended to beseech him with additional entreaties, she could not utter another word, and lowering her face, nearly destroyed by emotion and tears, she let her head rest upon the Count's breast. The Count, who was a most loyal knight, began to reproach her severely for her insane passion and to repulse the lady, who was on the verge of throwing her arms around his neck; then with many an oath he swore that he would rather be drawn and quartered than allow such harm to be done to the honor of his lord, whether by himself or by anyone else.

When the lady heard this, she immediately forgot about her love for him and, flying into a fury of rage, she said:

"So, you villainous knight, I am to allow my desire to be spurned by you in such a manner? Since you would see me die, so help me God, I will have you killed or driven off the face of this earth!"

As she said this, she ran her hands through her hair, tearing it and messing it up, ripped open her clothes at her breast, and began to shriek:

"Help! Help! The Count of Antwerp is trying to rape me!"

When he saw what was happening, the Count was more concerned about the envy at court than he was reassured by his own clear conscience, and he feared that more faith would be placed in the lady's wickedness than in his own innocence; so he walked out of the room as quickly as he could, left the palace, and fled to his home, where, without further reflection, he put his children on a horse, mounted one himself, and set out toward Calais as fast as he could.

Many people came running in answer to the lady's screams,

and when they saw her and heard the reason for her cries, not only did they believe her story, but they now concluded that the Count had for a long time been exploiting his charm and elegant ways in order to achieve such an end. In a rage they rushed to the Count's home to arrest him; not finding him there, they ransacked the entire place and then razed it to the ground. The story, told in the worst possible light, reached the King and his son in the field; they were greatly disturbed, condemned the Count and his descendants to perpetual exile, and offered very large rewards to anyone who might deliver them up dead or alive.

The Count, sorry that in fleeing he had turned his innocence into guilt, reached Calais with his children, having managed to conceal his identity and presence there; he then quickly crossed over into England, where, dressed in shabby clothes, he traveled to London. Before entering the city, he admonished his two small children at great length regarding two things in particular: he told them, first, that they should suffer patiently the state of poverty in which Fortune had cast them, along with him, through no fault of their own; and second, that if they valued their lives, they should take every precaution against revealing to anyone where they came from or whose children they were. The boy, who was called Luigi, was perhaps nine years old, and the girl, whose name was Violante, was about seven; and considering their tender age, they both paid very close attention to their father's instructions, as they later demonstrated by their actions. To make it easier for them to achieve their task, the Count thought it best to change their names, which he did, calling the boy Perotto and the girl Giannetta. Then, arriving in London shabbily dressed, they set about begging for alms, like the French beggars we see around here.

By chance, one morning they were begging this way in front of a church when a great lady, who was the wife of one of the King of England's Marshals, happened to be leaving the church and caught sight of the Count and his two little children, who were begging for alms; she asked him where he had come from and if these were his children. To this the Count replied that they were from Picardy and that because of the misdeeds committed by one of his elder sons, who was a scoundrel, he had been forced to depart with his other two children. The lady, who was most compassionate, set her eyes upon the girl and was most pleased with her, for she was beautiful, noble-looking and charming, so she said:

"Worthy man, if you would be willing to leave this little

daughter of yours with me, I shall be happy to take care of her, for she seems like a good child, and if she turns out to be a worthy girl, at the proper time I shall arrange a proper marriage for her."

The Count was most pleased by this request and immediately replied that he would be willing, and in tears he gave the child to the woman, commending her more than once to the lady's care. And so, having provided a good home for his daughter with a proper lady, he decided to remain there no longer; he and Perotto begged their way across the island and finally, with much difficulty, for the Count was not accustomed to traveling on foot, they reached Wales. There another of the King's Marshals resided, who occupied a high position and had a large retinue, and to this man's courtyard the Count, alone or with his son, would often go to get something to eat. In the courtyard there was one of the sons of the aforementioned Marshal as well as other children of noblemen, playing different kinds of running and jumping games, and Perotto began to mix with them and to play as skillfully as any of the others, or even more skillfully than they, at every game they played. On several occasions, the Marshal happened to notice this, and admiring the boy's bearing and behavior, he took a liking to him and asked who he might be. When told that the child was the son of a poor man who sometimes came there to beg alms, the Marshal asked if he could have the boy. The Count, who had been praying for precisely this to happen, while he found it most distressing to have to part with the boy, willingly handed him over. Now that the Count had provided for his son and his daughter, he decided that he no longer wished to remain in England, and in one way or another he managed to cross the sea to Ireland; landing at Strangford, he entered the service of a knight who was a part of a rural count's household, performing all the usual duties of a servant or groom. And there, unknown to anyone, he lived for a long time in a great poverty and toil.

Violante, now called Giannetta, who lived with the noble lady in London, was growing in years, in body, in beauty and grace, delighting the woman and her husband and all the others in their household as well as anyone else who knew her—so marvelous a thing was she to behold; nor was there anyone, upon observing her behavior and her manners, who would not remark that she was worthy of the highest honor and wealth. And so the noblewoman, who had taken the girl from her father about whom she knew nothing except what he had told her, decided that she should marry the girl honorably and according to the social station she believed the girl occupied. But God, the just discerner of the merits of others, knowing her to be of noble birth and blamelessly suffering the penitence of another's sins, disposed matters differently; and we must believe from the events which followed that He out of His loving-kindness allowed all this to happen in order to prevent the noble young lady from falling into the hands of a man of inferior station.

The noblewoman with whom Giannetta lived had an only son by her husband, whom she and his father loved very dearly, not only because he was their own child but also because of his own virtue and merits. Being outstandingly well-mannered, courageous, and handsome, he was most worthy of their affection. He was about six years older than Giannetta, and seeing how very beautiful and gracious she was becoming, he fell so passionately in love with her that he had eyes for no one else. But because he believed her to be of low birth, he dared not ask his father and mother for her hand in marriage. Moreover, since he feared being reproached for making the object of his love someone of lower state, he did all he could to keep his love concealed, and as a result, his passion tormented him more greatly than if he had revealed it. This excessive pain caused him to fall most seriously ill; a number of physicians were called in to cure him, but even with one test after another, they were still not able to diagnose his illness and they all despaired of finding a cure for him. The worry and grief which the young man's father and mother had to endure could not have been greater, and on numerous occasions they would beg him piteously to tell them what the cause of his illness might be, to which he would reply only with deep sighs or by saying that he felt himself burning all over.

One day while a rather young doctor who was nevertheless very learned sat by his side and held his arm by the part where physicians take the pulse, it happened that for some reason Giannetta, who out of respect for the boy's mother was nursing him with great care, came into the bedroom where the boy was lying. When he saw her enter, he felt the passion of his love beat stronger in his heart, and though he said or did nothing, his pulse began to beat more quickly than usual; the physician noticed this immediately and was greatly amazed, but he remained silent in order to see how long this rapid pulse would last. When Giannetta left the bedroom, his pulse returned to normal; the physician, therefore, concluded that he had discovered some part of the reason for the young man's illness. He waited for a while, continuing to hold the sick boy by the hand, and then, with the excuse of wishing to ask Giannetta about something, he had her summoned, whereupon she immediately came to him; no sooner had she entered the bedroom than the young man's pulse began to beat rapidly again, and when she left, it returned to its normal beat.

As a result, the physician now felt certain of his diagnosis, and rising to his feet, he took the young man's father and mother aside and said to them:

"The health of your son is beyond the cure of doctors, for it rests in Giannetta's hands, who, as I have learned from certain unmistakable signs, the young man loves most ardently, although, so far as I can tell, she herself does not realize it. You know now what you have to do if you value his life."

The nobleman and his lady, upon hearing this, were very happy, for there was now a possible cure for their son, but if this was the case, they were also very disturbed at the prospect of having to give him Giannetta as his wife.

And so, once the physician had gone, they went to their sick son, and his mother said to him:

"My son, I would never have believed that you would conceal any of your wishes from me, especially when you saw that not obtaining what you wanted caused you to waste away; you should have known all along that there is nothing I would not do to make you happy, even if it meant doing something less than virtuous, something I would not do on my own account. Though you have acted in the way you have, the good Lord has proved to be more compassionate on your behalf than you have of yourself, and to prevent you from dying from this illness, He has revealed to me the cause of your sickness, which is nothing more than an excessive passion you feel for some young woman, whoever she may be. You really should not have been ashamed to reveal it, for this is normal at your age; had you not fallen in love, I should esteem you much the less. So, my son, trust me and reveal freely your every wish to me; put aside all your pining and anxiety which cause your illness, and take heart, for you can be certain that there is nothing in the world I would not do for your sake, if it be in my power to do it, since I love you more than my own life. Drive away your shame and your fear, and tell me now if there is something I can do to assist this love of yours. And if you do not find me eager to help you and to bring this matter to a successful conclusion, you may regard me as the cruelest mother that ever gave birth to a son."

When the young man heard his mother's words, at first he was ashamed; then, thinking to himself that no one better than she might satisfy his desires, he put aside his shame and spoke to her in this fashion:

"Madam, nothing made me keep my love a secret more than the fact that I have noticed that when most people reach a certain age, they no longer wish to remember when they were young. But now that I see such discretion in you, I shall not only cease to deny as true what you said you have discovered for yourself, but I shall also tell you frankly with whom I am in love—but with this condition: that you carry out your promise to the best of your ability, and in so doing, you will have me well once again."

To this remark the lady, quite sure of her ability to arrange things in a manner different from that which he was expecting, replied sincerely that in confidence he should reveal his every wish to her, for without any delay whatsoever she would set out to make sure he would obtain his desires.

"Madam," the young man then said, "the great beauty and the praiseworthy manner of our Giannetta, as well as the fact that I have not been able to make her take notice of my love, or even to arouse her compassion, not to mention the fact that I have not dared to reveal my love to anyone—all this has brought me to the state in which you see me; and if what you have promised me does not come true in some way or another, rest assured that my life will be a brief one."

The lady, who thought this was a time more suitable for comfort than for reproach, said with a smile:

"My poor son! Have you let a little thing like that make you sick? Take comfort; leave everything to me, and you shall be cured."

The young man, filled with renewed hope, showed signs of great improvement in the shortest time; the lady, delighted with this, decided that she would try as best she could to carry out the promise she had made. And one day, having called Giannetta in, she asked her courteously but with a joking tone if she had a lover.

Giannetta, blushing all over, replied:

"Madam, a poor young girl who has been driven out of her home, as I have, and who lives in the service of others does not expect to indulge in love, nor would it be proper."

To this the lady answered:

"Well, if you do not have a lover now, we want to give you one, so that you may live happily and enjoy your beauty all the more, for it is not fitting that such a beautiful young girl as you should be without a lover."

To this Giannetta replied:

"Madam, ever since you rescued me from the poverty of my father, you have raised me as if I were your own daughter, and because of this I ought to carry out your every wish, but in this matter I shall not follow your wishes, for I believe I am justified in refusing. If you wish to provide me with a husband, I certainly will love him; otherwise there is no other way: since I have no other inheritance from my ancestors save my honor, I intend to protect and preserve that as long as my life shall last."

Such a reply presented an obstacle to the lady's intentions of keeping her promise to her son, but being the wise woman she was, while in her heart she admired greatly the young girl's resolution, she said:

"Do you mean, Giannetta, that if our lord the King, who is a young knight just as you are a most lovely young girl, wished to enjoy your love, you would deny it to him?"

To this question Giannetta quickly replied:

"The King might force me to do so, but he would never have my consent unless his intentions were honorable."

The lady, realizing the nature of the girl's strength of character, set words aside and decided to put her to the test; and so, she told her son that when he was well again, she would put Giannetta and him alone in a bedroom, and he should try to take his pleasure with her, concluding that it seemed improper for her to go about as if she were a procuress begging on her son's behalf and imploring her own lady-in-waiting. This did not please the young man at all, and his condition immediately became much worse. When the lady observed this, she revealed her intentions to Giannetta. But finding her more resolved that ever, she told her husband what she had done, and though they were very much displeased, both agreed to give Giannetta to their son in marriage, for they preferred to have their son alive with a wife who was unsuitable for him than dead with no wife at all; and so after many a discussion, they gave their consent. Giannetta was very happy over the outcome, and with a devout heart she thanked God, who had not abandoned her; nor, in spite of it all, did she ever make herself out to be anything more than the daughter of a man from Picardy. The young man recovered, celebrated the most joyous marriage a man ever had, and began to enjoy himself with her.

Perotto, who had remained in Wales with the King of England's Marshal, had likewise gained his lord's good graces and had become as handsome and worthy a man as there was on the island, and there was no one in the land who was his equal in tournaments, in jousts, or in any feat of arms; therefore, he became renowned and famous and known to everyone as Perotto the Picard. And as God had not abandoned his sister, in like manner He demonstrated that He also kept Perotto in mind. A deadly plague broke out in that area, carrying off almost half of the population as well as causing a very large proportion of those who survived to flee out of fear to other areas, so that the country seemed completely deserted. In the plague's wake his lord the Marshal, the Marshal's wife, one of his sons, and a number of others, including brothers, grandchildren, and relatives, all perished, leaving alive only a daughter of marriageable age and a few family retainers, among whom was Perotto. When the pestilence had somewhat subsided, the young woman, knowing that Perotto was a brave and valiant man, and following the recommendations and advice given her by the few surviving inhabitants, took him as her husband and made him the master of everything she had inherited; nor was it long afterward that the King of England, receiving word of the death of his Marshal and recognizing the valor of Perotto the Picard, put Perotto in the place of the dead man and made him his Marshal. And this, in a few words, is what happened to the two innocent offspring of the Count of Antwerp, who was forced to give up his children for lost.

It was the eighteenth year now since the Count of Antwerp had fled from Paris. He was still living in Ireland, where he had endured a wretched life of hardships, when, feeling that he was growing old, there came to him the desire to learn, if he could, what had happened to his children. He could see for himself that his physical appearance was completely changed from what it had been, and because of his long years of hard work he felt he was now fitter than when he had lived as a young man in the lap of luxury, and so, very poor and badly clothed, he left the man in whose service he had long remained and went to England, and there he traveled on to where he had last left Perotto. He discovered that Perotto had become a Marshal and a great lord and saw that he was healthy, strong, and handsome. This pleased him very much, but he decided not to reveal his true identity until he had learned what had happened to Giannetta. Therefore, he set out and did not rest until he had reached London, where, after he had cautiously inquired about the lady to whom he had entrusted his daughter and about his daughter's condition, he discovered that Giannetta had become the wife of her son, and this news pleased him so very much that he began to consider all of his past adversity quite insignificant, now that he had found his children alive again and in such a good condition. So anxious was he to see his daughter that he began to hang around her house as if he were a beggar, and there one day he was noticed by Giachetto Lamiens (which was the name of Giannetta's husband), who felt compassion for him; and believing him to be a poor old man, he ordered one of his servants to take him into the house and, for the love of God, to give him something to eat. This the servant readily did.

Giannetta had already borne several children to Giachetto, the oldest of which was no more than eight years of age, and they were the most beautiful and sweetest children in the world. When they saw the Count eating some food there, all of them gathered around him and began to make a fuss over him, almost as though some hidden power inside them allowed them to sense he was their grandfather. Recognizing his grandchildren, he began to show them his affection and to caress them, as a result of which the children refused to leave his presence no matter how often their tutor called them away. When Giannetta learned of this, she came from her bedroom to where the Count was sitting and threatened to spank the children if they did not do what their tutor asked. The children began to cry and to complain that they wanted to stay with this good man, who loved them more than their own teacher, at which the lady and the Count smiled. Not like a father but rather like a poor beggar, the Count rose to his feet to honor his daughter as a lady, and he felt a marvelous joy in his heart to see her again; but not at that moment or even later on did she recognize him, so completely transformed was he from the way he once appeared— now old and gray, with a beard, thin and sunburned, he looked more like another person than the Count. When the lady saw how her children did not wish to leave him and how they cried when she tried to take them away from him, she told their teacher that they could stay with him for a while.

And while the children were there with the good man, Giachetto's father, who despised Giannetta, happened to come home, and when he learned from the children's tutor what had taken place, he remarked:

"Let them stay with him and all the bad luck God gave them, for, after all, they are only imitating what they themselves come from: descended from a beggar on their mother's side, it's not surprising that they find themselves at home in the company of beggars!"

The Count overheard these words, and they hurt him deeply, but he shrugged his shoulders in silence and bore this insult as he had endured many others. No matter how displeased Giachetto was when he heard of the joy his children had from the company of the good man—that is, the Count—he loved them so much that rather than see them cry, he gave orders that if the good man was willing to stay and perform some chore or another, he should be taken into his household. The Count replied that he would gladly stay there, but that he knew how to do nothing but care for horses, a job to which he had been accustomed for his entire life. He was, therefore, given a horse, and whenever he finished tending to it, he occupied himself by playing with the children.

While Fortune was dealing with the Count of Antwerp and his children in the manner just described, it happened that the King of France, having established a number of truces with the Germans, died and in his place was crowned his son, whose wife was the reason why the Count had been driven into exile. When the last of the truces with the Germans had expired, the new king started to wage a bitter war against them, and to his assistance his recently acquired relative, the King of England, sent a large body of troops commanded by his Marshal, Perotto, and by Giachetto Lamiens, the son of his other Marshal. With him went the good man (that is, the Count), and, still unrecognized by anyone, he remained with the army for a long time as a groom; and being an able man, he did more good with his timely advice and actual deeds than might have otherwise been required of him.

During this war the Queen of France happened to fall gravely ill, and realizing that she was at the point of death, she repented of all her sins and devoutly made her confession to the Archbishop of Rouen, who was reputed by everyone to be a most holy and good man. Among other transgressions she told him about the great wrong done to the Count of Antwerp because of her. Nor was she satisfied with telling only the Archbishop, for she related the entire story in the presence of many other worthy men, and she besought them to intercede with the King so that the Count, if he was still alive, or, if not, then some of his children, might be reinstated to their former position. Not long afterward she passed away from this life and was buried most honorably.

When her confession was related to the King, he heaved a painful sigh when he thought of the injuries he had wrongly done to the worthy man, and then he issued an edict which was circulated throughout his entire army and in many other places as well, proclaiming that whoever might provide him with information concerning the Count of Antwerp or any of his children would receive from him a princely reward for every member of the family that was located, for as a result of the confession made by the Queen, the King now held the Count innocent of the crime for which he had gone into exile and he intended to restore him to his former, and even greater, rank. When the Count, working as a groom, learned of these developments and confirmed that this was indeed the case, he immediately went to Giachetto and begged him to accompany him to Perotto, for he wished to provide them the information the King was seeking.

When all three of them were together, the Count said to Perotto, who was already thinking of revealing his own identity:

"Perotto, Giachetto here has taken your sister as his wife but has never received any dowry from her; in order, therefore, for your sister to remain without a dowry no longer I think that he and he alone should receive the reward promised by the King for you—this he should do by declaring that you are the son of the Count of Antwerp, that Violante is your sister and his wife, and that I am the Count of Antwerp, your father."

Perotto, hearing this, stared intently at the Count and recognized him immediately. Weeping, he threw himself at his father's feet and embraced them, exclaiming:

"Father, you are indeed welcome!"

Giachetto, having heard what the Count had to say and then seeing what Perotto had done, was so astonished and so delighted at the same time that he scarcely knew what to do with himself. Convinced that his story was true, he felt very much ashamed for the harsh words he had once used with the Count when he was a stableboy, and weeping, he, too, fell to his knees and humbly begged the Count's pardon for all past injury, and this the Count, after raising him to his feet, most kindly granted. And when the different adventures of each of them had been recounted, and they had all wept and rejoiced together, Perotto and Giachetto wanted to provide the Count with a new suit of clothes, but he would in no way permit this; on the contrary, he wanted Giachetto, once he was certain of receiving the promised reward, to present him dressed just as he was in the attire of a stableboy in order to make the King feel all the more ashamed.

And so Giachetto went before the King with the Count and Perotto and offered to present the Count and his children to him on the condition that, according to the proclamation, he receive the reward. The King immediately had the reward for all three of them placed before Giachetto's astonished eyes, and told him he could take it away as soon as he had truly shown him, as he promised he would, the Count and his children. Then Giachetto turned around, placed the Count and his son Perotto before him, and announced:

"My lord, here is the father and his son; his daughter, who is my wife and is not present, you will soon see with God's help."

When the King heard these words, he stared at the Count, and although he was very different from the way he once looked, he nevertheless, after looking for some time, recognized him, and then, barely holding back the tears in his eyes, he raised the Count, who was on his knees, to his feet, kissing and embracing him; and then he greeted Perotto most warmly and ordered that the Count immediately be refurbished with all the clothes, servants, horses, and equipment befitting his noble position—this was done at once. The King did more than this: he honored Giachetto most royally and wanted to know all about his past adventures, and when Giachetto received the rich rewards for having found the Count and his children, the Count said to him:

"Take these gifts from the munificence of his Royal Highness the King, and remember to tell your father that your sons, his and my grandchildren, are not descended from beggars on their mother's side."

Giachetto took the gifts and had his wife and his mother brought to Paris, and Perotto's wife came as well; there they all lavishly celebrated with the Count, to whom the King had by now restored his every possession and whom he had granted an even higher rank than he had previously enjoyed; afterward, with the Count's leave, they all returned to their homes. And the Count, until his death, lived in Paris more gloriously than ever before.

[Second Day, Ninth Story]

❦

Bernabò da Genoa is deceived by Ambruogiuolo, loses his money, and orders his innocent wife to be killed; she escapes and in the disguise of a man enters the service of the Sultan: she locates the one who deceived her husband and leads Bernabò to Alexandria, where she dons female attire once again, after the deceiver is punished, and returns to Genoa with her husband and their riches.

AFTER Elissa had fulfilled her duty by recounting her touching story, Filomena the Queen, who was tall, beautiful, more pleasing, and more cheerful in her appearance than anyone else, gathered her thoughts together and said:

"We must keep our agreement with Dioneo, and since only he and I are left to tell a story, I shall tell mine first and then Dioneo, who asked this favor, shall be the last to speak." Having said this, she began as follows:

There is a proverb often heard among the common people: that the deceiver is at the mercy of the one he deceives. This proverb would not seem possible to prove if it were not for the actual cases we have to demonstrate it. And therefore, while adhering to the proposed topic, at the same time, dearest ladies, I should like to show you that the proverb is as true as they say; nor should you object to listen to it, for by doing so you may learn to avoid deceivers.

There were a number of very prosperous Italian merchants staying at an inn in Paris, where they were accustomed to going for one reason or another; and as they were all happily eating together one evening, they began to discuss a number of things, and as one subject led to another, they finally began talking about their ladies, whom they had left at home.

In a joking tone one of them said:

"I don't know what my wife does, but I can tell you that when some young girl that pleases me falls into my hands here, I put aside the love I have for my wife and take what pleasure I can from her."

Another replied:

"And I do the same, for whether I believe my wife is enjoying some little affair or not, she's probably doing it just the same, so it's tit for tat: what the ass gets from butting a wall, he gives back."

A third man arrived at more or less the same conclusion: in short, they all seemed to agree that the ladies they had left at home had no intention of wasting any of their time.

Only one man, whose name was Bernabò Lomellin da Genoa, argued to the contrary, declaring that as a special grace from God he possessed a lady for his wife who was more richly endowed than any other woman in all of Italy with all those virtues that a lady should possess, and even, to a great extent, those virtues that a knight or a squire should possess: she was physically beautiful, still very young, dexterous and handy with her hands—there was no type of woman's work (such as working in silk and the like) that she could not do better than anyone else. Besides this, he asserted that it was impossible to find any servant or page who could better or more skillfully serve at a gentleman's table than she could, since she was most well mannered, educated, and most discreet. Moreover, he praised her for her ability to ride a horse, handle a falcon, read and write, and to keep accounts better than any merchant; after singing many of her other praises, he finally got around to the topic under discussion, declaring that he swore you could not find a more honest or chaste woman than she, and for this reason, he was firmly convinced that even if he stayed away from home for ten years or forever, she would never agree to have anything to do with another man.

Among the merchants who were talking among themselves this way, there was a young merchant named Ambruogiuolo da Piacenza, who at the last praise Bernabò bestowed upon his wife began to roar with laughter, and jokingly, he asked Bernabò if it was the Emperor who granted him, and him alone, such a privilege. A bit angered by this, Bernabò replied that it was not the Emperor but God himself—who is a bit more powerful than the Emperor—who had granted him this grace.

Then Ambruogiuolo said:

"Bernabò, I don't doubt for a moment you believe what you are saying to be the truth, but as far as I am concerned, you have very little understanding of the nature of things, for if you had examined the matter with care you couldn't be so thick-witted as not to have understood certain things about human nature that would make you speak more cautiously on this subject. So that you will not think that we, who have spoken about our wives very frankly, have wives any different from yours, I should like to reason with you a bit more on this subject and show you that we speak from common knowledge of their nature. I have always understood that man is the most noble animal among the living creatures created by God, and woman comes next; but man, as is generally believed and demonstrated through his actions, is more perfect; and since man possesses more perfection, without a doubt, he must have more strength of will, as he in fact does, for women are commonly held to be more fickle, and the reason why could be demonstrated by many natural causes, which at present I do not intend to discuss. If, therefore, man has a greater strength of will and yet cannot resist a woman who tempts him (a situation we shall not discuss), let alone not desire a woman who pleases him, and not only desire her but do everything in his power to be with her not just once a month but a thousand times a day, how, then, do you think a woman, fickle by nature, may resist the entreaties, praises, gifts, and the thousand other stratagems that a clever man who loves her will employ? Do you really believe she can resist? Surely, no matter how much you argue to the contrary, you cannot convince me that you truly believe this; you yourself say your wife is a woman and that she is made of flesh and blood like other women. If this is true, she must have the same desires as other women have or those same forces that other women possess to resist such natural appetites; so, it is quite possible, no matter how very virtuous she may be, that she does what other women do, and anything that is possible should not be so readily denied, nor should its opposite be affirmed, as you are doing."

To this Bernabò replied, saying:

"I am a merchant, not a philosopher, and I shall answer you as a merchant. Let me say that I realize what you say might be the case among foolish women in whom there is no shame whatsoever, but those women who are wise have so much concern for their honor that they become even stronger than men, who care very little for their own, in defending it; and my wife is one such woman."

Ambruogiuolo said:

"Certainly, if every time a woman managed to have an affair a horn sprouted from her head in testimony to what she had done, I imagine there would be few women who would do it; not only do such women not sprout horns, but the clever ones leave no track or trace of what they have done, and shame or loss of one's honor only occurs when there is the evidence to prove it; thus, if they can do it in secret, they do so, and if they do not, they are abstaining out of stupidity. You can be sure of this: the only chaste woman is either one who has never been propositioned by anybody or one whose own advances were refused. And although I know that natural and logical reasoning proves this to be the case, I certainly would not go on at such length about it as I am now doing, if I had not often proved this truth for myself with a number of women. And let me tell you this—if I were with this most holy woman of yours, it wouldn't take me more than a short time to bring her to do what I have already brought other women to do."

Now angered, Bernabò replied:

"This arguing with words could go on forever: you would speak and I would reply and at the end it wouldn't make a bit of difference. But since you declare that all women are so pliable and that your own wit is so great, in order to convince you of my wife's honesty, I am prepared to have my head chopped off if you can ever convince her to commit such a pleasurable act with you; and if you fail, I do not ask you to lose more than a thousand gold florins."

Ambruogiuolo, by now really warming up to the discussion, answered:

"Bernabò, I wouldn't know what to do with your blood if I won, but if you wish to see the proof of what I have just argued, put up five thousand gold florins of your own, which should cost you less dearly than your head, against my own thousand; and since you have not set a time limit, I will agree to go to Genoa and within three months from today I shall leave there, having had my way with your wife, and as proof of this I shall bring back with me some of her most intimate possessions, things that will provide you with such irrefutable proof that you yourself will have to confess it to be true—all this I will do on condition that you promise me on your word of honor not to go to Genoa or to write anything to your wife about this matter during the agreed period of time."

Barnabò announced that this arrangement pleased him very much; and no matter how hard the other merchants who were present tried to prevent this wager, realizing the great harm that could come from it, the spirits of the two merchants by this time were so inflamed that, against the wishes of the others, the two men even drew up in their own hand a written contract which was binding to both parties.

As soon as Bernabò signed the agreement, Ambruogiuolo was off to Genoa as quickly as he could while Bernabò remained where he was; after Ambruogiuolo had been there for several days and had with great discretion informed himself about the name of the lady's neighborhood and her habits, he realized that what he learned about her more than confirmed all that Bernabò had told him, and so he began to feel that he was on an insane mission. Nonetheless, he managed to get to know a poor woman who often visited the lady's house and for whom the lady had a great deal of affection, and since he was unable to persuade her to assist him otherwise, he bribed her with money to have her carry him concealed in a chest that he had especially made to order, not only into the worthy lady's house but even into her bedroom. Following the instructions she had received from Ambruogiuolo, the good woman gave the chest to the gracious lady for safekeeping for several days, pretending that she wanted to transfer it somewhere else later on.

The chest was in the bedroom, and it was nightfall when Ambruogiuolo, deciding the lady was asleep, opened the chest with special tools of his and quietly stepped out into the room, where a lamp was burning, and with the aid of the light he began to look around him and to fix in his memory the arrangement of the room, its painted decorations, and every other noteworthy item that it contained. Then he drew near to the bed, and finding that the lady and a little girl who was there with her were fast asleep, he drew all the covers back and saw that she was just as beautiful naked as she was clothed, but on her body he found no special mark of any description except, perhaps, one which she had under her left breast: a mole around which were some soft hairs as yellow as if they were of gold; after noting this, he quietly covered her again, for when he saw how beautiful she was, he had the urge to risk his life and lie down beside her. But having heard how harsh and severe she was in affairs of this sort, he did not dare risk it. After spending the better part of the night at his leisure in her bedroom, he took a purse and a long cloak from one of her strongboxes along with some rings and belts and put all this into his chest, and then he climbed back inside it and locked it up as it was before; and in this manner he spent two nights without the lady ever suspecting a thing. On the third day, according to her instructions the good woman returned for her chest and had it carried back to where she had picked it up; Ambruogiuolo climbed out of it, satisfied the woman in accordance with the promise he had made her, and carrying with him the articles he had stolen, he returned as quickly as possible, to Paris before his time was up.

There, after calling together those merchants who were present when the oaths and the wagers had been made, and in Bernabò's presence, he declared that he had won the bet between them because he had done what he had boasted he could do. And as proof that this was true, he first described the arrangement of the lady's bedroom and its painted decorations, and then he displayed the lady's belongings he had brought back with him, claiming that he had received them from her. Bernabò admitted that the bedroom was arranged in the way he had described it and, moreover, that he recognized those items as truly belonging to his lady, but he added that Ambruogiuolo could have found out how the bedroom was arranged from some of the household servants and could have also come by these belongings in a similar fashion; therefore, if he had nothing more to declare, this did not seem to him sufficient evidence to win the wager.

To this Ambruogiuolo answered:

"To tell the truth, this should have been enough, but since you want me to say more, I shall go on. Let me tell you that Madonna Zinevra, your wife, has under her left breast a rather large mole around which are some six soft hairs as yellow as if they were made of gold."

When Bernabò heard this, it was as if he had been stabbed in the heart by a dagger, so great was the sorrow he felt: his face changed so completely that there was no need for him to say a word—it was clear from his face that what Ambruogiuolo said was true; and after a time he said:

"Gentlemen, what Ambruogiuolo says is true; therefore, since he has won the wager, let him come whenever he pleases and he shall be paid." And so the following day Ambruogiuolo was paid in full.

Bernabò left Paris, and with a heart full of fury for the lady, he headed for Genoa. When he neared the city he decided not to go in, but to remain a good twenty miles away on one of his properties; instead, he sent one of his most trustworthy servants into Genoa with two horses and a letter, telling the lady he had returned and that she should come with the servant to meet him; meanwhile, he had secretly ordered his servant that when he reached a place which seemed to him the most suitable, he was to kill the lady, showing no pity, and then return to him. His servant arrived in Genoa, delivered the letter, and gave her the message, and he was most joyfully received by the lady; the following morning, she and the servant mounted their horses and set out for Bernabò's estate.

Riding along together and discussing various things, they came to a deep, solitary valley, closed in by high rocks and trees; this spot seemed to the servant to be the safest place to carry out his lord's orders, and drawing his dagger, he seized the lady by the arm and said:

"My lady, commend your soul to God, for this is where you must die."

When the lady saw the dagger and heard these words, she was terrified and cried:

"Have mercy, for God's sake! Before killing me, tell me what I did to offend you so that you feel you must murder me."

"My lady," replied the servant, "you have done nothing to me; how you have offended your husband I do not know, I know only that he has ordered me to kill you on this road and to show no mercy whatsoever, and if I do not do so he has threatened to have me hanged by the neck. You know very well how much I depend upon him and how I cannot say no to anything he commands—God knows I feel sorry for you, but I have no choice."

To this, the lady replied in tears:

"Ah! Have mercy, for God's sake! Don't let yourself become the murderer of someone who has never offended you just to serve another. God, Who knows all, knows that I have never done anything for which my husband should so reward me. But never mind that at the moment; now, if you are willing to do so, you can please God, as well as your master and me, all at the same time, in this way: take these clothes of mine and leave me only your doublet and a cloak, return to your lord and mine with these clothes and tell him you have killed me; I swear to you, by the life you have given me, that I shall disappear and go somewhere where neither he nor you nor anyone in these parts will ever again hear news of me."

The servant, who was by no means eager to kill her, was easily moved to compassion; so, having taken her clothes and given her his tattered doublet and cloak to wear, he gave her some money which he had on him, and begging her to disappear entirely from the area, he abandoned her on foot in the valley and returned to his master, to whom he reported that his orders had not only been carried out but that he had abandoned the body of the dead woman to a pack of wolves. Sometime afterward, Bernabò went to Genoa, and when the incident became known, he was severely criticized.

As night fell, the lady, alone and abandoned, disguised herself as best she could and went to a small nearby town; and there she managed to obtain what she needed from an old woman; she altered the doublet to her size by shortening it and made her shift into a pair of trousers, cut her hair in such a way that she looked just like a sailor, and then she headed for the sea, where by chance she came upon a noble Catalan, whose name was Señor En Cararh, who had just come ashore at Alba from one of his ships, which was some distance offshore, in order to refresh himself at a fountain. She struck up a conversation with him, arranged to enter his service, and went on board his vessel, calling herself Sicuran da Finale. There she was given better clothes by the gentleman, whom she began to serve so efficiently and so properly that he became very fond of her. Not long afterward the Catalan happened to dock in Alexandria with a cargo including some peregrine falcons which were for the Sultan. He received them and invited the Catalan to dine with him on more than one occasion, during which he observed the behavior of Sicurano (who was always there to wait upon her master) and was so pleased with her performance that he asked the Catalan for

Sicurano as his own servant, and while the Catalan was reluctant to do so, he did leave his servant behind with him.

It was not long before Sicurano acquired with her fine service as much favor and affection from the Sultan as she had had from the Catalan. Time passed, and now it happened to be the time of year when it was the custom to hold a great trade fair, a great gathering of both Christian and Saracen merchants at Acre (which was under the rule of the Sultan), and in order to guarantee the protection of the merchants and their goods, the Sultan usually sent, among his other officials, one of his most important representatives with enough soldiers who were to stand guard. And when this time of year came, the Sultan thought about sending Sicurano, who had already learned the language fluently; and so he did.

Thus, Sicurano arrived at Acre as the master and captain of the guards in charge of protecting the merchants and their goods, and as she went around on her inspection tours, efficiently and skillfully performing the duties of her office, she came in contact with many merchants—Sicilians, Pisans, Genoese, Venetians, and other Italians—with whom she gladly became friendly out of a nostalgic feeling for her homeland. Then, it so happened that on one of those visits, having dismounted in front of a stall of some Venetian merchant, she noticed to her great amazement among the other precious objects there a purse and a belt which she immediately recognized to be her own; without showing her emotions, she casually asked to whom they belonged and if they were for sale.

Now Ambruogiuolo da Piacenza was among the merchants who had come there on one of the Venetian ships with a great deal of merchandise, and when he heard the captain of the guard asking to whom these things belonged, he stepped forward and said with a grin:

"Sir, these things belong to me and they are not for sale, but if you like them, I shall gladly give them to you as a gift."

When Sicurano saw him laughing, she suspected that he had somehow seen through her disguise, but, keeping a straight face, she replied:

"Perhaps you are laughing because you see a soldier asking for such womanly things?"

Ambruogiuolo answered:

"Sir, I am not laughing at that but rather at the way in which I acquired them."

To this Sicuran said:

"Well, if it is not too personal, for the grace of God, explain how you managed to get hold of them."

"Sir," said Ambruogiuolo, "a noble lady from Genoa named Madonna Zinevra, the wife of Bernabò Lomellin, gave me these things among others one night when I slept with her, and she begged me to keep them for the sake of her love. I was laughing just now because they remind me of the stupidity of Bernabò, who was insane enough to wager five thousand gold florins against my one thousand that I could not convince his lady to fulfill my desires—which I did, winning the wager, while he, instead of punishing himself for his own stupidity rather than punishing her for doing what all women do, once he returned from Paris to Genoa, from what I have heard tell, had her killed."

Sicurano, hearing this, immediately saw the motive behind Bernabò's anger against her and clearly understood that this man had been the cause of all her trouble; then she decided that she would not let him get away without being punished. And so Sicurano pretended that she liked his story very much and so cleverly established a close relationship with him that when the fair was over, she persuaded Ambruogiuolo to go with her to Alexandria, bringing all his merchandise, where Sicurano established a shop for him and put a great deal of money at his disposal; and Ambruogiuolo, seeing that this was turning out to be very profitable for him, gladly decided to stay there. Sicurano wished to give clear proof of her innocence to Bernabò, and she did not rest until with the assistance of a few important Genoese merchants who were in Alexandria and by means of a number of other strange pretexts, she managed to bring him to that city. Bernabò was in the depths of poverty, and Sicurano secretly arranged for some of her friends to provide him with hospitality until such time as she felt she could accomplish what she intended to do.

Sicurano had already persuaded Ambruogiuolo to tell his story in the presence of the Sultan, who had enjoyed it a great deal, but now that Bernabò had arrived, she felt there was no time to lose, and at the earliest suitable occasion she asked the Sultan to bring both Ambruogiuolo and Bernabò before him, so that in Bernabò's presence he might be convinced—if not by gentle persuasion, then by harsher means—to tell the truth concerning the boast he had made regarding Bernabò's wife. Ambruogiuolo and Bernabò arrived, and in the presence of a great many people the Sultan with a stern face ordered Ambruogiuolo to tell the truth about how he had won five thousand gold florins from Bernabò; Sicurano, in whom Ambruogiuolo had the most confidence, was also there, but with an even more angry look she threatened him with the harshest of tortures if he did not speak. And so Ambruogiuolo, being threatened from both sides, after a little more pressure, in the presence of Bernabò and many others and not expecting any more punishment than the restitution of the five thousand gold florins as well as the things he had taken, told the whole story, recounting everything exactly as it had happened.

Whem Ambruogiuolo had spoken, Sicurano, as if she were acting as the Sultan's minister, turned to Bernabò at that moment and said:

"And you, what did you do to your lady as a result of this lie?"

To this Bernabò answered:

"Overcome by the anger of losing my money and by the injury of the shame which I thought I had incurred from my lady, I had her killed by one of my servants; and according to what he told me, she was quickly devoured by a pack of wolves."

All these things were thus said in the presence of the Sultan, who while he heard and understood them, did not, as yet, comprehend Sicurano's reasons for organizing and requesting this meeting. Then Sicurano told him:

"My lord, you can now see quite clearly what manner of lover and husband this good woman could boast of: for the lover deprives her of her honor with lies, thus ruining her reputation and destroying her husband, while her husband, believing more in the falsehoods told by others than in her truth, which he should have known himself through long experience, has her killed and eaten by wolves; besides this, the goodwill and the love both her lover and her husband bear for her is so great that, even though they have dwelt with her for a good deal of time, neither of them are even capable of recognizing her. But in order that you may clearly understand what each of these men deserves, and if you will grant me the special grace of punishing the deceiver and pardoning the deceived, I shall, here in your presence and theirs, make the lady appear."

The Sultan, who was ready to please Sicurano in everything in this affair, declared that he would grant the special grace and that Sicurano should make the lady appear. Bernabò, who felt certain that the lady had died, was amazed, and Ambruogiuolo, already with a foretaste of the evil in store for him, was afraid that something worse might happen to him than having to pay back the money; nor did he know whether to hope for or to fear the lady's coming there, and thus bewildered, he awaited her arrival.

As soon as the Sultan had agreed to Sicurano's request, in tears she fell to her knees at the Sultan's feet, and instantly abandoning her masculine voice and her no-longer-needed masculine guise, she said:

"My lord, I am the wretched, unlucky Zinevra, who has wandered over the world for six years disguised as a man, wickedly and falsely slandered by this traitor Ambruogiuolo, and then handed over to be killed by a servant and eaten by wolves by that cruel and unjust man standing there." Then ripping open her clothes and bearing her breasts, making it most clear to the Sultan and to everyone else there that she was indeed a woman, she turned to Ambruogiuolo and asked him abusively if he had ever, as he had earlier boasted, slept with her; but Ambruogiuolo, recognizing who she was, became mute with shame and said nothing.

The Sultan, who had always believed she was a man, observed and heard all this and was so amazed that the more he saw and heard, the more he believed that it could not be real and that he must be dreaming. But then, having recovered from his amazement and recognizing the truth, with the highest of praises he commended the life, the constancy, the behavior, and the virtue of Zinevra, until then called Sicurano. Then he gave her the most elegant feminine garments and a number of women to wait on her, and following her earlier request, he pardoned Bernabò the death he deserved. When Bernabò recognized her, he threw himself at her feet weeping and begging her pardon, which she, although he was unworthy of it, kindly bestowed upon him, and raising him to his feet, she embraced him tenderly as her husband.

The Sultan then immediately ordered that Ambruogiuolo be taken to some other part of the city, tied to a stake, and smeared with honey, and that he remain there and not be removed until he fell of his own accord; and this was done. Then he ordered that whatever Ambruogiuolo owned should be given to the lady, a sum which came to not less than the equivalent of ten thousand doubloons, and he himself organized a most handsome banquet at which Bernabò, husband of Madonna Zinevra, and Madonna Zinevra, his most worthy wife, were to be honored, and he gave them precious stones, gold and silver plate, and money which amounted to more than another ten thousand doubloons. When the banquet was over, he had a ship prepared for them and gave them his leave to return to Genoa whenever they pleased. They returned there extremely wealthy and with the greatest of joy, and they were received with the highest honors—especially Madonna Zinevra, whom everyone believed to be dead; and as long as she lived, because of her extraordinary virtue, she was always held in highest esteem by everyone.

The very day that Ambruogiuolo was tied to the stake and smeared with honey, after enduring the excruciating agony inflicted by the flies, wasps, and horseflies that were aswarm in that country, not only was he killed but every bit of his flesh was eaten to the bone and then his bleached bones, still hanging from their sinews, remained there for a good long while before they were removed, as testimony of his wickedness to all who beheld them. And thus it was that the deceiver lay at the mercy of the deceived.

[Second Day, Tenth Story]

✤

Paganino da Monaco steals the wife of Messer Ricciardo di Chinzica; when he finds out where she is, he goes there and becomes Paganino's friend; when he asks Paganino to give his wife back to him, Paganino agrees on the condition that she is willing to go; she refuses to return to him, and after Messer Ricciardo dies she becomes Paganino's wife.

EACH member of the virtuous group praised as most beautiful the story told by their Queen—especially Dioneo, who was the only person that day still left to tell a tale. After paying many compliments to the story, he said:

Lovely ladies, one part of the story told by our Queen has made me change my mind about a story I was going to tell and moves me to tell another, and that is the part which concerns Bernabò's stupidity (in spite of the fact that all ended well for him) and the stupidity of all those other men who allow themselves to think as he did; that is, that while they travel all over the world taking their pleasure first with one woman and then with another, they think that the ladies they have left at home are twiddling their thumbs, as if we who are born from them, grow up among them, and stay around them did not know what they are most fond of doing. By telling this story, I shall show you the foolishness of such people, and at the same time I shall demonstrate how even greater is the foolishness of those who thinking they are stronger than Nature, believe that with fictitious arguments they can do what they cannot do, and try to make others be like they themselves are, no matter how contrary it may be to the nature of those others.

There was once in Pisa a judge, more endowed with intelligence than with bodily strength, whose name was Messer Riccardo di Chinzica; perhaps because he believed he could satisfy a wife with the same sort of work that he performed in his studies and because he was very rich, with no little effort he began searching for a woman to take as his wife who was both beautiful and young, whereas had he known how to give himself the same advice he offered to others, he would have stayed far away from both the first and the second of those attributes. And this quest of his was successful, for Messer Lotto Gualandi gave him as his wife one of his daughters named Bartolomea, one of the most beautiful and charming young girls of Pisa (a city in which, by the way, most of the women look like gecko lizards). With the greatest of festivity the judge brought the girl into his home and celebrated a most beautiful and magnificent wedding, in spite of the fact that on the first night he managed to take only one go at her in consummating the marriage—barely managing to stay in the game for one round, and the next morning (since he was a skinny, wizened, feeble kind of man) he found he had to drink lots of Vernaccia wine, eat restorative confections, and use a number of other aids to get back on his feet.

Now this judge fellow, having formed a more accurate estimate of his forces than he previously possessed, began to teach the young girl the kind of calendars which schoolchildren consult—perhaps the type that was once used in Ravenna.* For according to what he showed her, there was not a single day which was not the feast day of one or even a number of saints, and by means of various arguments he showed her that out of respect to them, men and women should abstain from sexual coupling—and to these days he added all fast days, the four Ember weeks, the eves of the Apostles and a thousand other saints, Fridays, Saturdays, and the Sunday of Our Lord, every day of Lent, certain phases of the moon, and many other exceptions, thinking, perhaps, that one takes as long a vacation from going to bed with a woman as he often does away from pleading a case in court. And he continued in this fashion for a long time, not without serious ill humor on the lady's part, whose turn came up perhaps

---

*In Ravenna, there were once so many churches that almost any day of the year could be celebrated as a saint's day and, therefore, as a vacation for schoolchildren.

only once a month at best; nonetheless with great care he continuously watched over her to prevent anyone from teaching her to recognize the working days just as he himself had taught her the holidays.

Now it happened that during the hot weather, Messer Riccardo got the idea that it would be nice to spend an amusing day on one of his very beautiful estates near Monte Nero, where he would enjoy the fresh air for a few days, and with him he took his beautiful lady. While they were there, to provide her with a bit of entertainment one day, he arranged a fishing party consisting of two boats: he writes some fishermen would be in one boat and she with some other ladies who would come along to watch were to be in the second boat; and occupied by his amusement, without realizing it they sailed several miles out into the ocean. As they were all attentively watching the fishing, there suddenly appeared a galley commanded by Paganin da Mare, a very famous pirate of his time, and as soon as he caught sight of the boats, he headed in their direction, and though they fled as quickly as they could, Paganin caught the ship sailing with the ladies, and no sooner did he see the beautiful woman than he desired only her, and while Messer Riccardo, who had already reached the shore, watched on, he put her in his galley and sailed away. It goes without saying that our judge, who had witnessed all this, was sorely distressed—being the kind that was even jealous of the air surrounding his lady. And to no avail he would go about Pisa and other places lamenting the wickedness of pirates, though he had no idea who had taken his wife or where she had been carried off to.

Paganino considered himself quite fortunate when he saw how beautiful the lady was, and since he was not married, he decided to keep her with him forever, and since she was weeping so bitterly, he tried to console her tenderly. When night came, and Paganino saw that the words he had used during the day had not done much good, he began to comfort the lady with deeds, for he was not the kind of man who thought by calendars or paid any attention to holidays or working days; and so well did he console her in this fashion that before they reached Monaco, she had lost all recollection of the judge and his laws, and with the greatest joy in the world she began living with Paganino, who, after bringing her to Monaco, besides the consolations he provided for her both day and night, honored her as if she were his wife.

Some time afterward Messer Riccardo heard of his lady's whereabouts, and with a passionate desire, and convinced that no one else could do what had to be done as well as he, he made up his mind to go in search of her himself. And ready to spend any amount of money for her ransom, he boarded a ship and went to Monaco, and there he happened to catch a glimpse of her and she of him, and later on that evening the lady told Paganino about this and informed him of her husband's intentions. The following morning Messer Riccardo saw Paganino and went up to him, and in a very short time he was on quite familiar and friendly terms with him, while Paganino, who pretended not to recognize him, was waiting to see what he would propose to do; and when the time seemed right to Messer Riccardo, as best he knew how and as amiably as possible, he revealed his reason for having come, imploring Paganino to take any sum of money he wished as ransom for the return of his lady.

To this request Paganino responded in a cheerful way:

"Sir, you are most welcome here, and to answer you briefly, let me say this: it is true that I have a young lady in my home, but I cannot say if she is your wife or someone else's, since I do not know you nor do I know her either, except that she has been staying with me for some time now. But if you are her husband as you say, since you seem to me to be a likable gentlemen, I shall take you to her, and I am sure that she will recognize you immediately. If she says that what you claim is true and wishes to leave with you, then, since you are such an amiable person, you yourself shall give me for her whatever ransom you wish; but if this is not the case, you would do me a great wrong to take her from me, for I am a young man, and I should be as able to look after a woman as well as anyone else, especially this one, who is the loveliest I have ever seen."

Then Messer Riccardo said:

"She is surely my wife, and if you take me to where she is staying, you will soon see this for yourself: she will embrace me at once, and I could not ask for things to be arranged any better than you yourself have suggested."

"If that is the case," said Paganino, "let us proceed."

And so they went off to Paganino's home, where, as they stood in a large hall, Paganino had the lady summoned: all neatly attired, she came out of a room and joined Riccardo and Paganino where they were waiting, and said nothing to Messer Riccardo other than what she would have said to any other stranger who had come home with Paganino. When the judge, who had been expecting to be greeted with a great display of delight, saw what happened, he was quite astonished, and he thought to himself:

"Perhaps the melancholy and the long period of grief I have

suffered through from the time I lost her has changed my appearance so much that she does not recognize me."

So he said:

"Lady, it has cost me very dear to take you fishing, for no one has ever felt the sorrow I have felt from the day I lost you, and yet, from the cold greeting you have given me, it would seem you do not even recognize me. Do you not see that I am your Messer Riccardo, come here to pay whatever this gentlemen requests in whose home we now are in order to have you back again and to take you home with me? And he has graciously consented to return you to me for whatever amount of money I choose to pay him."

Turning to Riccardo with the slight suggestion of a smile, the lady replied:

"Sir, are you speaking to me? Be sure that you have not mistaken me for someone else, for as far as I know, I have no recollection of ever having seen you before."

Messer Riccardo said:

"Come now, careful what you say; take a good look at me; if you really wish to remember, you will see very well that I am your Riccardo di Chinzica."

The lady said:

"Sir, you must forgive me, for it may not be as proper as you think to look at you so closely; nonetheless, I have done so, and I am certain that I have never seen you before."

Messer Riccardo thought that she said this out of fear of Paganino, not wishing to admit in his presence that she knew him, and so after waiting a moment, he asked Paganino the favor of speaking to her in the room alone. Paganino agreed to this on the condition that he should not attempt to kiss her against her will, and ordered the lady to go into a room with him to hear what he had to say to her and to reply to him however she saw fit.

And so the lady and Messer Riccardo went into a room alone, and when they were seated, Messer Riccardo began to say:

"Ah, heart of my body, my sweet soul, my hope, now do you not recognize your Riccardo who loves you more than himself? How can this be? Am I so transformed? Ah, apple of my eye, just look at me a little."

The lady began to laugh and without allowing him to speak further she replied:

"You know very well I am not so absentminded that I do not realize you are Messer Riccardo di Chinzica, my husband; but while I was with you, you showed that you knew me rather poorly, for if you were as wise or as eager as you wished to be regarded, you should have had enough understanding to realize that I was a young, fresh, vigorous woman and, because of this, you should have realized what young women require besides clothes and food, even if they do not say, because they are modest, what it is they want—and just how well you provided that, you yourself know. And if the study of the law was more appealing to you than your wife, you should not have married—though you never seemed much of a judge to me, but more like a town-crier of holy days, holidays, fasts, and vigils, so well did you know them all. And I can tell you that if you gave as many holidays to the laborers who work on your estates as you gave to the man who was supposed to work my small little field, you would never have harvested a single grain of wheat. But as God, a compassionate observer of my youth, willed it, I happened upon this man here with whom I share this room where holidays are unheard of (I am speaking of the kinds of holidays that you, more devoted to the service of God than to the servicing of women, used to celebrate so often); and not only has that door been shut on Saturdays or Fridays or vigils or the four days of Ember or Lent (which lasts forever), but here work goes on and we beat our wool all day and night; in fact since matins rung this morning I can swear to you that this type of work was performed at least once already. And so I mean to stay here with him and to work while I am still young and to save the holidays, the indulgences, and the fasts for when I am older; as for you, I suggest you leave as quickly as you can, and with the best of luck to you, go celebrate as many holidays as you like, but without me."

Messer Riccardo, upon hearing these words, suffered unbearable grief, and when he saw that she had finished speaking, he said:

"Ah, my sweet soul, do you know what you're saying? Do you have no concern for your parents' honor or your own? Would you rather stay here as this man's whore and live in mortal sin than live in Pisa as my wife? When this man is tired of you, to your great shame he will throw you out; I shall always hold you most dear, and whatever happens you will always be the mistress of my house. Must you abandon your honor and me, who love you more than my life, because of this unbridled and dishonest appetite of yours? Ah, my dear hope, do not say another word but come away with me; from this moment on, now that I understand your desires, I shall try harder; so, my good sweet wife, change your mind and come away with me, for I have never been happy since the moment you were taken from me."

To this the lady replied:

"As for my honor, now that it is too late, I do not intend for anyone to be more jealous of it than I am. Would that my parents had been more concerned over it when they gave me to you! But since they were unconcerned about my honor then, I do not intend to be concerned about theirs now, and if I am at present living in mortar sin, I would also be so with a cold pestle,* so do not be any more tender with my honor than I am. And let me tell you this, that here I feel like Paganino's wife, whereas in Pisa I felt like your whore, remembering all the phases of the moon and the geometrical calculations that were necessary between you and me to bring the planets into conjunction, while here Paganino holds me in his arms all night, squeezes, and bites me, and just what he does for me only God can explain. And you claim that you will try harder! But how? By doing it in three shots and then getting it up again stiff like a rod? I didn't realize you had become so bold a knight since I last saw you! Go away and just try to stay alive, for you look so run-down and wretched that you're barely able to hang on to life! And furthermore, let me tell you this: even if Paganino abandoned me (which he does not seem to wish to do as long as I wish to remain), I do not intend ever to return to you, because I know that if I squeezed you all over, you couldn't come up with even a thimble full of juice—I stayed with you once, suffering the greatest loss and paying too high an interest rate, and now I shall seek my profits somewhere else. So, once more, let me tell you that here there are no holidays or vigils, and here I intend to remain; so, with God's blessing, be off with you as quickly as you can or I shall scream and say that you are trying to rape me."

Messer Riccardo, now seeing himself in a hopeless situation and realizing now how foolish he was to have married a young girl when he was so impotent, left the room unhappy and forlorn, and though he said a number of other things to Paganino, it all made no difference. Finally, without having accomplished anything, he abandoned his lady and returned to Pisa, where he fell into such a state of madness from his grief that whenever anyone greeted him or asked him something as he walked the

---

*A typical pun on words (mortar sin—mortal sin) which introduces the sexual image of the pestle immediately following.

city, he could only reply: "The evil hole observes no holidays"; and not long afterward he died.

When Paganin heard about this and realized how much the lady loved him, he took her as his legitimate bride, and with no concern whatsoever about observing holidays or vigils or Lent, the two of them worked together as long as their legs could support them, and they thoroughly enjoyed themselves. Because of this, my dear ladies, it seems to me that in arguing with Ambruogiuolo, Ser Bernabò was riding his goat ass-backwards."*

[Second Day, Conclusion]

✠

THIS story gave the entire company so much to laugh about that there was none of them whose jaws did not ache, and all the ladies unanimously agreed that what Dioneo had said was true and that Bernabò had been an ass. When the story was over and the laughter had subsided, the Queen, who saw that the hour was already late and that everyone had told a story, realizing that the end of her rule had come, according to the established order, removed the garland from her brow and placed it upon the head of Neifile, and with a smile on her face she announced:

"Now, dearest companion, the rule of this tiny nation is yours." And then she sat down again.

Neifile blushed a little from the honor she had received, so that her face resembled a fresh rose in April or May when it displays itself in the morning light, and her eyes, which she lowered in modesty, were no less charming and sparkling than the morning star. But after a courteous round of applause from her companions displaying their joyful approval of the Queen had subsided, she regained her composure and, sitting in a slightly higher position than usual, she said:

"Since I am to be your Queen, I shall not depart from the manner of those who have preceded me, whose rule you have commended by your obedience, and I shall make known to you in a few words my own proposal, and if it meets with your approval, we shall follow it. As you know, tomorrow is Friday and

---

*The original (*cavalcasse la capra inverso il chino*) asserts Dioneo's view that Bernabò's argument in II, 9 concerning women's fidelity was on the wrong track.

the following day is Saturday, both of which most people consider rather tedious days because of the food we usually eat on those days—not to mention the fact that Friday is worthy of our respect, since on that day, let us recall, He who died that we might live suffered His Passion, and therefore I would consider it fitting and most proper if for the sake of God's love we passed our time praying instead of telling stories on that day. On Saturday, it is the custom for women to wash their hair and to rinse away all the dust and grime that have accumulated through the course of the past week's labors; many women are, likewise, accustomed to fast out of their reverence for the Virgin Mother of the Son of God and to rest from all activity for the rest of the day out of respect for the ensuing Sunday; therefore, since we would not be able on that day to follow in full measure the plan we have chosen to live by, I think we should do well to refrain from our storytelling on that day as well. We shall then have been here four days, and if we wish to avoid other people joining us here, I think it would be an opportune time to leave here and to go elsewhere; in fact, I have already thought of a place to go and have made the arrangements. When we gather together there after our Sunday-afternoon nap—and you will have had more time for reflection, since today we have devoted sufficient time in our discussions to this day's topic—it will be more amusing if we restrict our freedom of choice in storytelling, let us say, to one of the many acts of Fortune, and I have decided that our subject shall be the following: stories about people who have attained something they desired through their ingenuity or who have recovered something they once lost. On this topic let each one of us think of something to say to the group that can be useful or at least amusing, always, of course, with the exception of Dioneo's privilege."

Everyone commended the Queen's speech and her proposal, and so they decreed that it should be done. After this, the Queen had her steward summoned, and she explained to him where he should set the tables in the evening and all that he was to do during the period of her reign; and when this was done, she rose to her feet with her companions and gave them her permission to do whatever most pleased each one of them.

The ladies and the men then made their way toward a small garden where they amused themselves for some time, and when suppertime arrived, with gaiety, they joyfully dined together; after leaving the table, as it pleased the Queen, Emilia began to dance and Pampinea to sing the following song while the rest joined in the chorus:

What lady is worthier than I to sing,
who is made happy in her every wish?

Come then, Love, cause of my every good,
my every hope, my every happy consequence,
let us sing together for a while,
not of sighs nor of bitter pain
which now makes sweeter for me your delight,
but only of that passionate clear flame
in which I live and burn in joyous feast
adoring you as if you were my god.

You, Love, set before my eyes
the first day that I fell into your fire,
a young man of such talent,
accomplishment, and valor
the likes of which no one could surpass
or could even be compared to;
so much have you inflamed me with him, Love,
that now in joy I sing with you of him.

What gives me my supreme delight is this:
that I please him as much as he does me,
Love, thanks to you,
for in this world I have
my wish, and in the next I hope for peace
through that unbroken faith
I bear for him—may God, who sees this, shed
his loving light on us from His high realm.

After this song, they sang others, danced a number of dances, and played a variety of tunes, but when the Queen decided it was time to go to bed, each of them retired to his or her bedroom carrying torches to light their way. And during the next two days, they devoted themselves to those matters the Queen had spoken of previously and eagerly looked forward to Sunday.

[Third Day, Title Page]

✤

Here ends the second day of The Decameron: *and the third begins, wherein under the rule of Neifile, stories are told about people who have attained something they desired through their ingenuity or who have recovered something they once lost.*

[Third Day, Introduction]

✤

THE dawn had already begun to turn from vermilion to orange with the approach of the sun, and the Queen on Sunday rose from her bed and awakened all her companions. Earlier the steward had sent ahead, to the spot where they were going to stay, many of the things needed there and servants enough to prepare them; and once he saw the Queen herself set out, he quickly had everything else loaded up, as if he were striking camp, and with the baggage and the remaining servants he departed, following the ladies and the gentlemen.

The Queen, meanwhile, joined and followed by her ladies and the three young men, and accompanied by the singing of perhaps twenty nightingales and other birds, strolled leisurely through a seldom-used path, one full of green grass and flowers all just beginning to open with the arrival of the sun; and taking the path toward the west, chatting, joking, and laughing with her group of companions, after walking less than two thousand paces, and before it was half past tierce, she took them to a most beautiful and rich palace, which was situated above the plain on a small hill. They went inside, and wandering all around it, they discov-

ered that the large rooms and the cleaned and ornately deco-
rated bedrooms were filled with everything that they might
need; they greatly admired the place and came to the conclusion
that its owner had to be a magnificent lord. Then, when they de-
scended to inspect its enormous and pleasant courtyard, and its
cellars full of the finest wines as well as the abundant source of
very cold water that was down there, they praised the place
even more. To rest awhile they sat down under a loggia over-
looking the entire courtyard, all of which had just been covered
with boughs and all the flowers that were in season, and their
discerning steward came to receive them with the most delect-
able of confections and the finest of wines as refreshment for
them.

Afterward, they were shown into a garden next to the palace
that was completely surrounded by walls, and the place at first
glance seemed so marvelously beautiful that they began to in-
spect its many sections more carefully. The garden had a num-
ber of very wide paths running all around it and through its
center, all as straight as arrows and covered with pergolas of
vines (which showed every indication of producing many grapes
that year), all of them in bloom, filling the garden with such
perfume that, mixed together with the odor of the many other
living things which smelled so sweet there, it seemed to them
that they were standing in the midst of all the spices that had
ever grown in the Orient. The sides of these paths were almost
entirely closed in by white and red roses and by jasmine, so that
not only during the mornings but also when the sun was at its
height one could stroll everywhere under a sweet-smelling and
delightful shade without being touched by the sun. It would take
too long to tell how many different varieties of plants there were
in that place, and how all of them were arranged, but every
plant of the pleasing sort our climate nourishes was present there
in great abundance. In the center of the garden there was some-
thing which they praised far more than any of its many other
praiseworthy features: a lawn of the finest grass, so deep a
green that it almost seemed black, and sprinkled all over with
perhaps a thousand kinds of flowers; and surrounding the garden
were the greenest of orange and lemon trees bearing mature as
well as ripening fruit and blossoms all at once, providing both a
pleasant shade for the eyes and a pleasing odor for the nostrils.
In the midst of this lawn there was a fountain of whitest marble
covered with marvelous carvings, and from a figure standing on
a column in the middle of the fountain a stream of water (I
know not whether from a natural spring or by artificial means),

powerful enough to turn a mill, gushed high into the air and then with a delightful sound, descended again into the crystal-clear water. The water which overflowed from the fountain ran through some hidden path through the lawn and then became visible again through finely constructed artificial channels which completely surrounded the lawn, and through similar channels it flowed to almost every part of the garden, finally collecting in a single place from which it emerged from the garden, flowing in a clear stream toward the plain. But before it reached that location, with the greatest of force and with no little profit to its owner, it turned two mills.

The sight of this garden, its exquisite plan, the plants, and the fountain with its little streams flowing from it pleased each of the ladies and the three young men so much that all of them decided that if Paradise were to be created on earth, they could conceive of it as having no other form than that of this garden, nor could they imagine what beauty might be added to the garden other than what it already possessed. As they happily wandered through it, making for themselves the most beautiful garlands from the branches of different trees while they listened to the songs of perhaps twenty different kinds of birds singing almost as if they were competing with each other, they discovered another delightful feature which, being so overwhelmed by the others, they had not yet noticed: for they saw that the garden was full of as many, perhaps, as one hundred varieties of beautiful animals, and they began pointing them out to one another— rabbits coming from one side, hares running in another direction; elsewhere deer were lying down, while in another spot young fawns were grazing—and besides this, there were many other varieties of harmless animals, happily running all about as if they were tame, all of which added even greater pleasure to their other delights.

Once they had wandered about long enough, now looking at one thing and now at another, they had the tables set up around the beautiful fountain and there, after singing six canzonets and dancing a number of dances, at the Queen's command they sat down to eat, and with exquisitely prepared dishes, they were elegantly served choice and delicate foods. Rising from the table, now even more merry than before, they turned once more to playing music, singing, and dancing until with the hottest part of the day approaching, the Queen felt it was time for those who wished to do so to take a nap. Some of the company did retire, while others, overwhelmed by the beauty of the place, did not wish to leave it, so instead they remained there, some reading romances, others playing chess or dice games while the rest slept.

But after nones, they all got up and refreshed their faces with the cool water, and as the Queen wished, they assembled on the lawn near the fountain, where having taken their seats according to the customary manner, they began waiting to tell their stories on the subject the Queen had proposed. The first of the group upon whom the Queen imposed this task was Filostrato, who began in this fashion:

[Third Day, First Story]

❦

Masetto da Lamporecchio pretends to be a deaf-mute and becomes the gardener for a convent of nuns, who all compete to lie with him.

MOST beautiful ladies, many are those men and women who are so stupid as to be thoroughly convinced that when a young woman places a white veil over her head and a black cowl upon her back, she no longer is a woman or she no longer feels feminine desires, as if the act of making her a nun had turned her into stone; and should they perhaps hear something contrary to this belief of theirs, they become very upset, as if some enormous and wicked evil had been perpetrated against Nature, never stopping to think about nor wishing to consider their own situation, in which they cannot satisfy themselves even though they possess complete freedom to do as they wish, nor do they consider the powerful influences of leisure and solicitation. And likewise there are many other people who believe only too well that the hoe, the spade, coarse food, and general discomfort eliminate entirely the lustful desires of those who work the soil, and make feeble their intelligence and discernment. But to show you clearly how badly deceived all those who think in this manner are—since the Queen has ordered me to speak without departing from the subject she has proposed—I shall tell a little story.

In this countryside of ours there was, and still is today, a nun's convent which is renowned for its sanctity and which I shall refrain from naming in order not to diminish to any degree its fame. Not long ago, there were only eight nuns and the

Abbess in the convent, all of whom were young women; there was also a good, sturdy man who took care of their very beautiful garden, but since he was not happy with his salary, he settled his accounts with the nun's steward and returned to Lamporecchio, from where he had come. There, among the others who cheerfully welcomed him back, was a young worker, strong and hardy, who, considering that he was a peasant, was nevertheless a handsome man, and his name was Masetto. He asked the good man, whose name was Nuto, where he had been for so long a time, and Nuto told him, and when Masetto asked him what he did at the convent, Nuto answered:

"I worked in one of their beautiful big gardens, and sometimes I went to the woods for firewood; I also would get the water from the well, and other such services, but the ladies gave me such a small salary that I had barely enough to buy shoes for myself. What's more, they were all young, and I thought they had the devil in their bodies, for there was nothing you could do to please them; in fact, when I would be in the orchard, sometimes one of them would tell me, 'Put this here,' and another would say, 'Put this there,' and another would take the hoe from my hand, saying, 'That's not the way.' They pestered me so much that I stopped working in the garden, and for one reason or another I decided I didn't want to work there any longer, and I came back here. When I left, their steward made me promise to send someone from here who knew how to garden, and I promised him that if I found someone I would send him. But the man I look for or manage to send him God better have built sound of loins!"

When Masetto heard what Nuto had to say, he was consumed with desire to be with these nuns, for he understood from Nuto's words that he would be able to do what he wished there; he also realized that things would not work out for him if he told Nuto about his plans, and so he said:

"Well, you did right to come home. What's a man reduced to when he's around women? He's better off around devils; six out of seven times they don't know what they want!"

But later on after their conversation, Masetto began thinking about how he should act in order to get the job with the nuns. He knew he could do the work Nuto did just as well as Nuto himself, so he was not afraid of being turned away on that account; he was afraid, rather, of not being hired because he was too young and good-looking. After considering a number of plans, he thought to himself:

"The place is far away from here and no one knows me there;

if I can pretend to be deaf and dumb, they'll certainly take me in."

With this in mind, he took up his ax and without telling anyone where he was going, he went to the convent dressed as a poor man; he arrived there, and when inside the courtyard he found, by chance, the steward, to whom he made gestures as mutes do, asking him in sign language for a bite to eat for the love of God, and in turn offering to chop some wood if they needed any.

The steward gladly gave him something to eat, and then he showed him some logs which Nuto had not been able to split, and he split them in no time at all, for he was very strong. Then the steward had to go to the forest, so he took Masetto with him, and there he had him cut some firewood, then load it on the donkey, and, by means of gestures, made him understand that he should carry it back to the convent. Masetto did this so well that the steward kept him around for several more days to do some chores that needed to be done. One day the Abbess happened to see him and she asked the steward who he was. He replied:

"My lady, he is a poor deaf and dumb man who came by here one day begging for alms, and I helped him out and, in return, made him do many of the chores that had to be done. If he knows how to do gardening and wants to remain here, I think we would have a good servant in him. He is just what we need: he's strong, and we can make him do what we wish, and besides this, you wouldn't have to worry about the possibility of his joking with your young ladies."

To this the Abbess replied:

"By God's faith, you speak the truth. Find out if he knows how to garden and try to keep him here; give him a pair of shoes and an old cloak, praise him, pamper him, and give him plenty to eat."

The steward said he would do so. Masetto, who was not far away, was pretending to clean the courtyard while he listened to everything that was said, and with much delight he said to himself:

"If you put me in there, I'll work your garden as it's never been worked before!"

Now, when the steward saw that he knew how to work very well, he asked him with gestures if he would stay on, and Masetto, with gestures, answered that he was willing to do whatever the steward wanted; so the steward told him to work in the garden and showed him what he had to do; then he left him alone and went off to attend to the other chores of the convent. As Masetto worked day after day, the nuns began to pester him and to make fun of him, as often happens to deaf-mutes; they would use the foulest language they knew with him, certain that he could not understand them; and the Abbess thought little or nothing about it, perhaps because she thought that he was as much without a tail up front as he was without a tongue in his mouth. Now one day it happened that two young nuns walking through the garden approached him while he was resting after much hard work, and, as he pretended to be asleep, they began to stare at him; one of them, the boldest of the two, said to the other:

"If I thought that you could keep a secret, I would tell you a thought that has passed through my mind many times, something which you might find profitable too."

The other nun replied:

"You can tell me, for I shall certainly tell no one else."

Then the bolder one began:

"I don't know if you have ever thought about how carefully we are watched here and how no man ever dares enter here except the steward, who is old, and this deaf-mute, and I have often heard it said by many of the women who come here that all the pleasures of the world are a joke compared to what happens when a woman gets with a man. Because of this, I have been thinking about seeing if that could be true by trying it with this deaf-mute, since no one else is available; and he is the best person in the world for this purpose, since even if he wanted to, he could not or would not know how to speak about it; as you can see, he is a stupid youth, mature in everything but his wits. I should very much like to hear what you think about the idea."

"Oh," said the other nun, "what are you saying? Don't you know that we have promised our virginity to God?"

"Oh," answered the first, "how many promises do we make Him every day which we can't keep? If we have made Him promises, let Him find others to keep them for us."

To this her companion said:

"But if we become pregnant, what'll we do?"

"You're beginning to worry about the worst before it even happens," the bolder one replied. "Worry about it when and if it happens; there are a thousand ways to keep it a secret, if we don't talk about it ourselves."

When her companion heard this, she wanted more than the other to find out what kind of beast a man was, and she said:

"Well, all right, how shall we proceed?"

The other answered her:

"As you see, it is almost nones, and I think that all the sisters are asleep except for us; let's look to see if anyone is in the garden, and if there is no one around, all we have to do is take him by the hand and lead him over to that hut where he goes when it rains, and one of us can stay inside with him while the other keeps watch. He is so stupid that he'll do whatever we wish."

Masetto heard all this and was ready to obey, waiting only for the moment when one of them would lead him off. Both nuns looked around carefully, and when they saw that they could not be seen by anyone from anywhere, the sister who had first made the suggestion approached Masetto and woke him; quickly he rose to his feet. Then, she took him by the hand, while he made ridiculous giggling noises, and with flattering gestures she led him to the hut, where Masetto did what she wished without waiting for an invitation. After she had what she wanted, being a loyal friend, she gave her place to the other nun, and Masetto, still playing the fool, did what she wanted. And before they left, both sisters wished to see what it would be like to have the deaf-mute ride them once more; then later on, discussing it with each other, they decided that it really was as pleasant as they had heard, even more so; so, whenever they found it convenient, from then on they would amuse themselves with the mute.

One day it happened that one of the other nuns saw what was going on from one of the windows of her cell, and she showed two others; at first they decided to denounce the two girls to the Abbess, but then they changed their minds and came to an agreement with them instead: they became partners in Masetto's farm; and because of other various incidents, the convent's remaining three nuns soon joined their company.

Finally the Abbess, who still did not know about any of this, was walking in the garden one day all alone in the heat of the afternoon when she came upon Masetto, who tired easily during the day because of all the time he spent riding at night; he was stretched out in the shade of an almond tree, asleep, and the wind had blown the ends of his shirt up, leaving him quite exposed. Looking at it and realizing she was all alone, the Abbess fell victim to the same lustful cravings that had overtaken her nuns; she woke Masetto and led him to her room, where she kept him for several days, provoking much complaining from the nuns, since the gardener had not returned to work their garden, and the Abbess over and over again enjoyed that sweetness which before she used to condemn in others. At last, she sent him back to his room, but she called on him very often, taking more than her share, so that eventually Masetto was not able to satisfy so many, and he realized that his being mute might do him too much harm if he allowed it to continue any longer; therefore, one night when he was with the Abbess, he loosened his tongue and began to speak:

"My lady, I have heard that one cock is enough to satisfy ten hens, but that ten men can poorly, or with difficulty, satisfy one woman, and I have to satisfy nine of them. I can't stand it any longer; from doing what I've done I have reached the point of no longer being able to do anything! So either let me go, in God's name, or find some solution to this problem."

When the lady heard the deaf-mute speak, she was completely dumbfounded, and she answered:

"What is this? I thought you were a mute."

"My lady," Masetto said, "I really was, not from birth but rather because of an illness that took my speech from me, and tonight, for the first time, it was restored to me, and for this I give all my thanks to God."

She believed him, and asked him what he meant when he said he had nine women to satisfy. Masetto told her everything, and when the Abbess heard this, she realized that all of her nuns were wiser than she; but, being a discreet person, she decided to find a way, together with her nuns, to keep Masetto from leaving and prevent the convent from suffering any scandal. With Masetto's consent, they unanimously agreed (now that what everyone had done behind one another's backs was evident) to make the nearby inhabitants believe that by their prayers and the merits of the saint after whom the convent was named, the power of speech had been restored to Masetto, who had for a long time been mute, and since their steward had passed away a few days earlier, they decided to give him that position; and his labors were shared in such a way that he was able to perform them. In performing them, he generated a large number of little monks and nuns, but the matter was so discreetly handled that no one heard anything about it until after the death of the Abbess, when Masetto was nearing old age and was anxious to return home with the money he had made; he easily got what he wanted when his wishes became known.

So Masetto returned home old and rich and a father, without ever having to bear the expense of bringing up his children, for he had been smart enough to make good use of his youth: hav-

ing left with an ax on his shoulder, he returned affirming that
this was the way Christ treated all those who put a pair of horns
upon his crown.

[Third Day, Second Story]

❧

*A groom lies with the wife of King Agilulf, and Agilulf discovers
this but says nothing; he finds the man and shears his hair; the
shorn man shears all the others and thus avoids coming to a bad
end.*

When Filostrato's story, some parts of which had made the
ladies blush a bit while others moved them to laughter, came to
an end, it pleased the Queen for Pampinea to continue the story-
telling; and with a smiling face, she said:

Some people, having discovered or heard something which they
are better off not knowing, are so anxious at any cost to reveal
what they know that sometimes when reproaching the hidden de-
fects of others with the purpose of lessening their own shame,
they in fact increase it out of all proportion; and that such is
the case, fair ladies, I intend to demonstrate to you by its con-
trary, showing you how the cleverness of a man of even lower
station than Masetto matched the wisdom of a valiant king.

Agilulf, King of the Lombards, as his predecessors did, es-
tablished the capital of his kingdom in Pavia, a Lombard city,
having taken as his wife Teudelinga, the widow of Auttari, the
former King of the Lombards. She was a very beautiful woman,
wise and virtuous, but she had an unfortunate experience with
love. For during a time when the affairs of Lombardy were pros-
pering and there was peace because of the virtue and the wis-
dom of King Agilulf, it happened that the Queen's groom, a man
of the lowest birth but, in other respects, far too talented for
such a humble trade, as handsome and as tall as even the King
himself was, fell madly in love with the Queen. And his humble
station in life did not prevent him from realizing that this love
of his lay beyond the boundaries of every propriety, and he was
wise enough never to reveal his love to anyone, nor did he ever
dare reveal it even to his lady through his eyes. And while he
lived without any hope of ever winning the lady's favor, he
could at least take joy in the fact that he had directed his

thought toward such a lofty goal. Since he was a man burning all over with Love's amorous flame, more than any of his companions he eagerly did everything he felt might please the Queen. Thus it came about that whenever the Queen went riding, she preferred to ride the palfrey under his care rather than any of the others, and whenever this happened, the groom considered it a very special favor and never left her stirrup, considering himself blessed whenever he could as much as touch her clothes.

But as we very often observe, when hope lessens love becomes that much stronger, and this was the case with the poor groom, so much so that with the aid of some glimmer of hope, he found it most difficult to control the burning desire he kept concealed, and since he was unable to free himself from this passion, on many occasions he thought about killing himself. As he thought about this, he came to the conclusion that he would have to die in such a manner that through his death, the love he had borne and was still bearing for the Queen would become evident; and he proposed to act in such a way as to try his luck and see if he could totally, or at least in part, fulfill his desires. Nor did he attempt to say anything to the Queen or to reveal his love for her through letters, for he knew that it would be useless to speak or write. Instead he thought about attempting to lie with the Queen by means of a trick; and he knew that the only way to get to her, the only trick that might possibly work, was to impersonate the King, whom he knew did not lie with her every night, and in this way gain entrance to her bedroom.

And so in order to observe how the King acted and how he dressed when he went to her, many times during the night the groom would hide himself in one of the great halls of the King's palace, the one which was midway between the King's bedroom and that of the Queen. On one of these nights he observed the King leaving his room wrapped in a large cloak, carrying a lighted torch in one hand and a small rod in the other; he went to the Queen's bedroom and, without saying a word, knocked once or twice with the rod at the entrance to the room, whereupon the door was immediately opened to him and the torch was taken from his hand.

Having observed all this as well as the way the King would after a while return to his own quarters, the groom decided that he would have to do the same thing. He found a way to get a cloak similar to what he had seen the King wearing, a torch, and a small rod, and having thoroughly washed himself in a hot bath so that the odor of horse manure might not offend the Queen or cause her to suspect a trick, he took these objects with him and hid in his usual place in the great hall. When he sensed that everyone was asleep and it seemed that the time had come either to fulfill his desire or to open the way to his long-desired death and perish for this noble cause, he lighted his torch by striking a light with the flint and steel he brought with him for this purpose and, wrapping himself up in the cloak, made his way to the door of the bedroom and knocked twice with his rod. The door was opened by a sleepy chambermaid, who took the light and put it aside; then without speaking a word, the groom passed behind the bedcurtain, took off his cloak, and climbed into the bed where the Queen was sleeping. He knew that whenever the King was angry about something, it was his habit to refrain from conversation, so taking her lustfully in his arms, he pretended to be angry, and without uttering a word to her or her saying anything to him, he made the carnal acquaintance of the Queen several times. Though it was most painful for him to leave, he nevertheless feared that staying too long might turn the pleasures he had experienced into grief, so he left the bed, took up his cloak and light once more, and without saying a thing went away. As quickly as he could, he returned to his own bed.

He had no sooner reached it when the King, having arisen, went to the Queen's room, and to her great surprise, he climbed into her bed and greeted her cheerfully; she, taking courage from his good humor, exclaimed:

"Oh, my lord, what is this novelty tonight? You have only just left me, having taken your pleasure more passionately than usual, and now you are already back to start all over agin! Do be careful what you do!"

The King, hearing these words, presumed at once that the Queen had been deceived by a person of similar dress and size, but as he was a wise man, and since he saw that neither the Queen nor anyone else had noticed, he immediately decided not to reveal this to her. Many a fool would have acted differently, exclaiming instead: "That wasn't me! Who was the man who was here? What happened? How did he get here?" But this would have given rise to a number of complications that would have distressed the lady unnecessarily and also, perhaps, given her reason to desire once again what she had just experienced. By remaining silent no shame could accrue to him, whereas by talking about it he would have brought disgrace upon himself.

The King, angrier in his own mind than he allowed himself to reveal through his face or in his words, answered her in this fashion:

"My lady, do I not seem to you to be the kind of man that is capable of being with you once and then returning to you again?"

To this the lady replied: "Of course, my lord, but I nevertheless do beg you to look after your health."

Then the King said: "I shall take your good advice and leave you this time without bothering you further."

Seething with anger and indignation over what he saw had been done to him, the King picked up his cloak and left the room, having decided to find out in secret who had done this to him, for he knew that it had to be someone who was a part of his household and, whoever he might be, he could not have gotten past the palace gates. Accordingly, he picked up a lantern with a dim light and went up into a very large room located over the palace horse stables where all of his servants slept in different beds. Since he guessed that whoever had done what his wife had told him would not yet have been able to calm his pulse or the beating of his heart caused by the emotional excitement, the King quietly began to walk from one end of the room, feeling the chests of each of his servants to see if his heart were still pounding.

Although everyone was sleeping soundly, the man who had been with the Queen was not yet asleep, and as he saw the King draw nearer to him and realized what he was looking for, he became very much frightened, so much so that besides the pounding heart which resulted from the effort he had recently expended, his fear increased his pulse even more, for he was well aware that if the King noticed this, he would have him executed immediately. A number of things he might do passed through his head, but when he saw that the King was unarmed, he decided to pretend to be asleep and to wait and see what the King would do. Having touched many of them without finding any whom he judged to have been the man he was seeking, the King finally reached the groom, and discovering that his heart was beating so rapidly, he said to himself: "This is the man." But since he did not want his intentions known, all he did for the moment was to cut off a lock of the groom's hair, which in those days was worn very long, with a pair of scissors he had with him so that the following morning he would be able to recognize him from that sign; after he did this, he left and returned to his bedroom.

The groom, who had seen everything and was, moreover, very clever, realized all too clearly why he had been marked this way; whereupon, without a moment to lose he got up, found some scissors (several pairs of which were fortunately there in the stable for tending to the horses), and quietly went along from man to man sleeping in the room and cut his hair above the ears exactly the same way his was; once this was done, he went back to bed without anyone's noticing a thing.

Upon arising the next morning, the King ordered that before the gates to the palace were opened, his entire retinue should gather before him; and so this was done. When they were all assembled there and stood before him without anything on their heads, the King began to look them over in order to identify the man he had sheared. When he saw that the better part of them had been sheared in the very same fashion, he was amazed and said to himself: "This man, the one I am looking for, may be of low station, but he evidently has his wits about him!" Then, realizing that he could not obtain what he wanted without causing a disturbance, and determined not to acquire great shame at the expense of trivial revenge, the King decided to give the culprit a word of warning and to show him that he had not gone unobserved, and turning to the group he announced: "Let whoever did it never do it again, and now, with God's blessing, be off with you."

Another man would have had them all up on the rack, tortured, examined, and interrogated, but in so doing, he would have uncovered something that people should try to conceal; and once it was out in the open, even if he had taken the fullest possible revenge, as a result he would not have removed his own shame but, rather, greatly increased it as well as soiled the reputation of his lady. The men who heard the King's words were astonished, and for many days to come they would be asking each other what he had meant by them, but no one understood their meaning except the man to whom they referred. And he, clever man that he was, never revealed their meaning as long as the King lived, nor did he ever again entrust his life to the hands of Fortune by performing a similar deed.

[Third Day, Third Story]

❋

Under the pretense of going to confession and being of the purest of minds, a lady, who is in love with a young man, induces a sanctimonious friar, who is unsuspecting, to arrange things to the entire satisfaction of her pleasure.

PAMPINEA was now silent, and the bravery and prudence of the groom were praised by a number of the company, who also commended the wisdom of the King, when the Queen, turning to Filomena, ordered her to follow; whereupon Filomena began gracefully to speak in this fashion:

I would like to tell you a story concerning a trick which was actually played by a beautiful lady upon a sanctimonious churchman and which should prove to be all the more pleasing to laymen inasmuch as most of the clergy are very stupid men with strange manners and habits who consider themselves more worthy and knowledgeable than everybody in everything, when they are, in fact, far inferior, and since they are too simpleminded to know how to look after themselves as everyone else does, they seek refuge wherever they can find something to eat, just like pigs. I shall tell you this story, dear ladies, not only in obedience to the order imposed upon me but also to make you aware that even the clergy, in whom we place too much trust out of our excessive credulity, are capable of being cleverly deceived, as actually they sometimes are, not only by men but also by some of us women.

In our own city, more a place of fraud than love or loyalty, not many years ago there lived a noble lady who was endowed by Nature with as much beauty, good manners, fine breeding, and shrewd mind as any woman ever had. Her name, as well as other names connected with this story, I do not intend to disclose (although I know them all), for there are still some people alive who would be covered with shame by this, whereas they would otherwise allow the story to pass off with a laugh.

This lady, therefore, being of high birth and finding herself married to some wool merchant, was unable to suppress her contempt for the fact that he was a common merchant, for she believed that no man of low condition, no matter how rich he might be, was worthy of a noble lady, and when she realized that with all his wealth he knew nothing except how to design a blend of cloth, or to set up a loom, or argue with a spinning girl about a yarn, she decided to put up with only those embraces which were not in her power to refuse, and to satisfy herself by finding someone who she felt was more worthy of her than a wool merchant. And she soon fell in love with a very worthy gentleman of about thirty-five, so much in love that when she did not see him during the day, she was unable to get through the night in peace; but the worthy man was not aware of all this, and paid no attention to her, and being a very cautious person, she dared not declare her love by sending a maidservant as messenger or by writing him a letter, fearing the possible dangers this might entail.

Then she found out that he often could be found in the company of a cleric who, though a fat and coarse individual, was nevertheless, because of the most holy life he led, regarded by everyone as a most able friar, and she felt that this man would make an excellent go-between for her and the man she loved. So after reflecting on how she might do this, she went at a suitable hour to the church where the friar was to be found, had him summoned, and then asked him if he would be willing to hear her confession.

The friar upon seeing her realized that she was a noble lady, and he listened to her confession most willingly. After she had confessed, the lady said:

"Father, there is a matter, as I shall explain to you shortly, about which I am obliged to consult you for assistance and advice. I know, having told you all about them, that you are acquainted with my family and my husband, who loves me more dearly than his own life, and who, being an extremely wealthy man who can do anything he wishes, never shows the slightest hesitation in giving me whatever I desire. For this reason I love him more than my own life, and at the mere thought, not to mention my behavior, of my doing anything contrary to his wishes and his honor, I would be more deserving of the flames of Hell than the wickedest woman in the world. Now there is a certain person (I really have no idea what his name is) who would seem to be a proper gentleman, and who, if I am not mistaken, is often in your company. He is handsome and tall, dresses in elegant brown clothes, and perhaps because he does not understand my intentions, he seems to have laid siege to me; I cannot go to my window or look out the door, nor can I leave the house without him instantly appearing before me—in fact, I am amazed that he is not here now. I am very upset about this, for such behavior often gives an honest, innocent woman a bad name. I had in mind, on several occasions, to talk to my brothers about this, but then I realized that men sometimes carry out these missions in such a manner as to provoke sharp responses, which lead to cross words, and words lead to blows. So, in order to avoid any unfortunate circumstances or scandal that might result from all this, I have kept silent, and made up my mind to tell this to you and to no one else, not only because you seem to be his friend but also because it seems only fitting that a man in your position censure both his friends as well as strangers for this kind of behavior. In God's name, therefore, I beg you to reproach him for this and to persuade him not to continue in this fashion. There are probably many other women who would find all this appealing and who would like to be looked at and courted by him—whereas to me all this is a very unpleasant nuisance, for in no way am I well disposed to it." Having said this, as if she wished to weep, she lowered her head.

The holy friar quickly and correctly understood to whom she was referring, and praised the woman highly for her good conduct. Firmly convinced that what she had said was true, he promised to see to it that she would never ever be bothered by that man again; and as he knew she was wealthy, he started going on and on about acts of charity and the giving of alms, informing her of his own needy condition.

To this the lady said:

"I beg you, for the love of God, should he deny all this, be sure you tell him that it was I who told you and who complained about it."

And then, having made her confession and received her penance, remembering the advice the friar had given her on acts of charity, the lady discreetly filled his hand with money and requested that he say Masses for the souls of her dead relatives; then she got up from where she was kneeling at his feet and returned home.

Not long afterward, as was his custom, the worthy gentleman came to see the holy friar; after the two of them had discussed one thing and another for some time, the friar drew him aside and reproached him in a very polite tone for his courting and the amorous glances the lady had given the friar to believe the gentleman was casting in her direction. The worthy gentleman was astonished, as he had never looked at her and only very rarely was he accustomed to pass before her house, and he began to proclaim his innocence, but the friar, not allowing him to say a word, said instead:

"Now don't pretend to be surprised or to waste your words denying it, because you won't get away with it. I didn't learn these things from your neighbors; she herself, complaining bitterly about you, revealed it all to me. And besides the fact that such foolishness does not suit you, let me tell you this about her: I have never come across a woman who was more disgusted by such foolishness than she, so, for the sake of your honor and her tranquillity I ask you to get hold of yourself and leave her in peace."

The worthy man, more perceptive than the holy friar, was quick to understand the lady's cleverness, and pretending to be somewhat embarrassed, he replied that from now on, he would mind his own business. Leaving the friar, he went to the house of the lady, who was always watching from a tiny little window to see if he might happen to pass by. When she saw him coming, she looked at him with such joy and delight that he understood without a doubt the actual meaning of the friar's words; and from that day on, with great caution and to his delight and the greatest pleasure and consolation of the lady, pretending that some other business was the reason, he began to pass through her neighborhood regularly.

But a while later after the lady had already discovered that she pleased him as much as he pleased her, anxious to arouse his passion further and to demonstrate the love she bore for him, at the first appropriate opportunity she returned to the holy friar, and kneeling at his feet in church, she began to weep. The friar, seeing this, asked her compassionately what new misfortune had befallen her.

The lady replied:

"Father, the new misfortunes that I suffer are none other than that accursed friend of yours, of whom I complained to you several days ago, for I believe he was born only to become my greatest torment and to tempt me into doing something I shall regret forever and which would never again allow me to kneel at your feet."

"What?" said the friar. "Hasn't he stopped annoying you?"

"He certainly has not," the lady replied. "On the contrary, he seems to have taken the fact that I complained to you rather badly, and ever since then, almost as if out of spite, for every time he used to pass by my house he now passes by it seven times over. And would to God that his visits or his amorous glances might suffice, but he has been so bold and so impudent that only yesterday he sent a woman to my home to deliver some silly message with some trinkets of his—as if I didn't already own purses or belts, he sent me one of each; this made me so angry, and it continues to do so, that if I had not considered the scandal as well as your friendship for him, I would have raised the very devil; but I controlled my temper, nor did I wish to do or say anything before I first informed you about it. And besides this, after giving back the purse and belt to the maidservant who had delivered them, instructing her to return them to him, and dismissing her curtly, it occurred to me that she might keep them for herself and tell him that I had kept them (as I understand such women sometimes do), so I called her back and angrily snatched them out of her hands, and I have brought them here to you so that you yourself may return them to him, telling him for me that I have no need of his things, for, thanks be to God and my husband, I've got enough purses and belts to drown in. Furthermore—and I beg your pardon for saying so, father—if he does not stop this, I shall tell my husband and my brothers and let whatever happens happen, for I much prefer that harm come to him, if harm must be done, than for me to be blamed on his account. So, there you have it, father!"

And after she said this, all the while weeping profusely, she drew forth from her long cloak a most beautiful and ornate purse along with a fine and precious little belt and threw them in the friar's lap; fully convinced by what the lady said and angered beyond all measure, he took them and exclaimed:

"My daughter, if you are angered by these things, I am not at all surprised, nor do I blame you; on the contrary, I commend you most highly for following my instructions. I reprimanded him the other day, and since he has failed to keep the promise he made me that day, partly for that reason and partly because of what he has just done, I think I shall warm his ears in such a way that he will give you no further trouble. But in the meantime you, with God's blessing, should not allow yourself to be so carried away by your anger as to tell any of your relatives about this, for too great a punishment may befall him on this account. Nor should you ever fear that because of this you will incur any blame, for I shall always, before God and before all men, bear strong witness to your chastity."

The lady pretended to be somewhat reassured and, knowing how greedy he and his fellow friars were, she changed the topic of conversation and said:

"Sir, during the past few nights a number of my dearly departed relatives have appeared to me, and they seem to be suffering the most terrible of punishments and they beg for nothing but alms, especially my mother, who appears to be in such an afflicted and miserable state that it is a pity to behold. I believe she is suffering such tremendous pain from seeing me so persecuted by this enemy of God; therefore, I should like you to say on my behalf the forty Masses of St. George and your own prayers for their souls so that God may release them from that tormenting fire." And having said this, she put a florin in his hand.

The holy friar happily took it, and after a few good words and with a number of exemplary tales to reinforce the devotion of the lady, he gave her his blessing and sent her away. After the lady had gone, the friar, unaware that he had been hoodwinked, sent for his friend, who, as soon as he arrived and saw the friar so upset, immediately understood that he was about to receive news from the lady, and he waited to hear what the friar had to say. The friar, repeating to his friend the things he had said to him earlier, speaking to him again in a harsh and angry tone, reprimanded him severely for what the lady told him he had done. The gentleman, as yet unable to see where the friar's words were leading, denied having sent the purse and the belt in a halfhearted way so as not to discredit the story, just in case the lady had given them to him.

But the friar, in a rage, exclaimed:

"How can you deny this, you wicked man? Here they are, she herself just gave them to me in tears: look and see if you recognize them!"

The gentleman, pretending to be very ashamed of himself, replied:

"Yes, indeed, I do recognize them, and I confess to you that I was wrong to do it, and now that I know how she feels about me, I swear to you that you will never hear another word about this."

The words that followed were many, and finally the fool of a friar gave the purse and the belt to his friend, warning him and begging him not to pursue such matters any further, and when his friend promised not to, he sent him on his way. The gentleman was extremely delighted both by the certainty of the lady's love he now possessed and by the handsome gift she had given him. No sooner had he left the friar than he went directly to a place which would discreetly allow him to show his lady that he now possessed both her one gift and the other, all of which made the lady very happy, especially since she felt that her plan was working better and better. All she waited for now in order to bring her labors to a successful ending was for her husband to go away somewhere, and not long afterward for one reason or another her husband had to go all the way to Genoa.

In the morning, after he had ridden off on his horse, the lady went to the holy frair and, lamenting on and on in tears, she said to him:

"Father, I tell you now that I can no longer endure this; however, since I promised you the other day to do nothing without telling you first, I have come here now to justify my actions. Should you have reason to doubt my right to weep and complain, let me tell you what your friend—or rather, this devil from Hell—did to me this morning a little before dawn. What unfortunate circumstances allowed him to discover that my husband was going away to Genoa yesterday morning, I do not know, but this morning at the time I just told you, he entered my garden and climbed up a tree to the window of my bedroom overlooking the garden. And he already had the window open and was about to enter the bedroom when I woke up, jumped out of bed, and began to scream, and I would have continued to scream if not for the fact that while he was still outside, he announced who he was and begged me for mercy both in God's name and in yours. So I listened to him and for your sake kept silent, and naked as the day I was born, I ran to the window and slammed it in his face, after which I think that he, in his wretchedness, must have gone away, since I heard no more from him. Now judge for yourself if such a thing is proper or should be allowed to persist; for my part, I do not intend to tolerate it any longer. In fact, I have already endured too much for your sake."

The friar, hearing this, was the angriest man in the world, and the only thing he could do was to ask her over and over again if she was certain it had not been someone else.

To this the lady answered:

"God knows that by this time I should be able to tell him from someone else! I am telling you that it was he, and if he denies it, don't you believe him."

Then the friar said:

"Daughter, all that I can say is that now he has gone too far. What he has done is unpardonable, and you were right in sending him away as you did. But since God has preserved you from shame the two times you followed my advice, I beg you to do so one more time and allow me to handle matters without complaining to any of your relatives. Let me see if I can restrain this unchained devil whom I believed once to be a saint. If I manage to cure him of this vileness of his, all well and good, and if I am unsuccessful, then at that time I give you permission, and with my blessing, to do whatever your conscience tells you should be done."

"Very well," said the lady, "this time I shall not anger or disobey you, but see that he keeps from ever bothering me again, for I swear to you that I shall come back to discuss the matter with you again." And without saying another word, she turned and walked away from the friar as if she were angry.

The lady was no sooner outside the church than the gentleman arrived and was called to one side by the friar, who proceeded to administer the strongest rebuke a man ever had, calling him disloyal, a perjurer, and a traitor. The man, who twice before had seen where the reproaches of the friar would eventually lead, waited and with his ambiguous answers attempted to make him talk more, first by saying:

"Why are you so angry, sir? Have I crucified Christ?"

To this the friar replied:

"Just look at this shameless individual! Listen to what he's saying! He talks as if one or two years, more or less, have gone by and the length of time has made him forget his wickedness and dishonesty. Have you forgotten how you outraged someone this morning at dawn? Where were you this morning a little before daylight?"

The gentleman answered:

"I don't know where I was, but it didn't take you long to find out!"

"That's true," answered the friar, "it didn't take me long to find out. I suppose you thought that since her husband was out of town the good lady would immediately open her arms to you. Well, just look what an honest little fellow he is! Turned into a night prowler, he has, an invader of gardens and a climber of trees! Do you think your impudence is going to conquer the chastity of this lady, by climbing up trees at night to reach her window? She finds nothing in the world more displeasing to her than what you are doing, yet you insist on trying again and again! Besides the fact that she has shown you this over and over again, you certainly were well warned by all my reproofs! But let me tell you this: until now, and not out of any love she bears for you but rather because of my entreaties, she has kept quiet about what you have done, but she will not keep quiet any longer, for I have given her my permission to do whatever she sees fit if you should displease her any further in any way. What will you do if she tells her brothers?"

Having understood very well what he needed to do, the gentleman calmed the friar as best he knew how with a flow of promises; he left the friar, and on the next day at dawn he entered her garden, climbed the tree, and finding her window open, entered her bedroom, and as quickly as he could he threw himself into the arms of his beautiful lady, who had been waiting for him with the greatest of desire, and, receiving him happily she said:

"A thousand thanks to our friend the friar, who has taught you so well the way to come here."

And then, while enjoying each other, they talked and laughed hilariously over the stupidity of Brother Ignoramus, and made many a jibe about wool-wicks, wool-combs, and wool-carders* as together they amused themselves to the great delight of both parties.

They then organized their affairs in such a manner that they never again had to return to their friend the friar, and they found themselves together on many other nights sharing the same happiness. And I pray God through the bounty of His mercy that He may soon bestow the same thing upon me and every other Christian soul who has such a desire.

[Third Day, Fourth Story]

❦

Dom Felice teaches Friar Puccio how to attain sainthood by performing one of his penances; Friar Puccio does this, and by this means Dom Felice has a good time with the friar's wife.

WHEN Filomena, having come to the end of her story, fell silent and Dioneo with a few well-chosen words had praised the lady's ingenuity as well as Filomena's closing prayer, the Queen turned toward Panfilo, and, laughing, she said:

"And now, Panfilo, add to our delight with one of your amusing little stories."

Panfilo immediately replied that he would be delighted to do so and began:

My lady, there are many people who, while striving to get to Paradise, without knowing it manage to send someone else there

---

*Their jibes concerning these technical terms from the woolen industry are naturally aimed at the now cuckolded woolen merchant.

instead of themselves; and this, as you are now about to hear,
happened to a lady from our city not long ago.

There once lived, according to what I have heard, near the
Convent of San Brancazio a good man, and rich too, called Puc-
cio di Rinieri, who, as he was completely devoted to spiritual
matters, became a tertiary of the Franciscan Order, taking the
name of Friar Puccio: and in pursuing this spiritual life of his,
since all the family he had consisted of a wife and a maidser-
vant, which meant that there was no reason for him to go out
and work, he would very often frequent the church. Since he
was a rather thick-witted, simpleminded man, he always said his
Our Fathers and went to Mass, attended sermons, and never
failed to show up when lauds were being sung by laymen, and he
fasted, and practiced other types of discipline. It was even
rumored that he was a member of the Flagellants. His wife,
whose name was Monna Isabetta, was still young, between
twenty-eight and thirty, and she looked as fresh and pretty and
plump as an apple from Casole, but because of her husband's
saintliness and perhaps his old age, she very often went on long-
er diets than she might otherwise have desired; and on those oc-
casions when she might have wanted to sleep with him and fool
around in bed, he would lecture her on the life of Christ, the
preachings of Brother Nastagio, or the lament of the Magdalen,
or other such things.

About this time a rather young and handsome monk named
Don Felice, sharp-witted and very learned, who was one of the
conventual brothers at San Brancazio, happened to return from
Paris, and Friar Puccio struck up a very close friendship with
him. And because the monk was able to resolve many of his
friend's religious questions and knowing the kind of person the
friar was, he would make himself appear to be a very saintly
man, so Friar Puccio began to bring him home from time to time
and offer him lunch or dinner, depending on the time of day;
and his wife, out of love for Friar Puccio, also became friendly
with the monk and was happy to entertain him. And so, as the
monk continued to visit Friar Puccio's home and took notice of
his fresh and plump little wife, he guessed what it was that she
lacked the most; and he thought to himself that in order to
spare Friar Puccio the trouble he might just provide her with it
himself. And he cleverly managed to give her the eye on one oc-
casion or another in such a way that he ignited in her mind the
same desire he had in his, and as soon as the monk realized this,
the first chance he got he spoke to her of his desires. Although
he found her well disposed to bringing his work to fruition, they

could find no way to do so, for she would not risk being with the monk anywhere in the world except in her own home, and it was not possible in her house because Friar Puccio never left town—a fact that caused the monk great distress. But after much thought the idea came to him of how he could be with the woman in her own house and without arousing suspicion, notwithstanding the fact that Friar Puccio was at home all the while.

One day Friar Puccio came to see him, and he spoke to him in this way:

"I have often thought, Friar Puccio, that your one desire was to become a saint, but it seems to me you are taking the longest route in that direction, whereas there is a much shorter one which the Pope and the other great prelates of his who, though they know and employ it themselves, do not wish to reveal to others, for the clergy, which lives for the most part on charity, would quickly fall into ruin because laymen would no longer support them by way of donations or other means. But since you are my friend and have been very good to me, if I could believe that you would never reveal this method to anyone else and that you were willing to try it, I would reveal it to you."

Having become anxious to learn it now, Friar Puccio began first by begging him with the greatest earnestness to show it to him and then swearing that he would never reveal it to anyone without Dom Felice's permission, and then affirming that if the method was one that he could manage to follow, he would put his mind to doing it.

"Since you have promised me in this manner," said the monk, "I shall reveal it to you. I want you to know that the holy Doctors of the Church maintain that anyone who wishes to become a saint should follow the penance you are now about to hear. But please understand: I am not saying that after doing the penance you will no longer be a sinner as you are now. For what happens is this: all the sins you have committed up until the hour of your penance will be completely purged and forgiven because of the said penance, and as for those you will commit afterward, they will not be written down to your damnation—no, on the contrary, they will be washed away with holy water as you do with your venial sins now. Then it is necessary, first of all, for the man to confess his sins with the greatest of diligence before beginning the penance; after this the penitent must begin a fast and a very strict abstinence which is to last forty days, during which time he must abstain from touching not only other women but even his own wife. In addition, the penitent must have in his

own home some place where he can go at night to see the sky,
and at the hour of compline he is to go to this place, where there
should have been prepared a very wide plank set up in such a
way that while the penitent is standing on his feet, he is able, at
the same time, to rest his back upon it, but always keeping his
feet on the ground and his arms stretched out in the crucified
position—and, ah yes, should you wish to rest your arms on
some kind of supports, feel free to do so; and in this position,
gazing at heaven, you must remain without moving an inch until
matins. If you were a learned man, in this case you would have
to learn certain prayers that I would give you to recite; but
since you are not, it will suffice for you to say three hundred Our
Fathers along with three hundred Hail Marys in honor of the
Holy Trinity; and as you look up to the sky, always remember
that God was the creator of heaven and earth and bear in mind
the Passion of Christ as you are fixed in the same position in
which He Himself was upon the cross. Then, when matins
sounds, you may, if you wish, go dressed as you are to your bed
and lie down and sleep. Later on in the morning you must go to
church and hear at least three Masses and say fifty Our Fathers
with as many Hail Marys; and after that you may humbly go
about your own business, if you have any. Then, if you wish,
you may eat lunch, but then you must be in church around ves-
pers in order to recite certain prayers which I shall write down
for you and without which this whole thing would never work;
and then around compline you must start going through the en-
tire process from the beginning. If you do this, just as I have al-
ready done, you should, before reaching the end of your penance,
feel the wonderful effects of eternal blessedness, if you put
enough devotion into it."

Friar Puccio then said:

"This is not such a difficult nor too long a task to perform,
and I should easily be able to do it; therefore, in God's name, I
shall begin on Sunday."

After leaving Dom Felice and returning home, having already
obtained the monk's permission, he carefully explained every de-
tail of it to his wife. The woman understood only too well what
the monk meant with the part about his remaining still without
moving until matins; since she thought it was a very good idea
indeed, she told him that she was pleased about it, as she was
about every other thing he did for the good of his soul, and in
order that God might make his penance profitable, she would
fast along with him, but more than this, no.

So they were agreed on this, and when Sunday came, Friar

Puccio began his penance, and Messer Monk, having reached an understanding with the lady, would come most every evening at a time when he could not be seen to dine with her, always bringing with him lots of good food to eat and things to drink; then he would lie with her until the hour of matins, at which time he got up and left before Friar Puccio returned to his bed. The place which Friar Puccio had chosen to perform his penance was situated next to the bedroom in which the lady slept, and it was not divided from that room by anything but a very thin wall; one night while Messer Monk was frolicking a bit too wildly with the lady and she with him, Friar Puccio thought he felt the floor of the house shaking, and having just recited his one hundredth Our Father, he stopped at that point, and without moving, he called to the lady and asked her what she was doing. The lady, who could be very witty, and who, at that moment, was probably riding St. Benedict's ass, or better still, St. Giovanni Gualberto's, replied:

"Faith, husband, I am shaking all I can."

Friar Puccio then said:

"Shaking? What is all this shaking about?"

Laughing, the lady (who was a jolly and lively sort of woman who probably had good cause to laugh) replied:

"How is it you don't know what this is all about? I have heard you say a thousand times, 'Whoever does not at evening supper take, all through the night will truly shake.'"

Friar Puccio, who actually believed that her fasting was the reason why she was unable to sleep and therefore the cause of her shaking in bed, said to her in good faith:

"Lady, I have told you many times, 'Do not fast!' But since you wanted to do so anyway, stop worrying about it and think about sleeping; you are tossing about in bed so much that you are making everything in the house shake."

Then the lady replied:

"Don't worry about it; I know very well what I'm doing. You just keep up your good work, and I will do the best I can with mine."

Friar Puccio said no more and returned to his Our Fathers, but from that night on, the lady and Messer Monk had a bed set up in another part of the house and for as long as the period of Friar Puccio's penance lasted, they spent their time together there having a fine time; and when it was time for the monk to leave, the lady would return to her own bed, to which, shortly afterward, Friar Puccio would return from his penance. Thus while the friar carried on performing his penance in this way, the lady carried on to her delight with the monk, to whom she would, from time to time, make the quip:

"You make Friar Puccio do the penance but we are the ones who go to Paradise!" Since her husband had always kept her on a diet and now she had become accustomed to the monk's good food, she thought she never felt as good as this before, and so when Friar Puccio's penance was over, she found a means of dining with him elsewhere, and for a long time she discreetly had her fill of pleasure.

And so, to make my last words correspond to my first, this is how it happened that Friar Puccio thought he would get himself into Paradise by doing a penance, when instead he got the monk in, who had shown him the quick road there, as well as his wife, who lived with him but sorely lacked the thing which Messer Monk, charitable man that he was, managed to supply her with in great abundance.

[Third Day, Fifth Story]

❦

Zima gives Messer Francesco Vergellesi one of his horses and in return for this he receives his permission to speak to his wife; she is unable to speak, and Zima replies on her behalf, and later on, things turn out according to his reply.

PANFILO came to the end of his story about Friar Puccio, and not without much laughter from the ladies, when the Queen graciously ordered Elissa to continue; and she began to speak in a rather sharp tone—and not intentionally but rather out of habit—in this manner:

Many people think just because they know a great deal, everyone else knows nothing, and it often happens that while people such as these think they are fooling others, they soon come to realize that they themselves have been fooled; therefore, I consider it the height of foolishness for anyone to test the powers of another's intellect when there is no need to. But since everyone may, perhaps, not share my opinion, I should like to tell you, for it is now my turn to tell a story, of what happened to a knight from Pistoia.

In Pistoia there was a knight of the Vergellesi family named Messer Francesco, a very rich, judicious, and clever man in many ways, but he was an unbelievably miserly person. On being appointed *podestà* of Milan, he had everything necessary and befitting his rank ready to make the journey, except that he could not find a horse which was handsome enough for him; and unable to find one which pleased him, he was most distressed about it.

There was at that time in Pistoia a young man whose name was Ricciardo, of humble birth but very rich, who went about town so well dressed and so neatly groomed that everyone used to call him Zima;* and for some time now he had been in love with, and courted unsuccessfully, Messer Francesco's wife, who was most beautiful and very virtuous. Now this man owned one of the most handsome horses in Tuscany, and he was very fond of it because of its beauty; since everyone knew that he was courting the wife of Messer Francesco, someone told Francesco that if he were to ask for the horse, he would certainly get it because Zima was so devoted to his lady. Messer Francesco, carried away by greed, sent for Zima and asked him if he would sell the horse, hoping, of course, that Zima would give it to him as a gift.

Zima, liking what he heard, answered the knight:

"Messer, if you were to give me everything you owned in the world, you could not buy my horse but you may certainly have it whenever you wish as a gift from me on one condition: that before you accept it, I may, with your permission and in your presence, have a few words with your lady in a place just far enough away not to be heard by anyone but her."

The knight, carried away by avarice and hoping to trick Zima, replied that this arrangement was acceptable to him and that he could talk as long as he wished; then he left him in the hall of his palace and went to the bedroom of his lady, and having told her how easy it would be for him to get the horse, he ordered her to come and listen to Zima but to be very sure that she did not reply in any way to anything he said. The lady highly disapproved of the whole affair, but, as she was obliged to follow the wishes of her husband, she said she would do so, and walking behind her husband she entered the great hall to hear what Zima had to say.

After reconfirming his agreement with the knight, Zima sat down with the lady in a section of the hall, far away enough for no one else to hear, and began to speak in this fashion:

*A nickname based on *azzimato*: "ornately dressed, decked out in one's best clothes."

"Worthy lady, I am sure that someone as intelligent as you must have been aware for some time now how much I am in love with you, not only because of your beauty, which without any doubt surpasses that of any other woman I have ever seen, but also because of your praiseworthy manners and your intrinsic singular virtues, any of which would have the power to captivate the noblest heart of any man—and thus, it is not necessary for me to prove to you with words that this love of mine is the greatest and the most fervent that a man ever bore for any lady, and that this love will continue as long as my wretched life will sustain this body and even longer, for if we are able to love in the afterlife as we do in this world, I shall love you throughout eternity. Because of this you can rest assured that you possess nothing, be it precious or of little value, that you can regard more as your own and, thus, depend upon in every instance than my very self, whatever I may be worth, and upon everything I possess as well. And to convince you that what I say is true, let me assure you that I would consider it a far greater honor for you to order me to do something which pleases you than to have the whole world under my control and ready to obey me immediately. Thus, as you can see for yourself, I belong entirely to you; it is not without reason that I yearn to offer my prayers to you on high, the only source from which, and from nowhere else, I derive all my peace, my every good, and my salvation: as your most humble of servants I beg you—my dearly beloved, sole hope of my soul, which, hoping in you, is nourished in the flame of love—to show me some kindness and mitigate your past harshness toward me, who am entirely yours, that comforted again by your mercy I shall be able to claim that as I once fell in love with your beauty, so, too, did I receive from it my life, which, if your proud spirit does not yield to my entreaties, will, without a doubt, be so diminished that I shall die, and you will be accused of my murder. Putting aside the fact that my death would do you no honor, I nevertheless do believe that your conscience would sometimes suffer remorse, you would grieve from having brought it about, and when, occasionally, you found yourself more compassionately disposed you would say to yourself, 'Ah, how wrong it was for me not to have taken pity on my Zima,' but this repentence of yours having never occurred, would cause you even greater distress. Therefore, so this may not happen, that I may not die, while there is still time for you to help me, take pity on me, for in you alone resides the power to make me either the happiest or the most miserable man alive. I hope your graciousness will be such that you will not allow me to receive death as my reward for so great a love as mine, but rather that with a joyous and passionate reply you will restore my spirits, which, now terrified, tremble in your presence." Then he fell silent and after heaving the deepest of sighs and allowing several tears to fall from his eyes, Zima began to await the noble lady's answer.

The lady, who had previously not been moved by Zima's long courtship, his jousting, the morning serenades, and all the other ways Zima had shown his love for her, was now moved by the words of affection spoken by her most ardent lover, and she began to feel what she had never felt before—that is to say, love itself. In obedience to the command imposed upon her by her husband, she remained silent, but not so silent that she was able to conceal a few faint sighs which might well have revealed what she herself would have most willingly replied to Zima.

Zima, having waited for some time and seeing that no reply was forthcoming, was very much amazed, but then he began to understand the clever trick played on him by the knight. Yet, as he gazed into her face he noticed a certain gleam in her eyes when she would look at him from time to time, and this together with the sighs she allowed to escape from her bosom with less than their complete force filled him with fresh hope and encouraged him to devise a new plan. And so, as if he were the lady herself, he began to answer for her, as she sat there listening:

"My Zima, certainly I have been aware for a long time that your love for me was most intense and perfect, and now I realize this even more through your own words and am most happy, as it is fitting I should be. And if I have seemed harsh and cruel to you, I would not have you believe that I felt in my heart what I showed you in my face; on the contrary, I have always loved you and held you dearer than any other man, but I was forced to act in this manner for fear of others and in order to preserve my good name. But now the time is coming when I shall be able to show you clearly that I love you and give you some reward for the love which you have borne and still bear for me; so, be of good cheer and continue to hope, for within a few days Messer Francesco will be going to Milan to serve as its *podestà*, as you well know, for it was you who out of love for me gave him your beautiful horse. When he has gone away, without fail, upon my faith and the true love I bear for you, I promise you that within a few days time you will find yourself with me and together we shall bring our love to a pleasurable and complete fulfillment. But because I shall have no other occasion to discuss this matter with you again, let me tell you that on the day you see two towels hanging in the window of my bedroom which overlooks our garden, that evening after dark, being very careful not to be seen, come to me through the entrance in the garden, where you will find me waiting for you, and together we shall spend the entire night taking all the pleasure we wish from one another."

Zima, having spoken in this way, as if he were the lady, then began to speak once more for himself, replying as follows:

"Dearest lady, your kind answer has caused my every faculty to overflow with so much joy that hardly am I able to compose a reply that could sufficiently express my gratitude; and even if I could go on speaking as I wished and for as long as I wished, it would still not be sufficient to thank you to the extent I should like to and ought to do; and thus I leave to your discreet consideration the task of imagining that which I would so much like to express but cannot express in words. I shall tell you only this, that I shall, without fail, carry out your commands and then, perhaps, when I am more reassured of such a gift as the one you bestow upon me, shall I be able to do what is necessary to show you the proper gratitude. Since at present there remains nothing more to be said, my dearest lady, may God grant you whatever happiness and good you desire the most, and I bid you farewell."

Through all this the lady did not utter a single word; whereupon Zima rose to his feet and began to walk back toward the knight, who, as he saw him rise, came over to him and said with a laugh:

"Well, how do you like the way I kept my promise?"

"I do not, sir," answered Zima, "for you promised me I could speak with your lady and you have had me speak to a marble statue!"

This phrase pleased the knight very much, for while he already had a good opinion of his lady, now he held an even better one; and he remarked: "The horse that once was yours is mine from now on."

To this Zima replied:

"Sir, that is so, but if I had imagined that the favor I asked of you was to produce such fruit, I should have given it to you without asking for anything in return; and would to God that I had done so, for now you have purchased a horse which I have sold for nothing."

The knight laughed at this remark, and now that he had his

horse, a few days later he set out for Milan to begin his term as *podestà*. The lady, who was now alone in her home, kept thinking about Zima's words, and the love he bore for her, and the horse which for her sake he had given away; and observing him from her house, which frequently he would walk by, the lady said to herself:

"What am I doing? Why should I waste my youth? This husband of mine has gone away to Milan and won't be returning for six months; and when will he ever make up for those lost months? When I'm an old lady? And besides this, when will I ever find such a lover as Zima? I am alone, and I have no one to be afraid of; I don't see why I shouldn't take advantage of such good opportunity. I may never have such a chance again! No one will ever know a thing about this affair, and even if, by chance, it should come out, it's better to act and repent than to do nothing and be sorry you didn't!"

And after this discussion with herself, one day she hung two towels at the window overlooking the garden, as Zima had said; Zima was filled with happiness when he saw them, and after nightfall and all alone, he secretly made his way toward the entrance to the lady's garden and found it open; and from there he went to another entrance which led directly into the house, and there he found the noble lady waiting for him. When she saw him coming, she rose to greet him and received him with the greatest delight; he embraced her, and kissing her a hundred thousand times, he followed her up the stairs and went straight to bed, where they enjoyed the ultimate pleasures of love. Nor was this time, which was the first, to be the last; for during the time the knight was in Milan and even after his return, Zima went back there many a time, to the greatest pleasure of both parties concerned.

[Third Day, Sixth Story]

❦

Ricciardo Minutolo is in love with the wife of Filippello Sighinolfi; hearing that she is jealous, he tells her Filippello is going to the baths to meet his own wife on the following day and persuades her to go there, and believing that she is lying with her husband, she finds out it was Ricciardo.

ELISSA had nothing further to say, and the Queen, after praising Zima's astuteness, called on Fiammetta to proceed with a story; and she, all smiling, replied:

"Most willingly, my lady," and began:

Let us move a bit outside the limits of our own city, which is no less plentiful in topics of every sort than in everything else, and, as Elissa did, talk about instead some of the things which have occurred in other parts of the world; therefore, moving to Naples, I shall tell you about how one of those prudes who pretend to be so disgusted with love was through the ingenuity of her lover first made to taste the fruits of love before she had known its blossoms, and my story should warn you about things which can happen to you, and at the same time, entertain you with things that actually took place.

In the ancient city of Naples, which is, perhaps, as attractive a place as any other city in Italy, or even more attractive, there once was a young man renowed for his nobility of blood and the magnificence of his great riches whose name was Ricciardo Minutolo. Notwithstanding the fact that this man had a most beautiful and delightful young lady as his wife, he fell in love with a woman who, according to the opinion of many people, far surpassed the beauty of all the other Neapolitan women, and she was called Catella, the wife of an equally noble young man named Filippel Sighinolfo, whom she, as a most virtuous woman, loved and cherished more than anything in the world. As a result, while Ricciardo Minutolo was in love with this Catella, and going through all those actions which should enable one to acquire the favor and the love of a lady, he was, in spite of all this, unable to satisfy his desires and was almost in desperation; and even if he knew how, he would not have been capable of freeing himself from the bonds of love, and he could neither die nor see any purpose in life.

And one day, as he languished in this mood, certain of his women relatives happened to urge him very strongly to stop pursuing such a love, since he was struggling in vain, for Catella loved no one except Filippello, of whom she was so jealous that she believed every bird flying through the air was about to steal him away from her. When Ricciardo heard about Catella's jealousy, he suddenly thought of an idea that might allow him to fulfill his desires: he began to pretend that he had despaired of Catella's affections and had fallen in love with some other noble lady, and that it was for the love of her that he now participated in tournaments and jousted and did all those things which he had always done for Catella. And it was not long before nearly everyone in Naples, including Catella, was of the opinion that he no longer loved Catella but was instead deeply in love with this second lady; and he persevered so long and hard in this deception and managed to convince so many people that even Catella, not to mention various others, abandoned their aversion for him which was the result of his love for her, and she began to greet him in a friendly, neighborly way, as she would anyone else she happened to meet around town.

Now one day it happened to be very hot, and several groups of ladies and knights, as is the custom of the Neapolitans, set out for an entertaining time at the seashore, where they would lunch and sup together. Knowing that Catella had gone there with her own group, Ricciardo also went with his friends and was soon invited to join Catella's party of ladies, which he did after feigning some reluctance to their invitation and pretending not to be all that interested in being there. Then, the ladies, and Catella along with them, began to tease him about his new love affair, and Ricciardo pretended to become very angry over this, thus providing them with even more material to talk about. Eventually, as usually happens on such occasions, one by one the ladies started wandering off in different directions until Catella was left in the company of just a few ladies and Ricciardo, who then made a vague allusion in a joking way to a love affair her husband Filippello was having, and this sent her into an immediate fit of jealousy, and she was all aflame with the desire to know what Ricciardo meant by his remark. For a while she managed to restrain herself, but then she could no longer hold herself back and started begging Ricciardo, in the name of that lady he loved more than any other, to be so kind as to explain what he meant about Filippello.

"You have beseeched me in the name of a person for whose sake I dare not deny you anything you ask," Ricciardo said to her, "and so I am ready to tell you all about it, but you must promise me never to mention a word about it either to Filippello or anyone else until you will have seen for yourself whether what I am about to tell you is true, and, whenever you like, I can show you how you can see it for yourself."

What Ricciardo suggested not only pleased the lady, but it also made her believe what he said even more, and she swore to him never to say a word. So Ricciardo took her to one side, so as not to be overheard by the others, and began to speak in this manner:

"My lady, if I were still in love with you as I once was, never would I dare to tell you something which I believed might cause you distress, but since that love has passed, I am less concerned over revealing the whole truth of the matter to you. I do not know if Filippello ever felt offended by the love which I bore you, or if he might have believed that I was ever loved by you, but in any case, he never showed he did as far as I could tell. But now, perhaps having waited for a time when he thought I would be less suspicious, he seems to want to do to me what I am afraid he fears I have done to him, that is, to have his pleasure with my wife; and as far as I have been able to discover, he has for some time now been urging her by secretly sending her messages, all of which she has shown to me, and to all of which she has replied according to my instructions. But just this morning, before I came here, I discovered my wife in secret conversation in my home with a woman whom I immediately recognized for what she was, and so I called my wife and asked her what the woman wanted. She told me: 'It's that nuisance of a Filippello, whom you, with your sending him replies and raising his hopes, have brought to plague me; he says that he wants to know definitely what I intend to do and that whenever I wish, he will arrange for me to meet him secretly at the baths in town; and he is begging and urging me on to do it. If it were not for your insisting that I keep up this exchange of messages (why, I don't know!), I would have rid myself of him in such a way that he would never have looked in my direction again!' At that point, it seemed to me, things were getting out of hand and were no longer tolerable and that you should be told, so that you might become aware of just how he has rewarded your impeccable honesty, which at one time was almost the death of me. And so that you will not think that all this is just words or gossip, and so as to let you see and touch the truth for yourself if you so wished, I had my lady tell the woman, who was still waiting for her answer, that she was prepared to be at those baths tomorrow, around nones, when people were sleeping; and the woman went off looking quite happy with herself. Now I do not think you believe I would send my wife there, but if I were in your place, I would arrange for him to find you there instead of the woman he believes he is going to meet, and when he has lain with you for a while, I would let him know with whom he has lain and then tell him off in the manner he deserves, and if you do this, I think he will be so ashamed that you would at one and the same time avenge the injury he is trying to do both you and me."

Catella, upon hearing this, without giving any consideration to the kind of person it was who was telling her these things or the

possibility of his deception, as jealous people often do, was quick
to believe his words and began to connect certain things that had
occurred in the past with the story he had just told her; then,
suddenly flying into a rage, she told him that she would certainly
do what he suggested, for it required no great effort to do, and
that if Filippello showed up, she would certainly make him feel
so ashamed of himself that he would never be able to look at
another woman again without remembering it. Ricciardo, pleased
with what she said and believing that his scheme was a good one
and proceeding nicely, went on to add other details to his story
in order to confirm even more her faith in him, and begged her
never to tell a soul that she had heard about this from him; this,
upon her faith, the lady promised him.

The following morning Ricciardo went to the good woman who
was in charge of the baths he had told Catella about, and he ex-
plained to her what he intended to do and asked her to be as
helpful as she could. The good woman, who was very much in
his debt, said that she would do so gladly and then proceeded to
arrange what she had to do and say with him. In the house
where the baths were located there was a very dark room, there
being no window in it that opened out to the light, and the good
woman, according to the instructions of Ricciardo, prepared the
room as best she could and made the bed upon which Ricciardo,
after lunching, stretched out and began to wait for Catella.

The lady, who had listened to Ricciardo's story and given his
words more credence than they deserved, returned home that
evening full of indignation, and, by chance, Filippello happened
to return home too, and occupied with other thoughts, he did not
treat her with his usual affection. When Catella noticed this, she
became even more suspicious than she had been and said to her-
self: "He really does have his mind on that woman he thinks he
is going to have fun and games with tomorrow, but this certainly
is not going to happen." And with this thought on her mind, and
going over what she was planning to tell him when they were to-
gether, she was awake nearly all night.

So then what happened? Well, come nones, Catella took her
maid, and without giving the matter another thought, she went
straight to the baths which Ricciardo had told her about and
there she found the good woman and asked her if Filippello had
been there that day.

To this the good woman, as instructed by Ricciardo, an-
swered: "Are you the lady who was supposed to come to speak
with him?"

Catella answered: "Yes, I am the one."

"Well, then," the good woman replied, "go right in, he's in there."

Catella, in search of something she would not have wished to find, had the woman take her to the room where Ricciardo was waiting and with her face covered by a veil she went inside and locked herself in. When Ricciardo saw her coming toward him, he rose to his feet in joy and taking her into his arms, he whispered softly: "Welcome, my soul!" Catella, to convince him that she really was that someone else, embraced and kissed him and made a great fuss over him but without saying a word, fearing that if she spoke, he would recognize her voice. The room was very dark, a fact which pleased both of the parties concerned— nor did the fact that they remained there for a long time enable their eyes to see any better. Ricciardo led her to the bed, and there, talking to her in such a way that his voice could not be recognized, he lay with her for the longest time and to the great delight and pleasure of both parties.

But then Catella felt it was time to release her pent-up indignation, and blazing with raging anger she said:

"Ah, how wretched is the fate of women and how misplaced is the love that so many of them bear for their husbands! Oh, poor wretch that I am, for eight years now I have loved you more than my life itself, and you, I'm told, are burning with passion for another woman, evil and wicked man that you are! Now whom do you think you have just been with? You have been with the same woman you have been deceiving for many a year with your false compliments, pretending to love her while all the time you were in love with someone else. I am Catella, you faithless traitor, I am not Ricciardo's wife. Don't you recognize my voice? Yes, it is really she. I can't wait to be in the light again, so that I can shame you the way you deserve, you lousy, filthy dog. Oh my God! Just look at what I have loved for so many years! This unfaithful dog who thought he was in the arms of another woman has given me more caresses and amorous attention in this short period of time that I have been here with him now than in all the rest of the time I spent with him as his wife. Today, you disowned dog, you were full of life doing it, and at home you're most of the time so weak and worn-out that you can't keep it up. But, praise be to God, it was your own field you were plowing and not someone else's, as you thought! No wonder you didn't come near me last night! You were waiting to unload yourself somewhere else, and you wanted to arrive fresh as a knight entering the battlefield; but thank God and my wits that the water ended up flowing in the right direction! Why don't you answer, you wicked man? Why don't you say something? Have you become mute listening to me? By God's faith, I don't know what is keeping me from sticking my fingers into your eyes and tearing them out! So you thought you were going to pull off this betrayal in complete secrecy? By God, you aren't the only smart one! You didn't get by with it, did you? Because I had better hounds on your tail than you thought."

Ricciardo, who was enjoying these remarks to himself without responding to any of the accusations, embraced and kissed her and caressed her more passionately than ever, which only made her go on with her tirade, and she said:

"So, now you think that with your phony caresses you can win me over, you dirty dog; if you think you can console me and make peace, you are mistaken: I shall never be consoled in this matter until I have shamed you in front of every relative, friend, and neighbor we have between us. You wicked man, am I not as beautiful as the wife of Ricciardo Minutolo? Am I not as noble a lady? Why don't you answer, you rotten beast? What does she have that I don't? Move over there and don't touch me. You've jousted too much for today anyway. In any case, since you know who I am, from this moment on anything you do would be forced; but with the grace of God, I shall make you starve to death for it; and I don't know what keeps me from sending for Ricciardo, who has loved me more than himself even though he could never boast that I ever gave him a second look; and I'm not sure it wouldn't be such a bad idea—after all, you thought you had his wife here, and as far as you're concerned, it was just the same as if you had; so, you see, you couldn't rightly blame me for having him!"

Now the lady's words were many and her vexation great; but finally Ricciardo, thinking how much trouble might ensue if he left her with her beliefs, decided to reveal who he was and thus undeceive her; so taking her in his arms and holding her tight so that she could not escape, he said:

"My sweetheart, do not be angry, for that which by simply loving you I could not have, Love showed me how to get through deception—I am your Ricciardo." When Catella heard this and recognized Ricciardo by his voice, she suddenly wanted to jump out of bed, but she couldn't, and then she tried to scream, but Ricciardo put his hand over her mouth, saying:

"My lady, it is impossible to undo now what has already been done, even if you were to scream for the rest of your life; and if you do scream or do anything to reveal what happened to anyone, two things will happen to you. The first, which ought to cause you more than a little concern, is that your honor and your good reputation will be ruined should you claim that I made you come here through some deceitful means, for I shall maintain that it is not true and that, on the contrary, I brought you here by offering you money and promising you gifts, and that now you are angry and are causing all this uproar and saying such things because I did not give you as much as you hoped for—and you know how people are more likely to believe something bad rather than good. So, you see, my story will be no less credible than yours. The second thing is that your husband and I will become deadly enemies, and things might turn out in such a way that he could just as easily be killed by me as I could by him, in which case you would never be happy or contented again. And so, heart of my heart, do not at one and the same time dishonor yourself and put your husband and me into conflict and danger. You are not the first woman to be deceived, nor will you be the last; nor did I deceive you in order to take anything from you but, rather, because of the excessive love I bear for you and which I am prepared to bear for you forever, becoming your most humble servant. For a long time now, I and all my possessions and everything that I can do or am worth have been yours and at your service, and henceforth I intend for them to be at your disposal more than ever. Now since you are a wise woman in other matters, I am certain that you will act just as wisely in this one."

While Ricciardo spoke these words, Catella wept bitterly, and although she was very annoyed and upset, she nevertheless realized that Ricciardo's words were true and that it was entirely possible for things to happen the way Ricciardo explained, and so she declared:

"Ricciardo, I do not know how God will give me the strength to bear the injury and the deceit that you have inflicted upon me. I do not wish to make a scene here, where my own stupidity and excessive jealousy have brought me, but you can be sure of this—I shall never be happy until, in one way or another, I see myself revenged for what you have done to me; and so get out of here and let me go; you got what you wanted from me, you have tortured me enough, and now you can go. Go, get out, I beg of you."

Ricciardo, seeing that she was still very angry, was determined not to let her go until he made peace with her, and using the sweetest of words to soften her, he spoke and cajoled and implored her so effectively that she eventually was defeated and made her peace with him; and by mutual consent they lay together again for a long time in great delight. And from that day on the lady, realizing how much more tasty the kisses of a lover were than those of a husband, changed her harshness toward Ricciardo into sweet love, and began to love him most tenderly, and by proceeding with the greatest of discretion, they many times over enjoyed their love together. And may God grant that we enjoy ours as well!

[Third Day, Seventh Story]

Tedaldo, angry with his lady, leaves Florence; returning there after some time disguised as a pilgrim, he speaks with the lady and makes her aware of her error, and he frees her husband, who had been condemned to death for murdering Tedaldo, and he reconciles him with his brothers; then he discreetly enjoys himself with his lady.

FIAMMETTA was silent now, and as everyone praised her, the Queen, in order not to lose time, immediately entrusted the storytelling to Emilia, who began:

I prefer to return to our native city from which the last two storytellers chose to depart and show you how one of our fellow citizens regained his lost mistress.

Now, in Florence there was a noble young man whose name was Tedaldo degli Elisei, who fell in love beyond all measure with a lady named Monna Ermellina, the wife of a certain Aldobrandino Palermini, and who, because of his praiseworthy manners, deserved to enjoy his desires. To this enjoyment Fortune, the enemy of all those who are happy, was opposed; for whatever the reason might have been, after having satisfied Tedaldo for some time, she suddenly decided to deny him any further pleasure, and she refused not only to listen to any of his messages but under no circumstances would she see him. As a result, he fell into a state of bitter and unbearable melancholy, but he had kept his love so well concealed no one thought that this love affair was the cause of his melancholy.

Since he had tried very hard on many occasions to reacquire the love he had lost through no fault of his own (it seemed to him) and since every attempt had proved in vain, he decided to retire from the world so as not to give the satisfaction to the lady who was the cause of his suffering of seeing him waste away. And so he took what money he had, and without saying a word to a friend or a relative (except for one close friend of his who knew about the whole affair), in secret he went off to Ancona, where he went by the name of Filippo di San Lodeccio. There he became acquainted with a rich merchant with whom he took up service and with whom he sailed to Cyprus on his own ship. His manner and his behavior pleased the merchant so much that not only did he assign him a good salary, but he also made him his partner in the business, entrusting him with a large part of his business affairs. Filippo managed the business so well and with such attention that in just a few years he became an able, prosperous, and famous merchant. In the midst of these affairs, he still thought very often about his cruel lady, and he burned passionately with his love for her and the desire to see her again, but he was so strong-willed that for seven years he won this battle. But then one day it happened that while he was in Cyprus listening to someone singing a song that he himself had once written about the love he bore for his lady and hers for him and the pleasure that he had from her love, thinking it was impossible for her to have forgotten him, he was seized with such a desire to see her again that, unable to bear this torture any longer, he decided to return to Florence.

After putting his business affairs in order, he went with a servant of his as far as Ancona, where he waited for all his possessions to reach him, and then sent them ahead to Florence to the home of a friend of his business associate in Ancona, while he disguised himself as a pilgrim returning from the Holy Sepulcher with his servant following behind him; when they reached Florence, he went to a small inn owned by two brothers which was near his lady's home. The first thing he did was to go straight to her house to see if he might catch a glimpse of her; but he saw that the windows and doors and everything else were shut tight, which filled him with fear that she might have died or moved somewhere else. Deeply perturbed, he made his way to his brothers' home, in front of which he saw all four of them dressed in black, which was a great shock to him. Since he knew that he could not be easily recognized, so changed was his physical appearance and dress from what it used to be, he confidently walked up to a shoemaker and asked him why these men were dressed in black.

To this the shoemaker replied:

"They're dressed in black because not fifteen days ago, one of their brothers named Tedaldo, who has not been seen around these parts for some time, was found murdered. As I understand it, they have proved to the authorities that a man called Aldobrandino Palermini, who has now been arrested, murdered him, because this Tedaldo fellow was in love with his wife and had returned here in disguise to be with her."

Tedaldo was very surprised to learn that someone could resemble him so much as to be mistaken for himself, and the news about Aldobrandino's misfortune distressed him. He also had learned that the lady was alive and well, and now that night was falling, he returned to the inn with his mind full of different thoughts; after he had eaten supper in the company of his servant, he was shown to his sleeping quarters close to the top of the building. There, probably because of the many thoughts which troubled him or because of the uncomfortable bed and the quality of his supper, which had been meager, even after half the night had passed, Tedaldo had not yet been able to fall asleep; as a result, since he was awake, around midnight he thought he heard people climbing down from the roof into the building, and then through the cracks in the door of his bedroom he saw a light approaching. Quietly drawing closer to the crack, he tried to see what was happening: he saw a rather beautiful young woman holding a light, and coming toward her were three men who had descended from the roof; after greeting each other, one of the men said to the girl:

"We can breathe easily from now on, praise be to God, for we know for sure that Tedaldo Elisei's death has been attributed by his brothers to Aldobrandino Palermini, who has confessed now; though his sentence has already been pronounced, it is absolutely necessary for us to keep quiet about the whole affair, for if anyone should find out that we were the ones who did it, we'd be in the same fix as Aldobrandino." Having said this (and the woman appeared to be delighted about the whole affair), they walked down the stairs and went to bed.

When Tedaldo heard this, he began to reflect upon how many different kinds of erroneous conclusions fill the minds of men, thinking at first of how his brothers had mourned and buried a stranger in his place and then how an innocent man had been accused on the basis of a false suspicion and then sentenced to death on the evidence of false witnesses, and he also pondered the blind severity of laws and magistrates who, in their eager investigation of error, very often by cruel means cause falsehood to be accepted for fact, calling themselves ministers of God's justice, whereas in reality they are nothing but executors of evil and of the Devil. He then turned his thoughts to Aldobrandino's safety and decided what he had to do.

When he got up the next morning, he left his servant behind and at a suitable hour made his way alone to the home of his lady. When by chance he discovered her door open, he went inside and found his lady sitting on the floor of a small room on the ground floor, looking so tearful and forlorn that he himself almost began to weep as he drew near her and said:

"Madonna, do not torture yourself: your peace is at hand."

When the lady heard him, she raised her head and said in tears:

"My good man, you appear to be a foreign pilgrim; what could you know of my peace or my trials?"

The pilgrim then replied:

"Madonna, I am from Constantinople and have just now arrived here, sent by God to change your tears to laughter and to free your husband from the threat of death."

"How is it," said the lady, "if you have just now arrived here from Constantinople that you know who my husband and I are?"

Starting from the beginning, the pilgrim recounted the entire history of Aldobrandino's tribulations and told her who she was, how long she had been married, and many other things about her affairs, all of which he knew very well. The lady was astounded by all this and, taking him for a prophet, she kneeled at his feet, praying in God's name that if he had come for the salvation of Aldobrandino he should make haste, for there was little time left.

The pilgrim, assuming a very holy air, replied:

"Madonna, arise, do not weep, listen closely to what I am about to tell you, and be sure never to repeat it to anyone. As God has revealed to me, the tribulation you now suffer is the result of a sin which you once committed and which God Almighty wished you to purge in part with this distress of yours, and He wants you to make full amends for this sin. Otherwise, you will, without a doubt, be cast down into much greater suffering."

Then the lady exclaimed:

"Sir, I have committed many sins, and how am I to know which sin rather than another God Almighty wishes me to make amends for? And so, if you know which one it is, tell me, and I shall do whatever I can to make amends for it."

"Madonna," the pilgrim then said, "I know very well which one it is, and I shall question you about it now, not in order to learn more about it but so that as you speak about it yourself, you shall feel more remorse over it. But let us come to the matter at hand. Tell me, do you remember if you have ever had a lover?"

Upon hearing this question, the lady heaved a great sigh and was most amazed, for she believed no one had ever known anything about her affair, although since the day the man who had been buried as Tedaldo was murdered, such a rumor had been whispered about as a result of certain indiscreet words spoken by that one friend of Tedaldo's who knew all about it; and she answered:

"I see that God reveals all of man's secrets to you, therefore, I am not disposed to conceal my own. It is true that in my youth I was very much in love with the unfortunate young man whose death has been blamed on my husband; I shed bitter tears over his death, so distressing it was to me, for no matter how unyielding and unkind I pretended to be toward him before his departure, neither his departure, nor his lengthy stay, nor even his unfortunate death has ever been able to remove him from my heart."

To this the pilgrim replied:

"You never loved the unfortunate young man who was murdered, but you certainly did love Tedaldo Elisei. But tell me, what was the reason you were angry with him? Did he ever offend you?"

To this the lady answered:

"Certainly not, never did he offend me, and the reason for my harshness was the words of an accursed friar with whom I once made my confession; for when I told him about the love I bore for Tedaldo and about the intimacy I enjoyed with him, he screamed at me so thunderously that the thought of it still frightens me today, telling me that if I did not end this affair, I would end up in the devil's mouth at the bottom of Hell and would be committed to its tormenting flames. I was so shaken with fear by all this that I decided never again to be intimate with him, and in order not to have the occasion to do so, I refused to receive either his letters or his messages; but had he persevered a while longer (instead, as I presume, he left in desperation), I am sure that my harsh resolution would have melted, and I had no greater desire in the world than to let it, for I could see that he was wasting away like snow in the sun."

Then the pilgrim declared:

"Madonna, it is this sin alone which torments you now. I know for certain that Tedaldo never coerced you in the least; when you fell in love with him, you did so of your own free will, for he pleased you, and as you yourself desired, he came to you and enjoyed your intimacy, which by your very words and deeds proved to be so delightful to you that if he had loved you before, you now increased his love a good thousand times over. And if this was the case, as I know it was, what reason made you tear yourself away from him so inflexibly? You should have thought about all these things beforehand, and if you felt you were going to be sorry for doing something you thought was wrong, you should never have done it. The fact is that when he became yours, you also became his. While he remained yours, you could do with him as you pleased, for he belonged to you; but wishing to tear yourself away from him when you were his—this was the improper thing to do.

"It was robbery, since it was done against his will. Now as you know, I am a friar, and thus familiar with all their ways, and it is not as inappropriate for me to speak about them as it would be for a layman, so if I speak somewhat freely about friars, I do so in your own interest. And if I do speak about them, I do so with pleasure, in order that from now on you may know them better than you seem to have known them in the past. Friars were once most holy and worthy men, but the people who call themselves friars today and want to be considered as such have nothing in common with friars except their habits, nor are these really friars' garments, for while the inventors of the friars ordered their habits to be tight-fitting, shabby, and made of coarse cloth (it was a reflection of the mind's disdain for temporal things to have their bodies wrapped in such humble apparel), today these friars have their habits cut wide, and they are lined, made with a smooth texture and the finest cloth, and they have them done in a smart, pontifical style in which they shamelessly parade around like peacocks in the churches and the squares the way the layman would show off his clothes. And just as a fisherman tries to take a number of fish in the river in a single cast of his net, so, too, these friars, wrapping themselves in the ample folds of their garments, try to take in many a sanctimonious lady, widow, and many another silly person, both men and women alike, and this concern of theirs they place above all other duties. To speak more plainly, I tell you that these friars do not possess friars' habits but merely the color of their habits. And where their ancestors desired the salvation of men, the friars of today desire women and wealth; they have wasted all their energy, and they still do, on frightening the minds of the

foolish with noisy sermons and frescoes* and in showing them
how one's sins can be purged with alms and Masses, for they
have taken refuge in becoming friars more out of meanness of
spirit than from devotion and in order to avoid hard work, for
there are always those people who will bring them bread, while
others will send wine, and still others serve them food for the
sake of the souls of their departed ones.

"It is certainly true that alms and prayers may purge sins,
but if only the people who did this were more familiar with the
sort of people they are paying, they would much rather keep the
money for themselves or cast it before as many swine. But since
these friars know that the fewer people there are to share great
treasure, the better off they are, each one of them with thunder-
ous sermons and terrifying threats tries to keep others away
from what he wishes to keep exclusively for himself. These fri-
ars denounce lust in men so that when those who are denounced
are out of the way, the women are left to those who denounced
them; they condemn usury and ill-gotten gains, so that once
people have entrusted them with their restitution, they can
widen their habits and pursue their bishoprics and other splendid
priestly offices with the money that they claim would have led
anyone else who had it to damnation. And when they are
reproached for such actions and the many other filthy things
they do, they say, 'Do as we say and not as we do,' thinking
that this is a proper excuse for every serious offense, as if it
were possible for sheep to be more constant and steadfast than
their shepherds! And many a friar knows that a majority of the
people to whom they direct this response do not take it to mean
what they do. Today's friars want you to do as they say; what
they mean is: fill their purses with money, confide your secrets
to them, remain chaste and practice patience, forgive injuries,
and avoid speaking evil—all of which are good, honest, and
saintly things to do. But why? So that they may do things which
if done by laymen, they would be unable to do. Who does not
know that without money, idleness cannot endure? If you were
to spend your money on your own pleasures, the friar could not
wallow in idleness in his monastery; if you chase after women,
there is no room left for the friars; if you are impatient or do
not forgive injuries, the friar would not have the courage to
come into your home and contaminate your family. But why go
into so much detail? Every time they use that do-as-we-say ex-

---

*A reference to scenes of the Last Judgment frequently painted
in churches of the period.

cuse of theirs, they accuse themselves in the eyes of every intel-
ligent man and woman. Why do they not remain in their
cloisters if they feel that they cannot be chaste and holy? Or if
they really wish to lead a virtuous life, why do they not follow
that other holy text from the Gospel—'Then Christ began to act
and to teach'?* Let them act first and preach later. In my own
time I have seen a thousand of them courting, loving, and visit-
ing not only laywomen but nuns in convents as well; yet some of
these friars made the loudest noises from the pulpits! Should we,
then, follow people like this? Whoever does so may do as he
wishes, but only God knows if he is acting wisely! But even sup-
posing we grant that the friar who rebuked you in this instance
spoke the truth—that is, that breaking the marriage vows is a
great sin—is it not a more grievous offense to rob a man? Is it
not a more serious matter to murder him or to send him into ex-
ile to wander throughout the world? Everyone would concede
that it is. When a woman enjoys the intimacy of a man, that is
a natural sin, but robbing him, murdering him, or driving him
away springs from a malicious will. That you robbed Tedaldo I
have already demonstrated to you earlier, when you tore yourself
away from him after you, of your own free will, had become a
part of him. Moreover, as far as you are concerned, you killed
him, by showing as you did how cruel you could be to him, and
it was a wonder that he did not take his own life, and the law
states that an accessory to a crime is as guilty as the one who
commits it. And that you were the cause of his exile and his
wandering about the world for seven years cannot be denied, so
you see that you are guilty of a much greater sin in each one of
the three cases I just mentioned than you are in your intimacy
with him. But let us see now: perhaps Tedaldo deserved those
things? Certainly he did not; you yourself have already admit-
ted this, and furthermore, I know that he loves you more than
his own life. Nothing was ever so honored, so exalted, and so
highly praised as you were by him above every other lady when-
ever he was somewhere he could do so honorably and without
suspicion. His every possession, his every honor, and all of his
freedom he completely entrusted to you alone. Was he not a
noble young man? Was he not as handsome as his other fellow
citizens? Was he not accomplished in all those things which suit
a young man? Was he not loved, held dear, and gladly welcomed
by everyone? This you cannot deny. How could you, then, based
on the words of an insane, stupid, and envious little friar, have

*A reference to Matthew 4:23, Mark 1:21, or Luke 4:18.

resolved to treat him so cruelly? I do not understand why women make the mistake of looking down on men and considering them of little worth, for if they would only consider their own natures as well as the quantity and the quality of the nobility God has bestowed upon man above any other creature, they would be proud to be loved by a man and hold him most dear, seeking to please him in every possible way, so that he would never stop loving them. But what you did was inspired by the words of some friar who must have been, without a doubt, some drooling pie-muncher, and who, in all probability, hoped to get himself into the place from which he intended to chase out another. This sin, then, is the one that divine justice, who weighs all her operations with an accurate scale and brings them to a fitting end, would not allow to go unpunished, and just as you sought to tear yourself away from Tedaldo without good reason, so, too, your husband has for Tedaldo's sake been taken away without good reason and is still in danger, while you yourself are in pain. If you wish to be freed from this suffering, what you must promise—more important, what you must do—is this: if it ever were to happen that Tedaldo returned here from his lengthy exile, you must restore him to your grace, your love, your goodwill, and your intimacy, and you must return to him the position he enjoyed before you foolishly listened to that idiotic friar."

The pilgrim finished his remarks, to which the lady listened most attentively, and because his arguments seemed very sound, she was now convinced that her affliction was due to the sin she heard him describe, and so she said:

"Friend of God, I know all too well that what you say is true, and from your demonstration I have learned a great deal about the kind of people friars are, all of whom until now I regarded as saints. I understand now I have committed a serious error in treating Tedaldo the way I did, and if I possibly could, I would gladly make amends in the way you have described. But how can this be done? Tedaldo can never return here again: he is dead, and so I do not understand why it is necessary for me to make you a promise which I shall never be able to keep."

To this the pilgrim replied:

"Madonna, Tedaldo is not dead at all, for as God has revealed to me, he is safe and sound, and he would be happy if only you would restore your favor to him."

Then the lady said:

"But how can you be sure? I saw him dead in front of my door, his body full of dagger wounds, and I held him in these very arms and bathed his dead face in all my tears, which was perhaps the cause of all the talk that some dishonest person has spread around."

Then the pilgrim answered:

"Madonna, no matter what you say, I assure you that Tedaldo is alive; and if and when you give me your word with the intention of keeping it, there is every hope that you will see him soon."

And then the lady said:

"I will do this, and most willingly; there is nothing which would give me more happiness than to see my husband freed without harm and Tedaldo alive."

At that point Tedaldo felt it was time to reveal himself to the lady and to comfort her with reassurances about her husband, so he said:

"Madonna, to console you concerning your husband, I must reveal a great secret to you which you, in turn, must keep and never reveal for as long as you live."

They were both in a very remote and secluded part of the house, and the lady had the fullest confidence in the apparent holiness of the pilgrim, when Tedaldo took out a ring he had guarded with the greatest of care, one that the lady had given him on the last night he spent with her, and he showed it to her, saying:

"Madonna, do you recognize this?"

When the lady saw it, she recognized it immediately and exclaimed:

"Yes sir, I do, I once gave it to Tedaldo."

Then the pilgrim rose to his feet, quickly flung the cloak from his back and the hood from his head, and speaking in a Florentine accent, he said: "And do you recognize me?"

When the lady saw him and recognized him to be Tedaldo, she was utterly astounded as well as terrified as one can be to see the dead walking around like the living; and she did not rush forward to welcome him as she would have done to a Tedaldo returning from Cyprus but, rather, she had the urge to flee, as if from a Tedaldo returning from the grave.

Whereupon Tedaldo said to her:

"Madonna, do not be afraid, I am your Tedaldo alive and well; I never died, nor was I ever dead as you and my brothers thought."

The lady, somewhat reassured but still trembling at the sound of his voice, gazed at him for a while longer, and once she had convinced herself that he was indeed Tedaldo, in tears she threw her arms around his neck and kissed him, saying:

"My sweet Tedaldo, welcome back!"

After kissing and embracing her, Tedaldo announced:

"Madonna, there is now no time for more intimate greetings. I must go and make sure that Aldobrandino is returned to you safe and sound, and I hope that before evening comes tomorrow you have news about him that will please you; and if, as I expect to, I have good news of his safety, I should like to come to you tonight and talk to you about it in a more leisurely way than there is time for at present."

After he put his cloak and hood back on, he kissed the lady another time, cheered her with good hopes, and left her, going from there to where Aldobrandino, who was more concerned over his impending death than the hope of future deliverance, was held a prisoner; and as if intending to comfort him, with the permission of the jailers, who thought he was there to provide spiritual comfort, he entered the cell, sat down with him, and then said:

"Aldobrandino, I am a friend of yours sent for your deliverance by God, Who has been moved to pity by your innocence; therefore, if out of reverence for Him you will grant me the small gift I now ask of you, without any doubt, before evening comes tomorrow, instead of hearing the sound of your death sentence, you will hear that of your acquittal."

To this Aldobrandino replied:

"Worthy man, since you are so concerned about my safety, even though I do not recognize you nor remember ever having seen you, from what you say, you must be a friend. It is true that the sin for which it is decreed I must be put to death I never committed, though I have committed a great many other sins in the past which have perhaps brought me to this state. But let me tell you this, and in all reverence to God: if He should now show compassion for me, I would not only promise but willingly agree to undertake any great enterprise, big or small, so ask of me whatever you please, for rest assured that if I get out of this, I will not break my promise."

Then the pilgrim said:

"What I want is nothing more than for you to forgive Tedaldo's four brothers for having placed you in this predicament, for they thought you were guilty of their brother's death, and I want you to treat them as you would your own brothers and friends as soon as they beg your forgiveness for what they did to you."

To this Aldobrandino answered:

"No one knows better how sweet a thing revenge is nor how intense the ardor with which it burns, if not the person who has received the injury. Nevertheless, so that God may provide for my salvation, I shall gladly forgive them—in fact, I forgive them at this very moment; and if I ever get out of here alive and free, I shall act in a way that will please you."

This reply pleased the pilgrim, and without revealing anything else to Aldobrandino, he urged him to be of good cheer, for there was no doubt that before the next day was over he would hear reliable news of his deliverance.

After he left him, Tedaldo went to the Signoria* and in private spoke to an official in charge there, saying the following:

"My lord, everyone should willingly do everything possible to arrive at the truth of a matter, especially those who hold an office such as yours, so that those who have not committed crimes may go free and the criminal may be punished; in order that this may be done, thus bringing honor upon yourself and punishment upon those who deserve it, I have come here before you. As you know, you have prosecuted Aldobrandino Palermini most severely, believing you have discovered convincing proof that he was the man who killed Tedaldo Elisei, and you are about to pronounce sentence upon him; this evidence is entirely false, and I believe I can prove it to you before midnight tonight by placing the murderers of that young man in your hands."

The worthy man, who felt sorry for Aldobrandino, gladly lent an ear to the pilgrim's words, and after the official discussed the various aspects of the case with him and heard the evidence the pilgrim had to offer, he had the two innkeeper brothers and their servant arrested without any resistance shortly after they had gone to bed; he wanted to have them tortured in order to get to the truth of the matter, but the prisoners, who could not face the prospect of being tortured, first separately and then together openly confessed that they had murdered Tedaldo Elisei without knowing who he was. Asked for their reasons, they stated that he had given a great deal of trouble to the wife of one of them while they were away from the inn and had tried to rape her.

When the pilgrim learned this, with the permission of the noble official he departed and in secret entered the home of Madonna Ermellina; since everyone else in the household had gone to bed, he found her alone and waiting for him, equally

*The chief executive branch and main deliberative body of the Florentine government.

anxious to receive good news about her husband and of being fully reconciled with her Tedaldo. Going up to her, smiling, he announced:

"My dearest lady, rejoice, for tomorrow you shall certainly have your Aldobrandino back here again safe and sound," and in order to give her greater assurance of this he told her everything he had done.

Faced with two such unforeseen and sudden events—that is, having Tedaldo back alive, whom she truly believed she had mourned as dead; and then seeing Aldobrandino delivered from danger, whom in a few days she thought she would have to mourn as dead—the lady was happier than any other woman had ever been, and embracing and kissing her Tedaldo affectionately, they went to bed together and in all goodwill, gladly and graciously made their peace with each other, to their mutual and delightful joy. And as day drew near, Tedaldo arose, having already informed the lady of his intentions and repeated his plea to keep everything most secret, and still dressed as a pilgrim, he left the lady's home so as to be ready, when the time arrived, to attend to the business of Aldobrandino.

When day came, the Signoria, convinced that it had all the information it needed on the matter, released Aldobrandino immediately, and a few days later it had the delinquents beheaded on the spot where they had committed the homicide. Aldobrandino, now set free, to his own great delight and that of his lady and all his friends and relatives, clearly understood that all this had come about as a result of the pilgrim's endeavors, and so he had him brought to their home and invited him to stay there for as long as he wished to remain in the city; and once there they were never tired of honoring and feasting him, especially the lady, who alone knew whom they were so treating.

But after a few days Tedaldo thought it was time to reconcile his brothers with Aldobrandino, for he heard they were not only being ridiculed because of Aldobrandino's release but that they had even armed themselves out of fear, and so now he asked Aldobrandino to keep his promise. Aldobrandino readily replied that he was prepared to do so. The pilgrim had him arrange for an elegant banquet to be held the following day to which he told him he was to invite his own relatives and their ladies as well as his own four brothers and their wives, adding that he himself, in fact, would go immediately to invite them to Aldobrandino's peaceful reunion and banquet on Aldobrandino's behalf. And since Aldobrandino was pleased with everything the pilgrim requested, the pilgrim immediately went to his four brothers, and addressing them with words suitable to the occasion, using irre-futable arguments he finally convinced them without much diffi-culty to ask Aldobrandino's forgiveness and to request his friendship; and when this was done, he invited them and their ladies to dine the following morning with Aldobrandino, and they, reassured by his good faith, gladly accepted the invitation.

The following morning, therefore, around breakfast time Ted-aldo's four brothers, still dressed in black and accompanied by a few of their friends, were the first to arrive at the home of Aldo-brandino, who was awaiting them; and there, in front of every-one who had been invited by Aldobrandino to join in the festivities, they threw their weapons upon the ground, and put-ting themselves in Aldobrandino's hands, they begged his pardon for what they had done to him. With tears in his eyes, Aldobran-dino received them compassionately and, kissing them all on the mouth, with just a few words he quickly forgave them all the in-jury they had done him. After them came their sisters and wives all dressed in brown, and they were graciously received by Madonna Ermellina and the other women.

Then all of them, gentlemen and ladies alike, sat down to a splendidly served meal, and they thought everything was most praiseworthy, except for one thing: the general silence brought about by the recent grief still reflected in the dark clothes of Tedaldo's relatives; in fact, some of them had criticized even the thought of such a banquet, and since Tedaldo was aware of this, just as he had planned to do, when the time was right to break his silence, he rose to his feet while the others were still eating their fruit and exclaimed:

"The only thing missing at this banquet to make it a happy one is the presence of Tedaldo; since he has been in your midst all this time and you have not recognized him, I will point him out to you."

Then throwing off his cloak and all his other pilgrim's garb, he was left standing in a tunic of green silk, and not without the greatest amazement did everyone there stare at him and not be-fore inspecting him for quite a while did anyone dare to believe that it was he. Tedaldo noticed this, and so he started to iden-tify their families in detail, telling them about certain things that had happened between them and then recounting his own adventures, as a result of which his brothers and the other men, with tears of joy, ran to embrace him, and the ladies did the same thing, relatives and nonrelatives alike, all except for Monna Ermellina.

When Aldobrandino saw this, he said:

"What's this, Ermellina? Why don't you greet Tedaldo as the other women are doing?"

To this, as everyone listened, the lady replied:

"There is no one who would have more willingly greeted him, or who would greet him more willingly now than I, for I am more obliged to him than anyone else, since it was through his efforts that I have regained you; but those dishonest rumors that were spread during the time we were mourning the man we thought to be Tedaldo hold me back."

To this Aldobrandino said:

"Go on, do you think I pay any attention to yapping gossip? By obtaining my release, Tedaldo has more than proved such rumors to be false—though I never believed them from the start. Get up now and embrace him."

The lady, who desired nothing else, was not slow to obey her husband in this; rising from her place, as the other ladies had done, she embraced Tedaldo and greeted him most joyfully. Aldobrandino's magnanimity very much pleased Tedaldo's brothers, as it did all the other ladies and gentlemen who were there, and every trace of doubt born in certain minds from past rumors was expelled by this gesture. Now that everyone had welcomed him, Tedaldo himself stripped his brothers of their black garments and the brown clothing worn by their wives as well as his own sisters, and he ordered different garments to be brought out; when they were all newly dressed in them, they celebrated merrily with songs and dances and other entertainments; thus the banquet, which had begun in the gloom of silence, ended in the joy of noise. Then, just as they were, in continual merriment, they all went to Tedaldo's home, where they ate supper, and for a number of days afterward, in this mood they continued the celebration.

For many days the Florentines regarded Tedaldo almost as if he were a man arisen from the grave, a miracle! And in the minds of many people, including his brothers, there arose a slight doubt as to whether or not he really was Tedaldo, for even now they were not completely convinced, and they would have never been entirely convinced for a long time to come, if not for a particular event that happened to make it clear to them just who the murdered man had been. And that event was this:

One day some soldiers from Lunigiana were passing by the house, and when they spotted Tedaldo they rushed up to him and said:

"How's it going, Faziuolo?"

Tedaldo, in the presence of his brothers, answered:

"You have taken me for someone else."

When the men heard him speak, they were embarrassed and begged his pardon, saying:

"It's incredible how two men could look so much alike! You look just like a buddy of ours called Faziuolo da Pontriemoli, who got here about fifteen days or so ago, and we haven't been able to trace him since. No wonder we were surprised by your clothes, because he was just an ordinary soldier like us."

Tedaldo's eldest brother, upon hearing this, stepped forward and asked them what this Faziuolo was wearing at the time. They told him, and it turned out that the dead man had been dressed exactly as they described; as a result of this and other information, it was recognized that the man who had been murdered was not Tedaldo but Faziuolo, whereupon, from then on, any doubts his brothers or anyone else had about him vanished.

Thus Tedaldo, who had returned home a very rich man, persevered in his love and his lady never became angry with him again, and by acting discreetly, they both enjoyed each other's love for a long time to come. And may God grant that we enjoy ours as well!

[Third Day, Eighth Story]

After eating a certain powder, Ferondo is buried for dead; and the Abbot, who is enjoying his wife, takes him out of his tomb, imprisons him, and makes him believe that he is in Purgatory; after he is resurrected, he raises as his own a son which his wife has had from the Abbot.

WHEN Emilia came to the end of her long story—which in spite of its length displeased no one; on the contrary, they considered it to be briefly told with respect to the quantity and variety of events that were recounted in it—the Queen, expressing her wishes with a single nod to Lauretta, gave her leave to begin, and she did so as follows:

Dearest ladies, I find myself faced with the task of having to recount an actual occurrence which sounds much more like an invention than it really was, and having heard about a man who was mourned for and buried in place of another has reminded me of it. I shall tell you, then, how a living man was buried for dead, how he was later resurrected, and how he himself, as well as many other people, thought he was actually dead rather than alive when he rose from his tomb, and how, as a result of this, he was worshiped as a saint instead of being condemned for stupidity.

In Tuscany, then, there was once and still is today an Abbey situated, as evidently many of them are, in a place not overly frequented by men, and the Abbot chosen for the place was a certain monk who was a most holy man in everything except where women were concerned: in this regard, he knew how to proceed so cautiously that no one knew about it or even suspected him of it, and so he was considered most holy and just in every respect. Now it happened that the Abbot was on very good terms with a very wealthy peasant named Ferondo, an extremely crude and coarse man whose acquaintance pleased the Abbot if for no other reason than the amusement he sometimes received from the silly things he did, and in associating with him the Abbot noticed that Ferondo had a most beautiful lady as his wife, and he fell so passionately in love with her that he could think of nothing else day or night. But when he realized that no matter how simpleminded or witless Ferondo might be in other matters, in loving this wife of his and in keeping a close eye on her he was most clever, the Abbot was almost driven to despair. Yet he was so shrewd that he got around Ferondo in such a way as to persuade him to come with his lady from time to time to amuse himself in the garden of the Abbey, and there the Abbot spoke humbly with them about the blessedness of eternal life and of those holiest of deeds performed by many men and women from the past, and the lady was so moved by all this that she wished to go to him as her confessor, and when she asked Ferondo's permission to do so, she received it.

The lady, then, to the Abbot's great delight came to make her confession, but before beginning, sitting at his feet, she stated:

"Sir, if God had given me a real husband or even none at all, perhaps with your guidance it would have been easier to enter into the road you were telling us about that leads others to eternal life. But considering the kind of person Ferondo is, and his stupidity, I might as well call myself a widow. And yet I am, indeed, married, inasmuch as while he is alive, I can have no other husband except this crazy man who with no cause whatsoever is so unreasonably jealous of me that my life with him is nothing but trouble and tribulation. And so, before I go on with my confession, I beg you in all humility to be so kind as to give me some advice on this matter, for if this is not the basis of any attempt on my part to live a better life, then my confession or other good deeds will do me little good."

Her speech filled the Abbot's heart with great pleasure, for now it seemed that Fortune had opened the way to his greatest wish, and he replied:

"My daughter, I believe it must be a great nuisance for such a beautiful and delicate lady as yourself to have an imbecile for a husband, but it is much worse, it seems to me, to have one who is jealous; therefore, since you have both one and the other, I can easily believe what you say about your suffering. But to be brief about it, the only advice or remedy I can give you is this: that Ferondo must be cured of his jealousy. I know quite well how to prepare the medicine to cure him, provided that you are capable of keeping secret what I am about to tell you."

The lady said:

"Father, don't worry about that, for I would sooner die than tell anyone anything you told me not to tell anyone else: but how can this be done?"

The Abbot replied:

"If we wish him to be cured, he will of necessity have to go to Purgatory."

"And how can he go there," inquired the lady, "while he is still alive?"

The Abbot answered:

"He has to die and then he will go there; and when he has suffered enough punishment to be chastised for his jealousy, we shall, with certain orations, pray to God that he be returned to this life, and He will see to it."

"Must I, then, remain a widow?" asked the lady.

"Yes," replied the Abbot, "for a certain length of time during which you should be very careful not to allow yourself to re-marry anyone else, for God would take that rather badly, and when Ferondo returned, you would have to go back to him, and he would be even more jealous than before."

The lady said:

"So long as he is cured of this horrible jealousy of his—I can't stand this eternal prison—it's fine with me. Do what you please."

Then the Abbot said:

"I shall do so, but what reward should I receive from you for such a service?"

"Father," said the lady, "whatever you please, provided that it is in my power, but what can a poor woman like me offer as a suitable gift to a man such as you?"

To this the Abbot replied:

"My lady, you can do as much for me as I am about to do for you; that is, since I am willing to do something for your own good and consolation, so you, too, should do something for the freedom and salvation of my life."

Then the lady asked:

"If that is the case, I am ready to do so."

"Well, then," said the Abbot, "grant me your love and allow me to enjoy you, for I am burning all over, I'm consumed with love for you!"

The lady, amazed to hear these words, replied:

"Alas, father, what is this you ask of me? I thought you were a saint! Is it now proper for holy men to request such things of women who come to them for advice?"

To this the Abbot said:

"Do not be surprised, my sweet one, for this in no way diminishes my holiness, since holiness resides in the soul and what I am asking of you is a sin of the body. But in any case, your appealing beauty is so powerful that love compels me to act this way and to tell you that when you consider that your beauty pleases even the saints who are accustomed to gazing upon the beauties of heaven, you have more reason to be proud of it than any other lady. Furthermore, though I am an Abbot, I am a man like other men and, as you can see, I am not yet old. It will not be hard for you to do; on the contrary, you should welcome it, for while Ferondo is in Purgatory, I will keep you company during the night and provide you with the kind of consolation that he should be giving you; nor will anyone ever find out about it, for they all think I am a saint and even holier than what you yourself thought a moment ago. Do not reject the grace God sends you, for there are many women who yearn for what you can have, and if you wisely accept my advice, you will have it. Moreover, I own some beautiful and precious jewels, which I do not intend to belong to anyone but you. Therefore, my sweet hope, do for me what I, most happily, am doing for you."

The lady lowered her head, for she did not know how to refuse him, nor did she think that giving in to him was the proper thing to do; in the meantime the Abbot, who realized that she had listened to him and was hesitating over her reply, believing he had already half converted her, went on to add to his first argument many other words, and by the time he finished talking, he had managed to put the idea into her head that it was all right to do what he said; and so she, with a blush on her face, announced that she was prepared to follow his every command, but that she could do nothing until Ferondo had gone to Purgatory. To this the Abbot, happy as could be, replied:

"We shall see to it that he goes there immediately; make sure that he comes here tomorrow or the day afterward to visit me." After saying this, he slipped a very beautiful ring into her hand and sent her off. The lady, delighted by the gift as well as the expectation of receiving more, returned to her lady friends and began to tell them marvelous accounts of the Abbot's holiness as they walked home together.

A few days later, Ferondo went to the Abbey, and as soon as the Abbot caught sight of him, he decided to send him off to Purgatory. He had in his possession a power of marvelous strength which had been given him by a great prince of the East who maintained that it was used by the Old Man of the Mountain whenever he wanted to put someone to sleep and send him to Paradise and then to bring him back again, and that according to the quantity of the dosage, the person who took it would sleep for a greater or lesser time without hurting himself, and that while its strength lasted, no one would ever believe the person to be still alive. Then, without letting Ferondo see what he was doing, the Abbot measured out enough of the powder to induce sleep for three days, put it in a glass of rather cloudy wine, and gave it to him to drink while they were still in his cell; then he took him into the cloister, where he and his monks began to amuse themselves at the expense of Ferondo's foolishness. But it was not long before the powder started to work, and all of a sudden such a powerful sensation of drowsiness struck Ferondo's head that he started to doze off on his feet and collapsed fast asleep. The Abbot, pretending to be upset over the accident, had Ferondo's clothing unfastened, sent for cold water and had it tossed on his face, and ordered many other remedies of his to be administered, as if he wished to restore the life and feeling which had been taken from him by this attack of stomach gas or whatever else had seized him; but when the Abbot and the monks saw that for all their efforts, Ferondo was not responding, and on taking his pulse and finding there no movement, they all agreed that, for certain, he was dead. So they sent word to his wife and relatives and all of them came rushing to the place, and after his wife and relatives had wept for a while, the Abbot had him placed in a tomb dressed in the clothes he was wearing at the time.

The lady returned home, and she reassured the little son whom she had had by Ferondo that she would never abandon him; thus she remained in Ferondo's house caring for the son and administering the wealth of her husband.

With a Bolognese monk whom he trusted completely and who had just come that day from Bologna, the Abbot got up during the night and quietly carried Ferondo from his tomb to a burial vault devoid of all light which had been used as a place of confinement for errant monks. There they removed his clothes, dressed him in a monk's habit, and, placing him upon a bundle of straw, they left him there until such time as he should come to his senses. In the meanwhile, unbeknownst to anyone, the monk from Bologna, having been instructed by the Abbot as to what he was to do, waited there for Ferondo to regain consciousness.

The following day, the Abbot and a few of his monks, with the excuse of paying a courtesy call, went to the home of the lady and found her dressed in black and full of grief; after comforting her for a while he quietly asked her to fulfill her promise. The lady, realizing that she was now a free person and unhindered by Ferondo or anyone else, and having caught a glimpse of another beautiful ring on the Abbot's finger, declared she was prepared to do so and arranged for him to come to her the following evening. And so, after dark, the Abbot, disguised in Ferondo's clothes and accompanied by his monk, went to her home and with the greatest delight and pleasure, he lay with her until matins, at which time he went back to the Abbey, and this was a road he traveled very often to perform such services. Once in a while it happened that people would run into him during his comings and goings, and they believed that he was Ferondo who was wandering about the countryside doing penance, and soon many tales sprang up among the common people of the village, and more than once Ferondo's wife was told about it, but she knew very well what it was all about.

As soon as Ferondo regained his senses to find himself in some unknown place, the monk from Bologna, accompanied by a terrifying cry, walked into the tomb and with some branches in his hand he seized him and gave him a good beating.

Ferondo, weeping and screaming, kept on asking:

"Where am I?"

To this question the monk would reply: "You are in Purgatory."

"What?" exclaimed Ferondo. "You mean I'm dead then?"

The monk answered: "Of course you are." Then Ferondo began whimpering about himself, and going on about his wife and his son, saying the strangest things in the world.

Then the monk brought him something to eat and drink, and when Ferondo saw this, he said: "Oh! Do the dead eat?"

The monk replied:

"Yes, and what I am bringing you is the food the lady who was once yours brought this morning to the church requesting that Masses would be said for your soul, and it is the wish of God Almighty that you be given it here."

Then Ferondo said:

"God bless her! I loved her very much before I died, so much so that I would hold her in my arms all night long and do nothing but kiss her, and I even did some other things when I got the urge"; and then, since he was very hungry, he began to eat and drink, but as the wine did not seem too good to him, he said: "God damn her! She didn't give the priest the wine from the cask by the wall."

And when he finished eating, the monk seized him again and with those same branches he gave him another hard beating.

After screaming for a long time, Ferondo asked him:

"Hey! Why are you doing this to me?"

The monk said:

"Because God Almighty has ordered me to do so two times a day."

"But for what reason?" inquired Ferondo.

The monk replied:

"Because you are jealous, even though you had the finest woman in the district as your wife."

"Alas," said Ferondo, "you speak the truth, and she was also the sweetest: she was sweeter than a sugar plum! But I had no idea that God Almighty took it badly when men were jealous, otherwise I would never have been so."

The monk said:

"You should have thought about that while you were up there and mended your ways; now if it ever happens that you should return to life, be sure that you remember what I am doing to you now and don't be jealous ever again."

Ferondo said: "Oh, do people who die ever return?"

"Yes," answered the monk, "if God wishes."

"Well," exclaimed Ferondo, "if I ever return, I shall be the best husband in the world; I shall never beat her, I shall never say a mean thing to her, except about the wine she sent me this morning; and by the way, she didn't send me any candles either, forcing me to eat in the dark."

The monk said:

"Yes, she did send some, but they were used up during the Masses."

"Oh," Ferondo replied, "that's right, and if ever I return, I will be sure to let her do whatever she likes. But tell me, who are you who is punishing me?"

The monk said:

"I am also dead, and I came from Sardinia; and because I once highly praised a master of mine for being jealous, I have been condemned by God to this punishment, which is to give you food and drink and these beatings until God decides what else to do with you and me."

Ferondo said: "Isn't there anyone here but us two?"

The monk replied: "Certainly, thousands, but you cannot see or hear them any more than they can see or hear you."

Then Ferondo remarked:

"How far are we from our homes?"

"Oh ho!" answered the monk. "Far more miles than you and I could ever take a shit on."*

"God's faith! That sure is far!" exclaimed Ferondo. "I'll bet it's so far, we're right out of the world itself!"

Thus, with such discussions and others like them, between eating and beatings, Ferondo was kept there for about ten months, during which time the Abbot paid frequent and vigorously adventurous visits to the beautiful lady and had himself the best time in the world with her. But as accidents will happen, the lady became pregnant, and as soon as she was aware of it, she told the Abbot. As a result they both felt that without any further delay Ferondo would have to be resurrected from Purgatory and returned to her, and that she would have to say that he had made her pregnant.

So, on the following night, with his voice disguised, the Abbot called to Ferondo in his prison cell, saying:

"Ferondo, be of good cheer, for God wishes you to return to the world; and when you return, a son will be born to you from your lady, and you shall name him Benedetto, for through the prayers of your holy Abbot and your wife and through the love of St. Benedict, this grace is given you by God."

Hearing this, Ferondo was very happy, and he said:

"Am I glad! God bless God Almighty, the Abbot, St. Benedict, and my cheesy-weesy honey-bunny of a wife."

Having poured enough powder into the wine to make Ferondo

---

*This off-color answer is not intended to make sense but is only said to confuse Ferondo all the more.

sleep for about four hours, the Abbot dressed him in his old clothes again and with the assistance of his monk quietly returned him to the tomb in which he had been buried. The next morning around the break of day Ferondo came to his senses again. He saw a bit of light coming through a crack in the tomb, and since he had not seen light for a good ten months, sensing he was alive again, he began shouting: "Open up! Open up!" and he himself started pushing with his hands so hard against the cover of the tomb that he had already begun to budge it by the time the monks, who had just said matins, ran to the tomb, recognized Ferondo's voice, and saw him emerging from the tomb. They were so terrified by this unexpected occurrence that they all fled, running to tell the Abbot.

The Abbot, who pretended to be rising from prayer at that moment, said:

"My sons, do not be afraid; take the cross and holy water, and follow me, and let's see what the power of God can do," and away he went.

Ferondo was as pale as any man who spends too much time away from the light of the sun is likely to be, and climbing out of the tomb, he spotted the Abbot, ran to him, and quickly threw himself at his feet, exclaiming:

"Father, I've been told that your prayers, as well as those of St. Benedict and my wife, have rescued me from the punishments of Purgatory and brought me back to life, and so I pray may God give you a good year, and good months too, and days, and forever."

The Abbot replied:

"Praised be the power of God! Go then, my son, since God has returned you here, and console your lady, who from the day you passed away from this life has always been in tears, and from now on act as a friend and servant of God."

Ferondo said:

"Sir, that's just what I've been told; leave everything to me: when I find her, I'll kiss her so hard, I love her so much."

The Abbot pretended to be most amazed over the whole affair, and as soon as he was alone with his monks, he devoutly had them sing the *Miserere*.* When Ferondo returned to his village, everyone who saw him ran away from him in horror, and he would call them back, trying to reassure them that he had merely come back to life; and his wife, too, was afraid of him.

*The opening word of Psalm 50, a prayer asking for God's forgiveness.

Once the people started feeling more comfortable around him, seeing that he really was alive, they began asking him a number of questions, all of which he answered as if he had returned to life as some kind of wise man, and he even told them stories about the souls of their relatives, and he himself made up some of the most beautiful fables about the workings of the world of Purgatory; with the entire populace present, he told of the revelation he personally received directly from the mouth of the Rankangel Bagel* just before he was brought back to life. Having returned home with his wife and taken possession of his property, he made his wife pregnant, or so he thought, and by chance it happened that in just enough time to support the opinion of the foolish populace who believe that a woman carries her baby for exactly nine months, his wife gave birth to a male child, who was named Benedetto Ferondi.

Since almost everyone believed he had really been resurrected from the dead, Ferondo's return and his tales greatly enhanced the fame of the Abbot's holiness; and Ferondo, who had received many whippings because of his jealousy, was now cured of it, and just as the Abbot had promised the lady, he was never jealous again; the lady was most pleased about this, and from then on she lived with Ferondo just as chastely as she had in the past, except that whenever she could, she was always happy to find herself with the holy Abbot, who had so skillfully and most diligently attended to her most pressing needs.

[Third Day, Ninth Story]

*

Giletta of Narbonne cures the King of France of a fistula; in reward she requests Beltramo di Rossiglione for her husband, who after marrying her against his will, goes to Florence out of indignation; there he courts a young woman whom Giletta impersonates and in this way sleeps with him in her place and bears him two children; as a result, he finally holds her most dear and accepts her as his wife.

WHEN Lauretta's tale was finished, there remained only the Queen to speak, for she did not wish to deny Dioneo his privi-

---

*Ferondo confuses the Rankangel Bagel with the Archangel Gabriel.

lege; and so, without waiting for any of her companions to urge her on, she began to speak in a most charming manner as follows:

After hearing Lauretta's story, who will ever be able to tell a story as good as that? It was certainly fortunate for us that her story was not the first. Otherwise, few of the others that followed hers would have pleased us, which is what I fear will happen to those tales still to be told this day. But be that as it may, I shall go on and tell you the story I have chosen to illustrate our proposed topic.

In the Kingdom of France, there was once a nobleman whose name was Isnardo, the Count of Rossiglione, who, because of his poor health, always kept by his side a physician named Master Gerardo of Narbonne. This Count had only one small son, who was most handsome and charming, named Beltramo, who was brought up with other children of his age, among whom was a daughter of the physician, named Giletta, and she felt for this Beltramo a boundless love, one which was far more passionate than was suitable for her tender age. When his father died and he was entrusted to the care of the King, Beltramo found that he had to go to Paris, and this plunged the young girl into the deepest despair; not long afterward her own father died, and had she been able to find a reasonable excuse, she would have gladly gone to visit Beltramo in Paris, but now that she was left alone in the world and was a wealthy girl, she was closely watched and could not see any plausible means of doing so. Even when she reached marriageable age, she never was able to forget Beltramo, and without giving any explanation she turned down many a man that her relatives wanted her to marry.

Now, while she burned more than ever with her love for Beltramo, having learned he had turned into a most handsome young man, the news happened to reach her that the King of France, because of a tumor on his chest which had been badly treated, had a fistula which caused him the greatest pain and anguish. Although he had tried many physicians, none of them had been able to cure him—on the contrary, all of them had made him worse; as a result, the King was driven to despair and no longer would consult with or seek assistance from any of them. The young girl was overjoyed with the news, for she realized that not only did it give her a legitimate reason to go to Paris, but if the illness was what she thought it was, she would easily be able to have Beltramo as her husband in marriage. Then, using the many things she had learned from her father in the past, she made a powder from certain herbs that were helpful in treating the illness she believed the King suffered from, and she took to her horse and left for Paris. The first thing she did was to devise a means of seeing Beltramo; then, after obtaining an audience with the King, she asked him if he would favor her by showing her his malady. Since she was such a young and pretty woman, the King could not refuse her, and he showed it to her.

As soon as the young girl saw it, she immediately felt confident that she knew how to cure him and said:

"My lord, whenever you please and without any pain or exertion on your part, I hope, with God's help, to have you cured of this illness in eight days."

The King scoffed at her words, saying to himself:

"How can a young woman like this know how to do what the best doctors in the world couldn't?" So, he thanked her for her goodwill and told her that he had promised himself never again to follow a doctor's advice.

To this the young lady said:

"My lord, you despise my art because I am young and a woman, but let me remind you that I practice medicine not only with my own knowledge but also with the help of God and with the knowledge of Master Gerardo of Narbonne, who was my father and a famous physician in his day."

The King thought to himself:

"Perhaps God has sent me this girl; why not find out what she knows how to do, since she claims she can cure me in a short time without any pain on my part?" And deciding to put her to the test, he said:

"Young lady, if you cannot cure us, thereby forcing us to break our resolution, what do you agree should be the penalty?"

"My lord," replied the young lady, "keep me under guard, and if I do not cure you within eight days, have me burned; but if I do cure you, what shall be my reward?"

To this the King answered:

"It seems that you are still without a husband; if you succeed, we shall provide you with a proper and noble husband."

To this the young woman said:

"My lord, it would truly please me if you were to provide me with a husband, but I desire as a husband only the man I shall now request of you, excluding, of course, any of your sons or the members of the royal family."

The King immediately gave her his promise. The young woman began her cure, and shortly thereafter, and with time to spare, she restored him to health; feeling himself cured, the King declared:

"Young woman, you have certainly earned a husband."

To this she replied:

"If that is the case, my lord, I have earned Beltramo di Rossiglione, whom I began loving as a child, and whom I have loved most passionately ever since."

The King felt that giving him to her was a serious matter, but he had given his promise, and not wishing to break it, he had Beltramo summoned to him and spoke to him in this manner:

"Beltramo, you are now full grown and have been educated; we wish for you to return and govern your lands and that you take with you a young woman whom we have chosen as your wife."

Beltramo inquired:

"And who is the young woman, my lord?"

To this question, the King replied:

"She is the young woman who, with her cures, has restored our health."

Beltramo knew her and had seen her, but no matter how beautiful she appeared to him, he knew her not to be of a lineage which adequately matched his own nobility, and he said in a most indignant manner:

"My lord, do you therefore wish to give me a woman doctor as a wife? God forbid that I should ever take such a female!"

To this the King said:

"Do you therefore wish us to break the promise we made the young woman who asked for you as her husband in reward for restoring our health?"

"My lord," said Beltramo, "you can take whatever I possess and give me over to anyone you please, for I am your vassal, but I assure you that I shall never remain content with such a marriage match."

"Yes, you will," answered the King, "for the young woman is beautiful and wise and loves you very much; we are, therefore, hoping that you will have a much happier life with her than you would have with a lady of higher lineage."

Beltramo fell silent, and the King had great preparations made for the wedding feast; when the appointed day arrived, Beltramo did, however unwillingly, in the King's presence, marry the young woman who loved him more than herself. Having already decided what he had to do, after the wedding he announced that he wished to return to his lands to consummate the marriage there, and so he asked the King for his leave, and

mounting his horse, he rode off not to his estates but rather to
Tuscany. And as he knew that the Florentines were waging war
against the Sienese, he decided to support them; whereupon he
was cheerfully received and was honorably made captain of a
number of men, and since they paid him a good wage, he re-
mained in their service for a long while.

The new bride, little pleased with such an outcome but hoping
that through her good administration of his estates he would be
drawn back to them, came to Rossiglione, where she was re-
ceived by everyone as their mistress. Since for so long a period
of time the place had been without its count, when she arrived
there she found everything in ruin and chaos, and being an intelli-
gent woman, she reorganized everything with great diligence and
care, thus making her subjects very happy indeed. They held her
most dear and felt a great love for her, while they most strongly
criticized the Count for not being satisfied with her.

After completely setting in order the Count's domain, she noti-
fied him of this fact by way of two knights, begging him to tell
her that if it was because of her that he was not returning to his
lands, he should inform her of this, and to please him she would
leave the place. To these emissaries, the Count replied harshly:

"She can do as she pleases; for my part, I shall return to live
with her the day she wears this ring on her finger and holds a
son of mine in her arms." He held his ring most dear, nor did he
ever take it off, because of some power that he had been told it
possessed. The knights realized how harsh were the conditions
imposed by these two almost impossible demands, but seeing that
their words were unable to dissuade him from his resolution,
they returned to their lady and reported his answer to her.

She was filled with sorrow, but after much thought she de-
cided to try to see if these two conditions might possibly be ful-
filled. Having decided what she must do in order to regain her
husband, she called together a number of the most eminent and
distinguished men in her domain, told them in great detail and
with piteous words all that she had done out of love for the
Count, and pointed out what had come of it; finally, she told
them that she had no intention of staying there any longer if
this meant the Count's perpetual exile and that, on the contrary,
she meant to spend the rest of her life on pilgrimages and in do-
ing charitable works for the salvation of her soul; and she
begged them to undertake the protection and government of her
lands and to inform the Count that she had left him his pos-
sessions free and clear and had departed with the intention of
never returning to Rossiglione. As she spoke, many tears were

shed by these worthy men, who begged her many times over to change her mind and stay; but all this was of no avail.

Having commended them to God, accompanied by a cousin of hers and one of her chambermaids and dressed in pilgrim's garb, she took a large sum of money and precious jewels, and without letting anyone know where she was going she set out on the road, not stopping until she reached Florence; there she happened by chance to find a small inn, which a kindly widow kept, and she remained there living modestly in the guise of a poor pilgrim, hoping to hear news about her lord. It so happened that on the following day, she saw Beltramo pass by the inn on horseback with his troops, and although she certainly recognized him, she nevertheless asked the good woman of the inn who he might be.

To her question the innkeeper replied:

"He is a foreign nobleman called Count Beltramo, an affable and courtly man who is much beloved in this city, and he is passionately in love with one of our neighbors, who is a noblewoman but poor. To tell the truth, she is a most virtuous young lady, and it is because of her poverty that she is not yet married but lives with her mother, who is the most wise and goodly woman; if her mother were not present, perhaps by now she would have already done the Count's pleasure."

The Countess listened to every word and weighed them carefully; after examining the situation in more detail, looking at every particular to be certain that she clearly understood everything, she decided on a course of action: having learned the name and address of the lady and her daughter whom the Count loved, one day dressed in her pilgrim's garb she quietly went there. She found the lady and her daughter poverty-stricken, and after greeting them, she asked the lady if she could speak to her at her convenience.

The noble lady, rising to her feet, said that she was ready to hear her and led her into another room, where the two of them alone sat down, and the Countess began:

"Madam, it seems to me that you are just as much an enemy of Fortune as I am: but, if you wish, you may perhaps be able to improve the conditions of both yourself and me."

The lady replied that she desired nothing more than to improve her condition by honest means.

The Countess continued: "I must have your trust, on which I shall rely, and if you deceive me, you shall spoil both your prospects and my own."

"You may tell me with confidence anything you wish," said

the noble lady, "for you shall never find yourself deceived by me."

Then the Countess, beginning from the first moment she fell in love, told her who she was and what had happened to her up until that very day, and she told her story in such a moving way that the noble lady, who had already heard parts of it from other people, was convinced by what she said and began to take pity on her. And the Countess, after telling of her misfortunes, continued:

"You may have heard, then, that among my other troubles there are two things I must possess if I am to regain my husband; I know of no person who could assist me in obtaining them other than you, if what I hear is true—that is, that the Count, my husband, is passionately in love with your daughter."

To this the noble lady said:

"Madam, I do not know if the Count loves my daughter, but he certainly acts as if he does; but what could I do to assist you in this matter?"

"Madam," replied the Countess, "I shall tell you, but first I want you to know what I intend for you to gain from all this, should you do me this favor. I see that your daughter is beautiful and old enough for a husband, and from what I have heard and from what I have seen for myself, the fact that you lack wealth to marry her forces you to keep her at home. In exchange for the service you will perform for me, I intend immediately to provide her, from my own resources, the dowry that you yourself estimate would be suitable to marry her honorably."

As the lady was in need, the offer was welcome, but still, since she had a proud spirit, she said:

"Madam, tell me what I can do for you, and if it is an honorable thing for me to do, I shall gladly do it, and then you may reward me in whatever way you please."

The Countess said:

"I want you, through some person whom you trust, to tell the Count, my husband, that your daughter is prepared to fulfill his every desire whenever she may be assured that he loves her as much as he claims; this she will never believe unless he sends her the ring which he wears on his hand and which she has heard he is so fond of; if he sends this to her, you will give it to me. And then you will send someone to say that your daughter is prepared to fulfill his desires, and you will have him come here in secret and let him lie, unsuspectingly, with me who will be disguised as your daughter. Perhaps God will grant me the grace of becoming pregnant, and later, having his ring on my finger and the son engendered by him in my arms, I shall have him back and live with him as a wife should live with her husband, and you shall be the cause of all this."

This seemed to the noble lady no small request, for she feared that some dishonor could, perhaps, fall upon her daughter; but she considered what an honorable thing it would be to assist the good woman in regaining her husband, for in doing this she would be working toward an honorable goal. And so, trusting the good and genuine affection of the Countess, she not only promised the Countess to help her, but within a few days' time, acting with secrecy and caution and following the plan devised by the Countess, she had the ring (in spite of the fact that the Count was most reluctant to give it away), and in the place of her daughter she had skillfully managed to put the Countess to lie with the Count. In the course of their first couplings, lovingly sought after by the Count, it pleased God that the lady became pregnant with two male children, as was clear when the time for her delivery arrived. It was not only on one occasion that the noble lady managed to please the Countess with the embraces of her husband, but many times, working so secretly that never a word was learned about it, the Count all the while believing himself to have been in bed not with his wife but rather with the lady he loved; and when it was time to leave her in the morning, the Count would always present her with beautiful and precious jewels, all of which the Countess guarded most carefully.

When she knew that she was pregnant, the Countess no longer wished to trouble the noble lady with such services any further, and she said to her:

"Madam, thanks to God and to you, I have what I wanted, and now it is time for me to do whatever you wish me to do, so that afterward I may take my leave."

The noble lady told her she was happy that the Countess had obtained what she desired, but that she had not acted in the hopes of receiving any recompense but only because she felt it was her duty to support a good cause.

To this the Countess said:

"Madam, your intentions please me very much, but for my part, I have no intention of giving you something as a reward; but rather, I give you whatever you ask for supporting a good cause, for I believe that things should be done in this fashion."

Constrained by necessity, and with the greatest embarrassment, the noble lady then asked the Countess for a hundred pounds in order to marry her daughter. The Countess, understanding her embarrassment and hearing her modest request, gave her five hundred pounds as well as a quantity of beautiful and precious jewels amounting, perhaps, to as much again; the noble lady, more than satisfied, thanked the Countess profusely. Then the Countess left and returned to the inn. So that Beltramo would no longer have any excuse to send messages or visit her home, the noble lady went with her daughter to the country home of her relatives, and shortly thereafter, Beltramo was recalled home by his vassals and, having heard that the Countess had left the place, he returned there.

When the Countess learned that he had left Florence and had returned to his domain, she was very happy; she remained in Florence until the time for her delivery arrived, and she gave birth to two sons, both of whom very much resembled their father. She had them carefully nursed, and when she thought the time was right, she set out without being recognized by anyone and reached Montpellier; she rested there for a few days, making inquiries about the Count and his whereabouts, and when she learned that on All Saints' Day he was to give a great banquet for his ladies and knights in Rossiglione, she made her way there, still dressed in the pilgrim's clothing she had worn the day she left home.

And hearing that the ladies and knights gathered together in the Count's palace were about to sit down at the table, without changing her clothes and with the two little boys in her arms, she entered the dining hall, and she moved from one guest to another until, finding the Count, she threw herself at his feet, saying in tears:

"My lord, I am your unfortunate bride, who in misery has wandered about a long time in order to allow you to return and live in your own home. I beg you in God's name to observe the conditions imposed upon me by the two knights whom I sent to you: here in my arms is not one of your sons but two, and here is your ring. So the time has come for you to accept me as your wife according to your promise."

When he heard this, the Count was much confused, but he recognized his ring and even his sons, for they resembled him so, but he still asked: "How could this have happened?"

To the utter astonishment of the Count and of all the others who were present, the Countess recounted in detail how everything happened; because of this, he knew she was telling the truth, and seeing her perseverance and her intelligence and, moreover, two such handsome sons, the Count, in order to keep his promise as well as please his men and their ladies, all of whom begged him to receive and honor her as his legitimate wife, set aside his obstinate severity, raised the Countess to her feet, and embracing and kissing her, recognized her as his legitimate bride and her children as his own sons. Then he had her dressed in more suitable garments, to the greatest pleasure of all who were present and of all his other vassals who heard the news, and he gave a magnificent banquet which lasted not only that entire day but several days afterward; and from that day on, always honoring her as his bride and wife, he loved her and held her most dear.

[Third Day, Tenth Story]

❧

Alibech becomes a recluse and a monk named Rustico teaches her how to put the Devil back into Hell. Then she is led away from there to become the wife of Neerbale.

DIONEO had listened carefully to the Queen's story, and when he realized it was finished and that he alone remained to speak, without waiting for orders he began with a smile:

Gracious ladies, perhaps you have never heard how the Devil can be put back into Hell, and so, without diverging in the least from the topic which all of you have talked about today, I shall tell you how this is possible. Perhaps when you learn how to do this, you may still be in time to save your souls; and you will also learn that while Love is more at home in delightful palaces and luxurious bedrooms than in poor huts, he nevertheless sometimes makes himself felt in dense woodlands, on rugged mountains, and in desert caves. It is not difficult to understand the reason for this, for, after all, there is nothing that is not subject to his power.

Getting to the point, then, let me tell you that there once lived in the town of Capsa in Tunisia a very wealthy man who had, in addition to several sons, a beautiful and charming daughter whose name was Alibech. She was not a Christian, but because she heard so many Christians in her town praising their faith and the service of God, one day she asked one of these Christians how she could best and most quickly serve God. This person answered that those best served God who denied the things of this world, following the example of those who had gone to live in the Egyptian desert. The young girl was rather naive, for she was no more than fourteen years old. Moved by childish impulse rather than deliberate decision, she set out for the Egyptian desert all alone, without a word to anyone, the next morning. Spurred on by her desire and with great difficulty, she reached those solitary parts after several days, and from afar she saw a small hut toward which she went, and there she found a holy man on the threshold. Amazed to see her, the man asked her what she was doing there. The girl replied that she was inspired by God and that she wanted to enter his service, but that she had not yet met anyone who might teach her how to serve God. Seeing how young and beautiful she was and fearing how the Devil might tempt him if he kept her near him, the good man praised her fine intentions and after having given her a quantity of grass roots, wild apples, and dates to eat and some water to drink, he said to her:

"My child, not so far from here there lives a holy man who is far more qualified than I to teach you what you wish to learn; you should go to him." And he showed her the way. And when she arrived, she heard the same words from this other man, and so she went further on until finally she came to the cell of a young hermit, a very devout and good person whose name was Rustico, and of whom she asked the same questions she had asked the previous two. Since Rustico was anxious to test his willpower, he did not send her away or tell her to search for someone else—on the contrary, he kept her with him in his cell. And when night came, he made a bed of palm leaves in one corner of the cell, and he asked her to sleep there. No sooner had he made the bed than temptation began to struggle with his willpower, and, discovering that he had greatly overestimated his ability to resist, he shrugged his shoulders and surrendered without a battle. Setting aside his holy thoughts, his prayers, and his flagellations, he began contemplating the youth and the beauty of the girl, and also how he ought to act with her, so that she would not become aware of his licentiousness as he went about getting what he wanted from her. After testing her out with some questions, he discovered that she had actually never slept with a man before and that she was really just as naïve as she appeared. And so he decided that she, under the pretext of serving God, might well be the one to satisfy his desires. He began with great eloquence to show her how much of an enemy the Devil was to God, and then he gave her to understand that no service could be more pleasing to God than to put the Devil back into Hell, the place to which God had damned him. The young girl asked him how this might be accomplished, to which Rustico replied:

"You will soon find out, but first you must do whatever you see me do." And he began to remove those few garments he possessed until he was stark naked. And the girl did the same. He then sank to his knees as if he wished to pray, and he made her kneel opposite him in the same fashion. Being in this position, and more than ever burning with desire from the sight of her kneeling there so beautiful, the flesh was resurrected. Alibech looked at it in amazement and said:

"Rustico, what is that thing I see sticking out in front of you and which I do not have?"

"Oh, my child," replied Rustico, "that is the Devil, about whom I told you. Now you can see him for yourself. He is inflicting such pain on me that I can hardly bear it."

"Praise be to God!" said the girl. "I am better off than you are, for I do not have such a Devil."

"That is very true," Rustico replied, "but you do have something else which I do not have, and you have it in place of this."

"Oh?" answered Alibech. "What is it?"

"You have a Hell," said Rustico, "and I firmly believe that God has sent you here for the salvation of my soul. Since this Devil gives me such pain, you could be the one to take pity on me by allowing me to put him back into Hell. You would be giving me great comfort, and you will render a great service to God by making Him happy, which is what you say was your purpose in coming here."

"Oh, father," replied the girl in good faith, "since I have Hell, let us do as you wish, and as soon as possible."

"May God bless you, my child," Rustico said. "Let us go then and put him back, so that he will at last leave me in peace."

And after saying this, he led the girl over to one of the beds and showed her what position to take in order to incarcerate that cursed Devil. The young girl, who had never before put a single Devil into Hell, felt a slight pain the first time, and because of this she said to Rustico:

"This Devil must certainly be an evil thing and truly God's enemy, father, for he not only hurts others, but he even hurts Hell when put back into it."

"My child," Rustico said, "it will not always be like that." And to prove that it would not be, they put him back in Hell seven times before getting out of bed; in fact, after the seventh time the Devil found it impossible to rear his arrogant head, and he was content to be at peace for a while. But the Devil's pride was to rise up many a time, and the young girl, who was always obedient and eager to take him in, began to grow fond of this sport. She said to Rustico:

"Now I certainly understand what those good men of Capsa meant when they said that serving God was so pleasurable; and I cannot really remember anything I have ever done which was more pleasing or satisfying than putting the Devil back into Hell. I even think that anyone who thinks of anything but serving God is a fool."

For this reason, she would often come to Rustico saying:

"Father, I have come here to serve God and not to waste my time. Let's go and put the Devil back in Hell!"

And sometimes, while they were doing this, she would say to him:

"Rustico, I don't understand why the Devil would ever want to escape from Hell; if he enjoys being there as much as Hell enjoys taking him in and holding him, why would he ever want to leave?"

Since she invited Rustico to partake of this sport too often, constantly encouraging him in the service of the Lord, she took so much out of him that he began to feel the cold where another man would have begun to sweat from the heat. And because of this, he tried to tell the young girl that the Devil should only be punished and put back into Hell when he had raised his arrogant head:

"But we, by God's grace, have so humiliated him that he begs God to leave him in peace."

With these words, he was able to keep the girl calm for a while, but when she realized that Rustico was no longer asking her to put the Devil back into Hell, she said to him one day:

"Rustico, it's all well and good that your Devil is punished and no longer bothers you, but my Hell will not leave me alone; so you ought to have your Devil help me quench the fires of my Hell—after all, I did help you humble the pride of your Devil with my Hell."

Rustico, who lived on nothing but grass roots and spring water, could not respond very well to her requests, so he told her that to quench the fires of her Hell would require a hell of a lot of devils, but that he would do what he could for her. Thus, sometimes he was able to satisfy her, but those times were few—it was like tossing a bean into the mouth of a lion. So, feeling that she was not able to serve God to the extent she would have liked, the young girl would constantly complain. During the battle between Rustico's Devil and Alibech's Hell, the result of too much desire and too little strength, it happened that a fire broke out in Capsa in which Alibech's father was burned in his house along wth his sons and the rest of his family; as a result, Alibech was left sole heir to all his worldly possessions. A young man named Neerbale, who had spent all of his wealth in sumptuous living, having heard that she was alive, set out to look for her and found her before the court had time to confiscate her father's properties on the assumption that there were no heirs. To Rustico's great relief, but against Alibech's wishes, he brought her back to Capsa and took her for his wife, inheriting, in the process, part of her large fortune.

But before Neerbale had slept with her, she was asked by some women how she had served God in the desert. The girl replied that she had served him by putting the Devil back into Hell and that Neerbale had committed a grave sin in having taken her away from such a service. The ladies inquired as to how one puts the Devil back into Hell. With words and gestures the girl showed them how it was done; and then the women laughed hard (and they are probably still laughing) as they said:

"Don't be sad, child. People here do the same thing, and just as well. Neerbale will be extremely helpful to you in serving God in such a fashion."

This story was told and retold by one woman to another all over the city until it actually became a popular proverb, stating that the most pleasurable means of serving God was to put the Devil back into Hell. This saying, which spread across the seas to all parts, can still be heard today. And so, young ladies, if you seek the blessing of God, learn to put the Devil back into Hell, for this is not only pleasing in the sight of God but also to the parties concerned. And much good may rise and come from it!

[Third Day, Conclusion]

❧

DIONEO's story made the virtuous ladies laugh a thousand times or more, so apt and clever were his words; when he came to the end of it, the Queen realized that the end of her reign had arrived, she removed the laurel crown from her head and very graciously set it upon Filostrato's, and she said:

"Soon we shall see if the wolves know how to guide the sheep better than the sheep have guided the wolves."

Hearing this remark, Filostrato laughed and replied:

"If you had listened to me, the wolves would have taught the sheep to put the Devil back into Hell no worse than Rustico did with Alibech; so you shouldn't call us wolves, for you have not acted like sheep; nonetheless, since you have entrusted the kingdom to me, I shall now begin my reign."

To this Neifile replied:

"Listen, Filostrato, if you ever hoped to teach us anything, first you would need to be taught some sense, just as Masetto of Lamporecchio was taught by the nuns, and not regain the use of your speech until your bones rattled like a skeleton's."

Recognizing that the ladies' sickles were as sharp as his arrows, Filostrato set aside his jesting and began to govern the kingdom entrusted to him; first, he called for the steward to find out how matters stood, and then he discreetly gave him orders, according to what he thought would be best and satisfy the company most for as long as his reign was to last; then, turning to the ladies, he said:

"Loving ladies, it has been my misfortune, ever since I learned to distinguish good from evil, owing to the beauty of one of your lot to be perpetually subjected to Love, nor has it ever been of any use to me to follow as I have, humbly or obediently, all of his rules as best I knew how, for I always find myself first being abandoned for another lover and then from that point on things going from bad to worse; and they will continue doing so until the day I die. And so it pleases me that the topic of our discussion for tomorrow should be one that conforms best to my state of affairs: that is, those whose loves come to unhappy ends; as for me, I expect my love to have a most unhappy ending, nor was it for any other reason than this that my name, by which you call me, was given to me by someone who knew quite well what it meant."* Having said this, Filostrato rose to his feet and gave everyone permission to leave until suppertime.

The garden was so beautiful and so delightful that no one chose to leave it and seek greater pleasure elsewhere; on the contrary, since the sun was now much cooler, making it a pleasure to hunt, some of the ladies gave chase to the deer and rabbits and all the other animals in that garden which had on scores of occasions leaped into their midst as they sat there talking. Dioneo and Fiammetta began to sing about Sir Giuglielmo

---

*Etymologically, the name Filostrato means "overcome, vanquished by love."

and the lady of Vergiù,* while Filomena and Panfilo began to play chess; and thus doing, as they were, one thing or another, the time passed so quickly that before they realized it, it was already time for supper; and as soon as the tables were set around the beautiful fountain, they sat down to eat with the greatest of delight.

When the tables had been removed, Filostrato, not wishing to deviate from the path followed by the ladies who had reigned before him, then asked Lauretta to lead a dance and sing a song, and she replied:

"My lord, I do not know the songs of others, nor are any of my own which I still remember suitable enough for such a merry group; however, should you wish to hear one of them, I shall gladly sing one to you."

To this the King answered:

"Nothing of yours could be anything but beautiful and delightful, so, sing whatever song you have."

Then, in a very sweet but rather melancholy voice, with the others singing the refrains, Lauretta began as follows:

> There is no helpless lady
> who has more cause to weep than I,
> who sigh in vain, wretchedly in love.
>
> Heaven's mover and that of every star
> made me for His delight
> so light and lovely, gracious to behold
> that I might show to every noble mind
> on earth some trace of that
> beauty which dwells forever in His presence;
> but mortal imperfection,
> which cannot comprehend,
> finds me undelightful and I am spurned.
>
> There was one man who held me dearly,
> and I was young when he
> embraced me with his arms and all his thoughts—
> my eyes had set him all aflame,
> and time, which flies away
> so lightly, he spent it all in courting me;
> and I, in courtesy,

*An Italian version of a French composition entitled *La Chastelaine de Vergi*, dating from the thirteenth century.

made him worthy of me;
but now, alas, I am deprived of him.

But then appeared before my eyes a vain,
presumptuous young man,
though known to be most valiant;
he made me his and through a false belief
he turned to jealousy;
and then, alas, I came near to despair,
for now I realized
that I who had come to this world to please
all men was now possessed by only one.

I curse my wretched fate
forever saying "Yes, I do";
so beautiful was I in widow's black,
so happy did I feel, but now in a wife's dress
the life I lead is harsh
and one with far less honor than before.
Oh, wretched wedding feast,
if only I had died
before I had experienced such a fate!

Oh, first sweet love with whom I once had been
more than content,
who now in Heaven stands before the One
Who made him, ah, take pity on this soul
of mine, who for another man
cannot forget you: make me feel
that the flame which for me in you burned
is not yet spent,
and pray that I may soon be there with you.

Here Lauretta ended her song, which everyone listened to with
care but understood in different ways: there were those who
wished to construe it in the Milanese fashion, to mean that a
good pig was better than a pretty girl;* other interpretations re-
flected a more sublime, finer, and truer understanding of it, but
there is no need to mention them here. Then, the King, having
had many torches lit and set upon the grass and amid the flow-

---

*That is—better a live husband, though he may be bad, than a
good husband who is dead.

ers, had the other ladies sing, and they did so until every star that had risen was beginning to set; afterward, thinking it time to sleep, he bid them goodnight and ordered all of them to return to their respective bedrooms.

[Fourth Day, Title Page]

❀

Here ends the third day of The Decameron: *and the fourth begins, during which, under the rule of Filostrato, stories are told about those whose loves come to an unhappy end.*

[Fourth Day, Introduction]

❀

DEAREST ladies, both from what I have heard wise men say and from things I have often seen and read about, I used to think that the impetuous and fiery wind of envy would only batter high towers and the topmost part of trees, but I find that I was very much mistaken in my judgment. I flee and have always striven to flee the fiery blast of this angry gale, by trying to go about things quietly and unobtrusively not only through the plains but also through the deepest valleys. This will be clear to anyone who reads these short stories which I have written, but not signed, in Florentine vernacular prose, and composed in the most humble and low style possible; yet for all of this, I have not been able to avoid the terrible buffeting of such a wind which has almost uprooted me, and I have been nearly torn to pieces by the fangs of envy. Therefore, I can very easily attest to what wise men say is true: only misery is without envy in this world.

There have been those, discerning ladies, who have read these stories and have said that you please me too much and that it is not fitting for me to take so much pleasure from pleasing and consoling you, and, what seems to be worse, in praising you as I do. Others, speaking more profoundly, have stated that at my age it is not proper to pursue such matters, that is, to discuss women or to try to please them. And many, concerned about my reputation, say that I would be wiser to remain with the Muses on Parnassus than to get myself involved with you and these trifles. And there are those still who, speaking more spitefully than wisely, have said that it would be more practical if I were to consider where my daily bread was coming from rather than to go about "feeding on wind" with this foolishness of mine. And certain others, in order to belittle my labors, try to demonstrate that the things I have related to you did not happen in the way I told you they did.

Thus, worthy ladies, while I battle in your service, I am buffeted, troubled, and wounded to the quick by such winds and by such fierce, sharp teeth as these. God knows, I hear and endure these things with a tranquil mind, and however much my defense depends upon you in all of this, I do not, nevertheless, intend to spare my own forces; on the contrary, without replying as much as might be fitting, I shall put forward some simple answer, hoping in this way to shut my ears to their complaints, and I shall do this without further delay, for if I have as yet completed only a third of my task, my enemies are numerous and presumptuous, and before I reach the end of my labors, they will have multiplied—unless they receive some sort of reply before that time; and if this is not done, then their least effort will be enough to overcome me; and even your power, great as it may be, would be unable to resist them.

But before I reply to my critics, I should like to tell not an entire tale (for in doing so it might appear that I wished to mix my own stories with those of so worthy a group as I have been telling you about) but merely a portion of a tale, so that its very incompleteness will separate it from any of the others in my book.

For the benefit of those who criticize me, then, let me tell you about a man named Filippo Balducci, who lived in our city a long time ago. He was of rather modest birth, but he was rich, well versed, and expert in those matters which were required by his station in life; and he had a wife whom he dearly loved, and she loved him, and together they lived a tranquil life, always trying to please one another. Now it happened, as it must happen to all of us, that the good woman passed from this life and left nothing of herself to Filippo but an only child, whom she had conceived with him and who was now almost two years old.

No man was ever more disheartened by the loss of the thing

he loved than Filippo was by the loss of his wife; and seeing himself deprived of that companionship which he most cherished, he decided to renounce this world completely, to devote himself to serving God, and to do the same for his little boy. After he had given everything he owned to charity, he immediately went to the top of Mount Asinaio, and there he lived in a small hut with his son, surviving on alms, fasts, and prayers. And with his son, he was careful not to talk about worldly affairs or to expose him to them; with him he would always praise the glory of God and the eternal life, teaching him nothing but holy prayers. They spent many years leading this kind of life, his son restricted to the hut and denied contact with everyone except his father.

The good man was in the habit of coming into Florence from time to time, and he would return to his hut after receiving assistance from the friends of God according to his needs. Now, one day, when his son was eighteen years of age, Filippo happened to tell him that he was going into the city, and his son replied:

"Father, you are now an old man and can endure hardship very poorly. Why don't you take me with you one time to Florence so that you can introduce me to your friends and to those devoted to God? Since I am young and can endure hardship better than you, I can, from then on, go to Florence whenever you like to tend to our needs, and you can remain here."

The worthy man, realizing that this son of his was now grown up and was already so used to serving God that only with great difficulty could the things of this world have any effect on him, said to himself: "He is right." And since he had to go away, he took his son along with him.

When the young man saw the palaces, the houses, the churches, and all the other things that filled the city, he was amazed, for he had never seen such things in his life, and he kept asking his father what this one and that one was called. His father told him, and no sooner was one question answered than he would ask about something else. As they went along this way, the son asking and the father explaining, by chance they ran into a group of beautiful and elegantly dressed young women who were returning from a wedding feast; when the young man saw them, he immediately asked his father what they were. To this his father replied:

"My son, lower your eyes and do not look, for they are evil."

Then the son asked: "What are they called?"

In order not to awaken some potential or anything-but-useful desire in the young man's carnal appetite, his father did not

want to tell his son their proper name, that is to say "women,"
so he answered:

"Those are called goslings."

What an amazing thing to behold! The young man, who had
never before seen a single gosling, no longer paid any attention
to the palaces, oxen, horses, mules, money, or anything else he
had seen, and he quickly said:

"Father, I beg you to help me get one of those goslings."

"Alas, my son," said the father, "be quiet; they are evil."

To this the young man replied:

"Are evil things made like that?"

"Yes," his father replied.

And his son answered:

"I do not understand what you are saying or why they are
evil. As far as I know, I have never seen anything more beauti-
ful or pleasing than they. They are more beautiful than the
painted angels which you have pointed out to me so many times.
Oh, if you care for me at all, do what you can to take one of
these goslings home with us, and I will take care of feeding it."

His father replied:

"I will not, for you do not know how to feed them!"

Right then and there the father sensed that Nature had more
power than his intelligence, and he was sorry for having brought
his son to Florence. But let what I have recounted of this tale
up to this point suffice, so that I may return to those for whom
it was meant.

Well, young ladies, some of my critics say that I am wrong to
try to please you too much, and that I am too fond of you. To
these accusations I openly confess, that is, that you do please me
and I do try to please you. But why is this so surprising to
them? Putting aside the delights of having known your amorous
kisses, your pleasurable embraces, and the delicious couplings
that one so often enjoys with you, sweet ladies, let us consider
merely the pleasure of seeing you constantly: your elegant gar-
ments, your enchanting beauty, and the charm with which you
adorn yourselves (not to mention your feminine decorum). And
so we see that someone who was nurtured and reared in the con-
fines of a small cave upon a lonely and uncivilized mountaintop
without any companions except for his father desired only you,
asked for only you, gave only you his affection.

Will my critics blame me, bite and tear me apart if I—whose
body heaven made most ready to love you with, and whose soul
has been so disposed since my childhood when I first experienced
the power of the light from your eyes, the softness of your hon-

eylike words, and the flames kindled by your compassionate sighs—will they blame me for trying to please you and for the fact that you delight me, when we see how you, more than anything else, pleased a hermit, and what's more, a young man without feeling, much like a beast? Of course, those who do not love you and do not desire to be loved by you (people who neither feel nor know the pleasures or the power of natural affection) are the ones who blame me for doing this, but I care very little about them. And those who go around talking about my age show that they know nothing about the matter, for though the leek may have a white top, its roots can still be green. But joking aside, I reply by saying to them that I see no reason why I should be ashamed of delighting in these pleasures and in the ladies that give them, before the end of my days, since Guido Cavalcanti and Dante Alighieri (already old men) and Messer Cino da Pistoia* (a very old man indeed) considered themselves honored in striving to please the ladies in whose beauty lay their delight. And if it were not a departure from the customary way of arguing, I certainly would cite from history books and show you that they are full of ancient and worthy men who in their most mature years strove with great zeal to please the ladies—if my critics are not familiar with such cases, they should go and look them up! I agree that remaining with the Muses on Parnassus is sound advice, but we cannot always dwell with the Muses any more than they can always dwell with us. If it sometimes happens that a man leaves them, he should not be blamed if he delights in seeing something resembling them: the Muses are ladies, and although ladies are not as worthy as Muses, they do, nevertheless, look like them at first glance; and so for this reason, if for no other, they should please me. Furthermore, the fact is that ladies have already been the reason for my composing thousands of verses, while the Muses were in no way the cause of my writing them. They have, of course, assisted me and shown me how to compose these thousands of verses, and it is quite possible that they have been with me on several occasions while I was writing these stories of mine, no matter how insignificant they may be—they came to me, it could be said, out of respect for the affinity between these ladies and themselves. Therefore, in composing such stories as these, I am not as far

---

*Cavalcanti (1250?–1300) was a friend of Dante and a poet known for his philosophical view of love; Dante Alighieri (1265–1321) was the author of *The Divine Comedy*; Cino (1270–1336) was a poet and distinguished jurist.

away from Mount Parnassus or the Muses as some people may think.

But what shall we say about those who feel so much compassion for my hunger that they advise me to find myself a bit of bread to eat? All I know is that if I were to ask myself what their reply would be if I were forced to beg them for a meal, I imagine that they would tell me, "Go look for it among your fables!" And yet, poets have found more of it in their fables than many rich men have in their treasures, and many more still, by pursuing their fables, have lengthened their lives, while, on the contrary, others have lost them early in the search for more bread than they needed. What more, then? Let these people drive me away if ever I ask bread of them—thanks be to God, as yet I have no such need. And if ever the need arises, I know, in the words of the Apostle, how to endure both in abundance as well as in poverty.* And let no one mind my business but myself!

And as for those who say that these things did not happen the way I say they did in my stories, I should be very happy if they would bring forward the original versions, and if these should be different from what I have written, I would call their reproach justified and would try to correct myself; but until they produce something more than words, I shall leave them to their own opinions and follow my own, saying about them what they say about me.

Most gracious ladies, let this suffice as my reply for the time being, and let me say that armed with the aid of God and that of yourselves, in which I place my trust, with patience I shall proceed with my task, turning my back on that wind and letting it blow, for I do not see what more can happen to me than what happens to fine dust in a windstorm—either it does not move from the ground, or it does move from the ground; and if the wind sweeps it up high enough, it will often drop on the heads of men, the crowns of kings and emperors, and sometimes on high palaces and lofty towers; if it falls from there, it cannot go any lower than the spot from which it was lifted up. And if I have in the past striven with all my might to please you in some way, now I shall do so even more, for I realize that no reasonable person could say that I and the others who love you act in any way but according to Nature, whose laws (that is, Nature's) cannot be resisted without exceptional strength, and they are often resisted not only in vain but with very great damage to the

*Philippians 4:12.

strength of the one who attempts to do so. I confess that I do not possess nor wish to possess such strength, and if I did possess it, I would rather lend it to others than employ it myself. So let those critics of mine be silent, and if they cannot warm up to my work, let them live numbed with the chill of their own pleasures, or rather with their corrupt desires, and let me go on enjoying my own for this short lifetime granted to us. But we have strayed a great deal from where we departed, beautiful ladies, so let us return now and follow our established course.

The sun had already driven every star from the sky and the damp shadow of night from the earth when Filostrato arose and made his whole company stand, and they went into the beautiful garden, where they began to amuse themselves; and when it was time to eat, they breakfasted there where they had eaten supper the previous evening. When the sun was at its highest, they took their naps and then arose, and in their usual manner, they sat around the beautiful fountain. Then Filostrato ordered Fiammetta to tell the first story of the day; and without waiting to be told again, she began in a graceful fashion as follows:

[Fourth Day, First Story]

❦

Tancredi, Prince of Salerno, kills the lover of his daughter and sends her his heart in a gold goblet; she pours poisoned water on it, drinks it, and dies.

TODAY our King has given us a sad topic for discussion, especially when you consider that having come here to enjoy ourselves, we are now obliged to tell stories about the sorrows of others, ones which cannot be told without arousing the pity of those who tell them as well as of those who listen to them. Perhaps he did this in order to temper somewhat the happiness we have enjoyed during the past few days; but, since it is not for me to question his motives or try to change his wishes, I shall tell you about an incident that is not only pitiful but also disastrous and one worthy of your tears.

Tancredi, Prince of Salerno, was a most humane lord with a kindly spirit, except that in his old age he stained his hands with lovers' blood. In all his life he had but one daughter, and he would have been more fortunate if he had not had her. This girl

was as tenderly loved by her father as any daughter ever was;
and this tender love of his prevented her from leaving his side;
and she had not yet married, in spite of the fact that she had
passed by many years the suitable age for taking a husband.
Then, finally, he gave her in marriage to a son of the Duke of
Capua, who a short time later left her a widow, and she returned
to her father. She was as beautiful in body and face as any
woman could be, and she was both young and vivacious, and
wiser, perhaps, than any woman should be. She lived like a great
lady with her loving father in the midst of great luxury, and
since she was aware that her father, because of the love he bore
her, was not concerned about giving her away in marriage again,
and since she felt it would be immodest of her to request this of
him, she decided to see if she could secretly find herself a
worthy lover.

In her father's court she was able to observe many of those
men, both noble and otherwise, who frequent such courts, and
after studying the manners and habits of many of them, one
more than any of the others attracted her—a young valet of her
father's whose name was Guiscardo, a man of very humble birth
but one whose virtues and noble bearing pleased her so much
that she silently and passionately fell in love with him, and the
more she saw him, the more she admired him. The young man,
who among other things was not slow of wit, soon noticed her at-
tention toward him, and he took her so deep into his heart that
he could hardly think of anything else but his love for her.

And so they were secretly in love with each other, and the
young girl desired nothing more than to find herself alone with
him, and since she was unwilling to confide in anyone about her
love, she thought of an unusual scheme for letting him know how
they could meet. She wrote him a letter, and in it she told him
what he had to do the following day in order to be with her;
then she put it in the hollow of a reed and, as if in jest, she
gave it to Guiscardo, saying:

"Make a bellows of this tonight for your serving girl to keep
the fire burning."

Guiscardo took it, and realizing that she would not have given
it to him and spoken as she did without some reason, he brought
it home with him and after examining the stick, he found that it
was hollow, and opening it, he found her letter inside; when he
read it and learned what he had to do, he was the happiest man
that ever lived, and he carefully prepared to meet her in the
way she had described to him in her letter. Near the Prince's
palace was a cave hollowed out of a hill a long time before, and

it was lit by a small opening in the side of the hill; the cave had been abandoned for so long that the opening was almost covered over by brambles and weeds. One could reach this cave by a secret stairway blocked by a strong door which led from one of the rooms on the ground floor of the palace which the young lady occupied. Hardly anyone alive remembered that the stairway existed, for it had not been used for so long a time. But Love, from whose eyes no secret can remain concealed, brought back the stairway to this young lady's enamored mind.

For many days, the young lady tried with tools to open that door in such a way that no one might suspect; finally she succeeded, and once the door was open, she was able to walk down into the cave and see the outer entrance; then she sent word to Guiscardo that he should try to come there, indicating to him the probable height from the opening to the floor of the cave below. In order to accomplish this, Guiscardo immediately prepared a rope with knots and loops in it so that he would be able to climb up and down with it; then, wrapped in a leather skin to protect himself from the brambles, without anyone knowing about it, the following night he made his way to the cave opening. He tied one of the loops of the rope firmly to a tree stump at the mouth of the opening, and with it he lowered himself into the cave and waited there for the lady.

The next day, pretending that she wished to rest, the young lady sent her ladies-in-waiting away and, alone, she closed herself in her bedroom. Then, opening the stairway door, she descended into the cave, where she found Guiscardo, and they welcomed each other with great joy; later, they went to her bedroom, where they remained most of that day, to their greatest pleasure. Having made arrangements to keep their love affair a secret, Guiscardo returned to the cave, and the lady locked the door and came out to rejoin her attendants. Then, when night came, Guiscardo climbed up his rope and left the cave through the same opening that he had entered and returned home. Having learned the way, he was to return frequently in the course of time.

But Fortune, jealous of so long and great a pleasure, turned the happiness of the two lovers into a sorrowful event: Tancredi was sometimes in the habit of visiting his daughter's bedroom to spend a little time talking to her, and then he would leave. One day after eating, while the lady (whose name was Ghismunda) was in her garden with all her attendants, he went there without being observed or heard by anyone and entered her bedroom. Finding the windows closed and the bed curtains drawn back, and not wishing to take her away from her amusement, Tancredi sat down on a small stool at the foot of the bed; he leaned his head back on the bed and drew the bed curtain around him—almost as if he were trying to hide himself on purpose—and there he fell asleep. Ghismunda, who unfortunately that day had sent for Guiscardo, left her ladies-in-waiting in the garden and quietly entered her bedroom, where Tancredi was sleeping; she locked her door without noticing that someone was there and opened the door to Guiscardo, who was waiting for her, and they went to bed together, as they had always done, and while they were playing together and enjoying each other, Tancredi happened to awaken, and he heard and saw what Guiscardo and his daughter were doing. It grieved him beyond all measure, and at first he wanted to cry out, but then he decided to be silent and remain hidden, if he could, so that he could do with less shame what he had already decided must be done. The two lovers remained together for a long time, as they were accustomed to do, without noticing Tancredi; when they felt it was time, they got out of bed and Guiscardo returned to the cave and the lady left her room. Although he was an old man, Tancredi left the room by climbing through a window down to the garden, and, unnoticed, he returned, grief-stricken, to his room.

That night while all were asleep, on Tancredi's orders Guiscardo was seized by two guards just as he was emerging, hindered by his leather skin, from the cave opening, and in secret he was taken to Tancredi, who, almost in tears when he saw him, said:

"Guiscardo, my kindness toward you did not deserve the outrage and the shame which you have given me this day and which I witnessed with my very own eyes!"

To this, Guiscardo offered no other reply but:

"Love is more powerful than either you or I."

Then Tancredi ordered him to be guarded secretly in a nearby room, and this was done. The following day, while Ghismunda was still ignorant of all this, and after Tancredi had considered all sorts of diverse solutions, shortly after eating, as was his custom, he went to his daughter's room; he had her summoned, and locking himself inside with her, he said to her in tears:

"Ghismunda, I thought I knew your virtue and honesty so well that it never would have occurred to me, no matter what people might have said, that you could submit to any man who was not your husband, or even think of doing so, if I had not witnessed it with my own eyes; and thinking of it, I shall grieve for the duration of that little bit of life my old age still allows me. Since you had to bring yourself to such dishonor, would to God you had chosen a man who was worthy of your nobility. From among all the men that frequent my court you chose Guiscardo, a young man of very low class, who was raised at our court from the time he was a small child until today almost as an act of charity. You have caused me the greatest of worry, for I do not know what to do: as he left the cave opening last night, I had him arrested and now he is in prison; I have already made my decision about what to do with Guiscardo, but with you—God knows what I should do with you! On the one hand, the love I have always felt for you—more love than any father ever had for a daughter—urges me in one direction; on the other hand, my righteous indignation over your great folly urges me in the other; my love tells me to forgive you and my wrath tells me, against my own nature, to punish you. But before I make a decision, I should like to hear what you have to say about the matter."

Having said this, he lowered his head, and wept like a child who had been severely beaten. Ghismunda, hearing her father's words and realizing not only that her secret affair had been discovered but that Guiscardo had been seized, felt measureless grief, which she was very near to showing with cries and tears, as most women do; but her proud spirit conquered this cowardice, and her face remained the same through her miraculous strength of will, and knowing that her Guiscardo was already as good as dead, she decided that rather than offering excuses for her behavior, she preferred not to go on living; therefore, without a trace of feminine sorrow or contrition for her misdeed, she faced her father as a brave and unafraid young lady, and with a tearless, open, and unperturbed face, she said to him:

"Tancredi, I am disposed neither to deny nor to beg, since the former would not avail me, and I do not wish to avail myself of the latter; moreover, in no way do I intend to appeal to your kindness and your love but, rather, I shall confess the truth to you, first defending my reputation with sound arguments, and then, with deeds, I shall follow the boldness of my heart. It is true that I loved and still do love Guiscardo, and as long as I shall live, which will not be long, I shall love him; and if there is love after death, then I shall continue loving him. I was moved to act this way not so much by my womanly weakness but by your own lack of interest in marrying me, as well as by Guiscardo's own worth. It is clear, Tancredi, that you are made of flesh and blood and that you have fathered a daughter made of flesh and blood, not one of stone or of iron; and though you

are old now, you should have remembered the nature and power
of the laws of youth; although, as a man, you spent the best
part of your years soldiering in the army, you should, neverthe-
less, know how idleness and luxurious living can affect the old as
well as the young.

"And I was fathered by you and am of flesh and blood, and
have not lived so long that I am yet old—for both these reasons
I am full of amorous desire, which has also been greatly in-
creased by my marriage, which taught me how pleasurable it is
to satisfy such desires. Unable to resist their power, and being
both young and a woman, I decided to follow where they led me,
and I fell in love. And though I had made up my mind to com-
mit this natural sin, I tried as best I could to avoid bringing
shame on you and on myself. Compassionate Love and kindly
Fortune revealed to me a secret way to fulfill my desires without
anyone knowing. And no matter who told you or how you found
out, I make no denial of any of this. I did not choose Guiscardo
at random, as many women do, but I chose him over all others
with deliberate consideration and careful forethought, and the
two of us have enjoyed the satisfaction of our desires for some
time now. Besides reproving me for having sinned in loving, you
reprove me even more bitterly—preferring, in so doing, to follow
a common fallacy rather than the truth—in stating that I con-
sorted with a man of lowly birth, as if to say you would not
have been angry had I chosen a man of noble birth as a lover.
You fail to see that it is Fortune you should blame and not my
sin, for it is Fortune that most frequently raises the unworthy to
great heights and casts down the most worthy.

"But let us leave all that aside and look rather to the princi-
ples of things: you will observe that we are all made of the
same flesh and that we are all created by one and the same
Creator with equal powers and equal force and virtue. Virtue it
was that first distinguished differences among us, even though we
were all born and are still being born equal; those who possessed
a greater portion of virtue and were devoted to it were called
nobles, and the rest remained commoners. And although a cus-
tom contrary to this practice has made us forget this natural
law, yet it is not discarded or broken by Nature and good
habits; and a person who lives virtuously shows himself openly
to be noble, and he who calls him other than noble is the one at
fault, not the noble man.

"Look at all your noblemen, and compare their lives, customs,
and manners on the one hand to those of Guiscardo on the
other; if you judge without prejudice, you will declare him most

noble and those nobles of yours mere commoners. I do not trust the judgment of any other person concerning the virtue and valor of Guiscardo—I trust only what you yourself have said about him and what I have seen with my own eyes. Who has praised him more than you in all those praiseworthy matters worthy of a valiant man? You were certainly not mistaken; and unless my eyes deceive me, you never praised him for anything he did not clearly achieve in a manner more admirable than your words could express. If in this matter I was deceived in any way, then I was deceived by you. Will you say, then, that I consorted with a man of lowly condition? Then you do not speak the truth; you may, by chance, say that he is a poor man, and this I grant you—but only to your shame, for that is the condition in which you kept a valiant servant of yours. Poverty does not diminish anyone's nobility, it only diminishes his wealth! Many kings and great rulers were once poor, and many of those who plow the land and watch the sheep were once very rich, and they still are.

"As for your last problem—what to do with me—in no way should you hesitate: if in your old age you are inclined to do what you did not do as a young man—that is, to turn to cruelty—then turn your cruelty upon me. I shall not beg for leniency, for I am the true cause of this sin, if it be a sin; and I assure you that if you do not do to me what you have done or plan to do to Guiscardo, my own hands will do it for you. Now go, shed your tears with women, and if you must be cruel, if you feel we deserve death, then kill both of us with one blow!"

The Prince recognized his daughter's greatness of soul, but he did not believe she was as resolute as her words implied; therefore, having left her and given up all thought of punishing her cruelly, he thought he could cool her burning love with different punishment: he ordered the two men who were guarding Guiscardo to go in secret and strangle him that night and to cut out his heart and bring it to him. They did just as they were ordered to do, and the following day, the Prince sent for a large, handsome goblet of gold, and in it he put Guiscardo's heart; he sent it to his daughter by one of his most trusted servants, who was instructed to say the following words when he gave it to her:

"Your father sends you this to console you for the loss of that which you loved the most, just as you have consoled him for the loss of what he loved the most."

Ghismunda, firm in her desperate resolution, had had poisonous herbs and roots brought to her as soon as her father departed, and she distilled and reduced them to a liquid, in order to have them available if what she feared actually did occur. When the servant arrived and delivered the Prince's gift and his words, she took the goblet with a determined look, uncovered it, and seeing the heart and hearing the words, she knew for certain that this was Guiscardo's heart. Turning to the servant, she said:

"There is no burial place more worthy for such a heart than one of gold; in this regard, my father has acted wisely."

And saying this, she raised the cup to her lips and kissed it, and then continued speaking to the servant:

"I have always found my father's love for me to be most tender in every respect as I do now, even in this extreme moment of my life, but here it shows itself to be even more so than ever; and thanking him for the last time on my behalf, I bid you tell him how grateful I am to him for so precious a gift as this."

Then, looking into the goblet, which she held firmly in her hand, gazing at the heart, she sighed and said:

"Ah! Sweetest abode of all my pleasures, cursed be the cruelty of he who has forced me to look at you with the eyes of my body! It was already too much to gaze upon you constantly even with the eyes of my mind. Your life has run the course that Fortune has bestowed upon you; you have reached the goal toward which all men race; you have abandoned the miseries and trials of the world and have received from your very enemy the burial that your valor deserved. Nothing is lacking in your last rites except the tears of the one who loved you while you were alive. So that you might have them, God moved my pitiless father to send you to me, and I shall give you those tears, even though I was determined to die without them, and I will give them with a serene face; as soon as I have wept for you, I shall act in such a way that my soul will join yours without further delay, and may you, heart, accept my soul which once was so dear to you. In what company could I go more happily or more securely to unknown places than in yours? I am sure that your soul is still here and continues to look upon the places where we took our pleasure, and as I am certain that your soul loves me still, may it wait for my soul, which loves it so deeply."

And when this was said, she bent over the goblet and without a womanly show of grief, she began to weep in a way marvelous to behold, pouring forth her tears as if from a fountain as she kissed the dead heart countless times. Her attendants, who stood all around her, did not understand whose heart it was or what her words meant, but overcome with compassion they all began to weep; they asked her most pityingly why she was weeping, and they sought to comfort her as best they knew how, but it was all in vain. Then, when she felt she had wept enough, she raised her head, dried her eyes, and said:

"Oh, most beloved heart, now that I have fulfilled all my duties to you, nothing more remains for me but to come to you and join my soul to yours."

When she had said this, she took the phial she had prepared the day before containing the liquid, and pouring it into the goblet where the heart was bathed with her many tears, with no trepidation whatsoever, she lifted it to her lips and drank all of it. Having done this, she climbed upon her bed, with the goblet in her hand, and as modestly as possible she arranged her body upon the bed and placed the heart of her dead lover against her own, and without saying another word she waited for death.

Although her ladies-in-waiting had seen and heard all these things, they did not understand, nor did they know that the liquid she had drunk was poison; they sent word to Tancredi about it, and he, fearing what might happen, immediately went down to his daughter's bedroom. He arrived there just as she was arranging herself on her bed; observing her condition, he tried to comfort her (only too late) with sweet words and began to weep most sorrowfully. And the lady said:

"Tancredi, save those tears for a less fortunate fate than this, and do not shed them on my account, for I do not want them. Who ever heard of someone weeping over what he himself wished for? But if you still retain anything of that love you once had for me, grant me one last gift: since it displeased you that I once lived quietly in secret with Guiscardo, let my body be publicly laid to rest beside his, wherever you choose to cast his remains."

The anguish of his weeping did not allow the Prince to answer. Then, when the young woman felt her death was near, she drew the dead heart to her breast and said:

"God be with you, for now I leave you."

And closing her eyes, her senses left her, and she departed from this sorrowful existence. Thus, just as you have heard it, the sad love of Guiscardo and Ghismunda came to an end; and then Tancredi, who wept much and repented of his cruelty too late, amid the grief of all the people of Salerno, had them buried together honorably in one tomb.

[Fourth Day, Second Story]

✤

Brother Alberto convinces a lady that the Angel Gabriel is in love with her; then, disguised as the angel, he sleeps with her many times; in fear of her relatives, he flees from her house and seeks refuge in the home of a poor man, who, on the following day, leads him into the piazza dressed as a wild man of the forest, and there he is recognized by his brother monks and is put into prison.

THE story told by Fiammetta had more than once brought tears to the eyes of her companions; but as soon as it was over, the King, showing no emotion, said:

"I should consider my life worth very little in comparison with half the pleasure Guiscardo enjoyed with Ghismunda; nor should any of you be surprised at this, for, though living, I feel as if I am dying a thousand deaths, and yet not one bit of pleasure is granted to me.* But leaving aside my own problems for the moment, I want Pampinea to continue with a story that is somewhat similar to my own sad fate; if she will proceed as Fiammetta has begun, I shall, without doubt, feel some dewdrops fall upon my own amorous fire."

Pampinea, hearing the command directed to her, felt the mood of the company more through her own sensitivity than through the King's words; because of this, she was more inclined to entertain the group rather than to please the King, except insofar as his order to begin was concerned—and so, she decided, without straying from his theme, to tell a humorous story. She began in this way:

The man who is wicked and thought to be good
Can do no wrong, for no one believes that he would.

This proverb provides me with ample material for the theme that has been proposed to me, and it also enables me to demonstrate the nature and extent of the hypocrisy of the monks, who

---

*Filostrato, true to the meaning of his name, is an unrequited and suffering lover.

259

go about with their long, flowing robes, their artificially pale
faces, their voices humble and sweet when they are begging
alms, but shrill and bitter when they are attacking their own
vices in others or when they declare how others gain salvation
by giving alms while they do so by taking them; and, moreover,
rather than men who have to earn Paradise like us, they act al-
most as if they were its very owners and rulers, granting to each
person that dies, according to the quantity of money they are
left by him, a more or less choice place up there, and in doing
this they first deceive themselves (if they really believe in it),
and then they deceive those who put faith in their words. If I
were permitted to do so, I would soon reveal to all those simple-
minded people exactly what it is that they keep hidden beneath
their bulging habits. But for now, may God grant that all their
lies have the same fate as a certain minor friar who, by no
means a young man, was considered in Venice to be one of the
best men that St. Francis ever attracted to the order, and it
pleases me a great deal to be able to tell you this story, for, per-
haps, it will cheer somewhat your hearts, which are now so full
of pity for the fate of Ghismunda.

Gracious ladies, there was once in Imola a man of wicked and
corrupt ways named Berto della Massa, whose evil deeds were so
well known by the people of Imola that nobody there would be-
lieve him when he told the truth, not to mention when he lied.
Realizing that his tricks would no longer work there, in desper-
ation he moved to Venice, that receptacle of all sorts of wicked-
ness, having decided to employ a different kind of trickery there
from what he had used anywhere else before. And almost as if
his conscience were struck with remorse for his evil deeds com-
mitted in the past, he gave every sign of a man who had become
truly humble and, indeed, almost religious; in fact, he went and
turned himself into a minor friar and took the name of Brother
Alberto da Imola; and in this disguise he pretended to lead an
ascetic life, praising repentance and abstinence, and never eating
meat nor drinking wine unless they were of a quality good
enough for him.

Never before had such a thief, pimp, forger, and murderer be-
come so great a preacher without having first abandoned these
vices—even though in private he might still be practicing them.
To top it all off, once he got himself ordained a priest, he would,
whenever he celebrated the Mass at the altar, in view of all the
congregation, shed tears when it came to that moment in the
Mass for the Passion of Our Lord, for he was a man whose tears
were cheap, and he could produce them whenever he liked.

And in short, between his sermons and his tears, he managed to beguile the Venetians to such an extent that he was almost always made the trustee and guardian of every will that was made, the keeper of many people's money, and confessor and adviser to the majority of men and women; and acting in this way, he changed from a wolf into a shepherd, and his reputation for sanctity in those parts was far greater than St. Francis's was in Assisi.

Now it happened that there was a foolish and silly young woman named Madonna Lisetta da Ca' Quirino (the wife of a great merchant who had sailed off with his galleys to Flanders) who, along with other ladies, went to be confessed by this holy friar. She was kneeling at his feet and, being a Venetian (and, as such, a gossip like all of them), she was asked by Brother Alberto halfway through her confession if she had a lover. To this question she crossly replied:

"What, my dear brother, do you not have eyes in your head? Do my charms appear to you to be like all those of other women? I could have even more lovers than I want, but my beauty is not to be enjoyed by just anyone. How many ladies do you know who possess such charms as mine, charms which would make me beautiful even in Paradise?"

And then she kept on saying so many things about her beauty that it became boring to listen to her. Brother Alberto realized immediately that she was a bit of a moron, and since he thought she was just the right terrain for plowing, he fell passionately in love with her right then and there; but putting aside his flatteries for a more appropriate time, and reassuming his saintly manner, he began to reproach her and to tell her that her attitude was vainglorious and other such things; and so the lady told him that he was a beast and that he did not know one beauty from another; and because he did not want to upset her too much, Brother Alberto, after having confessed her, sent her off with the other women.

After a few days, he went with a trusted companion to Madonna Lisetta's home, and, taking her into a room where they could be seen by no one, he threw himself on his knees before her and said:

"My lady, I beg you in God's name to forgive me for speaking to you as I did last Sunday about your beauty, for I was so soundly punished the following night that I have not been able to get up until today."

"And who punished you in this way?" asked Lady Halfwit.

"I shall tell you," replied Brother Alberto. "As I was praying that night in my cell, as I always do, I suddenly saw a glowing light, and before I was able to turn around to see what it was, I saw a very handsome young man with a large stick in his hand who took me by the collar, dragged me to my feet, and gave me so many blows that he broke practically everything in my body. I asked him why he had done this and he replied:

" 'Because yesterday you presumed to reproach the celestial beauty of Madonna Lisetta, whom I love more than anyone else except God.'

"And then I asked: 'Who are you?'

"He replied that he was the Angel Gabriel.

" 'Oh, My Lord,' I said, 'I beg you to forgive me.'

" 'I shall forgive you on one condition,' he said, 'that you go to her as soon as you are able and beg her forgiveness; and if she does not pardon you, I shall return here and beat you so soundly that you will be sorry for the rest of your life.' "

Lady Lighthead, who was as smart as salt is sweet, enjoyed hearing all these words and she believed them all; then, after a moment, she said:

"I told you, Brother Alberto, that my charms are heavenly; but, God help me, I feel sorry for you, and from now on, in order to spare you more harm, I forgive you on condition that you tell me what the angel said next."

Brother Alberto said: "My lady, since you have forgiven me, I shall gladly tell you, but I remind you of one thing: you must not tell what I tell you to anyone in the world, otherwise you will spoil everything, you who are the most fortunate woman in the world today. The Angel Gabriel told me to tell you that you are so pleasing to him that he would have come to spend the night with you on several occasions if he had not thought it might frighten you. Now he has sent me here with a message to inform you that he would like to come to you one night and spend some time in your company; but since he is an angel and you would not be able to touch him in the form of an angel, he says that for your pleasure he would like to come in the shape of a man, and he asks that you inform him when you would like him to come and in whose shape he should come, and he will come; therefore you, more than any other woman alive, should consider yourself blessed."

Lady Silly then said that it pleased her very much that the Angel Gabriel was in love with her, for she loved him as well and never failed to light a cheap candle in his honor whenever she found a painting of him in church; and whenever he wished to come to her, he would be most welcome, and he would find her all alone in her room, and he could come on the condition that he would not leave her for the Virgin Mary, whom, it was said, he loved very much, and it was obviously true, because everywhere she saw him, he was always on his knees before her; and besides this, she said that he could appear in whatever shape or form he wished—she would not be afraid.

"My lady," Brother Alberto then said, "you speak wisely, and I shall arrange everything with him just as you have said. And could you do me one great favor—it will cost you nothing; the favor is this: would you allow him to come to you in my body? Let me tell you how you would be doing me a favor: he will take my soul from my body and place it in Paradise, and he will enter my body, and as long as he is with you, my soul will be in Heaven."

Then Lady Dimwit replied: "That pleases me; I wish you to have this consolation for the beating he gave you on my account."

Brother Alberto then said: "Now arrange for him to find the door of your house open tonight so that he can come inside; since he will be arriving in the form of a man, he cannot get in unless he uses the door."

The lady replied that it would be done. Brother Alberto left, and she was so delighted by the whole affair that, jumping for joy, she could hardly keep her skirts over her rear end, and it seemed like a thousand years to her waiting for the Angel Gabriel to come. Brother Alberto, who was thinking more about getting in the saddle than of being an angel that evening, began to fortify himself with confections and other delicacies so that he would not be easily thrown from his horse; and then he got permission to stay out that night and, as soon as it was dark, he went with a trusted companion to the house of a lady friend of his, which on other occasions he had used as his point of departure whenever he went to ride the mares; and from there, when the time seemed ripe to him, he went in disguise to the lady's house, and went inside; and, having changed himself into an angel with the different odds and ends he brought with him, he climbed the stairs, and entered the lady's bedroom.

When she saw this white object approaching, she threw herself on her knees in front of him, and the angel blessed her and raised her to her feet, and made a sign for her to go into bed; and she, most anxious to obey, did so immediately, and the angel lay down alongside his devout worshiper. Brother Alberto was a handsome young man with a robust, well-built body; Lady

Lisetta was all fresh and soft, and she discovered that his ride was altogether different from that of her husband. He flew many times that night without his wings, which caused the lady to cry aloud with delight, and, in addition, he told her many things about the glory of Heaven. Then, as day broke, having made another appointment to meet her, he gathered his equipment and returned to his companion, who had struck up a very friendly relationship with the good woman of the house, who was afraid of sleeping alone at night.

After breakfast, the lady went with one of her attendants to Brother Alberto's and told him the story of the Angel Gabriel and of what she had heard from him about the glory of eternal life and of how he had looked, adding all sorts of extraordinary inventions of her own to her story. To this Brother Alberto said:

"My lady, I do not know what happened to you with him; I only know that last night, when he came to me and I delivered your message to him, in an instant he transported my soul to a place where there were more flowers and roses than I have ever seen before, and he left my soul in this most delightful spot until matins this morning. What happened to my body I do not know."

"But did I not tell you?" replied the lady. "Your body spent the entire night in my arms with the Angel Gabriel inside it, and if you do not believe me, look under your left nipple, where I gave the angel such a passionate kiss that he will carry its mark for many a day!"

Then Brother Alberto said: "Today I shall do something that I have not done for some time—I shall undress myself to see if what you say is true."

And after a good deal more chatter, the lady returned home; and Brother Alberto, with no trouble at all, often went to visit her, disguised as an angel. One day, however, Madonna Lisetta was discussing the nature of beauty with one of her neighbors, and she, showing off and being the silly goose that she was, said: "You would not talk about any other women if you knew who really appreciates my beauty."

Her neighbor, anxious to hear more about this and knowing quite well the kind of woman Lisetta was, replied: "Madam, you may be right, but since I do not know to whom you are referring, I find it difficult to change my opinion so easily."

"Neighbor," replied Madonna Lisetta, who was easily excited, "he does not want it to be known, but my lover is the Angel Gabriel, and he tells me that this is because I am the most beautiful woman that there is in all the world or even in all of the Maremma,* as a matter of fact."

Her neighbor had the urge to break into laughter right then, but she held herself back in order to make her friend continue talking, and she said: "For God's sake, madam, if the Angel Gabriel is your lover and he tells you this, it must really be so; but I had no idea that angels did such things."

"Neighbor," replied the lady, "that is where you are wrong; by God's wounds, he does it better than my husband, and he tells me that they do it up there as well; but since he thinks I am more beautiful than anyone in Heaven, he fell in love with me and comes to visit with me very often. So there you have it!"

When the neighbor had left Madonna Lisetta, it seemed to her as if a thousand years had passed before she could find someone to whom she was able to repeat what she had learned; and at a large gathering of women, she told them the story piece by piece. These women told it to their husbands and to other women, who passed it on to others, and thus in less than two days it was the talk of all Venice. But among those whom this story reached were also the woman's in-laws, and they decided, without telling her a word, to find this angel and to see if he knew how to fly; and they kept watch for him for several nights. It just happened that some hint of this got back to Brother Alberto, so he went there one night to scold the lady, and no sooner was he undressed than her in-laws, who had seen him arrive, were at the door of the bedroom ready to open it. When Brother Alberto heard this and realized what was going on, he jumped up, and seeing no other means of escape, he flung open a window which looked out onto the Grand Canal and threw himself into the water.

Because the water was deep there, and he was a good swimmer, he did not hurt himself; after swimming to the other side of the canal, he immediately entered a door that was opened to him and begged the good man inside, for the love of God, to save his life, and he made up a story to explain why he was there at that hour and why he was naked. The good man, moved to pity, gave him his own bed, for he had some affairs of his own to attend to, and he told him to remain there until he returned; then, having locked him in, he went about his business.

---

*Equating the entire world with this small, marshy region of Tuscany, the lady demonstrates her stupidity both to her neighbor and to the reader.

When the lady's in-laws opened the door to her bedroom and entered, they found that the Angel Gabriel had flown away, leaving his wings behind him; they abused the lady to no end and finally, leaving her alone and distressed, they returned to their home with the angel's equipment. In the meanwhile, at daybreak, while the good man was on the Rialto, he heard talk of how the Angel Gabriel had gone to bed that night with Madonna Lisetta and had been discovered there by her in-laws, and how he had thrown himself into the canal out of fear, and how no one knew what had happened to him; immediately he realized that the man in his house was the man in question. Returning home and identifying him, after much discussion, he came to an agreement with the friar: he would not hand him over to the in-laws if the friar would pay him fifty ducats; and this Brother Alberto did.

When this was done, Brother Alberto was anxious to get out of that place, and the good man told him:

"There is only one way out, if you are willing to go along with it. Today we are celebrating a festival in which men are led around dressed as bears, some as wild men, others in one costume or another, and the festival comes to a close with a sort of hunt in St. Mark's Square, after which everyone goes wherever he pleases, with whomever he brought there. If you wish, rather than run the risk of being discovered here, I would be willing to lead you along in one of these disguises to wherever you like—otherwise, I don't see any way for you to escape from here without being recognized; and the in-laws of the lady, knowing that you are hiding somewhere around here, have posted guards everywhere to trap you."

Though it seemed hard to Brother Alberto to have to leave in such a disguise, his fear of the lady's relatives persuaded him to go along with it, and he told the man where he would like to go and that whatever costume in which he might choose to lead him there would be fine with him. The man smeared him all over with honey, covered him with feathers, and put a chain around his neck and a mask on his face; in one of his hands he put a large club and in the other two huge dogs which he had gotten from the slaughterhouse; at the same time he sent someone to the Rialto to announce that anyone interested in seeing the Angel Gabriel should go to St. Mark's Square—so much for Venetian loyalty!

And as soon as this was done, he took the friar outside and holding him by a chain from behind, he had him take the lead—all of which caused quite a commotion, as many bystand-

ers would ask: "Who is it? What is it?" And in this way he led
him all the way up to the piazza, where, between those who had
followed him along and those who had heard the announcement
and had come running from the Rialto, a huge crowd was
gathering. When he arrived there, he tied his wild man up to a
column in a conspicuous and elevated spot, pretending to wait
for the hunt; meanwhile, the gnats and horseflies were giving
Brother Alberto a great deal of trouble, for he was covered with
honey. But when the good man saw that the piazza was full, pre-
tending to unchain his wild man, he tore the mask from his face
and announced:

"Ladies and gentlemen, since the pig did not show up for the
hunt, there is not going to be a hunt, but I would not want you
to feel that you have come for nothing, so, may I present to you
the Angel Gabriel, who descends by night from Heaven to earth
to console our Venetian ladies."

When his mask was removed, Brother Alberto was instantly
recognized by everyone, a great cry arose from the crowd, and
they shouted the most insulting, the foulest words ever hurled at
any scoundrel; besides this, one by one they all started throwing
garbage in his face, keeping him occupied in this way for a long
time until, by chance, the news reached his brother friars; six of
them came, and throwing a cloak over him, they unchained him,
and in the midst of a great commotion, they led him back to
their monastery, where he was locked up, and there, leading a
wretched existence, it is believed he eventually died.

So it was that a man who was thought to be good and who
acted evilly, not recognized for what he really was, dared to turn
himself into the Angel Gabriel, and instead was turned into a
wild man, and, in the end, was cursed at by all as he deserved to
be and made to lament in vain for the sins he had committed.
May it please God that the same thing happen to all others like
him!

[Fourth Day, Third Story]

❖

*Three young men are in love with three sisters and run away
with them to Crete: the eldest sister kills her lover out of jeal-
ousy; the second sister saves the first from death by giving her-
self to the Duke of Crete, but then she is murdered by her lover,*

who flees with the first sister; the third lover is accused of the
crime along with the third sister, and both- are arrested and
made to confess; fearing death, they bribe their guards and flee,
impoverished, to Rhodes; and there they die in poverty.

AT the end of Pampinea's storytelling, Filostrato became pensive
for a while and then he turned to her and said:

"The only good thing about your story that gave me some
pleasure was the ending; there was far too much mirth in it be-
fore the end, something I would have preferred not to be there."
Then, turning to Lauretta, he said:

"Madam, proceed with a better story, if you can possibly do
so."

Laughing, Lauretta replied:

"You are too cruel with lovers if your only wish is to see them
come to an unhappy end, but in obedience to you, I shall tell
you a story about three such lovers who all came to an equally
bad end after having enjoyed very little of their love."

And when this was said, she began:

Young ladies, as you are surely aware, every vice can do the
greatest harm to the person who practices it and in many cases
to others as well. And among these vices, I believe that the one
which leads us straight into danger is the vice of anger, which is
nothing other than a sudden and thoughtless impulse, which in-
cited by some unhappiness we feel, drives all reason from us,
blinds the eyes of the mind with darkness, and consumes our
souls with burning rage. And while this often occurs in men, and
in some more than in others, it has nonetheless been known to
cause even greater damage in women, for it flares up more easily
in them, burns with a brighter flame, and finds less resistance to
it there. This is not surprising, for if we examine the matter
more closely, we will discover that by its very nature fire kindles
more readily in light and soft materials than in hard and heavy
things; and we women are—with no offense to you gentlemen—
more delicate than you are and much more capricious. So then,
bearing in mind that we are inclined toward anger and that our
mildness and kindness are a great source of tranquillity and
pleasure to the men with whom we associate, and that anger and
fury are a source of great trouble and danger, I intend to
strengthen ourselves against such anger by telling you a story of
the love of three young men and as many young ladies, as I said
earlier, and how through the anger of just one of them their
happiness changed to misery.

Marseille, as you know, is situated in Provence on the

seacoast and is an ancient and most noble city which was once populated by more wealthy men and by far greater merchants than we find there today; among these there was a man named N'Arnald Civada, a man of humble origins but of outstanding honesty and business integrity, and wealthy beyond measure in property and in money; his wife had borne him a number of children, of whom the oldest were three girls, and the rest were boys. Of these three, two were twins, fifteen years of age, and the third sister was fourteen; and the only thing delaying the marriages their parents had arranged for them was the return of N'Arnald, who had traveled to Spain with his merchandise. The names of the first two sisters were Ninetta and Magdalena; the third was called Bertella.

There was a young but poor nobleman named Restagnone who was as in love as could be with Ninetta, and the young girl was in love with him, and they had managed to devise a way of taking pleasure from their love without arousing the suspicion of a single living soul. And they had been enjoying each other for quite some time now when two young friends, one of whom was named Folco and the other Ughetto, both of whose fathers had passed away and left them very wealthy, happened to fall in love, one with Magdalena and the other with Bertella. When Restagnone found out about this, having been informed of it by Ninetta, he thought that there must be some way their love for the two sisters might be able to ease his own poverty, and so he became friendly with them, and on occasion he would accompany both one and the other man on visits to their ladies as well as his own.

And finally when he felt he was on friendly enough terms with them, he invited them one day to his home and said:

"My dear young friends, our friendship must certainly assure you of the great affection I bear for you, and the fact that I would do for you anything I would for myself; since I am so fond of you, I want to tell you what I have in mind, and then you and I together can choose the course of action which seems to us the best. You, if your words do not lie, and if what I gather from the way you have been acting day and night is correct, burn with the greatest passion for the two young ladies, just as I do for their third sister. If you agree, I daresay I have found a very sweet and pleasing remedy for your passion. You are very rich young men, something I am not: if you are willing to pool your wealth, to allow me to share one third of it with you, and decide to what part of the world we should go and live happily with these ladies, then without any doubt, I promise to persuade the three sisters to come with us anywhere we wish to go and to take with them a hefty portion of their father's wealth, and there each one of us with his lady, just as if we were three brothers, would live happier than any other men in the world. Now it is up to you to decide whether you wish to make yourselves happy by adopting this plan or whether you wish to reject it."

As soon as the two young men, who were burning beyond belief with passion, had heard there was a chance they might have their young ladies, they did not trouble themselves to deliberate too long, but, rather, they replied that no matter where it took them, they were prepared to go along. Some days after receiving this answer from the young man, Restagnone found himself, and not without considerable difficulty, in the company of Ninetta; after he had been with her for some time, he told her what he had said to the young men, and, using many an argument, he tried to convince her that his plan was a good one. And this was not very difficult for him to do, for even more than he, she wanted to be able to meet with him without fear of being caught; so she told him frankly that she liked the idea and that her sisters, especially in this matter, would do whatever she wanted them to do, and she told him he should, as soon as possible, organize everything required to achieve this. Restagnone went back to the two young men, who questioned him at great length about what he had previously proposed to them, and he informed them that as far as their ladies were concerned, the deed was done.

Having decided among themselves to go to Crete, they sold some of their properties, under the pretext of going into some business with the proceeds, and after converting everything else they owned into cash, they bought a brigantine, which they lavishly provisioned in secret. Then they awaited the appointed time. In the meantime Ninetta, who was well aware of her sisters' desires, with her sweet words filled them with so much enthusiasm for the undertaking that they thought they would not live long enough to see it happen.

So, when the night came for them to embark on the brigantine, having opened a large chest of their father's and taken from it a very large quantity of money and jewels, all three of them quietly left the house according to their plan, and found their three lovers waiting for them; with no further delay they all went aboard the brigantine, gave orders to weigh anchor, and off they sailed, without stopping anywhere until the following evening, when they reached Genoa, where the new lovers first took joy and pleasure from their love. After taking on all the provisions they needed, they set sail, going from one port to another, until on the eighth day, without any difficulty, they arrived in Crete, where, not far from Candia, they purchased the most magnificent and vast estates on which they built the most beautiful and delightful mansions; and there with a large retinue of servants, their hunting dogs, their hawks and horses, they began to live like lords, giving banquets and making merry with their ladies. They were the happiest men in the world.

While they were living in this fashion, one day it happened (as we all know from our everyday experience that too much of a good thing can often bring grief) that Restagnone, who had loved Ninetta very much, and who now was able to have her whenever he liked without arousing any suspicion, began to have regrets, and, as a result, his love for her diminished. And then one day at a banquet he was most taken by a young lady of the island, a beautiful and noble lady, and began to pursue her most eagerly, paying her great compliments and giving banquets in her home; when Ninetta became aware of this, she was so overcome with jealousy that soon he was unable to make a move without her knowing about it and flying into a fit of anger, using violent language, and making his life, as well as her own, a misery.

But just as a surfeit of good things generates disgust, so in like manner the denial of something desired increases our appetite for it; thus, Ninetta's fits of anger increased Restagnone's burning passion for his new love. And, in the course of time, whether Restagnone did or did not receive the favors of the lady he loved, whoever reported this to Ninetta managed to convince her completely that he had; as a result she fell into a state of deep unhappiness and from that into a state of anger, which finally developed into such a furious rage that the love which she had once borne for Restagnone was now transformed into bitter hatred, and blinded by her anger, she decided to avenge all the shame she felt he had caused her by killing Restagnone. There was an old Greek woman, an expert in the preparation of poisons, whom she called in, and with promises and gifts she convinced her to make a deadly liquid; and without considering the matter further, one evening she gave the concoction to Restagnone, who happened to be very thirsty because of the heat and paid no attention to what he was drinking. The power of this liquid was such that before the morning dawned it had killed him. When Folco and Ughetto and their ladies learned of his death, not knowing that he had been poisoned, they together with Ninetta wept bitterly and had him honorably buried. But not many days later it happened that the old woman who had made the poison liquid for Ninetta was arrested for some other evil deed, and under torture, among her many crimes she gave a full confession of this particular one, explaining in detail how Restagnone's death had come about; as a result, the Duke of Crete, without a word to anyone, surrounded Folco's palace one night and without a sound he quietly arrested Ninetta and without a struggle took her away; and without having to resort to torture he very quickly learned all he wanted to know from her about Restagnone's death.

Falco and Ughetto heard secretly from the Duke why Ninetta had been arrested, and their ladies in turn learned it from them, a story which distressed them very greatly; and they did everything they could to save Ninetta from being burned at the stake, which would be the punishment, they realized, to which she would be condemned, as she well deserved; but everything they did was in vain, for the Duke was firmly resolved to see justice done. Magdalena, who was a beautiful young lady and who for some time now had been courted by the Duke but who never consented to do his pleasure, believing that in pleasing him she might save her sister from the fire, made known to him through a trusted messenger that she was ready to do whatever he wished on two conditions: first, that she have her sister back safe and sound; and second, that the affair be kept secret.

The Duke received the message and liked the sound of it, and after thinking it over for some time, finally agreed to do it and replied that he was ready. And so one evening, with the lady's consent, he had Folco and Ughetto detained overnight by the police on the pretext of finding out what they knew about the affair while he went secretly to spend the night with Magdalena. But first, however, he had Ninetta tied in a sack and pretended that he was going to toss her into the sea that very night, but actually he took her with him to her sister's house and gave Ninetta to her as the price for that evening, begging her as he departed the next morning not to allow this first night of their love affair to be the last; and he also insisted that she send her guilty sister away, so that he would not be blamed for it or have reason to take cruel measures against her once more.

The next morning Folco and Ughetto were released from prison. Having heard that Ninetta had been drowned in a sack during the night, and believing it was true, they returned to their homes to console their wives for the death of their sister, but no matter how hard Magdalena tried to keep her sister hidden from

Folco, he soon discovered much to his amazement that Ninetta was there. Immediately he became suspicious, for he had heard before that the Duke was in love with Magdalena, and he asked her how it was possible for Ninetta to be there. Magdalena invented a long story in an attempt to explain how it all had happened, but since he was a clever man, he believed little of what she said. He pressed her to tell him the truth, which, after a number of other explanations, she finally did. Folco was first overcome by grief and then went into a fury, and pulling out his sword, as she pleaded in vain for mercy, he killed her.

Fearing the anger and the justice of the Duke, he left her dead body in the bedroom and went to where Ninetta was hiding, and said to her with a feigned air of cheerfulness:

"Let us go to the place your sister has decided I should take you, so that you will not fall into the Duke's hands again." Ninetta believed this, and because she was afraid, she was most anxious to leave, and without bidding farewell to her sister, she and Folco set out while it was still dark, taking with them all the money Folco could lay his hands upon, which was very little. They went to the docks and boarded a small boat, and no one has ever heard from them since.

When the next day dawned and Magdalena was found dead, certain people, because of the envy and hatred they bore for Ughetto, immediately reported the news to the Duke, who, because he was so much in love with Magdalena, rushed angrily to her house and arrested Ughetto and his lady and forced them, though they knew nothing about the matter—that is, the departure of Folco and Ninetta—to confess that they, along with Folco, had been guilty of Magdalena's death. Because of their confession, they feared, and rightly so, for their lives, and accompanied by their guards, with no time to take any of their possessions with them, they boarded a ship by night and fled to Rhodes, where in poverty and misery they ended their days not too long afterward.

Such was the fate which the foolish love of Restagnone and the anger of Ninetta brought upon not only themselves but also upon others.

[Fourth Day, Fourth Story]

❦

Gerbino, violating a pledge made by his grandfather, King William, attacks a ship belonging to the King of Tunis in order to abduct his daughter; when she is killed by the men who are on board, he kills them, and then he is beheaded.

HAVING finished her story, Lauretta fell silent, while the members of the group turned to one another lamenting the calamity of the lovers, some blaming Ninetta's anger, others blaming one thing or another; the King, at this point, as if aroused from deep thought, raised his eyes, signaling to Elissa that she should speak next; and she politely began:

Lovely ladies, there are many who believe that Love shoots his arrows only when kindled by the eyes, and they scoff at those who maintain that one may fall in love with another's reputation; that such people as these are deceived will become quite evident from a story I intend to tell you, in the course of which you shall see how one's reputation can lead people who have never seen each other before not only to fall in love but also to their tragic death as well.

According to the Sicilians, William the Second, King of Sicily, had two children, one a boy called Ruggieri and the other a girl named Gostanza. Ruggieri, who died before his father, left a son named Gerbino, who was raised with care by his grandfather and grew up to become a very handsome young man, famous for his gallantry and chivalrous deeds. His reputation was not confined within the boundaries of Sicily but resounded abroad in many parts of the world, and above all his fame was renowned in Barbary, which was in those days a tributary to the King of Sicily. Among the people who had heard of Gerbino's magnificent reputation for valor and courtesy was a daughter of the King of Tunis, a lady who, according to those who had seen her with their own eyes, was one of the most beautiful creatures Nature ever created, as well as the most well-mannered, endowed with a noble and generous heart. Since she liked to listen to tales about valiant men, she greatly cherished what she heard one person or another say about the valorous adventures of Gerbino, and they pleased her so much that, imagining to herself what he must look like, she fell passionately in love with him and spoke more willingly of him than of anything else, listening to anyone who mentioned his name.

At the same time, extraordinary reports of her own beauty and excellence had likewise spread to Sicily as elsewhere, where not without great delight, nor without effect, did they reach Gerbino's ears; indeed, he was burning with desire for her as much as the young lady was for him. Since more than anything else he wanted to see her but had no plausible excuse to obtain his grandfather's permission to go to Tunis, he would beg all his friends who traveled there to make his great and secret love known to her in whatever way they could, and to bring him back news of her. One of these friends succeeded in doing so most cleverly by posing as a merchant who had jewels for the lady's inspection; and he revealed Gerbino's passion for her in great detail, declaring that Gerbino and all his possessions were at her disposal. The young lady, with happiness in her eyes, welcomed both messenger and message, replying that Gerbino burned with a love equal only to hers, and as proof of this she sent him one of her most precious jewels. Gerbino received this with as much happiness as one could possibly derive from such a precious gift, and he, using the same messenger, wrote to her on a number of occasions and sent very expensive gifts, and they made a pact between them that if Fortune would allow it, someday they would meet and touch.

While the affair continued in this fashion for somewhat longer a time than might have been desired, with the young lady burning with passion here and Gerbino there, it happened that the King of Tunis promised her in marriage to the King of Granada. She was terribly upset over this, for she realized not only that she would be separated by a long distance from her lover but that most likely she would be entirely out of his reach, and if only she could have found a means to prevent this from happening, she would have willingly run away from her father and gone to Gerbino. Gerbino, too, when he heard about this marriage, was extremely distressed, and often thought to himself that if she were to travel to her husband by sea and the opportunity presented itself, he would take her by force.

The King of Tunis had heard tell of this love and of Gerbino's intentions, and in fear of the young man's strength and courage, when the time was near for his daughter's departure, he sent word to King William concerning the young man's intentions, informing him that as soon as he had his assurance that neither Gerbino nor anyone acting on his behalf would interfere with his plans, he meant to carry them out. King William, who was an old man and had not heard a word about Gerbino's love affair, never imagining that this was the reason he was being asked for this assurance, freely granted his request, and as a token of his word he sent the King of Tunis one of his gloves. Once the King received this assurance, he had a very large and handsome ship fitted out in the port of Carthage, and saw to it that it was provisioned with whatever was necessary for those who were to sail on it, and he had it decorated and adorned in a style suitable for sending his daughter to Granada, after which there was nothing to do but wait for good sailing weather.

The young lady, who saw all this and understood what it meant, secretly sent one of her servants to Palermo, telling him to greet the valiant Gerbino on her behalf and inform him that within a few days she was to sail to Granada, and that now it would become clear whether he was as courageous a man as people said he was, and whether he loved her as much as he had so often declared he did. The man to whom she entrusted this task performed his mission admirably and returned to Tunis. When Gerbino heard this and realized that King William, his grandfather, had given his assurances for safe passage to the King of Tunis, he did not know what to do; yet driven by love, and having listened to what his lady had to say on the matter, he did not want to appear as a coward, so off he went to Messina, where he had two light galleys quickly fitted out for battle, and having manned each ship with a crew of brave men, he sailed off in the direction of Sardinia, knowing that the lady's ship would have to pass through that vicinity.

Nor did things turn out very differently from what he had thought, for he waited there only a few days before the ship, driven by a light wind, reached a spot not far from the place where he had anchored to meet her. As soon as Gerbino caught sight of the ship, he said to his companions:

"Men, if you are as brave as I consider you all to be, there cannot be one among you who is not or has not been in love, for I am convinced that no mortal man can ever possess true virtue or excellence without it; and if you have been or are now in love, you will easily understand what I desire. I am in love, and Love has led me to propose this undertaking to you; and the lady I love stands on the ship which you see there before you and which in addition to the object I most desire is loaded with the greatest of treasures; if you are brave and fight like men, with little effort we can have these riches. I seek as my share of such a victory only one lady, for whose love I do battle: every other thing I freely concede to you from this moment on. Now, let us go with Fortune favoring us and attack the ship; God favors our enterprise, for He stills the wind and holds the ship there for us."

The valiant Gerbino need not have wasted so many words, for his crew from Messina, greedy for plunder, was already fired up to do what his words were urging them to do; the crew sent up a great shout of approval at the end of his speech, and sounding the trumpets, they grabbed their weapons, and plying the oars with all their might, they bore down on the ship. The sailors aboard ship, who could see the galleys approaching from afar, realizing that they were unable to escape, began to prepare for their defense. The valiant Gerbino, upon reaching the ship, ordered her officers to come aboard his galleys unless they wanted to do battle. The Saracens, having announced who they were and learned what was demanded of them, declared that such an act was in violation of the King's pledge, and in witness to this fact they displayed the glove of King William while clearly affirming that they would never surrender or give up anything on board ship without being forced to do so in battle. Gerbino, who had caught a glimpse of his lady on the ship's poop, standing there looking even more beautiful than he had imagined, and who was more inflamed now than ever before, announced in reply to the glove that there was no need for a glove, since there were no falcons around at this particular time, and that if they did not wish to hand the lady over, they should prepare to do battle. Without further delay, they began to fight fiercely, shooting arrows and hurling stones at one another, and with casualties on both sides, they fought this way for a long stretch of time.

Finally, when Gerbino realized that he was not getting very far, he took a small boat he had towed from Sardinia and set it afire; then, with the help of his two galleys, he pulled it alongside the ship. When the Saracens saw this and realized that it meant either death or surrender, they had the King's daughter brought on deck from below, where she had been in tears, and leading her to the ship's prow, they called for Gerbino's attention. And as she screamed for mercy and help, in front of his very eyes, they slit her veins and tossed her into the sea with the words:

"Take her, we give her to you the only way we can and in the manner which your trustworthiness deserves!"

When Gerbino saw how cruel they had been, almost anxious to die and oblivious of arrows or stones, he came right alongside the ship, and climbing aboard in spite of the odds against him—not

unlike a starving lion falling upon a herd of yearling bulls, who
tears one apart first with his teeth and then another with his
claws, satisfying his wrath more than his hunger—with sword in
hand, slashing one and cutting down another, Gerbino without
mercy slaughtered many a Saracen; as the fire spread through-
out the burning ship, he ordered his sailors to carry off as much
as they could in payment for their services, and then he aban-
doned it, having achieved a less than happy victory over his ene-
mies. He then saw to it that the body of the beautiful lady was
recovered from the sea, and after he had mourned over it for
some time, shedding many a tear, he returned to Sicily, and on
the tiny island of Ustica, almost opposite Trapani, he had her
honorably buried, and then, more sorrowful than any man could
be, he returned to his home.

When the King of Tunis heard the news, he sent his ambassa-
dors dressed in black to King William to complain about the
promise which had not been kept. When they explained how this
had come about, King William, who was most perturbed and saw
no way of denying them the justice they demanded, had Gerbino
arrested; and he himself, while every one of his barons tried
with their pleas to dissuade him, condemned Gerbino to death
and in his very presence he had him decapitated, preferring to
remain without a grandson rather than to be considered a king
without honor.

So then, just as I described it to you, the two lovers in only a
few days' time died tragic deaths, without ever tasting any of
the fruits of their love.

[Fourth Day, Fifth Story]

✦

*Ellisabetta's brothers kill her lover; he appears to her in a
dream and tells her where he is buried; she secretly digs up his
head and places it in a pot of basil, over which she weeps every
day for a long time; her brothers take it away from her, and
shortly afterward she dies of grief.*

WHEN Elissa's story was finished and had been praised in some
respects by the King, Filomena was called upon to speak, who
full of compassion for the wretched Gerbino and his lady, after
a piteous sigh, began:

My story, gracious ladies, will not concern people of so high a station as those about whom Elissa has spoken, but perhaps it will be no less moving; I was reminded of it by the mention a moment ago of Messina, where the misfortune occurred.

In Messina there were three young brothers, all of them merchants, who became very rich after the death of their father (who was from San Gimignano), and they had a sister called Elisabetta, a very beautiful and accomplished young girl, who for some reason had not yet married. Besides the three brothers there was a young Pisan named Lorenzo who worked in their shop and saw to all of their business. He being so handsome and charming, Lisabetta, having gazed at him more than once, found him unusually attractive; and Lorenzo, too, after seeing her a few times, put aside all his other loves and set his heart on loving her; and since each found the other equally pleasing, not much time passed before they took courage and did what each of them desired to do the most.

And continuing this way, spending a great deal of time together in their pleasure, they were no longer able to conceal their love affair, for one night as Lisabetta was quietly making her way to where Lorenzo slept, the oldest of the brothers noticed her, though she did not see him. Since he was a wise young man, in spite of the fact that his discovery bothered him a great deal, he restrained himself from making a move or uttering a word until the next morning, after he had considered and weighed the various solutions to the matter in his mind. Then when day came, he told his brothers what he had seen happen between Elisabetta and Lorenzo the previous night, and after long deliberation, so that neither they nor their sister might suffer any loss of reputation, they all decided to pass over the matter quietly and to pretend to have seen or heard nothing until a more suitable time should arise in which they, without damage or dishonor to themselves, might be able to wipe away this shame before it went any further.

Having adopted this proposal, they continued to joke and laugh with Lorenzo as they always had, and one day, pretending to take a trip outside the city, they took Lorenzo with them. Having come to a very remote and deserted spot, they realized their chance had come: catching Lorenzo off guard, they killed him and buried him in such a way that no one would take notice. Then they returned to Messina and let it be known that they had sent Lorenzo somewhere on business—something which was easily believed, since they were in the habit of sending him here and there very often. When Lorenzo did not return, often Lisabetta would anxiously ask her brothers where he was, for his absence deeply grieved her. One day, when she had asked about him in a very insistent way, one of the brothers replied:

"What is the meaning of this? What do you have to do with Lorenzo that you keep asking about him? If you ask about him again, we shall have to give you the answer you deserve!"

And so the young woman, sad and grieving, full of fear and forebodings, stopped asking questions, and sometimes at night she would piteously call out to him begging him to return; sometimes she would burst into tears over his absence, and in this painful state of waiting she remained without ever cheering up. One night after she had wept so much over Lorenzo's absence that she finally cried herself to sleep, Lorenzo appeared to her in a dream, pale and all unkempt, with his clothes torn and rotting on his body, and it seemed to her that he spoke:

"Oh, Lisabetta, you do nothing but cry out to me and lament my long absence and bitterly accuse me with your tears; therefore, I want you to know that I can never return to you, for on the last day you saw me I was killed by your brothers."

He told her the spot where they had buried him and asked her not to call him any longer or to wait for him; then he disappeared. The young woman, having awakened, believed the vision and wept bitterly; after rising the next morning, not daring to say anything about this to her brothers, she decided to go to the place he had mentioned to see if what had appeared to her in her sleep was the truth. Having received permission from her brothers to leave the city for a while to amuse herself in the company of a woman who had on other occasions been with her and Lorenzo, and who knew all about her, she set out for that place as quickly as possible. She removed some dry leaves covering a portion of the ground that appeared to be soft and began to dig; she had hardly started when she discovered the body of her poor lover, which had not yet decomposed or decayed, and now she understood clearly the truth of her vision. More sorrowful than any woman alive, but realizing that this was no time for tears and that it would be impossible for her to carry away his entire body in order to give him a more proper burial (though had she been able, she would have willingly done so), with a knife she cut his head from the shoulders as best she could and wrapped it in a cloth; then, after covering the rest of the body with earth, she gave the head to her servant to carry, and without being seen by anyone, she left that place and returned to her home.

There, with this head, she shut herself in her bedroom, and

she cried bitterly and long over it, bathing it with all her tears, giving it a thousand kisses on every side. Then she took a large and handsome vase, the kind in which marjoram or basil is grown, and inside it she placed the head wrapped in a beautiful cloth; then, covering it with earth, she planted above it several sprigs of the finest basil from Salerno, and she watered it only with rose or orange water or with her own tears. She spent her time sitting close to the pot, turning all of her desire upon it, for it contained her beloved Lorenzo hidden within; and after gazing at it for a long time, she would bend over it and begin to weep and weep until all of the basil was bathed in her tears.

From the long and continuous care she gave it and because of the richness of the soil which came from the decomposing head within, the basil became most beautiful and very fragrant. And because the young woman incessantly followed this practice, she was often observed by her neighbors; they told her brothers (who were also amazed at the fact that her beauty was fading and her eyes seemed to be sinking into her head) what they had seen:

"And we have noticed that she does the same thing every day."

When the brothers had heard this and then discovered it for themselves, after reproaching the girl for this several times, but without success, they secretly had that pot removed from her room. When she found it was missing, over and over again she would ask for it, and because it was not returned to her, after incessant weeping, she fell ill, and in her sickness she asked for nothing but her pot of basil. The young men were amazed at her insistence and so they decided to see what was inside it; when they poured the earth out, they saw the cloth and in it the head that was not yet so decomposed that they did not recognize it as Lorenzo's from his curly hair. This amazed them even more, and they feared that the murder might be discovered; so they buried the head, and without a word to anyone, they cautiously concluded their business in Messina and left for Naples.

The young girl wept and wept, continuing to demand that her pot of basil be returned to her; and she died crying; thus her unfortunate love came to an end, but after a time the whole affair became known to many people, one of whom composed that song which is still sung today:

Who was that wicked man
who stole my pot of herbs,
etc.

[Fourth Day, Sixth Story]

✦

Andriuola loves Gabriotto; she tells him of a dream she has had and he in turn tells her another; he dies suddenly in her arms; while she is carrying him back to his home with the assistance of one of her servants, they are arrested by the authorities and she explains what happened; the podestà tries to make her lie with him, but she will not stand for it; when her father hears about this and she is found innocent and is released, she refuses to live in the world any longer and becomes a nun.

THE ladies found Filomena's story quite delightful, for they had heard that song sung many times but had never been able to determine, no matter how often they asked, the reason for its composition. When the King heard the concluding words of the story, he instructed Panfilo to follow in his turn. Panfilo then said:

The dream described in the last story gives me reason to tell you another story in which two dreams are mentioned, both concerning future events rather than, as in the other story, things which have already taken place; and no sooner were they described by those who dreamed them than they both came true. The truth is, dear ladies, that every living person has the sensation of witnessing different things in his sleep which all seem most real while the person is sleeping, but upon awaking, the sleeper judges some to be real, others likely, and a number of them to be beyond all belief, yet you will find that many of them do come true. As a result, many people have as much faith in their dreams as in the things they witness while awake, and their dreams alone can suffice to make them happy or sad according to whether their dream encouraged or frightened them; on the other hand, there are people who have no faith whatsoever in dreams, unless after the dream they actually do come into the danger prophesied by it; I do not recommend either of these views—that is, the opinion that dreams are either always true or always false. That they are not always true every one of us has experienced; and that they are not all false, Filomena's tale earlier has already demonstrated, and as I said earlier, I intend to demonstrate this in my own. For I believe that when a person lives and acts virtuously, he never has to fear a dream which is contrary to his behavior, nor should his good intentions be abandoned on this account; but in wicked and perverse matters, no matter how favorable one's dream may seem to such attitudes and no matter how they encourage the dreamer with good omens to believe in them, none of them should be believed, while those which point to the contrary should be totally accepted. But now let us come to our story.

In the city of Brescia there was once a nobleman named Messer Negro da Ponte Carraro, who among many other children had a daughter named Andreuola, a young and very beautiful woman who was not yet married but who, by chance, fell in love with a neighbor of hers named Gabriotto, a man of humble origins but endowed with many a good quality, and who was handsome and pleasant. With the assistance of her household servant, the young lady not only managed to make her love known to Gabriotto but also to have him brought many times over into a beautiful garden of her father's to the mutual delight of both parties concerned. And so that nothing except death might ever come between this pleasurable love of theirs, they secretly became husband and wife.

And they continued to make love this way in secret until one night while she was asleep, the young lady had a dream in which she seemed to see herself in the garden with Gabriotto, both of them deriving the greatest of pleasure as she held him in her arms; and while they were thus occupied, she thought she saw some dark and terrible thing come out of his body, the shape of which she was unable to distinguish, and it seemed that this thing seized Gabriotto, and in spite of her resistance, it pulled him out of her arms with amazing force and scurried off underground with him, and they never saw each other again. Her anguish was so great it awakened her, and though now she was awake and happy to see that what she had dreamed had not come to pass, nevertheless she was still afraid from her terrible dream. And so, knowing that Gabriotto was to come to her the next night, she did everything she could to prevent his coming; on the following night, however, seeing how anxious he was to come and in order not to make him suspicious, she received him in her garden. It was the season for roses, and after picking many white and red ones, she went to join him at the foot of a most beautiful fountain with clear flowing water situated in the garden, and there, after they rejoiced at length together over seeing each other, Gabriotto asked her what was the reason for her refusal to have him come the day before. Then the girl told him about the dream she had had the previous night and all about the premonitions it had aroused in her.

When Gabriotto heard this, he started laughing about it and saying that it was the height of folly to place any faith in dreams, for they were the result of either too much food or the lack of it, and that every day life showed how completely meaningless they were, and then he added:

"If I paid any attention to dreams, I would not have come here—not so much because of your dream but rather because of one I, too, had this past night. I seemed to be out hunting in a beautiful and delightful forest and there I caught the most beautiful and charming little doe you have ever seen; she seemed whiter than snow, and in a short time she became so fond of me that she would not leave me. I seemed to be so fond of her that in order to prevent her from leaving me, I put a gold collar around her neck and held her by a chain of gold. And then I dreamed that while the doe was asleep and resting its head on my breast, a greyhound, as black as coal, appeared from nowhere, looking famished and very terrifying; she came toward me, and I seemed to offer no resistance to it, for she thrust her muzzle into the left side of my breast and kept gnawing at it until she reached my heart, which it seemed she tore out and carried off with her. I felt such a pain from this that my sleep was broken, and when I was awake I immediately felt my side with my hands to see if anything had happened, but when I discovered no wound there, I laughed at myself for having done so. Now what do you think this meant? I have dreamed such dreams before, many of which were even more frightening, but nothing in the world has ever happened to me as a result; therefore, let us put aside our dreams and think about enjoying each other."

The girl, already quite terrified by her own dream, became even more frightened when she heard about his; but in order not to displease Gabriotto, she concealed her fear as best she could. And as she enjoyed herself embracing and kissing him while being embraced and kissed by him, she was afraid without knowing why, and she found herself gazing at his face much more than usual and sometimes she would look around the garden to see if something black might be approaching from somewhere.

And while they were doing this Gabriotto, heaving a deep sigh, clutched her and said:

"Alas, my love, help me, I am dying!"

And having said this, he fell back onto the grass.

On seeing this, the girl drew her fallen lover to her bosom and said, almost in tears:

"Oh, my sweet lord, what is the matter?"

Gabriotto did not reply, but gasping heavily and sweating all over, in no time at all he passed from this life.

How insufferable and sorrowful this was to the young lady, who loved him more than herself, everyone can well imagine. She wept over him for a long while, calling out to him over and over again, but in vain; then, after she felt all over his body and discovered he was completely cold, she realized that he really was dead; not knowing what to do or say, tearful as she was and full of anguish, she ran to call her servant, who was aware of her love affair, and she poured out to her all her misery and her sorrow.

After they had wept miserably together over Gabriotto's dead face, the girl said to her servant:

"Since God has taken him away from me, I do not intend to live any longer; but before I kill myself, I want to do everything possible to preserve my honor and the secret love that existed between us, and to see that his body, from which his noble spirit has departed, is properly buried."

To this the servant replied:

"My daughter, do not speak of killing yourself, for if you have lost him here, by killing yourself you will also lose him in the next world, for you would go to Hell, where I am convinced his soul has not gone, since he was a good young man; it is much better to console yourself and to set your mind to helping his soul with prayers and good works in case he needs such assistance for some sin he may have committed. As for burying him, the quickest way would be to do it right here in this garden where no one will ever discover him, since no one knows he comes here; but if you prefer not to do this, we can place him outside the garden and leave him there: tomorrow morning he will be discovered, carried to his home, and buried by his relatives."

Although the girl was full of sorrow and could not stop weeping, she nevertheless listened to the advice of her servant; she could not agree to her maid's first suggestion, and she replied to her second one, saying:

"God could not wish me to permit such a dear young man, one I love so much and who is my husband, to be buried like a dog or to be left lying in the street. He has received my tears, and so far as I am able I shall see to it that he receives those of his relatives as well, and I already have in mind what we must do to bring this about."

She quickly sent the servant to fetch a piece of silk cloth, which she kept in one of her strongboxes; when she returned, they spread it out on the ground and placed Gabriotto's body upon it, and setting his head upon a pillow, weeping all the while she did this, she closed his eyelids and his lips, and then she made a wreath of roses for him, and all around him she spread the other roses they had gathered together as she said to her servant:

"From here to the door of his house is not far away; therefore you and I, just as we have arranged him, will carry him there and leave him in front of the door. It will not be long before daybreak and he will be taken in; although this will provide little consolation to his loved ones, yet to me, in whose arms he died, it will give some small pleasure."

Having said this, in tears once again, she threw herself over his face and wept for a long while; after numerous entreaties from her servant, as day was breaking, she arose, and removing from her finger the very ring with which she had been wed to Gabriotto, she slipped it onto his finger, saying as she wept:

"My dear lord, if your spirit now witnesses my tears and if any awareness or feeling remains in the body after the departure of the soul, receive kindly this last gift from the woman whom you loved so much while you were alive"; and after she had said this, she fainted and fell upon his body once more.

After a while she recovered her senses and arose, and with her servant she picked up the cloth upon which the body lay and left the garden with it, walking toward his home. And by chance, as they were making their way along, some officers on guard, who happened to be walking about at that hour because of some other mishap, discovered them with the dead body and arrested them. Andreuola, more anxious to die than to live, recognizing the guards, resolutely declared:

"I know who you are and realize that it would be futile to escape; I am prepared to come with you before the authorities and to tell them what has occurred; and since I shall obey you, if any of you dare to touch me, or remove anything from this man's body, I shall denounce him." And so no one touched her, and with Gabriotto's body they all went to the palace of the *podestà.**

When the *podestà* heard about the affair, he got out of bed

*See explanatory note in II, 1.

and had Andreuola brought to his chambers, where he questioned her about what had occurred; he had certain physicians check to see if the good man had been murdered by poison or in some other manner, and they all affirmed that he had not been, but that some abscess near his heart had burst and had suffocated him. When the *podestà* learned this, he still felt she was guilty to some small degree, and pretending to offer her a favor which he had no right to sell, he claimed that if she would be willing to yield to his pleasures, he would set her free. But since these words got him nowhere, setting aside all propriety, he began to employ force; Andreuola, however, who burned with indignation, her strength greatly increased, defended herself boldly, pushing him away from her with scornful, haughty words.

When day had come and Messer Negro was informed of the whole affair, distressed almost to the point of death he went with many of his friends to the palace, and there, having been informed of everything by the *podestà* himself, he sorrowfully requested that his daughter be restored to him. The *podestà*, wishing to excuse himself for the force he had tried to use on the girl before the girl herself accused him, began to praise the young woman for her constancy, and then explained what he had done to test it; and on seeing how resolute she was, he had fallen passionately in love with her, and if it was agreeable to him, who was her father, and to her, he would gladly take her for his wife, notwithstanding the fact that she had previously been married to a man of humble origins.

While they were talking in this fashion, Andreuola came into her father's presence and threw herself, in tears, before him, saying:

"Father, I do not think there is any need for me to tell you the story of my bold love and the tragedy of it all, for I am sure you have heard it and know all about it; and so, as best I know how, I humbly beg your forgiveness for my sin—that is, to have chosen, without your permission, someone for my husband who most pleased me. I do not ask your pardon in order to spare my life but so that I may die as your daughter and not as your enemy." Then, weeping, she fell to his feet.

Messer Negro, who had a kind and loving nature and who was getting old, began to cry when he heard these words of hers, and still weeping, he raised his daughter gently to her feet and said:

"My child, it was my fondest hope for you to take such a husband as I deemed suitable for you, but if you had chosen for yourself a man who pleased you, he would have necessarily pleased me; only the fact that you kept him hidden from me because of your lack of confidence in me saddens me, especially since you lost him before I even knew anything about it. But since this is the way things stand, now that he is dead, I intend to do what I would have gladly done for him for your sake when he was alive—that is, honor him as my son." And turning to his sons and relatives, he ordered them to arrange a magnificent and honorable funeral for Gabriotto.

Meanwhile, the relatives of the young man had heard the news and were gathering there together with nearly all the men and women of the town; and so the body of Gabriotto, which lay in the middle of the courtyard upon Andreuola's cloth, surrounded by all her roses, was not only mourned by her and by all her relatives, but it was publicly mourned by almost all the women of the town and many of the men; and then he was taken from the palace courtyard, not like a commoner but more like a lord, upon the shoulders of the noblest citizens, and carried to his burial place with the greatest of honor. Then, after a few days, the *podestà* pursued his request, but when Messer Negro spoke about it to his daughter, she would hear nothing of it; and her wishes being her father's will, she and her servant entered a convent most renowned for its sanctity, and there as nuns they lived in virtue for many years.

[Fourth Day, Seventh Story]

❦

Simona loves Pasquino; they are together in a garden; Pasquino rubs his teeth with a sage leaf and dies; Simona is arrested, and while she is explaining to the judge how Pasquino died, she rubs one of the leaves against her teeth and dies in the same manner.

PANFILO had just reached the end of his story when the King, showing no compassion at all for Andreuola, looked at Emilia, giving her to understand that he wished her to follow those who had spoken; without any delay, she began:

Dear companions, the tale told by Panfilo leads me to tell you one which is unlike it in every respect except for the fact that just as Andreuola lost her lover in a garden, so too did the woman of whom I shall speak. She too was arrested, as was Andreuola, but she managed to free herself from the authorities not by force or virtue but rather by her unexpected death. And as we have had occasion to remark in the past, no matter how willingly Love dwells in the homes of noblemen, he does not, because of this, scorn to rule in those of the poor; on the contrary, he sometimes demonstrates his powers in such places in order to make himself feared as the most powerful lord by the more wealthy. This will, if not completely at least in large part, become evident in my story, with which I shall have the pleasure of returning to our own city whence we have wandered so far during this day, speaking as we have about many different subjects in various parts of the world.

Not too long ago, then, there lived in Florence a girl named Simona, the daughter of a poor father, and she was quite beautiful and charming, considering her social condition, even though she was forced to go out and earn her bread with her own two hands, supporting herself by spinning wool. She was not, in spite of this, so poor in spirit that she did not long to receive love into her heart, which for some time now had been wanting to enter there through the pleasant words and deeds of a young man of no higher social status than herself, who worked for a wool merchant delivering wool to spin. Having thus received Love into her heart in the pleasing form of this young man, whose name was Pasquino, and being filled with passionate desires, but not daring to reveal them, she heaved a thousand sighs, more burning than fire itself, with every yard of woolen thread she wrapped around her spindle, recalling the one who had given her the wool. Pasquino, for his part, became very concerned in seeing that his master's wool was well spun, and acting as though the finished fabric were to consist of only the wool Simona spun and that of no one else, he supervised her more closely than the other girls. And so it happened that while one was being attentive and the other was enjoying the attention, one of them grew bolder than was his custom, while the other set aside her usual timidity and modesty, and together they were united in mutual pleasure, which was so enjoyable to both parties that rather than one waiting to be invited by the other, it was, whenever they would meet, a case of who could be the first to make the invitation.

And thus, as this pleasure of theirs continued from one day to the next, growing always more passionate as it endured, it happened that Pasquino told Simona that he would like very much for her to find some way of getting to a certain garden where they could meet, and be together more freely and arouse less suspicion. Simona replied that she would be happy to do so; and one Sunday, after lunch, having led her father to believe that she wanted to go to the Indulgences of San Gallo,* she went with a companion of hers named Lagina to the garden Pasquino had told her about, and there she found him with a friend of his named Puccino but who was called 'Stramba."† Stramba and Lagina quickly fell for each other, so Pasquino and Simona went off to one part of the garden to pursue their own pleasures, leaving Stramba and Lagina to theirs in another.

There was in the part of the garden where Pasquino and Simona had gone a very large and beautiful sage bush at the foot of which they settled down to a long session of pleasure taking and talk of a picnic they were planning to have in that garden as soon as they were rested from their pleasure. Then Pasquino, turning toward the sage bush, plucked a leaf from it and began to rub his teeth and gums with it, declaring that sage was a good way of cleaning off everything that got stuck to your teeth and gums after eating. After rubbing them this way for a while, he returned to discussing the picnic they had just been talking about, but he had not said much before his whole face began to change, and following this change, in no time at all he lost his sight and his speech, and an instant later he was dead. When Simona saw this, she began to cry and scream, calling Stramba and Lagina; they quickly ran up to her, and when Stramba saw that Pasquino was not only dead but was already swollen and covered with dark blotches all over his face and body, he immediately cried:

"Ah, you wretched female, you've poisoned him!" He was making a great deal of noise and was heard by many of the people who lived near the garden; they ran toward the sound, and what with finding Pasquino dead and swollen and hearing Stramba on the one hand, lamenting and accusing Simona of having tricked Pasquino into taking poison, and Simona, on the other, not knowing how to explain things—for she was beside herself with grief from this unexpected misfortune that had taken away her lover—everyone there believed that things had happened just the way Stramba claimed they had.

*Before its destruction in 1530, it was a Florentine custom to attend Mass every first Sunday of the month here.
†IV, 7, is a story filled with the uncourtly nicknames of the many plebeian characters it contains, a reflection of Emilia's aristocratic disdain for the class they represent and a foil to the nobler atmosphere of IV, 6 (Andreuola and Gabriotto). Puccino, a diminutive form of Jacopo (Jacopuccino), is disparagingly called Stramba— "crooked." Later in the story, Pasquino's other companions have equally ignoble nicknames—Atticciato ("husky, stocky, overweight") and Malagevole ("ill at ease").

And so she was arrested, and weeping all the while, she was taken off to the palace of the *podestà*. And once there, Stramba, Atticciato, and Malagevole (all friends of Pasquino who had arrived on the scene) made the accusations, at which point a judge was put on the case forthwith and began to question her on the matter; but since he was unable to persuade himself that she had committed a criminal act or that she was guilty from the way she described the whole affair, he decided that he wanted to examine the dead body for himself and inspect the scene while in her presence, to see if it had happened the way she told it. Without any commotion, then, he had her brought to where Pasquino's body still lay, as swollen as a barrel, and then he went there himself, and gazing at the body in astonishment, he asked her how all this had come about. She went over to the sage bush, and having gone through every detail of the story once more, so that the judge might have all the facts concerning the misfortune which had occurred, she did just as Pasquino had done and rubbed one of those sage leaves against her teeth. While Stramba, Atticciato, and all of Pasquino's other friends and companions sneered in the judge's presence at her actions, shouting that it was all frivolous play-acting on her part and with even more insistence accusing her of being evil, declaring that nothing less than burning at the stake would be a fitting punishment for such evilness, the miserable girl, who was confused from her grief over her lost lover as well as from the fear of the punishment demanded by Stramba, went on rubbing her teeth with the sage, and then the same misfortune that happened to Pasquino, to the utter amazement of everyone who was present there, happened to her.

Oh, happy souls, whose fervent love and mortal lives both ended on the same day! And happier still, if you journeyed together to the same destination! And most happy of all, if Love exists in the next world, and you love each other as much as you did here on earth! But happiest of all is the soul of Simona, insofar as we who remain alive and have survived her are able to judge, for Fortune did not allow her innocence to fall before the accusations of Stramba, Atticciato, and Malagevole—who were nothing more than wool carders or even less—but instead, with a death similar to that of her lover, Fortune found for her a more appropriate way of freeing her from their infamous accusations and letting her follow the soul of her Pasquino, whom she loved so dearly.

The judge, as well as everyone else who was there, was so stunned by what had just occurred that he was at a loss for

words and stood there for a long time; then, coming to his senses
again, he said:

"It is clear that this sage bush is poisonous, which is quite un-
usual for a sage. And so that this bush may not harm anyone
else in similar fashion, cut it down to the roots and set it on
fire."

The man in charge of the garden did so in the judge's
presence, and no sooner had he cut down the thick bush than the
reason for the death of the two poor lovers became apparent.
Under this sage bush was a toad of amazing size, whose venom-
ous breath, they concluded, must have poisoned the sage bush.
And since no one dared to go near this toad, they surrounded it
with an enormous pile of firewood and burned it along with the
sage bush; and thus ended the inquest of his lordship the judge
into the death of poor Pasquino.

Pasquino, along with his Simona, swollen as they were, were
buried by Stramba, Atticciato, Guccio the Mess,* and
Malagevole in the Church of San Paolo, of which they were, as
chance would have it, parishioners.

[Fourth Day, Eighth Story]

❧

*Girolamo loves Salvestra; he is persuaded by his mother's en-
treaties to go to Paris; he returns to discover Salvestra married;
he secretly enters her home and dies there by her side; his body
is taken to a church, and Salvestra dies by his side.*

WHEN Emilia's tale came to an end, Neifile, on the King's com-
mand, began in this manner:

Worthy ladies, in my opinion there are some people who think
they know more than other people and who, in fact, know less;
and because of this, they presume to oppose their intelligence not
only against the counsel of other men but even against the very
nature of things as well. Such presumption has at times resulted
in the most serious of misfortunes, and no good has ever come
from it. Now, since there is nothing in all of nature that is less
amenable to advice or to interference than Love, whose nature is
such that it is more likely to consume itself rather than be divert-

---

*This strange character will appear again in VI, 10.

ed by someone else's foresight, it has occurred to me to tell you the story of a lady who, trying to be wiser than was fitting to her (or than she actually was) and far more than the matter in which she attempted to demonstrate her intelligence required, believing that she could actually remove from her enamored son's heart the love which had, perhaps, been kindled there by the influence of the stars, managed instead to drive out both love and life from his body at the same time.

There was once, then, in our native city, according to the tales our elders tell, a very powerful and wealthy merchant, whose name was Leonardo Sighieri, who had by his wife a son named Girolamo, and who, following his son's birth, leaving his affairs in good order, departed from this life. The child's guardians along with his mother carefully and loyally watched out for the boy's interests. The boy grew up with the other children of families in the neighborhood and became very friendly with a little girl of his own age, the daughter of a tailor; as they grew more mature, their friendship was transformed into so great and passionate a love that Girolamo was unhappy unless he was able to see her, and certainly she did not love him any less than she was loved by him.

The boy's mother, when she became aware of this, scolded him many times and even punished him for it, but unable to dissuade Girolamo, she complained to the boy's guardians, and believing because of her son's great wealth that she could, as it were, change a prune into an orange tree, she said to them:

"This son of ours, who is hardly fourteen years old, is so much in love with our neighbor, the tailor's daughter named Salvestra, that if we do not take her from his sight, perhaps one day, without anyone knowing it, he will take her as his wife, and then I would never be happy again; or there is the chance that were he to see someone else marrying her, he would simply waste away; so, in order to avoid this, it seems to me you should send him off to some faraway place on business, for if he is kept from seeing her again, she will be forgotten, and then we can see to his marrying a young lady of good breeding."

The guardians agreed that the woman was entirely correct, and that they would do whatever they could; they had the young man come to the shop, and one of them began to say rather affectionately to him:

"My son, you are by now quite grown up; it would be a good idea for you to begin looking after your affairs in person; it would make us very happy if you were to go to stay in Paris for a while, where you will not only be able to see how a large por-

tion of your wealth is managed, but you will also, by observing
the lords, barons, and noblemen who live there in great numbers,
learn their customs and become a much better, more polished,
and experienced man than you would ever become by staying
here; then you can return home."

The young boy listened attentively and replied briefly that he
wanted nothing to do with it, since he thought he could just as
well live in Florence as anyone else. Hearing his reply, the
worthy gentlemen tried again with yet more arguments, but they
were unable to extract a different answer, and they reported this
to his mother. She was furious about it—not about his refusal to
go to Paris but rather about his infatuation—and she gave him a
severe scolding; but then, soothing him with sugary words, she
began to praise him and to beg him sweetly to do what his
guardians wanted him to do; and she knew how to speak so
cleverly to him that he agreed to go and stay there for one year
but not more; and so it was all arranged.

Girolamo, then, still deeply in love, went off to Paris, where
they managed to detain him for two years by postponing his re-
turn trip from one day to the next; when he finally did return
home, more in love than ever, he found his Salvestra married to
a worthy young man who was a tentmaker, and this made him
sorrowful beyond all measure. But since he realized that there
was nothing he could do about it, he tried to resign himself to
the situation; and once he found out where her home was lo-
cated, as is the custom of all young men in love, he began to
walk back and forth in front of her house, believing that she
could not have forgotten him just as he had not forgotten her.
But things turned out quite differently. She no more remembered
him than if she had never seen him before, and if she did
remember something, she showed precisely the opposite. And to
his great anguish, the young man came to realize this in a short
space of time; nevertheless, he went on trying to do everything
he could to bring himself back into her mind, but when nothing
seemed to work, he decided, even at the risk of his own life, to
speak to her himself.

After he had learned from one of the neighbors how the rooms
of her house were arranged, one evening while she and her hus-
band were out with some neighbors to a wake, he secretly en-
tered the house and hid himself in her bedroom behind some
sheets of canvas that were hanging there; there he waited until
they had returned and gone to bed, and as soon as he heard her
husband sleeping, he went over to the place where he had seen

Salvestra lie down, and placing his hand over her breast, he said in a whisper:

"Oh, my love, are you sleeping already?"

The girl, who was not sleeping, was about to cry out, but the young man quickly said:

"For God's sake, do not scream, for I am your Girolamo."

When she heard this, she replied, trembling all over:

"Oh, for God's sake, Girolamo, go away: those days when we were young and much in love are gone forever. As you can see, I am married, and for this reason it is no longer fitting for me to love any man other than my husband. Therefore, in God's name I beg you to leave here, for if my husband hears you, even if no harm were to come from it, it would surely follow that I could never live in peace and quiet with him again, whereas now, beloved by him, I am able to live happily and tranquilly with him."

When the young man heard these words, he felt great pain, but he tried to recall to her moments from the past and the fact that his love for her had never diminished, in spite of the distance which had separated them, and he begged and beseeched her and promised her everything, but he got nowhere with her. And now, his only wish being to die, as a last resort, he begged her in the name of his immense love to allow him to lie down beside her and warm himself a bit, for he had become chilled while waiting for her, promising her that he would neither say a word to her nor touch her, and that after warming himself a little, he would depart. Salvestra, feeling compassion for him, granted his request but only on the conditions he proposed. So the young man lay down beside her without touching her, and concentrating into a single thought his long love for her, her present cruelty, and his lost hope, he decided to live no longer, and without saying a word, he clenched his fists, suppressed his vital spirits, and died right there by her side.

After some time had passed, the young lady, wondering at his behavior and fearing that her husband might awaken, began to say: "Oh, Girolamo, why don't you leave?" Receiving no response, she thought he must have fallen asleep, and so, stretching out her hand to touch and awaken him, to her great amazement she discovered as she touched him that he was as cold as ice; she then poked him harder, and when she saw that he did not move after shaking him over and over again, she realized that he was dead. She lay there for some time, distressed beyond belief, not knowing what to do.

Finally, she decided to see what her husband might say should be done if she told him that this had happened to some other person; so she awakened him and told him how what had just happened to Girolamo had happened to someone else, and then she asked him what steps he would take if the same thing had ever happened to her. The good man said that he thought that the man who had died should be quietly carried to his home and left there, and that no blame should be attached to the lady, whom he felt had done nothing wrong.

Then the young lady said:

"Then this is exactly what we must do." Taking his hand, she made him touch the dead young man. Completely bewildered by it all, he jumped to his feet, and after lighting a light, without discussing it further with his wife, he dressed the dead body in its own clothes, and encouraged by their own innocence in the affair he lifted the body without further delay onto his shoulders and carried it to the door of the dead man's home, where he put it down and left it.

When morning came and the dead body of the young man was discovered in front of his door, there was a great commotion raised, especially by his mother; the corpse was examined and checked all over, but since no wound or mark whatsoever could be found by the physicians, it was assumed that he had died of grief, as, in fact, he had. His body was then taken to a church, to where his grieving mother together with many other women, both relatives and neighbors, went, and they all began to weep and grieve over his body, as is our custom.

While this mourning was taking place, the good man in whose home Girolamo had passed away said to Salvestra:

"Now put a cape over your head, go to the church where Girolamo has been taken, mingle with the women, and listen to what they are saying about this matter; I shall do the same among the men, so that we may find out if anything is being said against us."

The girl, who too late had become compassionate, was most willing to do it, for she wished to see in death the man she refused in life to grant even a single kiss; and so she went there.

How astonishing it is when we consider the difficulties of analyzing the powers of Love! The very heart which Girolamo's good fortune was unable to open was now unlocked by his own misfortune, and while she, concealed by her cape, wandered among the women, she happened to catch sight of his dead face, and her ancient flames were rekindled and suddenly transformed into so much compassion that she did not stop until she had reached the very corpse itself; and there, with a piercing scream, she threw herself upon the dead young man, whose face she hardly had time to bathe in tears, for no sooner had she touched his body than she died, as the young man had, from so much grief. But the women, who had not yet recognized her, tried to comfort her and to get her on her feet again, and when she did not get up, they tried to raise her themselves only to discover that she was motionless, and finally, when they did manage to lift her up, they saw at one and the same instant that she was Salvestra and that she was dead; and now, all the women who were there, filled with twice as much pity, began their weeping again, this time even louder than before.

The news spread through the church and outside among the men, and when it reached the woman's husband, who was among them, he wept for a long while, paying no attention to the consolation or solace offered by those around him; then, later on, he told a number of people who were present the story of what had happened between the young man and his wife the night before, and everyone seemed to understand quite clearly the reason for their death, and they were filled with great sorrow. Once the dead girl had been taken away and dressed in the manner in which we prepare our dead, she was placed beside the young man on the same bier, and after mourning over her for a long time, the two bodies were buried in the same tomb: thus, those whom Love was unable to unite in life were joined by death in inseparable companionship.

[Fourth Day, Ninth Story]

♣

Sir Guiglielmo Rossiglione makes his wife eat the heart of her lover, Sir Guiglielmo Guardastagno, whom he has killed; when later she discovers this, she throws herself from a high window to the ground and dies, and she is buried with her lover.

WHEN Neifile's story came to an end, not without moving all of her companions to great compassion, the King, who did not intend to infringe upon Dioneo's privilege, since there were no other storytellers left, began:

I am reminded, compassionate ladies, of a tale which, since you are so moved by examples of love's misfortunes, will require on your part no less compassion than did the previous story, because those of whom I shall speak happened to be of much nobler rank and the misfortunes they suffered were far more cruel.

You must know, then, that according to what the Provençal people say, in Provence there once lived two noble knights, both of whom possessed castles and vassals: one was named Sir Guiglielmo Rossiglione and the other Sir Guiglielmo Guardastagno. Since both men were most skilled in bearing arms, they became very good friends and would always accompany each other to all the tournaments, jousts, or other contests of arms, both wearing the same emblem. Though each man lived in his own castle, separated from the other by a distance of a good ten miles, Sir Guiglielmo Guardastagno happened, nonetheless, to fall totally in love with the very beautiful and charming wife of Sir Guiglielmo Rossiglione, and notwithstanding the friendship and brotherhood that existed between them, he managed in one way or another to bring his love to the lady's attention: and she, knowing him to be a most valiant knight, was pleased by this and began to fall so much in love with him that her only desire, her only love, was for him, nor did she look forward to anything more than being approached by him in person—which happened not long afterward, and from then on they met frequently and made passionate love to each other.

But they were not sufficiently discreet about their lovemaking, and one day they happened to be seen by her husband, who became so incensed by it that the great love he bore for Guardastagno was transformed into mortal hatred; and concealing his hatred for him better than the two lovers knew how to conceal their love, he made up his mind to kill him at all costs. Having made this decision, Rossiglione happened to hear of a grand tournament that was to be held in France, and immediately he sent word of this to Guardastagno, asking him also if he would like to come to his place and there they could decide together whether or not they wished to attend and how they would get there. Guardastagno was delighted to reply he would be there to dine with him, without fail, on the following day.

When Rossiglione heard this, he decided that this would be the time to murder him; the next day he armed himself and, accompanied by a few of his men, he rode off and lay in ambush about a mile away from his own castle in the woods where Guardastagno was sure to pass. Having waited for a good long time, he saw him approaching, unarmed and accompanied by two unarmed men, for they suspected nothing; and when he got to where he wanted him to, with a heart full of rancor and his lance held high, ferociously he rushed out at him, crying: "Traitor, now you are dead!" And before he had finished saying this, he had driven the lance through his chest.

Guardastagno, pierced through by the lance, was unable to defend himself or even to utter a word; he fell from his horse and shortly thereafter died. His men, not having recognized who it was who had done this, turned their horses around and, as quickly as they could, fled in the direction of their master's castle. Rossiglione dismounted, and with a knife he cut open Guardastagno's chest, then with his own hands he tore out his heart, and wrapping it up in a pennant from a lance, he ordered one of his men to carry it; then he issued orders to his men never to utter a word about what had occurred, and by the time he remounted his horse and returned to his castle night had already fallen.

The lady, who had heard Guardastagno was supposed to come that evening to dinner, was waiting for him with the greatest of desire, and when she did not see him arrive, she was very perplexed and said to her husband:

"How is it, my lord, that Guardastagno has not come?"

To this question her husband replied:

"My lady, I have received word from him that he cannot come here until tomorrow," a reply which left the lady a bit annoyed.

After dismounting, Rossiglione had his cook summoned and said to him:

"Take this boar's heart and see that you make of it the best and the most delectable dish that you are capable of making; and when I am at the table, send it to me in a silver dish." The cook, who took it and devoted all his skill and care to it, mincing it and mixing it with many savory spices, produced a very tasty dish indeed.

When it was time for dinner, Sir Guiglielmo sat down at the table with his lady. The food was brought in, but because the crime he had committed weighed so heavily on his mind, he ate very little. The cook sent in the special delicacy, which he had placed before his lady, remarking on his own lack of appetite that evening but commenting on how delicious the dish looked. The lady, who did not lack an appetite, began to eat it, and since she seemed to like it, she ate every bit of it.

When the knight saw that the lady had eaten it all, he said:

"Madam, what did you think of that dish?"

The lady replied: "My lord, in good faith I liked it very much."

"I hope to God you did," exclaimed the knight, "and I am not surprised that what you liked more than anything else when it was alive you liked when it was dead."

When the lady heard this, she was taken aback for a moment; then she said:

"What do you mean? What is this you have made me eat?"

The knight answered:

"What you have eaten was actually the heart of Sir Guiglielmo Guardastagno, whom you, treacherous female that you are, loved so much; and you may be certain that it was his, for with my very own hands I tore it from his breast just before returning."

No need to ask how grieved the lady was when she heard this news about the man she loved more than anything else; but after a while, she said:

"You have acted as only a treacherous and wicked knight would, for if I, of my own free will, made Guardastagno the lord of my love and outraged you by so doing, not he but I should have suffered this punishment. But God forbid that any other nourishment should ever pass my lips after such a noble food as that of the heart of so worthy and courtly a knight as Sir Guiglielmo Guardastagno!"

Rising to her feet, without the slightest hesitation, she jumped out of the window which was directly behind her. The window was high above the ground, so the lady's fall not only killed her but also shattered her body. Sir Guiglielmo was terribly shaken by what he had just seen and felt that he had done wrong; and fearing what the Count of Provence as well as the peasants might do to him, he had his horses saddled and fled.

By the following morning the news of what had happened spread throughout the district, and people from Sir Guiglielmo Guardastagno's castle as well as those from that of the lady came to gather up the two bodies. Then, amid great grief and mourning, they were placed in one and the same tomb in the chapel of the lady's own castle, and on the tombstone were inscribed verses telling who was buried there and the manner and cause of their deaths.

[Fourth Day, Tenth Story]

❦

The wife of a physician, believing her lover to be dead after he has fallen asleep from taking a drug, puts him inside a chest, which is carried off with the man inside by two usurers to their home; when the lover comes to his senses, he is arrested as a thief; the lady's servant tells the authorities that she was the one who put him inside the chest stolen by the usurers, whereupon the lover escapes the gallows and the moneylenders are condemned to pay a fine for making off with the chest.

Now that the King had told his story, only Dioneo remained to speak; knowing this already, and having been requested by the King, he began as follows:

The sorrowful accounts of unhappy lovers have so saddened not only your eyes and hearts, my ladies, but my own as well, so much so that I have anxiously longed for the end to come. Now, praise be to God, for unless, God forbid, I should wish to add another sad tale to this unfortunate lot, these stories are over with, and instead of pursuing such a sorrowful topic, I shall initiate a somewhat happier and more agreeable theme, perhaps providing thereby a good indication of what topic should be discussed tomorrow.

I want you to know, loveliest of ladies, that not long ago in Salerno there lived a very famous surgeon whose name was Doctor Mazzeo della Montagna. When this man reached the very last years of his life, he took for his wife a beautiful and noble young lady from his native city, and he saw to it that she had the most elegant and expensive clothing, the most precious jewels—more than any other lady in that city—and everything else that a woman might desire; but the truth is that most of the time she suffered from a chill, for the doctor did not cover her sufficiently in bed. And just as Messer Riccardo di Chinzica, of whom we have previously spoken,* taught his wife to observe all the holidays, so, too, did Doctor Mazzeo point out to his wife that sleeping with a woman one time required who knows how

*See II, 10.

301

many days to recover, and other similar nonsense; as a result, she lived in the depths of discontent.

But since she was intelligent and high-spirited, she decided, in order to conserve what goods she had at home, to take to the high road and make use of someone else's merchandise; and after looking over a number of young men, she finally found one who pleased her and in whom she placed all her hope, all her heart, and all her happiness. When the young man noticed this, he was extremely pleased, and he, too, turned all his love toward her. He was called Ruggieri d'Aieroli, a man of noble birth but of so disreputable and censurable a character that he no longer had a single relative or friend who wished him well or even wanted to see him; and throughout Salerno he was infamous for his thievery and most other disgraceful crimes, but this mattered very little to the lady, for he pleased her for quite another reason; and with the help of one of her maidservants, she arranged things so that they could be together. And after they had been making love for some time, the lady began to criticize him for the way he lived and to beg him, for the sake of her love, to change his way of life; and in order to encourage him to do so, she began to furnish him with sums of money now and again.

Very discreetly, they continued to carry on together in this way, when it happened that a sick patient with a festering leg was placed under the surgeon's care: after the doctor had examined his diseased leg, he told the man's relatives that unless a gangrenous bone in the leg was removed, it would be necessary to amputate the entire limb, or he would die, and since there was no way of guaranteeing them that with the removal of the bone the patient would be cured, he advised them that he would not take the case unless they were willing to consider the man as already a lost cause; his relatives, having agreed to these conditions, then placed him in the surgeon's care. The doctor realized that the patient would not bear the pain of the operation or even allow himself to be treated without first being drugged, and since he had to wait until evening to perform this operation, that morning he had a liquid distilled from one of his special prescriptions which, when drunk, would make a person sleep for as long as the doctor thought was necessary to operate on him; and he had this liquid sent to his home, and there he put it in his bedroom without mentioning what it was to anyone.

When the hour of vespers arrived and the surgeon was about to go to his patient, some very good friends of his in Amalfi sent word that he should drop everything he was doing and go there at once because there had just been a violent brawl in which many people had been wounded. Postponing until the following morning the operation on the leg, the surgeon took a boat and sailed to Amalfi; when his wife learned he would not return home that night, she, as she would usually do, secretly sent for Ruggieri and hid him in her bedroom, locking him in there until certain other people in the house had gone to bed.

While Ruggieri was waiting in the bedroom for the lady, either because of the work he had done during the day, or the salty food he had eaten, or simply because of his nature, he became very thirsty, and having caught sight, there on the windowsill, of the small carafe of liquid the surgeon had prepared for the patient, and believing it to be drinking water, he raised it to his lips and drank it all down. Not long afterward he became very drowsy and he fell fast asleep. As soon as she could, the lady came to her bedroom, and when she discovered Ruggieri sleeping, she began touching him and asking him in a soft voice to get up; but all this was in vain, for he neither answered nor did he move at all; so the lady, who was somewhat upset, started pushing him more vigorously, saying:

"Get up, sleepyhead; if you wanted to sleep, you should have gone home instead of coming here."

Pushed about in this fashion, Ruggieri fell to the floor from a chest on which he was lying, and he showed about as much life as a dead body. The lady, now rather frightened, began trying to raise him up and to shake him more forcefully, and she twisted his nose and pulled his beard, but all this was useless: he was sleeping like a log. The lady began to fear he was dead, but she still continued to pinch him hard and even burn him with a lighted candle, but all was of no avail; though she was married to a doctor, she was no doctor herself, but she knew without any doubt that he had to be dead. There is no need to ask how distressed she was, for she loved him more than anything else; and not daring to make a sound, she began to weep quietly over his body and lament her great misfortune.

But after a while, the lady, fearing to add dishonor to her loss, realized that she had to find a quick means of getting him, dead as he was, out of the house; not knowing what to do, she quietly called her servant, pointed to her unfortunate problem, and asked her advice. The servant was very much astonished, and when she had pulled and pushed and pinched Ruggieri and saw that he had no feeling, she agreed with what the lady had said—that is, that the man was dead—and she advised her to get him out of her house.

To this advice the lady replied:

"But where can we place him so that when he is discovered in the morning no one will suspect he has been carried out of here?"

To this the maid answered:

"My lady, late this evening behind the shop of the carpenter who is our neighbor, I saw a chest which was not too large and which, if he hasn't put it back inside, will be perfect for our needs: we can put him in it, give him two or three stabs with a knife, and leave him there. Regardless of who discovers him inside the chest, I don't see why they would think he was placed inside it here rather than somewhere else; on the contrary, since he was such a wicked young man, people will believe that as he was on his way to commit some crime or other, an enemy of his killed him and then put him in the chest."

The lady liked the advice her servant gave her, except for the part about stabbing Ruggieri a few times, for this, she declared, she would not allow for anything in the world; then she sent the servant to see if the chest was still where she had first seen it, and the servant returned to say that it was. Then the servant, who was young and strong, with the lady's assistance got Ruggieri onto her shoulders, and with the lady walking in front of her to make sure no one saw them, they reached the chest, placed him inside, locked it, and left him.

A few days earlier two young men who loaned money at usurious rates had moved into the house down the street; they, who were just as eager to make a lot of money as they were not to spend it, were in need of furniture, had noticed the same chest on the previous day, and had agreed that if it was still there that night, together they would take it home with them. At midnight, they left their home, found the chest, and without examining it very closely—though it did seem somewhat heavy to them—they quickly carried it inside and left it right near the bedroom where their wives slept, and not bothering to check if it was secure where it was, they just left it there, and went to bed.

Ruggieri, who had slept for a very long time, had, by now, digested the potion and used up its strength, when he awakened close to the hour of matins; and though he had broken his sleep and recovered his senses, his brain still remained in a bit of a stupor—as it did, in fact, for a number of days afterward; when he opened his eyes and found that he was unable to see anything, he started feeling about with his hands here and there, and when he realized that he was in a chest, he began wondering and muttering to himself:

"What's happening? Where am I? Am I asleep or am I

awake? I seem to remember going into the bedroom of my mistress this evening, but now I seem to be inside a chest. I wonder what it's all about? Perhaps the doctor returned or some other unforeseen event occurred and the lady hid me here while I was sleeping. Sure, that must be it, that's the way it happened."

And so Ruggieri kept quiet and tried to listen for any noise he might hear; after remaining there for a long while, he began to feel uncomfortable inside the chest, which was rather small, and feeling the side of his body he was lying on beginning to get sore, he decided to turn over on his other side, and this he managed to do with such dexterity that while leaning his back against one side of the chest, which had not been placed firmly on the ground, he made it tip over and it fell to the floor, making such a loud noise that the women who were sleeping in the next room woke up in fear, and out of fear they did not utter a word.

Ruggieri was terrified by the fall of the chest, but when he realized that it had opened from the fall, he thought he would be better off, if anything else were to happen, outside and not inside the chest. And what with his not knowing where he was and one thing and another, he began groping about the house trying to find stairs or a door so that he could leave. His fumbling about was heard by the women, who began calling out: "Who's there?" Ruggieri did not recognize their voices, so he did not answer; the women then started calling the two young men, who, because they had stayed up very late that night, were sound asleep and did not hear a thing. The women, who had become even more frightened, then jumped out of bed and rushed to the windows screaming, "Thieves, thieves!" This brought neighbors rushing in from all parts, some through the roof, others through one door or another—and even the young men woke up to the sound of all this noise.

When Ruggieri saw himself in the midst of all this confusion, he was absolutely flabbergasted and had no idea how to get out of there; so he was seized and placed in the custody of the magistrate's guards, who had also been brought to the scene by all that racket; then he was taken before the magistrate, and since he was reputed by everyone to be a very wicked person, he was immediately put to the torture and made to confess that he had broken into the home of the moneylenders with the intention of robbing them; as a result, the magistrate decided to have him hanged by the neck as soon as possible.

The next morning, the news was all over Salerno that Ruggieri had been arrested for robbing the home of some moneylenders; when the lady and her servant heard this, they were so bewildered and astonished that they almost began to believe that they had not really done what they thought they had done the night before, but that they had dreamed the whole thing up. And besides this, the lady was going almost out of her mind with grief, thinking of the danger Ruggieri was in.

Not long after half past tierce the doctor, having returned from Amalfi, asked that his liquid potion be brought to him, for he wished to treat his sick patient; when he discovered that the carafe was empty, he made a great fuss about how nothing in his house could ever be left where he put it.

The lady, who had other troubles on her mind, angrily said to him:

"I hate to think, doctor, how you would handle a serious problem if you make such a fuss over a little carafe of water being spilled! Was that the last drop of water in the world?"

To this the doctor replied:

"Lady, you assumed that this was normal water, but that is not the case; on the contrary, it was a liquid designed to put people to sleep," and then he explained to her why he had prepared it.

When the lady learned this, she realized that Ruggieri must have drunk it and that was why they had thought he was dead, and she remarked:

"We know nothing about this, sir, so you will simply have to prepare some more of it." The doctor, realizing that there was nothing else he could do, had some more made.

Shortly afterward, the servant who on the lady's orders went off to hear what people were saying about Ruggieri returned and told her:

"My lady, everyone is speaking very badly about Ruggieri, and so far as I could find out, he hasn't got a single friend or relative who will raise a finger to help him or even someone who intends to do so, and everyone is convinced that tomorrow the judge will have him hanged for sure. And besides this, I have something new to tell you, and that is that I think I know how he came to be in the moneylenders' home. Let me tell you how. You know the carpenter next door in front of whose shop we found the chest to stick him in? Well, he was just now having the hottest argument in the world with a man who appears to have owned that chest and who was demanding money for his chest while the carpenter was insisting that he had not sold it and, quite the opposite, that it had been stolen the night before.

And then the other man said: 'That's not so, you sold it to the two young moneylenders, because they themselves told me so when I saw the chest in their home after Ruggieri was arrested.' 'They are lying,' the carpenter said, 'I never sold it to them. They must have stolen it from me last night. Let's go and see them.' And so they all agreed to go to the home of the moneylenders, and I came back here; as you can see, it is easy to understand how Ruggieri was transported to where he was discovered, but how he came back to life there—that I don't see."

The lady now understood exactly how everything had happened, and after telling the maidservant what she had heard from the doctor, she begged her to help her rescue Ruggieri, and the lady told her that she could, if she were willing, not only set Ruggieri free but also preserve the lady's reputation at the same time.

The servant answered:

"My lady, show me how, and I shall gladly do anything."

The lady, who was pressed for time, quickly decided what had to be done, and then informed her servant in great detail about it.

The servant first went to the doctor and, in tears, she began saying:

"Sir, I must beg your pardon for a great wrong I have done you."

"What is it?" the doctor asked.

The servant, continuing to weep, replied:

"Sir, you know the kind of person young Ruggieri d'Aieroli is, and when he took a liking to me, between my fear of him and my love for him, I became his mistress not too long ago. Last night he knew that you would not be here and persuaded me to bring him into your home and into my bedroom to sleep with me, and as he was thirsty and there was nowhere I could quickly get my hands on some water or wine, and since I didn't want your wife, who was in the parlor, to see me, I remembered seeing in your bedroom a jug of water, and so I ran to find it, gave it to him to drink, and put the container back where I found it; and then I found out that you made a great fuss about it! Now I do confess I did wrong, but, then, who doesn't from time to time? And I am very sorry for doing it, especially since Ruggieri may lose his life as a result of this, and so I really do beg you to forgive me, and would you give me permission to go and help Ruggieri in whatever way I can?"

When the doctor heard all this, even with all the anger he felt, he replied wittily:

"You already have the pardon you deserve: for you thought you were going to have a young man who would warm your wool for you last night, but all you got was a sleepyhead; so off with you and go and save your lover, but from now on take care not to bring him into the house again, or I shall punish you for both this time and the next!"

The maid, who felt that she had brought off the first phase of the plan quite well, went as quickly as she could to the prison where Ruggieri was held and persuaded the jailer to allow her to speak with Ruggieri. After telling him exactly what to say to the judge if he wished to be released, she managed to obtain an audience with the chief magistrate himself.

But before the judge would hear her out, since she was a fresh and lusty girl, he meant to get his hook into such a delightful one of God's creatures, and in order to receive a better hearing, she found this not at all distasteful; and once he got her off his hook, she picked herself up and said:

"Sir, you have arrested Ruggieri d'Aieroli as a thief, but there is no truth in it." And starting at the beginning, she went through the whole story right to the end, explaining how she, his mistress, had brought him into the doctor's house and how she had given him the drugged liquid to drink without realizing it, and how she had thought he was dead and put him in the chest; then she told him what she had overheard the carpenter and the owner of the chest say in order to show him how Ruggieri must have ended up in the house of the moneylenders.

The judge, knowing how easy it was to verify her story, first asked the doctor if what she said about the liquid was true and discovered that it was; then he summoned the carpenter, the owner of the chest, and the moneylenders, and after a lot of talk, he found out that the moneylenders had stolen the chest and put it in their house the night before. Finally, he sent for Ruggieri and asked him where he had been the past night, and he replied that he didn't know but that he remembered quite well how he had gone to spend the night with Doctor Mazzeo's maidservant, in whose bedroom he had drunk some water because he was so thirsty—but afterward, what happened to him from that moment until he awakened and found himself inside a chest in the home of the moneylenders, he did not know. The judge, who was much amused by the explanations they gave, made the servant, Ruggieri, the carpenter, and the moneylenders all repeat their stories a number of times.

Finally, finding Ruggieri innocent and fining the moneylenders who had stolen the chest ten gold florins, he released Ruggieri—and there is no need to ask how happy this made him, and how it delighted his mistress to no end, who, later on, in the company of Ruggieri and her dear maid, the one who earlier had wanted to give him a few stabs with a knife, would laugh and make merry over the whole affair, and their love and their pleasure always increased, getting better and better—something I wish would happen to me—but not the part about being put inside a chest!

[Fourth Day, Conclusion]

❦

IF the first few stories had saddened the hearts of the fair ladies, this last one of Dioneo's gave them all such a good laugh, especially the part where he told how the judge got his hook in, that they quite recovered from all the melancholy aroused by the other stories. But when the King saw that the sun was already beginning to turn yellow and that the end of his rule had come, he addressed some graceful remarks to the beautiful ladies, begging their pardon for what he had done—that is, to have made them speak on so sad a topic as the misfortunes of lovers; then, after making his apology, he stood up and removed the laurel crown from his head, and as the ladies waited to see upon whom he would bestow it, he cheerfully placed it upon the golden-blond head of Fiammetta as he said:

"I now bestow upon you this crown, for you better than anyone else will know how to console these companions of ours for the harsh storytelling of today with what you will order for tomorrow."

Fiammetta, with her long and curly golden hair falling about her delicate white shoulders, her nicely rounded face glowing all over with a mixture of the true color of white lilies and red roses, her eyes black as falcons, and a sweet little mouth with lips that looked like twin rubies, answered with a smile:

"Filostrato, I gladly accept it, and so that you may better perceive what you have done, I wish and decree forthwith that each one of us be prepared tomorrow to tell stories about lovers who, after unhappy or misfortunate happenings, attained happiness."

Fiammetta's proposal pleased everyone, and after summoning the steward and making all the necessary arrangements with him, she arose and gladly gave the entire group leave to do as they pleased until suppertime.

So some of the group wandered through the garden, of whose beauties one did not easily tire, while others went beyond the garden and toward the turning windmills, and still others went here and there, following their various whims, amusing themselves until suppertime. When it was time for supper, they all gathered, as was their custom, near the beautiful fountain and with the greatest of pleasure they ate an excellently served meal. Then, having gotten up from the table, they turned to dancing and singing in their customary fashion, and while Filomena was leading the dancing, the Queen said:

"Filostrato, I do not intend to depart from the ways of my predecessors: like them, I, too, intend to command that a song be sung, and since I am certain that your songs will resemble your stories, so that no other day besides this one may be disturbed by your tales of misfortunes ever again, I want you to sing whichever one of them most pleases you."

Filostrato replied that he would be happy to do so, and without hesitating he began to sing in the following manner:

> With my own tears, I show
> how rightly grieves the heart
> when Love's faith is deceived.
>
> Love, when you first
> placed in my heart the one for whom I sigh
> hopelessly in vain,
> you showed her so full of grace
> that I considered every torment light
> which came through you into my mind,
> which now is left bereaved;
> but now I recognize
> my error, and not without great pain.
>
> I learned of the deceit
> when she in whom alone I placed
> my hope abandoned me,
> for when I thought myself to be
> most in her grace and in her service
> and could not see the coming

of all my future pain,
I found that she had welcomed to her heart
another and had driven me away.

Once made aware I had been spurned,
there was born in my heart the pain of sorrow,
and it still dwells therein;
and often do I curse the day and hour
when first appeared to me her lovely face,
adorned with every charm,
more radiant than ever!
My faith, my ardor, and all my hope
my dying soul will never cease to curse.

Just how bereft of comfort is my grief,
Love, you know, for you hear how forcefully
my grieving voice calls you.
I tell you that I burn with such fierce pain,
that I crave death as a far lesser pain.
Let death come, then, and end
my cruel and painful life,
the madness of it all, with its swift blow
—wherever I may go, I'll suffer less.

No other way, no other means of solace
remains to soothe my grief save death.
Grant it to me now
and with it put an end, Love, to my woes,
and take away my heart from this vile life.
Ah, do so now, for wrongly have I been
deprived of my happiness and of my solace.
And Lord, make her as happy with my death
as you made her when you gave her a new love.

My song, if no one learns to sing you,
I do not care, for no one ever could
sing you as well as I.
One task alone I charge you with:
find Love for me and tell him, him alone,
how worthless to me is
my sorry, bitter life,
and beg him in the name of his own honor
to guide me to a better port than this.

The words to this song quite clearly expressed Filostrato's state of mind and the reason for it, and perhaps the face of a certain woman dancing would have made it even clearer if the shadows of the oncoming night had not concealed the blush upon her cheeks, and when his song was over, many other songs were sung until it was time for them to go to bed, when at the Queen's command, they all retired to their bedrooms.

[Fifth Day, Title Page]

❦

Here ends the fourth day of The Decameron *and the fifth be-gins, during which, under the rule of Fiammetta, stories are told about lovers who, after unhappy or misfortunate happenings, at-tained happiness.*

[Fifth Day, Introduction]

❦

THE eastern sky had already whitened and the rays of the rising sun lightened all our hemisphere when Fiammetta was awakened by the sweet songs of birds happily singing their greetings from the bushes to the first hour of the day; she arose and had all the other ladies and the three young men summoned and then she slowly walked with her company to the fields below, where, pass-ing through the open plain and over the dewy grass, she amused herself conversing about one thing and another with them until the sun had risen well into the sky. But feeling the sun's rays were becoming too intense, she turned her steps in the direction of their residence, and once they had returned there, she saw to it that they were all refreshed from their gentle exertion with the finest of wines and confections, after which they all amused themselves within the delightful garden until dinner-time. With every detail of the meal seen to by their resourceful steward, af-ter singing a number of canzonets and one or two ballads, as it pleased the Queen, they all merrily sat down to eat. Having en-joyed each course of the meal, now mindful of their custom of dancing, they danced several times accompanied by instruments and songs. Then the Queen gave them their leave until after the siesta hour, so some went to sleep while others remained in the beautiful garden pursuing their pleasure. But shortly after nones, at the Queen's bidding, they all gathered near the fountain as was their custom; and the Queen, having occupied her throne *pro tribunali*,* turned to Panfilo and smiling at him, ordered him to begin the stories which were to end happily. He agreed most gladly and spoke in this fashion:

[Fifth Day, First Story]

❧

Cimone acquires wisdom by falling in love with Efigenia, his lady, whom he abducts on the high seas; he is imprisoned in Rhodes, from where he is freed by Lisimaco, with whom he once again abducts both Efigenia and Cassandrea during their marriage celebrations, fleeing with them to Crete; there the ladies become their wives, and then they are all summoned back to their own homes.

CHARMING ladies, there are many tales I can think of to tell to begin such a joyful day as this one shall be, but of these many tales, one pleases me more than any other, for through it you will not only be able to perceive the happy ending which is to be the goal of our stories but also how holy, how weighty, and how beneficent are Love's powers, which many people, who do not know what they are saying, condemn and vituperate quite wrongly, all of which, if I am not mistaken, inasmuch as you are all, I believe, in love, you should find most pleasing.

Well, then, as we know from the ancient chronicles of the Cypriots, there once lived on the island of Cyprus a very noble gentleman by the name of Aristippo, who was wealthier in worldly goods than any of his countrymen; and if Fortune had not saddened him in one particular matter, he might have been happier than anyone else. And this was that one of his children, who was taller and more handsome than all the others, was for all intents and purposes an imbecile whose case was hopeless; his real name was Galeso, but since neither his tutor's efforts nor

---

*A legal term meaning "in a position of honor"—such as a judge would take before a tribunal.

the entreaties and beatings of his father nor the stratagems of anyone else succeeded in putting the slightest bit of learning or good manners into his head—on the contrary, it left him even more coarsely inarticulate and with manners more suitable to a beast than a man—he was contemptuously called Cimone by everyone, which in their language sounded something like "numbskull" in ours. His wasted life worried his father a great deal; and as he had already given up hope for him, in order not to have the reason for his sorrow always before his eyes, he ordered his son to go to his country villa and to live there with his peasants; this pleased Cimone very much, for the customs and the manners of unpolished countryfolk suited him better than those of city people.

So Cimone went off to the country, and as he occupied himself with those matters suitable to that kind of life, it happened that one day after noon, while he was going from one of the properties to another with his stick on his shoulder, he happened to enter a beautiful wood which was in that area, and it being the month of May, everything was in full bloom. As he walked through the wood, guided, as it were, by Fortune, he happened to come to a meadow surrounded by the tallest of trees, in one corner of which there was a very beautiful young lady sleeping upon the green grass, dressed in clothing so transparent that it concealed almost nothing of her fair flesh and covered from her waist down by a pure white and transparent quilt; at her feet were sleeping two women and a man, all servants of this young lady.

When Cimone saw her, as if it were the first time he had ever seen the feminine form, he leaned upon his stick and without saying a word, he began to gaze upon her most intently with the greatest of admiration; and within his rustic bosom, in which a thousand lessons failed to leave any impression at all of refined delight, he felt a thought awaken which within his material and uncouth mind told him that this lady was the most beautiful thing that had ever been seen by any living man. And from that moment he began to examine her features, praising her hair, which he thought was made of gold, her face, her nose, her mouth, her neck, her arms, and especially her breasts, yet still undeveloped. And having been suddenly transformed from a peasant into a connoisseur of beauty, he desired most fervently to see her eyes, which were closed in her deep slumber; and more than once he wanted to awaken her in order to see them. And since he thought she was more beautiful than any other woman he had ever seen, he felt she might be some goddess; but he possessed enough good sense to know that godlike things should be regarded with more respect than those of this world, and so he hesitated, waiting for her to awaken by herself; and even though the waiting seemed unending, he nevertheless was so taken by this new sensation of his that he was unable to leave her.

After a long while the young lady, whose name was Efigenia, happened to awaken before any of her servants, and opening her eyes and raising her head, she saw Cimone before her leaning upon his staff, and in great amazement she said:

"Cimone, what are you doing in the woods at this time of day?"

Cimone, who was known to almost everyone in the whole countryside for his good looks and brutishness as well as his father's nobility and wealth, made no reply to Efigenia's question, but rather began to gaze into her eyes, which were now open, and he seemed to sense such a sweetness coming from them that he was filled with a pleasure he had never before experienced.

When the young lady noticed this, she began to fear from the way he stared at her that his rustic instincts might induce him to commit an act which could bring her dishonor; and so, after calling her maidservants, she rose to her feet and said: "Cimone, God be with you."

To this Cimone replied: "I shall come with you."

Although the young lady tried to refuse his company, for she was still afraid of him, not until he had accompanied her to her home did she manage to get rid of him; and from there Cimone went to his father's home, where he announced that he never wished to return to the country under any circumstances. Though his father and family were troubled by this, they nevertheless allowed him to remain, waiting to see what the reason for his change of mind could be.

And now that Cimone's heart, into which no teaching had ever been able to enter, was pierced by Love's arrow through Efigenia's beauty, in the briefest of time he passed from one way of thinking to another, to the amazement of his father, his relatives, and anyone else who knew him. First he asked his father if he could wear the same kinds of clothes and all the other kinds of ornaments his brothers wore, a request which his father was most happy to grant. Next he began to associate with worthy young men, and observing the manners appropriate to gentlemen, especially to gentlemen in love, in a very short time, to the greatest astonishment of everyone, not only did the first traces of learning emerge, but he even became most skillful among those who practiced philosophy. Moreover—the cause of it all being the love which he bore for Efigenia—not only did he change his coarse and rustic manner of speaking, adopting a more suitable and refined tone, but he also became an accomplished singer and musician, as well as most skillful and daring in horsemanship and the martial arts whether on sea or land. And in brief (without going into the details of his many accomplishments), the fourth year from the day he fell in love had not passed before he had succeeded in becoming the most charming, well-mannered, and accomplished young man on the island of Cyprus.

What then, charming ladies, should we say of Cimone? Surely nothing more than that the lofty virtues infused by heaven into his valiant spirit had been bound and shut away in the smallest part of his heart with the strongest of chains by invidious Fortune, all of which Love, who is much more powerful than she, had broken and unchained; and as an awakener of dormant talents, Love had drawn them forth with his power into the light of day from the cruel darkness which had concealed them, clearly displaying from where he draws those minds subject to his rule and where he may lead them with the light of his rays.

Now, while Cimone in his love for Efigenia would go to extremes in some respects, as young men in love often do, Aristippo, reflecting on how Love had transformed Cimone from a muttonhead into a human being, not only suffered these excesses patiently, but he even encouraged Cimone to pursue his every pleasure. But Cimone, who refused to be called Galeso, since he recalled that Efigenia had addressed him in this fashion, wished to bring his desire to an honorable end, and many times over he tried to persuade Cipseo, Efigenia's father, to give her to him as his wife, but Cipseo always replied that he had promised her to Pasimunda, a noble man from Rhodes, and that he did not intend to break his word.

When the time came for the marriage arranged for Efigenia to be honored and her husband had sent for her, Cimone said to himself:

"Now is the moment to show you, oh Efigenia, how much I love you. Because of you, I became a man, and if I can succeed in winning you, I believe I can become more glorious than a god, and I shall have you or surely I shall perish."

Having sworn this, he quietly enlisted the help of some noble young men who were his friends, had a ship secretly fitted out with everything needed for a naval battle, and put out to sea, where he awaited the ship which was to be carrying Efigenia to

her husband in Rhodes. Once the friends of her husband had
been richly entertained by Efigenia's father, their ship put to
sea, pointed its prow in the direction of Rhodes, and sailed
away. Cimone, who was not caught napping, overtook them on
the following day with his own ship, and standing on the prow,
he shouted loudly to the crew on board Efigenia's vessel:

"Cast your anchor and lower your sails, or expect to be taken
and sunk!"

Cimone's opponents had brought their weapons up from the
hold and were preparing to defend themselves, so Cimone fol-
lowed up his words by seizing an iron grappling hook and hurling
it onto the stern of the Rhodians' vessel just as it was swiftly
pulling away, thus connecting it hard to the prow of his own
ship; as fierce as a lion, and as if his adversaries would be no
problem to him at all, he leaped aboard the Rhodians' ship with-
out even waiting for any of his men to follow him; and spurred
on by Love, he set upon his enemies with amazing strength, and
cutlass in hand, he slaughtered them, one after another, like so
many sheep. When the Rhodian sailors saw this, they threw their
arms down on the deck and virtually in one voice gave them-
selves up as his prisoners.

Cimone then said to them:

"Young men, neither desire for spoils nor hatred for you made
me leave Cyprus armed in order to attack you here on the high
seas. What moved me is something the acquisition of which I
value most highly and which is something you could easily and
peacefully concede to me: and that is Efigenia, whom I love
more than anything else, and whom, since I could not obtain her
from her father as a friend and in peace, Love has forced me to
acquire from you as an enemy and with my weapons. I intend
to be for her what your Pasimunda was to have been. So give
her to me and be off with God's grace."

The young sailors, constrained more by necessity than by gen-
erosity, handed the weeping Efigenia over to Cimone, and when
he saw her weeping, Cimone exclaimed:

"Noble lady, do not be disconsolate; I am your Cimone, whose
long love for you makes me far more deserving to have you than
does a promise made to Pasimunda."

Having seen to it that Efigenia was carried aboard his ship,
Cimone, without touching any of the Rhodians' other possessions,
returned to his companions and allowed the Rhodians to sail
away. And then, delighted more than anyone could ever be over
the acquisition of such a valuable prize, after spending a goodly
amount of time in consoling his weeping mistress, Cimone per-

suaded his companions not to return to Cyprus for the moment, and they all agreed to turn the prow of their vessel in the direction of Crete, where almost all of them, and especially Cimone, had old as well as more recent family ties and many friends and where they believed they, along with Efigenia, would be safe.

But Fortune, which had quite willingly granted to Cimone the conquest of the lady, fickle as she is, quickly changed the boundless happiness of the young man who was in love into an unhappy and bitter sorrow. Not four hours had passed since Cimone left the Rhodians when, with night approaching, a time during which Cimone awaited keener pleasure than any other he had ever experienced, a violent and tempestuous storm blew up, filling the sky with clouds and the ocean with dangerous winds. As a result, no one was able to see what he was doing or where he was going, not to mention that there was no one on board ship able to stand on his feet to perform his duties. How distressed Cimone was, there is no need to ask. He felt that the gods had granted him his wish only in order to make his death more agonizing, for without her he would have cared little about dying. Cimone's companions were also distressed, but Efigenia was more distressed than all the rest, weeping loudly and fearing every blow of the waves; and in her weeping she cursed bitterly Cimone's love and condemned his passion, claiming that the cause of this raging storm was precisely the fact that the gods did not want him, whose wish it was to take her as his wife against their will, to enjoy his presumptuous desire and that they intended for him first to witness her demise, after which he would himself die a miserable death.

With such laments and even stronger ones, and with the wind growing fiercer and the sailors not knowing what to do or even where they were heading, the ship neared the island of Rhodes; not recognizing it to be Rhodes, they did everything in their power to reach land and save their lives. Fortune was favorable to their efforts and guided them to a small bay to which the Rhodians whom Cimone had released a short time ago had brought their vessel; dawn was breaking and turning the heavens a little brighter, and no sooner were they aware of landing on the island of Rhodes than they saw perhaps no more than a bowshot away the very ship which they had set free the day before. Cimone was distressed beyond all measure by this fact, and fearing that very fate which was eventually to overtake him, he ordered his men to make every effort to flee from that spot, allowing Fortune to take them wherever she pleased, since they could not have been in a worse place than that. They tried with all their might to escape from there, but all was in vain: a very strong gale was blowing against them, so that not only were they unable to leave the tiny inlet, but of necessity they were driven onto the shore.

When they landed there, they were recognized by the Rhodian sailors, who had already left their ship; one of them quickly ran to a nearby village where the young Rhodian nobles had gone and told them that through the workings of Fortune, the ship carrying Cimone and Efigenia had, just as their own had done, landed on the shore. They were overjoyed to learn this, and gathering together many of the men in the village, they immediately went to the beach; Cimone and his sailors, who had already disembarked and had decided to flee to some nearby woods, were all captured along with Efigenia and taken to the village; and there they were held until Lisimaco, who during that year was serving as the highest magistrate of Rhodes, arrived from the city escorted by a very large body of armed men, and took Cimone and his companions all off to prison, as Pasimunda had arranged by filing a complaint with the Senate of Rhodes as soon as he heard the news.

And so it happened that the wretched and enamored Cimone lost his Efigenia only a short time after he had won her, with nothing more to show for it than a few kisses. Efigenia was welcomed and consoled by many of the noble ladies of Rhodes both for the suffering she had undergone during her capture and for the hardships she had endured on the stormy sea; and she remained with these ladies until the day appointed for her wedding. Because the day before they had released the young men from Rhodes, the lives of Cimone and his companions were spared (in spite of the fact that Pasimunda did everything he could to have them executed), and they were condemned to life in prison; and there, as one might well imagine, they languished without any hope of ever knowing happiness again. In the meantime Pasimunda was urging that his forthcoming marriage be arranged as soon as possible.

Fortune, almost as if she were repenting for the sudden injury she had inflicted upon Cimone, was busy arranging a new and unexpected turn of events for his salvation. Pasimunda had a younger brother, no less worthy than himself, whose name was Ormisda and who for a long time had been trying to marry a young and beautiful noble lady of the city named Cassandrea, with whom Lisimaco was very much in love, but the marriage, because of a number of different and unexpected events, was postponed several times. Pasimunda, realizing that he would be celebrating his own marriage with a great banquet, thought it would be an excellent idea if he could arrange for Ormisda as well to take his wife at the same time and at the same banquet, this way avoiding double expenses and celebrations; and so he reopened the negotiations with Cassandrea's parents, successfully completing them, and he and his brother agreed with them that on the same day Pasimunda married Efigenia, Ormisda would marry Cassandrea.

When Lisimaco learned about this, he was distressed beyond measure, for he saw himself deprived of all the hope he had placed in the fact that if Ormisda did not marry Cassandrea, he would be the one to possess her. But he was intelligent enough to keep the agony he suffered concealed and began to think about how he might prevent the marriage from coming about, and he concluded that the only possible means was to abduct her. This seemed simple enough to him because of the office he held, but he felt it would have been a far less dishonorable thing to do had he not occupied such a position; but finally his honor gave way to love, and he determined, no matter what happened, to kidnap Cassandrea. And when it came time to consider what accomplices he might need to do this and the strategy he would have to devise, he remembered Cimone and his companions, whom he held in prison; and he could think of no one else who might be a better or more loyal accomplice to have in such an enterprise than Cimone.

So, the next night, he had Cimone brought secretly to his bedroom and he spoke to him in this manner:

"Cimone, even as the gods are great and very generous bestowers of gifts to men, they are in like manner also the wisest judges of our merits, and those men whom they discover to be unchanging and constant under all sorts of conditions, they consider the most worthy of the highest rewards, for they are the more valiant. The gods wished for more certain proof of your valor than you might be able to demonstrate within the confines of the home of your father, whom I know to be an extremely wealthy man. They first, as I have been told, transformed you with the compelling stimulus of Love from an insensitive beast into a human being; now it is their intention to see whether with this bad luck of yours and the pain of imprisonment your spirit has changed from what it was a short time ago when you were happy over the prize you had won. And if your courage is still what it once was, nothing will make you as happy as what they are now preparing to grant you: this I intend to show you, so that you may regain your spent strength and become courageous again. Pasimunda, delighted over your misfortune and intent upon securing your death, is urging the quick celebration of the wedding ceremony with your Efigenia, so that he may enjoy the prize which smiling Fortune once conceded to you and then in anger quickly snatched away. How much this makes you suffer (if you are as much in love as I believe you are), I, too, can understand, for his brother, Ormisda, is preparing to do me as much harm on the same day by marrying Cassandrea, whom I love above all things. To escape such injury and pain from Fortune, I see no means open to us other than the courage of our convictions and the strength of our right hands, with which we must seize our swords and cut away a path to these two ladies of ours—you to your second abduction and I to my first; and so, if you desire to possess your lady again, not to speak of your liberty, which I would think is of little concern to you without her, the gods have placed the means in your own hands, if you are willing to follow me in my own undertaking."

These words completely restored Cimone's low spirits, and without taking very long to form his reply, he answered:

"Lisimaco, if things turn out the way you say they must, you could have no stronger or more faithful companion in such an enterprise than I; therefore, command me to do whatever you wish, and you will see with what astonishing force I shall follow your wishes."

To this Lisimaco said:

"Two days from now the new brides will enter their husbands' homes for the first time; as night falls, you with your armed companions and I with some of my own in whom I place the highest trust shall enter the houses and from the midst of the guests carry the ladies off to a ship which I shall have secretly made ready, killing anyone who dares to try to stop us."

Cimone liked the plan, and he remained quietly in prison until the appointed time.

The day for the wedding came, and it was one of great pomp and splendor, with every corner of the two brothers' homes filled with joyous celebration. Lisimaco, having made all the necessary preparations, provided Cimone and his companions as well as his own friends with weapons, which they concealed under their clothes, and then, first urging them on to their enterprises with many a fiery word, he then, when the time was ripe, divided them into three groups, one of which he prudently sent to the port so that no one could prevent them from going aboard their ship when the need arose. With the other groups he went to Pasimunda's quarters, posting one group at the door so that no one inside might prevent their entrance or cut off their exit, while with the remaining group of men, including Cimone, he charged up the stairs. When they reached the room where the new brides were nicely seated with many other ladies all around the table just about to begin the meal, they rushed in and overturned the tables, and each of them seized his lady and handed her over to his companions, ordering the men to escort them at once to the waiting ship.

The new brides began crying and screaming, and so did the other women and servants, and in an instant the entire place was in a uproar and filled with wailing. But Cimone, Lisimaco, and their companions, having drawn their swords, as everyone made way for them, headed for the stairs with no one to oppose them. Descending the stairs, they ran into Pasimunda, who with a large club in his hand was hastening toward the commotion, but Cimone struck him so fierce a blow over the head that he nearly cut it in half and Pasimunda fell dead at his feet. The wretched Ormisda ran to his brother's assistance, and he too was killed by one of Cimone's blows, while a number of other men who tried to approach were wounded and beaten back by the companions of Lisimaco and Cimone. Leaving the house full of blood, noise, weeping, and sorrow, the two men, keeping close together as they carried their prizes, made their way, unimpeded, to the ship. Having seen to it that their ladies were taken aboard, they, too, along with their comrades, embarked just as the shore was crowding up with armed men who had rushed to the rescue of the two ladies, and setting their oars in the water, they departed, delighted with their exploits.

Upon arriving in Crete, they were joyously welcomed by many of their friends and relatives, and after they had married their ladies and celebrated a grand wedding feast, they turned to enjoying the delights of their spoils. In both Cyprus and Rhodes their exploits gave rise to great uproar and commotion which lasted for quite a long time. Finally, their friends and relatives, having interceded for them in both these places, found a way, after a certain period of exile, for Cimone to return happily to Cyprus with Efigenia and for Lisimaco to return with Cassandrea to Rhodes; and each lived happily ever after with his lady in his own homeland.

[Fifth Day, Second Story]

❧

*Gostanza is in love with Martuccio Comito, and when she hears
that he is dead, in desperation she sets out alone in a boat which
is carried by the wind to Susa; she discovers Martuccio alive in
Tunisia and makes herself known to him; whereupon he, who
had become a great favorite of the King because of certain ad-
vice with which he had provided him, returns home with the lady
to Lipari, a rich man.*

THE Queen, having heard Panfilo's story come to an end, after
praising it highly, ordered Emilia to continue with another, and
she began as follows:

It is only right that each one of us take pleasure in those
things in which we see rewards follow from our desires; and
since in the long run love should merit pleasure rather than pain,
it gives me much greater pleasure to obey the Queen now by
speaking on the present topic than it did yesterday when I
obeyed the King.

Let me tell you, then, fine ladies, that near Sicily is an island
named Lipari upon which not long ago there lived a very beauti-
ful girl named Gostanza born into one of the island's noblest
families; a young man on the island named Martuccio Gomito,
who was most handsome, well-mannered, and skilled in his pro-
fession, fell in love with her. In like manner Gostanza fell so
passionately in love with him that she never felt happy when he
was out of her sight, and wishing to have her for his wife, Mar-
tuccio asked her father for her hand, but was told that since he
was poor, he could not give her to him. Indignant over being re-
jected for his poverty, Martuccio swore to some of his friends
and relatives that he would never return to Lipari unless he was
rich, and leaving the island, he turned to piracy and sailed the
coasts of Barbary, plundering any vessel that was weaker than
his own, and Fortune would have continued to smile on him in
this enterprise, had he only known how to limit his ambition.
But it was not enough for him and his companions to have be-
come very rich in a short space of time. As they were trying to
become even richer, it happened that after engaging a number of
Saracen vessels in long battle, his ship was taken and plundered,

the better part of his crew massacred by the Saracens, and the boat sunk, while Martuccio was taken to Tunisia, where he was thrown in prison and remained for a long time in a wretched state.

Back in Lipari, the news arrived not merely by one or two but many different people that all the men with Martuccio aboard his ship had drowned. The girl, who had been sorrowful beyond all measure over Martuccio's departure, upon hearing now that he, along with the others, was dead, wept over him for a long while and then made the decision that she no longer wished to live; not possessing sufficient courage to take her own life by violent means, she devised a rather strange but sure way of killing herself: one night in secret she left her father's house and went to the port, where by chance she found, set somewhat distant from the other vessels, a small fishing boat, which, since its owners had just gone ashore, she found was still equipped with a mast, sail, and oars. And since like most women on the island she was somewhat familiar with the rudiments of navigation, she quickly climbed aboard and rowed out into the sea. Then she set the sail, threw away the oars and the rudder, and completely abandoned herself to the wind, calculating that what was bound to happen was either that the boat without a cargo or a pilot would be capsized by the wind, or that it might strike some reef and be smashed, in which case she had no choice but to drown; and wrapping a cloak around her head, she lay down upon the deck of the boat and wept.

But things turned out quite differently from what she had imagined: for since the wind blowing from a northern direction was rather gentle, there was hardly a wave, so that the ship maintained an even keel and toward evening of the following day, she drifted ashore near a town called Susa, a good hundred miles beyond Tunis. The girl did not know whether she was on land or at sea, for she had made up her mind to lie there with her head down and never to raise it, no matter what happened.

When the boat struck the shore, there was by chance a poor old woman on the beach who was taking in the nets left to dry in the sun by the fishermen for whom she worked. The woman saw the boat and was amazed by the fact that it had been allowed to run aground under full sail; believing that the fishermen were probably asleep inside, she went over only to find the young woman inside sound asleep. Calling her a number of times, at last she managed to awaken her, and recognizing from her dress that she was a Christian, she spoke to her in Italian, asking her how it happened that she had arrived there all alone in the boat. The girl, hearing Italian spoken, was afraid that she had perhaps been blown back to Lipari by a contrary wind, and rising quickly to her feet, she looked all around her; but not recognizing the countryside, and seeing that she had run aground, she asked the good woman where she was.

The good woman replied:

"My daughter, you are near Susa in Barbary."

When the girl heard this, distressed that God had not wished to send her to her death and fearing for her honor and not knowing what to do, she sat alongside the boat and began to cry. The good woman, upon seeing this, took pity on her and persuaded her after much coaxing to follow her to her little cottage, where she convinced the girl to tell her how she had arrived there. Realizing that the girl must be hungry, the good woman prepared some of her dry bread, fish, and water for her, and managed to persuade her to eat a little. Then Gostanza asked who the good woman was and how she came to speak Italian so well, whereupon she replied that she was from Trapani, was called Carapresa, and that she worked for some Christian fishermen. When the young lady heard the name Carapresa, she took it as a good omen—why she did so she did not know—and, although she was still feeling sorry for herself, she began to have more hope, with no apparent reason, and she was less eager to do away with her life. Without revealing who she was or from where she had come, she earnestly begged the good woman for the love of God to have pity on her youth, and to advise her on how to safeguard herself from any harm that might befall her.

When Carapresa heard her request, like the good woman she was, leaving Gostanza in her cottage, she quickly gathered in her nets, then returned and wrapped the girl up in her own cloak and took her to Susa; when they arrived there, she said:

"Gostanza, I am taking you to the home of a very kind Saracen lady, whose needs I very often serve. She is an elderly and most compassionate lady, and I shall commend you to her as best I can, and I am very certain that she will gladly welcome you and treat you as her daughter. You stay with her, and do everything in your power to acquire her favor by serving her well until God provides you with a better fortune." And she did just as she said she would.

When the lady, who was quite along in years, heard Gostanza's story she looked into the girl's eyes and began to weep, and then, embracing her, she kissed her forehead and led her by the hand into her home, where she lived with several other women but without any men, and there they all worked with their hands, making various articles from silk, palm, and leather. After a few days, the girl learned to make some of them and began to work along with the others, winning, in so doing, an amazing amount of goodwill and affection from the old lady as well as the others, and after a brief period of time, she even managed to learn their language from them.

Now while the girl was living in Susa, having long ago been given up by her family as lost and dead, the King of Tunis, whose name was Meriabdela, happened to be threatened by a powerful young man from an important family who came from Granada, claiming that the kingdom of Tunis belonged to him, and having assembled a huge army, he was marching against the King of Tunis in order to drive him from his kingdom.

When Martuccio Gomito came to learn of these developments in prison, since he knew Arabic very well, hearing that the King of Tunis was making vast preparations for his own defense, he said to one of the jailers who was guarding him and his companions:

"If only I could speak to the King, I know in my heart that I could give him the advice he needs to win this war of his."

The guard reported these remarks to his superior, who quickly relayed them to the King; as a result, the King ordered Martuccio to be brought before him, and having been asked what his advice might be, Martuccio replied in this fashion:

"My lord, since I am familiar with this country of yours, if I have correctly observed the tactics you employ in your battles, it seems to me that you make more use of your archers than you do of anything else; therefore, if you could discover a means whereby your adversary's archers were to run out of arrows while your own archers were to have an abundance of them, I know that this battle of yours would be won."

To this, the King replied: "If this could be done, without a doubt, I would be confident of winning."

To this Martuccio added:

"My lord, if you wish, it can be done, and here is how. You must have bowstrings for the bows of your archers made which are much thinner than those usually produced, and then have arrows made, the notches of which will be useless except for these thin bowstrings; this must be done in complete secrecy so that your adversary knows nothing about it, otherwise he would be able to take countermeasures. And the reason why I say this is the following: when the archers of your enemy have shot all their arrows and our archers have shot theirs, as you know, your enemies will have to collect the arrows you have shot, while our men will have to gather up theirs in order for the battle to continue, but the enemy will not be able to use the arrows shot by your archers, for their thin notches will not fit their thick bowstrings, while the opposite will occur with the arrows of the enemy, for our thin bowstrings will quite easily fit their arrows with their wider notches; and so your archers will enjoy an abundance of arrows, whereas the others will run short of them."

The King, who was a wise leader, liked Martuccio's advice, and following it to the letter, he found that as a result he had won his war; consequently, Martuccio rose high in his favor and as a result occupied a quite powerful and wealthy position.

The news of these events spread throughout the country, and Gostanza came to learn that Martuccio Gomito, whom she had long believed to be dead, was alive; and so her love for him, which had already begun to cool in her heart, was suddenly rekindled, and it became greater, reviving all her dead hopes. As a result, she revealed every detail of her misfortunes to the good woman with whom she was staying, and she told her that she wished to go to Tunis so that she might satisfy her eyes with the sight of what her ears had made her desirous of seeing through the reports she had received. The lady praised her desire most highly, and as if she were her own mother, she went with her on a boat that sailed to Tunis, where she and Gostanza were honorably received in the home of one of the lady's relatives. And since Carapresa had traveled with them, they sent her around to find out all she could about Martuccio; when she returned with the news that she had discovered he was alive and occupying a high estate, the kind lady was delighted to be the one to inform Martuccio that his Gostanza had arrived there.

And one day she went to where Martuccio was staying and said to him:

"Martuccio, a servant of yours from Lipari has turned up in my home and would like to speak with you there in private; since he did not wish me to trust another with this task, I came to tell you this myself." Martuccio thanked her and then followed her back to her house.

When the girl saw him, she was so happy that she nearly died, and unable to contain herself, with open arms she ran up to him and embraced him, and overcome by the memory of her past misfortunes as well as her present joy, unable to utter a single word, she began to cry tenderly. When Martuccio saw the girl, he stood for a moment in astonishment, and then with a sigh he exclaimed:

"Oh, my Gostanza, are you really alive? Some time ago I heard that you were lost and that you were never heard of again at home." After saying this, crying tenderly, he embraced and kissed her. Gostanza told him everything that had happened to her and about the welcome she had received from the kind lady with whom she was living.

After talking to her for a long time, Martuccio left her and went to his master, the King, and told him the whole story—that is, all that had happened to him and to the girl—adding that with the King's permission, it was his intention to marry her in accordance with our religion. The King was amazed by this account, and he sent for the girl, and having heard from her own lips that everything had happened just as Martuccio had reported, he said: "Well then, you have certainly earned Martuccio for your husband." He then had sumptuous and regal gifts brought forth, some of which he gave to Gostanza and some to Martuccio, granting them his permission to arrange their affairs between themselves in whatever way pleased them most.

After highly honoring the kind lady with whom Gostanza had been living and thanking her for all she had done to help her, Martuccio bestowed upon her such gifts as were suitable to her station, and commending her to God, and not without many tears on Gostanza's part, he and the girl departed. Then with the King's permission they embarked on a small boat, taking Carapresa with them, and accompanied by a favorable wind they sailed back to Lipari, where the rejoicing was so great that words could never describe it. And there, Martuccio married her and gave a grand and beautiful wedding feast; and thereafter they enjoyed each other's love in peace and quiet for a long time to come.

[Fifth Day, Third Story]

Pietro Boccamazza runs away with Agnolella; they encounter some brigands; the young girl flees through a forest and is taken to a castle, while Pietro is captured but escapes from their clutches, and after a number of adventures he happens upon the castle where Agnolella is staying; he marries her and returns with her to Rome.

THERE was no one among them in the group who did not praise Emilia's story; when the Queen saw that she was finished, turning to Elissa, she ordered her to continue; anxious to obey her, Elissa began:

Charming ladies, the tale that comes to mind concerns a miserable night spent by two young people who were rather unwise; but since many happy days followed that night, thus conforming to our topic, I should like to tell you about it.

In Rome, which today is the rump of the world just as once it was its head, there lived not long ago a young man called Pietro Boccamazza, who belonged to one of the most distinguished families in Rome and who fell in love with a very beautiful and charming young lady called Agnolella, the daughter of a man called Gigliuozzo Saullo, who, though a plebeian, was very much beloved by the Romans. And loving her as he did, Pietro succeeded in making the girl love him no less than he loved her. Tormented by his burning love and convinced that he could no longer endure the harsh pain of his desire to have her, Pietro asked for her hand in marriage; but when his relatives found out about this, they all went to him and reproached him sharply for what he wanted to do; and at the same time they gave Gigliuozzo Saullo to understand that in no way should he heed Pietro's entreaties, for if he did, they would never accept him as a friend or an in-law.

When Pietro saw that the only way he could conceive of attaining his desire was blocked, he wanted to die from grief; and if Gigliuozzo had only consented, he would have gone ahead and married his daughter even against the wishes of every last relative he had. But in any case, he was determined, provided the girl was willing, to fulfill his wishes, and having heard through a third party that she was indeed willing, he arranged with her to elope with him from Rome. So, after making preparations for this, early one morning Pietro arose, and mounting their horses, they rode off together in the direction of Anagni, where Pietro had certain friends whom he trusted implicitly; and since they were afraid of being followed, they did not take time to stop and celebrate their nuptials, but rode along together talking about their love and now and then kissing each other.

Now it happened that Pietro was not very familiar with the road, and so, about eight miles from Rome, when they should have taken a right turn on the road, they went, instead, to the left; and they had not ridden more than two miles before they found themselves near a small castle from which, once they had been sighted, twelve soldiers quickly sallied forth. And they were almost upon them by the time the girl saw them, and crying out, she said: "Pietro, let's flee, they are attacking us!" And as best she knew how, she turned her horse in the direction of a vast forest, and digging her spurs into its flanks, she hung on to the saddlehorn. When her horse felt the bite of her spurs, he galloped away, carrying her off into the forest.

Pietro, who was riding along, gazing into her face more than watching the road, was not as quick as she to notice the arrival of the soldiers, and while he was still looking around to see where they were coming from, he was overtaken by them, seized, and made to dismount from his horse. They asked him who he was, and as soon as he told them, the soldiers began discussing the matter among themselves, saying: "This fellow's a friend of our enemies; there's no better way of showing our contempt for the Orsini family than by taking his clothes and his horse, and stringing him up from one of these oak trees!"

And having all agreed to this plan, they ordered Pietro to strip off his clothes; and as Pietro, by now well aware of his fate, was taking off his clothes, all of a sudden, an ambushing party of at least twenty-five soldiers happened to descend upon them, crying: "Kill them, kill them!" Surprised by this attack, they abandoned Pietro and turned to their own defense, but when they saw they were greatly outnumbered by their attackers, they began to flee, with their pursuers at their heels. When Pietro saw this, he quickly grabbed his clothes, jumped on his horse, and as fast as he could he made his escape down the road he had seen the girl take. But finding no road or path through the woods, nor even a single hoofprint, the moment he was safe and out of reach of both the soldiers who had captured him as well as the ones who had attacked the others, unable to find his young lady, he felt like the most miserable man in the world, and he began to cry and meander about, calling out her name. But no one answered him, and while he dared not go back, he had no idea of where he would end up by going ahead; and then also he was afraid both for himself and for the girl of the wild beasts that lurked in the forests, and he kept imagining the girl being torn apart by a bear or a wolf.

And so the unfortunate Pietro went wandering through the forest the entire day, crying out and calling, sometimes going around in circles when he thought he was moving straight ahead, until finally, what with his crying out, his weeping, his fear, and his long lack of food, he was so exhausted that he could not go on any farther. Finding that night had fallen and not knowing what else he could do, he got off his horse and tied it to a large

oak tree that he had discovered, and then, so as not to be de-
voured during the night by wild animals, he climbed up the tree.
Then, once the moon had risen and the sky was very clear, Pie-
tro did not dare to fall asleep for fear of falling—even though
his sorrow and his preoccupation over his young lady would not
have permitted him to do so even if he had wanted to—so he
stayed awake, sighing and crying and cursing his misfortune to
himself.

In the meanwhile, as we said before, the girl was fleeing with-
out knowing where she was heading but only that her horse was
carrying her wherever he pleased, and soon she had gone so far
into the forest that she could no longer see where she had en-
tered it; so not unlike what Pietro had done, she spent the whole
day going this way and that through that wild forest, now stop-
ping, and now galloping on, weeping, calling out, and lamenting
her miserable fate. Finally, with evening approaching and Pietro
nowhere to be found, she happened upon a path which her horse
started to follow, and after riding no more than two miles, she
saw a little cottage off in the distance, and toward it she rode as
quickly as she was able. There she came upon a kindly-looking
man who was very old and his wife, who appeared to be just as
old.

When the couple saw her there all alone, they said:

"Oh, child, what are you doing all alone in the country at this
hour?"

Weeping, the young girl replied she had lost her escort in the
forest and asked whether Anagni was nearby; to this the kind
man replied:

"My child, this is not the road to Anagni; it is more than
twelve miles from here."

Then the girl said: "Is there any place near here where I can
stay the night?"

To this question, the kind man answered: "There is no place
near here you could reach before dark."

Then the girl said: "Would you, for the love of God, be so
kind, since I am unable to go anywhere else, to let me stay here
tonight?"

The kind man answered:

"Young lady, we would be delighted for you to stay with us
this evening, but we must warn you that day and night around
these parts there are men of bad sorts, friends and foes alike,
who very often do bad things and cause serious harm; with you
being here, if by some misfortune one of them happened along
and saw such a beautiful young girl as yourself and did you

harm or caused you shame, there is no way we could help you. We wanted to warn you about this, so that if it were to happen you would not blame us for it."

Though she was terrified by the old man's words, seeing that the hour was late, the girl said:

"Please God, He will safeguard both you and me from such harm here; yet, if such a thing should happen to me, it is far less of an evil to be abused by men than to be torn apart in the woods by wild animals."

Having said this, she dismounted from her horse and went inside the poor man's cottage, where she ate with them what little food they had, and then, fully dressed, she lay down with them on their little cot; and all through the night she never stopped sighing and weeping over her misfortune and that of Pietro, about whom she was unable to imagine anything but the worst.

And then, close to daybreak, she heard a loud sound of people stamping around; she got up and went into a large courtyard which was behind the small cottage, and noticing a large pile of hay to one side of it, she decided to hide there, so if those people were to come, they would not find her so easily. And no sooner had she hid herself than a large band of brigands were at the door of the cottage; they opened it, went inside, and discovered the girl's horse still fully saddled, and they wanted to know who was there.

When the kindly man saw that the young girl was not around, he answered: "There's no one here but us; this horse, which must have run away from somebody, wandered here this evening, and we put it inside the cottage so that the wolves would not devour it."

"Well, then," said the leader of the band, "it will do quite well for us, since it has no owner."

The men then spread out all over the little cottage, and some of them went into the courtyard, where they set down their lances and wooden shields; but one of them, having nothing better to do, just happened to throw his lance at the pile of hay, very nearly killing the girl, who was hiding inside, and almost causing her to give herself away, for the tip of the lance grazed her left breast so close that it tore her clothes, whereupon she was about to let out a loud scream from fear of being wounded; but remembering where she was, she controlled herself and remained silent. The band of men, some here and some there, cooking goat's meat as well as other meat they had with them, ate and drank and then took off about their own affairs, taking with them the girl's horse.

Once they were quite some distance away, the kindly man asked his wife:

"What happened to that young lady of ours who came last night? I haven't seen her since we got up."

The good woman replied that she did not know, and off they went to look for her.

Having heard the band of men leave, the girl climbed out from under the hay, and the kindly man was very pleased, for now he knew that she had not fallen into their hands, and since it was already getting light, he said to her:

"Now that the day is dawning, if you wish, we shall accompany you to a castle about five miles from here where you will be safe, but we shall have to go on foot, for that bunch of rogues that just left here took your horse with them." The girl was not concerned over this but begged him, for the love of God, to take her to this castle; so they started out and reached it about half past the hour of tierce.

It was a castle belonging to a member of the Orsini family who was called Liello di Campo di Fiore, and fortunately his wife, who was a very fine and saintly woman, happened to be staying there at the time, and as soon as she saw the girl, she instantly recognized her. After giving her a cheerful welcome, she insisted on knowing every detail of how she had come to arrive there. The girl told her everything. The woman, who also knew Pietro, because he was a friend of her husband's, was most distressed over what had happened, and when she heard that he had been taken prisoner, she was convinced that he must have been killed. Then she said to the girl:

"Since you do not know what happened to Pietro, you shall stay with me until I am able to send you safely to Rome."

Meanwhile, Pietro was sitting in the oak tree, as unhappy as he could be, and about the time everyone else was falling asleep he saw circling around him at least twenty wolves that had caught sight of his horse. When his horse heard them, it tossed its head, broke its reins, and started to gallop off, but since it was surrounded, it was unable to get away and so it defended itself with its teeth and hooves, holding them at bay for quite some time; but finally they brought it to the ground, killed it, and after tearing out its innards, they all quickly devoured it, and leaving nothing but the bones behind, they ran off. Pietro lost heart over the sight of this, for he had always considered his horse to be a sort of companion, a comfort in his afflictions, and now he thought he would never be able to escape from the forest.

And just before daybreak as Pietro sat in his oak tree, nearly freezing to death from the cold, continuing to keep watch, he saw a huge fire about a mile away; so when it was daylight, not without some apprehension, Pietro climbed down from the oak tree and started walking in the direction of the fire until he reached it. Around it he discovered some shepherds who were eating and making merry, and they took pity on him and invited him to join them. Having eaten and warmed himself and told them about his misfortunes, including how he happened to be there all alone, he asked them if in those parts there was some villa or castle where he might go. The shepherds told him that about three miles away there was the castle of Liello di Campo di Fiore and at the moment Liello's wife was living there; Pietro was very pleased to hear this and asked if any of them would accompany him to the castle. Two of the shepherds did so most willingly.

On reaching the castle Pietro met some people that he knew there, and while he was attempting to organize some way of searching for the young girl in the forest, he was summoned by Liello's wife; he went to her immediately, and when he saw Agnolella with her, there was nothing quite like the happiness he felt. He was dying to take her in his arms, but he was too embarrassed to do so in front of the lady; and if his joy was so great, the girl's was certainly no less upon seeing him.

After receiving him and making him welcome, and having listened to all that had happened to him, the noble lady strongly reproached him for wanting to go against the wishes of his relatives, but when she realized that he was determined to do so nonetheless, and that the girl was most willing, she said to herself:

"Why should I waste my breath? They love each other, they understand each other, and both of them are good friends of my husband, and their intentions are honorable, and, I believe, they have God's blessing, for one of them escaped the gallows and the other death from a lance, and both from the jaws of wild beasts, so let them do as they please." And then turning to them, she said:

"If you truly wish to become husband and wife, then it is my wish too, and so be it; the wedding will be celebrated here at Liello's expense, and later on I shall arrange to make peace between you and your relatives."

Pietro was delighted and Agnolella even more so, and there they married, and the noble lady gave them as elegant a wed-

ding feast as was possible in her mountain home, and there it
was that they first tasted the sweetest fruits of their love.

And then, some days later, accompanied by the lady, they
mounted their horses and under heavy guard they returned to
Rome, where, having discovered that Pietro's relatives were very
angry over what he had done, the lady managed to restore him
to their good graces; and afterward Pietro lived with his Agno-
lella in much peace and pleasure until a ripe old age.

[Fifth Day, Fourth Story]

❦

*Ricciardo Manardi is found by Messer Lizio da Valbona with his
daughter, whom he marries, and he remains on good terms with
her father.*

ELISSA fell silent and listened as her companions praised the tale
she had told, and then the Queen ordered Filostrato to tell an-
other story; laughing, he began:

I have been criticized so many times by so many of you for
imposing upon you a tragic topic and for making you weep that
it seems to me I should now in some measure make amends to
you for the displeasure I have given you by telling you a story
that will make you laugh a bit; so I intend to tell you in a
rather short little story about a love which, except for a few
sighs mixed with a brief moment of fear resulting from shame,
came to a happy end.

Not long ago, worthy ladies, there lived in Romagna a most
wealthy and esteemed knight called Messer Lizio da Valbona,
who had the good fortune as he approached old age to have a
daughter born to his wife, Madonna Giacomina. His daughter
grew up to become the most beautiful and charming girl in those
parts; and because she was their only child, they loved and cher-
ished her dearly, and they watched over her with the greatest of
care, for they hoped to arrange a distinguished marriage for her.

Now there was a handsome and attractive young man from
the Manardi da Brettinoro family, named Ricciardo, who would
often come to Messer Lizio's house, and he was much liked by
Messer Lizio, and neither he nor his wife thought any more of
keeping an eye on him than they would have on their own
son.

And as Ricciardo noticed more and more how beautiful and graceful the girl was, how accomplished and charming, and that she was of a marriageable age, he fell madly in love with her, and it was only with the greatest of difficulty that he managed to conceal his love. But the young girl was aware of this, and far from rejecting his attentions, she, too, began to fall in love with him, which, of course, pleased Ricciardo very much. Although he often felt the need to speak to her, he kept silent because he was timid. But one day he found the opportunity and courage to say to her:

"Caterina, I beg you not to let me die of love."

"God grant that you do not make me die of it first!" the young girl quickly answered.

This answer greatly increased Ricciardo's ardor and eagerness, and he said to her:

"Ask of me anything you wish, but it is up to you to find a means of saving both your life and my own."

The young girl replied:

"Ricciardo, you see how closely I am watched. I do not see how you can come to me nor I to you, but if you can find a way that will not bring shame upon me, tell me and I will do it."

Ricciardo thought of several solutions, and then suddenly he said:

"Caterina, my sweet—I can see no way unless you can manage to be on the balcony overlooking your father's garden, and sleep there. If I knew that you would be there at night, I would find a way to climb up there, no matter how high it might be."

"If you are brave enough to climb up there," Caterina answered, "I believe that I can find a way to sleep there."

Ricciardo agreed; they hastily kissed each other and departed. It was around the end of May, and on the following day, the young girl began to complain to her mother that she had not been able to sleep the night before because of the excessive heat. Her mother replied:

"What heat are you talking about, daughter? It was not at all hot."

To this Caterina answered:

"Mother dear, if you had added 'in my opinion,' then perhaps you would be right. But you ought to remember that young girls get hotter than older women do."

"That is true, my child," said her mother, "but I cannot make it hot and cold whenever I wish, just to please you. You must put up with whatever weather the season brings. Perhaps tonight it will be cooler and you will sleep better."

"I hope to God that you are right," said Caterina, "but usually the nights do not get cooler as summer approaches."

"Well," said her mother, "what do you want me to do about it?"

"If you and father would not mind," said Caterina, "I would like to have my bed on the balcony which is beside father's bedroom, overlooking his garden, and there I would sleep; and listening to the nightingale sing and being in a cooler place, I would be much better off than in your room."

"Cheer up, my child," said her mother, "I will talk to your father, and we shall do whatever he wishes."

When old Messer Lizio heard this, he became somewhat cross and said:

"What is this nonsense about being serenaded to sleep by a nightingale? I'll make her sleep to the tune of the crickets in broad daylight!"

When Caterina learned of his reply, more out of spite than because of the heat, not only did she refuse to sleep at all the following night, but she also kept her mother from sleeping by constantly complaining about the heat. Next morning, her mother went to Messer Lizio and said:

"Sir, do you care so little about your daughter? What does it matter if she sleeps on that balcony? She could not sleep a wink last night because of the heat, and besides that, why does it surprise you to know that she would like to hear the nightingale sing? After all, she is a young girl! Young people like things that are like themselves."

After hearing her out, Messer Lizio said:

"Very well, then, make whatever bed you want for her out there and hang a curtain around it, and let her sleep there and listen to the nightingale's song as much as she likes!"

When the young girl learned that her father had given his permission, she immediately had a bed made up on the balcony, and since she was to sleep there that night, she waited until she saw Ricciardo and gave him a prearranged signal by which he understood what he had to do.

When Messer Lizio heard the young girl go to bed, he locked the only door leading from his bedroom to the balcony, and he, too, retired for the night. And when Ricciardo saw that everything was quiet throughout the house, with the help of a ladder he climbed up a wall; then, by climbing up the stones that jutted from the house, he pulled himself, with great difficulty and great danger of falling, up onto the balcony. Once there, he was quietly but joyfully received by the young girl. After kissing many times, they lay down together, and for almost the entire night they took delight and pleasure in one another, and as they did, they made the nightingale sing time and time again.

The night was short and their pleasure was great, and although they were not aware of it, it was almost day when they finally fell asleep without a thing on their bodies, exhausted from the hot weather as they were from their play. Caterina had her right arm under Ricciardo's neck, and her left hand was grasping that thing which you ladies are ashamed to mention in the company of gentlemen.

And in this position they slept, but as day broke it failed to awaken them. Messer Lizio got up, and remembering that his daughter was sleeping on the balcony, he quietly opened the door and said:

"Let us see if the nightingale made Caterina sleep last night."

And walking out onto the balcony, he lifted up the curtain around the bed and saw Ricciardo and Caterina sleeping completely naked in each other's arms and in the position just mentioned above. After recognizing Ricciardo, he quietly slipped away and went to his wife's bedroom, and he called to her, saying:

"Hurry, woman, get up and come see how enchanted your daughter is by the nightingale she has caught and is still holding in her hand!"

"How can this be?" asked his wife.

"You'll see," said Messer Lizio, "if you come quickly."

The lady quickly dressed herself and quietly followed Messer Lizio, and when they both reached the bed and lifted the curtain, Madonna Giacomina saw for herself exactly how her daughter had managed to catch and hold on to the nightingale which she had so longed to hear sing.

Feeling that she had been treacherously deceived by Ricciardo, the lady wanted to scream at him and to insult him, but Messer Lizio told her:

"Woman, if you value my love, do not say a word, for since she has snared him, he shall be hers! Ricciardo is a noble and rich young man; we have only to gain from such a match. If he wishes to leave this house with my blessing, he will have to marry her first; thus he shall have put his nightingale into his own cage and not into anybody else's!"

This comforted his wife, for she saw that her husband was not angered by what had taken place, and having considered the fact that her daughter had spent a good night, that she had rested well and caught a nightingale, she kept silent.

Hardly had they spoken these words when Ricciardo woke up, and when he saw that it was day, he thought that he was a dead man for sure, and calling to Caterina, he said:

"Oh, my love, what shall we do now that day has come and trapped me here?"

At the sound of these words, Messer Lizio stepped forward, raised the curtain, and said:

"We shall do very well."

When Ricciardo saw him, he felt as if his heart had been ripped from his body, and sitting up straight in the bed, he exclaimed:

"My lord, in God's name have mercy on me! I realize that I deserve to die for being so disloyal and wicked; therefore, do with me what you will. But I beg you to have pity on me and if it is at all possible, spare my life."

To this Messer Lizio answered:

"Ricciardo, this is not the reward I should receive from my love and trust in you. But since this is the way things stand, and since it was your youth that made you commit this error, so that you may save my honor and your own life, before you leave here, take Caterina for your lawful wife. And in so doing, she will be yours for as long as she may live, just as she has been yours this night. And in this way, you shall have both my pardon and your own safety. But if you do not agree to this, then I suggest you commend your soul to God."

While all of this was being said, Caterina let her hold on the nightingale slip, and covering herself up, she burst into tears, begging her father to forgive Ricciardo; at the same time she implored Ricciardo to do as Messer Lizio wished, so that from then on, they might enjoy without fear other such nights together. But there was no need for such pleas, since on the one hand, there was the shame of the error committed and the desire for atonement, and on the other the fear of death and the desire to escape it; and above all, there was Ricciardo's burning love and his desire to possess his beloved; so, freely and without any hesitation whatsoever, Ricciardo agreed to do what Messer Lizio wished.

Messer Lizio then borrowed one of Madonna Giacomina's rings, and right then and there in the presence of her parents, without getting out of bed, Ricciardo took Caterina for his wife. When this was done, Messer Lizio and his wife left them, saying:

"Now go back to sleep, for you probably need sleep more than you do getting up."

When they had left, the two young people embraced each other, and since they had not gone more than six miles that night, they did two more before getting out of bed—and that was it for the first day.

Once they got out of bed, Ricciardo made more conventional arrangements with Messer Lizio, and a few days afterward, as was proper, in the presence of their friends and relatives he married the young girl all over again, and with great fanfare he took her home to celebrate their marriage at a magnificent wedding feast. And for a long time afterward he lived with her in peace and quiet, trapping the nightingale, night and day, as much as he liked.

[Fifth Day, Fifth Story]

❧

Guidotto da Cremona leaves Giacomin da Pavia in charge of his daughter and passes away; in Faenza, Giannol di Severino and Minghino di Mingole fall in love with her; the two men fight over her; when the girl is recognized to be Giannole's sister, she is given to Minghino as his wife.

LISTENING to the story of the nightingale made every lady there laugh so hard that it was some time after Filostrato had ended his storytelling before they were able to control themselves. Then, when they were done laughing, the Queen said to Filostrato:

"If you depressed us yesterday, today you have, without a doubt, managed to tickle us so that we can no longer hold it against you." And turning to Neifile, she ordered her to continue the storytelling, and Neifile cheerfully began in this manner:

Since Filostrato entered the region of Romagna with his story, I, too, should like to roam around those parts awhile with my own storytelling. Let me say, then, that in the city of Fano there once lived two Lombards, one of whom was called Guidotto da Cremona and the other Giacomin da Pavia, both of whom were men well along in age and who had spent a good deal of their youth engaged mostly in feats of arms and soldiering. As a result, when Guidotto was on the point of death, having no son or friend or relative that he trusted more than Giacomin, he left in Giacomin's care a daughter, who was about ten years old, and all his worldly possessions, and having told Giacomin many particulars of his past life, he died.

Now it happened in those days that the city of Faenza, which had long been engaged in wars and had experienced bad times, was returned to somewhat more stable conditions, and anyone who wished to return there was freely granted permission to do so; because of this, Giacomino, who had lived there previously and had liked it, returned there with all his possessions, and with him he took the daughter left to him by Guidotto, whom he loved and treated as if she were his very own daughter.

As she grew older, the girl became a very beautiful young lady, more beautiful than any other who lived in the city at that time, and she was as well-mannered and as virtuous as she was beautiful; because of this she began to attract the attention of a number of men, especially that of two young men, both very handsome and both from good families, and they fell so much in love with her that their jealousy and hatred for each other went beyond all limits. One of these men was called Giannole di Severino and the other was Minghino di Mingole. Neither of them, since the girl now had reached the age of fifteen, would have been anything but willing to take her as his wife if his parents had permitted it, but when each one of them was refused permission to marry, each of them set about to take possession of her by any means they could find.

Giacomino had in his home an old serving woman as well as a manservant whose name was Crivello, a very pleasant and sociable fellow indeed; Giannole became very friendly with him, and when the time seemed right to him, he revealed his love to Crivello, begging the servant to help him in obtaining his desires and promising him a great many things if he would do so. To these promises Crivello replied:

"Look here, the only way I can help you in this affair is by letting you, on that occasion when Giacomino goes out somewhere for supper, into the room where she may be at the time, for if I were to speak to her on your behalf, she would never listen to me. If you like this idea, I give you my word to do it for you: then it is up to you to do whatever you think best."

Giannole said that he could wish for nothing better, and they remained in agreement.

Minghino, on the other hand, had become friendly with the serving woman and had worked on her in such a way that he succeeded in getting her to take several messages to the young girl and had almost managed to kindle her with Minghino's love; moreover, the serving woman had promised Minghino to let him inside the house whenever, for some reason, Giacomino happened to be out of the house for the evening.

And so it happened that not long after these arrangements were made, thanks to Crivello, Giacomino was persuaded to go out with a friend of his to dine; and after notifying Giannole about this, Crivello arranged that on receiving a certain signal Giannole was to come to the house, where he would find the door open. At the same time, the maidservant, unaware of all this, let Minghino know that Giacomino was not eating supper at home and told him to stay close to the house so that when he saw her give the signal, he could come to the house and be let inside. Evening came, and the two lovers, neither of whom knew what the other was doing but both of whom were suspicious of the other, arrived escorted by a number of armed companions so as to be certain of carrying off the girl. Minghino with his men waited for his signal in a friend's home near the girl's house, while Giannole also waited with his companions not too far away.

As soon as Giacomino left, Crivello and the maidservant did their best to get rid of each other. Crivello said to the maidservant: "Haven't you gone to bed yet? What are you doing still wandering about the house?"

And the maidservant answered him back: "And why don't you go and fetch your master? What are you hanging around for now that you've eaten?"

And so neither one was able to persuade the other to leave. But when Crivello realized that the hour agreed upon with Giannole had come, he said to himself:

"What do I care about her? If she doesn't keep quiet, she'll get what's coming to her." And having given the signal they had agreed upon, he went to open the entrance to the house, and Giannole quickly arrived with two of his companions and went inside, and finding the girl in the main hall, they seized her to take her away. The girl began to resist and to scream at the top of her voice, and the maidservant did the same; when Minghino heard this, he immediately ran to the spot with his own companions, and seeing the girl already being dragged out the door, they drew their swords and cried: "Ah, you traitors, you're as good as dead; you won't get away with this—what do you mean by this outrage?" And having shouted this, they began to do battle.

Meanwhile, the neighbors, the moment they heard the uproar, came rushing from their houses bearing torches and weapons, and condemning this violence, they began helping Minghino. As a result, after a long struggle, Minghino managed to get the girl away from Giannole and take her back to Giacomino's house. The brawl had not ended before the *podestà*'s guards arrived and arrested a great number of them, and among those arrested were Minghino, Giannole, and Crivello, all of whom were taken to prison. Later on, when things had quieted down and Giacomino, who was most distressed by the incident, returned home and inquired how the whole thing happened, he realized that the girl was in no way to blame, and somewhat relieved, he thought to himself that in order to avoid a similar occurrence, he should marry her off as soon as possible.

The following morning, the relatives of both young men, having heard what had actually happened and knowing what harm might come to the young men who had been arrested if Giacomino decided to do what he had every legal right to do, went to Giacomino and with smooth words they begged him not to pay as much attention to the injury he had received from the young men's lack of good sense as to the love and the goodwill they all believed he bore for themselves, his suppliants; then, afterward, they offered, on behalf of themselves as well as the young men who had committed the crime, to make whatever amends he wished them to.

Giacomino, a good-hearted man who had seen worse things happen in his day, quickly replied:

"Gentlemen, even if I were in my own native city and not here, I would consider myself such a friend of yours that I would never do anything that would displease you either in this present matter or in any other; besides, in this matter I must bend to your wishes, for you have wronged one of your own, as this girl is not from Cremona or Pavia as many of you think but from Faenza—though neither I nor she nor the man who entrusted her to me ever knew whose daughter she was; therefore, in this affair I am entirely disposed to do anything you request of me."

The worthy men, learning that the girl was a native of Faenza, were very much surprised; and having thanked Giacomino for his generous reply, they begged him to be kind enough to explain to them how she came into his hands and how he knew her to be from Faenza; and to these questions Giacomino answered:

"When Guidotto da Cremona, who was my friend and comrade at arms, was about to die, he told me that when this city was captured by the Emperor Frederick and everything was being plundered, he and his companions entered a house which he found full of booty and abandoned by its inhabitants, except for this young girl, at the time about two years of age, who while he was climbing up the stairs called out 'Father' to him. This aroused his compassion, and together with all the possessions in the house, he brought her away with him to Fano; and there, on his deathbed, he left me everything he had, including her, with the understanding that when the time came I would see that she was married and that I would give her what had been his as her dowry. And while she has reached the age for taking a husband, I have not, as yet, succeeded in finding her a person whom I like; and I would be happy to do this before another incident like the one last night happens to me all over again."

Among the group there was a certain Guiglielmino da Medicina, who had been with Guidotto at the time this happened and who knew very well which house it was that Guidotto had plundered; seeing the owner present there among the others, he went up to him and said: "Bernabuccio, do you hear what Giacomin is saying?"

And Bernabuccio replied: "Yes, and I was just thinking about it, since I remember that during those tumultuous times, I lost a little daughter who was about the age that Giacomin mentioned."

Then Guiglielmin said to him:

"Surely this is the girl, for I was once in a place where I heard Guidotto describe the house he had plundered, and I realized that it had to be yours; try to remember, then, if she had some mark by which you could identify her and have them look for it, and I am certain you will discover she is your daughter."

After thinking for a while, Bernabuccio remembered that she had a scar in the shape of a small cross above her left ear caused by an abscess which he had had lanced a short time before the incident occurred, and so, without further delay, he went up to Giacomino, who was still there, and implored him to take him into his house and allow him to see the girl. Giacomino took him quite willingly and had the girl brought before him. When Bernabuccio saw her, he thought he saw before his eyes the very face of the girl's mother, who was still a beautiful woman; but not satisfied with this, he asked Giacomino if he would be so kind as to allow him to lift up the hair over her left ear, to which Giacomino consented. Drawing near to the girl, who was standing there rather embarrassed, Bernabuccio, raising her hair up with his hand, caught sight of the crossmark; whereupon, realizing that she truly was his daughter, he began to weep tenderly and to embrace her, although the girl seemed to object to this.

Turning to Giacomino, Bernabuccio declared:

"Brother, this is my daughter; my house was the one plundered by Guidotto, and in the sudden excitement she was forgotten inside the house by my wife, the child's mother, and until now we thought she had burned to death inside our house, which later that day was set on fire."

On hearing all this and seeing that he was an old man, the girl believed his explanation, and moved by some mysterious power, she yielded to his embraces and began to weep tenderly along with him. Bernabuccio immediately sent for her mother, some of her other relatives, as well as her sisters and brothers; and having presented her to all of them and explained the whole story, and amid great rejoicing and the exchanging of a thousand embraces, he took her home with him, to Giacomino's great delight.

When the *podestà*, fine man that he was, learned about this development and realized that Giannole, whom he was holding as a prisoner, was Bernabuccio's son and the girl's blood brother, he decided that he would deal with him leniently and ignore the crime he had committed; and he became the intermediary in this affair, arranging, along with Bernabuccio and Giacomino, for peace to be made between Giannole and Minghino; and to the great satisfaction of all his relatives, he gave the girl, whose name was Agnesa, to Minghino as his wife, and along with the two young men he released Crivello and the others who had been implicated in the affair.

And then, Minghino, delirious with joy, after a big and beautiful wedding, took his wife to his home, where he lived with her in peace and prosperity for many years to come.

[Fifth Day, Sixth Story]

Gian di Procida is discovered with the girl he loves, who had been handed over to King Frederick, and with her he is tied to a stake and is about to be burned when he is recognized by Ruggier de Loria; then he is freed and they are married.

WHEN Neifile's tale, which had pleased the ladies very much, came to an end, the Queen ordered Pampinea to prepare to tell the next one; lifting her shining face, without hesitating she began:

The powers of Love, dear ladies, are very great indeed, inducing lovers to endure immense hardships as well as extraordinary and unimaginable dangers, as can be seen from many of the stories told both today and on other occasions; but nevertheless, I should like to demonstrate his powers still further with a story about the courage of a young man in love.

Among all the girls living on Ischia, an island very near Naples, there was one who was a very beautiful and charming young girl named Restituta, the daughter of a nobleman of the island whose name was Marin Bolgaro; and living on an island near Ischia called Procida was a young man named Gianni who loved this girl more than his own life, and she, in turn, loved him. Not satisfied with going from Procida to Ischia to see her by day, he would often cross over at night, even swimming at times all the way from Procida to Ischia when he could not find a boat, so that if he could do nothing else, he could at least stare at the walls of her home.

And during the course of this passionate courtship, it happened that one day while the girl was all alone on the seashore, going from rock to rock gathering seashells, which she pried off the rocks with a small knife, she chanced upon a cove hidden among the rocks. In that spot were a number of young Sicilians who had sailed from Naples and had landed from their frigate in order to take some shade and cool water from a fountain nearby. When they saw how beautiful she was and that she was all alone and had not seen them yet, they decided to seize her and carry her off, and no sooner had they decided than the deed was done. Though she kept screaming, they took her and put her aboard their ship, and sailed away. Once they reached Calabria, they began to discuss who was to take possession of the girl, and, to put it briefly, everyone seemed to want her; and so, since they were unable to reach any agreement among themselves, fearful of making things worse and ruining their business over her, they decided to give her to Frederick, King of Sicily, who was then a young man who delighted in such beautiful things as she, and as soon as they reached Palermo, they did just that.

The King saw how beautiful she was and held her most dear; but since he was somewhat unwell, he ordered that until such time as he had regained his strength, the girl was to be lodged in one of his sumptuous apartments located in a garden of his called La Cuba, and there be waited upon; and this was done.

The uproar in Ischia over the girl's abduction was enormous, and the worst part of it was that no one was able to find out who it was that had carried her off. But Gianni, who was more distressed than anyone else about this turn of events, did not wait around Ischia for news of the girl but, having learned the direction which the captors' boat had taken, had his own frigate fitted out and set sail as quickly as he could, searching the entire coast from Minerva down to Scalea in Calabria, and making inquiries everywhere about the girl, until finally in Scalea he was told that she had been taken by Sicilian sailors to Palermo. Then, as fast as he was able, Gianni sailed to Palermo, and arriving there, he discovered after much searching that the girl had been given to the King and was being kept by him in La Cuba, all of which distressed him greatly, causing him to give up all hope not only of getting her back but even of ever seeing her again.

But yet, Love kept him there, and since no one there recognized him, he sent his frigate away and remained. One day during his many walks past La Cuba, he happened to catch a glimpse of her at a window and she saw him, and both of them were overjoyed. And when Gianni saw that the place was deserted, he managed to get as close to her as he could, and speaking to her, he learned from her what he must do in order for them to speak to each other in the future. Then he left, but not before studying the layout of the area. Biding his time until well into the night, he then returned there, and hanging on to parts of the wall that even a woodpecker could not have perched upon, he managed to climb over, and once inside the garden he found a plank, which he propped up against the window which the girl earlier had pointed out to him, and by this means he easily climbed up it.

Since she believed that her honor by now was as good as lost, the girl, who had been rather uncharitable toward Gianni in the past in preserving it, now made up her mind to fulfill his every desire, for she felt that there was no one to whom she could give herself that was more worthy than he, and that this might persuade him to get her out of there, and so she left the window open for him to reach her more quickly. So then, when Gianni found the window open, he quietly entered and lay down beside the girl, who was not sleeping. Before they did anything else, the girl revealed her every intention to him, begging him with all her heart to free her and take her away from there; and Gianni replied that nothing would please him more, and that when he left her, without fail he would arrange things in such a way that he would take her away with him the next time he returned. Then, embracing each other with the greatest of delight, they took that pleasure which is the greatest Love may provide, and they repeated it a number of times, before, without realizing it, they fell asleep in each other's arms.

The King, who had liked the girl from the first moment he saw her, remembered her, and now that he was feeling better, he decided, even though it was before dawn, that he wanted to spend some time with her; and with one of his servants he quietly went to La Cuba and, entering the apartments, he had them unlock the door of the bedroom in which he knew the girl was sleeping. Then he entered, preceded by a large, blazing torch. When he looked at her bed, he saw them there together, the girl with Gianni, both asleep and naked in each other's arms. He was so outraged by this sight and quickly he became so furious that he could hardly restrain himself from killing them both with a dagger he wore by his side without saying a word about it. But realizing how cowardly a thing it would be for any man, not to mention a king, to murder two naked people who are asleep, he held back and decided, instead, to have them publicly executed at the stake. Turning to the sole companion he had brought with him, he said: "What do you think of this wicked female in whom I once placed all my hopes?" Then he asked him if he was acquainted with this young man who had been so bold as to come to the King's own house to commit such an outrage and give him such displeasure.

The man whom he had questioned replied that he could not remember ever having seen him before. Then, in a rage, the King left the room and ordered that the two lovers, naked as they were, should be seized and tied up, and when daybreak came, taken to the square in Palermo and, back to back, bound to a stake, where they were to be held until the hour of tierce, so that they could be viewed by everyone; and then they were to be burned at the stake as they deserved. Having given these orders, he returned to Palermo and retired to his chambers, furious with anger.

After the King had departed, a number of his men burst in on the two lovers and not only woke them up but swiftly seized and bound them, showing them no pity; when the two young people realized what was happening to them, grief-stricken, and fearing for their lives, they wept and reproached themselves, as might well have been expected. Following the King's command, they were taken to Palermo and bound to a stake in the square, and before their very eyes the wood was stacked in preparation for burning them at the time appointed by the King.

All the people of Palermo, both men and women, immediately rushed to see the two lovers: while the men stood in a group

gazing at the girl, all of them praising the beauty of all her parts
and how well-built she was, so in like manner, all the women,
who had raced to look at the young man, were expressing their
highest approval for his good looks and good body. But the un-
fortunate lovers, deeply stricken with shame, hung their heads
low and wept over their unhappy fate, expecting from one mo-
ment to the next a cruel death by fire. And while they were
being held there until the appointed hour, the news of the crime
they had committed, which was shouted all over town, reached
the ears of Ruggier de Loria, a man of inestimable worth and, at
that time, the King's Admiral. Curious to see who they were, he,
too, headed for the place where they were tied up. And arriving
there, first he looked upon the girl and found her most beautiful
indeed; then, coming to the young man, without much trouble he
soon recognized who he was, and drawing closer to him, he asked
him if he was not Gianni di Procida.

Gianni raised his head, and recognizing the Admiral, he said:

"My lord, I am indeed the man about whom you are inquir-
ing, but I am not going to be so for very much longer."

Then the Admiral asked him what crime had brought him to
such a state, and to this Gianni answered: "Love and the wrath
of the King."

The Admiral had him recount his story in more detail; and
having heard how everything had happened, he was about to
leave when Gianni called him back and said to him:

"Ah, my lord, if it is possible, can you obtain one favor for
me from the man who put me here?"

"And what favor is that?" asked Ruggieri.

Gianni replied: "I see that I must die and very soon, and so I
wish to ask this favor—that since I have been tied here back to
back with this girl, whom I have loved more than my own life
just as she has loved me, allow us to be turned around, so that
while I am dying, I may look upon her face and can pass away
contented."

Laughing, Ruggieri said that he would gladly do so: "I'll see
to it that you see her so much before you die, you will regret it."

After leaving Gianni, he ordered the men who had been placed
in charge of the execution not to do anything further until they
had received additional orders from the King; and without wait-
ing any longer, he went to the King. Although Ruggieri saw that
the King was very angry, he did not hesitate to speak his mind,
and he said to him:

"Sire, how have the two young people whom you have ordered
to be burned at the stake in the square offended you?"

The King told him, and Ruggieri continued:

"The crime they committed certainly deserves punishment, but not from you; and just as crimes deserve punishment, so, too, good deeds deserve rewards, not to mention favor and compassion. Do you realize who these people are that you wish to have burned at the stake?"

The King replied that he did not know them; then Ruggieri declared:

"Then I want you to know, so that you may see how unwise it would be for you to allow yourself to be carried away by your impetuous anger. The young man is the son of Landolfo di Procida, the dear brother of Messer Gian di Procida, through whose efforts you are now King and lord of this island; the girl is the daughter of Marin Bolgaro, whose power even today keeps your rule from being driven out of Ischia. Moreover, these young people have been in love with each other for a long while, and not in order to show disrespect for your royal highness but rather compelled by love did they commit this sin, if what young people do in the name of love can be called a sin. Why would you, then, wish to put them to death, when you ought to be honoring them with the greatest of gifts and favors?"

When the King heard these words and was certain that Ruggieri was speaking the truth, not only did he stop himself from taking worse action, but he felt great remorse for the actions he had already taken; and so he immediately ordered that the two young people be released from the stake and brought before him, and this was done. And after he inquired thoroughly into their condition, he decided to make amends with honors and gifts for the injury he had caused them; so he had them dressed in courtly fashion, and knowing that they both consented, he married the girl to Gianni. And having given them magnificent gifts, he sent them happily home, where they were received with the greatest of celebrations, and there they lived together for a long time in pleasure and joy.

[Fifth Day, Seventh Story]

❦

Teodoro, in love with Violante, the daughter of Messer Amerigo, his master, causes her to become pregnant and is condemned to be hanged; but while he is being whipped along the way to the gallows, he is recognized by his father, and given back his freedom, he takes Violante as his wife.

ALL the ladies were nervously waiting to learn whether or not the two lovers would be burned at the stake, and when they heard that they had escaped, rejoicing, they thanked God; then, having heard the end of the tale, the Queen imposed the task of telling the next one upon Lauretta, who cheerfully began as follows:

Lovely ladies, during the time when good King William ruled Sicily, there was on the island a nobleman called Messer Amerigo Abate da Trapani who, with other worldly goods he possessed, was well furnished with many children. Therefore, he was in need of servants, and when certain galleys arrived from the Levant belonging to Genoese pirates who had captured many young boys during coastal raids in Armenia, believing that these boys were Turkish, he bought some of them. While they all looked like they were of peasant stock, there was one among them whose noble and better appearance seemed to reflect some other origin, and he was called Teodoro. Although he was treated as a servant, he was nevertheless raised in the house together with Messer Amerigo's sons, and as he grew up, Teodoro, who inclined more to his own nature than to the accident of his condition, became so well mannered and likable and he pleased Messer Amerigo to such an extent that Amerigo made him a free man. Believing he was a Turk, Amerigo had him baptized, giving him the name of Pietro, and he entrusted him with all his important affairs, placing the greatest of faith in him.

Along with Messer Amerigo's other sons, there also grew up a daughter of his called Violante, a beautiful and delicate young girl who, because her father was in no hurry to marry her off, happened to fall in love with Pietro; but though she loved him and had the greatest of esteem for his manner and his achievements, she was, nevertheless, too shy to reveal her love to him. But Love spared her this burden, for Pietro, who more than once had cast a furtive glance at her, fell so much in love with her that he never felt happy unless she was somewhere in his sight; but he was very much afraid that someone would notice this, feeling as he did that what he was doing was less than proper. But the girl, who enjoyed his company, was aware of how he felt, and in order to reassure him, she made it appear that she was delighted with it, as indeed she was. And their relationship continued this way for some time, the one not daring to say anything to the other, no matter how much they wished to do so.

But consumed this way, each by the flames of the other's love, Fortune, as though deciding that this was her wish, found a way for them to drive away the apprehension and fear which stood in their way. Approximately a mile outside of Trapani, Messer Amerigo owned a very beautiful property, to which his wife and daughter along with other ladies and maidservants would often go for a change of scene; having gone there one day when the weather was extremely hot, taking Pietro with them, they found that the sky, as it does from time to time in the summer, suddenly became covered with dark clouds; so the lady, not to be caught there by the bad weather, set out with her companions to return to Trapani, going as fast as they could.

But Pietro and the girl, both being young, found themselves far ahead of the mother and their other companions, perhaps encouraged to do so no less by Love than by fear of the weather; and when they had gone so far ahead of the mother and the others that they could no longer be seen, there were a number of thunderclaps followed immediately by a heavy hailstorm, from which the lady and her companions sought shelter in the house of a peasant. Pietro and the girl, not having such a ready shelter, entered an old and quite dilapidated cottage in which no one lived any longer; and having both managed to squeeze in under a bit of the roof which still remained standing, they huddled together, forced by the necessity of the insufficient cover overhead to touch one another; and such contact was cause enough for them to find the courage to reveal their amorous desires.

Pietro began first by saying:

"Now would that God never stop this hailstorm, forcing me to remain here forever!"

And the girl said: "I would like that very much!"

And these words led to holding each other's hands and squeezing them and then to embracing each other and then to exchanging kisses, all while it continued to hail; and so that I shall not have to recount every little detail, the weather did not improve until they had tasted the ultimate delights of Love and arranged to meet again secretly to further their mutual pleasure. When the bad weather passed, they went and waited for the girl's mother at the entrance of the city, which was nearby, and all together they returned to the house. And from time to time with the utmost secrecy and discretion, they would meet there again to their mutual great delight. Things went on this way until finally the girl became pregnant, which was most distressing to both of them; whereupon she took a number of measures to go against the course of nature and miscarry, but none of them had any effect.

Because of this, Pietro, fearing for his life, decided to flee, and he told the young girl so, but when she heard this, she said to him: "If you leave me, I will certainly kill myself!"

To this remark Pietro, who loved her very much, replied:

"How can you expect me to stay here, my lady? Your pregnancy will reveal our transgression: they will forgive you without much difficulty, but I shall be the poor wretch to suffer the punishment for your sin and my own."

To this the young girl said:

"Pietro, my sin will be apparent, but rest assured that yours, unless you confess it yourself, will never be revealed."

Then Pietro replied:

"Since you have made me this promise, I shall stay; but be sure you keep it."

The young girl kept her pregnancy concealed for as long as she could, but one day when she saw that her body was swelling up to the point that she could no longer hide it, she went in tears to her mother and confessed it, begging her to save her life. Her mother, sorrowful beyond measure, gave her a good tongue-lashing, demanding to know how all of this had happened. So that no harm might come to Pietro, the girl made up some story of her own, altering the truth of the affair. Her mother believed her, and in order to hide her daughter's condition, she sent her off to one of their country estates.

The time was near for the girl to give birth, and she was screaming as women usually do at those times; the girl's mother never thought Messer Amerigo would come there, for he seldom did so, but one day on his way back from a hawking trip he just happened to walk by the room where his daughter was screaming, and astonished at the sound, he immediately entered the room and asked what was happening. When the lady saw her husband come in, she rose to her feet full of sorrow and told him what had happened to their daughter; but since he was less credulous than his wife had been, he declared it was impossible for his daughter not to know who had made her pregnant and that he wanted to know the whole story, for only if she told him everything might she be restored to his favor; and if she refused, she could expect to die with no pity at all. His wife tried as best she could to convince her husband to accept the story the girl had told her, but he would have nothing to do with it.

Flying into a rage, with his drawn sword in hand he rushed toward his daughter, who while her father was talking to her mother had given birth to a male child, and exclaimed: "Either you tell me who fathered this child or you shall die this instant!"

In fear of death, the girl broke the promise she had made to Pietro and confessed everything that had happened between them; when the gentleman heard this, he immediately became incensed and could hardly restrain himself from killing her; but after he spoke his mind according to the dictates of anger, he climbed back onto his horse and went to Trapani, straight to a certain Messer Currado, the King's military governor, and told him of the injury Pietro had done him. Since Pietro was unaware of what was going on, the governor promptly had him arrested; and when he was put to the torture, he confessed to everything.

After a few days Pietro was sentenced to be whipped as he passed through the city and then hanged by the neck, and in order to rid the world of the two lovers and their son all at the same time, Messer Amerigo, whose anger had not been abated any by having Pietro condemned to death, poured some poison into a goblet of wine and handed this to one of his servants along with a unsheathed dagger, saying:

"Take these two things to Violante and tell her for me that she is to choose quickly which death she prefers—the poison or the blade; if she refuses, I shall have her burned at the stake before the eyes of all the town just as she deserves, and this done, I shall take the son she gave birth to several days ago, and after smashing its head against a wall, I shall throw it to the dogs to eat." After the cruel father had passed so harsh a sentence on his own daughter and grandson, the servant, who was more disposed to doing evil than good, departed.

The condemned Pietro was being led by some soldiers who were whipping him as he made his way to the gallows, when the leaders of this troop decided to go past an inn where there happened to be lodged three Armenian noblemen who had been sent by the King of Armenia as ambassadors to Rome to negotiate with the Pope on important matters concerning a crusade which they were supposed to undertake. Having stopped at the inn to refresh themselves and rest for a few days, they were entertained most honorably by the noblemen of Trapani, and especially by Messer Amerigo. When they heard the men who were escorting Pietro pass by, they went to a window to see.

Pietro was naked from the waist down and had his hands tied behind his back; as one of the three ambassadors, an older man with a great deal of authority named Fineo, looked at Pietro, he

noticed a large bright red birthmark on his chest, not painted on
but rather implanted naturally upon the skin, the kind women
there would call "roses." When he saw it, he was immediately
reminded of a son of his who, more than fifteen years before,
had been kidnapped by pirates on the coast of Laiazzo and had
never been heard of since. And as he estimated the age of the
poor wretch who was being whipped along, he came to the con-
clusion that if his son was still alive, he would be about the
same age as this fellow appeared to be; and because of the
birthmark, he began to suspect that he was really his own son;
and he thought to himself that if this was so, he should still be
able to remember his own name and that of his father as well as
the Armenian language.

And so, when he came close enough to him, he cried out: "Oh,
Teodoro!"

When Pietro heard his voice, he quickly raised his head, then
speaking in Armenian, Fineo said: "Where do you come from?
Whose son are you?"

Out of respect for this worthy gentleman, the soldiers who
were dragging Pietro along came to a halt so that Pietro could
answer: "I come from Armenia, the son of a man named Fineo,
and I was brought here as a small boy by people I did not
know."

When Fineo heard this, he was certain that this was the son
he had lost, and in tears he ran down with his companions
through the soldiers to embrace Pietro; and taking off his cloak,
which was made of the finest fabric, he threw it over Pietro's
shoulders and requested that the man leading him to execution
please wait there until he received further orders. The man re-
plied that he would gladly do so.

Fineo already knew the reason why Pietro was being led to his
death, for the news had spread all over town; and so he, along
with his companions and their retinue, went straight to Messer
Currado and said to him:

"Sir, the man whom you are sending to his death as a slave is
a free man and my son, and he is prepared to take as his wife
the woman whose virginity he is said to have stolen; therefore,
may it please you to delay his execution long enough to learn if
she would be willing to take him as her husband, so that if she is
indeed willing to do so, you will not find yourself breaking the
law."*

---

*It was customary for a condemned man to be released if some
woman would agree to marry him.

Messer Currado was very surprised to learn that Pietro was Fineo's son, and apologizing for the injustice of Fortune, he admitted that what Fineo was saying had to be true and then quickly convinced him to return to his inn, after which he sent for Messer Amerigo and told him all that had happened. Messer Amerigo, who thought his daughter and grandson were already dead, was the unhappiest man in the world because of what he had done, for he realized that everything could have been set right again if only she were still alive; but nevertheless, he sent someone racing off to the place where his daughter was being held so that just in case his order had not been carried out yet, it could be withdrawn. The man he sent discovered that the servant Messer Amerigo had dispatched earlier, having placed the dagger and the poison in front of the girl, was trying to force her to choose between the two and was abusing her because she was not making up her mind quickly enough; but when he heard his master's order countermanded he left her alone, returned to Messer Amerigo, and reported to him where matters stood. Messer Amerigo, who was happy to hear this, went to the place where Fineo was staying and on the verge of tears, as best he knew how, he begged his forgiveness for what had happened and asked his pardon, declaring that if Teodoro was willing to take his daughter as his wife, he would be more than happy to give her to him.

Fineo gladly accepted his apologies and then said:

"I intend that my son marry your daughter, but if he is not willing to do so, then let the sentence pronounced upon him be carried out."

Fineo and Messer Amerigo, being thus in agreement, went to Pietro, who, while happy over finding his father again, was still afraid of dying, and they asked him what his wishes were in this matter. When Teodoro heard that Violante would be his wife if he so wished, his joy was such that he felt as though he had leaped from Hell into Paradise, and he said that he would consider it the greatest of favors, if both of them looked favorably upon it. Then they sent word to the girl to learn of her wishes, and when she heard what had happened to Teodoro and what was now about to happen to him, Violante, once the saddest woman in the world who expected nothing but death, after a while, putting trust in the messenger's words, began to take heart. She replied that if she followed her own desires in this matter, nothing would make her happier than to be Teodoro's wife, but that she nevertheless would do whatever her father ordered. And so by mutual agreement the girl's betrothal was announced and celebrated with a great feast to the immense pleasure of all the townspeople.

After giving her small son to a wet nurse, she began recuperating, and before long the girl appeared more beautiful than ever; no longer confined to her bed, she presented herself to Fineo, whose return from Rome had been expected, and she paid him all the respect due to a father. And Fineo, most delighted at having such a beautiful daughter-in-law, saw to it that their marriage was celebrated with the greatest of festivity and feasting, and he accepted her as if she were his own daughter, and always considered her as such from that time on. A few days afterward, Fineo embarked on a galley with his son, the lady, and his little grandson, and took them with him to Laiazzo, where the two lovers remained in peace and tranquillity for as long as they lived.

[Fifth Day, Eighth Story]

💮

Nastagio degli Onesti, in love with a girl from the Traversari family, squanders all his wealth without being loved in return; his relatives beg him to leave for Chiassi; there he sees a knight hunting down a young lady, who is killed and devoured by two dogs; he invites his relatives and the lady he loves to dine with him, and when she sees this same young lady torn to pieces, fearing a similar fate, she takes Nastagio as her husband.

WHEN Lauretta fell silent, at the Queen's command Filomena began as follows:

Charming ladies, just as our compassion is praised, so, too, is our cruelty punished severely by divine justice. In order to prove this to you and to give you reason to drive all such cruelty completely from your hearts, I would like to tell you a story which is no less moving than it is entertaining.

In Ravenna, that most ancient city of Romagna, there once lived many a noble gentleman, among whom was a young man named Nastagio degli Onesti, who was left rich beyond all measure by the deaths of his father and one of his uncles. And as often happens to young men who have no wife, he fell in love with one of the daughters of a certain Paolo Traversaro, a girl of a far nobler family than his own, but whose love he hoped to win by means of his accomplishments. But no matter how magnificent, splendid, and praiseworthy these were, they not only did him little good but, on the contrary, they seemed to do him harm—so cruel, harsh, and unfriendly did the young girl he loved act toward him; perhaps because of her singular beauty or perhaps because of her exalted rank, she became so haughty and disdainful that she disliked everything about him and anything he liked. Such behavior was so difficult for Nastagio to bear that he often considered, after grieving much over it, taking his own life in despair; but yet he held back, at times deciding to give her up altogether or to learn to hate her just as she hated him. But such resolutions were taken in vain, for it appeared that the less hope of success he enjoyed, the more his love increased.

And so then, as the young man persisted in loving and in spending lavishly, there were certain friends and relatives of his who thought that he was on the brink of wasting away both himself and his fortune; and so they would often beg and advise him to leave Ravenna and to stay for a while in some other place, for in doing this, both his passion and his expenses might be diminished. Nastagio consistently made fun of their advice, but they begged him so insistently that he was no longer able to refuse, and so he agreed to do as they said; and having made great preparations, as if he were going to France or Spain or some other faraway land, he climbed upon his horse, and accompanied by his many friends, left the city and went about three miles outside Ravenna to a place called Chiassi, where he had his pavilions and tents set up, informing those who had ridden with him that he wished to stop there and that they were free to return to Ravenna. So then Nastagio, having established himself there, began to lead the finest and most elegant life that anyone could possibly lead, inviting different groups of friends to dine or lunch with him, as was his custom.

Now it happened to be around the beginning of May and the weather was beautiful when Nastagio began to brood over his cruel lady, and having ordered all his servants to leave him alone so that he could think about her at his pleasure, step by step, lost in his thoughts, he wandered into the pine woods. And it was already past the fifth hour of the day* when, having walked at least half a mile into the pine forest, not mindful of eating or anything else, he suddenly seemed to hear a terrible cry and the most horrible shrieks of a woman; his sweet train of thoughts being thus interrupted, he raised his head to see what it

*This is, between 11:00 A.M. and noon.

was and discovered to his astonishment that he was in a pine forest. Moreover, as he looked straight in front of him, he saw a very beautiful girl, naked, her hair all disheveled, her flesh torn by the briars and thorns, running toward him through a wood thick with bushes and briars, weeping and crying out for mercy; then he saw running behind her two huge and ferocious mastiffs that every so often would catch up with her and bite her savagely; and even farther behind her, he could see a dark-looking knight, his face flushed with anger, riding a black steed and holding a sword in his hand, threatening her with death in horrible and abusive language.

This sight filled his soul with both wonder and fear as well as with compassion for the unfortunate woman, and from his compassion was born a desire to save her, if he could, from such anguish and threat of death. On finding himself without weapons, he used the branch of a tree as a club and prepared to confront the dogs and the knight.

But when the knight saw this, he shouted to him from a distance:

"Nastagio, don't interfere; leave it to me and these dogs to give this wicked female what she deserves!"

No sooner had he said this than the dogs seized the girl firmly by her thighs and stopped her, and the knight, reaching that spot, dismounted from his horse, as Nastagio went up to him and said:

"I do not know who you are or how you happen to know me, but let me tell you how base an act it is for an armed knight to try to kill a naked woman and to set dogs upon her as if she were a savage beast. I certainly shall defend her to the best of my ability."

The knight then said:

"Nastagio, I was from the same town as you, and you were still a small child when I, Messer Guido degli Anastagi, fell too passionately in love with this woman, far more so than you are with this Traversari girl of yours; her arrogance and cruelty led me to such a wretched state that one day with this very sword you see in my hand, I killed myself out of desperation, and I am now condemned to eternal punishment. Nor was it long afterward that this woman, who rejoiced at my death beyond all measure, also died, and for the sin of her cruelty and for the delight she took in my sufferings, unrepentant as she was and convinced that she deserved to be rewarded rather than punished for them, she, too, was and continues to be condemned to the pains of Hell. When she descended into Hell, both of us received a punishment: she was to flee from me and I, who had loved her so much, was to pursue her as if she were my mortal enemy and not the woman I loved; and every time I catch up to her, with this sword, the one I used to kill myself, I kill and split her back open, and that hard and cold heart, into which neither love nor compassion ever entered, I tear from her body along with her other entrails, as you will see presently, and give them to these dogs to devour. Then, after a short space of time as decreed by the justice and power of God, she is resurrected, as if she had never been dead, and she begins her painful flight all over again, with the dogs and me pursuing her. And every Friday around this time I catch up with her at this spot, and here I slaughter her as you are about to witness; but do not think that we rest on other days, for I catch up with her then in other places where she thought or acted cruelly toward me; and having changed from her lover to her enemy, as you see, in this role I must pursue her for as many years as the number of months she was cruel to me. Now, allow me to carry out the sentence of divine justice and do not try to oppose what you are helpless to prevent."

When Nastagio heard these words, he became quite frightened, and there was not a hair on his head which was not standing on end, and stepping back, he watched the wretched girl and waited in fear to see what the knight would do to her; when the knight finished speaking, with sword in hand, like a mad dog, he pounced on the girl, who was kneeling and screaming for mercy as the two mastiffs held her tightly, and with all his might, he stabbed her in the middle of her breast, the blade passing through to the other side. When the girl received this blow, she fell to the ground, still weeping and screaming, and the knight, having laid hold of a dagger, slit open her back, ripped out her heart and everything else around it, and threw it all to the two mastiffs, who, ravenous with hunger, devoured it instantly. Nor was it long before the girl, almost as if nothing had happened, suddenly rose to her feet and began to run off in the direction of the sea with the dogs still tearing at her flesh; and the knight, having remounted his horse and taken up his sword again, also began to chase her, and in a short time, they were so far away that Nastagio could no longer see them.

After witnessing these events, Nastagio remained in that spot for a long while, caught up in his feelings of compassion and fear, but after a while it occurred to him that this spectacle, since it took place every Friday, might well be useful to him; and so, after marking the spot, he returned to his servants, and then, when the time seemed right, he sent for a number of his relatives and friends and said to them:

"For a long time now, you have been trying to persuade me to stop loving this hostile lady of mine and to put an end to my spending, and this I am prepared to do on condition that you do one favor for me, which is this: that on this coming Friday, you arrange for Messer Paolo Traversari, his wife and daughter, and all their womenfolk, as well as anyone else you wish, to dine in this spot with me. Why I wish to do this, you will see when the time comes."

They all felt that this was not much to ask of them, and returning to Ravenna, at the appropriate time, they invited the people Nastagio requested, and although it was not at all easy to convince the girl Nastagio loved to go with them, she nevertheless went along with the other ladies. Nastagio arranged for a magnificent banquet to be prepared, and he had all the tables placed under the pine trees near the spot where he had seen the slaughter of the cruel lady; and in seating the men and the ladies at the table, he organized things in such a way that the girl he loved was placed directly in front of the place where the event was to occur.

And so it was that just after the last course was served, everyone began to hear the desperate cries of the girl who was being pursued. Everyone was very astonished and asked what it was, but since nobody seemed to know, they all got up to see what was happening for themselves, and they caught sight of the suffering girl, the knight, and the dogs; and in a matter of no time at all, they found them in their very midst.

They began screaming loudly at the dogs and the knight, and many of them stepped forward to help the girl, but the knight, speaking to them just as he had spoken to Nastagio, not only forced them to draw back but filled them with terror and amazement; and after he had done to the girl what he had done the other time, all of the ladies present (many of whom were relatives either of the suffering girl or of the knight and who remembered his love affair and his death) began to weep piteously, as if what they had witnessed had actually been inflicted upon themselves. When the scene came to an end and the lady and the knight had vanished, they all began to discuss what they had observed, with many different interpretations. But among those who were the most terrified was the cruel girl Nastagio loved, for she had clearly seen and heard every detail and realized that these things concerned her far more than anyone else who was present, inasmuch as she recalled the cruelty she had always inflicted upon Nastagio; as a result, she already felt herself fleeing from his rage and the mastiffs lunging at her sides.

So great was the terror aroused in the lady by this spectacle that in order to avoid a similar fate herself, she changed her hatred into love, and as soon as the proper occasion presented itself (which was that very evening), in secret she sent one of her trusted maidservants to Nastagio, begging him on her behalf to be so kind as to come to her, for she was now prepared to do everything he wished. To this request, Nastagio sent a reply saying that this was most gratifying but that he preferred to take his pleasure, preserving her honor; that is, to take her as his wife in marriage, if she would agree. The girl, who knew she alone was to blame for the fact that she and Nastagio were not already married, sent him a message that she would be delighted. And so, acting as her own intermediary, she told her father and mother that she would be happy to become Nastagio's bride, which pleased them immensely.

And so on the following Sunday, Nastagio married her, and having celebrated their nuptials, they lived happily together for a long time to come. Nor was this the only good that came from this terrible apparition, for all the ladies of Ravenna became so frightened that from then on they became a good deal more amenable to men's pleasure than they ever had been in the past.

[Fifth Day, Ninth Story]

❧

Federigo degli Alberighi, who loves but is not loved in return, spends all the money he has in courtship and is left with only a falcon, which, since he has nothing else to give her, he offers to his lady to eat when she visits his home; then she, learning of this, changes her mind, takes him for her husband, and makes him rich.

FILOMENA had already finished speaking, and when the Queen saw there was no one left to speak except for Dioneo, who was exempted because of his special privilege, she herself with a cheerful face said:

It is now my turn to tell a story and, dearest ladies, I shall do so most willingly with a tale similar in some respects to the preceding one, its purpose being not only to show you how much power your beauty has over the gentle heart, but also so that you yourselves may learn, whenever it is fitting, to be the donors of your favors instead of always leaving this act to the whim of Fortune, who, as it happens, on most occasions bestows such favors with more abundance than discretion.

You should know, then, that Coppo di Borghese Domenichi, who once lived in our city and perhaps still does, a man of great and respected authority in our times, one most illustrious and worthy of eternal fame both for his way of life and his ability much more than for the nobility of his blood, often took delight, when he was an old man, in discussing things from the past with his neighbors and with others. He knew how to do this well, for he was more logical and had a better memory and a more eloquent style of speaking than any other man. Among the many beautiful tales he told, there was one he would often tell about a young man who once lived in Florence named Federigo, the son of Messer Filippo Alberighi, renowned above all other men in Tuscany for his prowess in arms and for his courtliness.

As often happens to most men of gentle breeding, he fell in love, with a noble lady named Monna Giovanna, in her day considered to be one of the most beautiful and most charming ladies that ever there was in Florence; and in order to win her love, he participated in jousts and tournaments, organized and gave banquets, spending his money without restraint; but she, no less virtuous than beautiful, cared little for these things he did on her behalf, nor did she care for the one who did them. Now, as Federigo was spending far beyond his means and getting nowhere, as can easily happen, he lost his wealth and was reduced to poverty, and was left with nothing to his name but his little farm (from whose revenues he lived very meagerly) and one falcon, which was among the finest of its kind in the world.

More in love than ever, but knowing that he would never be able to live the way he wished to in the city, he went to live at Campi, where his farm was. There he passed his time hawking whenever he could, imposing on no one, and enduring his poverty patiently. Now one day, during the time that Federigo was reduced to these extremes, it happened that the husband of Monna Giovanna fell ill, and realizing death was near, he made his last will: he was very rich, and he left everything to his son, who was just growing up, and since he had also loved Monna Giovanna very much, he made her his heir should his son die without any legitimate children; and then he died.

Monna Giovanna was now a widow, and every summer, as our women usually do, she would go to the country with her son to one of their estates very close by to Federigo's farm. Now this young boy of hers happened to become more and more friendly with Federigo and he began to enjoy birds and dogs; and after seeing Federigo's falcon fly many times, it made him so happy that he very much wished it were his own, but he did not dare to ask for it, for he could see how precious it was to Federigo. During this time, it happened that the young boy took ill, and his mother was much grieved, for he was her only child and she loved him dearly; she would spend the entire day by his side, never ceasing to comfort him, asking him time and again if there was anything he wished, begging him to tell her what it might be, for if it was possible to obtain it, she would certainly do everything in her power to get it. After the young boy had heard her make this offer many times, he said:

"Mother, if you can arrange for me to have Federigo's falcon, I think I would get well quickly."

When the lady heard this, she was taken aback for a moment, and then she began thinking what she could do about it. She knew that Federigo had been in love with her for some time now, but she had never deigned to give him a second look; so, she said to herself:

"How can I go to him, or even send someone, and ask for this falcon of his, which is, as I have heard tell, the finest that ever flew, and furthermore, his only means of support? And how can I be so insensitive as to wish to take away from this nobleman the only pleasure which is left to him?"

And involved in these thoughts, knowing that she was certain to have the bird if she asked for it, but not knowing what to say to her son, she stood there without answering him. Finally the love she bore her son persuaded her that she should make him happy, and no matter what the consequences might be, she would not send for the bird, but rather go herself to fetch it and bring it back to him; so she answered her son:

"My son, cheer up and think only of getting well, for I promise you that first thing tomorrow morning I shall go and fetch it for you."

The child was so happy that he showed some improvement that very day. The following morning, the lady, accompanied by another woman, as if they were out for a stroll, went to Federigo's modest little house and asked for him. Since the weather for the past few days had not been right for hawking, Federigo happened to be in his orchard attending to certain tasks, and when he heard that Monna Giovanna was asking for him at the door, he was so surprised and happy that he rushed there; as she saw him coming, she rose to greet him with womanly grace, and once Federigo had welcomed her most courteously, she said:

"How do you do, Federigo?" Then she continued, "I have come to make amends for the harm you have suffered on my account by loving me more than you should have, and in token of this, I intend to have a simple meal with you and this companion of mine this very day."

To this Federigo humbly replied: "Madonna, I have no recollection of ever suffering any harm because of you; on the contrary: so much good have I received from you that if ever I was worth anything, it was because of your worth and the love I bore for you; and your generous visit is certainly so very dear to me that I would spend all over again all that I spent in the past, but you have come to a poor host."

And having said this, he humbly led her through the house and into his garden, and because he had no one there to keep her company, he said:

"My lady, since there is no one else, this good woman, who is the wife of the farmer here, will keep you company while I see to the table."

Though he was very poor, Federigo until now had never realized to what extent he had wasted his wealth; but this morning, the fact that he had nothing in the house with which he could honor the lady for the love of whom he had in the past entertained countless people, gave him cause to reflect: in great anguish, he cursed himself and his fortune, and like someone out of his senses he started running here and there throughout the house, but unable to find either money or anything he might be able to pawn, and since it was getting late and he was still very much set on serving this noble lady some sort of meal, but unwilling to turn for help to even his own farmer (not to mention anyone else), he set his eyes upon his good falcon, which was sitting on its perch in a small room, and since he had nowhere else to turn, he took the bird, and finding it plump, he decided that it would be a worthy food for such a lady. So, without giving the matter a second thought, he wrung its neck and quickly gave it to his servant girl to pluck, prepare, and place on a spit to be roasted with care; and when he had set the table with the whitest of tablecloths (a few of which he still had left), he returned, with a cheerful face, to the lady in his garden and announced that the meal, such as he was able to prepare, was ready.

The lady and her companion rose and went to the table together with Federigo, who waited upon them with the greatest devotion, and they ate the good falcon without knowing what it was they were eating. Then, having left the table and spent some time in pleasant conversation, the lady thought it time now to say what she had come to say, and so she spoke these kind words to Federigo:

"Federigo, if you recall your former way of life and my virtue, which you perhaps mistook for harshness and cruelty, I have no doubt at all that you will be amazed by my presumption when you hear what my main reason for coming here is; but if you had children, through whom you might have experienced the power of parental love, I feel certain that you would, at least in part, forgive me. But, just as you have no child, I do have one, and I cannot escape the laws common to all mothers; the force of such laws compels me to follow them, against my own will and against good manners and duty, and to ask of you a gift which I know is most precious to you; and it is naturally so, since your extreme condition has left you no other delight, no other pleasure, no other consolation; and this gift is your falcon, which my son is so taken by that if I do not bring it to him, I fear his sickness will grow so much worse that I may lose him. And therefore I beg you, not because of the love that you bear for me, which does not oblige you in the least, but because of your own nobleness, which you have shown to be greater than that of all others in practicing courtliness, that you be pleased to give it to me, so that I may say that I have saved the life of my son by means of this gift, and because of it I have placed him in your debt forever."

When he heard what the lady requested and knew that he could not oblige her because he had given her the falcon to eat, Federigo began to weep in her presence, for he could not utter a word in reply. The lady at first thought his tears were caused more by the sorrow of having to part with the good falcon than by anything else, and she was on the verge of telling him she no longer wished it, but she held back and waited for Federigo's reply once he stopped weeping. And he said:

"My lady, ever since it pleased God for me to place my love in you, I have felt that Fortune has been hostile to me in many ways, and I have complained of her, but all this is nothing compared to what she has just done to me, and I shall never be at peace with her again, when I think how you have come here to my poor home, where, when it was rich, you never deigned to come, and how you requested but a small gift, and Fortune worked to make it impossible for me to give it to you; and why this is so I shall tell you in a few words. When I heard that you, out of your kindness, wished to dine with me, I considered it only fitting and proper, taking into account your excellence and your worthiness, that I should honor you, according to my possibilities, with a more precious food than that which I usually serve to other people. So I thought of the falcon for which you have just asked me and of its value and I judged it a food worthy of you, and this very day I had it roasted and served to you as best I could. But seeing now that you desired it another way, my sorrow in not being able to serve you is so great that never shall I be able to console myself again."

And after he had said this, he laid the feathers, the feet, and the beak of the bird before her as proof. When the lady heard and saw this, she first reproached him for having killed a falcon such as this to serve as a meal to a woman. But then to herself she commended the greatness of his spirit, which no poverty was able, or would be able, to diminish; then, having lost all hope of getting the falcon and thus, perhaps, of improving the health of her son, she thanked Federigo both for the honor paid to her and for his good intentions, and then left in grief to return to her son. To his mother's extreme sorrow, whether in disappointment in not having the falcon or because his illness inevitably led to it, the boy passed from this life only a few days later.

After the period of her mourning and her bitterness had passed, the lady was repeatedly urged by her brothers to remarry, since she was very rich and still young; and although she did not wish to do so, they became so insistent that remembering the worthiness of Federigo and his last act of generosity—that is, to have killed such a falcon to do her honor—she said to her brothers:

"I would prefer to remain a widow, if only that would be pleasing to you, but since you wish me to take a husband, you may be sure that I shall take no man other than Federigo degli Alberighi."

In answer to this, her brothers, making fun of her, replied:

"You foolish woman, what are you saying? How can you want him? He hasn't a penny to his name."

To this she replied: "My brothers, I am well aware of what you say, but I would much rather have a man who lacks money than money that lacks a man."

Her brothers, seeing that she was determined and knowing Federigo to be of noble birth, no matter how poor he was, accepted her wishes and gave her with all her riches in marriage to him; when he found himself the husband of such a great lady, whom he had loved so much and who was so wealthy besides, he managed his finanicial affairs with more prudence than in the past and lived with her happily the rest of his days.

[Fifth Day, Tenth Story]

❦

Pietro di Vinciolo goes out to eat supper; his wife has a young man in, and when Pietro returns, she hides him under a chicken coop; Pietro says that a young man was discovered in Ercolano's home, where he was eating supper, having been hidden there by Ercolano's wife; Pietro's wife criticizes Ercolano's wife severely; unfortunately, a donkey steps on the fingers of the young man hidden beneath the coop, and he cries out; Pietro runs there, sees him, realizes his wife's deception, but finally reaches an arrangement with her in accordance with his own depravity.

WHEN the Queen's story had come to its conclusion and everyone had praised God for having given Federigo his just reward, Dioneo, who was never in the habit of waiting for orders, began:

I do not know whether it is an accidental failing, originating from our own debased customs, or whether it is, instead, a result of an innate failing in us, but the fact is that we are more likely to laugh over bad things than over virtuous deeds, especially when we ourselves are not directly involved. And since the task which I have undertaken on previous occasions and which I am about to take up again now has no other goal than to drive away your melancholy and provide you with laughter and joy, although, loving ladies, the subject matter of the story I am about to tell you may be somewhat less than virtuous, since it may amuse you, I shall tell it to you. And as you listen to it, you should do with it what you are accustomed to do when you enter a garden and stretch out your delicate hands to pluck the roses but leave the thorns where they are: you may do this by leaving the wicked man to his misfortune and dishonorable behavior, while you laugh merrily at the amorous deceptions of his wife and, whenever the occasion warrants, feel sorry for the misfortunes of others.

There was in Perugia, not so very long ago, a rich man named Pietro di Vinciolo who took a wife, perhaps to fool others and to alter the general opinion all the Perugians held about him rather than out of any real desire on his part; and Fortune so conformed to his desire that the wife he took was a robust young woman with red hair and complexion, who would have preferred to have a pair of husbands rather than just one, whereas she now found herself with a husband who was more interested in other men than in her.

When in the course of time she came to understand this, realizing that she was so fresh and pretty, and since she felt so healthy and lusty, at first she was very upset about this and would quarrel with her husband from time to time, leading a rather miserable life; but then, as soon as she realized that by doing this she was going to ruin her health rather than mend her husband's ways, she said to herself:

"This sorry man abandons me to go up the dry path in clogs, but I shall see about taking someone else aboard ship for the wet.* I took him as my husband and brought him a big, fat dowry, thinking he was a man and believing he was fond of what men are and should be fond of, and if I had any idea that he was not a man, I would never have married him. He knew I was a woman, so why did he marry me if women were not to his liking? I won't put up with it! If I had not wanted to live in the world, I would have become a nun; but since I chose to live in it, here I am, but if I have to wait for thrills and joy from him, I'll probably still be waiting when I'm an old woman; and in my old age, what good will it do me then if I have to look back and complain about wasting my youth, which my husband, fine teacher that he is, has shown me how to enjoy by enjoying what he himself is enjoying now? Such enjoyment is commendable in me, whereas in him it is most blameworthy, for I would only be breaking the law, but he breaks both that law and the law of Nature as well."

And so, the good woman, having come to such a conclusion and having thought it over on more than one occasion, with the idea of putting her plan into effect secretly, made friends with an old woman who seemed more saintly than Saint Verdiana feeding the serpents and who constantly went about with her rosary beads in her hand, attending every general indulgence service and talking about nothing but the lives of the Holy Church Fathers and the stigmata of Saint Francis, so that everyone took her to be a saint. And when the time seemed right, the wife re-

---

*Two equivocal expressions referring respectively to unnatural love ("the dry path") and natural love ("the wet").

vealed her intentions to her in great detail, to which the old woman said:

"My child, God knows, for He knows everything, that you are acting for the best; and if you did it for no other reason, you and every other young woman should do it in order not to waste the opportunities your youth affords you, for to a person who has experienced it, there is no pain equal to that of knowing you have wasted time. And what the devil are we women good for when we are old anyway, only to sit around the fire and stare at the ashes? If there is a woman who can testify to this, I am certainly that one: now that I am old, not without the greatest and most bitter pain in my heart (but all to no avail) I realize how many opportunities I allowed to slip past me—though I assure you I didn't waste them all (I wouldn't want you to think I was that foolish!)—yet, when I think of the things I could have done and see myself reduced to the state in which you see me now, where no one would ever deign to give me so much as a light, only God knows the agony I feel. It's not the same with men: they are born fit to do a thousand things, not just this one, and the majority of them are better at it when they're old than when they're young; but women are not good for anything but doing that one thing and giving birth to children, and for this reason we are held so dear. And if you are not convinced by anything else, this ought to persuade you, and that is that a woman is always ready to do it, but the same is not true with men; what's more, a woman can wear out a number of men, while a number of men cannot wear out one woman. And since we're born to do it, let me tell you once more that you are right to give your husband tit for tat, for at least in your old age your heart will have no reason to reproach your flesh. In this world, you've got to grab what you can get, and especially a woman, who needs, even more than men, to take advantage of every opportunity that presents itself. For as you can see, when we get old, no husband or anyone else cares to look at us; on the contrary, we are chased into the kitchen to tell stories to the cat or to count the pots and pans—and even worse, they write songs about us like: 'When they're young, give 'em plenty, when they're old, leave 'em empty'; and many others in the same vein. But not to keep you any longer with my talk, let me assure you that there is no one in the world you could have revealed your thoughts to who could be more helpful to you than I, for there is no man refined enough to stop me from telling him what he needs, nor is there a man so uncouth and uncultivated that I cannot easily soften him up and bring him around to my way of

thinking. Just show me the man you want, and then leave every-
thing up to me; but let me remind you of one thing, my child: I
am a poor woman who needs looking after, and from now on I
want you to have a share in all my indulgences and in as many
Our Fathers as I recite, so that God may look kindly upon your
dearly departed." And with this she stopped speaking.

And so the young woman came to an agreement with the old
woman that if she came across a certain young man who quite
often passed through that part of the city, and she described him
in full to her, the old woman would know what to do; and hav-
ing given her a piece of salted meat, she sent her on her way
with God's blessing. After not too many days had passed, the old
woman secretly saw to it that the man she had told her about
got into her bedroom, and later, from time to time, she provided
whatever types the young woman fancied; and though she lived
in constant fear of her husband, she never lost an opportunity to
do what she could.

And then one evening it happened that while her husband was
out to supper with a friend of his whose name was Ercolano, the
young woman commissioned the old woman to bring her one of
the most handsome and most agreeable young lads in Perugia;
this she immediately did. But no sooner did the lady sit down to
supper with the young lad than there was Pietro shouting from
the entrance for her to open the door. When the lady heard him,
she thought she was as good as dead; but all the same, if pos-
sible, she wanted to conceal the young man, but not having
enough sense to make him hide somewhere else in the house, she
had him crawl under a chicken coop which was in a shed near
the room in which they were eating, and then over the coop she
threw a piece of sackcloth she had emptied that day; and after
she had done this, she quickly went to open the door for her hus-
band.

As soon as he entered the house, she said: "You sure did gulp
down that supper of yours in a hurry."

Pietro answered: "We didn't even taste it."

"How's that?" the lady asked.

Pietro then replied:

"I'll tell you. While we were sitting around the table—that is,
Ercolano, his wife, and I—we heard the sound of a sneeze
nearby, which none of us paid any attention to the first or sec-
ond time; but when the person who sneezed did so a third,
fourth, and fifth time, and even more besides, we were all some-
what amazed, to say the least; and so Ercolano, who was rather
upset with his wife for having made us wait so long at the door

before opening it, said in a fury: 'What's going on here? Who is it sneezing like that?' And getting up from the table, he went over to the stairs close by, under which there was near the foot of the stairs an enclosure made from planks usually used to store things when people tidy up their house. And since Ercolano seemed to feel that the sound of the sneezing was coming from inside this cupboard, he opened a small door which was in it, and when he did, the worst stink of sulphur you can imagine came pouring out, the smell of which he happened to notice earlier and which, when he had complained of it, the woman had said: 'That's because I was bleaching my veils earlier in the day with sulphur, and sprinkled it in a wide bowl so that they would soak up the fumes better and put it under the stairs, and it still seems to be giving off an odor.' Once Ercolano opened the door and the stink dissipated a bit, looking inside he saw the man who had sneezed and was still sneezing from the strength of the sulphur; and no matter how much he sneezed, the sulphur had already choked his chest to such an extent that had he stayed there much longer, never again would he have sneezed or done anything else for that matter. When Ercolano saw him, he shouted: 'Woman, now I see why when we arrived earlier, we were kept waiting so long outside before you opened the door for us; but I'll pay you back for this if it's the last thing I do!' On hearing this his wife, realizing now that her sin had been discovered, got up from the table, and without trying to make excuses she fled, and I have no idea of where she went. Ercolano, not noticing that his wife had run away, repeatedly ordered the man who was sneezing to come out; but the man did not have the strength to do so, and in spite of what Ercolano said he did not move; whereupon Ercolano took him by one of his legs and pulled him out, and then ran to grab a knife to kill him. But fearing for my own neck should the police get involved, I jumped up and prevented Ercolano from murdering the man or doing him any harm; in fact, it was my shouting and defending him that brought the neighbors on the scene, who, in turn, took the already unconscious young man and carried him someplace outside the house; so all this made for a somewhat turbulent supper, and so, as I said before, not only did I not gulp it down, I didn't even taste it."

When his wife heard this story, she realized that there were other women as clever as she, even though some of their schemes did on occasion meet with misfortune, and she would have gladly spoken out in defense of Ercolano's wife, had she not thought that criticizing the faults of others would make it easier to cover her own, so she said:

"Now aren't these some fine goings-on! Well now, there's a good and holy woman for you! There's the faith of an honest woman, and I was ready to confess my sins to her, she always seemed so saintly to me. And what's worse is that at her age, she should be giving a good example to younger women! Damn the hour that she was born into this world, and damn her as well for carrying on this way, allowing herself to live, deceitful wicked female that she is, the universal shame and disgrace of every woman in this city. Not only has she cast aside her virtue, the fidelity she promised her husband, her good name in society, and all this for another man, but she hasn't even a sense of shame for bringing disgrace upon herself and her husband too, and he is such a good man, such an honorable citizen, and he always treated her with such kindness. So help me God, women like this should be shown no mercy; such women deserve to be killed, to be burned alive and reduced to ashes!"

But then, remembering that her lover was hidden under the chicken coop just in the next room, she began urging Pietro to go to bed, telling him that it was getting late. But Pietro wanted to eat more than to sleep, and so he asked if there was anything left for supper, to which his wife replied:

"If there's anything left for supper? So now we are cooking supper for you when you're not even home to eat it? Sure, I'm just like Ercolano's wife, I am! Look, why don't you just go to bed for tonight? You'll be a lot better off."

Now earlier in the evening, a number of Pietro's workers had happened to be delivering certain things to him from the country, and they tied up their donkeys, without giving them anything to drink, in a little stable beside the shed, and one of these donkeys, who had the most terrible thirst, broke its tether, left the stable, and was wandering about, sniffing to see if it could find some water, and as it happened to be wandering around, the ass stumbled up against the chicken coop under which the young man was hiding. Since the young man was forced to remain on all fours, the fingers of one of his hands resting on the ground were sticking out from underneath the chicken coop, and as his luck would have it (we should really say bad luck), this donkey with one of its hooves stepped on his fingers. In his excruciating pain, the man let out a loud scream.

Pietro, when he heard this, was astonished, for he realized that it had come from inside the house; and so, rushing from the room, the young man's screaming still ringing in his ears, for the donkey had as yet not raised its hoof from his fingers but was still pressing down firmly on them, Pietro shouted: "Who's there?" And when he ran over to the chicken coop and lifted it up, he saw the young man, who, besides the pain he was experiencing from having his fingers crushed by the ass's hoof, was trembling for fear that Pietro might do something to hurt him. Pietro recognized the young man, for he was someone Pietro himself had been chasing after for his own wicked ends for some time now, and when Pietro asked him, "What are you doing here?" rather than answer his question, the young man begged Pietro, for the love of God, not to do him any harm.

To this, Pietro answered:

"Get up, don't worry, I won't hurt you; just tell me how you happen to be here and why."

The young man told him everything; Pietro, no less delighted over discovering him there than his wife was upset, took him by the hand and led him into the room, where his wife awaited him with all the fear in the world.

Sitting down directly in front of her, Pietro said:

"Just a moment ago when you were carrying on, cursing Ercolano's wife in such a fashion and saying that she should be burned and that she was the disgrace of all you women, why didn't you say the same about yourself? If you wanted to keep yourself out of it, how did you have the nerve to talk about her, when you had done the same thing she did? Certainly nothing made you do it other than the fact that all you women are alike, and you like to cover up your own transgressions with the faults of others. I just wish a fire would descend from Heaven and burn the whole disgusting lot of you up!"

Realizing from the moment he opened his mouth that Pietro was going to inflict nothing worse than words upon her, and seeing how delighted he was to hold such a handsome young man by the hand, the woman took heart and said:

"I'm sure you'd like fire to descend from Heaven and burn us all up, for you are about as fond of women as a dog is of a whipping; but by God's Holy Cross, you won't see it happen! But let's discuss this thing a bit, because I'd like to know what it is you have to complain about. It's all well and good for you to compare me to Ercolano's wife, but at least that old holier-than-thou hypocrite gets what she wants from her husband, and he holds her as dear as a wife should be, which doesn't happen to me. Sure, I'll admit that you clothe me decently and provide me with shoes, but you know very well how I fare in something else and how long it's been since you last slept with me; I'd

rather go around barefoot dressed in rags and get the proper
treatment in bed than have all those clothes and be treated the
way you treat me. Understand me very well, Pietro, I'm a
woman like any other woman and I want what they want, and if
I don't get it from you, you can't blame me for chasing after it
elsewhere. At least I do you the honor of not getting involved
with stableboys and scrubby types."

Pietro realized that she could go on talking like this for the
rest of the night, and since he was not much interested in her
anyway, he answered:

"Now that's enough, woman: I'll see to it that you're satisfied
in this matter. Be so kind as to make something for us to eat,
since it appears that this young man, like myself, has not yet
eaten supper."

"Of course he hasn't eaten supper yet," said the woman, "we
were about to sit down at the table to eat when you had to come
home!"

"Go on now and see that we get something to eat," said Pie-
tro, "and then I will see to it matters are arranged in such a
way that you won't have anything to complain about."

The lady got up, and seeing her husband so contented, she
quickly set the table again and brought in the supper she had
prepared, and she, the young man, and her wicked husband had
a merry meal all together.

What exactly Pietro had thought up to satisfy all three of
them after supper now slips my mind; but I do know this much,
though: on the following morning when the young man was re-
turned to the main square, he found himself not quite sure about
which one he had been with more that night, the husband or the
wife. And so my advice to you, my dear ladies, is that whoever
sticks it to you, stick 'em back, and if you can't, keep it in mind
until you can; this way whatever the ass gives in butting a wall,
he gets back in return.

[Fifth Day, Conclusion]

❧

DIONEO's story thus ended, and if the ladies' laughter seemed re-
strained, it was more out of modesty than lack of amusement,
and the Queen, realizing that her reign had come to an end, rose

to her feet, and removing the laurel crown from her head, she placed it gracefully on Elissa's head, saying to her:

"Now, my lady, it is your turn to rule."

Accepting the honor, Elissa did as those before her had done by first giving orders to the steward concerning what was needed during her reign, and then, to the satisfaction of the group, she said:

"We have already frequently heard how many people, by means of clever remarks, ready replies, or with quick wits, have been able to repel the biting remarks of others with one of their own, or avert impending dangers; and since this is such a good topic and one that may be useful to us, I wish, with God's help, that our stories tomorrow be restricted to these matters; that is, stories about those who, having been provoked by some witty remark, have defended themselves with the same or who, with a ready reply or some other shrewd move, have managed to escape danger, loss, or ridicule."

This suggestion was highly approved of by everyone, and the Queen, having risen to her feet, gave them all her leave until the supper hour. When they saw the Queen arise, the virtuous company of men and women stood up, and according to their usual practice, they all turned to doing what pleased them the most.

But when the singing of the cicadas could no longer be heard, everyone was summoned, and they sat down to supper; they finished it with merry festivity and then all turned to singing and playing music. And no sooner had Emilia, with the Queen's permission, begun a dance than Dioneo was ordered to sing a song. He immediately struck up "Monna Aldruda, lift up your tail, for I bring you good tidings." Whereupon all the ladies began to laugh, especially the Queen, who ordered him to stop and to sing them another.

Dioneo replied:

"My lady, if I had a tambourine, I'd sing you 'Raise your skirts, Monna Lapa,' or 'The grass grows under the olive tree,' or would you like me to sing 'I'm sick from the waves of the ocean's motion'? But I don't have a tambourine, and so you'll have to tell me which of these others you prefer. Would you like 'Come out and be cut down, like a maypole in the country'?"

"No," said the Queen, "sing us another one."

"Well, then," replied Dioneo, "shall I sing you 'Monna Simona, fill up your cask, it isn't the month of October'?"

Laughing, the Queen said:

"Oh no! Please sing us a nice song, we don't want to hear that one."

Dioneo replied:

"No, my lady, do not take offense. Now, which do you prefer? I know more than a thousand of them. Would you like 'This treat of mine cannot be beat,' or 'Not so fast, husband dear,' or 'I bought a cock for one hundred lire'?"

Though all the others were laughing, the Queen now became a bit angry with him and she said:

"Dioneo, stop being funny and sing us a pretty song; if you don't, you'll find out how angry I can get."

When Dioneo heard this, he abandoned his foolishness and promptly began to sing in this fashion:

> Love, the lovely light
> which shines from out my lady's lovely eyes
> has made me both your slave and hers.
>
> The splendor of her lovely eyes
> first kindled your flame in my heart,
> as it transfixed my own;
> And all the greatness of your power
> was shown to me through her sweet face,
> which when I have it in my mind,
> I feel myself bringing together
> every virtue, yielding them to her,
> which is new reason for my sighs.
>
> Thus, one among your followers
> I have become, dear lord, and in obedience
> I await the mercy of your power;
> but yet I do not know if my high hope,
> which you have set within my breast,
> or my unbroken faith,
> is fully known to her,
> who so possesses all my mind, that I would not have,
> nor would I want, any other happiness.
>
> And so I pray you, gentle lord of mine,
> to show her this, and make her feel
> something of your fire
> in grace to me, for you can see that I
> already waste away in love, and in its torments
> bit by bit wither;
> then, when the time is ripe,

commend me to her as you should—
how gladly would I come to do it with you!

When Dioneo by his silence showed that his song had come to an end, the Queen, after praising it most highly, ordered many others to be sung. But after a good part of the night had passed, the Queen, feeling the heat of the day had by now been quenched by the cool of the evening, bade them all go and sleep as long as they wished till the following day.

[Sixth Day, Title Page]

✠

Thus ends the fifth day of The Decameron, *and the sixth begins, in which, under the rule of Elissa, stories are told about those who, having been provoked by some witty remark, have defended themselves with the same, or who, with a ready reply or some other shrewd move, have managed to escape danger, loss, or ridicule.*

[Sixth Day, Introduction]

✠

THE moon, set in the center of the heavens, had lost its radiance, and every part of our hemisphere was already lighting up with the fresh light of dawn, when the Queen arose and called her company together, and leaving their fair abode behind, slowly strolling over the dew, they talked about different things, discussing the relative merits of the stories they had told and, at the same time, laughing again over the various situations recounted therein, until, with the sun rising higher and the air getting warmer, everyone agreed that it was time to return home; and so, turning around, they went back to the house. And there they found that the tables had already been set and sweet-smelling herbs and lovely flowers had been scattered all about, and at the Queen's command, they all sat down to eat before the heat of the day grew stronger. After a happy lunch together, before doing anything else, they sang some gay and lively songs, and then some went to rest while others played chess or dice games; and

Dioneo, accompanied by Lauretta, began to sing a song about Troilus and Cressida.

And when the time came for them to reassemble, the Queen called them all together, and they sat down around the fountain as was their custom; and the Queen was just about to call for the first story to begin, when something happened which had never happened before, namely that the Queen and everyone else heard a great commotion coming from the kitchen among the maids and menservants. Whereupon the steward was summoned, and when he was asked who was screaming and what the noise was all about, he replied that there was a quarrel between Licisca and Tindaro but he did not know the reason for it, for just as he had arrived on the scene to silence them, he had been summoned by the Queen. So the Queen ordered that Licisca and Tindaro be brought before her immediately, and when they arrived, she asked them what was the cause of their argument.

Tindaro was about to answer, but Licisca, who was no spring chicken and on the arrogant side, all warmed up for the argument, turned on him, declaring with an angry look:

"See here, you beast of a man, how dare you speak before I do when you see me standing right here before you! Let me talk!"

And turning to the Queen, she said:

"My lady, this fellow thinks he knows Sicofante's wife better than me, as if I had no idea of who she was, and he has the nerve to try to make me believe that the first night Sicofante slept with her, Messer Hammerhead took the Black Mountain by force and with some loss of blood; but that's not true and, on the contrary, I say he entered with ease and to the general delight of all the troops stationed there. This man is such an idiot, he thinks that girls are foolish enough to waste their opportunities waiting for their fathers or brothers, who six out of seven times take from three to four years longer than they should to marry them off. Brother, they would be in a fine state if they waited that long! I swear to Christ—and I don't swear like that if I don't know what I'm saying—I never had a neighbor who was a virgin when she got married, and as for the married women, I know all too well the many different kinds of tricks they play on their husbands. And this big knucklehead wants to teach me about women, as if I was born yesterday!"

While Licisca was speaking, the women laughed so hard that you could have pulled all their teeth out, and although the Queen tried to silence her at least six times, it was impossible: she would not stop until she said all she wanted to say.

But when Liscisca finally had had her say, the Queen laughed, and turning to Dioneo, said:

"Dioneo, this is a question for you to settle, and so, when our storytelling is over, you shall pronounce the final judgment on this matter."

To this request, Dioneo quickly replied:

"My lady, judgment may be pronounced without hearing another word: I declare that Licisca is right and I believe that things are just the way she says they are, and that Tindaro is an ass."

When Licisca heard this, she began to laugh, and turning to Tindaro, she said:

"There, I told you so! Now be off with you and stop thinking you know more than I do—why, you're still wet behind the ears! I'll have you know I haven't lived for nothing, not me!" And if it weren't for the fact that the Queen with a stern face imposed silence upon her, ordering her not to say another word or make another sound, unless she wished to be whipped and then sent away along with Tindaro, there would have been no time left to do anything for the rest of the day except listen to her. And when the two servants had left, the Queen ordered Filomena to begin the stories, and she cheerfully began in the following way:

[Sixth Day, First Story]

✦

A knight offers Madonna Oretta a ride on a story; but he tells it so poorly that she begs him to put her down.

Young ladies, just as on clear nights the stars decorate the heaven, and in the spring the flowers and budding shrubs adorn the green meadows and the hills, so, too, are good manners and polite conversation enhanced by witty remarks; and being brief, these remarks are even more suitable for women than for men, since it is less becoming in women than in men to speak at great length. The truth is, whatever the reason may be, whether it be our lack of intelligence or a singular enmity of the heavens to our times, today few, if any, women remain who know how to utter a witty remark at the opportune time or who understand one properly when it is delivered, and this is to the universal shame of every one of us. But since Pampinea has already spo-

ken on this subject at some length, I do not intend to say any
more about it; but in order to show you how beautiful such say-
ings can be when uttered at the appropriate time, I would like to
tell you about a courteous remark made by a noble lady which
imposed silence on a certain knight.

As many of you know, either by sight or by what you have
heard said of her, not long ago in our city there lived a noble,
gracious, and accomplished lady whose worth was such that her
name does not deserve to go unmentioned. She was then called
Madonna Oretta and was the wife of Messer Geri Spina; and
one day she happened to be in the country, as all of us are right
now, enjoying herself by going from one place to another with a
party of ladies and knights who earlier that day had come to
dine at her house, and because the road which would take them
to the place they wished to reach was rather long to do on foot,
one of the knights in the group said:

"Madonna Oretta, if you like, I shall tell you one of the most
beautiful stories in the world, which will make a good part of
our journey as easy for you as if you were riding a horse."

To this offer, the lady replied:

"Sir, I beg you most heartily to do so, for I would truly ap-
preciate it."

This knight, whose sword by his side was probably no more
effective than his tongue was in telling stories, upon hearing this
remark, began his story, which in truth was in itself very good,
but by repeating the same word three, four, or even six times,
and then going back to the beginning to start the story all over
again, and remarking from time to time, "I'm not telling this
very well, am I?" and frequently getting the names of the char-
acters wrong and even mixing them up with one another, the
knight managed to make a dreadful mess of it all—not to men-
tion how badly out of keeping his delivery was with the charac-
ters and incidents he was describing.

As she listened to him, Madonna Oretta began to perspire pro-
fusely and every so often she felt her heart sink, as if she were
ill and about to pass away; when she could suffer this no longer
and realized that the knight was riding deeper into his own dung
heap, from which he was not about to extricate himself, she said
pleasantly:

"Sir, this horse of yours has too rough a trot, so I beg you,
please, to set me down."

The knight, who was fortunately much better at taking a hint
than at telling stories, understood her witty remark, and taking

it cheerfully and in a joking spirit, he began to talk of other things, putting aside the story he had begun and continued to tell so badly.

[Sixth Day, Second Story]

✦

With a single phrase, Cisti the baker shows Messer Geri Spina that he has made an unreasaonble request.

MADONNA Oretta's remark was praised most highly by every lady and gentleman in the company, and then the Queen ordered Pampinea to continue; and so she began as follows:

Fair ladies, I myself am unable to decide which of the two is more at fault: Nature when she joins a noble spirit to an inferior body, or Fortune when she provides a body endowed with a noble spirit with an inferior occupation, as happened in the case of Cisti, our fellow townsman, as well in many other instances which we have had occasion to observe; for this Cisti, a man endowed with the noblest of spirits, Fortune made into a baker. I would certainly curse both Nature and Fortune alike, if I were not aware of the fact that Nature is most discerning and that Fortune has a thousand eyes, although fools picture her as being blind. It is my opinion that Nature and Fortune, both being very clever, do what many mortals often do who, uncertain of future events, for their own protection bury their most precious possessions in the most unimposing part of their houses (for it is the least likely to be suspected), and then in the time of greatest need, they bring them out from there, a humble hiding place having guarded them more securely than the most splendid chamber might have done. And in like fashion, the twin arbiters of the world frequently conceal their most cherished treasures beneath the shadow of occupations which are reputed to be the most demeaning, so that when the need arises and they are drawn into the light, their splendor will appear all the more striking. This is made evident in an episode, in itself of little importance, concerning how Cisti the baker moved Messer Geri Spina to reflection, and of which I was reminded by the tale about Madonna Oretta, who was Geri's wife, and which I would like to tell you in a rather brief little story.

Let me begin by saying that when Boniface, who held Messer

Geri Spina in the highest of esteem, was Pope, he sent certain of his noble ambassadors to Florence on urgent papal business, and they lodged at Messer Geri's home, where they would discuss the Pope's affairs together. Almost every morning, for some reason or another, Messer Geri, along with the Pope's emissaries, would happen to pass on foot by the Church of Santa Maria Ughi, where Cisti the baker had his oven and carried on his trade. Although Fortune had endowed Cisti with a rather inferior profession, she was so kind to him in this work that he had become extremely wealthy from it, and with no desire at all to abandon this trade for any other, he lived most splendidly, always enjoying, among the other good things he possessed, the best white and red wines that could be found in Florence or the surrounding districts.

When Cisti saw that Messer Geri and the Pope's ambassadors would pass by his door every morning, since it was very hot outside, it occurred to him that it would be a fine act of courtesy on his part to offer them some of his good white wine to drink; but since he was conscious of his own station and that of Messer Geri, presuming to invite Messer Geri did not seem the honorable thing to do, and so he thought of a way by which he might induce Messer Geri to invite himself. And every morning, always wearing a shiny white doublet and a freshly washed apron, which made Cisti look more like a miller than a baker, around the hour he thought Messer Geri would be passing by with the emissaries, at the entrance of his shop he would have set up a shiny tin pail of fresh water and a new but small Bolognese flask of his good white wine along with two glasses that gleamed so brightly they looked like silver; and there he would sit, and as they passed by, he would clear his throat once or twice, and then begin to drink this wine of his with such gusto that he would have made even a dead man thirsty.

Messer Geri noticed this one or two mornings, and on the third day he said:

"How is it, Cisti, is it good?"

Springing to his feet, Cisti replied:

"Sir, yes it is, but how can I make you understand just how good it is if you do not taste it?"

Whether because of the day's heat, or because he had exerted himself more than usual, or perhaps even because he saw Cisti drink the wine with such gusto, Messer Geri developed such a thirst that turning to the ambassadors with a smile, he declared:

"My lords, we would do well to taste this worthy man's wine;

perhaps it will be of such a quality that we shall not regret it";
and he walked, together with the ambassadors, toward Cisti.

Cisti immediately had a fine-looking bench brought from in-
side the bakery and begged them to be seated; and as their ser-
vants were stepping forward to wash the glasses, he said: "Step
aside, my friends, and leave this service to me, for I am no less
skilled at pouring wine than I am at baking; but don't expect to
taste a single drop!" Having said this, he himself washed four
beautiful new glasses and had a small decanter of his good wine
brought forth, and then with meticulous care he poured the wine
for Messer Geri and his companions, who thought it was the best
they had tasted for a long while and praised it very highly; and
for as long as the ambassadors remained, almost every morning
Messer Geri would accompany them there to drink it.

When the ambassadors had concluded their business and were
about to depart, Messer Geri gave a magnificent banquet, to
which he invited many of the town's most honorable citizens as
well as Cisti, who would not agree to attend on any condition.
And so Messer Geri ordered one of his servants to take a flask
and ask Cisti to fill it with his wine, and then to serve a half
glass of it to each person with the first course at the banquet.
The servant, perhaps angry because he had never been allowed
to taste the wine before, took with him a huge flask.

When Cisti saw this, he said: "Son, Messer Geri did not send
you to me."

The servant kept insisting that he had, but he was unable to
get any other answer from Cisti, and returning to Messer Geri,
he told him what he had said, and Messer Geri answered:

"Go back there and tell him that I did, indeed, send you, and
if he still answers you in this manner, ask him to whom I am
sending you."

The servant returned and he said: "Cisti, I assure you that it
is to you and no one else that Messer Geri sends me."

To which Cisti replied: "And I assure you he did not, my
boy."

"Well, then," the servant asked, "to whom does he send me?"

Cisti answered: "To the River Arno."

When the servant reported this to Messer Geri, his eyes were
immediately opened to the truth, and he said to the servant:

"Let me see the flask you took him." When he saw it, he de-
clared: "Cisti is right"; and having given his servant a sound
tongue-lashing, he made him take back a more suitable flask.

When Cisti saw the flask, he said:

"Now I am sure that it is Messer Geri who sends you to me," and he gladly filled it up for him.

Later on that very same day, Cisti had a small cask filled with a wine of the same vintage and had it carefully transported to Messer Geri's home, and he followed behind it; and when he reached Messer Geri's place, he said to him:

"Sir, I would not have you think the huge flask this morning shocked me, but feeling, perhaps, that you might have forgotten when I demonstrated to you in the past few days with these little flasks of mine—that is, that this wine is not a wine for servants—I wanted to remind you of that this morning. Now, because I do not intend to store all this wine for you any longer, I have brought you every last drop of it, and from now on, do with it what you please."

Messer Geri held Cisti's gift most dear, and he rendered to him the kind of thanks he believed most suitable, and from then on he held Cisti in high esteem and considered him a friend forever.

[Sixth Day, Third Story]

✤

With a quick reply, Monna Nonna de' Pulci silences the less than honorable witticisms of the Bishop of Florence.

WHEN Pampinea had completed her story and everyone had praised most highly both Cisti's reply and his generosity, it pleased the Queen to have Lauretta speak next, and so she happily began in this fashion:

Charming ladies, there is much truth in what first Pampinea and then Filomena touched upon in speaking about the beauty of repartee and our lack of skill in using it. While it is not necessary to repeat their arguments, I should like to remind you, in addition to what has already been said about repartee, that the nature of wit is such that it should have the bite of a lamb rather than that of a dog, for if the witty remark bite like a dog, it would not be a witty remark at all but rather an insult. Madonna Oretta's remark and Cisti's retort illustrate the point extremely well. It is true that if in his reply a person bites back like a dog after having been, so to speak, bitten by a dog, he is not to be blamed for retorting as he otherwise would be; and so one must be careful as to how, when, and with whom, as well as where, one chooses to employ his wit. There was once a prelate of ours who, paying little attention to such matters, received back no less of a bite than he gave, and I should like to tell you about it with a little story.

During the time when Messer Antonio d'Orso, a worthy and wise prelate, was the Bishop of Florence, there came to Florence a Catalan nobleman named Messer Dego della Ratta, the Marshal of King Robert; he was most handsome and very much the ladies' man, and there happened to be among the ladies of Florence one who pleased him greatly: she was a very beautiful lady and the niece of a brother of the said Bishop. Having heard that her husband, although he came from a good family, was extremely greedy and corrupt, the Marshal made arrangements to pay him five hundred gold florins for allowing him to sleep with his wife for one night; and so the Marshal had some ordinary silver *popolini* coins* which were in circulation at that time gilded, and after lying with the man's wife, which he did against her will, he handed over the money to the husband. Subsequently the story became known to everyone and the loss and joke were on the bad husband; and the Bishop, wise man that he was, pretended to know nothing at all about the affair.

The Bishop and the Marshal frequently found themselves in each other's company, and one day during the feast of Saint John they happened to be riding side by side, and as they were looking over the ladies lining the street down which the *palio*† was run, the Bishop spotted a young woman, whom this present plague of ours took away from us in her later years, whose name was Monna Nonna de' Pulci, a cousin of Messer Alesso Rinucci, whom you all must know. She was at that time a fresh and beautiful girl with a ready tongue and a lively spirit just married not too long before in the Porta San Piero district, and the Bishop pointed her out to the Marshal, and then, when they were near enough to her, the Bishop, putting his hand on the Marshal's shoulder, said:

"Nonna, what do you think of this fellow? Do you think you could win him over?"

Nonna felt that the Bishop's words were damaging to her good reputation or were, at least, bound to sully it in the eyes of the

---

*Coins similar in shape to the florin but worth only two cents.
†A horserace held in the streets of medieval Italian towns and still celebrated today in Siena.

many people there who heard him say this; and so, less concerned with vindicating her honor than returning blow for blow, Nonna quickly replied:

"Sir, in the unlikely event that he should win me over, I should wish to be paid in real money."

When the Marshal and the Bishop heard her reply, they were both equally struck to the quick, the former as the perpetrator of the dishonest deed involving the niece of the Bishop's brother, and the latter as the recipient of the shame brought upon his own brother's niece; and without as much as a glance at each other, the Marshal and the Bishop, ashamed and silent, rode away, without saying another word to Nonna that day. And so, in this instance, since the girl had been bitten first, it was not inappropriate for her to bite back with a witty remark.

[Sixth Day, Fourth Story]

✤

Chichibio, Currado Gianfigliazzi's cook, turns Currado's anger into laughter with a quick word uttered in time to save himself from the unpleasant fate with which Currado had threatened him.

When Lauretta was silent and everyone had praised Nonna to the skies, the Queen ordered Neifile to continue, and she said:

Loving ladies, while a quick wit will often provide the speaker with words that are both to the point and well phrased as required by circumstances, sometimes Fortune, occasional assistant to people in distress, will suddenly put words into their mouths which they would never have been able to come up with in a calmer moment: this is what I intend to show you with this story of mine.

As each of you will have heard or seen for yourself, Currado Gianfigliazzi has always been a notable figure in our city: generous and magnificent, he always led a gentlemanly life, enjoying hunting with his hounds and his falcons, not to mention his numerous and more important activities. One day while he was hunting with his falcon in the vicinity of Peretola, he killed a crane, and discovering the bird to be plump and young, he had it sent to one of his fine cooks, who was a Venetian called Chichi-

bio, with instructions to roast the bird for supper and to see to it
that it was prepared with great care.

Chichibio, who was no less simpleminded than he looked,
plucked the crane, set it over the fire, and began to roast it with
great care. But when the bird was nearly cooked and was giving
off a most delicious smell, there happened into the kitchen a
country girl called Brunetta with whom Chichibio was pas-
stionately in love, and sniffing the smell of the crane and seeing
it roasting there, she pleaded lovingly with Chichibio to give her
one of the legs.

Chichibio answered her in a singsong way, saying:

"You won't get it from me, Lady Brunetta, you won't get it
from me!"

This angered Lady Brunetta, and she said to him:

"I swear to God, if you don't give it to me, you'll never get
what you want from me again!" And to make a long story short,
they had a lengthy argument, and finally, in order not to anger
his lady love, Chichibio pulled off one of the crane's legs and
gave it to her.

Later, the crane with the missing leg was set before Currado
and his guests, and Currado, astonished at the sight of this, sum-
moned Chichibio and asked him what had happened to the
crane's other leg. To this question, the lying Venetian answered:

"My lord, cranes only have one leg and one foot."

Now angered, Currado declared:

"What the devil do you mean, only one leg and one foot? Do
you think this is the only crane I have ever seen?"

Chichibio continued:

"Sir, that's the way it is; and whenever you like we'll go and
see some live ones, and I'll show you."

Out of consideration for his guests, Currado did not wish to
continue the argument, but he remarked:

"Since you insist that by taking me to see the live ones, you
can prove something that I never saw or ever heard existed
before now, well then, tomorrow morning, I want to see it for
myself, and then I'll be satisfied; but I swear to you on the
body of Christ that if things are not as you say, I'll fix you so
that you'll remember my name as long as you live!"

And with that the discussion was closed for that evening, but
on the following morning at daybreak, Currado, whose rage was
not calmed with sleep, arose still seething with anger and ordered
his horses to be saddled up; and making Chichibio mount a nag,
Currado led him off, riding in the direction of a river whose
banks were always crowded with cranes at daybreak, saying:

"We shall soon see who lied last night, you or me!"

Realizing that Currado was still angry and that he would have to substantiate his lies, Chichibio, not knowing what he could do about it, rode beside Currado in a state of absolute terror, and he would gladly have run away if only he could have done so; but since he could not, he would look around him: ahead, behind him, everywhere he turned, he thought he was seeing cranes standing on two legs.

But just as they were nearing the river, Chichibio happened to be the first to catch sight of at least twelve cranes, on the bank, all resting on one leg, as cranes usually do when they are sleeping; and so Chichibio, quickly pointing them out to Currado, announced:

"As you can plainly see, sir, last night I was telling you the truth: cranes do have only one leg and one foot—you need only observe those standing over there."

Currado looked at them and replied: "Just wait a while, and I'll show you they have two of them," and having moved somewhat closer to the birds, he shouted: "Hey! Hey!" and at the sound of his cry, the cranes lowered their other leg, and after taking a few steps thay all began to fly away; whereupon Currado turned to Chichibio and exclaimed: "What do you think of that, you rogue? Do they, or do they not, have two legs now?"

Chichibio, in his confusion, not knowing himself where the words for his answer came from, said:

"Yes, sir, but last night you didn't shout 'Hey! Hey!' at the crane we had; if you had shouted like that, it would have pushed its other leg and foot out just as these did."

Currado liked this reply so much that all of his anger was changed into merriment and laughter, and he said:

"Chichibio, you are right: that's exactly what I should have done."

So then in this way, with a quick and amusing reply, Chichibio managed to escape an unpleasant fate and make peace with his master.

[Sixth Day, Fifth Story]

❦

Messer Forese da Rabatta and Maestro Giotto, the painter, make fun of each other's poor appearance while returning from Mugello.

THE ladies were thoroughly amused by Chichibio's reply, and as soon as Neifile was silent, Panfilo, at the Queen's command, began:

Dearest ladies, just as quite often Fortune has been known to conceal great treasures of virtue in the humble artisan, as Pampinea showed us a moment ago, so, too, amazing genius is often found to have been placed in the ugliest of men. This was clearly the case in two of our citizens, of whom I intend to tell you a short tale. One of these men was called Messer Forese da Rabatta. He had a small, deformed body, and a flat, pushed-in face which would still be considered horrible even when compared to the ugliest of the Baronci family;* nevertheless, he was such a learned jurist that many worthy men considered him a walking library of knowledge when it came to civil law. The other, whose name was Giotto, was a man of such genius that there was nothing in Nature—the mother and moving force behind all created things with her constant revolution of the heavens—that he could not paint with his stylus, pen, or brush, making it so much like its original in Nature that it seemed more like the original than a reproduction. Many times, in fact, while looking at paintings by this man, the observer's visual sense was known to err, taking what was painted to be the very thing itself.

Now, since it was he who had revived that art of painting which had been buried for many centuries under the errors of various artists who painted more to delight the eyes of the ignorant than to please the intellect of wise men, he may rightly be considered one of the lights of Florentine glory; and even more so, when one considers his great modesty, for he always refused to be called "Maestro," even though he was the master of all living artists and had rightfully acquired the title. And this title which he refused shone all the more brightly in him in that it

*This remark will be clarified in the next story (VI, 6).

was eagerly usurped by those who knew far less than himself, or by his own disciples. But for all the greatness of his art, neither was he physically more handsome, nor had he a face more pleasing in any way, than Messer Forese.

But turning to our story now, let me start by saying that both Messer Forese and Giotto owned land in the region of Mugello; it was summertime, the courts were closed for their vacation, and Messer Forese had gone to visit his estate; by chance, as he rode the sorry-looking nag he had rented, he came across the aforementioned Giotto, who was also returning to Florence after inspecting his own property. Giotto was no better mounted or dressed than Messer Forese, and since the two of them were getting on in years, they traveled at a leisurely pace, moving along side by side.

As often happens in the summer, it started to rain all of a sudden, and caught in the downpour, they quickly took shelter in the home of a peasant who was a friend and acquaintance of both of them. But after a time, as the rain gave no signs of stopping and because each of them wished to be in Florence that day, they borrowed two old woolen capes from the peasant and two hats, worn with age, for there was nothing better, and continued on their way again.

Now, they had gone some distance, soaking wet and covered with mud from the many splashings their nags had given them (something which is not likely to improve a person's appearance), when the weather started to clear a bit, and after a long period of silent traveling, they began to talk to each other again. And as he rode and listened to Giotto, who was a very fine storyteller, Messer Forese began to look him over from top to bottom; and seeing him so unkempt and wretched-looking, he began to laugh, and giving no thought at all to his own appearance, he said:

"Giotto, what if we were to run into a stranger who had never seen you before, do you think he would believe you were the best painter in the world, as you really are?" To this Giotto quickly replied:

"Sir, I think he would believe it if, after looking you over, he were to think you knew your ABCs!"

When Messer Forese heard this, he realized his mistake, and found himself paid back in the same coin for which he had sold the goods.

[Sixth Day, Sixth Story]

✠

Michele Scalza proves to certain young men that the Baronci are the noblest gentlemen in the world (or in the Maremma) and wins a supper.

THE ladies were still laughing over the well-phrased and quick reply made by Giotto when the Queen ordered Fiammetta to go on with the next story, and she began to speak in this fashion:

Young ladies, having been reminded by Panfilo of the Baronci, a family you may perhaps not know as well as he does, brings to mind a story which shows how great was their nobility, and since it does not stray from our topic, I should like to tell it to you.

Not long ago in our city there was a young man named Michele Scalza, one of the most charming and entertaining fellows in the world, a person who could always come up with the most bizarre stories at the drop of a hat, and because of this, the young Florentine men, whenever they got together, loved to have him in their company. Now one day he happened to be with some of them at Montughi and they started arguing over which was the noblest and most ancient family in Florence. Some claimed the Uberti were, others the Lamberti, some this one and some that one, suggesting whatever name came to mind.

When Scalza heard this, he began grinning and said:

"Go on, get out of here, you idiots, you don't know what you're talking about! The most noble and the most ancient family not only in Florence but in the entire world (not to mention the Maremma) is the Baronci, and all the philosophers agree on this as would anyone who knows the Baronci as I do. But in case you happen to be confusing them with some other family, I am speaking of the Baronci who are your neighbors from the Santa Maria Maggiore quarter."

When the young men, who were expecting him to say something entirely different, heard this, they all made fun of him, saying:

"You're pulling our leg, as if we didn't know the Baronci as well as you do!"

Scalza answered:

"I swear by the Gospel I'm not—on the contrary, I am speaking the truth. If there is anyone who wishes to wager a supper on it for the winner and any six friends he may choose, I'll gladly take him up on it; and I'll do even better: I'll abide by the decision of any judge you select."

One of the young men in the group, who was named Neri Vannini, said:

"I am ready to win this supper." And after all of them had agreed to appoint as their judge Piero di Fiorentino, in whose house they had gathered that day, they went to find Piero, accompanied by all the others, who were anxious to see Scalza lose the bet so that they could make fun of him, and explained everything to him.

Piero, who was an intelligent young man, first heard Neri's side of the argument, then turned to Scalza and said:

"And how will you prove what you claim?"

Scalza replied:

"How? I'll prove it in such a way that not only you but he, who denies it, will have to admit that what I say is true. As you may all know, the older a family is, the nobler it is, and this you all agreed upon just a moment ago; and if the Baronci are older than any other family, they must also be the noblest; so, if I can prove to you that they are the oldest, I shall, without doubt, have won the argument. The fact is that the Baronci were created by the Good Lord when He was first learning how to paint, whereas the rest of mankind was created after the Good Lord had already learned how. If you do not believe me, think about the Baronci compared to the rest of mankind. If you do, you will see that whereas other men have well-formed, and properly proportioned faces, a number of the Baronci have a very long and narrow face, while others have faces wide beyond all measure; still others have very long noses, some of them short ones, and some have chins that stick out and turn up with jaws like that of an ass; and there are even some who have one eye bigger than the other, and there are even a few who have one eye lower than the other, which all gives them faces like the ones children usually make when they are first learning how to draw. And so, as I said before, it seems quite obvious that the Good Lord was still learning to paint when he created them; therefore, since they are older than anyone else, they are the most noble."

After Piero, who was the judge, and Neri, who had made the wager, and everyone else recalled how the Baronci looked and had listened to Scalza's delightful argument, they all began to laugh and to agree that Scalza was right, that he had won the supper, and that the Baronci were most certainly the noblest and the most ancient family that existed, not only in Florence, but in the entire world and even in the Maremma for that matter.

And so in trying to describe the ugliness of Messer Forese's face, Panilo was quite right in stating that he would have looked hideous alongside one of the Baronci family.

[Sixth Day, Seventh Story]

✣

Madonna Filippa is discovered by her husband with a lover of hers, and when she is called before a judge, with a ready and amusing reply she secures her freedom and causes the statute to be changed.

FIAMMETTA had finished speaking, and everyone was still laughing over the strange argument Scalza had used to ennoble the Baronci above every other family when the Queen called upon Filostrato to tell a story; and he began, saying:

Worthy ladies, it is good to know how to say the right thing at the right time, but I think it is even better when you know how to do so at a moment of real necessity. There was a noble lady, about whom I intend to tell you, who accomplished this so well that she not only provided her listeners with amusement and laughter, but she also managed to slip out of the clutches of a shameful death, as you shall hear.

In the city of Prato, there was once a statute—in truth, no less harsh than it was worthy of criticism—which, without any extenuating circumstances whatsoever, required that any woman caught by her husband committing adultery with a lover should be burned alive, just the way a woman who goes with a man for money would be. And while this statute was in effect, it happened that a noble lady named Madonna Filippa, who was beautiful and more in love than any woman could be, was discovered in her own bedroom by her husband, Rinaldo de' Pugliesi, in the arms of Lazzarino de' Guazzagliotri, a noble and handsome young man from that city, whom she loved more than herself. When Rinaldo discovered this, he was extremely angry and could hardly restrain himself from rushing at them and murdering them, and had he not been so concerned over what might happen to him if he were to follow the impulse of his anger, he would have done so. While able to restrain himself from doing this, he was, however, unable to refrain from claiming the sentence of Prato's statute, which he was not permitted to carry out by his own hand, that is, the death of his wife.

And so, in possession of very convincing evidence of his wife's transgression, when day broke, without thinking further about the matter, he denounced the lady and had her summoned to the court. The lady, who was very courageous, as women truly in love usually are, was determined to appear in court, and in spite of the fact that she was advised against this by many of her friends and relatives, she decided that she would rather confess the truth and die with a courageous heart than, fleeing like a coward, live in exile condemned *in absentia* and show herself unworthy of such a lover as the man in whose arms she had rested the night before. Escorted by a large group of women and men, all of whom were urging her to deny the charges, she came before the *podestà* and, with a steady gaze and a firm voice, demanded to know what he wanted of her. Gazing at the lady and finding her to be most beautiful and very well-bred as well as most courageous, indeed, as her own words bore witness, the *podestà* took pity on her and was afraid she might confess to something which would force him, in order to fulfill his duty, to condemn her to death.

But since he could not avoid questioning her about what she had been accused of doing, he said to her:

"Madam, as you can see, your husband Rinaldo is here and has lodged a complaint against you, in which he states that he has found you in adultery with another man; and because of this he demands that I punish you by putting you to death in accordance with the statute which requires such sentence here in Prato. But since I cannot do this if you do not confess, I suggest you be very careful how you answer this charge; now, tell me if what your husband accuses you of is true."

Without the slightest trace of fear, the lady, in a lovely tone of voice, replied:

"Sir, it is true that Rinaldo is my husband and that this past night he found me in Lazzarino's arms, where, because of the deep and perfect love I bear for him, I have many times lain; nor would I ever deny this; but, as I am sure you know, the laws should be equal for all and should be passed with the consent of the people they affect. In this case these conditions are not fulfilled, for this law applies only to us poor women, who are much better able than men to satisfy a larger number; furthermore, when this law was put into effect, not a single woman gave her consent, nor was any one of them ever consulted about it; therefore, it may quite rightly be called a bad law. And if, however, you wish, to the detriment of my body and your own soul, to put this law into effect, that is your concern; but, before you proceed to any judgment, I beg you to grant me a small favor: that is, to ask my husband whether or not I have ever refused, whenever and however many times he wished, to yield my entire body to him."

To this question, without waiting for the *podestà* to pose it, Rinaldo immediately replied that without any doubt, the lady had yielded to his every pleasure whenever he required it.

"So then," the lady promptly continued, "I ask you, Messer *Podestà*, if he has always taken of me whatever he needed and however much pleased him, what was I supposed to do then, and what am I to do now, with what is left over? Should I throw it to the dogs? Is it not much better to give it to a gentleman who loves me more than himself, rather than let it go to waste or spoil?"

The nature of the case and the fact that the lady was so well known brought almost all of Prato's citizens flocking to court, and when they heard such an amusing question posed by the lady, after much laughter, all of a sudden and almost in a single voice, they cried out that the lady was right and had spoken well; and before they left the court, with the *podestà*'s consent, they changed the cruel statute, modifying it so that it applied only to those women who were unfaithful to their husbands for money. And Rinaldo, confused by the whole mad affair, left the courtroom, and the lady, now free and happy, and resurrected from the flames, so to speak, returned to her home in triumph.

[Sixth Day, Eighth Story]

❈

Fresco advises his niece not to look at herself in the mirror if, as she has declared, she finds the sight of disagreeable people annoying.

As the ladies were listening to the story Filostrato was telling, at first their hearts were touched with a slight sense of shame, made evident by a blush of modesty which appeared on their cheeks, but then, starting to exchange glances with each other, they could hardly keep themselves from laughing, as they listened to the rest of the tale with half-concealed smiles. And when the story came to an end, the Queen turned to Emilia, and ordered her to continue; and as if she had just been awakened from sleep, Emilia, with a sigh, began to speak:

— Charming ladies, having been for quite a while now caught up in thoughts which have carried me far away from here, I shall now obey our Queen and hasten to tell you a story (much shorter, perhaps, than I otherwise might have told, had I not been so preoccupied with my thoughts), of how the foolish error of a girl was corrected by means of an amusing remark made by one of her uncles, though she herself was not intelligent enough to understand it.

Once there was a man named Fresco da Celatico who had a niece whose pet name was Cesca, a term of endearment. While this girl had a beautiful face and figure—yet not in the same class with those angelic faces we often see—she had such a high and mighty opinion of herself that she had become accustomed to criticizing every man, woman, and thing she laid eyes on, never noticing her own shortcomings, even though she was in fact the most disagreeable, tedious, and insipid person herself, and nothing anybody ever did could please her; moreover, she was so conceited that even in a member of the French royal family, such arrogance would have been considered excessive. And whenever she walked down the street, she would twist her nose up in disgust, as though everyone she happened to see or run into was emitting some horrible smell.

Now, leaving aside her many other disagreeable and unpleasant habits, one day she happened to return to the house to find Fresco, and sitting down beside him, she started fretting and fussing, doing nothing but huff and puff, until Fresco finally asked her:

"Cesca, what's happened? Why have you come home so early on a holiday?"

And Cesca, dripping with affectation, replied:

"It is true. I have returned home early, but I do not ever remember seeing so many disagreeable and unpleasant men and women on our city streets as there were today, and there was not a single one among them that did not strike me as being more loathsome than bad luck itself. I do not believe there is a woman in this world who is more upset at the sight of unpleasant people than I am, and so, in order to spare myself the sight of them, I came home early."

To this remark Fresco, who was extremely displeased by his niece's disgusting attitude, replied:

"My girl, if you find disagreeable people as disagreeable as you say you do, I suggest for your own happiness that you never look at yourself in the mirror again."

But Cesca, whose head was more hollow than a reed, though she thought she was as wise as Solomon, understood the true meaning of Fresco's witty remark as well as some dumb animal might, and said that she intended to look at herself in the mirror just as other women would. And so she remained as stupid as she ever was, and continues to remain so to this day.

[Sixth Day, Ninth Story]

✢

With a witty remark, Guido Cavalcanti quite rightly rebukes certain Florentine gentlemen who had come upon him by surprise.

WHEN the Queen realized that Emilia had so quickly finished her story, and that apart from the person who was to speak last by special dispensation there was no other left to speak but her, she began in this fashion:

Fair ladies, although you have deprived me of recounting at least two of the stories I meant to tell you today, I still have one left to tell, at the end of which there is a remark so well put that it is perhaps more subtle than any that we have heard so far.

You must remember that in past times, our city was known for its very charming and praiseworthy customs, all of which today, thanks to the avarice with which wealth has been accumulated, have been driven away. Among these was the custom for a group of a certain number of gentlemen in various districts of the city to gather together in different places in Florence, the company consisting of only those who could easily afford the expenses involved, and so each member took his turn at entertaining the entire company on his appointed day, and at these banquets they often honored distinguished visitors, when they came to town, as well as other fellow citizens; also, at least once a year, they all wore the same kind of clothes, and on the most important holidays, they rode through the city together and sometimes they jousted, especially on the major feast days or when good news, such as a military victory or the like, reached the city.

Among these companies there was one headed by Messer Betto Brunelleschi, and Messer Betto along with his associates had tried very hard to attract to their group Messer Cavalcante de' Cavalcanti's son, Guido, and not without reason, for besides the fact that he was one of the best logicians in the world and a superb natural philosopher (things for which the group cared very little), Guido was a most charming and courteous man, and a gifted conversationalist who could do everything he set his mind to and who, better than any other man, knew how to undertake those things which were befitting a gentleman; and besides all this, he was extremely wealthy, and thus capable of entertaining as lavishly as you can imagine anyone whom he felt was worthy of such treatment. But Messer Betto had never succeeded in persuading him to join their group, and he and his companions thought this was because of his philosophical meditations, which often seemed to cut Guido off from his fellow man; and because he leaned somewhat toward the opinions of the Epicureans, it was said among the common folk that these philosophical speculations of his were solely directed toward the possibility of discovering that God did not exist.

Now one day Guido happened to walk from Orto San Michele past the Corso degli Adimari until he reached the Baptistry of San Giovanni, which was a walk he frequently took, because it took him past those great marble tombs which are now located in Santa Reparata, as well as many other graves that lie around San Giovanni; and while he was wandering among the tombs, between the porphyry columns that stand in that spot and the entrance to San Giovanni, which was locked, Messer Betto with his company came riding through the piazza of Santa Reparata, and when they caught sight of Guido there among those tombs, they said: "Let's go and give him a hard time." Spurring their horses, as if they were making a playful attack, they were upon him before he had time to notice them, and they began saying to him:

"Guido, you refuse to join our company; but listen here, what good will it do you when you finally manage to discover that God doesn't exist?"

Guido, finding himself surrounded by them, quickly replied: "Gentlemen, in your own house you may say to me whatever you wish"; then, placing a hand on one of those tombstones, which were very high, nimble as he was, he leaped over the top onto the other side, and having escaped them, he went on his way.

The men were all left looking at each other. And then they began to claim that Guido was out of his mind and that what he had replied meant nothing, since the spot where they were standing had no more to do with them than with any of the other citizens, and least of all with Guido.

Messer Betto turned to them all and said:

"It is you who have lost your minds if you did not understand him: Guido has elegantly and in only a few words paid us the worst insult imaginable, for if you think about it carefully, these tombs are the houses of the dead, for here is where the dead are laid to rest, it is where they live; when he claimed that we are at home here, he was telling us that in comparison to him and other learned men, we and other ignorant people like us who are not learned are worse than the dead, and so, standing as we are, here in this place, we are in our own house."

Now that they understood what Guido had meant to imply, each of them was most ashamed, and they never gave him a hard time again, and from then on they considered Messer Betto to be a gentleman who possessed a subtle and intelligent mind.

[Sixth Day, Tenth Story]

✦

Brother Cipolla promises some peasants that he will show them a feather from the Angel Gabriel; but finding only bits of charcoal in its place, he tells them that these were the ones used to roast Saint Lorenzo.

EACH member of the company having told a story, Dioneo realized that it was now his turn, and so, without waiting for any formal command, he imposed silence upon those who were praising Guido's clever reply and began:

Pretty ladies, although I enjoy the privilege of speaking on whatever subject I please, I have no intention of straying from the topic on which all of you have spoken so admirably today; on the contrary, I intend to follow in your footsteps and show you how one of the friars of Saint Anthony managed with a quick solution to avoid a trap set for him by two young men. Nor should it bother you if, in order to tell the story as it should be told, I have to speak at some length, for if you will look up at the sun, you will discover it is still mid-heaven.

Certaldo, as you may have heard, is a fortified city in the Valdelsa, within our own territory, which, no matter how small it may be now, was inhabited at one time by noble and well-to-do people. Because it was such good grazing ground, one of the brothers of Saint Anthony used to go there once a year to collect the alms that people were stupid enough to give him. He was called Brother Cipolla,* and was warmly welcomed there no less, perhaps, because of what his name stood for than for religious reasons, since that area of the country produced onions which were famous throughout Tuscany.

Brother Cipolla was short, redheaded, with a cheerful face, and he was the nicest scoundrel in the world; and despite the fact that he had no education, he was such a skillful and quick talker that whoever did not know him would not only have taken him for a great master of eloquence but would have considered him to be Cicero himself or perhaps even Quintilian; and if he was not the godfather of almost everyone in the district, he was at least their friend or acquaintance.

Now, as was his custom, he went there for one of his regular visits in the month of August; and one Sunday morning, when all the good men and women of the surrounding villages were gathered together in the parish church to hear Mass, Brother Cipolla stepped forward at the proper time and said:

"Ladies and gentlemen, as you know, it is your practice every year to send some of your grain and crops—some of you more and others less, according to your capacity and your piety—to the poor brothers of our blessed lord Saint Anthony, so that the blessed Saint Anthony may keep your oxen, your donkeys, your pigs, and your sheep safe from all danger; furthermore, you are used to paying, especially those of you who are enrolled in our order, those small dues which are paid once a year. To collect these contributions, I have been sent by my superior, that is, by Messer Abbot; and so, with God's blessing, after nones, when you hear the bells ring, you will come here to the front of the church, where in my usual manner I shall preach my sermon and you will kiss the cross. Moreover, since I know you all to be most devoted to my lord Messer Saint Anthony, as a special favor, I shall show you a most holy and beautiful relic which I

---

*It is interesting to note that this virtuoso storyteller (whose name, *Cipolla*, means "onion" in Italian) came from Certaldo, possibly Boccaccio's birthplace.

myself brought back from the Holy Land, overseas: it is one of
the feathers of the Angel Gabriel, precisely the one which was
left in the Virgin Mary's bedroom when he came to perform the
Annunciation before her in Nazareth."

He said this, and then he stopped talking and returned to the
Mass. When Brother Cipolla was making this announcement,
there happened to be, among the many others in the church, two
young men who were most clever: one called Giovanni del Bra-
goniera and the other Biagio Pizzini, both of whom, after quite a
bit of laughing over Brother Cipolla's relic, decided to play a
trick on him and his feather, even though they were old and
close friends of his. They found out that Brother Cipolla would
be eating that day in the center of town with a friend; when
they figured it was around the time for him to be at the table,
they took to the street and went to the inn where the friar was
staying. The plan was this: Biagio would keep Brother Cipolla's
servant occupied by talking to him while Giovanni was to look
for this feather, or whatever it was, among the friar's possessions
and steal it from him, in order to see just how he would be able
to explain its disappearance to the people later on.

Brother Cipolla had a servant, whom some called Guccio the
Whale, others Guccio the Mess, and still others Guccio the Pig;
he was such a crude individual that even Lippo Topo* himself
would not have been able to do him justice. Brother Cipolla
would often joke about him with his friends, and say:

"My servant has nine qualities, and if any one of them had
existed in Solomon, Aristotle, or Seneca, it would have sufficed to
spoil all of their virtue, intelligence, and holiness. Just think,
then, what kind of man he must be, having nine such qualities,
but no virtue, intelligence, or holiness!"

And when he was asked what these nine qualities were, he
would recite them in a kind of doggerel verse:

"I'll tell you. He's lying, lazy, and lousy; negligent, disobedi-
ent, and foul-tongued; heedless, careless, and bad-mannered;
besides this, he has other various little defects that are best left
unmentioned. And what is most amusing about him is that wher-
ever he goes, he wants to take a wife and set up housekeeping;
and because he has a big, black, greasy beard, he thinks he is
very handsome and attractive—in fact, he imagines that every
woman who sees him falls in love with him, and if it were up to
him, he'd lose his pants chasing after them all. And it is true
that he is of great assistance to me, for he never lets anyone

*Probably a reference to a mediocre painter of the period.

burden me with secrets without getting his share of an earful, and if someone happens to ask me a question about something, he is so afraid that I will not know how to reply that he quickly answers yes or no for me as he sees fit."

Brother Cipolla had left his servant back at the inn and had ordered him to make sure that no one touched his belongings, and especially his saddlebags, for the sacred objects were inside them. But Guccio the Mess was happier to be in a kitchen than a nightingale was to be on the green branches of a tree, especially if he knew that some servant girl was also there. When he noticed the innkeeper's maid, who was a fat, round, short, and ill-shapen creature with a pair of tits that looked like two clumps of cowshit and a face like one of the Baronci family,* all sweaty, greasy, and covered with soot, Guccio left Brother Cipolla's room unlocked and all his possessions unguarded as he swooped down into the kitchen just like a vulture pouncing on some carcass. Although it was still August, he took a seat near the fire and began to talk with the girl, whose name was Nuta, telling her that he was a gentleman by procuration, that he had more than a thousand hundreds of florins† (not counting those he had to give away to others), and that he knew how to do and say so many things more than even his very master ever dreamed of doing and saying. And with absolutely no concern for his cowl, which was covered with so much grease it would have seasoned all the soup kettles in Altopascio, or his torn and patched-up doublet, covered with sweat stains all around his collar and under his arms and in more spots and colors than a piece of cloth from India or China ever had, or his shoes, which were all worn out, or his hose, which were full of holes, he spoke to her as if he were Milord of Châtillons, talking about how he wanted to buy her new clothes and take her away from all this drudgery and into the service of someone else, and how he would give her the hope for a better life, even if he did not have much to offer, and he told her many others things in this very amorous way, but, like most of his undertakings, this one, too, amounted to nothing but hot air.

And so, when the two young men found Guccio the Pig busy with Nuta (something which made them very happy, since this meant that half of their task was done), without anyone to stop

*See VI, 6.
†Guccio invents this amount, as well as the previous phrase "by procuration," in order to impress his lady.

them, they entered Brother Cipolla's bedroom, which they found unlocked, and the first thing they picked up to search through was the saddlebag in which the feather was kept; they opened it, and discovered a little casket wrapped in an extravagant length of silk, and when they lifted the lid, they found a feather inside, just like the kind you find on a parrot's tail; and they realized that it had to be the one that Brother Cipolla had promised the people of Certaldo. And it certainly would have been easy for him to make them believe his story, for in those times the luxurious customs of Egypt had not yet made their way to any great degree into Tuscany, as they were later to do throughout all of Italy, much to its ruin; and if these feathers were known to just a few, those few certainly were not among the inhabitants of that area. On the contrary, as long as the crude customs of their forefathers endured there, not only had they never seen a parrot, but most of the people there had never heard of one.

The young men were happy to have discovered the feather. They took it out, and in order not to leave the container empty, they filled it with some charcoal that they found in a corner of the room.

They shut the lid and arranged everything just as they had found it, and unnoticed, they merrily departed with the feather and then waited to hear what Brother Cipolla would say when he found charcoal in place of the feather. The simpleminded men and women who were in church, having heard that they were going to see one of the Angel Gabriel's feathers after nones, returned home when the Mass was finished; friends and neighbors spread the news from one to another, and when everyone had finished eating, so many men and women rushed to town to see this feather that there was hardly enough space for them all.

After a hearty meal and a short nap, Brother Cipolla got up a little after nones, and when he heard that a great crowd of peasants was gathering to see the feather, he ordered Guccio the Mess to come along with him to ring the church bells and to bring the saddlebags with him. With great reluctance, he left Nuta and the kitchen and made his way there very slowly; he arrived there panting, for having drunk so much water he had bloated his stomach. But on Brother Cipolla's order, he went to the door of the church and began to ring the bells loudly.

When all the people were gathered together, Brother Cipolla began his sermon, unaware that any of his belongings had been tampered with, preaching in a way that served his own personal ends, and when it came time to reveal the Angel Gabriel's feather, first he had the congregation solemnly recite the *Confiteor* and had two candles lighted, then after drawing back his cowl, he very gently unwound the silk and took out the box; after pronouncing several words of praise about the Angel Gabriel and his relic, he opened the box. When he saw it was full of charcoal, he did not suspect that Guccio the Whale had done this to him, for he knew him too well to believe he was capable of such tricks, nor did he even blame him for not keeping others from doing this; he merely cursed himself silently for having made him guardian of his belongings when he knew him to be so negligent, disobedient, careless, and absent-minded—nevertheless, without the slightest change of color on his face, he raised his face and hands to heaven, and spoke so that all could hear him:

"O Lord, may Thy power be praised forever!" Then he closed the box and turned to the people, saying:

"Ladies and gentlemen, I want you to know that when I was very young, I was sent by my superior to those parts of the earth of the rising sun, and I was charged by express order to discover the special privileges of the Porcellana, which, although they cost nothing to seal, are much more useful to others than to ourselves. I set out on my way, leaving from Venice and passing through Greekburg, then riding through the kingdom of Garbo and on through Baldacca, and I came to Parione, whereupon, not without some thirst, I reached, after some time, Sardinia.

"But why do I go on listing all the countries that I visited? After passing the straights of St. George, I came to Truffia and Buffia, lands heavily populated with a great many people, and from there I came to Liarland, where I discovered many of our friars and those of other orders who scorned a life of hardship for the love of God, who cared little about the troubles of others, following their own interests, and who spent no money other than that which had not yet been coined in those countries; and afterward I came to the land of Abruzzi where men and women walk around on mountaintops in wooden shoes and dress their pigs in their own guts. And farther on I discovered people who carry bread twisted around sticks and wine in goatskins; then I arrived at the Baskworms' mountains, where all the streams run downhill.

"To make a long story short, I traveled so far that I came to Parsnip, India, where I swear by the habit I wear on my back that I saw feathers fly, an incredible thing to one who has not witnessed it; and Maso del Saggio, whom I found there cracking nuts and selling the husks retail, was witness to the fact that I do not lie about this matter. But, not able to find there what I was seeking, and since to travel further would have meant going by sea, I turned back and came to the Holy Land, where cold bread in the summer costs four cents and you get the heat for nothing; and there I found the venerable father Messer Blame-menot Ifyouplease, the most worthy patriarch of Jerusalem, who, out of respect for the habit of our lord Messer Saint Anthony, which I have always worn, wanted me to see all the holy relics he had there with him; and they were so numerous that if I had counted them all, I would have finished up with a list several miles long; but in order not to disappoint you, let me tell you about some of them.

"First he showed me the finger of the Holy Spirit, as whole and as solid as it ever was, and the forelock of the seraphim which appeared to Saint Francis, and one of the nails of the cherubim, and one of the ribs of the True-Word-Made-Fresh-at-the-Windows, and vestments of the holy Catholic faith, and some of the beams from the star which appeared to the three wise men in the East, and a phial of the sweat of Saint Michael when he fought the Devil, and the jawbones from the death of Saint Lazarus, and many others.

"And since I was happy to give him copies of the *Slopes of Monte Morello* in the vulgar tongue as well as several chapters of the *Caprezio*,* for which he had been hunting a long time, he gave me in return part of his holy relics, presenting me with one of the teeth of the Holy Cross, and a bit of the sound of the bells from the temple of Solomon, in a little phial, and the feather from the Angel Gabriel which I already told you I have, and one of the wooden shoes of Saint Gherardo da Villamagna, which I gave, not long ago in Florence, to Gherardo de' Bonsi, who holds it in the greatest reverence. And he also gave me some of the charcoal upon which the most holy martyr Saint Lorenzo was roasted alive. All these articles I most devoutly brought back with me, and I have them all.

"The truth is that my superior has never permitted me to show them until they were proven to be authentic, but now, because of certain miracles that were performed through them and letters received from the Patriarch, he is now sure that they are authentic, and he has allowed me to display them to you. And since I am afraid to trust them to anyone else, I always carry them with me. As a matter of fact, I carry the feather from the Angel Gabriel in one box, in order not to damage it, and the

---

*These imaginary book titles have been seen by some scholars as a veiled reference to sodomitic practices.

coals over which Saint Lorenzo was roasted in another, and both boxes are so much alike that I often mistake the one for the other, and this is what happened to me today; for while I thought that I had brought the box containing the feather here, instead I brought the one with the charcoal. But I do not consider this to be an error; on the contrary, it is the will of God, and He Himself placed the box in my hands, reminding me in this way that the Feast of Saint Lorenzo is only two days away; and since God wished me to show you the charcoal in order to rekindle in your hearts the devotion that you owe to Saint Lorenzo, rather than the feather that I had wanted to show you, He made me take out these blessed charcoals that were once bathed in the sweat of that most holy body. And so, my blessed children, remove your cowls and come forward, devoutly, to behold them. But first, I want each of you to know that whoever makes the sign of the cross on himself with this charcoal will live for one year safe in the knowledge that he will not be cooked by fire without his feeling it."

And after he said those words, he sang a hymn in praise of Saint Lorenzo, opened the box, and displayed the charcoal. The foolish throng gazed upon it in reverent admiration, and they crowded around him and gave him larger offerings than they ever had before, begging him to touch each one of them with the coals. And so Brother Cipolla took these charcoals in his hand and on their white shirts and doublets and on the women's veils he made the largest crosses possible, announcing that, as he had proved many times, no matter how much the charcoals were consumed in making those crosses, afterward they would always return to their former size no sooner than they were placed back in the box.

And in this manner, and with great profit for himself, Brother Cipolla turned the entire population of Certaldo into crusaders and, by means of his quick wit, tricked those who thought they had tricked him by stealing his feather. The two young men, having been present at his sermon and having heard the fantastic story he had invented, laughed so hard that they thought their jaws would break, for they knew how farfetched his story was; and after the crowd dispersed, they went up to him and got the greatest joy in the world out of telling him what they had done; then they gave him back his feather, with which, by the way, he happened to rake in for himself all during the following year no less than the charcoal had that day.

[Sixth Day, Conclusion]

+

THIS story greatly pleased and entertained each and every member of the company, and they all laughed heartily over Brother Cipolla, especially at his pilgrimage, and at the relics he had seen or brought back with him; and when the Queen realized that the story was finished, as was the duration of her reign, she rose to her feet, removed her crown, and, laughing, she placed it upon Dioneo's head, stating:

"The time has come, Dioneo, for you to experience just how difficult it is to have to rule and guide women: therefore, be King and rule us in such a manner that at the end of your reign, we shall have cause to praise it."

After accepting the crown, Dioneo replied with a laugh:

"I daresay you have often seen kings worth a great deal more than myself—I mean kings on a chessboard; now, if you were to obey me as a true king ought to be obeyed, I would certainly see to it that you tasted pleasure of a kind without which no festive occasion is truly completely happy! But enough of such words: I shall rule as best I know how." And Dioneo, following the usual practice, had the steward summoned, and told him in some detail what he was to do during the duration of his reign, and then announced:

"Worthy ladies, we have discussed so often and in a variety of ways the subject of human endeavor as well as its different kinds of adventures that if Mistress Licisca had not arrived on the scene a short time ago and said something which gave me material for a new topic tomorrow, I am afraid I would have found it very difficult to turn up a theme for us to talk about. As you heard, she declared she never knew a girl in her neighborhood who went to her husband a virgin, and she added that she was well acquainted with the many kinds of tricks married women played on their husbands. But leaving aside the first part of what she said, which is child's play, I think the second should make for pleasant discussion, and so, since Mistress Licisca has provided us with the clue, tomorrow I want you to tell stories about the tricks which, either out of love or for their own self-preservation, wives have played on their husbands, whether these tricks were discovered or not."

Telling stories on such a topic seemed unsuitable to some of the ladies, and they begged Dioneo to revise the theme he had just proposed; to these entreaties, the King replied:

"Ladies, I am aware, no less than you are, of what I have ordered, but the objection you have raised is insufficient to move me to change my mind, for I believe that times are such that as long as ladies and gentlemen take care not to act immorally, every form of speech is permitted. Now, are you not aware that because of the corruption of these times, judges have abandoned their tribunals, the laws, both of God and man, have fallen silent, and everyone is granted free rein to protect his own life? And so, if you were to stretch the bounds of your chastity somewhat with your storytelling, never meaning to follow this with improper actions, but only with the intention of providing pleasure for yourselves and for others, I do not see how in the future any plausible argument could be used to criticize anyone. And besides, from the first day until this very moment, our company has behaved most honorably, regardless of what has been said here, and it does not seem to me that any act whatsoever has sullied our honor, nor, with God's help, will it ever be sullied. Moreover, everyone knows how virtuous you are, and in my opinion no amusing little stories or even the terror of death, for that matter, could make you any less virtuous than you are. And, to tell you the truth, if anyone were to find out that you had refrained from talking about these little matters on any occasion, they might suspect that you actually had a guilty conscience and, because of this, did not wish to discuss them. Not to mention the fact that you would be paying me a pretty compliment indeed if after I have obeyed you all, you, now that you have made me your King, decide to take the law into your own hands by refusing to speak on the topic I have imposed. So, set aside these false scruples which are more befitting a wicked mind than they are our own, and let each one of you do your best to think of some beautiful story to tell." Hearing this argument, the ladies agreed to do as he wished, and then the King gave all of them his permission to do as they pleased until the supper hour.

The sun was still high because the storytelling that day had been brief, and so when Dioneo sat down to play dice with the other young men, Elissa called the other ladies aside and said:

"Since the day we arrived here, I have wanted to take you to a place very nearby where I believe none of you has ever been, a place called the Valley of the Ladies, but until today, since the sun is still high, I did not see how I might be able to do so; and so, if you would like to go there, I have no doubt that when you get there, you will be most delighted for having gone."

The ladies replied that they were ready to go; and without saying anything about it to the young men, they sent for one of their maidservants and set out; and they had not gone more than a mile before they reached the Valley of the Ladies. They entered this valley through a very narrow path, along one side of which flowed a crystal-clear little stream, and they found it to be as beautiful and delightful, especially during that time when the weather was so hot, as one might possibly imagine. And according to what some of them told me afterward, the plain in the hollow of the valley was as round as if it had been drawn with a compass, in spite of the fact that it was the work of Nature and not the hand of man: it was a little more than half a mile in circumference, surrounded by six little hills, none of which was very high, and on the summit of each could be seen a palace built like a charming little castle.

The sides of these little hills sloped downward toward the plain like tiers in an amphitheater, arranged so that they gradually descended from the summit to the lowest row, continuously diminishing their circles. And as for these slopes, the side facing south was covered with vines, as well as olive, almond, cherry, fig, and many other varieties of fruit-bearing trees, so copious that there was not a foot of land which remained uncultivated. The slopes that looked north were thick with woods filled with oaks, ashes, and other trees, all as green and straight as they could possibly be. The plain which touched the slopes, lacking any other entrances except that one through which the ladies had come, was full of firs, cypresses, laurels, and a number of pine trees, all so well arranged and organized that they might well have been planted by the most skillful gardener. And when the sun was high overhead, little or no sunlight at all reached through these trees to the ground below, which was composed of a meadow of the most delicate grass, full of flowers of purple and many other colors.

And besides all this there was something else which delighted them no less: a small stream which splashed, cascading down the living rock of the gorge dividing two of these little hills, creating a noise which was most delightful to hear, and it appeared from a distance as though it were propelled by some hidden pressure as it sprinkled a fine spray of quicksilver. And when it reached the small plain of the valley, it flowed swiftly along down a pretty little channel to the center, where it collected to form a tiny lake, like those which city dwellers sometimes build in their gardens to use as a fishpond if they have the means to do so. This little lake was no deeper than the height of a man to his chest, and since it was free of all impurities, its bed clearly showed a stretch of the finest gravel, which could have been counted to the last grain by anyone who had nothing better to do; and the bottom of the lake was not the only thing that could be seen through the water, for there were also many fish darting here and there, all both delightful and wondrous to behold. The lake was enclosed by no other banks than the terrain of the meadow, which was so much the more beautiful all around the lake because it was kept damp by its water. And the water which overflowed drained through another small channel, and flowed out of the little valley, running toward the lowlands.

This, then, was the place the young ladies had come to, and after looking all around it and praising the place highly, since it was very hot and was right there in front of them, having no fear of being seen, they decided to go for a swim. After ordering their maidservant to stand above the path through which they had entered the valley to make sure to warn them if anyone came, all seven of them undressed and went into the water, which concealed their milk-white bodies not unlike the way a crystal glass conceals a pink rose. And when the ladies were in the water, which became no less clear because of their presence, they began as best they could to swim here and there chasing the fishes, which were sorely pressed to hide, trying to catch them with their bare hands. After amusing themselves for quite a while with such sport, having captured several of the fishes, they emerged from the water and put their clothes on once more, and unable to praise the place any more highly than they had already praised it, they thought it was time to return home, and at a leisurely pace, still speaking at length about the beauty of this spot, they started off.

It was still quite early when they arrived at the palace, and finding the young men where they had left them, still playing dice, Pampinea said to them laughingly:

"We have certainly deceived you today."

"How is that?" said Dioneo. "Have you begun to do those things even before you tell stories about them?"

"Yes, your majesty," Pampinea replied, and she went on to tell him in detail where they had gone, describing the valley, telling him how far away it was, and what they had done there.

Hearing the beauty of the place described, the King became

anxious to see it for himself, and so he quickly ordered supper to be served, and after everyone had eaten with a great deal of pleasure, the three young men accompanied by their servants left the ladies and went to this valley; none of them had ever been there before, and after examining the place, they concluded that it was one of the most beautiful sights in all the world. And after they had gone for a swim, and dressed again, since the hour was getting late, they returned home, where they found the ladies dancing a *carola* to a song being sung by Fiammetta; and when the *carola* was over, the men began to talk to them about the Valley of the Ladies, of which they all spoke very highly, praising its beauties. Then the King called the steward and ordered him to see that on the following morning, arrangements be made to bring beds to the valley in the event that anyone might wish to sleep or lie down there in the middle of the day. Then he ordered torches, wine, and confections and when they had refreshed themselves a bit he ordered everyone to join in the dancing, and at his request Panfilo began leading a dance, while the King turned toward Elissa and said pleasantly to her:

"Beautiful young lady, as today you honored me with this crown, so this evening I should like to give you the honor of singing us a song; therefore, sing us the one you like the most."

Smiling, Elissa replied that she would gladly do so, and in a soft voice she began singing in this way:

> Love, if I could ever escape your claws,
> I hardly can believe
> that any other hook would ever catch me again.
>
> I entered just a maiden in your war,
> believing it was perfect peace, benign,
> and all my arms I laid upon the ground,
> as any trusting person would have done,
> but you, treacherous tyrant, harsh and fierce,
> were quick, instead, to leap on me
> with your cruel claws and all your arms.
>
> And then, you had me bound up with your chains,
> to that man who was born to make me die,
> and I in bitter tears and suffering
> was given to him as a prisoner;
> his lordship is so cruel
> that not a sigh or cry from me,
> who waste away, can make him change.

The wind keeps sweeping all my prayers away;
no one will listen, nor do they even care,
and so, my torment constantly increases,
I hate my life, but how to end it all?

Ah, lord, have pity on my pain,
and do for me what I cannot:
deliver him to me, bound in your chains.
If you cannot grant me this wish, at least
loosen the knot that binds my hope so tight.
Ah, lord, I beg you, grant me this request;
for if you do, I trust that I can still
return to all my former beauty,
and, sorrow banished, I shall deck
myself in flowers white and scarlet.

When Elissa had brought her song to a close with a very moving sigh, although they all were puzzled by its words, no one there could imagine why she chose to sing such a song. But the King, who was in good humor, called for Tindaro and had him bring out his bagpipes, to the sound of which Dioneo had them do several dances; and it was well into the night before he bade them, one and all, to go to bed.

[Seventh Day, Title Page]

✤

Here ends the sixth day of The Decameron: *and the seventh begins, in which, under the rule of Dioneo, stories are told about the tricks which, either out of love or for their own self-preservation, wives have played on their husbands, whether or not these tricks were discovered.*

[Seventh Day, Introduction]

✤

EVERY star had by now vanished from the eastern skies, except the one we call Lucifer, which was still glimmering in the whitening dawn, when the steward arose and made his way with a large quantity of baggage to the Valley of the Ladies in order to arrange everything according to the orders and instructions of his master. And after his departure, it was not long before the King, too, arose, for the noise caused by the loading of the carts and animals had awakened him; and he saw to it that the ladies and the young men were also called. The rays of the sun were scarcely shining forth when they all started on the way; and it seemed to them that never had they heard the nightingales and the other birds sing so gaily as they seemed to be singing that morning; they enjoyed the company of their songs until they reached the Valley of the Ladies, where they were greeted by the singing of even more birds, who seemed to be rejoicing at their arrival. As they roamed around the valley examining it once again, it appeared to them even more beautiful than it had the day before, especially at this hour of the day, which displayed its beauties more effectively. And when they had broken their fast with good wine and confections, in order not to be outdone by the songs of the birds, they, too, began to sing, and the valley resounded with its sound, echoing the songs they were singing; and all the birds, as if unwilling to be outsung, added their new, sweet notes to theirs.

But when it came time for dinner and the tables had been set beneath the laurel and the other splendid trees near the beautiful little lake, as the King desired, they all sat down, and as they ate, they watched large schools of fishes swimming about the lake, which not only attracted their attention but gave rise to discussion. Once the meal had ended and the food and tables had been removed, even happier than they were before, they began to sing. Then their discerning steward had beds made up in various places in the small valley, all of which were surrounded with curtains and enclosed by canopies made from light, printed French fabrics, and with the King's permission, anyone who wished to could use them to rest, and those who did not wish to sleep were free to choose any of the other amusements to which they were accustomed. But when they were all up and about again, and it was time for them to gather together to tell their stories, according to the King's wishes, they all sat down on carpets which had been spread out over the grass near the lake not far away from the place where they had eaten, and then the King ordered Emilia to start. Smiling, she happily began to speak as follows:

[Seventh Day, First Story]

❧

Gianni Lotteringhi hears a knock at his door during the night; he awakens his wife, and she makes him believe it is a ghost; they go and exorcise the ghost with a prayer, and the knocking stops.

My lord, I would have much preferred it had you chosen some other person than myself to introduce so fine a topic as the one we are to speak about; but since you wish me to serve as an encouragement to all the other ladies, I shall do so most willingly. And I shall attempt, dearest ladies, to speak about something which may be useful to you in the future, for if other women are like myself, they are easily frightened, especially of ghosts—and God knows, I have no idea what they are, nor have I ever found a woman who did, yet all of us fear them just the same—but if ever you run into a ghost you will be able to drive it away, for by listening carefully to my story, you will learn a fine and holy prayer made precisely for this purpose.

There once lived in the San Brancazio quarter of Florence a wool weaver who was called Gianni Lotteringhi, a man who was more successful in his trade than he was sensible in other matters, for although he was something of a simpleton, he was quite often elected leader of the laud-singers of Santa Maria Novella and had to oversee their performances and was frequently called upon to fulfill a number of other relatively unimportant duties, and as a result, he thought quite highly of himself; and yet the only reason these duties were given to him so often was that, being a man of means, he could provide the friars with some good meals. And since they often managed to get a pair of hose or a cloak or a scapular out of him, they taught him some good prayers and gave him copies of the *Paternoster* in the vernacular, as well as the song of Saint Alexis, the lament of Saint Bernard, the laud of Lady Matelda, and other such nonsense, all of which he valued very highly and used most diligently for the salvation of his soul.

Now this man had a most beautiful and charming wife, a very wise and discerning lady, whose name was Monna Tessa, and she was the daughter of Mannuccio dalla Cuculia, a very wise and experienced man; his wife, having realized the simpleminded nature of her husband, fell in love with Federigo di Neri Pegolotti, who was a handsome and lusty young man, and he fell in love with her. She had one of her maidservants bring Federigo to a very beautiful villa which her husband Gianni owned in Camerata and where Tessa would spend the whole summer; Gianni would occasionally go there to eat supper and spend the night, and in the morning return to his shop or sometimes to his laud-singers. Federigo, who desired nothing better, on a day which was prearranged, took the occasion and around vespers he made his way there, and since Gianni was not coming that evening, he ate supper and completely at ease and to his great delight he spent the night with the lady; and as Tessa lay in his arms that night, she taught him at least half a dozen of her husband's lauds. But since she did not intend for this first time to be the last time they would spend together, and since Federigo felt the same way, in order to avoid having to send her maidservant for him every time, they agreed on the following: that every day, whenever he went to or returned from one of his properties which was a short way up the road, he would keep an eye on a vineyard alongside her house where he would see the skull of an ass on one of the poles in that vineyard. If he saw its face turned toward Florence, that meant he could come in safety and should come without fail to visit her that evening when it was dark, and if he did not find the door open, he should knock three times, and she would open it for him; and when he saw the skull's face turned toward Fiesole, he was not to come, since Gianni would be there. And by using this method, they were able to see each other quite often.

But on one of these occasions when Federigo was supposed to have supper with Monna Tessa and she had cooked two fat capons for him, it so happened that Gianni, who was not supposed to come home, did so late that evening, which distressed the lady greatly, and she and her husband supped on a bit of salted meat which she had boiled separately. Meanwhile, she had her maidservant take the two boiled capons in a large white napkin, together with a quantity of fresh eggs and a flask of good wine, down to her garden (which could be reached without going through the house) where she would on occasion dine with Federigo, and she ordered the maidservant to put everything at the foot of a peach tree which grew by the edge of the small meadow. But the lady was so upset by what had happened that she forgot to tell her servant to wait until Federigo arrived so as to let him know that Gianni was at home and that he should take the food in the garden away with him. And so after she and Gianni and the maidservant had gone to bed, it was not long before Federigo arrived and knocked gently once at the door, which was so close to the bedroom that Gianni heard it at once, and so did the lady, but she pretended to be asleep so that Gianni would have no reason to suspect her.

After waiting awhile, Federigo knocked a second time, and Gianni, who began wondering what it was, nudged his wife a bit, and said:

"Tessa, do you hear what I hear? It sounds as if someone is knocking at our door."

The lady, who had heard the noise much better than he had, pretended to wake up, and replied:

"What did you say? Mm?"

"I said," Gianni answered, "it sounds as if someone is knocking at our door."

The lady said:

"Knocking? Oh, my dear Gianni, don't you realize what that

is? That's the ghost that's been scaring me so these past few nights that whenever I heard it, I stuck my head under the sheets and never dared to come back out until the break of day."

Then Gianni said:

"Go on, woman, if that's what it is, there's no need to be afraid, for I said the *Te lucis* and the *Intemerata* and many another powerful prayer before we went to bed, and I also made the sign of the cross from one corner of the bed to the other in the name of the Father, the Son, and the Holy Ghost, so there's no need to be afraid. No matter how powerful this ghost may be, it cannot do us any harm."

To prevent Federigo from becoming suspicious and getting angry with her, the lady decided that she should get out of bed and let him know that Gianni was there; and so she said to her husband:

"That's all well and good for you to have said your prayers, but as for me, I'll never feel safe or sound unless we exorcise it, and seeing that you're here, why don't we?"

"And how can the ghost be exorcised?" asked Gianni.

The lady answered:

"I know exactly how to exorcise it, because the day before yesterday, when I went to the indulgence services in Fiesole, one of those lady hermits, who is, Gianni dear, the holiest person in the world, as God is my witness, seeing how afraid I was of this ghost, taught me a holy and useful prayer and told me she had tried it many times before becoming a hermitess and that it had always worked. But God knows I would never have dared try it alone; now that you are here, let's go and exorcise it together."

Gianni said that he liked the idea, and getting out of bed, they both went quietly over to the door, outside of which, Federigo, whose suspicions by this time were aroused, was waiting; and when they got to the door, the lady said to Gianni: "Now you spit when I tell you to."

"All right," replied Gianni.

And the lady began to exorcism by saying:

"Ghost, ghost, who walks by night, who came here with your tail up tight, keep it up and go; go to the garden, and at the foot of a large peach you'll find some oily greasy mess and lots of chicken droppings there; then take a swig of wine and go, and harm me not nor Gianni mine." And after she had said this, she told her husband: "Spit, Gianni!" and Gianni spat.

Federigo, who was outside and heard all this, had stopped

feeling jealous, and in spite of his disappointment, he could hardly stop himself from laughing out loud, and when Gianni spat, Federigo found himself whispering "Your teeth!" The lady, after she had exorcised the ghost in this fashion three times, returned to bed with her husband.

Federigo, who had not yet eaten supper because he had expected to do so with the lady, understood the words of the prayer very well, and so he went into the garden and at the foot of the large peach tree he discovered the two capons, the wine, and the eggs, and he took all of it home with him and ate supper at his leisure; and when he found himself with his mistress on many a later occasion, he laughed hilariously with her over that incantation of hers.

It is true that some people claim the lady had actually turned the skull of the ass toward Fiesole but that a worker in the vineyard who was passing by stuck a stick inside it and turned it all around and left it facing Florence, and so Federigo, thinking that he was being summoned, went to the house; and they also claim that the lady's prayer went something like this: "Ghost, ghost, leave us be, the ass head wasn't turned by me; God's curse upon the one who turned it round, I'm right here with my Gianni safe and sound"; and so Federigo would have left without a bite to eat or a place to stay. But one of my neighbors, a very old woman, tells me that both versions are true, according to what she learned as a young girl, but that the second version happened not to Gianni Lotteringhi but to a man called Gianni di Nello instead, who lived in the Porta San Piero district and was no less of a pea-brain than Gianni Lotteringhi was. And so, my dear ladies, I leave it up to you to choose whichever of the two incantations pleases you the most, or perhaps you like them both, for as you have just seen for yourselves, they can be very effective in certain situations. Learn them by heart, for they may come in handy in the future.

[Seventh Day, Second Story]

❧

Peronella hides her lover inside a barrel when she discovers that her husband is coming home; she tells the husband, who has sold the barrel, she had already sold it to someone who is inside of it checking to see if it is sound; when her lover jumps out of the

*barrel, he has her husband clean it and then carry it off to his
home for him.*

EMILIA'S story was received with roars of laughter, and the
prayer was praised as useful and holy by everyone; and when
the tale came to its conclusion, the King ordered Filostrato to
continue; and he began:

My very dear ladies, the tricks men play on you are so nu-
merous, and especially those that husbands play, that when a
woman on occasion does as much to her husband, you should not
only rejoice over it and be happy that you heard it talked about,
but you should also go around telling it to everyone yourself, so
that men may come to learn that women, for their part, know
just as much about these things as they do. This cannot be any-
thing but useful to you, for when someone knows that others
know about such matters, he will not easily wish to deceive you.
Who can doubt, therefore, that when men learn what we have to
say about this subject today, this will serve as a very good rea-
son for them to refrain from such deceits, since they will dis-
cover that you, too, know how to deceive them, if you wish? It
is therefore my intention to tell you how a young woman, al-
though she was of low birth, deceived her husband and on the
spur of the moment managed to save herself.

Not long ago in Naples a poor man took as his wife a beauti-
ful and charming young girl named Peronella; he, with his
mason's trade, and she, as a spinner of wool, earned very little,
but they managed their lives as best they could. One day a
handsome young man caught sight of Peronella and was so
charmed by her that he fell in love with her, and he managed to
get around her in one way or another so that soon he was on in-
timate terms with her. And in order to be together, between the
two of them they agreed on a plan: when her husband would get
up early every morning to go to work or to look for a job, the
young man would hide until he saw him leave; and as the dis-
trict where they lived (which was called Avorio) was not a busy
place, when the husband left, he would enter her house; and this
they did many times.

But one morning, out of many mornings, when the good man
had left and Giannello Scrignario, the young man, had entered
her house and was with Peronella, after a little while the hus-
band, who usually stayed out all day, happened to come home
after a short time, and when he discovered the door locked from
the inside, he knocked, and after knocking, he began saying to
himself:

"O God, may you be praised forever, for though you have made me poor, at least you have consoled me with a good and honest young wife! See how she immediately locked the door from the inside when I left, so that nobody would come in and bother her."

When Peronella heard this and understood that it was her husband from the way he knocked, she said:

"Oh, Giannel, my love, I'm done for! It's my husband! He's come home, God damn him, and I have no idea what's going on, for he never comes back at this hour. Maybe he saw you when you came in! But for the love of God, whatever the reason, get in that barrel over there, and I'll open the door for him and find out what brings him home so early."

Giannello quickly jumped into the barrel, and Peronella went to the door and opened it for her husband, and with a frown on her face she said:

"Now what's the idea of coming home so early this morning? I see you have come back with your tools in hand; it seems to me you don't want to do a thing; and if you keep on this way, how are we going to live? How will we buy our bread? Do you think I'm going to let you pawn my best dress and my other odds and ends of clothes? I do nothing all day but spin wool and work my fingers to the bone just to have enough oil to light our lamp. Husband, I tell you, husband, there's not a neighbor here that isn't amazed and doesn't make fun of me for all the work that I put up with, and you come home with your hands dangling when you should be out there working!"

And saying this, she began to cry and to start the whole story over again:

"Oh, poor me, miserable me, why was I ever born! Under what unlucky star did I come into this world! I could have married a good young man, but I didn't want him, and I settled for this one, who thinks nothing of the woman he took into his home! Other women have a good time with their lovers (and there's not a single one without two or three of them), and they enjoy them and make their husbands believe the moon is the sun. And me, poor me! Because I'm good and don't care to do such things, I'm the one who has to suffer with bad luck. I don't know why I don't get myself a lover as the rest of them do. You listen good, husband mine, if I wanted to sin, I could easily find someone to do it with; there are some handsome young men who love me and wish me well and who have offered me lots of money, clothes, and jewelry, if I want; but not being the daughter of that kind of a woman, my heart wouldn't allow me to do such a thing. And you come home to me when you should be at work!"

"Hey, for God's sake," said her husband, "don't get so excited; believe me, I know you and what you are like, and this morning I have even seen some evidence of it. True, I was going to work, but what you say shows that you did not realize any more than I that today is the Festival of Saint Galeone, and since there's no work today, I came home early; but I have nevertheless provided for you: I have found a way to keep us in bread for more than a month. I sold the barrel which, as you know, has been taking up room in the house for some time now, to this man you see with me here, and he is giving me five silver coins for it."

Peronella replied:

"And all this is also part of what makes me mad! You are a man, you get around, and you should know how the world is run—you sold a barrel for five silver coins—while I, a woman, when I saw the trouble it was giving us in the house, I, who almost never gets out of this house, sold it for seven silver coins to a good man who, just before you walked through the door, climbed inside to see if it was in good enough shape."

When the husband heard this, he was overjoyed, and he told the man who had come for the barrel:

"My good man, God be with you. You heard my wife; she sold it for seven, and you wanted to give me only five."

"Very well," the good man replied, and he left.

Then Peronella said to her husband:

"Now that you're home, get up here, and see to our business with him."

Giannello, who had his ears cocked to hear whether there was need to be afraid or to take precautions, heard what Peronella said, and he quickly jumped out of the barrel; and pretending to know nothing of the husband's return he said:

"Where are you, my good woman?"

"Here I am; what can I do for you?"

"Who are you?" asked Giannello. "I should like to speak to the woman with whom I made the deal for this barrel."

And the good man answered:

"Don't worry, you can deal with me; I am her husband."

Then Giannello said:

"The barrel seems sound enough to me, but it looks as if you have stored wine dregs in there, for it's completely coated over with some kind of dry stuff that I can't scrape off with my nails, and I will not take it if it isn't cleaned up first."

And Peronella said:

"No, the deal won't be called off for that; my husband will clean the whole thing for you."

And her husband said, "Of course." Laying down his tools and rolling up his sleeves, he lit a lamp and picked up a scraper, crawled into the barrel, and began to scrape it. And Peronella, pretending to be interested in what he was doing, put her head, one shoulder, and an arm into the mouth of the barrel, which was not very large, and began saying to her husband:

"Scrape here, and here, and also over there, and—see there where you left a little."

And while she stood in this position instructing and directing her husband, Giannello, who had hardly satisfied his desire that morning before the husband returned, contrived to satisfy it as best he could, for he could not do it as he really wanted to. He went up behind Peronella, who, by standing there, was blocking off the mouth of the barrel, and just as the unbridled stallions of Parthia mount the mares in the open meadows when they are hot with love, so he, too, satisfied his youthful lust, reaching his climax at almost the same time as the scraping of the barrel came to an end; after which he withdrew, and Peronella removed her head from the barrel's mouth, and her husband came out. Then Peronella said to Giannello:

"Take this light, my good man, and see if it is cleaned well enough for you."

Giannello looked inside, replied that everything was fine and that he was satisfied, and paying the husband seven silver coins, he had him carry the barrel to his home.

[Seventh Day, Third Story]

✦

Brother Rinaldo lies with the mother of his godchild; when her husband discovers him in her bedroom, they lead him to believe that he is exorcising his godson's worms.

FILOSTRATO's reference to the Parthian mares was not so veiled that the discerning ladies did not laugh over it, though they pretended to be amused by something else. But when the King realized that his story was finished, he ordered Elissa to continue the storytelling; she gladly obeyed and began as follows:

Pleasing ladies, the exorcism of Emilia's ghost has brought to mind a story about another exorcism which, although not as entertaining as her story was, I shall nevertheless recount, since nothing else dealing with our topic comes to me at this moment.

I want you to know that in Siena there once was a rather charming young man from an honorable family, by the name of Rinaldo, who happened to be passionately in love with a very beautiful lady who was the wife of a wealthy neighbor of his, and hoping, if only he could find a means of talking to her without arousing suspicion, to obtain from her everything he wanted, since the lady was pregnant, he decided that he had no other choice but to become her child's godfather; so having become friends with the lady's husband, in the most honorable way possible, he made his request to the husband, and it was accepted. Thus Rinaldo became the godfather to Madonna Agnesa's child, and now that he had a somewhat more plausible reason for speaking with her, he grew more confident, and with his words, he apprised her of his intentions, which she had long before guessed from the look in his eyes, but it did him little good, in spite of the fact that the lady did not find his declaration displeasing.

Not long afterward, for some reason or another, Rinaldo became a friar, and regardless of how he found these pastures, he stuck to them. Although he had from the time he became a friar put aside the love he bore his godchild's mother, as well as a couple of his other worldly vices, yet in the course of time, without abandoning his friar's habit, he reverted to his old ways, and he began to take pleasure in the way he looked, in expensive material for his habits, in being gallant and elegant in everything he did, in composing songs, sonnets, and ballads, in singing, and in spending his time in all sorts of similar activities.

Why do I go on this way about this Brother Rinaldo of ours? Is there a friar that does not act this way? Oh, scandal of this corrupted world that they are! They're not at all ashamed of being so fat and flushed-faced, or so effeminate in their dress and all their affairs, and they strut around not like doves but, rather, like proud cocks with their crests raised on display. And what's worse (not to mention the fact that their cells are stocked with bottles of ointments and creams, with boxes full of assorted confections and phials and flasks containing perfumes and oils, and casks overflowing with Malmsey and Greek and other vintage wines, so that anyone who saw their cells would be more likely to take them for apothecary or perfume shops than for friar's quarters), they are not ashamed to let others know they suffer from the gout, actually believing that people are unaware that regular fasting, a simple meager diet, and living a sober way of life produce thin, lean, and for the most part healthier men; or if such men do fall ill, at least it is not from the gout, for which the medicine usually prescribed is chastity and other things befitting the life of a simple friar. And besides, they think others do not realize that a simple life, long vigils, prayer, and self-discipline should make men pale and drawn, and that neither Saint Dominic nor Saint Francis ever owned four cloaks apiece, nor did they ever dress up in finely dyed, elegant garments but, rather, in coarse, woolen robes of natural colors made to keep out the cold rather than to appear stylish. May God see to it that they and all those simpleminded souls who supply their needs get what they deserve!

And so, to go on, Brother Rinaldo reverted to his old cravings, and he began to visit his godchild's mother quite often; growing more and more bold, he began to urge her with more insistence than ever to give him what he wanted. The good lady, finding herself solicited this way, and thinking that Brother Rinaldo was perhaps more handsome than he had first appeared to be, one day while being more insistently pestered by him resorted to a stratagem which all women adopt when they wish to concede what is being requested of them, and she said:

"Really, Brother Rinaldo, do friars do this sort of thing?"

To this question, Brother Rinaldo replied:

"Madam, the moment I remove this cloak, which I can remove quite easily, you will see me as a man made just like all the others and not as a friar."

The lady pretended to laugh and said:

"Oh dear, poor me! You are the godfather of my son; how could you do such a thing? It would be terribly wicked, and I have always been told that it is a very serious sin; if it weren't for that, I would be happy to do what you like."

To this, Brother Rinaldo said:

"You are a foolish woman if you pass this up for that reason. I'm not saying it's not a sin, but God forgives even greater sins as long as you repent. But tell me something: who is a closer relative to your son, I who held him at his baptism, or your husband by whom he was begotten?"

The lady answered: "My husband is more closely related."

"That is correct," remarked the friar, "and doesn't your husband sleep with you?"

"Of course he does," the lady replied.

"Therefore," concluded the friar, "since I am less closely

related to your son than your husband is, I should also be able
to sleep with you the way your husband does."

The lady, who was unskilled at logic and was in need of very
little persuasion, either really believed or pretended to believe
that what the friar said was true, and she answered: "Who
could ever refute such wise words?" And then, in spite of their
spiritual relationship, she proceeded to fulfill all his desires. Nor
did this happen only once, for concealed under the cover of this
special relationship with her son, which gave him better oppor-
tunity with less suspicion, they met together more and more
often.

On one of these many occasions that they met, Brother
Rinaldo had come to the lady's home with a companion of his,
and realizing that there was no one else in the house except the
lady's very beautiful and charming maidservant, he sent his
friend off with her up to the pigeon coop on the roof to teach her
the Lord's Prayer while he and the lady, who was holding her
small child by the hand, went into the bedroom, and locking
themselves inside, they settled down on a divan that was there
and began having fun with each other. And while they were do-
ing this, the child's father happened to come home, and without
any of them hearing him, he reached the entrance to the bed-
room, knocked, and called his wife.

When Madonna Agnesa heard this sound, she said:

"I'm as good as dead, my husband's here; now he's bound to
see what's behind our friendship."

Brother Rinaldo was undressed (that is, no cloak and hood,
standing there in just a vest), and hearing the noise, he said:
"That's for sure! If only I were dressed, there might be some
way to get out of this; but if you open the door to him now and
he finds me like this, there's no way to explain."

The lady, assisted by a sudden inspiration, replied:

"Now you get dressed, and when you're dressed, take your
godson in your arms and listen very carefully to what I am go-
ing to say to him, so that what you say will back me up, and
leave the rest to me."

The good man had hardly finished knocking before his wife re-
plied: "I'm coming," and getting up, she composed herself and
went over to the bedroom door, and she opened it, exclaiming:

"Oh, husband, let me tell you that if Brother Rinaldo, our
godfather had not come—had he not been sent by God—we
would have surely lost our son today."

When the poor fool of a husband heard this, he turned all pale
and asked: "What?"

"Oh, husband," the lady went on, "a while ago, the child suddenly fainted and I thought he was dead and I didn't know what to do or say, but Brother Rinaldo, our godfather, arrived at that very moment, took him in his arms, and said '*Comare,** these are worms he has in his body, and if they come any closer to his heart they could easily kill him, but have no fear, for I shall exorcise them and kill them all, and before I leave you, you shall see your son as healthy as you have ever seen him.' He needed you to recite certain prayers, but since our servant couldn't find you, he had his companion recite them in the highest part of our house, and he and I went into the bedroom. And since no one but the child's mother can perform this function, to keep others from interrupting us, we locked ourselves inside: Brother Rinaldo is still holding the child in his arms, and now all he is waiting for, I think, is for his companion to finish saying the prayers, and then the exorcism will be complete, for the child has already regained his senses."

Believing all this, the simpleton was so moved by his affection for his son that he did not notice the trick his wife was playing on him, and heaving a great sigh, he said: "I want to go see him."

The lady replied:

"Don't go in, or you will spoil everything that has been done until now; wait and let me see if you can go in, and I'll call you."

Brother Rinaldo, who had overheard everything that was said while he finished dressing himself quite leisurely, picked up the child in his arms, and after he had arranged things to suit him, he called out:

"Oh, *comare*, do I hear my *compare* out there?"

And the simpleton answered: "Yes, sir."

"Well, then," said Brother Rinaldo, "come right in." The simpleminded husband went inside, and Brother Rinaldo said to him:

"Take your son, restored to health through God's grace, although there was a moment when I thought you would not see him alive by vespers; you should have a life-size wax statue of the child made, and for the glory of God, placed before the

*In this context, *comare* and *compare* are friendly terms of address still in use in the south of Italy, and they have no real equivalent in English. Literally, the words mean "godmother" and "godfather." In this instance, it just happens that the *compare* and family friend, Brother Rinaldo, really is the godfather of the child in question.

statue of Messer Saint Ambrose, through whose merits God has granted you this grace."

When the young boy saw his father, he ran toward him and, as little boys do, made a fuss over his arrival; his father took him in his arms, weeping as if he were taking the boy from his grave, and he began to kiss his son and to thank the godfather for having cured him. Brother Rinaldo's companion, in the meantime, had taught the young servant girl not one but perhaps as many as four Our Fathers and had given her a purse of white linen which had been given to him by a nun, thus making the young girl his devotee; when he heard the simpleton calling at his wife's door, he had quietly slipped downstairs to a spot where he could see and hear everything that was going on, and when he saw that things were going quite nicely, he came downstairs, entered the bedroom, and announced:

"Brother Rinaldo, I've said all four of those prayers you ordered me to say."

To this Brother Rinaldo replied:

"Brother, you're in good form, and you've done a good job. As for me, when the father of my godson arrived, I had only recited two of them, but through your labors and my own, God Almighty has granted us this grace and has cured the child."

The simpleton sent for some good wine and confections, and he treated his *compare* and his companion with the kind of refreshments they needed more than anything else; then he left the house with them, commended them to God, and without the slightest delay he had the wax image made and sent to be hung with all the others in front of the statue of Saint Ambrose—but not the one in Milan.*

[Seventh Day, Fourth Story]

✦

One night, Tofano locks his wife out of the house, and when she finds, in spite of all her entreaties, that she is unable to get back inside, she pretends to throw herself down a well by dropping a huge stone into it; Tofano leaves the house and runs to the well,

---

*Not Milan's famous Church Doctor but rather a Domenican from Siena (1220–86) to whom the city dedicated a chapel in 1288.

while in the meantime, she enters the house, locks him outside,
and shouts insults at him.

WHEN the King saw that Elissa's story had reached its conclu-
sion, he immediately turned toward Lauretta, indicating that he
wished her to tell the next story; whereupon, without hesitation,
she began as follows:

Oh Love, how numerous and how great are your powers, what
resource of counsel, what insight you have! What philosopher,
what artist ever could display such intelligence, such insight, or
such explanations as you spontaneously bestow on those who fol-
low in your footsteps? Every other doctrine is most certainly be-
hind the times with respect to your own, a fact which can be
clearly seen from the cases which have been previously dis-
cussed; to these, loving ladies, I should like to add a story
concerning what a simple woman accomplished by using an expe-
dient which I believe could only have been revealed to her by
Love.

Well then, there once lived in Arezzo a rich man who was
called Tofano. This man took as his wife a most beautiful lady
whose name was Monna Gita, of whom he immediately became
jealous without any reason whatsoever, a fact which offended the
lady when she discovered it; she asked him on repeated occa-
sions for some explanation for his jealousy but she received
nothing but vague and confused replies, and so the lady decided
to make her husband die of the very disease which he had no
reason at all to dread so. And having noticed that a young man,
a very fine person in her opinion, was casting amorous glances in
her direction, she discreetly began to come to an understanding
with him; when things had advanced so far between the two of
them that nothing remained but to translate their words into
deeds, the lady thought of a means to do this. Since among her
husband's bad habits she had discovered that he liked to drink,
she began not only to commend him for it, but she would en-
courage him in clever ways to do so very often. And she went
about it so well that she was able to get him drunk almost
anytime she wished; and when she saw that he was good and
drunk, she would put him to bed and off she would rush to meet
with her lover, and in this way they continued to meet safely on
many occasions, and the lady had so much confidence in her
husband's drinking habits that not only did she dare to take her
lover into her own house, but sometimes she would even go with
him for a good part of the night to his own home, which was not
so far away.

The enamored lady had been doing this for some time when it happened that the unfortunate husband came to notice that whenever she encouraged him to drink, she never drank anything herself; this made him suspect (which was, indeed, the case) that she got him drunk so that she could afterward do as she pleased while he was sleeping. And determined to know whether this was, in fact, the case, he pretended by the way he spoke and acted one evening, not having drunk a drop all day, to be the drunkest drunk possible, and so the lady, taken in by his act, was sure that he required no more to drink in order to sleep soundly, and quickly put him to bed. And after she did so, as was her custom on many other occasions, she left the house and went to the home of her lover, and there she remained until midnight.

When Tofano no longer heard his wife in the house, he got up, went over to the door, and locked it from the inside, and then he stationed himself at the window, so that he could see his wife when she returned and show her that he had discovered what she was up to. He stayed there until the lady came home, and when she reached her house to discover that she was locked out, she was most upset indeed, and began to try forcing the door open. Tofano allowed this to continue for a while, before saying:

"Lady, you're wasting your energy, you'll never get back in here. Go back to wherever you have been until now, and rest assured that you'll never return to this house until, in the presence of your relatives and neighbors, I have paid you the kind of honor you deserve."

The lady began to beg him for the love of God to let her in, insisting that she was not returning from where he imagined but, rather, from sitting up with one of her neighbors, who was unable to sleep because the nights were long and she was the only one in the house. Her pleas got her nowhere, for this fool was perfectly willing to let everyone in Arezzo learn of his shame, when as yet no one actually knew a thing about it.

When the lady realized that her begging would do her no good, she resorted to threats and said:

"If you don't open the door for me, I'll make you the unhappiest man alive!"

To this Tofano replied: "And what can you do to me?"

The lady, whose wits had been sharpened by the counsel of Love, replied:

"Before I suffer the shame you wrongly wish to inflict on me, I shall throw myself down that well over there, and then when they find me dead down there, there will be no one who will not think that in your drunkenness, you threw me down there; and so you shall either have to flee for your life, lose everything you own, and live in exile, or you'll have your head chopped off for murdering me, which is, in effect, what you will have really done."

But these words had no effect on changing Tofano's foolish mind; and so the woman said:

"Now see here, I will not let you torment me any longer. May God forgive you! I am leaving my spindle here for you to put back where it belongs." The night was so pitch-black that a person could hardly see another on the street, and having said these words, the woman made her way toward the well, and picking up a big stone which was lying near it and crying "Lord, forgive me!" she dropped it into the well.

As the stone struck the water it made a loud noise, and when Tofano heard it, he was convinced that she had thrown herself in; and so he quickly grabbed the well pail and the rope and ran outside the house to help her, racing to the well. When the woman, who had concealed herself near the door of her house, saw him running toward the well, she rushed into the house, locked herself in, went over to the window, and began to shout:

"You ought to water down your wine when you drink it and not so late at night."

When Tofano heard her, he realized she had made a fool of him, and when he returned to the door and found he was unable to get in, he began ordering his wife to open the door for him.

His wife, who until then had been speaking to him in little more than a whisper, was now on the verge of screaming as she said:

"By God's cross, you lousy drunk, you won't get in here tonight; I can't stand this behavior of yours any longer: it's time for me to show the world just what kind of a man you really are and what time you come home at night."

Tofano, who by now was also in a rage, started yelling insults at her, and all the neighbors, hearing the noise, got out of bed, men and women alike, opened their windows, and asked what was happening.

In tears, the woman began to explain:

"It's this wicked man, who comes home drunk in the evening or falls asleep in taverns and then returns at this time of night; I have put up with this for a long time, but it has done me no good, and since I could take it no longer, I decided to shame him by locking him out of the house to see if he would mend his ways."

The silly fool of a Tofano, instead, was trying to explain how the whole thing really happened as he threatened her violently.

Then the lady said to her neighbors:

"Now do you see what kind of a man he is? What would you say if it were me out in the street there the way he is instead of here in the house as I am? By God's faith, I'm sure you'd think he was telling the truth. You do see how clever he is, don't you? He claims I have done the very thing I say he has done. He thought he could frighten me by tossing I don't know what into the well, but now I wish to God he had really thrown himself down and drowned, so in that way at least the wine he drank so much of would have been well watered down!"

The neighbors, men and women alike, all began to reproach Tofano, to lay the blame on him, and to abuse him for the things he had accused his wife of doing, and in short, the news spread from neighbor to neighbor until it finally reached the woman's relatives. They arrived on the scene, and when they heard what had happened from one or another of the neighbors, they grabbed Tofano and gave him such a whipping that he was left with bruises all over; and then they went into the house, gathered together the woman's belongings, and took her back to their own home, threatening Tofano with even worse treatment to follow. Seeing himself reduced to such a sorry state brought about by his jealousy, Tofano, since he really did love his wife, turned to several of his friends, asking them to act as intermediaries on his behalf, and managed to arrange for her to come home to him in peace, promising her he would never be jealous again; besides this, he gave her permission to do whatever she pleased but to do it so discreetly that he would never notice. And so, like some crazy peasant, first he got mad and then turned pleasant. So long live Love and all our company and death to every tightwad!

[Seventh Day, Fifth Story]

❋

A jealous husband disguised as a priest hears his wife's confession, and she gives him to believe that she loves a priest who comes to her every night, and while the jealous husband keeps watch hiding by the door, the lady has her lover come through the roof and lies with him.

AFTER Lauretta had concluded her story and everyone had praised the lady for having treated her wicked husband exactly as he deserved, the King, in order not to lose time, turned to Fiammetta, and in a pleasing fashion imposed upon her the task of telling a story; and so she began:

Most noble ladies, the previous story prompts me to tell a similar story about a jealous husband, for I believe that whatever their wives do to them, especially when they become jealous without cause, is well done. And if lawmakers had considered the matter fully, it is my opinion that the punishment they established for wives should have been no different from the punishment they established for someone who attacks another person in self-defense, for jealous husbands are treacherous plotters against the lives of young wives and are most diligent seekers of their demise. Like everyone else, after being closed inside the house all week, attending to the needs of the family and the household, these young girls wish to enjoy the peace and quiet of a holiday and to enjoy themselves, as do the laborers in the fields, the artisans in the cities, and the magistrates in the courts, and just as God Himself did when He rested from all His labors on the seventh day, and as it is prescribed in both canon and civil law, which, in consideration of the reverence due to Him and for the common welfare of everyone, has distinguished days of labor from those of rest. But jealous husbands will have nothing of this; on the contrary, on those days when other women are happy, they keep their wives not only in their houses but even locked in their rooms, making such days even more miserable and painful; how exhausting all this is only those wretched creatures who have experienced it know. And so to conclude, whatever a wife does to a husband who is jealous without a reason is certainly to be praised rather than to be condemned.

So then, there once lived in Rimini a merchant who was very wealthy in land and money, who had a most beautiful wife and who became jealous of her beyond all measure; he had no reason to be so except for the fact that because he loved her greatly and considered her to be extremely beautiful and knew that she tried to do everything she could to please him, he assumed that every man must love her, that she must seem beautiful to them all, and even that she would, as a result, try to please other men besides himself—an argument worthy of a wicked man of little sensitivity. And as jealous as he was, he guarded her so closely and kept her under such tight reins that even those sentenced to death are not so closely watched by their captors. Not even to mention the fact that he would not allow her to go to weddings, festive occasions, or church, or even to set her foot outside the house, nor did she dare to show herself at a window or to look outside the house for any reason; and so her life was most miserable, and she endured this pain all the more impatiently since she knew that she was guiltless.

And so, seeing herself wrongfully injured by her husband, she decided that for her own consolation she would discover a means, if at all possible, of arranging things so that he would have some real cause for his jealousy. And since she could not show herself at the windows, she was thus unable to reveal her delight at the attentions of anyone who might have courted her while passing through the area. But since she knew that in the house next to hers there lived a handsome and pleasant young man, she thought that if she could find an opening of some sort in the wall which separated her house from the next one, she might be able to look through it from time to time, just enough to see the young man and to be able to speak to him and to offer him her love, if he were willing to accept it, and, if there were some means of doing so, to meet with him on occasion and in this way be able to endure her wretched life until this evil spirit of jealousy left her husband.

And so, when her husband was not at home, she went from one part of the house to the next, examining the walls until she happened to find in a rather remote part of the house a spot where the wall was opened slightly by a crack; and so, looking through this crack, even though she had trouble seeing through to the other side, she was, nevertheless, able to see that the spot where the crack was located looked into a bedroom, and she said to herself:

"If this is Filippo's bedroom,"—that was the name of the young man who was her neighbor—"I'm practically all set." She had one of her maidservants, who felt sorry for her, keep watch cautiously through the hole, and she came to discover that the young man, in fact, did sleep by himself in that room. And so, by paying frequent visits to the crack whenever she heard the young man on the other side, and by pushing little pebbles and tiny pieces of straw through it, she finally managed to get him to come over to the wall in order to see what was happening. The lady called quietly to him, and since he recognized her voice, he replied; and, taking this opportunity, she quickly revealed her heart to him. The young man was delighted by this, and from his side of the wall he started to enlarge the hole, but in such a way that no one would take notice of it. And there on numerous occasions they would talk together and touch each other's hands, but they were unable to go any further because of the close watch kept by her jealous husband.

Now, as the Christmas holiday was growing near, the lady told her husband that if he agreed, she would like to go to church on Christmas morning, to make her confession, and to take Communion as other Christians do; to this request, the jealous husband replied:

"And what sins have you committed that make you want to go to confession?"

The lady answered:

"What? Do you think I am a saint just because you keep me locked up here? You know very well I commit sins just like other people who live in the world; but I do not wish to tell them to you, for you are not a priest."

The jealous husband became suspicious from her remarks, and he decided he would try to find out what sins she had committed. So he replied that he would allow her to do this but that he did not want her to attend any other church than their own chapel, and that she should go there early in the morning and make her confession either with their own chaplain or with whatever priest the chaplain might provide for her and with no one else, and that after this she should return home immediately. The lady had more or less guessed his intentions, but asked no questions and replied that she would do what he asked.

When Christmas morning came, the lady got up close to dawn, prepared herself, and went to the church her husband had chosen. The jealous husband also had gotten up and gone to the same church, arriving there before she did. Having already arranged everything with the priest there, he quickly put on one of the priest's robes with a hood that came down to his cheeks, like those we often see priests wearing, and after pulling it forward a bit, he went to sit down in one of the pews. Arriving at the church, the lady asked for the priest. The priest came, and when she told him she wished to be confessed, he told her he could not do it, but that he would send a fellow priest; and leaving her, he sent the jealous husband in, much to his misfortune. The husband walked solemnly up to her, and although there was not much light and he had pulled his cowl well over his eyes, he was unable to disguise himself well enough and was instantly recognized by the lady; and when she saw who he was, she said to herself:

"Praise be to God, he's been transformed from a jealous husband into a priest; but never mind, I'll see that he gets what he's looking for." And so, pretending not to recognize him, she sat down at his feet. Messer Jealous had put a few pebbles in his mouth to change his voice a bit and to prevent his wife from recognizing him, and he believed his disguise was convincing enough in every respect that there was no way she could identify him. Now, getting to her confession, the lady told him, among other things, after first noting that she was married, that she had fallen in love with a priest who came to sleep with her every night.

When the jealous husband heard this, he felt as though he had been stabbed through the heart with a dagger, and if it had not been for the fact that he wanted to know more about it, he would have abandoned the confessional and left the chapel; holding his ground, he asked the lady: "What? Doesn't your husband sleep with you?"

The lady replied: "Yes, father."

"Well, then," said the jealous husband, "how can the priest sleep with you too?"

"Father," answered the lady, "how he manages to do it I do not know, but I tell you there is not a locked door in the house which does not open when he touches it; he tells me that when he comes to the door of my bedroom, before he opens it, he says certain words which put my husband right to sleep, and as soon as he hears him sleeping, he opens the door, comes inside, and lies with me: and this method never fails."

Then the jealous husband declared:

"Madam, this is a sorry affair, and it must cease immediately!"

To this the lady said:

"Father, I do not think I could ever do that, for I love him so much."

"Then," replied the jealous husband, "I cannot give you absolution."

To this the lady replied:

"I am sorry about that, but I did not come here to tell you lies; if I thought I could do what you ask, I would tell you."

The jealous husband continued:

"Madam, I am, indeed, sorry for you, because by taking such a decision, I see you losing your soul; however, in order to help you, I shall labor on your behalf by saying some of my special prayers to God, which may do you some good. And from time to time I shall send you one of my seminarians whom you are to tell whether these prayers are doing any good or not, and if they work, we shall proceed from there."

To this the lady said:

"Father, do not send anybody to the house, for if my husband learns about it, he is so insanely jealous that nothing in the world could remove the notion from his head that the man who had come was up to no good, and he would give me no peace for the rest of the year!"

To this the jealous husband replied:

"Madam, do not worry about that, for I shall arrange things in such a way that you will never hear a word about it from him."

Then the lady concluded:

"If you can manage to do that then I agree." And after she had made her confession, she received her penance, and getting up from where she had been kneeling at his feet, she went off to hear Mass.

The hapless husband, boiling with anger, took off his priest's robes and went back home, anxious to find some means of catching the priest and his wife together so that he could do them both a bad turn. The lady returned from church and saw quite clearly from the expression on his face that she had spoiled his Christmas holiday; but he, as best he could, tried to conceal what he had done and what he thought he knew.

And since he had made the decision to keep a close watch at the main entrance that night to see if the priest would come, he said to his wife:

"This evening, I shall be eating supper and spending the night elsewhere, and so be sure you lock up the front door well, the door on the landing, and the bedroom door, and you may go to bed whenever you like."

"I shall do so," said the lady.

As soon as she had the chance, she went to the crack in the wall and made the usual signal, and when Filippo heard it, he came over there; the lady told him everything she had done that morning and what her husband had told her after breakfast, and then she said:

"I am certain he will not leave the house but will, instead, stand guard by the front door, and so find some way to climb in here through the roof tonight, so that we can be together."

Thoroughly delighted by this proposal, the young man replied:

"My lady, leave everything to me."

When night came, the jealous husband concealed himself with his weapons in a room on the ground floor. And after his wife had locked all the doors tightly, especially the one at the landing so that the jealous husband would not be able to come up, it was soon time and the young man very cautiously came over from his side of the building; then they got into bed and had a good time with each other until daybreak, when the young man returned to his home.

The jealous husband, miserable, supperless, and freezing to death, remained for almost the entire night with his weapons close to the front door, waiting for the arrival of the priest; and near daybreak, unable to stay awake any longer, he went to sleep in a room on the ground floor. A few minutes before tierce, he got up, and finding the front door of the house was already open, he pretended to be arriving from somewhere else, went upstairs, and ate breakfast. Shortly thereafter, he sent one of his servant boys, disguised as if he were the seminarian of the priest who had confessed his wife, to ask her if the man whom she knew about had come to pay her a visit again. The lady, who quite easily recognized the messenger boy, replied that he had not come that evening and if things continued this way, she might very well forget him, even though she had no desire to do so.

Now what more can I tell you? The jealous husband remained at the entrance of the house for many a night in order to catch the priest, and the lady continued to have a good time with her lover. Finally, the jealous husband, who could put up with it no longer, angrily asked his wife what she had told the priest on the morning she had made her confession. The lady answered that she did not wish to tell him, since doing so was neither honest nor proper.

To this response, the jealous husband declared:

"Wicked bitch, despite your refusal, I know exactly what you told him, and I absolutely insist that you tell me who this priest is with whom you are so much in love and who sleeps with you every night by means of his incantations, or I shall slit your throat!"

The lady replied it was untrue that she was in love with a priest.

"What?" asked the jealous husband. "Isn't that what you told the priest who heard your confession?"

The lady answered:

"As a matter of fact, I did tell him that, and you couldn't have known it any better than if you had been there yourself."

"Never mind," said the jealous husband, "tell me right now who this priest is."

The lady began to smile as she said:

"I am always delighted to observe a simple woman leading an

intelligent man around by the nose as if he were a ram being led by the horns to the slaughter—not that you are intelligent, nor have you ever been so from the moment you allowed the evil spirit of jealousy to enter your heart without good reason. And the more foolish and stupid you are, the less is my accomplishment. Husband, do you really believe that my eyes are as blind as the eyes of your brain? Certainly not! When I saw you, I knew who the priest confessing me was, I knew it was really you; but I made up my mind to give you exactly what you were looking for, and that I did. But if you had been as smart as you think you are, you never would have resorted to such a trick in order to learn the secrets of your honest wife, nor would you have succumbed to groundless suspicion, for you would have realized that what she confessed to you was the truth and that she had in no way sinned. I told you that I was in love with a priest, and weren't you, whom I love so unwisely, a priest? I told you that none of the doors in my house could remain locked when he wanted to sleep with me, and what door in your house was ever kept closed to you when you wished to come to me? I told you that the priest slept with me every night, and was there ever a night when you did not sleep with me? And as you know, as many times as you sent your seminarian to me, and you were not sleeping with me, I sent him back to you to tell you that the priest had not been with me. What other fool but you, who allowed yourself to be blinded by your jealousy, would not have understood all these things? You who stay at home all night to keep watch at the front door and try to make me believe you have gone somewhere else to eat supper and to spend the night! Isn't it time you took a good look at yourself, and return to being the kind of man you used to be? Stop allowing someone who knows you as well as I do to make such a fool of you, and stop keeping the close watch over me that you do; for I swear to God, if I wanted you to wear the horns of a cuckold, had you a hundred eyes instead of the two you do have, I could find a way of taking my pleasure without your ever noticing it!"

The poor jealous husband, who thought he was so clever in finding out his wife's secret, upon hearing this felt himself put to shame; and without saying anything by way of reply he began to think of his wife as a good and wise woman, and thus, just as he had worn the mantle of a jealous man when there was no need to, now he discarded it completely. And so the clever wife, practically given a license, as it were, to do what she pleased, no longer had her lover come through to visit her over the roof as cats are accustomed to do, but had him enter, instead, by the front door, and from that day on, by acting discreetly, she was able to enjoy herself with him on many an occasion and to lead a happy life.

[Seventh Day, Sixth Story]

🏵

While she is with Leonetto, Madonna Isabella, who is loved by a certain Messer Lambertuccio, is visited by him just as her husband is about to return home; she sends Messer Lambertuccio out of her house with a dagger in his hand, and later on her husband accompanies Lionetto home.

FIAMMETTA's story was enormously enjoyed by everyone, and they all declared that the lady had acted quite rightly and had treated her stupid husband exactly as he deserved. But now that the story was finished, the King ordered Pampinea to continue, and she began by saying:

There are many people who, speaking foolishly, maintain that Love impairs one's intelligence and that anyone who falls in love turns into somewhat of a fool. This seems to me to be a silly notion, as the stories told earlier have amply shown, and now I intend to show it once more.

In our city, which abounds in all the good things of life, there was a noble and very beautiful young lady, who was the wife of a very brave and excellent knight. And as often happens, just as people grow tired of eating the same food day after day and wish to vary their diet, in like manner, this lady, not being completely satisfied with her husband, fell in love with a young man whose name was Leonetto, an extremely pleasing and well-mannered person, though he was not of noble birth, and Leonetto, too, fell in love with her; and since, as you know, only very rarely does some result not come from it when both parties are willing, very little time passed before they consummated their love.

Now, because the lady was such a beautiful and charming woman, a knight named Messer Lambertuccio fell passionately in love with her, but since she considered him to be an unpleasant and boorish person, she was not disposed to love him for anything in the world; but he continued to entreat her with messages, which did him no good, however, and since he was a

man of influence, he proceeded to threaten to ruin her reputation
if she did not fulfill his desires. Because of this, the lady was
afraid, and realizing what kind of a man he was, she brought
herself to do what he wished.

And having gone to stay in one of her beautiful country es-
tates, as is our custom to do in the summer, the lady, whose
name was Madonna Isabella, sent word to Leonetto to come to
stay with her, since her husband had ridden off somewhere that
day and would be away for several days; and he, who was
overjoyed, did so immediately. In the meantime, Messer Lam-
bertuccio, hearing that the lady's husband was not at home,
mounted his horse and, unaccompanied, rode to her place and
knocked at the door. When the lady's maidservant saw him, she
quickly ran to Isabella, who was in the bedroom with Lionetto,
and calling to her, she exclaimed:

"My lady, Messer Lambertuccio is downstairs all by himself."

When the lady heard this, she was most distressed indeed;
since she was terrified of Messer Lambertuccio, she begged Le-
onetto not to object to concealing himself for a while behind the
bedcurtains until Messer Lambertuccio had left. Leonetto, who
was no less afraid of him than was the lady, hid himself there;
and the lady ordered her maidservant to go and open the door
for Messer Lambertuccio, which she did, and having ridden into
the courtyard he dismounted his palfrey, tied it to a hook, and
climbed up the stairs. Putting on a cheerful expression, she came
to the head of the stairs, and as best she could she welcomed
him with a smile and asked him why he had come. Embracing
and kissing her, the knight explained:

"Love of my life, I heard that your husband was not at home,
so I came to be with you for a while." After he said this, they
went into the bedroom and locked themselves inside, and Messer
Lambertuccio began to take his pleasure with her.

And while he was with her, contrary to her expectations, it
happened that the lady's husband returned; when her maidser-
vant saw him approaching the house, she quickly ran to the
lady's bedroom and cried:

"Madam, it is the master who is returning; I think he is al-
ready downstairs in the courtyard!"

When the lady heard this and realized she had two men inside
the house (and knew that she could not conceal the knight, since
his palfrey was standing in the courtyard), she thought she was
as good as dead; nevertheless, leaping out of bed, she instantly
made up her mind what to do and said to Messer Lambertuccio:

"Sir, if you love me in the least and wish me to escape certain death, you will do as I tell you. Take out your dagger and with it in hand, with anger and outrage all over your face, rush down the stairs, shouting as you go: 'I swear to God I'll catch up with him someplace else'; and if my husband tries to stop you or to ask you something, say nothing except what I told you to say, then get on your horse and on no account let him stop you."

Messer Lambertuccio said that he was willing to do this, and drawing his dagger, his face all flushed by his recent exertion as well as by his anger over the knight's return home, he did just as the lady had instructed him. The lady's husband, having already dismounted in the courtyard, was puzzled at the sight of the palfrey, and just as he started to climb the stairs, he saw Messer Lambertuccio coming down, and being most amazed by his words and expression, her husband said: "Sir, what is going on here?"

Messer Lambertuccio, after putting his foot in the stirrup and mounting his horse, said nothing but: "I swear to God I'll catch up with him someplace else!" And off he rode.

The gentleman climbed the stairs and found his wife at the top of the landing, bewildered and full of fear, and he asked her:

"What's going on here? Who is Messer Lambertuccio threatening in such an angry fashion?"

Withdrawing toward the bedroom where Leonetto was listening, the lady replied:

"Sir, I have never been so afraid in all my life. A young man whom I do not even know ran in here with Messer Lambertuccio pursuing him with a dagger in hand. By chance he discovered this bedroom open and trembling all over, he said: 'Madam, for God's sake help me, or I shall be murdered in your very arms.' I got right up and was about to ask him who he was and what the argument was about when Messer Lambertuccio came in shouting: 'Where are you, traitor?' I stood in the doorway of the bedroom, and although he wanted to come inside, I restrained him, and at least he was courteous enough that when he realized I did not want him to come inside, he merely made a number of remarks and rushed downstairs as you saw for yourself."

Then her husband said:

"Lady, you did the proper thing: it would have been too great a dishonor for us if anyone had been killed under our own roof, and Messer Lambertuccio committed a most villainous act in pursuing someone who had taken refuge within our home."

Then he asked where the young man was.

The lady replied: "Sir, I do not know where he has hidden himself."

The knight then asked:

"Where are you? You may safely come out."

Leonetto, who had overheard everything, came out from where he had concealed himself, trembling with fear like someone who really was afraid.

Then the knight asked:

"What do you have to do with Messer Lambertuccio?"

The young man replied:

"Sir, not a thing in the world, and that is why I am thoroughly convinced that the man is not in his right mind, or perhaps that he mistook me for someone else, because not far from this house, spotting me in the street, he put his hand to his dagger and shouted: 'Traitor, you're as good as dead!' I did not stop to ask why, but began to run as fast as I could and reached here, where, thanks be to God and to this gracious lady, I was saved."

Then the knight said:

"Come now, have no fear, I shall see you to your home safe and sound, and later you can try to find out what this is all about."

And after they had supper, the husband escorted him back to Florence on horseback and left him at his home; then, following the instructions he had received from the lady, that very evening the young man spoke in secret with Messer Lambertuccio, arranging matters with him in such a way that even though there was a great deal of talk about the affair, the knight never found out about the trick his wife had played on him.

[Seventh Day, Seventh Story]

✦

Lodovico reveals to Madonna Beatrice the love he bears for her, whereupon she sends her husband Egano into a garden disguised as herself while she lies with Lodovico; then, afterward, Lodovico gets out of bed, goes into the garden, and gives Egano a beating.

MADONNA Isabella's clever trick as recounted by Pampinea was considered marvelous by every member of the company; but now Filomena, upon whom the King had called to continue the storytelling, said:

Loving ladies, if I am not mistaken, I think I can tell you a tale just as good as the last, and it won't take long.

I want you to know that in Paris there once lived a Florentine nobleman, who because of his poverty had become a merchant, and he was so successful in his business that he became extremely wealthy from it; and from his wife he had but one son, whom he named Lodovico. And because his son inclined more toward the father's nobility than to business, the father did not wish to place him with any commercial establishment but had, instead, sent him to live with other noblemen in the service of the King of France, where he learned a great deal about good manners and other important matters.

And while he was living there, certain knights returning from the Holy Sepulcher happened to come across a group of young men, one of whom was Lodovico, arguing about the relative beauty of the women of France, England, and the other parts of the world, and after listening to these young men, one of the knights began to tell them that in all the parts of the world he had visited and of all the women he had ever seen, there had certainly never been any woman equal in beauty to Madonna Beatrice, the wife of Egano de' Galluzzi from Bologna; and all his companions, who had seen her with him in Bologna, were in agreement. When Lodovico heard this, since he had not yet fallen in love with anyone, he was inflamed by such a powerful desire to see her that he could think of nothing else; absolutely determined to go all the way to Bologna to see her and even to remain there if he found her pleasing, he gave his father to believe that he wanted to go to the Holy Sepulcher, and only with the greatest of difficulty did he obtain his permission.

He then took the name of Anichino and went to Bologna; and, as Fortune would have it, on the following day he saw this lady at a banquet, and he decided that she was even more beautiful than he had been told; and so, falling most passionately in love with her, he determined never to leave Bologna before winning her love. And having thought about the different means he might use to achieve this goal, he decided, having rejected every other plan, that if he could join her husband's staff as one of the many servants he employed, this would be the only way to achieve what he desired. After he had sold his horses and arranged for his servants to be adequately housed, having first ordered them to pretend they did not know him, he became friendly with his innkeeper and told him he would gladly join the service of a nobleman of standing, should he be able to find one, and to this the innkeeper replied: "You are exactly the kind of retainer that would please a certain nobleman of this city whose name is Egano and who employs a great many servants and likes them all to be as impressive-looking as you are; I'll speak to him about you."

The innkeeper did just as he said he would and before taking his leave of Egano, he had arranged for Anichino to be hired, and this pleased him greatly. Now that he lived with Egano and had ample opportunity to see his wife quite often, he began to serve Egano so well and came to please his master so much that Egano thought very fondly of him and could not do without him; and he entrusted to Anichino the administration not only of his household but of all his possessions.

Now one day it happened that Egano having gone falconing and Anichino remaining at home, Madonna Beatrice, who was not yet aware of Anichino's love for her (although she had on more than one occasion observed him and his behavior and found that they pleased her), engaged Anichino in a game of chess; wishing to please her, Anichino with some subtle moves allowed the lady to win, which thrilled the lady no end. And when the ladies-in-waiting who had been watching the game had gone and left them to play alone, Anichino heaved a deep sigh.

Looking at him, the lady asked:

"What is the matter, Anichino? Does it hurt so much when I win?"

"My lady," replied Anichino, "a much greater matter than that is the cause of my sigh."

Then the lady said:

"Ah! Tell me, in the name of the love you bear for me."

When Anichino heard that he was being implored "in the name of the love you bear for me," and by the lady whom he loved more than anything else in the world, he heaved an even deeper sigh than he had before; and so the lady asked him yet again to please tell her what was the cause of his sighs; to this question Anichino replied:

"My lady, I am very much afraid that you might be displeased if I told you; and I fear that later on you might repeat what I say to someone else."

To this the lady said:

"It shall certainly not displease me, and you may rest assured that whatever you tell me, if it be your wish, I shall never repeat to anyone else."

Then Anichino declared:

"Since you make me this promise, I shall tell you." Almost with tears in his eyes, he told her who he was, what he had heard about her, where and how he had fallen in love with her, and why he had become a servant in her husband's household; and then he humbly begged her, if she could do so, to have pity on him, and to fulfill this secret and so fervent desire of his; and that if she did not wish to do so, she allow him to remain in her service and be content that he should love her.

Ah, the exceptional sweetness of Bolognese blood! How highly you are always to be praised in such affairs! Neither tears nor sighs ever found your favor, but you were always compliant to entreaties and susceptible to amorous passions; if I possessed the eloquence to praise you as you deserve, my tongue would never grow weary.

As Anichino spoke, the noble lady looked at him, and believing his every word, the power of his prayers so moved her heart that she, too, began to sigh, and after sighing a number of times, she replied:

"My sweet Anichino, be of good cheer; neither gifts, nor promises, nor the courtships of noblemen, lords, or anyone else has ever been able to move my heart to such an extent that I loved them in return (and I have been and am still pursued by many men), but in the brief space of time that it has taken you to utter these words, you have made me belong far more to you than I do to myself. I think that you have most certainly earned my love, and so I give it to you and promise you that I shall make it yours to enjoy before this night is over. And to bring this about, arrange to come to my bedroom around midnight; I shall leave the door open, and you know on which side of the bed I sleep; come there, and if I am sleeping, touch me enough to awaken me, and I shall console you for your long desire. And so that you may believe what I say is true, I want to give you a kiss as a pledge." Then, throwing her arms around his neck, she kissed him passionately, and Anichino did the same to her.

Having said these things, Anichino left the lady and went to attend to his duties, looking forward to the coming of night with the greatest joy in the world. Egano returned from his hawking, and after eating supper, since he was exhausted, he went to bed and then later the lady did the same and, just as she had promised, left the door of her bedroom open. And at the hour he had been told, Anichino came there and quietly entered the room, and after locking the door behind him, he went to the side of the bed where the lady slept, and placing his hand upon her breast, he discovered that she was not asleep. As soon as the lady felt his presence, she took his hand with both of hers, held it tightly, and began twisting and turning in the bed until Egano was awakened from his sleep. She said to him:

"I didn't want to say anything to you about it last night, since I thought you looked tired, but tell me, Egano, as God is your salvation, of all those servants you employ in your household, which of them do you consider to be the best, the most loyal, and the one who loves you the most?"

Egano answered:

"Lady, what is this that you are asking me? Don't you know who he is? I do not have nor have I ever had a servant whom I ever trusted or now trust and love as much as I trust and love Anichino; but why do you ask?"

When Anichino heard that Egano was awake and could hear them talking about him, more than once he tried to pull his hand away and leave, being terrified that the lady was going to trick him; but she held him so tightly in her grip that he was unable to do so. The lady, replying to Egano, said:

"I'll tell you. I thought that things were just as you said and that he was more worthy of your trust than anyone else, but he has undeceived me, for when you left to go hawking today, he stayed behind, and when the time seemed ripe to him, he had no shame in asking me to consent to fulfill his desires; and so without having to gather an excessive amount of evidence and to let you see it for yourself, I told him that I would be delighted to do so and that this evening, after midnight, I would go into our garden and wait for him by the foot of the pine tree. Now, for my part, I have no intention of going there, but if you wish to observe your servant's loyalty for yourself, you can do so very easily by putting on one of my skirts, covering your head with a veil, and going downstairs to see if he comes, and I am certain he will."

When Egano heard this, he said: "I certainly must go and see this." After getting out of bed, as best he could in the dark, he put on one of the lady's skirts and a veil on his head, and went into the garden, and at the foot of the pine tree he waited for Anichino.

When the lady heard him get up and was sure he had left the bedroom, she got up and locked the door from the inside. Anichino, who had just experienced the worst scare of his life, who had tried with all his might to escape from the lady's clutches, and who had cursed a thousand times over both her, her love, and himself for trusting her, was, at the end of it all when he heard what she had done, the happiest man that ever lived; and then the lady got into bed, and at her request he took off his clothes, and joined her, and for a good long time they lay together taking their mutual pleasure and delight. Then, when the lady thought that Anichino had stayed long enough, she had him get up and dress, and said to him:

"Sweet lips of mine, now you must go down to the garden with a good, strong stick, pretending that you had propositioned me in order to test me, and shower him with abuse, as if he were me, and then give him a good thrashing with the stick—what joy and sheer delight it will give the both of us!"

Anichino got up, and down into the garden with a willow branch in his hand he went, and when he was near the pine tree and Egano saw him coming, he stood up, as if he wished to greet him with the greatest delight, and stepped forward to meet him, but Anichino said to him:

"Ah, you wicked woman, so you really came thinking that I could have or really would have wronged my master this way? A thousand curses on you!" And lifting the stick, he began to beat him.

As soon as Egano heard this and saw the stick, without saying a word he began to run away, and Anichino ran after him, shouting continuously: "Run, you wretched woman, and may God punish you; I'm going to tell Egano tomorrow about this for sure!"

After receiving quite a few good licks, Egano returned to his bedroom as quickly as he could, and the lady asked him if Anichino had come to the garden. Egano declared:

"I wish he hadn't, for he thought I was you, and he beat me all over with a stick, calling me the foulest names any wicked woman has ever been called. I certainly would have thought it strange if he had said such things to you with the intention of dishonoring me; instead, since he found you were so merry and gay, he merely wished to test you."

Then the lady said:

"Praise be to God that he tested me with words and you with deeds, for I think he will be able to say that I was better able to bear his words than you his deeds. But since he is so faithful to you, we should hold him most dear and do him honor."

Egano replied: "You are certainly right."

Because of what had happened, Egano was convinced that he possessed the most faithful wife and the most loyal servant that any nobleman could ever possess; as a result, on numerous later occasions, he and his wife along with Anichino laughed over what had happened, while at the same time it became much easier for Anichino and the lady to enjoy more freedom than they would have otherwise enjoyed, and to do what they both found delightful and pleasurable for as long a time as Anichino chose to remain with Egano in Bologna.

[Seventh Day, Eighth Story]

❦

A man becomes jealous of his wife, and she ties a string to her toe during the night, so that she will know that her lover has come to visit her; the husband notices this, and while he is off chasing her lover, the wife puts another woman in her place in bed, whom her husband beats and whose hair he cuts off; then he goes to fetch his wife's brothers, and when they discover what her husband claims is not true, they revile him.

EVERYONE felt Madonna Beatrice had been unusually clever in tricking her husband, and they all agreed that Anichino's fear must have been tremendous all the while the lady was holding him tightly and he heard her claim that he had solicited her love. But when the King saw that Filomena had finished talking, he turned to Neifile and said: "Now you tell a story." And with a faint smile on her lips Neifile began:

Lovely ladies, a difficult task faces me if I am to please you with as beautiful a tale as those with which my predecessors have amused you, but with God's help, I hope to do my job well.

You should know, then, that in our city there once lived a very wealthy merchant named Arriguccio Berlinghieri, who quite foolishly, and as we still see merchants doing today, thought that he could ennoble himself by marrying into an aristocratic family, and he chose a young noblewoman very badly suited to him, whose name was Monna Sismonda. Since he was often on the road, as most merchants are, and could spend little time with his lady, she fell in love with a young man named Ruberto, who had been courting her for quite a while now. And having become his mistress and having, perhaps, acted somewhat less discreetly than usual, since he did please her enormously, it happened that Arriguccio, either because he heard rumors of an affair or for some other reason, turned into the most jealous man in the world, and abandoning all his comings and goings and a good deal of his other business affairs, he spent all his time keeping a

close watch on her. Nor did he ever fall asleep before he had
heard her climb into bed, and this the lady found most dis-
tressing, for she was unable to find a means of being with her
Ruberto.

Now, having given a great deal of thought to finding some
way of being with him, and constantly urged on to do so by her
lover, she finally came up with the following scheme: since her
bedroom ran along the street, and since on many occasions she
had noticed that while Arriguccio took a long while to fall
asleep, once asleep he slept very soundly, she decided to have
Ruberto come to the door of her house around midnight, and she
would go down to open it and spend some time with him while
her husband was sound asleep. And so that she would know
when he had arrived, she arranged, in a way that no one would
notice it, to have a string dangling outside the window of the
bedroom, one end of which would almost touch the ground out-
side, while the other would run along the bedroom floor leading
up to her bed and then under the sheets, and when she got into
bed, she would tie it to the big toe of her foot. She then sent a
message about this to Ruberto and told him that when he ar-
rived, he should pull on the string, and if her husband was
asleep, she would release the string and come down to open the
door; and if he was not asleep, she would hold tight to the string
and then pull it toward her, so that he would know that he was
not to wait for her. This arrangement pleased Ruberto, and he
went there on many an occasion, sometimes succeeding in being
with her and other times not.

They continued using this system until finally one night while
the lady was sleeping, Arriguccio happened to be stretching him-
self in bed when his foot touched the string; and following it
along with his hand and finding it tied to his wife's foot, he said
to himself: "This must be some trick." Then, noticing that the
string went trailing out the window, he was convinced that it
was a trick; and so, quietly cutting the string from his wife's
toe, he tied it to his own and waited, ready to see what this was
all about. It was not long before Ruberto came and pulled on
the string, as he usually did, and Arriguccio felt it; but because
he had not tied it tightly enough, when Ruberto pulled hard on
it, the string dropped into his hands, and he understood that he
was supposed to wait, which is what he did.

Jumping out of bed and grabbing his weapons, Arriguccio ran
to the door to see who the fellow was and to do him harm. Now
Arriguccio, though only a merchant, was a brave and strong
man. But when he got to the door and did not open it as quietly

as the lady usually did, Ruberto, hearing the noise while he was waiting there, and realizing what had happened—that is, that the person who had opened the door must be Arriguccio—took off instantly with Arriguccio behind him in hot pursuit. Eventually, after running for quite a distance with Arriguccio still chasing him, Ruberto, who was also armed, drew his sword and turned about, and the one attacked while the other defended himself.

When Arriguccio opened the bedroom door, the lady awakened to find that the string had been cut from her toe, and she knew at once that her trick had been discovered; hearing Arriguccio running after Ruberto, she quickly got out of bed, and realizing what was likely to happen, she called her maidservant, who knew everything about the affair, and prevailed upon her to take her own place in the bed, imploring her not to reveal her identity and to receive patiently all the blows Arriguccio might inflict upon her, for which service she would be rewarded so handsomely that she would have no cause for regret. And having extinguished the light in the bedroom, the wife left the room and hid in another part of the house to wait for what was bound to happen.

While Arriguccio and Ruberto were fighting, the neighbors in the district heard the noise, which got them out of bed and made them start cursing at them, and Arriguccio, for fear of being recognized, was forced to abandon Ruberto and head for home, which he did boiling mad with rage, for he had not even discovered who the young man was or managed to do him the slightest injury. Entering his bedroom in a rage, he asked: "Where are you, you wicked woman? You put out the light so I wouldn't find you, but you are mistaken!" Going over to the bed, thinking he was seizing his wife, he grabbed the maidservant, and he gave her so many slaps and kicks with his hands and feet that her face was black and blue all over; and to finish it off he cut off her hair, all the while calling her the worst names ever heard by the foulest of women.

The maidservant cried at the top of her voice, and she had good reason to; and though she screamed from time to time "Oh my God, have mercy!" or "No more!" her voice was so changed by her crying, and Arriguccio was so blinded by his anger, that he did not realize this was the voice of another woman and not his wife's. And so, having beaten the living daylights out of her and cut off her hair, as we said earlier, Arriguccio declared:

"Wicked woman, I have no intention of laying another hand on you; instead, I shall go to your brothers and tell them about your fine deeds, and then let them do with you what they believe their honor demands, and take you away from here, for you shall surely never live in this house again." And after saying this, he left the bedroom, locked the door from the outside, and went off all alone.

When Monna Sismonda, who had overheard everything, saw that her husband had left, she opened the bedroom door, relit the light, and discovered her maidservant all beaten up and crying her eyes out; she consoled her as best she could and took her back to her own quarters, where afterward in secret she had her nursed and waited upon, and she rewarded her with enough of Arriguccio's own money to make the girl quite happy. And having returned the maidservant to her quarters, she quickly made up her own bed, tidied up the whole room so that it seemed as if no one had slept there that night, and then she relit the lamp and fixed herself up to appear as if she had never gone to bed; then she lit another lamp, took some clothes, sat down at the head of the stairs, and began to sew and to wait to see how things would turn out.

After leaving home, Arriguccio went as fast as he could to the home of his wife's brothers, and arriving there, he kept knocking at the door until he was heard and let in. The lady's brothers, three of them, and her mother, hearing that it was Arriguccio, got out of bed and with the lamps lit, they came down to ask him what he was doing there all alone and at that hour of the night. Beginning with the string which he had found tied to the toe of Monna Sismonda's foot, Arriguccio told them everything he had discovered and all that he had done up to that point; and to provide them with conclusive proof of what she had done, he handed over to them the hair which he thought he had cut off his wife's head, adding that they were to come for her and do what they believed their honor required, for as far as he was concerned, she would never come into his home again. The lady's brothers, who believed every word of the story, were furious over what they had heard, and full of anger at her, they called for torches to be lit and then set out with Arriguccio for his home with the intention of severely punishing their sister. When their mother saw what was happening, with tears in her eyes she began following them, begging now one of them and now another not to be too hasty in believing these things without first seeing more evidence or learning more about the circumstances, for her husband might well have become angry with her for some other reason and treated her badly, and he could be blaming her in order to excuse himself. She also said that she was most amazed that such a thing could happen, especially since she felt she knew her daughter very well and had raised her from the time she was a small child, as well as many other similar remarks.

And so they arrived at Arriguccio's house, went inside, and began to climb the stairs; when Monna Sismonda heard them coming, she asked: "Who's there?"

One of her brothers replied: "You know very well who it is, you wicked woman!"

Then Monna Sismonda said: "Now what does this all mean? God help us!" And standing up, she declared: "Brothers, you are most welcome; what are all three of you doing here at this hour of the night?"

When her brothers saw her sitting there sewing, not a visible mark of a beating on her face though Arriguccio claimed to have given her a sound thrashing, they were at first somewhat surprised, and their anger began to cool a bit; then they asked her for an explanation of the affair which Arriguccio was accusing her of, threatening her severely if she did not tell them the whole story.

The lady said: "I have no idea what I am supposed to say, nor do I understand why Arriguccio should be complaining to you about me." Arriguccio gazed at her, staring as if he had lost his wits, for he remembered how he had slapped her in the face perhaps a thousand times, had scratched her all over, and had given her the worst beating in the world, and yet he saw her now looking as if not a thing had happened to her. To make a long story short, her brothers told her what Arriguccio had told them, including the string, the beating, and all the rest.

Turning to Arriguccio, the lady exclaimed:

"Oh, husband, what is this I hear? Why, to your own great shame, do you make me out to be such a wicked woman, when I am not, and yourself to be such a wicked and cruel man, when it is not so? When were you ever in the house tonight with me? And when did you beat me? For my part, I have no remembrance of it."

Arriguccio began to protest:

"What, you wicked woman, did we not go to bed together? Did I not return here after chasing your lover away? Did I not give you a good beating and cut off your hair?"

The lady replied:

"You did not go to bed in this house tonight. But let us forget that, since I cannot provide you with proof of this except for my own true words, and come to what you claim, that you beat me and cut off my hair. You never beat me, and you as well as everyone present here can check to see if I have any marks from a beating on any part of my body; nor would I advise you to be so foolhardy as ever to lay your hands on me, for, by God's cross, I would scratch your face to pieces. Nor, as far as I can feel or see, did you ever cut off my hair, unless, perhaps, you did it when I wasn't looking: let me see whether it is cut off or not." And she lifted the veils from her head to show them that it was all there and that not one hair had been cut.

When her brothers and mother saw and heard these things, they turned to Arriguccio, saying:

"What does this mean, Arriguccio? This does not fit the story you came to tell us, and now tell us how you plan to prove the rest of it."

Arriguccio stood there as though in a trance, trying to speak, but seeing that what he thought he could prove was not the case, he made no attempt to say anything.

The lady turned to her brothers and said:

"Well, my brothers, I see now that he is asking for it; he is forcing me to let you in on a secret I would never have revealed concerning his miserable and wicked way of life, and I shall tell you about it. I am firmly convinced that what he told you did actually happen and that he did do everything he said he did, and let me tell you how. This worthy man to whom in my most unfortunate hour you gave me in marriage, a man who calls himself a merchant and wishes to be respected as such, who would like to be thought of as being more temperate than a monk and more virtuous than a maiden—this man comes home drunk from the taverns most evenings, playing around now with one whore and now with another, and I have to stay up until midnight, and sometimes until morning, waiting for him just the way you found me now. I am sure that when he was good and drunk he went to bed with one of his sorry whores and when he woke up, he found the string on her foot, and then proceeded to perform the brave deeds he recounted, and finally turning against her, he beat her and cut off her hair; and not quite having come to his senses yet, he believed, and I am sure he still does believe, that he did all these things to me. If you take a good look at his face, you can see he's still half-drunk. But all the same, whatever he has said about me I want you to take as nothing more than the words of a drunkard, and since I forgive him, you should forgive him as well."

When her mother heard these words, she started to make a racket and said:

"By God's cross, my daughter, we shall do nothing of the kind; on the contrary, we ought to murder this pesty dog of a nobody who is not worthy of having a girl such as you! Just look here! This would have been too much to take even if you had picked her up out of the gutter! He can go to Hell before you'll put up with the rotten slander of an insignificant little trader in donkey dung, one of those yokels from the country, right out of some pigsty, who dress in shabby clothes, with their short baggy stockings and their quill pens sticking out of their asses. As soon as they've gotten a few cents in their pockets, they want the daughters of noblemen and worthy ladies for their wives, and they make up a coat of arms, and then they claim: 'I'm one of the so-and-so family' or 'The people in my family do such-and-such.' I really wish my sons had followed my advice, for they could just as honorably have found you a home with one of the Counts of Guidi with no more than a piece of bread as a dowry, but they preferred to give you away to this fine jewel of a fellow, you, the best and most virtuous daughter in Florence, whom he has the impudence to call, and in the middle of the night, too, a whore, as if we didn't know you. But by God's faith, if it were up to me, I'd see to it he got such a beating that he stunk from hurting." Then, turning to her sons, she said:

"My boys, I told you this couldn't be true. Have you heard now how your fine brother-in-law has treated your sister, this twerp of a two-bit merchant that he is? If I were you, after hearing what he said about her and what he did, I wouldn't be happy or satisfied until he was wiped clean from the face of the earth; and if I were a man instead of a woman, I wouldn't let anyone stop me either! Good God, punish this wretched man, this foul drunkard that has no shame!"

The young men, having seen and heard all this, turned to Arriguccio and reviled him, calling him the worst names ever called a criminal; and they concluded by saying:

"We'll forgive you this time because you were drunk, but if you value your life, from now on you'd better make sure we never hear any more such stories, for if we ever hear another like it, we'll pay you back for sure, and not only for this one but for the next as well." And having said this, they left.

Arriguccio stood there like an idiot, not knowing himself whether what he had done he had actually done or if he had been dreaming, and so he said no more about it and left his wife in peace; and thus, through her cleverness, not only did she

avoid an impending danger, but she also opened the way to ful-
filling her every pleasure in the future, without ever having to
fear her husband again.

[Seventh Day, Ninth Story]

꙳

*Lidia, the wife of Nicostrato, is in love with Pirro; in order to
test her love, Pirro asks her to perform three tasks, all of which
she does for him; besides this, in Nicostrato's presence, she
makes love to him, and gives Nicostrato to believe that what he
has seen is not true.*

NEIFILE's story was so delightful that the ladies could not keep
from laughing and talking about it, even though the King several
times had ordered them to be quiet and had commanded Panfilo
to tell his tale; but finally when they were silent, Panfilo began
as follows:

I do not believe, revered ladies, that there is anything, no
matter how difficult or dangerous, which those who are pas-
sionately in love will not dare to do; and in spite of the fact
that this has been demonstrated in many of our stories, never-
theless I believe I can show this still more clearly with a story I
intend to tell you, wherein you shall hear about a lady whose
deeds were favored far more by Fortune than by her common
sense. And because of this, I would not advise any of you to risk
following in the footsteps of the lady about whom I mean to tell
you, since Fortune is not always so favorably disposed, nor are
all the men in the world equally stupid.

In Argo, that most ancient city of Greece, a place more
renowned for its past rulers than its size might imply, there once
lived a nobleman who was called Nicostrato, upon whom, when
he was reaching his old age, Fortune bestowed as his wife a lady
of nobility who was no less bold than beautiful, by the name of
Lidia. Since he was a wealthy and noble man, he kept many ser-
vants, dogs, and hawks, and he took the greatest delight in hunt-
ing; and among his many servants there was a young man
named Pirro, a charming, elegant, and handsome person who was
capable of doing anything he put his mind to doing and whom
Nicostrato loved and trusted more than any of his other ser-
vants. Lidia fell passionately in love with this man, so much so

that neither day nor night could she think about anything else; but either because he was unaware of this or because he wished not to show that he did know, Pirro paid no attention to her, and this filled the lady's heart with unbearable sorrow.

Ready to do anything to make known her feelings to him, Lidia summoned one of her servants, named Lusca, whom she trusted a great deal, and said to her:

"Lusca, the favors you have received from me ought to make you obedient and loyal, and so, take care that what I am about to tell you is never heard by anyone except the person to whom I order you to repeat it. As you can see, Lusca, I am a fresh young woman, abounding in all those things a young woman might desire, and in short, I have no complaints except for one, which is that my husband is far too old compared to me, and I am not well satisfied with that thing which gives other young ladies the greatest pleasure. And since I desire this thing as much as other women, for some time now I have made my mind up, since Fortune has been such a poor friend in providing me with such an old husband, not to be my own worst enemy and to find some means of providing for my own pleasures and salvation. And in order to be as well provided for in this matter as I am in all others, I have decided, since he is more worthy than anyone else, to choose our Pirro to fulfill my needs with his embraces, and I have begun to love him so much that I am not happy unless I see him or am thinking about him—and if I cannot have him soon, I know I shall die. And so, if my life is dear to you, by whatever means you think best, tell him of my love and beg him on my behalf to favor me with his presence when you go to fetch him."

The maid replied that she would gladly do so; and at the first opportunity she took Pirro aside and delivered her lady's message as best she knew how. When Pirro heard this, he was most amazed, for he had never noticed anything of the kind, and he was afraid the lady was doing this to test him; and so he answered her abruptly and rudely:

"Lusca, I cannot believe that these words come from my lady, so be careful what you say; and even if they did come from her, I cannot believe she meant them to be taken seriously; and even if she were speaking sincerely, I would never commit such an outrage against my master, who treats me with more esteem than I deserve, not even if my life depended on it; so take care never to speak to me about such matters again."

Unshaken by his severe manner, Lusca said to him:

"Pirro, I shall speak to you about these matters and about

anything else and as often as my lady orders me to, no matter
how much pleasure or bother it may give you—but you really
are a fool!"

Somewhat angered by Pirro's words, the servant returned to
the lady, who wanted to die the moment she heard his reply;
and after several days had passed, she spoke to her maid again
and said:

"Lusca, as you know, the oak tree does not fall at the first
blow; therefore, it seems to me you should return once more to
this fellow who has such a strange way of proving his loyalty to
me at my expense; and when you feel the time is right, make a
full declaration of my burning desire, and do everything you can
to make it work, for if it should fail I shall die, and he will
think that he has been made a fool of, and in seeking love, we
shall have won his hatred."

The maid comforted the lady, and then when she saw Pirro,
finding him cheerful and in good mood, she said:

"Pirro, a few days ago I revealed to you how your mistress
and mine was burning from the love she bears for you, and now,
once again, I reassure you that if you persist in the harshness
you showed the other day, you can be sure she will not live
much longer. Therefore, I implore you to give her the solace she
desires; and while I have always considered you a very intelli-
gent man, if you persist in being so obstinate, I'll be forced to
think of you as a fool. What greater honor could befall you than
to be loved more than anything else by so beautiful and noble a
lady? And besides this, don't you realize how grateful you should
be to Fortune, when you think that she offers you a remedy
suitable to the craving of your youth as well as a refuge for
your material needs? How many of your equals do you know
who would be better off when it comes to such pleasure than
yourself—that is, if you're smart enough? Who could ever match
you in weapons, horses, clothes, and money—if only you concede
her your love? So open your heart to my words and come back
to your senses; remember that Fortune usually comes but once
with smiling face and open arms to any man and no more; and
when such a man does not know how to welcome her and later
finds himself impoverished and a beggar, he has only himself,
and not her, to blame. And besides this, the loyalty between ser-
vants and masters should not be equated with that between
friends and equals; on the contrary, servants should treat their
masters, insofar as they can, just as they are treated by their
masters. If you had a beautiful wife, mother, daughter, or sister
that Nicostrato took a liking to, do you think he would be con-

cerned with loyalty the way you are with respect for his wife?
You really are a fool if you believe that he would! You can be
sure that if his flattery and entreaties were not sufficient, no
matter what you may think, he would resort to force. So, let's
treat them and their belongings just as they treat us and ours.
Accept Fortune's favor: do not drive her away; meet with her
and welcome her, for if you do not, not only will you most
surely bring about the death of your lady, but you will regret
what you did so often that you will want to die yourself."

Pirro, who more than once had thought over what Lusca had
first told him, had already made up his mind that if she ap-
proached him again, he would change his reply and do every-
thing he could to satisfy the lady, provided he could be sure that
she was not merely testing him; and so he answered:

"Look, Lusca, everything you are telling me I know to be
true; but on the other hand, I also know that my master is very
shrewd and clever, and because he has entrusted me with all his
affairs, I am very much afraid that Lidia, with her husband's
advice and consent, is doing this in order to test my loyalty; but
if she is willing to do three things I ask of her in order to reas-
sure me, there is nothing, I assure you, that she may command
me to do that I shall not do instantly. And the three things I ask
for are these: first, in Nicostrato's very presence she must kill
his best sparrow hawk; then, she must send me a lock of Nicos-
trato's beard; and finally, she must send me one of his teeth, one
of the best he has."

These things seemed difficult to Lusca and extremely difficult
to the lady, but Love, who is a good comforter and great master
of guile, nevertheless made her decide to do it, and so, by means
of her maid, she sent Pirro a message saying that she would do
everything he had asked and would do so as soon as possible;
moreover, since he thought Nicostrato was so smart, she said
that in her husband's very presence, she would make love to
Pirro and make Nicostrato believe that what he was seeing was
not true.

Pirro then waited to see what the noble lady would do. A few
days later, while Nicostrato was entertaining certain noblemen at
a grand banquet as he would often do, when the tables had been
cleared away, Lidia, wearing a green velvet dress and many jew-
els, came out of her bedroom and entered the hall where all the
guests were; and with Pirro and everyone else watching, she
went to the perch upon which the sparrow hawk which Nicos-
trato loved so much was sitting, and unchaining the bird as if

she wanted to take it on her hand, she seized it by its jesses, dashed it against the wall, and killed it.

And Nicostrato screamed at her: "Oh, woman, what have you done?" She did not answer him, but rather, turning to the gentlemen with whom he had dined, she said:

"My lords, I could hardly take my revenge on a king who might insult me, if I lacked the courage to do the same to a sparrow hawk. I want you to know that this bird has for a long time now deprived me of all that time which a man should dedicate to the pleasure of his woman; for usually, at the break of dawn, Nicostrato arises, mounts his horse, and with his sparrow hawk on his hand rides off to the open meadows to watch it fly; and I, such as you see me here, am left alone and discontent in bed; because of this, on more than one occasion I have wanted to do exactly what I have just done, and the only thing that kept me from doing it sooner was that I wanted to do it in the presence of men who would judge my case impartially, which I trust you will do."

Believing that Lidia's affection for Nicostrato was no less genuine than her remarks implied, all the gentlemen laughed, and turning to Nicostrato, who was angry, they said: "Ah, how right the lady was to avenge her wrong with the death of the sparrow hawk!" And with a number of other witty remarks on this same subject, once the lady had returned to her bedroom, they managed to turn Nicostrato's anger into laughter.

When Pirro saw this, he said to himself:

"The lady has launched my happy love with a lofty beginning; may God help her to persevere!"

So, not many days after she had killed the sparrow hawk, Lidia happened to be in her bedroom with Nicostrato, playing around and caressing him, when, just for fun, he pulled her gently by the hair, and this gave her an excuse to fulfill the second task Pirro had imposed on her; she quickly took hold of a small curl of his beard, and while she was laughing, she pulled on it so hard that it came right out of his chin. And when Nicostrato complained about this, she replied: "Now what's the trouble, why make such a face, just because I pulled no more than six hairs from your beard? It couldn't have hurt you as much as it hurt me when a moment ago you pulled my hair." And so, one word led to another while they continued their playful games, and the lady carefully preserved the curl of the beard she had pulled out and, that very day, she sent it to her beloved.

The third task gave the lady a bit more to think about; nevertheless, being a woman of sharp wit, which Love had made even sharper, she succeeded in thinking of a way to achieve it. Nicostrato had two young boys who, since they were of noble birth, had been entrusted to him by their fathers so that their sons might learn courtly manners; and whenever Nicostrato ate, one of them would cut his food, while the other would pour his drink; and so the lady, having summoned them both, made them believe that their breath smelled bad, and she instructed them that whenever they served Nicostrato, they were to hold their heads back as far as they could, and that they were never to mention this to anyone. Believing her, the young boys began to do as she had told them; as a result, on one occasion she was able to ask Nicostrato:

"Have you noticed how these young men act when they wait on you?"

Nicostrato said:

"Indeed, I have, and as a matter of fact, I wanted to ask them why they were acting like that."

To this the lady replied:

"Don't do that, for I can tell you why; I've kept quiet about it for a good long time now so as not to bother you; but now that I realize other people are beginning to notice, I see no reason to conceal it from you any longer. There's no other explanation except that your breath smells terribly bad, and I can't imagine what could be causing it, because it didn't use to be like that; this is a horrible thing to happen, especially since you are always in the company of gentlemen, and so we must find a means of curing it."

Then Nicostrato said:

"How could this be? Could I have a rotten tooth in my mouth?"

Lidia replied: "Perhaps you do." After leading him over to a window she made him open his mouth, and after she had examined first one part of his mouth and then the other, she announced:

"Oh, Nicostrato, how could you have put up with it for so long? You have a tooth on this side which, as far as I can see, is not only decayed but completely rotten, and if you keep it in your mouth any longer, it will surely ruin the two teeth on either side; so I would advise you to have it pulled out before it gets any worse."

Then Nicostrato said:

"If that's what you think, then I agree to it; without further delay, send for a doctor who can pull it out for me."

To this the lady replied:

"God forbid that we call a doctor for this. I think the tooth is such that I can easily pull it out for you without a doctor. Besides, these doctors are so cruel when they perform such operations that I could not bear to see or hear you suffering in the hands of somebody else; so I want to do everything myself, for at least then, if it is too painful for you, I can stop at once—something which no doctor would ever do."

And so she sent for the appropriate instruments, and cleared everyone out of the bedroom, except for Lusca, whom she kept with her. After locking themselves inside, she made Nicostrato stretch out on a table, inserted the pincers into his mouth, and took hold of one of his teeth. Though he screamed with pain, while one of them held him down firmly, the other with great force pulled out a tooth; concealing that tooth, she replaced it with another which was horribly decayed, one which she had been hiding in her hand, and Lidia, showing it to her husband, who was in excruciating pain and half-dead, said: "Look what you've had in your mouth for all this time!" Nicostrato believed her, and in spite of the terrible pain he was suffering and complaining bitterly about, when the tooth was pulled out, he thought he was cured, and once his pain had diminished and they had comforted him in one way and another, he left the room. The lady took the tooth and promptly sent it to her lover, who, now convinced of her love, declared himself ready to do her every pleasure.

The lady was anxious to reassure him still further, and even though every hour seemed like a thousand until she could be with him, she wished to maintain the promise she had made to her lover, and so she pretended to be ill, and one day while Nicostrato was visiting her after lunch, accompanied only by Pirro, she begged him to help her into the garden in order to break the monotony of her day. And so, while Nicostrato supported her on one side and Pirro did the same on the other, they carried her out into the garden and put her down on the grass at the foot of a beautiful pear tree, and after sitting there altogether for a while, the lady, who had already informed Pirro of what she was about to do, said to him:

"Pirro, I have a longing for one of those pears, so climb up there and throw some of them down."

Pirro quickly climbed the tree and began throwing down some pears, and while he was throwing them, he began to say:

"Oh, sir, what are you doing? And you, my lady, aren't you ashamed to allow this to happen in my presence? Do you both think I'm blind? A moment ago you were ill! How could you be

well enough so quickly to do these things? And if you want to do
it, you have plenty of good rooms; why not choose one and do it
in there? That would be more fitting than to do it under my
very eyes."

The lady turned to her husband and asked: "What's Pirro
saying? Is he going crazy?"

Then Pirro replied: "I'm not crazy, my lady; don't you think
I can see?"

Nicostrato was most amazed, and he said: "Pirro, I truly be-
lieve you are dreaming."

To this, Pirro replied:

"My lord, I'm not dreaming at all, and neither are you; on
the contrary, you are pumping so hard that if you pumped this
tree that way, there wouldn't be a pear left hanging up here."

Then the lady said:

"What can he mean? Could he really believe that what he is
saying is true? God help me, if I were as well as I used to be, I
would climb up there and see these marvels which Pirro claims
to be seeing."

Up in the pear tree, Pirro went on telling the same story; then
Nicostrato said to him: "Climb down here," and he climbed
down; and next Nicostrato asked him: "Now, tell me what you
saw."

Pirro replied:

"I think you both take me for either an idiot or a day-
dreamer: I tell you I saw you on top of your lady, since you
want the truth; and when I climbed down, I saw you get off her
and sit down where you are sitting right now."

"Clearly," declared Nicostrato, "you are out of your mind, be-
cause from the moment you climbed the pear tree, we have not
moved an inch from where you see us now."

To this, Pirro replied:

"Why are we arguing about this? I certainly did see you; but,
even if I did see you, I saw you on your own property."

Nicostrato was more and more intrigued, so much so that he
said, "I certainly would like to find out if this pear tree is en-
chanted, and if such marvels can be seen from up there!" And he
climbed up the tree; as soon as he was up there the lady and
Pirro began to make love, and when Nicostrato saw this, he
shouted down: "Ah, you wicked woman, what's this you're do-
ing? And you, Pirro, whom I trusted more than anyone else?"
And as he said this, he began climbing down the tree.

The lady and Pirro replied: "We're just sitting here"—and as
they saw him climbing down the tree, they returned to the posi-

tion in which he had left them. When Nicostrato reached the ground and saw them there where he had left them, he began insulting them.

Pirro answered:

"Nicostrato, now I must truly confess that what you said earlier was true and that I saw wrongly when I was up in the pear tree; and the only way I have of knowing this is the fact that I know you, too, have seen wrongly. There is no better proof of the truth of what I am saying if you stop and think for a moment whether your wife, who is most virtuous and wiser than any other woman, if she wished to commit such an outrage against your honor, would bring herself to do so right before your very eyes; I say nothing of myself, for I would sooner be drawn and quartered than even think about such a thing, much less do it in your very presence. And so, whatever the cause of this illusion may be, it must come from the pear tree; for nothing in all the world would have kept me from believing that you were not lying carnally here with your wife, if I had not heard you say you thought I had done the very same thing, which I most certainly never did, nor did I ever have the slightest thought of doing so."

Then the lady, who appeared to be quite angry, stood up and began saying:

"Damn you if you think I'm so stupid as to want to do the wicked things you claim you saw me do right before your eyes! You can be certain of this: should the desire ever arise in me, I wouldn't come and do it here; on the contrary, I think I would be capable of arranging to do it in one of our bedrooms, and in such a way that I would be very much surprised if you ever found out a thing about it."

Nicostrato, who actually seemed to believe that what both of them were saying was true, that they would never have committed such an act before his very eyes, set aside his complaints and recriminations, and began to speak of the novelty of this phenomenon and of the miracle of the vision which changed things so substantially for anyone who climbed up the tree.

But the lady pretended to be angry over the opinion Nicostrato held of her, and she said:

"This pear tree is certainly not ever again going to be the cause of shame for me or any other woman, if I can help it; therefore, run and fetch an ax, Pirro, and avenge the both of us by chopping down this tree—though it would be a much better idea to smash Nicostrato over the head with it, since without any reason whatsoever, he allowed the eyes of his intellect to be so easily blinded; for no matter how much you thought you saw what you said you did, Nicostrato, you never should have allowed the judgment of your mind to imagine or admit that it was true."

Pirro immediately went for an ax and cut the pear tree down, and when the lady saw it fall, she said, turning to Nicostrato: "Now that I have seen the enemy of my virtue struck to the ground, my anger is gone"; and as Nicostrato pleaded with her to forgive him, she graciously did so, insisting that never again should he entertain such thoughts about his lady, who loved him more than her very own life.

And so the wretched and derided husband returned with her and her lover to the palace, where many times thereafter Pirro and Lidia took pleasure and delight from each other with much greater ease. And may God grant us all the same thing.

[Seventh Day, Tenth Story]

✛

Two Sienese are in love with the same woman, and one of them is the godfather of her child; the godfather dies and returns to his friend, as he promised he would, and he describes how people live in the next world.

THE King was the only person left to tell a story, and when he saw that the ladies had stopped mourning over the innocent pear tree which had been cut down, he began:

It is absolutely clear that every just king must be the first to follow the laws he himself has set down, and if he does otherwise, he should be considered a servant deserving of punishment rather than a king: nevertheless, I, your King, am almost forced to fall into this very error, thus incurring your disapproval. It is true that yesterday, when I prescribed the rules for our story-telling today, I did not intend to exercise my privilege during the day but, instead, I was going to subject myself, along with all of you, to this rule and speak on the topic you all have spoken about. However, not only has the tale I thought of telling you already been told, but what is more, so many other and more entertaining ones have been told that for my part, no matter how hard I rack my brain, nothing comes to mind on such a topic that could in any way equal the stories that have already been told. And therefore, since I am forced to break the very law I myself established, I confess to be deserving of punishment and am prepared, at this time, to make any amends which may be demanded of me, and now I shall fall back upon my customary privilege. Let me say that the story told by Elissa about the god-father and the mother of his godchild, and also about the stupidity of the Sienese, offers such appealing subjects, my dearest ladies, that setting aside the tricks played upon silly husbands by their clever wives, I am tempted to tell you another little story about them; and while my story is all filled with things you will find hard to believe, nevertheless, there are at least parts that you will find entertaining to hear.

There once lived in the Porta Salaia section of Siena two young men of the lower class, one of whom was called Tingoccio Mini and the other Meuccio di Tura; and they were almost always together and, as far as anyone could tell, they were very fond of each other. Like everyone else, they attended church, and listened to the sermons which often dealt with the rewards and punishments of souls after death according to their merits. Wishing to have solid proof of this, but seeing no way of having it, they promised each other that whichever of them died first would return to the one who remained alive, if he was able, and would tell him whatever he wanted to know; and this promise was sealed with a solemn oath.

After this promise had been made and as they continued to be close friends, it happened that Tingoccio became godfather to the son of one Ambruogio Anselmini of Camporeggi and his wife, Monna Mita. Tingoccio, in the company of Meuccio, would visit his godchild's mother rather frequently, and in spite of their spiritual relationship, he fell in love with her, for she was a beautiful and charming woman; and since Meuccio found her pleasing and because he would often hear Tingoccio praise her, he fell in love with her too. And each one avoided speaking about his love to the other, but for different reasons: Tingoccio kept from revealing it to Meuccio because of the wickedness he himself saw in loving his own godchild's mother, and he would have been ashamed if anyone had learned of it; Meuccio did not do so because he noticed that she pleased Tingoccio so much; whereupon he said to himself:

"If I reveal this to him, he will become jealous of me, and since he can speak to her whenever he likes, for he is the godfather of her child, he might make her dislike me, and so I may never get what I want from her."

Now these two young men kept on loving in the manner just

described, and then it happened that Tingoccio, who was more skillful at revealing his feelings to the lady, was so clever in word and deed that he had his pleasure of her; Meuccio was well aware of this, and although it displeased him very much, he still hoped to fulfill his own desires, and he pretended not to know anything about the affair, so as not to give Tingoccio an excuse or a reason to spoil or to impede any of his plans.

And so the two companions were in love, one more happily than the other. The fact was that Tingoccio found himself in possession of the lady's fertile terrain, and he so spaded and plowed it over that an illness struck him which, after several days, grew worse; and unable to bear it any longer, he passed from this life. On the third day after his death (perhaps because he could not get there any sooner), he came one night, as he had promised, to Meuccio's bedroom and called to him as he slept soundly. When he woke up, Meuccio said:

"Who are you?"

To this he replied:

"I am Tingoccio, and according to the promise I made you, I have returned to give you news of the other world."

Meuccio was somewhat frightened at the sight of him, but he pulled himself together and said:

"You are welcome here, my brother!"

And then he asked him if he was lost, to which Tingoccio replied:

"What is lost cannot be found; and if I stand here before you, how could I be lost?"

"That's not what I mean," replied Meuccio, "I'm asking you if you are among the damned souls in the eternal fires of Hell."

Tingoccio answered:

"That, no, but I am suffering terrible punishment and am in the greatest of anguish for the sins that I committed."

Then Meuccio asked Tingoccio which punishments were given in the next life for which sins committed during this life on earth, and Tingoccio explained each of them to him. Then Meuccio asked him if he could do anything for him while he was there in Purgatory; Tingoccio replied that he could have Masses and prayers said for him and he could give alms, for such things helped them very much. Meuccio said that he would do this gladly, and as Tingoccio was leaving him, Meuccio remembered the woman, and lifting his head a bit, he said:

"I just remembered, Tingoccio: for sleeping with your godchild's mother, what punishment did they give you?"

To this Tingoccio replied:

"Brother, when I arrived there, there was someone who seemed to know every one of my sins by heart, and he ordered me to go to a place in which I lamented my sins in extreme pain and where I found many companions condemned to the same punishment as I was; and standing there among them and recalling what I had done with my godchild's mother, I trembled with fear, for I expected an even greater punishment for that than the one I had already received—although, in fact, I was at that moment standing in a huge and very hot fire. And as one of those who were suffering at my side noticed this, he asked me:

" 'Why do you tremble, standing in the fire? Have you done something worse than the others who are here?'

" 'Oh, my friend,' I answered, 'I am terrified of the judgment which I expect to be passed on me for a great sin that I have committed.'

"Then that soul asked me what sin it was, and I replied:

" 'The sin was this: I slept with the mother of my godchild, and I made love to her so much that I wore it to the bone.'

"Then, laughing at me, he said:

" 'Go on, you idiot, don't worry, for down here they don't count the mother of a godchild for very much!' And when I heard this, it made me feel much better."

And this he said as dawn was breaking; then he added:

"Meuccio, God bless you. I cannot stay with you any longer." And he quickly went away.

When Meuccio heard that in the other world they did not care whether or not you did it with the mother of your godchild, he began to laugh at his stupidity for having already spared a number of such women and, abandoning his ignorance, he became wiser in such matters from that time on. If Brother Rinaldo had known these things, there would have been no need for him to go about dreaming up syllogisms when trying to convert the worthy mother of his godchild to his pleasures.

[Seventh Day, Conclusion]

❦

As the sun descended in the west a light breeze had risen, and the King, having completed his story, removed the laurel crown from his head, and since there was no one else left to tell a tale, he placed it upon Lauretta's head, saying: "Madam, with your

own namesake I crown you Queen of our company, and now as
our mistress, it is up to you to give such orders that you feel will
provide us all with entertainment and pleasure"; and he returned
to his seat.

Having become Queen, Lauretta summoned the steward and or-
dered him to set up the tables in the delightful valley somewhat
earlier than usual, so that after the meal, they could return to
the palace with more leisure; then she also instructed him as to
what he was to do for as long as she was in command. Having
done this, she turned to the company and said:

"Yesterday, Dioneo wanted us to talk today about the tricks
played by wives on their husbands; but, if it were not for the
fact that I have no desire to be thought of as belonging to that
breed of ill-tempered dogs who quickly snap back at people, I
would say that tomorrow we ought to tell stories about the tricks
played by husbands on their wives. But instead of this, I would
like each of you to think of a story about the tricks which
women always seem to be playing on men or men on women or
men on other men; I believe that this subject will be no less
amusing to discuss than this day's topic has been." And having
spoken in this manner, she rose to her feet and gave the com-
pany the liberty to do as they pleased until the supper hour.

And so, all of them, ladies and gentlemen alike, arose, and
some of them began to wade barefoot in the clear water, while
others for their amusement roamed through the green meadow
beneath the beautiful tall trees. Together, Dioneo and Fiam-
metta sang a long song about Arcita and Palemone, and so in a
number of different ways all of them delightfully whiled away
the time until the supper hour. When it was time for supper,
they sat down at tables along the little lake, and accompanied
by the singing of a thousand birds and refreshed by a constant,
gentle breeze rising from the small hills surrounding them, in joy
and leisure they ate their meal without a fly to bother them. The
tables had been cleared, and they were strolling around the de-
lightful valley, since the sun was still high at half past vespers,
when at the Queen's request, they retraced their steps at a lei-
surely pace homeward; laughing and joking about at least a
thousand things, not only those discussed during the day but
other matters as well, they reached their beautiful palace very
close to nightfall. There they refreshed themselves from the ex-
ertion of their little walk with the freshest of wines and confec-
tions, and soon they began dancing around the lovely fountain,
accompanied sometimes by the music of Tindaro's bagpipes and

sometimes by a mixture of other instruments. Finally, the Queen ordered Filomena to sing a song, and she began in this manner:

Alas, ah luckless life of mine!
And can it be I shall return
to where a bitter parting took me from?

I am not certain, within my heart,
of ever returning, alas, where once I was.
Oh, my sweet love, oh, my sole peace,
who hold my heart so tightly,
ah, tell me, for I dare not ask another,
nor do I know another I could ask.
Alas, my lord, alas, give me some hope,
so that my wandering spirit may be relieved.

I can't describe how sweet was the delight
which has inflamed me so
that night or day I can find no repose,
For hearing, touching, seeing, each of them
with unaccustomed force
has kindled stronger fires on their own,
and in them I am burning;
and no one but yourself can comfort me
or bring my shaken senses back to life.

Ah, tell me if and when the time shall come
for me to find you once again
where I can kiss those eyes which murdered me;
tell me, sweet love of mine, my soul,
when will you come to me,
and comfort me by using the word "soon."
May all that time be short
from now until you come, but long while you remain,
for I care not, I am so much in love.

If ever I should hold you once again,
I shall not be so foolish
as once I was to ever let you go.
I'll hold you tight, and then let come what may;
and on your lovely mouth
I'll let desire take its satisfaction
and say no more about the rest;

come quickly, then, come and embrace me—
I sing with just the thought that you may come!

This song led the entire company to suspect that Filomena
was held captive by some new and pleasing love; and because
the words of the song seemed to imply she had gone beyond the
stage of mere amorous glances, they considered her most fortu-
nate, and some of those present could not help but feel jealous.
But as her song came to an end, the Queen remembered the next
day was Friday, and so she cheerfully announced to them all:

"As you know, noble ladies and you young men, tomorrow is
the day consecrated to the Passion of our Lord, which, if I
remember correctly, when Neifile was Queen, we devoutly conse-
crated by refraining from our delightful storytelling; and we did
the same thing on the following Saturday. Since I wish to follow
the excellent example Neifile has provided for us, I believe it
would be the proper thing for us tomorrow and the day after to
abstain, as we did in the past, from our pleasant storytelling, re-
calling to mind, instead, what occurred on those days for the sal-
vation of our souls."

The devout remarks of their Queen pleased everyone, and
since a good part of the night was already spent, she dismissed
the company, and all of them retired.

[Eighth Day, Title Page]

❖

Here ends the seventh day of The Decameron; *and the eighth day begins, in which, under the rule of Lauretta, stories are told about the tricks which women always seem to be playing on men or men on women or men on other men.*

[Eighth Day, Introduction]

❖

ON Sunday morning, the rays of the rising sun had already appeared among the highest mountaintops, every shadow had departed, and all things were clearly visible, when the Queen and all her company arose from their beds; first they wandered over the dewy grass, and then around half-past tierce, they paid a visit to a little church nearby, where they heard the holy services. Then, returning home, in a joyful, festive mood they ate, and then after singing and dancing for a while, they were given their leave by the Queen, so that anyone who wished to rest could do so. But when the sun had passed mid-heaven, at the Queen's request, they all took their seats near the beautiful fountain for the customary storytelling, and at the order of the Queen, Neifile began in this manner:

[Eighth Day, First Story]

✤

Gulfardo borrows a sum of money from Guasparruolo, and he makes an arrangement with Guasparruolo's wife to sleep with her for the sum of money he has received; later, in her presence, he tells Guasparruol he has returned his money to his wife, and she has to admit that this is true.

SINCE God has ordained that I am to be the one to open this day with my story, I am happy to do so. And so, loving ladies, since we have said a great deal about the tricks played by wives on their husbands, I should like to tell you about a trick played by a man on a woman, not because I intend to criticize with this story what the man did or to claim that the woman was not well served, but rather in order to praise the man and to criticize the woman and to show that men also know how to play tricks on those who trust them, just as much as they are tricked by those whom they trust. But strictly speaking, what I am about to tell you should not be called a trick but rather a just reward, and the reason is this: a woman should always be extremely virtuous and protect her chastity as she would her life, nor should anything induce her to stain it (though it is not always possible to observe this to the fullest, because of our frailty). And so I insist that any woman who yields herself for a price deserves to be burned at the stake, while a woman who does so for love, recognizing its most powerful forces, deserves to be forgiven by a judge who is not too severe, just as Filostrato several days ago pointed out to us in the case of Madonna Filippa in Prato.

Now, there once was a soldier of fortune in Milan whose name was Gulfardo, a valiant man who was extremely loyal to those in whose service he enrolled, which is rarely the case with Germans. And since he could be highly trusted in paying back money that he borrowed, he was able to find many a merchant who would lend him any amount of money at a low rate of interest. While living in Milan, he fell in love with a very beautiful woman named Madonna Ambruogia, the wife of a rich merchant by the name of Guasparruol Cagastraccio, of whom he was quite a good friend; and since he was most discreet about his love for this lady, without her husband or anyone else becoming aware,

475

one day he sent someone to speak with her, begging her please to
be willing to treat his love favorably, and that for his part, he
was ready to do whatever she ordered him to do. After many
equivocations, the lady came to the conclusion that she was
ready to do what Gulfardo wanted when two conditions were ful-
filled: first, that he must never reveal this affair to anyone; and
second, that since he was a rich man and she was in need of two
hundred gold florins to purchase something, he give her that sum,
and then she would be at his service always.

When Gulfardo, who thought her a worthy lady, learned of
her greediness, he was outraged by her baseness of spirit, and his
burning love turned almost to hatred as he thought of some way
to deceive her: and he sent word to her, saying he would be de-
lighted to grant her request and to do anything else in his power
to make her happy, and so she should go right ahead and let him
know when she wanted him to come to her, and he would bring
her the money himself, and no one would ever hear a word
about the affair, except for a friend of his whom he trusted a
great deal and who was in on all his affairs. The lady, or more
accurately, the wicked woman, was delighted when she heard
this, and she sent him a message, saying that Guasparuolo, her
husband, in a few days had to go all the way to Genoa on some
business of his and that she would let him know when it was
time and send for him.

When the time seemed ripe, Gulfardo went to Guasparuolo
and said to him: "I'm about to close a business deal for which I
need two hundred gold florins and I would like to borrow them
from you at the same interest rate you usually give me."
Guasparuolo said that he would be delighted to do so, and he
counted the money out for him immediately.

A few days later, Guasparuolo left for Genoa, just as the lady
had said he would, and so the lady sent word to Gulfardo for
him to come to her and to bring the two hundred gold florins.
Taking his companion along, Gulfardo went to the lady's house;
when he found her waiting for him, the first thing he did was to
place in her hands the two hundred gold florins in the presence
of his companion, and then he said to her: "My lady, take this
money and give it to your husband when he returns."

The lady took the money, but had no idea why Gulfardo said
what he did; she believed he did it so that his companion would
not think he was giving the money to her as a payment; and so
she replied: "I'll gladly do so, but first let me see how much
there is"; pouring the coins out on a table and finding that
there really were two hundred florins there, quite pleased with

herself, she put them away. She returned to Gulfardo, and taking him to her bedroom, not only that night but on many other nights before her husband returned from Genoa she provided him the satisfaction of her body.

When Guasparuolo came back from Genoa, Gulfardo immediately went to see him, and when he was sure that he was with his wife, in her presence he announced:

"Guasparuolo, the money, that is, the two hundred gold florins which you lent me the other day, were not necessary, since I was unable to close the deal for which I borrowed them; and since I brought them straight back here and gave them to your wife, will you cancel my debt?"

Guasparuolo turned to his wife and asked her if she had received the money; since she saw the witness right there before her, there was no way she could deny it, and she said: "Of course I received it, but I forgot to tell you about it."

Then Guasparruolo said:

"Gulfardo, that settles it; feel free to go; I'll see to it that your debt is canceled."

Gulfardo left, while the woman who had been made a fool of returned to her husband the dishonest price of her wickedness; and thus the clever lover had enjoyed his greedy lady free of charge.

[Eighth Day, Second Story]

❦

The priest of Varlungo goes to bed with Monna Belcolore, leaving his cloak with her as a pledge; after borrowing a mortar from her, he sends it back to her and asks that she return the cloak he left as a pledge; the good woman returns it to him with a few well-chosen words.

BOTH the men and the ladies were still approving of what Gulfardo did to the greedy Milanese woman when the Queen turned with a smile to Panfilo and ordered him to continue the storytelling; and so Panfilo began:

Lovely ladies, it occurs to me to tell you a little story aimed against those who constantly offend us without our being able to offend them back, that is, against priests, who have proclaimed a crusade against our wives, and who seem to think that when

they can lay one under them, they have earned the forgiveness
of their sins and faults, just as surely as if they had dragged the
Sultan back from Alexandria to Avignon* in chains. We poor
laymen cannot do the same to them, even though we may vent
our anger upon their mothers, sisters, mistresses, and daughters
with no less passion than they employ in assaulting our wives.
Be that as it may, I mean to tell you about a country love af-
fair, more amusing for its ending than for its length, from which
you should be able to pluck the fruitful moral that everything a
priest tells you is not to be believed.

Let me begin by saying that in Varlungo, a town quite close to
here, as you all know or may have heard, there was a valiant
priest, physically well endowed for servicing the ladies, who, al-
though he was not too good at reading, did, however, manage to
entertain his parishioners at the foot of an elm tree on Sundays
with many a good and holy saying; and whenever the menfolk
went off somewhere, he managed to be better at visiting their
wives at home than any priest that served before him had ever
been, bringing them items from religious festivals, holy water, or
even a few candle ends on occasion, and giving them his
blessing.

Now, it happened that among his many women parishioners
whom he fancied from the very first, there was one in particular
who attracted him, named Monna Belcolore, the wife of a farm-
worker called Bentivegna del Mazzo. She was, to tell the truth,
quite a pleasing, saucy country wench, brown-skinned, buxom,
and better at the art of grinding than anyone else; furthermore,
when she had occasion to play the tambourine, to sing "The
water runs down the ravine," and lead a reel or jig, holding a
delicate little handkerchief in her hand she was better than any-
body else around there. Because of all this, Messer Priest was so
taken by her that he was driven to a frenzy, and he loitered
about the entire day just to be able to catch a glimpse of her;
and when he spotted her in church on Sunday morning, he would
recite a *Kyrie* or a *Sanctus*, trying with all his might to sound
like a great cantor when in fact he was braying like a jackass,
whereas whenever he did not see her, he would merely mouth the
words; yet he was so clever in the way he acted that neither
Bentivegna del Mazzo nor any of his neighbors ever caught him.
And in order to get to know Monna Belcolore better, every now
and then he would give her presents: sometimes he sent her a

*At the time Boccaccio wrote *The Decameron*, the papacy was in
Avignon, France, not in Rome.

bunch of fresh garlic, of which he grew the finest in the area and in his own garden which he worked with his own hands, or sometimes he sent a basket of beans, while on other occasions he sent a bunch of fresh onions or shallots. And whenever he had the chance, he would look at her with a sad expression on his face and reproach her amorously while she, awkwardly reluctant, would pretend not to understand and go her way with her nose in the air; as a result, Messer Priest was unable to get anywhere with her.

Now one day the priest happened to be wandering about the neighborhood at precisely midday, when he ran into Bentivegna del Mazzo driving before him a donkey loaded with merchandise, and calling him over, the priest inquired where he was going.

To this Bentivegna replied:

"Why, sir, to tell the truth I'm going to town on some bisqueness of mine, and I'm taking this stuff to Ser Bonaccorri da Ginestreto, so that he'll help me answer the premature summings I've received from the persecuting attorney to appear before the climeral judge."*

Delighted, the priest said:

"That's fine, my son; now go with my blessing and return soon; and if you run into Lapuccio or Naldino, don't forget to tell them to bring me those leather thongs for my grain flails."

Bentivegna said he would do that; and when the priest saw him heading off toward Florence, he thought that now was the time to visit Belcolore and to try his luck; running off, he did not stop until he reached her house; and as he went inside, he said: "God bless this house, is anyone at home?"

Belcolore, who had gone out on the balcony, answered when she heard him: "Oh, father, you are most welcome. What are you doing wandering about in this heat?"

The priest replied:

"With God's grace, I've come to spend a little time with you, since I noticed your husband was heading into town."

Belcolore came downstairs, sat down, and began to sift some cabbage seeds her husband had gathered earlier. Then the priest said to her: "Well now, Belcolore, tell me, are you going to keep torturing me this way?"

Belcolore began to laugh as she replied: "Oh, what is it I am doing to you?"

---

*The comic language of this passage in which words are distorted ("bisqueness" for "business," "climeral" for "criminal," and so on) underlines the hapless peasant's fruitless attempts to speak eloquently.

The priest said: "You're not doing anything to me, but the trouble is you won't let me do what I want to you—something God has ordained."

Belcolore exclaimed: "Ah! Go on with you; do priests do things like that?"

The priest replied:

"Of course, we do it better than other men, and why not? And I'll tell you something else: we're better at this work, and do you know why? Because we do our grinding only at harvest time; but, to tell you the truth, you'll be better off, if you just lie back and let me get on with it."

Belcolore inquired:

"Ah, what is this I'll be 'better off' business all about? You priests are all tighter than the devil himself!"

Then the priest said:

"I don't know, you tell me; go ahead and ask. Do you want a pair of pretty little shoes, or a silk kerchief, or a belt of fine wool, or what is it you want?"

Belcolore answered:

"Father, that's some choice! But I've got all those already. If you really like me so much, why don't you just do me one favor, and then I'll do whatever you want?"

Then the priest replied:

"Tell me what you want, and I'll gladly do it."

Then Belcolore explained:

"Saturday, I have to go to Florence to deliver some wool I've spun and to have my spinning wheel fixed; if you will lend me five lira, which I know you've got, I can go to the pawnbroker's and pick up my dark skirt and my waistband which I got married in, for you see, without them I can't possibly go to church or to any other nice place—and then I'll do anything you want, always."

The priest replied:

"As God is my witness, I don't have any money on me, but believe me, before Saturday, I'll be very happy to see that you get it."

"Sure," said Belcolore, "all you priests are great promisers, but then you never keep any of them. Do you think you're going to treat me the way you did Biliuzza, who ran off pregnant with promises?* By God's faith, you won't do that to me—she had to

---

*The original reads *che se n'andò col ceteratoio*, which has been interpreted either as "ran off with unkept promises" (*ceteratoio*: a distortion of *eccetere*) or as "pregnant as the shape of a guitar"

walk the streets because of that! If you don't have the money on you, go home and get it."

"Ah," the priest complained, "you're not going to send me all the way home now, not right now when my luck is good and up, as you can see, and nobody's around; and by the time I get back, there could be somebody here to ruin our plans. And besides, I've never seen it rise to an occasion better than this."

But Belcolore replied: "That's fine by me. If you want to go get it, go on; if not, do without it."

Realizing that she was not ready to do anything to please him unless she had a *salvum me fac*, whereas he wanted to do it *sine costodia*,† the priest answered:

"Look here, you don't believe I'll bring you the money, do you? To make you believe me, I'll leave you this blue cloak of mine as a guarantee."

Belcolore looked up and said: "Well, now, this cloak—how much is it worth?"

The priest answered:

"What do you mean, how much is it worth? I will have you know it is made of Douai cloth, even Treai, and some of our parishioners insist that it's made of Fourai;‡ less than fifteen days ago it cost me seven whole lire to get it from Lotto, the old-clothes dealer, and according to Buglietto, who you know is an expert judge of such fabrics, I saved five whole lire on the deal."

"Really?" remarked Belcolore. "So help me God, I would never have thought so; but hand it over to me first."

Messer Priest, whose crossbow was already cocked, took off the cloak and gave it to her; and after putting it away, she told him:

"Father, let's go out to the shed. Nobody ever goes out there"; and so they did.

As soon as the priest got there, he smothered her with all the kisses in the world, adding her to the family of God Almighty, as he took his pleasure with her for a good long time; afterward,

---

(*ceteratoio*: a distortion of *chitarra*). The woman's speech, like that of her husband, reflects her class origins. In our translation, we have tried to combine both interpretations.

†These Latin expressions are employed in a jocular manner to mean, respectively, "guarantee" and "without a pledge of guarantee."

‡Here we see more playful tampering with language, beginning with the reference to Flemish cloth from Douai, the sound of which (*duagio*) recalls the number two and gives rise to imaginary kinds of cloth based on the numbers three and four (Treai, Fourai).

dressed only in his cassock, which made him appear as if he were returning from celebrating a wedding, he left her and went back to his church.

Back at the church, when he realized that all the candle tips he could gather up from the offerings of an entire year would not come to one half of five lire, he felt he had made a mistake, and regretting having left the cloak behind, he began to think of some way to get it back without having to pay. And since he was quite the little sharpster, he came up with a great way of getting it back, and it couldn't have worked better: since the following day was a holiday, he sent the son of one of his neighbors to this Monna Belcolore's house, asking her to be kind enough to lend him her stone mortar, for he was eating that morning with Binguccio dal Poggio and Nuto Buglietti and he wanted to prepare some sauce. Belcolore sent it to him.

And around mealtime, when the priest was certain that Bentivegna del Mazzo and Belcolore would be sitting down to eat, he called his sacristan and said to him: "Take this mortar and return it to Belcolore, and say: 'Father says to thank you very much and asks you to return the cloak which the boy left as his guarantee.' The sacristan went off with the mortar to Belcolore's house and found her with Bentivegna at the table eating; he put the mortar down on the table and delivered the priest's message.

As soon as Belcolore heard him asking for the cloak, she tried to say something, but Bentivegna said with a scowl:

"So, you asked for a guarantee from the priest? I swear to Christ I feel like punching you in the nose; go give it back to him right now, and a pox take you! And make sure that from now on, whatever the priest wants, even if he asks for our ass, you don't ever tell him no!"

Complaining loudly, Belcolore got up, went to her linen chest, took out the cloak, gave it to the sacristan, and said:

"Tell the father this on my behalf: 'Belcolore says she swears to God you will never grind any more sauce in her mortar after the way you messed her up this time."

The sacristan returned with the cloak and delivered the message to the priest; laughing, the priest said to him:

"Tell her, when you see her, that if she won't lend us the mortar, I won't lend her my pestle—that seems a fair exchange."

Bentivegna thought his wife was making these remarks because he had scolded her, and he thought nothing more about it; but Belcolore was furious with the priest and refused to speak to him until the grape harvest, during which time the priest had threatened to consign her to the very mouth of Lucifer himself, and so she, good and scared, made peace with him over a bottle of new wine and some hot chestnuts, and from then on and more than once, they had a good guzzle together. And to make up for the five lire, the priest had her tambourine reskinned and hung a tiny little bell on it, and Belcolore was satisfied.

[Eighth Day, Third Story]

❖

Calandrino, Bruno, and Buffalmacco go down to the Mugnone River in search of heliotrope, and Calandrino thinks he has found it; he returns home loaded with stones; his wife scolds him, and he, losing his temper, beats her up, and tells his companions what they already know better than he.

WHEN Panfilo finished his story, at which the ladies laughed so hard they must still be laughing at it now, the Queen ordered Elissa to continue; still laughing, she began:

Delightful ladies, I do not know if I can make you laugh as much with one of my little tales, which is no less true than it is amusing, as Panfilo did with his story, but I shall do my best.

Not long ago in our city, which has always abounded in unusual customs and strange people, there was a painter called Calandrino, a simpleton of bizarre habits who spent most of the time with two other painters called Bruno and Buffalmacco, men who were pleasant enough but also very shrewd and sharp, and they spent their time with Calandrino because they found his ways and his simplemindedness often very funny.

There was also at that time in Florence a most attractive and charming young man named Maso del Saggio, who was able and fortunate in whatever he wished to do and who, when he heard the many tales about Calandrino's simplicity, decided to amuse himself by playing a trick on him or persuading him to believe some fantastic notion. And one day, by chance in the Church of San Giovanni, he came upon Calandrino, who was staring at the paintings and the bas-reliefs of the canopy which had been built recently over the altar of that church, and he decided that this was the right time and place to put his plan into action. After informing one of his companions of what he intended to do, they walked over to where Calandrino was sitting alone, and pretending not to see him, they began to talk to each other about the hidden powers of various stones, about which Maso spoke with the conviction of a famous authority on precious stones; Calandrin perked up his ears at the sound of this conversation, and when he decided that the secret part of their talk had come to an end, he rose to his feet and went over to join them, much to the delight of Maso, who was asked by Calandrin, picking up their conversation, where such magical stones might be found.

Maso replied that most of them were found in Berlinzone, the land of the Basques, in a region which is called Bengodi, where they tie up vineyards with sausages and where you can have a goose for a penny and a gosling thrown in for good measure, and that there was a mountain there made entirely of grated Parmesan cheese upon which there lived people who did nothing but make macaroni and ravioli which they cook in capon broth and later toss off the mountain, and whoever picks up more gets the most; and nearby there flowed a stream of dry white wine, the best you ever drank, without a drop of water in it.

"Oh," said Calandrino, "that sounds like a great country, but tell me, what do they do with all the capons they cook?"

"The Basques eat them all," answered Maso.

"Were you ever there?" asked Calandrino.

"You ask if I was ever there?" replied Maso. "If I've been there once, I've been there a thousand times!"

Then Calandrino asked: "And how many miles is it from here?"

Maso replied: "More than ten times a hundred, I would say—and that's traveling night and day."

"Then," concluded Calandrino, "it must be farther off than the Abruzzi."

Since Maso said all this with a straight face, never laughing, the simpleminded Calandrino believed every word of his, and so he said:

"It's too far away for me, but if it were a little closer, I can tell you I'd give it a try once just to see the macaroni come tumbling down and to stuff myself full of it. But tell me, if you will, can't you find any of those magical stones around these parts?"

To this Maso replied:

"Yes, two types of stones with great magical power are found here: there are the sandstones of Settignano and Montisci from which we get our flour when they are made into millstones—that's why they say in these parts that grace comes from God and millstones from Montisci; but there are so many of these sandstones around here that we value them as little as they value their emeralds, of which they have an entire mountain higher than Monte Morello, and it shines at night, by God! And did you know that anyone who polishes the millstones and sets them in a ring and presents them to the Sultan, before a hole is bored in them, can have anything he wants for them? The other is a stone which we lapidaries call the heliotrope, a stone of extraordinary powers; for while a person carries it around with him, as long as he has it on him, he cannot be seen, no matter where he is."

Then Calandrin said:

"That's some power! But this second stone, where can you find it?"

To this question, Maso answered that they are usually found in the Mugnone valley.

Then Calandrino asked:

"How large is this stone and what color is it?"

Maso replied:

"There are all different sizes, some more, some less big, but they are all a kind of blackish color."

Calandrino took note of all these things to himself, and then pretending to have something else to do, he left Maso, having made up his mind to search for the stone; but he decided not to start looking until he told Bruno and Buffalmacco, who were his special friends. And so he wasted all the rest of that morning looking for them, so that they might all go searching for the stones together and without delay and before someone else discovered them. Finally, some time after nones, he remembered that they were working in the convent of the nuns of Faenza, and dropping everything he was doing, he was off and running in spite of the great heat of the day; and calling them outside, he said this to them:

"My friends, if you are willing to trust me, we can become the richest men in Florence, for I have heard from a trustworthy man that in the Mugnone there is found a stone that makes you invisible when you carry it; so I think we ought to go there quickly, before someone else does, and look for it. We'll find it for sure, because I know what it looks like; and when we've found it, we won't have to do anything but put it in our pockets and go to the bankers, whose tables, as you know, are always full of silver and florins, and take as much as we like. No one will see us, and in this way we can get rich quick and not have to spend the whole day daubing the walls like snails."

When Bruno and Buffalmacco heard this, they began laughing

to themselves, and looking at each other, they pretended to be greatly amazed, and they praised Calandrino's suggestion; then Buffalmacco asked what the name of the stone was. Calandrino, whose brain was soft as pasta, had already forgotten it, and so he answered:

"What do we care about its name when we know its powers? I think we ought to go look for it right away."

"All right," Bruno said, "but what does it look like?"

Calandrin answered:

"They come in all shapes and sizes, but all are kind of black; so what we do is pick up all the black stones we see, until we hit on the right one; so let's get going and stop losing time."

To this Bruno said: "Wait a minute." And turning to Buffalmacco he remarked:

"It seems to me Calandrino has a good idea, but I don't think that this is the best time for it; since the sun is high and blazing down on the Mugnone, it will have dried out all the stones, so that the stones which look black in the morning before the sun has dried them out, now will all look white; and besides, there are sure to be a lot of people around for one reason or another, since it's a working day along the Mugnone, and if they see us, they might guess what we are doing there and perhaps might start doing the same thing; and they might uncover the stone before we do, and then the whole thing would have been a waste of time. If you agree, I think that this job should be done in the morning when the black stones can be distinguished better from the white ones, and on a holiday when there won't be anyone around to see us."

Buffalmacco praised Bruno's advice, and Calandrino agreed to it, and they also agreed that the following Sunday morning all three of them would go together to look for this stone; but above all else Calandrino begged them not to tell anyone in the world about this, for it had been confided to him in the strictest of confidence. And once they had all agreed, he proceeded to tell them what he had heard about the country of Bengodi, swearing that what he had heard was true. As soon as Calandrino left them, they decided between themselves what they were going to do.

Calandrino waited anxiously for Sunday morning to come, and when it came, he got up at daybreak and called his friends, and leaving the city by the San Gallo gate, they went down to the Mugnone and started seaching for the stone. As they moved downstream, Calandrino took the lead, since he was the most eager, and darting to this side and to the other, whenever he saw some black stone he pounced upon it, picked it up, and put it inside his shirt. His companions followed behind, gathering a stone here and there, but Calandrino had not gone very far before he found his shirt was full; so he pulled up the folds of his tunic (which was not cut in the narrow Flemish fashion) and securely fastened them to his waist all around him, forming a large bag, which he also filled in a short time; and, again, turning his cloak into a bag, he soon filled this too with stones. Buffalmacco and Bruno saw that Calandrino was loaded with stones and that it was nearly time to eat, and so, according to their plan, one said to the other:

"Where's Calandrino?"

Buffalmacco, who could see him standing right there, turning in every direction to look for him, replied:

"I don't know, but he was right here in front of us just a minute ago."

Bruno answered:

"A minute ago—that's a laugh! By now he's probably home eating, that's for sure, and he's left us with this crazy idea of his to look for black stones in the Mugnone."

"Well, then," said Buffalmacco, "he was right to trick us and leave us here, since we were stupid enough to believe him. Who, besides us, could be so dumb as to believe that you can find such a valuable stone in the Mugnone?"

When Calandrino overheard this, he believed he had found the stone and though he stood right there in their presence, its powers were now preventing them from seeing him. Overjoyed by his good fortune, without saying a word to them he decided to return home, and turning around, off he went. Seeing this, Buffalmacco said to Bruno:

"What shall we do? Why don't we go home?"

To this Bruno answered:

"Let's go, but I swear to God that Calandrino will never play another trick on me again; and if ever again I get as close to him as I was all morning, I'll give him such a blow on the shins with this stone that he'll remember this trick for at least a month!"

And all at once, saying these words, he drew back his arm and hit Calandrino in the heel with a stone. Calandrino, feeling the pain, raised his foot high as he began to gasp, but he remained silent and kept on going. Then Buffalmacco picked up one of the sharper stones he had collected and said to Bruno:

"Hey, do you see this nice pointed stone? This is how I'd like to toss it at Calandrino!"

And letting it fly, he gave Calandrino a real whack with it right in the kidneys, and to make a long story short, in this manner, now saying one thing and then another, they stoned Calandrino all the way from the Mugnone to the San Gallo gate. There they threw away all the stones they had gathered and stopped to let the customs guards in on the trick, and the guards, pretending not to see Calandrino, let him pass as they roared with laughter. Without stopping, Calandrino went straight to his home, which was near Canto alla Macina, and Fortune so favored this trick that all the while Calandrino was walking from the river through the city, no one said a thing to him, for it was dinnertime and there were few people in the streets. And so Calandrino entered his home with his load. By chance his wife, a beautiful and worthy woman named Monna Tessa, was at the head of the stairs, somewhat annoyed because he had stayed out so long, and as soon as she saw him come in, she began to scold him:

"Where the devil have you been? Everyone's done eating and you're just arriving!"

When Calandrino heard this, he realized that he was visible now, and full of anger and grief he screamed:

"Damn you, woman, is that you up there? Now you've done it! But by God, I'll fix you for it."

He went upstairs and dumped the stones he had gathered in a room, then ran at his wife like some wild beast, and taking her by the hair, he threw her on the ground at his feet and began kicking and beating her all over as hard as he could, not leaving a hair on her head untouched or a bone in her body without a bruise, and the fact that she was begging for mercy with clasped hands did her no good whatsoever.

Buffalmacco and Bruno laughed over the trick with the customs guards for a while and then, at a slow pace, they began to follow Calandrino, keeping quite a distance between them and him; and when they reached his door, they heard the terrible beating he was giving his wife and they called to him, pretending that they had just returned. Calandrino appeared at the window all sweaty, flushed, and out of breath, and asked them to come up. Pretending to be a bit angry, they came up the stairs and saw the room full of stones, and his wife in one corner crying in pain, all disheveled, her clothes torn, and her face bruised and beaten; in the other corner of the room they saw Calandrino sitting, out of breath and with his clothes messed up. After looking at all this for a moment, they said:

"What's this, Calandrino? Have you become a mason with all

these stones we see here?" To this, they added: "And what's the matter with Monna Tessa? It looks like you've beaten her up. What's going on here?"

Worn out by the weight of the stones he had carried and from the anger with which he had beaten his wife, as well as his grief over the good fortune which he felt he had now lost, Calandrino could not catch enough breath to utter a single word in reply; and since he hesitated to answer, Buffalmacco continued:

"Calandrino, if you were angry, you shouldn't have taken it out on us by tricking us the way you did; you talked us into going to look for this precious stone with you, and then without even saying 'God be with you' or 'Go to Hell,' you left us like two idiots in the Mugnone and came back here, and we're not happy about it at all! This is the last trick you're ever going to play on us, and that's for sure!"

Gathering up his strength, Calandrino made an effort to reply:

"Friends, don't be angry. Things aren't the way they seem. Unlucky me, I actually found the stone; do you want to hear the truth? When you first asked each other where I was, I was not more than ten yards from you, and when I noticed that you were coming home but did not see me, I kept a little ahead of you and continued to do so all the way home."

And beginning from the beginning, he told them everything they had done or said until their arrival; he even showed them his back and his heels, how they had been bruised by their stones, and then he continued:

"And I tell you that as I entered the city gate with all these stones on me—these you see here—no one spoke to me, and you know how unpleasant and what pains those customs guards can be, wanting to look through everything and all; and besides this, on my way home I met many of my friends and neighbors who would normally speak to me and invite me for a drink, but no one even said half a word to me—it was just like they didn't see me. Finally, when I arrived home, this devil of a damned woman appeared before me and caught sight of me and as you know, being a woman she can cause everything to lose its power; and so just as once I could have considered myself the luckiest man in Florence, now I am the unluckiest, and because of this I beat her as much as my hands could stand, and I don't know what kept me from slitting her throat. Damn the moment I first laid eyes on her and the moment she first put foot into this house!"

And flying into a rage once more, he was about to get up and start beating her all over again. As Buffalmacco and Bruno listened to his story, they pretended to be very much amazed, and

from time to time they would confirm what Calandrino said, and
it was all they could do to keep from bursting with laughter!
But seeing him so angry that he was about to get up and beat
his wife a second time, they rushed over to hold him back, tell-
ing him that it was not her fault but rather his, for he knew that
women cause everything to lose its power and that he had not
told her to stay away from him that day and that his precaution
had been denied him by God either because such good luck was
not to be his or perhaps because he had it in mind to trick his
friends, to whom he should have shown his discovery as soon as
he had made it.

And after many words and a good deal of trouble, they man-
aged to reconcile the weeping wife with her husband and de-
parted, leaving him in a mood of gloom and a house full of
stones.

[Eighth Day, Fourth Story]

*The Rector of Fiesole is in love with a lady who is a widow; he
is not loved in return by her, and while he is in bed with one of
her maidservants, thinking that he is in bed with her, the lady's
brothers arrange to have him discovered there by his Bishop.*

WHEN Elissa came to the end of her story, which she had told
not without great delight to the entire company, the Queen
turned to Emilia and made her understand that she wished her
to tell her tale after Elissa; and so Emilia, without hesitation,
began in this fashion:

Worthy ladies, while many of the stories we have told, I seem
to recall, have shown how insidiously priests, friars, and clerics
of all types test our virtue, since it would be impossible to ex-
haust this subject no matter what we add to it, I now intend to
tell you, adding to the stories already told, another one about a
Rector who, come what may, wanted a noble widow lady to love
him, whether she was willing to do so or not; and since she was
very intelligent she treated him just as he deserved.

As you all know, Fiesole, whose hilltop we can see from here,
was once a very ancient and famous city, and even though it is
completely in ruins today, it has never been, because of this,
without a Bishop, nor is it without one today. And there, near

the main church, a noble lady, a widow named Monna Piccarda, once owned a piece of property with not too large a house on it; and since she was not the most wealthy woman in the world, she lived there for most of the year with her two brothers, both very respectable and polite young men. Now it happened that since the lady, who was still a very attractive and delightful young woman, would often attend services at this church, the Rector of the church fell so passionately in love with her that he could think of nothing else; and after a while, he grew so bold as to inform the lady himself of his desires and begged her to be content with his love and to love him as he loved her.

This Rector was a man well on in years, but he still had the mentality of a child: he was impudent and presumptuous, he held a mighty high opinion of himself, and he had such a picky and unpleasant way about him and was in general so boring and pompous that he was disliked by everybody, and if anyone liked him the least, that person was Monna Piccarda, who not only disliked him, but hated him worse than a headache; nevertheless, since she was a wise woman, she replied to him:

"Sir, the fact that you love me is very dear to me, and I am bound to return your love, and I shall love you most willingly, but nothing unseemly must ever befall your love or my own. You are my spiritual father and a priest, and you are nearing old age, all of which should make you virtuous and chaste; and, on the other hand, I am no longer a young girl to whom such love affairs are still suitable, I am a widow, and you know how much virtue is required of widows; and so you must excuse me, for I shall never be able to love you, nor would I wish to be loved that way by you."

Although he was unable to get more than that from her this time, the Rector was not frightened off or defeated by a single blow, but rather, employing his usual arrogance, he begged her over and over again with letters and messages, and even in person whenever he saw her go into church. As a result, when the lady felt this annoyance had become too serious and bothersome to bear, she made up her mind to rid herself of this nuisance with the kind of treatment he deserved, for it seemed she had no other choice; however, she would not do anything until she had first discussed the matter with her brothers. After informing them of the Rector's comportment with her and what she proposed to do about it, and receiving their full consent, a few days later she went to the church as she usually did, and when the

Rector caught sight of her, he walked over to her and began speaking to her in his customary insinuating way.

When the lady saw him coming and looked in his direction, she gave him a cheerful glance; and after he had taken her to one side and whispered a number of things to her in his usual manner, the lady, heaving a deep sigh, said:

"Sir, I have often heard it said that no castle is so impregnable that it cannot be taken by siege at least once if it is attacked every day; I see quite clearly that this is what has happened to me. You have surrounded me so completely with your sweet words, with one charming gesture and another, that you have broken my resolve: since I am so pleasing to you, I am now ready to be yours."

Overjoyed, the Rector declared:

"Oh, thank you so much, my lady; but to tell you the truth, I was rather amazed to see you hold out so long—a thing that has never happened to me with any woman before; in fact, I have been known to say on occasion: 'If women were made of silver, you couldn't mint them into coins, for none of them hold up to the hammer.' But enough of that for the moment. When and where can we be together?"

To this the lady replied:

"My sweet lord, the time can be whenever you wish, since I have no husband to whom I must justify how I spend my nights; but I can't think of where."

The Rector said: "What do you mean, you can't? What about your house?"

The lady replied:

"Sir, you know I have two younger brothers, who day and night are in and out of the house with their friends, and my house is not a very large one; so it cannot be there, not unless we want to spend our time there like deaf-mutes, not uttering a word or a whisper in the dark as if we were blind; in this case, it would be possible, since my brothers never come into my bedroom, even though their room is right beside my own, and you can't even whisper without being heard."

Then the Rector said:

"Madam, this shouldn't be a problem for one or two nights; in the meanwhile I shall think of a place where we can be together more comfortably."

The lady said:

"Sir, that will be your task, but there is one thing I beg of you: that you keep this a secret, and that no one ever hear a word about it."

The Rector then said:

"Madam, have no fear on that count; but if at all possible, do arrange things so that we can be together this evening."

The lady answered, "Very well," and after telling him how and when he was to visit her, she left him and returned home.

This lady had a maidservant who was not too young, and she had the ugliest and most contorted face that you ever saw: her nose was smashed flat, her mouth twisted, with thick lips and enormous, crooked teeth, she squinted, her eyes were always running, and her complexion had a green and yellow tint to it which made her look as if she had spent the summer in Sinagaglia* rather than in Fiesole—and besides all this, she was lame and a bit crippled on her right side; her name was Ciuta, but since her face was so yellowishly ugly, everyone called her Ciutazza; and while her body was misshapen, she was, nevertheless, a rather mischievously clever girl. The lady sent for her and said:

"Ciutazza, if you are willing to do me a favor tonight, I shall give you a brand-new blouse."

As soon as Ciutazza heard her mention the blouse, she said:

"My lady, if you were to give me a blouse, I would be willing to jump into a fire, to say the least."

"Fine," said the lady. "I want you to sleep with a man in my bed tonight and to make love with him, but you must be careful not to utter a word, so that you will not be overheard by my brothers, who, as you know, sleep next door; and then I shall give you the blouse."

Ciutazza said: "Sure, I'll even sleep with six men, let alone one, if I have to!"

So when evening came, the good Erector† arrived just as he had been told to, and the two young men, just as the lady had arranged with them, were in their bedroom making enough noise to be heard. So the Rector entered the lady's bedroom quietly, and in the dark, as she had instructed him, he went over to her bed to the side where Ciutazza, who had been carefully coached by the lady as to what to do, was lying. The good Erector, thinking that he had the lady by his side, drew Ciutazza into his arms and began to kiss her without making a sound, and Ciutazza did the same and then the Rector began taking his

---

*Sinagaglia (today Senigallia) was famous for its malaria, which may explain the woman's strange appearance.

†Here Boccaccio is playing with the word for Rector (*proposto* he makes *ploposto*), and in so doing he prepares the scene for the amusing downfall of the prelate. He will use this term two more times before the end of the story.

pleasure with her, taking possession of the property that he had desired for so long a time.

Having done this much, the lady then had her brothers put the rest of the plan into effect: quietly leaving their bedroom, they made their way to the public square; and Fortune was even kinder to them than they had hoped, for, since it was very hot that evening, the Bishop had been searching for the two young men just to spend some time with them at their house over a leisurely drink. And as soon as he saw them coming he told them what he had in mind, and they were on their way; then, entering the cool little courtyard of their home, all lit up with many lights, the Bishop to his great delight drank some of their excellent wine.

After they had finished drinking, the two young men said:

"Sir, since you have been so gracious as to honor with your presence this humble abode of ours, to which we were about to invite you, we would like you to do us the courtesy of looking at a little something we wish to show you."

The Bishop replied that he would be happy to do so, and so one of the young men with a lighted torch in his hand led the way, and with the Bishop and everyone else following, he headed toward the bedroom where the good Erector was sleeping with Ciutazza. So eager was the Rector to arrive at his destination that he put all he had into his gallop, and before the group reached the bedroom, he had already ridden more than three miles, and being a little tired from his ride, and in spite of the hot weather, he had fallen asleep holding Ciutazza in his arms. So when the young man entered the bedroom, torch in hand, and the Bishop and all the others followed him, what they saw was the Rector with Ciutazza in his arms. With this, the good Rector woke up, and seeing the torchlight and all these people around him, he hid his face under the covers, feeling thoroughly ashamed and quite afraid; the Bishop reviled him bitterly and forced him to come out from under the covers and to reveal with whom he had been sleeping. Because of the realization of the trick the lady had played on him and of the dishonor he had brought upon himself, the Rector quickly became the most wretched man who ever lived; and having put on his clothes at the Bishop's command, he was sent to his own house under close guard, where he was to endure a severe penance for the sin he had committed. Then the Bishop wanted to know how all this had happened and how he had come to sleep with Ciutazza. The young men explained everything to him in detail; having heard the whole story, the Bishop had nothing but praise for the lady

and her young brothers, who, without staining their hands with
the blood of a priest, had treated the Rector as he deserved.

The Bishop made the Rector do forty days' penance for this
sin, while Love and indignation made him sorry for at least
forty-nine—not to mention the fact that for a long time after-
ward, the Rector could never show his face outdoors without the
children pointing a finger at him and saying: "He's the one who
slept with Ciutazza"; this bothered him so much that it nearly
drove him insane. And this then was how the worthy lady man-
aged to rid herself of the bother of an impudent Rector and
Ciutazza earned herself a blouse.

[Eighth Day, Fifth Story]

❀

*Three young men pull down the breeches of a judge, who had
come to Florence from the Marches, while he is on the bench
administering the law.*

WHEN Emilia had finished telling her story, and the widow lady
had been praised by everyone, the Queen turned to Filostrato
and said: "It is now your turn to speak." And Filostrato, an-
swering immediately that he was ready to do so, began:

Delightful ladies, mention of the young man, Maso del Saggio,
by Elissa a while ago, persuades me to abandon a story I had
intended to tell you in order to tell you another one about him
and a few of his companions; and while it is not an unseemly
story, it does contain some words which you might be ashamed
to use, but since it is so very amusing, I shall tell it to you just
the same.

As you all know, many of the magistrates of our city very of-
ten come from the Marches, and these men are for the most
part so mean-hearted and lead such a miserly and miserable ex-
istence that everything they do is lousy with stinginess. And be-
cause of their innate wretchedness and avarice, they bring along
with them judges and notaries who seem more like men trained
behind a plow or a cobbler's bench than men educated in a
school of law. Now, one of these men came to Florence as
podestà, and among the many other judges he brought with him,
there was one who called himself Messer Niccola da San Lepi-
dio, who looked more like a tinker than anything else, and this

man was assigned to the group of judges that heard criminal cases. Now, as often happens, citizens will visit the law courts who have no business to be there at all, and this was the case with Maso del Saggio, who went there one morning to look for a friend of his; and when he arrived, he glanced up to where this Messer Niccola was seated, and looking him over very carefully, he came to the conclusion that he was a gullible-looking pigeon indeed. And as he scrutinized him, he noticed that his hat trimmed with vair was all black with smoke, that his quill case was dangling from his belt, that his tunic was longer than his judge's robe, and a number of other strange things, all unbecoming to a tidy and well-mannered gentleman, but the most outstanding feature of all, in Maso's opinion, was the judge's pair of breeches, the crotch of which, when the judge sat down with his robes pulling open in front of him because they were too tight, seemed to be hanging almost down to his knees.

And so, Maso saw all he needed to see of these breeches to make him abandon what he had come there to do and to take up another quest: he found two of his friends, one called Ribi and the other Matteuzzo, each of whom was no less high-spirited than Maso himself, and he said to them: "If you value my friendship, come along with me to the courthouse, and I'll show you the strangest-looking half-wit you ever saw."

So he went with them to the courthouse and showed them this judge and his breeches. Even at a distance, they began laughing at what they saw, and then, when they got closer to the bench upon which Messer Judge was seated, they discovered that a person could very easily crawl under it; and besides this, they noticed that the plank upon which Messer Judge was resting his feet was split open and a person could very easily reach a hand and an arm up through it.

So Maso said to his friends:

"Let's pull those breeches right off him—it'll be so easy!"

Each of his friends had already figured out a way to do it, and so, after planning what each one was to say and do, the following morning they returned to court, and with the courtroom full of people, Matteuzzo, without anyone's noticing him, crawled under the bench and went to the exact spot where the judge was resting his feet.

Maso went up to Messer Judge on one side and started tugging at the hem of his robe, while Ribi went up to him on the other side and did the same, and then Maso began saying:

"Your honor, your honor: I beg you in the name of God— don't let that petty thief on the other side of you leave here without making him give back the pair of boots he stole from me; he denies he did it, but it was not even a month ago that I saw him having the boots resoled."

And Ribi was, on the other hand, shouting at the top of voice:

"Your honor, don't believe him, for he's a lousy crook, and when he found out that I was coming here to file a complaint against him for stealing a saddlebag of mine, he shows up here with this story about his boots, which I'm supposed to have had in my house for ages; and if you don't believe me, I can call as witness my neighbor, the grocerwoman, or Grassa, the tripe-vendor, and even the garbageman from Santa Maria a Verzaia, who saw him on his way home from the country."

Maso, for his part, was not about to let Ribi do all the talking, so he began to yell, and Ribi yelled ever louder. And when the judge stood up and was starting to edge up closer to them in order to hear them better, Matteuzzo saw his chance, and sticking his hand through the broken plank, he grabbed the seat of the judge's breeches, and pulled down very hard, and the breeches were off in a flash, for the judge was skinny and had no flesh on his buttocks. When the judge felt what had happened, though he had no idea how it could have happened, he tried to cover himself in front by pulling his robes around and sitting down, but on either side of him he had Maso and Ribi still holding on to him and yelling with all their might: "Your honor, it's an outrage your not listening to my case and trying to get out of here this way! In a small case like this there is no need for written evidence!" And while all this was being said, they kept pulling at his robes until everyone in the courtroom saw that he did not have his breeches on. As for Matteuzzo, who felt he had hung on to them long enough, he dropped them and crawled out from under the bench, making his escape without being noticed.

Ribi, who felt things had gone far enough, announced:

"I swear to God I'll take my case to a higher court!"

Maso, on his side, let go of the judge's robe and declared:

"Not me, your honor, I'll keep coming back here until I find you less distracted than you appear to be this morning," and as quickly as they could, one of them took off in one direction and the other in the opposite direction.

Messer Judge, finally catching on to what had happened, pulled up his breeches in the presence of everyone, as if he were just getting up from bed, and demanded to know where the men who had quarreled over the boots and the saddlebag had gone; but since they were nowhere to be found, he began to swear on the guts of Christ that he would appreciate knowing if it was the

custom in Florence to pull down a judge's breeches while he was
seated on the bench of the law. The *podestà*, on the other hand,
when he heard this, made a great stink about it; but then, when
his friends pointed out to him this had only been done to show
him the Florentines realized he had brought idiots along with
him instead of real judges in order to save money, he thought it
best to remain silent, and on this occasion, nothing more was
said about the matter.

[Eighth Day, Sixth Story]

❦

*Bruno and Buffalmacco steal a pig from Calandrino; pretending
to help him find it again by means of a test using ginger cookies
and Vernaccia wine, they give him two such cookies one after
the other, made from cheap ginger seasoned with bitter aloes,
thus making it appear that he stole the pig himself; then, they
force him to pay them a bribe by threatening to tell his wife
about the affair.*

FILOSTRATO'S story, which gave the group a good laugh, had no
sooner reached its conclusion than the Queen ordered Filomena to
continue the storytelling; and she began:

Gracious ladies, just as Filostrato was moved by the mention
of Maso's name to tell the story you have just heard, in like
manner, I am inspired by the mention of the names of Calan-
drino and his companions to tell you another tale about them
which, I believe, will amuse you.

There is no need for me to explain to you who Calandrino,
Bruno, and Buffalmacco were, for you have already heard a
great deal about them in an earlier tale; and so getting on with
my story, let me say that Calandrino owned a little farm not far
from Florence, which he had acquired by way of his wife's
dowry, and from it, along with the other produce which he col-
lected there, every year he received a pig; and it was his regular
custom to go to the country around December with his wife to
slaughter the pig, and to have it salted there.

Now it happened once, at a time when his wife was not
feeling very well, that Calandrino went by himself to slaughter
the pig; when Bruno and Buffalmacco heard about this and
learned that his wife was not going to be there with him, they

went to stay for a few days with a priest who was a great friend of theirs and who lived near Calandrino. On the very morning of their arrival, Calandrino had slaughtered the pig; seeing them with the priest, he called them over and said: "I bid you welcome. I would like you to see what a good farmer I am," and he took them into the house and showed them this pig.

When they saw what a fine pig it was and learned from Calandrino that he intended to salt it for his family, Bruno said to him:

"Hey! You must be crazy! Sell it and let's enjoy the money and tell your wife it was stolen from you."

Calandrino replied:

"No, she won't believe me, and she'll run me out of the house. Stay out of this. I'd never do anything like that."

They tried to convince him with all sorts of arguments, but it was no use. Then Calandrino invited them to supper, but so begrudgingly that they refused to eat with him, and off they went, leaving him there.

Bruno said to Buffalmacco: "What would you say to stealing that pig of his tonight?"

Buffalmacco replied: "And how could we do that?"

Bruno replied: "I've already figured out how to do it, provided he doesn't move it from where it was just now."

"Well," concluded Buffalmacco, "let's do it; why shouldn't we do it? And then we can all enjoy it here together, you, me, and the priest."

The priest declared that this plan was very much to his liking; then Bruno said:

"Now this calls for a bit of skill. Buffalmacco, you know how greedy Calandrino is and how happy he is to have a drink when somebody else pays the bill; let's go and take him to the tavern; let the priest pretend to be our host and pay for all the drinks; we won't let him pay for anything, and Calandrino will drink himself silly, and then the rest will be easy, since there is no one else in the house."

And so they did just as Bruno suggested. Calandrino, seeing that the priest would not allow him to pay, began to drink in earnest, and while usually it never took much to get him drunk, this time he drank a great deal. It was already late in the evening when he left the tavern, and, not wishing to eat supper, he went home, and thinking that he had locked the door, he left it open and went to bed. Buffalmacco and Bruno went to eat supper with the priest; after they had eaten, they collected the tools they needed to get into Calandrino's house the way Bruno had planned, and they quietly made their way there; but when they found the door open, they went straight in and carried the pig off to the priest's home, where they stowed it away and then went off to bed.

In the morning, after the wine had cleared from his brain, Calandrino got up, and when he went downstairs, he looked around and saw that his pig was gone and the door wide open; and so he asked a number of people if they knew who had taken his pig, but unable to find it, he began making a racket, crying, "Ah, poor me, my pig has been stolen." When Bruno and Buffalmacco got out of bed they went straight over to Calandrino's to hear what he would have to say about his pig. When Calandrino saw them, he called them over and on the verge of tears he said: "Oh, my friends, my pig has been stolen from me!"

Bruno drew close to him and whispered: "I'm amazed; so you finally got smart for once in your life."

"Oh, no," said Calandrino, "I'm really telling the truth."

"That-a-boy, that's the way," Bruno said, "tell it loud and clear so it looks the way it should."

Then Calandrino started shouting louder and saying:

"God's body, I'm speaking the truth, it has been stolen from me!"

And Bruno replied:

"Well put, that's perfect, just right, scream louder, make yourself heard, it'll seem truer that way!"

Calandrino insisted:

"You'll drive my soul to the devil: I'm telling the truth and you don't believe me, but I swear, may I be hanged by the neck, if my pig hasn't been stolen!"

Then Bruno said:

"Ah, how can this be? I saw it here just yesterday; do you think you can make me believe it just flew out of here?"

Calandrino answered: "It's just like I'm telling you."

"Ah," remarked Bruno, "how can that be?"

"That's it, yes sirree" declared Calandrino, "and now that's the end of me, and I don't know how I can go home now. My wife will never believe me, and even if she does, I'll have no peace from her for a year."

Then Bruno said:

"God help me, if it's true, this is a serious matter; but you know, Calandrino, this is exactly what I told you to say yesterday. You wouldn't be trying to fool your wife and us at the same time, would you?"

Calandrino began to scream and say:

"Ah, why are you driving me crazy and making me curse God, His saints, and everything else? I'm telling you that the pig was stolen from me last night."

Then Buffalmacco said:

"If that's the case, we must try to find some way to get it back again if possible."

"And what way," asked Calandrino, "is there?"

Then Buffalmacco replied:

"Well, for sure, nobody came all the way from India to steal this pig from you; one of these neighbors of yours must have done it, and so, if you can bring them all together, I can perform the bread-and-cheese test,* and then we'll see at once who has the pig."

"Just great," said Bruno, "you'll do splendidly with your bread-and-cheese test, especially with the fine people that live around here! It's clear that one of them stole it, and they would catch on to what we're doing and refuse to come."

"What can we do, then?" asked Buffalmacco.

Bruno relpied:

"We could do it with some nice ginger cookies, and some good Vernaccia wine, and invite them all for a drink. They won't think anything of it and will come, and then we can bless the ginger cookies just as if they were bread and cheese."

Buffalmacco said:

"Yep, that's it for sure! And you, Calandrino, what do you say? Are we going to do it?"

Calandrino replied:

"By all means, I beg you, for the love of God, go ahead and do it; I wouldn't feel half so bad, if only I knew who took my pig."

"Well, that's it," Bruno said, "I'm prepared to go all the way into Florence for the things you need, if you give me the money."

Calandrino had around forty copper pennies, which he gave to Bruno. And Bruno went to Florence to a friend of his who was an apothecary and bought a pound of excellent ginger cookies, having him prepare two of them from cheaper ginger, which he had mixed into a confection of fresh hepatic aloes. Then he had them sprinkled with sugar just like the other cookies and in order not to lose them or mix them up with the others, he had

---

*According to some traditional beliefs, special prayers or spells could be performed over bread and cheese, making it impossible for thieves to swallow the morsels which had been so treated.

them marked with a certain sign, by which he could easily recognize them; and after purchasing a flask of good Vernaccia wine, he returned to the country and said to Calandrino:

"You must invite all those you suspect to come and have a drink with you tomorrow morning: it's a holiday, and everyone will be happy to come, and this evening, along with Buffalmacco, I'll cast the spell on the ginger cookies and bring them to your house tomorrow morning, and for your sake, I, myself, will give them out and do and say what must be done and said."

Calandrino did just that. And the next morning, after he gathered together around the elm in front of the church a considerable group of farm laborers and whatever young Florentines happened to be staying in the country at the time, Bruno and Buffalmacco came around with the box of cookies and the flask of wine; and getting them all to stand in a circle, Bruno announced:

"Gentlemen, I must tell you the reason why you are here, so that if anything happens to cause you displeasure, you will not blame it on me. Last night, Calandrino, who is right here, was robbed of one of his fine pigs, and he has not been able to discover who took it; and since it could have been stolen only by someone here, in order to find out who has taken it, he is going to give each of you in turn one of these cookies to eat and something to drink. I warn you in advance that the one who stole the pig will be unable to swallow the cookie. On the contrary, it will taste more bitter than poison to him, and he will spit it out; and so, in order not to disgrace himself in the presence of so many people, perhaps it would be better for the person who stole the pig to confess now to the priest, and I can forget the entire affair."

Everyone there said they would gladly eat one of the cookies, and so Bruno lined them up, placing Calandrino among them, and beginning at one end of the line, he started giving a ginger cookie to each of them; and when he reached Calandrino, he took one of the special cookies and put it in his hand. Calandrino, without hesitating, popped it into his mouth and began to chew, but his tongue had no sooner tasted the bitter aloes than Calandrino, unable to stand the bitter taste, spit it out. Everyone was looking at everyone else to see who was going to spit his out; Bruno, who had not yet finished handing them out, pretended not to notice anything, when he heard a voice behind him say: "Hey, Calandrino, what's the meaning of this?" He quickly turned around and, seeing that Calandrino had spit his out, he declared: "Wait a minute, perhaps something else caused him to spit; try another one." Picking out the second one, he stuck it into Calandrino's mouth and then went on to finish handing out the rest of them. If the first one had seemed bitter to Calandrino, this second one seemed even more bitter; but since he was ashamed to spit it out, he chewed it a bit and kept it in his mouth, until his eyes began to produce tears the size of hazelnuts; and finally, when he could bear it no longer, he spit it out as he had done with the first one. Buffalmacco was pouring out drinks for the group, as was Bruno, and when they and all the others saw what happened, everyone said that it had to be Calandrino himself who had stolen the pig; and there were even some in the group who reproached him harshly.

But when the crowd had broken up, leaving Bruno and Buffalmacco behind with Calandrino, Buffalmacco began to say:

"I was certain right from the start that it was you who stole it yourself, and that you were trying to make us believe that it had been stolen from you just so you wouldn't have to stand us to a round of drinks with the money you received from the profits."

Calandrino, who had still not spat out the bitterness of the aloes, began swearing he had not taken it.

But Buffalmacco said, "Come on now, buddy, tell us how much you got out of it. Did it fetch six florins?"

When Calandrino heard this, he was at the point of despair, but then Bruno said to him:

"Listen to this, Calandrino. There was a fellow in the group we were eating and drinking with today who told me you had a young girl up here you were keeping for your amusement and that you gave her whatever you could scrape together, and he was convinced you had sent her this pig. You've really become quite a trickster! There was that time you led us along the Mugnone River to pick up those black stones, and after leading us on a wild-goose chase, you took off for home and then tried to make us believe you had really made the discovery! And now, once again, you think with your oaths you can make us believe that this pig, which you either gave away or sold, was actually stolen from you. We've caught on to your tricks by now; you can't fool us anymore! And to tell you the truth, that's why we took so much trouble to cast the spell, and now, unless you give us two brace of capons we mean to tell Monna Tessa everything."

Seeing that they would not believe him, and feeling that he had enough trouble as it was without letting himself in for a battle with his wife's temper, Calandrino gave them the two brace of capons; and after they had salted the pig they took back everything with them to Florence, leaving Calandrino behind with a loss and the expense of their laughter.

[Eighth Day, Seventh Story]

✦

A scholar is in love with a widow, who loves another man and makes the scholar stand one winter night under the snow waiting for her; later on, as the result of following his advice, she is forced to stand for an entire day in mid-July on top of a tower, naked and exposed to the flies, horseflies, and the sun.

THE ladies laughed heartily over poor Calandrino, and they would have laughed even more, if not for the fact that they felt sorry to see him robbed of the capons by the people who had also stolen the pig. But when the story came to a close, the Queen ordered Pampinea to tell her tale, and she immediately began in this manner:

Dearest ladies, it often happens that one cunning deed will outdo another cunning deed, and for this reason, it shows little intelligence to take pleasure in deceiving others. In a number of the stories that have been told, we have laughed a great deal over the tricks which have been played, but in these stories, there has never been any mention of retaliation having taken place; so now I intend to arouse some compassion in you for the just revenge dealt to a woman of our own town whose trick, when turned around and used against her, almost caused her death. Nor will it be unprofitable for you to hear this tale, for it will make you more cautious about playing tricks on others, and so you will be that much the wiser.

Not many years ago, there once lived in Florence a young woman named Elena, who was beautiful of body, proud of spirit, and of rather noble lineage, and who was well provided with the blessings of Fortune. Left, as she was, a widow, she decided she would never marry again, for she had fallen in love with a handsome and charming young man of her own choosing; and since now she was free of all other cares, with the assistance of a maidservant of hers, whom she trusted a great deal, she was able to spend much time enjoying him, to her wondrous delight. Now in those days, it happened that a young nobleman of our city

amed Rinieri, who had studied for a long while in Paris—not
or the purpose of selling his learning later on for profit, as oth-
ers do, but rather to learn the reason and the cause of things (a
esire which highly becomes a nobleman)—returned from Paris
o Florence; and there, honored as much for his nobility as for
is learning, Rinieri lived in a manner befitting a gentleman.

But as often occurs, those who have a keener understanding of
rofound matters are more easily snared by Love's noose, and
his happened to our Rinieri. For one day, in the mood for some
ntertainment, he went to a banquet where this Elena appeared
efore his eyes, dressed in black (as our widows usually are),
nd she seemed to him to be so graced with beauty and charm,
ore so than any other woman he had ever seen; and he
hought to himself that the man to whom God should grant the
race of holding her naked in his arms could truly consider him-
elf to be blessed. Gazing at her cautiously on one occasion and
nother, and realizing that great and precious things cannot be
von without effort, he decided to himself that he would concen-
rate his every care and attention on pleasing her, so that in this
nanner he might acquire her love and, in so doing, might be able
o possess her fully.

The young lady, who had a higher opinion of herself that she
ad a right to, was not in the habit of keeping her eyes fixed on
he ground, but with artful glances she looked around and
uickly singled out who it was who regarded her with such de-
ight. When she noticed Rinieri, laughing to herself, she said: "I
ave not come here today in vain, for if I'm not mistaken, I've
ot this bird by the beak." And she began to look at him from
ime to time out of the corner of her eye, doing her best to show
im that he mattered to her, thinking for her part that the more
nen she beguiled and snared with her beauty, the more highly
er beauty would be prized, especially by the man to whom,
long with her love, she had given it.

The wise scholar, setting aside his philosophical reflections,
urned all his thoughts toward her, and since he believed it
vould please her, after he had learned where her house was lo-
ated, he began walking past it, inventing various reasons for
aving to pass by there. The lady, for the reason already given,
hat is, that she gloried in her own vanity, pretended to view his
assings-by with great pleasure; and so the scholar found some
vay to strike up a friendship with her maidservant, after which
e revealed his love to her, and begged her to use her good of-
ices so that he might enjoy her mistress's favor.

The maidservant made him grand promises and recounted all

this to her lady, who in turn, howled with laughter when her maid told her, and then she said: "You see how the fellow has lost all that wisdom he brought back with him from Paris? Well, now, let's give him what he's looking for. Whenever he speaks to you again, tell him I love him much more than he loves me, but that I must protect my honor, so that I may hold my head high in the company of other ladies; and if he is as wise as they say, he ought to hold me even dearer because of this." Ah, the naughty girl, the naughty girl! She had no idea, my dear ladies, what getting involved with a scholar is all about! When she found him, the maidservant did as her lady ordered. The happy scholar graduated to more impassioned entreaties, to writing her letters, and to sending her gifts, and while she accepted everything, the only responses which came back in return were vague ones; and in this manner, she kept him grazing on his own hopes for quite a while.

Finally, revealing everything to her lover, who became rather angry and then a bit jealous over the affair, in order to show him that he was wrong to be suspicious of her, she sent her maidservant to the scholar, who was becoming more insistent in his entreaties, to tell him on her behalf that although she had not yet had the opportunity to satisfy his desires from the moment she had learned of his love, she hoped to be with him sometime during the Christmas holidays, which were near at hand. Further, she told him that if he was willing, on the night after Christmas he should come to her courtyard, where, as soon as she could, she would go to meet him. The scholar was the happiest man in the world, and at the appointed time he went to the lady's house; and after being let into the courtyard by the maidservant and locked inside, he began waiting for the lady.

The lady, who that evening had summoned her lover to come to her and who was happily eating supper with him, told her lover what she intended to do that evening, and added: "And now you'll be able to see just how much I love this man of whom you have become so foolishly jealous." These words the lover took in with great satisfaction, and now he was anxious to witness through her actions what her words gave him to believe. By chance, it had snowed heavily the day before, and everything was covered with snow. Because of this, the scholar had not remained long in the courtyard before he began to feel the worst chill he had ever experienced; but as he was expecting relief to come at any moment, he suffered the cold patiently.

After a while, the lady said to her lover:

"Let's go into the bedroom, and we can watch from a little

window what this fellow of whom you have become so jealous is
doing and see what he has to say to my maidservant, whom I
have just sent to speak with him."

And so they both went over to the little window where they
could see the scholar without being seen by him and where they
could overhear the maidservant, speaking to the scholar from an-
other window, who said:

"Rinieri, my mistress is the most sorrowful woman that ever
lived, for this evening one of her brothers arrived, and he talked
on and on to her, and then he wanted to eat supper with her,
and he still hasn't left yet, although I think he will be going
soon; and so she hasn't been able to come to you, but she'll be
here before long; she begs you not to mind the waiting."

The scholar, who believed this to be the truth, replied:

"Tell my lady she should not give any thought to me until she
is able to come at her convenience, but to do so as soon as she
can."

The maidservant went back into the house and then to bed;
the lady then said to her lover: "Well, what do you have to say?
Do you think that if I loved him as you fear, I would allow him
to stand down there and freeze?" And having said this, with her
lover, who was already partially satisfied, she went to bed, and
there they played and took their pleasure for the longest time,
laughing and making fun of the poor scholar.

The scholar was walking back and forth in the courtyard in
order to keep warm, and because he had no place to sit down or
to take shelter, he cursed the brother for staying so long with the
lady; and every time he would hear a noise, he thought it was
the sound of the lady opening the door for him, but he hoped in
vain.

After enjoying herself with her lover until almost midnight,
the lady said to him:

"What do you think of our scholar, my love? Which do you
think is greater, his knowledge or the love I bear for him? Will
the cold I am causing him to suffer expel from your heart the
chill of jealousy which entered it because of my remarks in jest
about him the other day?"

Her lover replied:

"Heart of my body, of course, I know it as well as I know
you are my happiness, my repose, my delight, and all my hope,
and I, too, am yours as well."

"Well, then," said the lady, "kiss me now at least a thousand
times, and let me see if you are telling the truth." And so her

lover embraced her tightly, kissing her not a thousand but more than a hundred thousand times.

After pursuing this venture for quite some time, the lady remarked:

"Why don't we get up for a moment and see if the fire, which this new lover of mine said in his letters was consuming him totally all day long, is thoroughly extinguished?"

And getting up, they went over to the same little window. Looking out into the courtyard, they saw the scholar dancing a jig in the snow to the tune of his own chattering teeth, and never had they seen a dance quite like it, so quickly and lively did he move. Then the lady said: "What do you say to that, my sweet hope? Do you agree that I know how to make men dance without the sound of trumpets or bagpipes?"

Laughing, the lover replied: "Yes, you do, delight of my delight."

The lady said:

"Let's go downstairs to the door; you be quiet, and I'll speak to him, and we'll hear what he has to say and perhaps we'll have just as much fun as we do watching him from here." Leaving the bedroom quietly, they went downstairs to the door, and there, without opening it at all, in a muted voice, the lady called to the scholar through a tiny crack in the door.

When the scholar heard himself being called, he praised the Lord, believing too quickly that he was about to get inside, and drawing close to the door, he said:

"Here I am, my lady: for God's sake, open up, I am dying from the cold."

The lady replied:

"Ah, yes, I imagine it must be chilly out there, but are you really all that cold, just because of a little snow? I've heard that there are much worse snows in Paris. I can't open up for you yet, for this damned brother of mine, who came to have supper with me last night, has not left yet; but he'll leave soon, and then I shall come at once and let you in. It was all I could do just now to slip away from him and come down here to cheer you up for having to wait so long."

The scholar answered:

"Oh! My lady, I beg you, for the love of God, to open the door for me, so that I can take shelter inside, for the thickest snow I've ever seen started falling a while ago, and it's still coming down; then I shall wait for you as long as you please."

The lady said:

"Alas, my sweet, I cannot, for this door makes such a noise

when it is opened that my brother would surely hear it if I were to open it for you; but let me go now and persuade him to leave, so that I can come back and let you in."

The scholar said:

"Go quickly, then; I beg you to have a warm fire prepared so that when I do come, I can warm myself up, for I'm so cold, I hardly have any feeling left."

The lady said:

"How can this be so, if what you wrote to me on numerous occasions is true, that is, that you burn all over because of your love for me? But I am sure you say this in jest. I'm going now; wait here and keep your courage up."

The lover, who heard everything and took the greatest delight in it, went back to bed with the lady, and they slept very little that evening; on the contrary, they spent almost the entire night saisfying their desires and making fun of the scholar.

The poor wretch of a scholar, whose teeth chattered so hard it was as though he had turned into a stork, realized he had been tricked and tried the door several times to see if he could open it, and then he looked all around him for a way by which he might escape; but not seeing any, he paced about like a lion in his cage, as he cursed the bad weather, the treachery of the lady, and the length of the night along with his own stupidity, and so furious was he with her that the long-standing and fervent love he had borne for her quickly turned to cruel and bitter hatred, and he began to mull over in his mind various complicated schemes for getting revenge, which he now desired more than he had ever desired earlier to be with the lady.

After a long and painful wait, night drew to an end and dawn began to appear; and the lady's maidservant, following her instructions, came downstairs and opened the door to the courtyard, and pretending to feel sorry for the scholar, she said:

"Curse that brother of hers for coming here last night! He kept us in suspense all night long and made you freeze; but you know how it is! Cheer up. Be patient, and you'll see that what couldn't be for tonight will have to be for another time; I know that nothing could have displeased my mistress more than what happened here last night."

Although the scholar was furious, like the intelligent man he was, he realized that threats were nothing but weapons for those who are threatened, and he locked within his breast the anger which would have expressed itself, were it not for the restraint of his strong willpower; and in a low voice, without showing himself in the least angry, the scholar replied:

"To tell you the truth, I spent the worst night I ever spent, but I clearly realize that this was not the lady's fault in any way, since she herself, taking pity upon me, came all the way down here to excuse herself and to comfort me; and as you say, what couldn't be for tonight will have to be for another time. So commend me to your mistress and goodbye."

Nearly paralyzed by the cold, the scholar returned home as best he could. When he was home, feeling exhausted and dying from lack of sleep, he threw himself upon his bed to rest, and he awakened to discover that he hardly had any strength in his arms and legs; and so, having sent for several doctors and explaining to them the chill he had suffered, he placed his health in their hands. Although the physicians treated him with the most prompt and effective remedies, it was some time before they were able to cure his muscles, allowing them to straighten out his limbs, and if it had not been for the fact of his youth and the arrival of warmer weather, he could never have been able to recover. But after regaining his health and vigor, concealing his hatred within himself, he pretended to be far more in love with his widow than ever before.

Now it happened, after a certain period of time, that Fortune provided the scholar with an opportunity to satisfy his desire for revenge. For the young man who was loved by the widow, no longer caring about the love she bore for him, fell in love with another lady, and since he was absolutely resolved to do nothing to please her, nothing at all, she was wasting away in tears and bitterness. But her maidservant, who felt very sorry for her because she was unable to find a way to dispel the lady's sorrow over the loss of her lover, upon seeing the scholar passing through the neighborhood the way he usually did, came up with a foolish idea, and this was that her mistress's lover might be induced to love her again as he once had through some form of the art of magic, and that the scholar was probably well versed in such an art. Then she communicated the idea to her mistress. Not realizing that had the scholar been an expert in magic he would have used it to advance his own cause, the rather unwise lady took her servant's advice and told her to find out from him at once whether he would agree to do this and to promise him faithfully that in return for his assistance, she would do whatever he wished.

The servant was perfect in delivering her message, and when the scholar heard it, filled with joy, he said to himself: "God be praised, now the time has come, and with His help, I shall be able to punish this wretched woman for the wrong she did me in

xchange for the great love which I bore her"; then he said to
ae servant: "Tell my lady not to be concerned about this, for
ven if her lover were in India, I would see to it that he were
ack here at once begging her mercy for having acted against
er wishes, and if she will set a time and place suitable to her, I
ill tell her myself how she is to handle the matter. Tell her this
or me and do give her my best wishes." The maid delivered his
eply, and the lady arranged for them to meet at the Church of
anta Lucia by the Prato gate.

The lady and the scholar met there, and as they spoke in pri-
ate together, having forgotten that this was the man whom she
ad brought almost to the point of death, she openly revealed all
er troubles to him, telling him what she wanted and begging
im for his assistance; to her plea, the scholar replied:

"Madam, it is true that magic, about which I know all there
s to know, was among the many subjects I studied in Paris, but
ince God finds this art most displeasing, I have sworn never to
nake use of it, either for my own profit or for that of others. It
, also true that the love I bear for you is so great I do not
now how I can refuse anything you request of me; and so, even
f I were condemned to Hell for this deed alone, I am most
eady to do it, since it is your wish that I do so. But I remind
ou that this is a more difficult thing to do than you perhaps re-
lize, especially when a lady wishes to regain the love of a man,
r a man the love of a lady, for this cannot be done except by
he very person who is involved; and it is essential that the per-
on who does it be brave, for this magic must be done at night,
n lonely spots, and with no one else around, and I do not know
whether you are disposed to do such things."

To this the lady, more in love than she was intelligent, replied:

"The love that spurs me on is so strong that there is nothing I
vould not do to get back the man who has wrongly abandoned
ne, but please tell me, if you will, why I must be brave."

The scholar, who was as clever as the Devil, said:

"Madam, I shall need to make a tin image of the man you
vish to get back, and when you have received it you must take
t and go all by yourself, as the moon begins to wane, around the
.our you would normally fall asleep, and completely naked, im-
nerse yourself with this image seven times in a stream of flow-
ng water; after this, still naked, you must climb up a tree or to
ome deserted rooftop, and facing the north with the image in
our hand, you must recite certain words I shall give you in
vriting, and once you have recited them, two young maidens, the
nost beautiful you have ever seen, will greet you and ask you

politely what it is you wish them to do. Be sure you express you
wishes fully and clearly to these two maidens (being careful no
to mix up one name with another), and once you have explained
everything, they will go away and you will climb back down t
the place where you left your clothes, put them back on, and re
turn home. And without a doubt, before the following night i
half over, your lover will return to you and beg you in tears fo
your pity and forgiveness, and you may be sure that from tha
moment on, he will never abandon you for another woman."

It was as if the lady, having heard these words and believed
them completely, already had her lover back in her arms, an
now that she felt somewhat comforted, she said:

"Rest assured, I shall follow your instructions to the last de
tail, and I have the best place in the world to do this, for I ow
a farm along the upper valley of the Arno which is very close t
the banks of the river; and in early July bathing there will b
delightful. And I also recall that not far from the river there i
a tower which is abandoned, except for the shepherds who occa
sionally climb up its wooden stairs to reach a terrace from whic
they can look for their lost sheep; it is in a very solitary an
out-of-the way place and I hope by climbing to the top to per
form perfectly all you require me to do."

The scholar, who knew very well the location of both the
lady's land and the tower, was delighted that things were going
as he had planned and said:

"Madam, I have never been in that part of the country be-
fore, and therefore I am not acquainted with your farm or the
tower; but if it is as you describe it, there can be no better spot
in the world. And so, when the time is right, I shall send you the
image and the incantation; but I most strongly urge you that
once your desire has been fulfilled, you realize how well I have
served you and remember to fulfill your promise to me."

The lady said that she would do so without fail, and having
taken leave of him, she returned to her home.

Overjoyed because his plan seemed to be taking effect, the
scholar constructed an image with some cryptic lettering upon it
and composed some nonsensical lines as an incantation; and
when he felt the time had come, he sent them to the lady and
instructed her that without further delay she should do what he
told her to do on the very next night; and then with one of his
servants, he secretly went to the home of a friend of his, which
was very near the tower, in order to put his plan into action.

Meanwhile, the lady set out with her maidservant and went to
her farm; and when night fell, pretending that she was ready to

retire, the lady sent her servant to bed, and in the dead of night she quietly left the house and went to the banks of the Arno near the tower, and having looked all about her and seen or heard no one, she then took off her clothes and hid them under a bush, and went into the water seven times, holding the image in her hand; then, still naked and holding the image, she walked over to the tower. The scholar, who at nightfall had hidden with his servant among the willows and the other trees near the tower, observed all these things, and when she walked right past, so close to him, naked as she was, he gazed at the whiteness of her body penetrating the shadows of the night, and at that moment, as he stared at her breasts and the other parts of her body, thinking how beautiful they were and realizing to himself what was about to happen to them, he felt a twinge of pity for her. Moreover, suddenly attacked by the desires of the flesh which caused a certain part of him which had been resting to stand up straight, he was tempted to leave his hiding place, seize her, and fulfill his desires—and caught between pity and lust, he was almost overcome. But when he recalled who he was, the injury that was done him, why he had received it, and from whom, his indignation was fired up again, both his compassion and his lust were driven away, and he remained firm in his resolution, allowing her to pass by him. After climbing up the tower and facing the north, the lady began to repeat the incantation the scholar had given her; meanwhile, the scholar shortly thereafter entered the tower and slowly and quietly removed the ladder which led up to the terrace upon which the lady was standing, and then he waited to see what she would say and do.

The lady repeated the incantation seven times and began to wait for the appearance of the two maidens, and she waited for such a long time that apart from the chill, which she felt far more than she might have liked, she was still there to witness the arrival of dawn; and then, upset by the fact that things had not turned out as the scholar had told her they would, she said to herself: "I fear he wanted to give me a night like the one I gave him, but if that was what he had in mind, he has not avenged himself very well, for my wait has only been a third as long as his, not to mention that the cold was of another magnitude altogether." And so as not to be caught out there on the terrace in daylight, she prepared to climb down from the tower only to discover that the ladder was no longer there. Then, almost as if the earth had collapsed beneath her feet, the lady fainted and fell onto the terrace of the tower. Later, when she returned to her senses, she began to cry miserably and to lament, realizing only too well that this was the work of the scholar, and she began to feel sorry for first having offended him and then for trusting too confidently in a person whom she should rather have treated as an enemy; and in this state of mind, she remained for the longest time.

Then she looked around to see if there might be some other means of climbing down, but she was unable to find any and began her weeping all over again, for a bitter thought entered her mind as she said to herself:

"Oh, luckless creature, what will your brothers, your relatives, your neighbors, and all the Florentines say when they discover that you have been found here naked? Your good reputation will be revealed as false; and even if you could come up with lies to excuse yourself, this damned scholar, who knows all about you, will not let you lie. Ah, poor wretch that you are, you have at the same time lost both the young man you loved so unwisely and your honor!" After uttering these words, she was so overcome by grief that she nearly threw herself from the tower to the ground below.

Since the sun had already risen, she moved a bit closer to the wall on one side of the tower, hoping to be able to see some shepherd boy nearby with his animals whom she could call and send to her maidservant, but it just happened that the scholar, who had been asleep for a while under a bush, awakened and saw her just as she caught sight of him; the scholar said to her: "Good morning, madam, have the maidens arrived yet?"

When the lady saw and heard him, she burst into tears once more, begging him to come into the tower so that she might speak to him. The scholar was very courteous in granting her request.

Lying face down on the terrace, only the lady's head showed through the trapdoor as she said tearfully:

"Rinieri, if I gave you a bad night, you have certainly avenged yourself quite well, for although it is July, since I was naked I thought that I was going to freeze up here last night, not to mention the fact that I have wept to such an extent over both the trick I played upon you and my own foolishness in believing you that it is a wonder I still have any eyes left in my head. Therefore, I beg you, not for love of me, for you have no reason to love me, but for your own self-esteem as a gentleman, to let what you have done to me suffice as revenge for the injury I did you, and bring me my clothes so that I can climb down from here. Please do not take away from me that which you could never restore to me even if you wished, that is, my good name, for even if I deprived you of spending that one night with me, I can pay you back whenever you please with many such nights in exchange for that one. Let this suffice for you, then, and, as a gentleman, be satisfied with the revenge you have taken and with having made me aware of it. Do not exercise your strength against a woman: an eagle wins no glory in overcoming a dove; therefore, for the love of God and your own honor, have mercy upon me."

The scholar, indignantly remembering the injury he had suffered and at the same time seeing her weep and beg, felt both pleasure and pain in his heart—pleasure from the revenge which he desired above all else, and pain which his humanity moved him to feel in compassion for her misery; nevertheless, his humanity was not enough to conquer the harshness of his desire for revenge, and he answered:

"Madonna Elena, if my prayers, which, in truth, I was unable to bathe in tears or to sweeten with honeyed words as you do so well now with your own, had obtained for me on the night I was dying from cold in your snow-filled courtyard the slightest bit of shelter from you, it would be an easy matter for me now to comply with your own request; but if you care more now for your good name than you did in the past and find it so uncomfortable to be up there naked, why not direct your prayers to the man in whose arms, as you will recall, you did not mind lying naked all that night, while you listened to my chattering teeth as I paced up and down outside in your courtyard full of snow? Let *him* help you, let *him* return your clothes, and let *him* replace the ladder so that you may climb down, and try arousing some concern in *him* for your reputation, since it was for this man, not only now but on a thousand other occasions, that you never hesitated to place your honor in jeopardy. Why do you not call upon him to come and help you? To whom does this task belong more than to him? You are his, and whom should he protect or help if not you? Call for him, you foolish woman, and find out if the love you bear him, and your intelligence combined with his, are enough to free you from my foolishness; when you were enjoying yourself with him, did you not ask him which seemed to him to be the greater, my stupidity or the love you bore for him? You are too generous in offering me what I no longer desire, or what you could not deny to me if I did still desire it; save your nights for your lover, if you manage to leave here alive, let them be for you and him—I had more than enough of one of them, and being tricked once is enough for me! And yet again with cunning speech, you try by flattering me and calling me a valiant gentleman to regain my kindness, secretly attempting to dissuade me from punishing your wickedness by praising my magnanimity; but your words of praise will not obscure the eyes of my intellect now as once your treacherous promises did. I know myself, for you made me learn more about myself in a single night than I learned during the entire time I lived in Paris. But even supposing that I were really magnanimous, you are not the sort of person toward whom magnanimity should be shown. The only fit punishment and revenge for a savage beast like yourself is death, whereas, if I were dealing with a human being, what you mentioned before would be punishment enough. And so, while I am not an eagle, I also know that you are not a dove but, rather, a poisonous serpent, and I intend to persecute you with all my hatred and all my strength, as if you were man's oldest enemy,* even though what I am doing to you cannot accurately be termed revenge but, rather, punishment, for revenge should be greater than the offense, and this punishment of mine will not even equal it. And so, when I consider in what peril you placed my life, it would not be enough for me to take your life by way of revenge, nor the lives of a hundred other women like you, for I would be killing only one vile, evil, and wicked woman. And except for this pretty little face of yours, which in a few years will be ruined and covered with wrinkles, how the devil are you any different from just any common servant girl? But you did not mind at all trying to murder a gentleman (as you called me a moment ago) whose life could be of more value to the world in a single day than one hundred thousand women like you could be for as long as the world lasts. Therefore, I shall teach you with this pain you are suffering what it means to ridicule a man's feelings, and especially those of a scholar; and I shall give you good cause never to stoop to such folly again, that is, if you manage to escape alive this time. But if you are so anxious to come down, why not just throw yourself to the ground? With God's help, by breaking your neck, you will, at the same time, escape from the suffering you seem to be enduring and make me the happiest man in the world. Now, I don't wish to speak to you any further. I was smart enough to make you climb up there; let us see if you are as clever now in getting down by yourself as once you were in tricking me."

While the scholar was saying all this, the wretched woman wept continuously, time was passing, and the sun was rising

---

*Man's most ancient enemy is the Devil, who took the form of a serpent in the Garden of Eden.

higher and higher in the sky; but when she heard him speak no more, she said:

"Ah, cruel man, if that cursed night made you suffer so, and my fault seemed so great that neither my youthful beauty nor my bitter tears nor my humble prayers can move you to feel any pity, at least you should be moved a little and your stern severity lessened by the fact that I finally did place my trust in you and revealed my every secret to you, which allowed you to fulfill your desire to show me the error of my ways, for if I had not trusted you, you would have had no way of taking revenge on me, which you obviously so eagerly desired. Ah, set your anger aside and forgive me now! If you are willing to forgive me and allow me to climb down from here, I am ready to abandon completely this faithless young man and take you as my lover and master, no matter how much you disdain my beauty and call it fleeting and of little value; and even though my beauty, as well as that of any other woman, may be as fleeting as you say, I tell you this: it should be valued, if for no other reason, for the fact that it represents the pleasure, amusement, and delight of a man's youth; and you are not an old man. And no matter how cruelly you have treated me, I cannot believe that you wish to see me suffer such a dishonorable death as that of throwing myself down from here like a desperate woman before your very eyes, those eyes which, if you were not then the liar you have now become, were once so greatly pleased by my beauty. Ah, have mercy on me in the name of God and for pity's sake. The sun is getting too hot, and is beginning to hurt me as much as the unbearable cold did last night."

The scholar, who was delighted to exchange words with her, replied:

"Madam, you put your trust in my hands not for any love you bore for me but, rather, in order to get back what you had lost, and therefore, you deserve nothing if not harsher treatment. And you are quite mad if you believe this was the only means I had of getting the revenge I desired. I had a thousand different possibilities, and I wound a thousand snares around your feet while pretending to love you. And even if this one had failed, before long you would have inevitably fallen into another trap— though you could not have fallen into one which would have caused you greater suffering or shame than this, but then again I did set this trap not to make things easier for you but, rather, more enjoyable for me. And even if all my plans had failed me, my pen would not have done so, and with it I would have written so many things about you and in such a fashion that when you came to learn about them, which you would have, you would have wished a thousand times a day that you had never been born. The powers of the pen are far mightier than those people suppose who have not known them through experience. I swear to God (and may He allow the revenge I am taking on you to be as sweet right up to the end as it has been from the beginning), I would have written such things about you that you yourself, not to speak of other people, would have been so ashamed that you would have gouged your eyes out rather than look upon yourself again; and so do not blame the sea for being enlarged by a tiny stream. As concerns your love and your belonging to me, as I said before, I care not in the least: go on belonging to the man who possessed you before, if you can; just as I once hated him, I now love him, for I see what he has done to you. You women go around falling in love with younger men, and wanting them to fall for you because their complexions are fresher and their beards a bit blacker, and they walk straighter, and because they dance and joust; somewhat more mature men once possessed all these attributes, but they also know things younger men still have to learn. Moreover, you believe that younger men are better riders and able to do more miles in a day's ride than more mature men. True, I will admit that they can warm your wool with greater energy, but mature men who are more experienced are better acquainted with all those places where the flea hides; a small but spicy serving can be far better than a big but tasteless one; hard riding will break and tire anyone, no matter how young he is, but a slow ride, though you may come somewhat later to your destination, at least will get you there in good shape. Senseless creatures that you are, you women do not see how much evil lurks beneath that little bit of handsomeness. Young men are not satisfied with one woman, they desire as many as they see, and they think they deserve to have just that many, so their love cannot be stable, and you yourself can now testify quite well to this fact through your own experience. And they think they deserve to be pampered and worshiped by their ladies, and their greatest glory is in boasting about all the women they have had—a defect which has made many a woman end up under a friar, who never opens his mouth about such matters. And although you claim no one knew about your love affairs except your maidservant and me, you are mistaken and quite wrong if you believe this: all of your lover's neighbors, as well as your own, speak of almost nothing else, but the person who is the most concerned with such affairs is usually the last to know these things. Also, young men will steal from you, while more mature men give you gifts. Therefore, you, who made a bad choice, belong to the man to whom you gave yourself, and you must leave me, whom you scorned, for another, for I have found a lady who is worth much more than you are, one who understands me much better than you ever did. And if you want greater assurance of the desire of my eyes in the next world than you have from my words in this world, throw yourself down here now, and your soul, which I firmly believe has already been welcomed into the Devil's arms, will be able to testify if my own eyes, on having witnessed your fall, were at all tearful or not. But I do not think you wish to make me this happy, and so, I say that as the sun begins to burn you, remember the cold you made me suffer, and if you mix this hot with that cold, you will certainly feel the sun burn less."

When she realized that the scholar's words were pointing to a cruel fate, the disheartened lady began to weep again and said:

"Wait; since nothing I have said moves you to pity me, perhaps you will be moved by the love which you bear for that lady whom you have found to be wiser than myself, and who you say loves you. Forgive me for the sake of her love, bring me back my clothes, let me dress myself again, and help me climb down from here."

With that the scholar began to laugh, and noticing it was well past the hour of tierce, he replied:

"Well, in that case, how could I refuse you, since you beg me in the name of such a lady? Just tell me where your clothes are, and I shall get them and see to it that you get down from up there."

Believing what he said, the lady felt somewhat reassured, and she told him where she had left her clothes. Coming out of the tower, the scholar ordered his servant not to leave that spot but to stay close at hand and to do all he could to see that no one went into the tower before he returned; and after giving these orders, he went to the house of a friend of his, and there he ate a leisurely meal, and then when it was time, he took a nap.

The lady, still up there on the tower, and somewhat comforted by her foolish hope, started moving over to the part of the wall where there was a bit of shade, and there, sad beyond measure and accompanied by the bitterest of thoughts, she began to wait, now brooding, now weeping, now hoping, now despairing of the scholar's ever returning with her clothes, her mind jumping from one thought to another; and being so overcome with grief and not having slept at all the night before, she fell asleep. The sun, which had by now reached its noonday zenith, was blazing hot, and it beat straight down upon the woman's tender, delicate body and upon her uncovered head with such force that not only did it scorch part of her flesh that was exposed to its rays but it caused her skin to crack with countless blisters; and her roasting was so intense that she was forced to wake up, though she was fast asleep.

She moved a bit when she felt the burning, and when she moved, it seemed as if all of her cooked skin was cracking and splitting, like a piece of scorched parchment being pulled apart; besides this, her head ached so much she thought it was going to split in two, which was no surprise at all. The platform of the tower was so hot that she was unable to find a place where she could stand or sit, so she kept moving about now here and now there as she wept. Moreover, since there was not a breath of wind, the place was teeming with flies and horseflies that settled on her open flesh and stung her so fiercely that every sting felt like the wound from a long spear; and so she kept her hands in perpetual motion, swatting all around her, continually cursing herself, her life, her lover, and the scholar. And being thus tortured, goaded, and pierced by the inestimable heat of the sun, by flies and horseflies, and by hunger and still more by thirst, as well as by a thousand distressing thoughts, she got to her feet, and ready to try anything that might save her life, she began to look around her with the hope of seeing or hearing someone nearby to whom she might call out for help. But Fortune, her enemy, deprived her of even this possibility.

The peasants had all abandoned the fields because of the heat, and in any case, no one had been working near the tower that morning, because all of them were around their homes, threshing the corn. So she heard nothing but the cicadas and saw nothing but the Arno River, whose inviting waters did not quench her thirst but rather made it worse. She could see here and there woods, shaded areas, and homes, all of which increased her anguish, since she longed for them. What more can we say about this unfortunate widow? The sun above her, the heat of the floor below, the stings of the flies and horseflies on all sides of her had so changed her that whereas the night before the whiteness of her skin shone through the shadows of the evening, now her flesh had become redder than anger itself and was spotted all over with blood, and to anyone who saw it, it would have seemed the ugliest thing in the world.

And so there she remained with no hope or help, expecting death more than anything else, until after half-past nones had already struck, when the scholar, waking from his sleep, remembered his lady, and returned to the tower to see what had become of her, and to send his servant, who had not yet eaten, off for his meal; when the lady heard him, weak and overcome by her great pain, she crawled over to the trapdoor and sat down, and in tears, she said:

"Rinieri, surely you have taken more than enough revenge, for if I had you freeze in my courtyard at night, you have roasted me, or, rather burned me on top of this tower by day, and besides this, you are killing me with hunger and thirst; therefore, I beg you in the name of God's love to climb up here and, since I do not have the courage to kill myself, do it for me, for I desire death more than anything else, so great is the torment that I am suffering. And if you will not grant me this favor, at least give me a cup of water so that I can wet my mouth (my tears are insufficient to do so), such is the dryness and the burning I have within me."

The scholar was well aware from the sound of her voice that the lady's condition was weakening, and he also could see all those parts of her body that were scorched by the sun, and because of what he saw, as well as her humble entreaties, he felt a bit of compassion toward her; nevertheless, he answered:

"Wicked woman, you shall never die by my hands but, rather, by your own, if what you wish is to die; and you shall receive from me as much water to relieve your heat as I received fire from you to lessen my cold. I regret very much that the illness I contracted from my cold had to be treated with heat from stinking dung, while your own illness caused by the heat can be treated with the coolness of sweet-smelling rose water; and whereas I almost lost the use of my limbs and my very life, you have only been skinned by this heat and you will return just as beautiful as you ever were, like the snake that sheds its old skin."

"Oh, wretched me," exclaimed the woman, "may God bestow beauty acquired at such a price only upon my enemies; but you, who are crueler than any savage beast, how can you bear to torture me in this way? What greater punishment could you or anyone else inflict upon me, even if I had murdered every last one of your relatives using the cruelest of tortures? I am certain there is no greater cruelty you could inflict upon a traitor guilty of having slaughtered an entire city's population than this one to which you have subjected me, roasting me in the sun and having me eaten by the flies; moreover, you will not even give me a cup of water, whereas even a condemned murderer on the way to his execution is often given some wine to drink if only he asks for it. However, now that I see you are unwavering in your bitter cruelty and that my suffering can in no way move you, I am now ready to meet my death with resignation, so that God may have mercy on my soul, and I pray that He will take note of this deed of yours with His just eyes."

Having uttered these words, in great pain she dragged herself toward the middle of the platform, despairing of ever being able to escape the scorching heat, and not one but a thousand times she thought she would faint from thirst, not to mention her other torments, and all this time she wept bitterly and moaned about her misfortune.

It was now evening, and the scholar felt he had done enough, so he had her clothes picked up and wrapped in his servant's cloak, and then he set out for the wretched lady's house; when he arrived there, he found her servant sitting on the doorstep looking sad and forlorn and desperate, and he said to her: "What has happened to your mistress, my good woman?"

The servant answered him:

"Sir, I do not know. This morning, I thought I would find her in bed, where I thought I saw her go last night, but I did not find her there or elsewhere, and I do not know what has become of her, and I am very worried about her. Would you by any chance have news for me about her?"

To this, the scholar replied:

"I only wish I could have put you where I put your mistress, so I could have punished you for your sins just as I have punished your mistress for hers! But you can be sure I shall not allow you to escape my clutches without paying you back for what you did in such a way that never will you play a trick on another man again without remembering me first." And after he said this, he told his servant: "Give her these clothes and tell her to go to her mistress, if she wishes."

The servant obeyed his order; after taking the clothes and recognizing them, the maidservant, in light of what she had heard said, was terrified that they had killed her mistress, and she could hardly restrain herself from screaming; and once the scholar had left, she suddenly burst into tears and started running toward the tower, carrying with her the lady's clothes.

That same day, one of the lady's workers had the misfortune of losing two of his pigs, and searching for them, he reached the tower a short while after the scholar's departure, and while he was looking all around to find his pigs, he heard the unfortunate lady's miserable moaning; climbing up the tower as far as he could, he shouted: "Who's crying up there?"

The lady recognized the voice of her peasant, and calling him by name, she said to him:

"Ah, go and find my maid and tell her to come up here to me."

Recognizing her voice, the peasant said:

"Good God, my lady, who brought you all the way up there? Your maid has been running around looking for you all day, but who would ever have guessed you were up there?"

Taking the two sides of the ladder, the peasant set it in its proper position and began to tie on the rungs with cords; while he was doing this, the maidservant arrived and entered the tower, and no longer able to control her emotions, she slapped both sides of her head with her hands and screamed: "O my poor, sweet mistress, where are you?"

When the lady heard her, she said as loudly as she could:

"Oh, sister, I am up here: do not cry, just bring me my clothes, and quickly."

When the maidservant heard her speak, she was greatly comforted and climbed up the ladder, which by then had been repaired by the peasant, and assisted by him, she reached the platform of the tower; when she saw her mistress, lying there naked on the floor, utterly exhausted and destroyed, her body looking more like a burned-out log than a human form, she dug her nails into her face and began to weep over her mistress as if she were dead. But the lady begged her in God's name to be quiet and to help her get dressed; and then when she learned from her maid that no one was aware of where she had been, except for the peasant and those who had brought her clothes, she was somewhat relieved, and she begged her servant in God's name never to say a word about it to anyone. After much discussion, the peasant lifted the lady onto his shoulders, since she was unable to climb down by herself, and carried her safely out of the tower. The poor little maidservant, who was left behind them, climbed down less skillfully, for she lost her footing and fell from the ladder down to the ground and broke her leg, and the pain she felt made her groan like a lion.

After the peasant had set the lady down upon a patch of grass, he went to see what was the matter with the maidservant, and finding her with her leg broken, he also carried her out and placed her beside her mistress on the grass; when the lady saw that in addition to her other troubles, the woman from whom she expected the most assistance had just broken her leg, sorrowful beyond all belief, she began her weeping once again, and she wept so piteously that not only was the peasant unable to console her, but he, in fact, began to weep himself. And as the sun was by then beginning to set and they did not want to be caught there by nightfall, at the lady's request, the peasant went back to his house, got his wife and two brothers, and returned to the tower with a plank, upon which they placed the maidservant and carried her back to the house, and after comforting the lady with some cool water and encouraging words, the peasant hoisted her onto his shoulders and carried her into his wife's bedroom. After giving the lady some bread-soup to eat, the peasant's wife undressed her and put her to bed; and then they arranged for her and the maidservant to be taken back to Florence that night, and this was done.

When she arrived there, the lady, who had an abundance of wiles at her command, spun a yarn which had nothing to do with what had actually occurred, convincing her brothers, sisters, and everyone else there that what had happened to her and her maidservant was the result of some diabolic witchcraft. Physicians were quickly summoned, and only at the cost of great suffering and discomfort—for more than once she shed her skin, which stuck to the bedsheets—did they manage to cure her of a burning fever and all her other maladies; and they did the same for the maidservant's leg. And so, having forgotten her lover, from that time on the lady wisely refrained from playing any more tricks or from falling in love; and the scholar, hearing that the maidservant had broken her leg, felt his revenge was now quite complete, indeed, and he happily went about his business never saying another word about the matter.

So, then, this is what became of the foolish young woman and her tricks when she thought she could play around with a scholar the way she might with any other man, for little did she know that scholars—not all of them, I say, but the majority—know only too well where the Devil hides his tail. And so, ladies, beware of playing such tricks, especially on scholars.

[Eighth Day, Eighth Story]

✦

Two men are intimate friends, and one goes to bed with the other's wife; when the other man discovers this, he arranges with his wife to lock the first man inside a chest, upon which he makes love to the wife of the man who is trapped inside.

GRIEVOUS and painful as Elena's misfortunes were for the ladies to hear, they listened to them with restrained pity, since they felt she had in part deserved them, although at the same time they did consider the scholar to have been somewhat rigid, and fiercely relentless, not to mention cruel. But now that Pampinea had come to the end of her story, the Queen ordered Fiammetta to continue, and she, eager to obey, said:

Charming ladies, since you seem to be somewhat distressed by the outraged scholar's severity, I believe it would be fitting to sweeten your soured spirits with something that is a bit more delightful; and so I intend to tell you a little story about a young man who had a gentler reaction to an injury he received, and took his revenge in a more moderate way; through this story, you will come to learn that a man ought to be satisfied with giving only as good as he gets and not wish to go beyond the boundaries of a just revenge whenever he decides to avenge himself for an injury he has received.

So let me begin by telling you, then, that in Siena, as I have heard tell, there once lived two rather well-to-do young men from respectable but common families, one of whom was called Spinelloccio Tavena, and the other Zeppa di Mino, and they were next-door neighbors in the district of Camollia. These two young men always went around together, and judging from appearances, they were as close to each other as two brothers—or even more so—and both of them had very beautiful wives.

Now it happened that Spinelloccio spent a great deal of time in Zeppa's home, and not only when Zeppa was there but also when he was not there, and in so doing he became friendly with Zeppa's wife and began sleeping with her; he continued to do this for a good long time before anyone caught on. Eventually, however, one day when Zeppa happened to be at home without his wife's knowing it, Spinelloccio came to pay him a visit. The lady shouted down that Zeppa was not at home, and so Spinelloccio at once went upstairs, and finding the lady there in the main room and seeing that there was no one else around, he took her in his arms and began to kiss her, and she him. Zeppa, who saw all this, did not make a sound but remained hidden, waiting to see where this game of theirs would end; then shortly afterward, he saw his wife and Spinelloccio, arm in arm, going into the bedroom, and they locked themselves inside—a sight which made Spinelloccio very angry. But realizing that making a fuss over this would in no way lessen the damage done him, but would, on the contrary, only add to his shame, Zeppa began to think of the kind of revenge he could take for the injury done him that would not make the affair public knowledge and that would give him peace of mind; after giving the matter much thought, he believed he had discovered the way to do it, and he remained there in hiding as long as Spinelloccio stayed with his wife.

Then, when Spinelloccio had left, he went into the bedroom and found his wife still adjusting the veils on her head, which had fallen off while Spinelloccio was making love to her, and he said: "Madam, what are you doing?"

To which the lady replied: "Can't you see?"

Zeppa said: "I certainly can, and I've seen some other things as well, that I wish I hadn't seen!" and then he began to argue with her over the things she had done; after finding a number of excuses, finally, in great fear, she confessed to him what she could not easily deny about her affair with Spinelloccio, and weeping, she begged Zeppa's forgiveness.

To this, Zeppa said:

"Now listen to me, woman, you have done wrong, and if you want me to forgive you, you will have to do exactly what I tell you to do, which is this: I want you to tell Spinelloccio that tomorrow morning around the hour of tierce, he is to find some excuse to leave me and to come here to be with you; once he is here, I will return home, and when you hear me coming in, you are to make him climb inside this chest and then you lock him inside; after you have done this, I will tell you what else you must do; and don't be afraid to do this, for I promise you I won't hurt him in the least." In order to satisfy him, the lady said she would do it, and she delivered the message.

The next day, while Zeppa and Spinelloccio were together around the hour of tierce, Spinelloccio, who had promised the lady he would visit her at that hour, said to Zeppa:

"This morning, I must eat with a friend of mine, and I don't want to keep him waiting, so goodbye."

Zeppa said: "But it's not time to eat yet."

Spinelloccio replied: "That doesn't matter; I also have to talk to him about a business deal of mine, so I really have to get there early."

So Spinelloccio left Zeppa, circled around, and headed for the house of his friend's wife; and it was not long after he entered her bedroom that Zeppa came home again; when his wife heard him, she pretended to be very frightened and made him hide inside the chest which her husband had pointed out, and locking him inside it, she left the bedroom.

When Zeppa reached the top of the stairs, he said: "Lady, is it time to eat?"

His wife answered: "Yes, it is."

Then Zeppa said:

"Spinelloccio went to eat with a friend of his this morning, and he left his wife all alone; go to the window and call her, and tell her to come over to eat with us."

Zeppa's wife, who still feared for herself and had thus become very obedient, did what her husband told her to do. After much insistence from Zeppa's wife, Spinelloccio's wife, when she heard that her husband was not going to be eating at home, decided to go over and join them; and when she came in, Zeppa made a great fuss over her, and taking her tenderly by the hand, after quietly ordering his wife to go into the kitchen, he led the woman into the bedroom, where once inside, he turned around and locked the door. When the lady saw him locking the bedroom from the inside, she said:

"Oh my, Zeppa, what is the meaning of this? Is this what you had in mind when you invited me over? Now what about the love you bear for Spinelloccio and your loyal friendship for him?"

Moving closer to the chest in which her husband had been locked, holding her tightly, Zeppa said:

"Lady, before you start complaining about this, listen to what I am going to tell you. I loved Spinelloccio, and I still do, as if he were my own brother; but yesterday, unknown to him, I discovered that the trust which I had placed in him had come to this: that he sleeps with my wife just as he does with you. Now, because I do love him, I do not intend to take any more revenge upon him than his offense requires: he has possessed my wife, and I intend to have you. And if you are not willing, you can be certain that one day I shall catch him in the act, and since I do not intend to allow this outrage to go unpunished, I shall punish him in such a way that neither you nor he will ever be happy again."

When the lady heard this, after asking him a number of questions, which Zeppa answered, she was persuaded to believe him, and said:

"My dear Zeppa, since I am the one upon whose shoulders this revenge of yours must fall, so be it, but only on condition that your wife will remain on good terms with me in spite of what we are about to do, just as I intend to do with her in spite of what she has done to me."

To this request, Zeppa replied: "I shall certainly see to it, and

I shall also give you as precious and as beautiful a jewel as any other that you have ever owned." After he had said this, embracing her, he began to kiss her, and then he laid her upon the chest inside of which her husband was locked, and there, to his heart's content, he enjoyed himself with her and she with him.

Spinelloccio, who was inside the chest, heard everything Zeppa said as well as his wife's reply, and to top it off he also heard the jitterbugging* going on over his head: for the longest time he was filled with such great anguish that he thought he would die; and if it had not been for the fact that he was afraid of Zeppa, he would have called his wife every name under the sun, in spite of the fact that he was locked in the chest. But then, considering it was he who had initiated the outrage, Spinelloccio thought that Zeppa was right to do what he was doing, and that Zeppa had comported himself humanely and like a true friend, and so he decided to himself that if Zeppa was willing, he would become even more of a friend to him now than he ever was before.

After taking his fill of the lady, Zeppa got off the chest, and when the lady asked him for the jewel he had promised her, opening the bedroom door, he had his wife come inside, whose only words were: "Madam, you have given me tit for tat," and as she said this, she laughed.

Then Zeppa said: "Open this chest," and his wife did so; and inside the chest, Zeppa showed the lady her Spinelloccio.

It would take quite a while to decide which of the two was the more embarrassed: Spinelloccio, who was looking up at Zeppa and who realized that Zeppa knew what he had done, or Spinelloccio's wife, who saw her husband down there and realized he had heard and felt what she had been doing to him right over his head.

Zeppa said to Spinelloccio's wife: "Here's the jewel I shall give you."

Spinelloccio, having climbed out of the chest, without wasting words, said:

"Zeppa, we're even now, and it's good, as you said a moment ago to my wife, that we remain friends just as we have always been, and since we have always shared everything in common except our wives, let us now share them as well."

Zeppa was happy to go along with this, and all four of them dined together in the most amicable fashion imaginable, and

---

*The original reads *danza trivigiana*, a dance from Treviso apparently on the lewd side.

from that day on, each of those ladies had two husbands and each man had two wives, with nary an argument or squabble ever arising between them about the arrangement.

[Eighth Day, Ninth Story]

❦

Master Simone, the doctor, in order to become a member of a supposed club of expeditioners, is persuaded by Bruno and Buffalmacco to go one night to a certain spot, where he is thrown by Buffalmacco into a ditch full of filth and left there.

AFTER the ladies had chatted awhile about the wife-swapping the two men from Siena had agreed to, the Queen, the only one left to speak, so as not to infringe upon Dioneo's privilege, began:

Loving ladies, Spinelloccio was most deserving of the trick Zeppa played upon him; and therefore, it is my belief, as Pampinea tried to show a little while ago, that the man who plays a trick on someone who is asking for it or who truly deserves it should not be judged too harshly. Spinelloccio deserved his trick, and now I intend to tell you about a man who was just asking for his, and I feel that those who played the trick on him are to be praised more than blamed. The man upon whom the trick was played was a doctor who had come to Florence from Bologna, and like the ass that he was, he returned to Florence all covered with vair.*

We have occasion to see every day how our fellow citizens return to us from Bologna, some as judges, some as doctors, and others as notaries, all decked out in long, flowing robes of scarlet and vair and a good deal of other pompous paraphernalia, and every day we see the results of all this.

Among such men was a Master Simone da Villa, richer in family inheritances than in learning who not long ago returned to Florence, dressed in scarlet robes and wearing a doctor's hood—a doctor of medicine, according to what he called himself—and he took a house in a street which we today call Watermelon Row. Now this Master Simone, newly returned to town, as was just

---

*It was customary in Boccaccio's time for university graduates, such as the judge in VIII, 5, or Master Simone here, to deck their robes with vair (squirrel fur).

mentioned, would always, among his numerous notable habits, ask whomever he happened to be with at the time all about anyone he happened to see passing on the street; as if what a man did were to determine the ingredients for the medicines he prescribed his patients, he would observe these people and collect all the information he could about them.

And among the people who most aroused his interest were two painters, about whom we have already talked here today on two occasions, Bruno and Buffalmacco, who were his neighbors and who were always together. And since these two men appeared to Master Simone to be the most carefree people in the world and living the gayest of lives, which, in fact, they did, he made a number of inquiries as to how they made their living; but when he had heard everyone say that these two men were painters and that they were poor, he took it into his head that it was impossible to be so poor and lead so happy a life, and he decided, since he had heard they were clever men, that they must be making enormous profits from some unknown source; and because of this, he became anxious to make friends with them—if not both of them, at least one of them—and he managed to strike up a friendship with Bruno. And as soon as Bruno realized from the few times he had been around this doctor that he was an ass, he began to take the greatest delight in the world from his stupidity, and the doctor, too, began to take the most wondrous delight in Bruno's company. Having invited Bruno to eat with him several times, the doctor felt because of this that he could speak with him on a familiar basis, and so he explained his astonishment over how he and Buffalmacco, who were poor, managed to live so merrily, and he begged Bruno to show him how they did it.

Bruno took the doctor's request to be just another one of his usual inane, ridiculous questions, and he began to laugh, and deciding that a stupid question deserved a stupid answer, he replied:

"Master, I wouldn't tell many people how we do it, but since you are my friend, and I know you won't tell anyone else about it, I'll share the secret with you. It's true: my friend and I do live as merrily and as well as it appears—and even more so in fact; but if we had to live from our painting or from the income from what we own, we wouldn't have enough money to pay our water bill. I wouldn't want you to think, however, that we go around stealing—what we do is simply go about on expeditions, and without harming a soul, we get from this everything we need and all that makes us happy, and from this profession comes our merry way of life which you have observed."

When the doctor heard this, though he did not understand what it meant, he believed it and was greatly amazed, and he instantly felt a burning desire to know what going on expeditions entailed, swearing that he would certainly never tell anyone else what it meant.

"Good grief!" said Bruno. "Master, what are you asking of me? What you wish to know is such a dark secret that if anyone else found out about it, I could be ruined, driven from the face of the earth, even cast into the jaws of San Gallo's Lucifer;* but the love which I bear for your exquisite ineptitude and the faith I have in you is so intense that I cannot deny you anything you wish; and so I shall tell you on this one condition: that you will swear to me by the cross at Montesone that you will never, as you promised, tell anyone about this."

The doctor swore he would never tell.

"Let me tell you, then, dull-sit† doctor," continued Bruno, "that not long ago in this city, there lived a renowned expert in necromancy whose name was Michael Scott‡ (since he was from Scotland), and he was treated with the greatest of honor by many noblemen, few of whom are alive today; and when it came time for him to leave Florence, at their insistence, he left them two of his most able disciples, whom he ordered to be at all times ready to fulfill every wish of these so noble gentlemen who had paid him so great an honor. So these two men assisted the aforementioned gentlemen in particular love affairs and other trifling matters; then, as they grew to like the city and the ways of its people, they decided to remain here permanently, and they formed a good number of very close friendships with various people, without regard to whether they were noblemen or commoners, rich or poor—provided only that the interests of these men conformed to their own. And in order to please these friends of theirs, they organized a club of approximately twenty-five men, who at least twice a month were to meet together at some

---

*At San Gallo (already mentioned earlier in IV, 7), there was an enormous painting of the Devil, with several mouths, on the building's façade.

†The original Italian (*dolciato*) is actually an insult; while appearing to mean sweet ("dulcet"), it actually means "without salt" or "insipid," hence "stupid."

‡A famous thinker and astrologer of the thirteenth century, placed by Dante in Hell (*Inferno* XX, 116) for his prowess in magic.

place of their choosing; and when they are gathered there, each member makes a wish and the two magicians quickly fulfill their wishes that very evening. Since Buffalmacco and I were on especially good terms with these two men, they allowed us into the club, and we still belong to it. And let me tell you, whenever we happen to meet together, it is always a marvelous experience to behold the tapestries covering the walls of the banquet hall where we eat, the tables set in a regal manner, the number of fine and handsome servants, both male and female, all at the beck and call of every member of the club, and the bowls, jugs, flasks, goblets, and the other vessels of gold and silver from which we eat and drink! And besides all this, there is a variety of different kinds of foods, prepared to suit the taste of each member and served one after the other. I could never describe to you the range and diversity of sweet sounds coming from countless musical instruments and the melodious songs we hear there, nor could I tell you how much wax is consumed by the candles used at these banquets, nor the quantity of confections eaten, nor the number of fine wines drunk there. Nor would I have you believe, my wise-less drear one,* that we go there dressed in the clothes you see us in now; even the poorest one there looks like an emperor, for we all wear expensive robes and other beautiful things. But above all the other pleasures offered us, there is that of the beautiful women who are immediately brought to us from all parts of the world whenever we want them. Why you're liable to see there the Lady of the Barbarnicals, the Queen of the Basks, the wife of the Sultan, the Empress Orabitch, the Changeacrap of Noway, the Samaway Asa Before, and the Scalpuka of Nausea. But why list them all? Why every queen in the world is there, I mean right down to Quick John's skinkymurralady!† Now there's a sight for you! And once they have eaten some sweets and had a drink, these ladies perform a dance or two, and then each of them retires to the bedroom of the man who had her brought to him. And let me tell you that these bedrooms are so beautiful that it's like being in Paradise, and they are as fragrant as the spice jars in your shop when you're pounding your cumin; these rooms have beds in them that are

*Like the earlier *dolciato*, this phrase, *zucca mia da sale* in the original, is a complimentary-sounding insult. See previous note.

†Another list of fantastic names, similar in tone and comic effect to those listed by Brother Cipolla (VI, 10) or Maso del Saggio (VIII, 3). Prester John, a legendary Christian ruler in a nation supposedly located in the region occupied today by the Sudan and Ethiopia, was called in Florence Presto Giovanni ("Quick John").

more beautiful than the bed belonging to the Doge of Venice, and on such beds they sleep. And just how these lady weavers work their treadles and pull your loom reeds for you nice and tight right up to themselves to produce a fine, close fabric I leave to your own imagination! But among the luckiest, in my opinion, are Buffalmacco and myself, for on most occasions Buffalmacco has the Queen of France brought to him, while I send for the Queen of England for myself, and they are two of the most beautiful women in the world; and we know how to handle them so well that they don't have eyes for anyone else but us. And so you can see for yourself how and why we live better and are happier than other men, for we enjoy the love of two such queens—not to mention the fact that when we have need of one or two thousand florins, there's never a time they won't give them to us. And this is what we call going on an expedition: like pirates on an expedition, we steal the property of other men; but we are a bit different from them, for while they never give back what they take, we do give it back, after we have used it. So, now, my simply fine master, you know what we call going on an expedition is all about, and you can see for yourself how secret this must remain; so there's no need for me to tell you or even ask you to keep it a secret."

The doctor, whose knowledge probably did not extend any further than the treatment of milk rashes in suckling children, took Bruno's remarks to be the gospel truth, and he burned with such desire to join this club as if it were the highest goal toward which a man might aspire. Because of this, he told Bruno that he was certainly no longer astonished that they always went about so happy, and it was all he could do to restrain himself from asking to be made a member of the club right then and there, rather than waiting until after he had done more nice things for Bruno, so that he could make his request with greater confidence of success. And having thus restrained himself, he began cultivating Bruno's friendship more and more by having him over to eat with him in the evening or in the morning, and by displaying a limitless amount of affection toward him; and they spent so much of their time in each other's company that it began to appear that the doctor could no longer live, nor would he have wanted to, without Bruno.

Since Bruno felt he was well off, in order not to seem ungrateful for all the hospitality the doctor showed him, he painted a Lenten mural in his dining room, a Lamb of God over the entrance to his bedroom, and a urinal* over the front door to the shop, so that people who needed his help could tell his house from the others; and in one of his loggias, he painted for him the battle between the mice and the cats, which according to the doctor, was too beautiful for words; besides this, Bruno would sometimes say to the doctor, on those occasions when he had not eaten supper with him: "Last night, I was at the club, and I got a little bored with the Queen of England, so I had the Adumba of the Genghis Khan of Alterego brought to me."

The doctor said:

"What does 'Adumba' mean? I don't understand these names."

"Oh well, my good master," said Bruno, "I am not at all surprised, for I have been told that Hypotomus and Aviseenyou have nothing to say about them."

"You mean Hippocrates and Avicenna,"† replied the doctor.

Bruno said:

"Cripes sake, I don't know: I know as little about your names as you do about mine; but 'Adumba' in the language of the Genghis Khan means the same as 'Empress' in your own language. Oh, she was really a gorgeous wench! I'll tell you this: she sure would make you forget your medicines, your enemas, and all your poultices."

Telling him these things from time to time, Bruno kept the doctor's interest burning until it happened that one evening while he was up late holding the light for Bruno, who was painting the battle of the mice and the cats, the Master Doctor felt that Bruno was sufficiently in his debt by now, because of all he had done for him, that he was ready to bring his feelings out in the open, and since they were alone, the doctor said to him:

"Bruno, God knows there's not another living soul for whom I would do all the things I would do for you; even if you asked me to go from here to Peretola,‡ I believe I would do it; and so I don't want you to be surprised if I ask something of you as a friend and in the strictest of confidence. As you know, not long ago you talked to me about the activities of your merry club, and since then, I've wanted so very much to become one of your

---

*Since the analysis of urine was a major tool in making a diagnosis in Boccaccio's day, the image of a container for the specimen would alert any passerby to the fact that this was the home of a doctor.

†Two physicians of classical antiquity often cited as models of proper medical procedure in Boccaccio's day.

‡Peretola is only a few miles from Florence.

group that I never wanted anything more in all my life. And this is not without good reason, as you will see for yourself if I happen to be admitted to your club, for if I don't have summoned up for me the most beautiful wench you've ever seen, you can call me an idiot; I spotted her a while back, last year in Cacavincigli, and since then I have been madly in love with her; by Christ's body, I was willing to give her ten fat Bolognese silver coins if she would agree to make me happy, but she refused. And so, I beg you, as best I know how, to tell me what I have to do to become a member, and also to do what you can and use your influence to get me in, and you will have truly made yourself a good, loyal, and honorable friend. First of all, you can see how handsome a man I am, what a fine pair of legs I have, and that my face is as fresh as a rose; besides this, I am a doctor of medicine, and I doubt that you have any of them as members, and I know lots of interesting stories and a number of fine little songs—in fact, let me sing one for you right now," and all of a sudden he was singing.

Bruno had such an urge to laugh he could hardly contain himself, yet he managed to do so, and when the song was over, the doctor said: "What do you think?"

Bruno replied: "Fantastic! The cacophonous archisticness of your voice would put the best reed whistle to shame."*

The doctor said: "Didn't I tell you that you'd never believe your ears if you didn't hear it for yourself?"

"You were certainly telling the truth," remarked Bruno.

The doctor said:

"I also know a good many more, but that's enough for now. Just as you see me here before you, my father was a nobleman, though he lived in the country, and my mother's people come from Vallecchio; and, as you have been able to observe, I possess the loveliest books and the most elegant wardrobe of any doctor in Florence. By God's faith, I have a robe which, including everything, cost nearly one hundred lire in small change, and that was more than ten years ago! And so I beg you with all my might to make me a member of your club, and by God's faith, if you do so, you can get as sick as you like, and I'll never take a lira from you for my services."

When Bruno heard what he said, he was now convinced of

---

*Here, as elsewhere in this story, the compliments paid to the Bolognese doctor are actually insults. The Italian reads *sì artagoticamente stracantate*, which sounds quite complimentary indeed, but only to the foolish doctor.

what he had thought earlier: the doctor was a dope! And he said:

"Master, give me a little more light up here and wait until I finish painting the tails on these mice, then I'll answer you."

After he finished the tails, pretending that the doctor's request was troubling him, Bruno said:

"Master, there is no limit to what you would do for me, and I realize this. Nevertheless, what you are asking of me, while it may seem small to a man of your great intellect, is still, as far as I am concerned, a very large request, and I don't know of another person in the world for whom I would do it, if I could, than you, both because I love you as much as you deserve, and also because your remarks are seasoned with so much wisdom that they could shock any old pious woman right out of her boots, not to mention make me change my mind; and the more time I spend with you, the wiser you seem to me. And let me also say this, that even if I had no other reason to love you, I would do so because I see you are in love with a woman as beautiful as the one you have described. But I must tell you this: I am not as influential in such matters as you may think I am, so I cannot do what is necessary on your behalf; but if you promise me upon your sacred and tainted word to keep this a secret, I shall give you the means of undertaking this task yourself, and since you own so many fine books and all those other things you told me about earlier, I feel certain you will succeed."

To this the doctor replied:

"Feel free to speak; I can see that you don't know me well enough to know how well I can keep a secret. There were very few things which Messer Gausparuolo da Saliceto did, when he was the *podestà*'s judge at Forlimpopoli, about which he did not confide in me, for he knew I was a man who could keep a secret. Do you want proof of this? Well, I was the first man he told that he was going to marry Bergamina. Can you imagine that?"

"Well, that's good enough for me, then," said Bruno, "if a man like that trusted you, I, too, can certainly trust you. What you have to do is this. We always have a captain with two counselors in this club of ours, who are changed every six months, and from the first of next month, there is no doubt that Buffalmacco will be the captain and I his counselor, and that's for sure; and whoever the captain is, he can do a great deal in getting anyone he wants into the club; so it seems to me that you should do everything in your power to make friends with Buffalmacco and to give him the royal treatment. He is a man who, as soon as he sees how wise you are, will fall in love with you immediately, and once you have cultivated his friendship a bit more, employing all that wisdom of yours as well as all the fine possessions that you own, you can ask him, and he won't know how to say no to you. I have already spoken with him about you, and he's as fond of you as he can be, and when you've done all this, leave the rest to me and him."

Then the doctor said:

"What you advise pleases me to no end, and if Buffalmacco is a man who delights in wise men, then let him converse with me awhile, and I'll have him constantly seeking out my company, for so well endowed with wisdom am I that I could supply an entire city with it and still remain the wisest of all."

Having arranged this, Bruno explained everything in detail to Buffalmacco, and to Buffalmacco it seemed like a thousand years before he could give this Master Sap what he was looking for. The doctor, who wanted above all else to go on an expedition, did not rest until he became Buffalmacco's friend, which he easily succeeded in doing; and he began to treat Buffalmacco to the most sumptuous suppers and meals in the world, inviting Bruno along with him as well, and scratching their bellies with joy, they stuck close to him like those lords who can smell out the finest vintage wines, the fattest capons, and many other delicious things, and now even without the coaxing of too many invitations, and constantly making it a point to remind him that they would not do as much for anyone else, they never left his side.

Then finally, when the doctor thought the time seemed ripe, he made the same request to Buffalmacco he had made earlier to Bruno; Buffalmacco pretended to be extremely angry over this, and he screamed at Bruno, saying:

"I swear by the tall God of Pasignano* that it is all I can do to keep from punching your head in and knocking your nose to your heels, you traitor, for nobody else but you could have revealed these things to the doctor."

But the doctor bravely defended Bruno, declaring and swearing he had learned about them from another source, and with a great many of his words of wisdom, the doctor managed finally to pacify Buffalmacco.

Turning to the doctor, Buffalmacco said:

"My dear doctor, it is quite clear you have been to Bologna and have brought back with you to this city a pair of well-sealed

---

*High above the entrance of the church at Pasignano there was apparently a painting of God the Father, to which this comic oath refers.

lips; and let me tell you more. You are not the type who learned his ABCs by writing them on an apple, as many dunces did, no sir, you learned them perfectly by writing them on a melon, which, you see, is much longer;* and if I'm not mistaken, you were baptized on a Sunday. Even though Bruno told me that you studied medicine in Bologna, I am convinced that you studied how to captivate men's minds, because using your wisdom and eloquence, you do this better than any other man I've ever met."

The doctor, interrupting him in midsentence as he turned toward Bruno, declared:

"Do you see what it means to converse with intelligent men and to keep their company? Who else could have immediately understood every aspect of my feelings as this worthy man has just done? You did not perceive my worth quite as quickly as he did; but now tell him at least what I told you when you explained to me that Buffalmacco admired intelligent men. Do you not think I lived up to it?"

"Better than I expected," Bruno said.

Then the doctor said to Buffalmacco:

"If you had seen me in Bologna, you would have even more to say, for there was no man—important or unimportant, professor or student—who didn't think the world of me, so admirable did they find my wisdom and my wits. And let me tell you more: I never uttered a word there which did not make everyone laugh, so much did I please them; and when I had to leave, they made the biggest fuss about it and wanted me to stay—they even campaigned to keep me there, and they went so far as to offer to let me alone do all the lecturing to the students studying medicine; but I refused, for I had already decided to return to an enormous estate I have here which has always been in my family; and that is what I did."

Then Bruno said to Buffalmacco:

"What do you think? You didn't believe me when I told you. By the Holy Gospel! There's not a doctor in this country who understands donkey urine better than he does, and you surely won't find another man like him between here and the gates of Paris. Now how can you refuse to do what he wants?"

The doctor said:

"Bruno is telling the truth, but I am not really appreciated

---

*It appears that teachers and parents used to encourage children to learn the alphabet by carving letters on apples, rewarding the child with the fruit. Melons, in Boccaccio's language, usually connote stupidity and foolishness.

here in Florence. On the whole you people are all more or less ignorant, but if you could only see me among my own kind, among learned men!"

Then Buffalmacco replied:

"Doctor, you know far more than I would ever have imagined: therefore, speaking to you as one should speak to men as learned as yourself, let me tell you that underexaggeratedly I shall see to it that you are admitted, without fail, to our club."

The amount of hospitality lavished by the doctor on the two men after receiving this promise now multiplied: they had the greatest time making him believe the greatest absurdities in the world, promising to give him as his mistress the Countess of Latrine,* who was the most beautiful thing to be found in the entire ass-sembly of the human race.

The doctor asked who this countess was; to his question, Buffalmacco replied:

"Bless my seminal cucumber, why she is a very great lady, for there are few homes in the world in which she does not have some jurisdiction, and even the Franciscans, not to mention the others she receives, render their tributes to her to the sound of kettledrums. And let me tell you this, that whenever she is in the vicinity, she makes her presence smelled, even though she usually stays aloof; but it was not long ago that she passed by your door one night on her way to the Arno to wash her feet and to take a breath of fresh air; but her usual residence is in the town of Latrina. You see her retainers around here quite often, and as a sign of her authority, they carry a pole and a drain cleaner. Her barons are everywhere to be found; there is Baron Turdgate, Don Dung, Count Handel of the Bristlebrush, Sir Dia Rrhoea, and others, all of whom I believe you know but do not recall at this moment. Such, then, is the grand lady into whose sweet arms we shall place you, if our plan succeeds, and then you can forget all about that girl from Cacavincigli."

The doctor, who had been born and bred in Bologna, did not

---

*The reference to the Countess Latrine (literally "the Countess of Civillari," a reference to a spot in Florence near the Monastery of San Jacopo a Ripoli, which was customarily used as an open toilet) begins a series of comic and scatological or obscene references, all of which are informed by the location of this beautiful nobelady: the *ass*sembly of the human race (*culattario*); the bodily function similar to drums, the foul smells, the town of Latrina (Laterino in the Italian), the poles and drain cleaners, and her noble court consisting of ridiculous noblemen. The promise to place the doctor into this nobelady's embraces is an ironic warning of what is to come, even though the doctor is incapable of understanding it.

understand the meaning of their words, and so he told them he was satisfied with the lady; nor did he have long to wait after all this before the two painters brought him the news that he had been accepted into the club. And on the day before the evening the club was to assemble, the doctor invited both men to dinner; and after they had eaten, the doctor asked them how he was supposed to get to the club; and Buffalmacco, answering this question, said:

"Now look, doctor, you have to be very courageous, for if you aren't, you might meet with some obstacle and cause us a great deal of harm. Now let me tell you the reason why you must be very brave: this evening around the time one normally goes to bed, you must find a way to climb up onto one of those raised tombs, the ones just recently constructed outside Santa Maria Novello, wearing one of your most handsome robes, so that not only will you make a noble impression when you appear before the club for the first time but also because, you being nobly bred, the Countess (from what we have been able to gather, not being present at the time) intends to make you a Knight of the Bath at her own expense; and you are to wait for us there on the tomb until the man we send comes for you. So that you may be informed about everything that will take place, I warn you now that you will be met by a black horned creature, not very large, which will leap about the piazza in front of you making a loud hissing noise in order to frighten you; but when it sees you are not afraid, it will quietly approach you. And when it is close enough to you, without displaying any fear, you climb down from the tomb and, without invoking God or the saints, you get on it, and when you are mounted firmly on its back, fold your arms across your chest in courtly fashion and never touch the beast again. Then the beast will slowly move off and bring you to us; but until the moment that it does, if you call upon God or the saints, or if you show fear, let me warn you that the beast could throw you off or get you into a real stinker of a mess. And so, if your courage isn't up to it, don't come, for you would only be doing us a bad turn and yourself no good."

Then the doctor said:

"You don't know me yet. Perhaps the fact that I wear gloves and long robes worries you. But if you only knew the things I used to do with my friends at night in Bologna, when we were out for women, you would be amazed. By God's faith, there was that one night when one of them refused to come with us (she was a skinny little wench, and what's worse, she was no taller than the palm of your hand), but after I gave her a few punches and picked her up off the ground, I think I must have carried her a stone's throw before convincing her to come with us. And then there's the time I was walking alone except for a servant of mine, shortly after the *Angelus* prayer, and I passed right by the cemetery of the Franciscans, and in spite of the fact a woman had been buried there that very day, I wasn't at all afraid; so do not doubt my courage, for I have courage and strength to spare. And as concerns being nobly dressed for the occasion, let me tell you that I shall wear the scarlet robe in which I received my doctorate, and you will soon seen how the club will rejoice to see me and whether I am elected captain before long. You just wait and see how things go when I get there, for even the Countess, who has not laid eyes on me, has already fallen so much in love with me that she wants to make me a Knight of the Bath. But perhaps you think knighthood will suit me badly, or that I won't know how to handle it well or badly! You just leave everything to me!"

Buffalmacco said:

"Very well put, but be careful you don't play a trick on us and not come, or that you aren't to be found when we send for you; I say this because it is cold, and you men of medicine are sensitive to cold weather."

"God forbid!" exclaimed the doctor. "I'm not sensitive to the cold, and I don't pay any attention to it; whenever I get up during the night to relieve my bodily needs, as men sometimes do, I never put a thing on except for a fur coat over my doublet; so, I'll be there for sure!"

The two men left, and when nighttime came, the doctor made up some excuse for leaving his wife at home, and after secretly getting his handsome robe out of the house, when he thought the moment had come, he put it on and climbed up onto one of those tombs; and sitting there huddled on the marble, for it was bitter cold, he began to wait for the beast. Buffalmacco, who was tall and husky, managed to get one of those masks which were worn during certain celebrations no longer held today, and putting on a black fur coat inside out, he disguised himself to look like a bear, except for his mask, which had a devil's face and sported horns. Disguised this way, Buffalmacco went to the new square of Santa Maria Novella with Bruno following close behind him to see what would happen; as soon as he saw that the learned doctor was there, he began to leap up and down, hissing, yelling, and screaming like a man who was possessed.

When the doctor saw and heard all this, every hair on his body stood on end, and he began to tremble all over, worse than a frightened woman; and for an instant, he wished he were in his own home rather than where he was. But since he had come, he managed to control his fear, for his desire to see the marvels Bruno and Buffalmacco had told him about overcame his fright. After Buffalmacco had performed his devilish feats for a while in the manner just described, pretending now to calm down, he drew closer to the tomb upon which the doctor was huddled and stood still. The doctor, trembling with fear, could not make up his mind to get on or to stay right where he was. Finally, afraid that the beast would hurt him if he did not get on his back, he allowed his second fear to drive out the first: climbing down from the tomb, whispering to himself "God help me!" he got on the beast and fixed himself firmly on its back; still trembling, he crossed his arms over his chest, just as he had been told to do.

Then Buffalmacco slowly began to move off toward Santa Maria della Scala, and he crawled on all fours, carrying the doctor nearly all the way to the convent at Ripoli. In those days, there were ditches in those parts into which the farmers poured their offerings to the Countess of Latrine in order to enrich their fields. When Buffalmacco neared this spot, he drew close to the edge of one of these ditches, and choosing the right moment, he put his hand under one of the doctor's feet and pushing up, he threw him clear off his back and headfirst into the ditch, and then he began to snarl ferociously and leap and rage all over the place, and then to take off alongside Santa Maria della Scala in the direction of the meadow of Ogni Santi, where he came upon Bruno, who had dashed off because he was unable to keep from laughing. Both of them danced with joy when they saw each other, and then they set about observing from a distance what the besmirched doctor might do. His lordship the doctor, finding himself in such an abominable place, made every effort to stand up and attempt to climb out, and falling now here and now there, totally besmirched from head to toe, sorrowful and wretched, having choked down several drams of the filthy liquid and lost his doctoral hoods, he finally managed to get out of there. Cleaning himself off with his hands as best he could, and not knowing what else to do, he made his way back home and kept knocking at the door until he was let in.

No sooner had he entered the house, stinking all over, and the door shut behind him, than Bruno and Buffalmacco were there at the door listening to hear what kind of welcome his wife would give him. As they stood there listening, they heard his wife giving him the worst tongue-lashing any poor wretch could possibly receive, as she said:

"Well, it serves you right! So you went running after some other woman and you wanted to look your best in your scarlet robe? Now, aren't I enough for you? Brother, there's enough of me to satisfy a whole parish, not to mention you. Well, I wish they'd drowned you instead of tossing you where you deserved to be tossed! Here's a fine doctor for you, wife and all, and he goes around at night chasing other men's wives!"

And with these and many more words, while the doctor went on washing himself all over, the lady did not cease tormenting him until midnight.

Then, the next morning, after painting bruises all over their bodies under their clothes, as if they had gotten them from a beating, they went to the doctor's house, where they found him already up and around; as they went inside to greet him, they could smell the stink, for it had been impossible to get the stench out of everything so soon. When the doctor heard them coming, he went to greet them, bidding them good day; as Bruno and Buffalmacco had agreed to do earlier, they replied with angry expressions:

"We can't say the same to you; on the contrary, we pray to God that He grants you so many bad days that you end up put to the sword—you're the worst, the most disloyal traitor that ever lived, and it's no thanks to you that we, who tried to honor you and entertain you, were not killed like dogs. Because of your treachery, last night we got beaten up and punched so many times that you could have driven an ass to Rome with fewer blows—not to mention the fact that we were in danger of being thrown out of the very club into which we had arranged for you to be admitted. And if you don't believe us, just look at the state our bodies are in." They opened the front of their shirts in the dim light, showed the doctor their chests all painted up, and then instantly closed them up again.

The doctor attempted to excuse himself, explaining his own misfortunes, and how and where he had been thrown off, but to this Buffalmacco said:

"I wish he had been thrown off the bridge right into the Arno! Why did you call upon God or the saints? Didn't we tell you beforehand that you were not to?"

The doctor protested: "In God's faith, I didn't do it."

"What?" asked Buffalmacco. "You didn't call on them? You don't have a very good memory, do you? For our informant told us you were shaking like a leaf and that you didn't even know where you were. You've really fixed us up good this time, but we'll never let anyone do it to us again, and we shall see to it that from now on you get what you deserve from us."

The doctor begged them to forgive him, and he tried with all the persuasive eloquence he had at his command to make peace with them, begging them in the name of God not to disgrace him; and out of fear that they would make this disgrace of his public knowledge, from that time on he entertained them and pampered them with banquets and other things. And so, now you know how wisdom is learned by those who have not acquired much of it in Bologna.

[Eighth Day, Tenth Story]

A Sicilian woman masterfully relieves a merchant of all the goods he has brought to Palermo; pretending to have returned to Palermo with even more goods than he had the first time, he borrows money from her and leaves her with nothing but water and hemp.

THERE is no need to ask how certain parts of the Queen's story made the ladies laugh: there was not one among them who did not have tears in her eyes at least a dozen times from too much laughter. But as soon as she finished, Dioneo, who knew it was his turn now, said:

Gracious ladies, it is clear that the more cunning a person is, the more delight we take in seeing that cunning trickster artfully tricked. And while all the stories you have told were very good, I intend to tell you one which should please you more than any of the others, for the woman who was tricked at the end was a far greater artist in tricking others than any of the other men or women you have spoken about.

In all the coastal cities which have a suitable seaport, it was common practice, and perhaps still is today, for any merchant arriving there with cargo to unload it and then transport it to a warehouse, which in many places is called a customshouse and is under the control of the commune or the ruler of the place, and there, after those in charge have been supplied with a written list of all the merchandise and its value, they provide the merchant with a storehouse in which his goods are placed under lock and key; and then the customs officers record in their account book all the goods belonging to the merchant, and later on, as he withdraws his goods, all or in part, he is made to pay the required duties. And it is from this customshouse account book that the brokers quite often learn about the quantity of the merchandise stored there, as well as the identity of the merchants who own it; later, when the opportunity presents itself, these brokers discuss exchanges, barters, sales, and other transactions with the merchants.

Among the many places where this practice existed was Palermo in Sicily, which was also known, and still is today, for its numerous women who are beautiful in body but enemies of virtue, who, to anyone unfamiliar with their ways, would appear to be, and are reputed to be, grand and respectable ladies. And since these women are completely dedicated not just to shaving men but rather to skinning them alive, whenever they spot a foreign merchant, they manage to inform themselves from the account book in the customshouse just what the merchant has in deposit and how much he is worth. And in their charming, amorous ways, and with the sweetest words, they do their best to beguile these merchants and to entice them into loving them, and in so doing they have cheated many such merchants, some out of a hefty part of their merchandise, others out of the entire lot, while some others of them have even left behind not only their cargos and their ships but their very flesh and bones as well, so skillfully has the lady barber known how to wield her razor.

Now, not very long ago, one of our young Florentines named Niccolò da Cignano, better know as Salabaetto, happened to be sent to that city by his employers, with a quantity of woolen cloth left over from the fair at Salerno that was valued at five hundred gold florins; having given the invoice for these goods to the customs officials, he put them in storage, and since he was in no great hurry to sell them, he began to search for something amusing to do in town. And since he was quite handsome, fair-skinned and with blond hair, and very dashing, one of these lady barbers, who called herself Madam Jancofiore, just happened to hear tell of his affairs and began to cast an eye in his direction; and when he noticed this, he assumed that she was a fine lady who had fallen in love with his good looks and decided to conduct this love affair very carefully; without saying anything about it to anyone, he began to walk back and forth in front of her house. When Jancofiore noticed this, after several days of casting fiery glances at him, pretending to be burning with passion for him, she secretly sent him one of her women servants who was most skillful in the art of pandering. This woman, after

much talk and almost in tears, informed him he had so over-
whelmed her mistress with his good looks and his pleasing man-
ner that she was unable to rest, day or night; and so she hoped
more than anything else that he would agree to meet her secretly
at a public bath; and then, taking a ring from her purse, she
gave it to him on behalf of the lady. When he heard this, Sala-
baetto was the happiest man who ever lived; taking the ring and
touching it to his eyelids, he kissed it and placed it on his finger,
telling the good woman that if Madam Jancofiore loved him,
then she was well repaid, for he loved her more than life itself
and was willing to go anywhere with her at any time she wished.

Shortly after the go-between returned to her mistress with his
reply, Salabaetto was told at what public bath he was to await
her arrival the following day after vespers. Without a word to
anyone, Salabaetto quickly went there at the appointed hour and
found the bathing room already engaged by the lady. He was not
there long before two slave girls arrived, loaded down with
things: one balanced a beautiful large cottonwool mattress on
her head, while the other was carrying a big basket full of differ-
ent objects. After setting down the mattress on a bed in one of
the private rooms of the bath, they spread over it a pair of the
thinnest sheets edged with silk, and then a bedcover of the
whitest Cyprian buckram and two marvelously embroidered pil-
lows; having done this, they undressed, got into the bath, and
washed and scrubbed it thoroughly. Nor was it long before the
lady with two more slave girls arrived at the bath; the first
thing she did was rush to greet him effusively, and following the
deepest sighs in the world, and much hugging and kissing, she
said to him: "There is no one who could have led me to do this;
you have set my heart on fire, my darling Tuscan."

After this, at her request, they both entered the bath naked,
attended by two of the slave girls. There, without allowing any-
one else to lay a hand upon him, the lady herself, taking mar-
velous care, washed Salabaetto all over using soaps scented with
musk and cloves, and then she had herself washed and rubbed
down by the slave girls. And when this was done, the slave girls
brought two of the whitest and thinnest sheets, from which there
arose so strong an odor of roses that everything in the room
seemed made of roses; having wrapped Salabaetto in one and
draped the lady in the other, they lifted both of them up and
carried them to the bed made ready for them. And there, when
they stopped perspiring, the sheets were removed by the slave
girls, and they were left naked between the other sheets. The
most beautiful silver perfume bottles appeared from the basket,

some full of rose water, some with water from orange blossoms, others from jasmine blooms, and still others with various kinds of citron extract, and the slave girls sprinkled all these lotions over them; and later on came boxes of confections and bottles of the most precious wines with which they refreshed themselves. Sala-baetto felt as if he was in Paradise, and he must have looked at the lady a thousand times, so very beautiful was she, and every hour that passed seemed like a hundred years to him until the slave girls would leave them so that he might find himself alone in her arms. Then finally, at the lady's command, the girls with-drew, leaving a small light burning in the room, and she em-braced Salabaetto as he did her, and to the greatest delight of Salabaetto, who thought the lady was madly in love with him, they spent quite some time together there.

But then the lady decided it was time to get up; she called in the slave girls while the two of them dressed, and once again they refreshed themselves with a bit of wine and confections; after washing their hands and faces with those sweet-smelling waters, as they were about to leave, the lady said to Salabaetto: "If you are willing, you would be doing me a great favor if you would join me for supper this evening and then spend the night with me."

Salabaetto, who was by now snared by the lady's beauty and her cunning charm, firmly convinced that she loved him as much as the heart of her own body, replied:

"My lady, your very wish is my greatest pleasure, and so this evening and forever I intend to do whatever pleases you and whatever you order me to do."

So the lady returned home, and seeing to it that her finest gowns and other possessions were all on display in her bedroom and that a delicious supper was prepared, she waited for Sala-baetto; as soon as it was dark, he went to her house, where he was joyously welcomed and given a cheerful supper royally served. Then they went into her bedroom, where he could smell a marvelous aroma of Oriental wood and Cyprian incense birds, and he saw the luxurious bed and the many beautiful gowns hanging from pegs. All these things, taken together and sep-arately, make Salabaetto think that she must be a great and rich lady. And though he had heard gossip to the contrary concerning her way of living, he would not believe it for anything in the world, and even if he suspected that she might have taken ad-vantage of another man, nothing in the world could make him think it might happen to him. He lay with her that night with the greatest of delight, his love for her growing all the more passionate.

When morning came, she fastened a handsome and stylish little silver belt around his waist with a beautiful purse attached to it, and she said to him:

"My sweet Salabaetto, I beg you to remember that just as my body is yours to enjoy, so everything I possess and everything I can do is at your command."

Overjoyed, Salabaetto embraced and kissed her, and then he left her house and went to the merchants' gathering place.

As he frequently consorted with the lady, his visits costing him nothing, he became more and more involved with her, and then one day he happened to sell his cloth for cash at a handsome profit. The good woman immediately heard about this, not from him but from someone else, and one evening when Salabaetto had gone to see her, she began to joke and frolic with him, and with her kisses and embraces she pretended to be so passionately in love with him that it seemed as if she were about to die of love in his arms. She even wanted to give him two of the most precious silver goblets that she owned, but Salabaetto did not want to accept them, for on one occasion or another he had received gifts from her which were worth at least thirty gold florins, never having managed to make her take a silver coin's worth in return. Finally, after she had aroused his passion for her sufficiently by showing herself so full of excitement and generosity for him, one of the slave girls came into the room, as she had ordered her to do earlier, and called on her to come out. Having left the bedroom and been gone for quite a while, she returned in tears, and throwing herself face down upon the bed, she began the most piteous lamentation a woman ever made.

The amazed Salabaetto took her in his arms and began to weep with her, as he said:

"Ah, heart of my body, what happened to you so suddenly? What is the cause of such grief? Ah, tell me, my love!"

After allowing him to beg her for quite some time, the lady replied:

"Alas, my sweet lord, I don't know what to do or what to say! I just received some letters from Messina, and my brother writes me that unless I sell and pawn everything I own, sending him eight days from today without fail a thousand gold florins, they are going to chop off his head; and I don't know what to do, and I have no idea how to get the money in such a short time; if I had at least fifteen days, I could find ways of getting it from a source which owes me much more than that, or I would sell one of our estates; but I cannot, and I would rather have died than receive such bad news!" And having said this, pretending to be very upset, she kept on sobbing.

Salabaetto, who had already lost a good part of his wits to his amorous passion, believed her tears were most sincere and that her words were even truer, and he said:

"Madonna, I could not give you a thousand gold florins, but I can certainly spare five hundred if you think you can return them to me within fifteen days from now; you are in luck, for just yesterday, I happened to sell my cloth, and if that had not happened, I could not lend you as much as a silver coin."

"Oh my," exclaimed the lady, "you mean you were in financial straits? Why didn't you tell me? I may not have a thousand florins, but I certainly had a hundred or even two hundred to give you—now I no longer have the heart to accept the assistance you are offering me."

Taken in even deeper by these remarks of hers, Salabaetto said:

"Madonna, I would not have you refuse because of this, for if my need were as great as yours is, I would certainly have asked you."

"Ah, my Salabaetto," the lady said, "how well I see that yours is a true and perfect love for me; why, without waiting to be asked, you generously offer to give me such a large sum of money in my hour of need. And while you can be sure I was completely yours before this offer, with it I shall be even more yours than ever; nor shall I ever fail to recognize that it is to you I owe my brother's life. But God knows I am taking this money unwillingly, considering that you are a merchant and that merchants do all their transaction with cash: but since my need is pressing and I have every hope of returning the money to you soon, I shall take it, and as for the rest of what I need, if I cannot find a quick way of getting it elsewhere, I shall just have to pawn all of my belongings," and having said this, in tears, she fell into Salabaetto's arms.* Salabaetto began to comfort her; and after spending the night with her, in order to prove his most generous devotion to her, without waiting to be asked, he brought her back five hundred fine gold florins, which she, with a heart full of laughter and eyes full of tears, accepted, giving Salabaetto in return nothing but a simple promise of repayment.

As soon as the lady had the money, the terms of their rela-

---

*We translate "arms" for *viso* ("face") even though the text actually reads: *sopra il viso di Salabaetto si lasciò cadere.*

tionship began to change; whereas before, Salabaetto had been free to visit the lady anytime he wished, now all kinds of excuses began to crop up, so that he got in to see her about one time in seven, nor did he get from her the same caresses and smiles or happy welcomes he used to get before. One month and then two passed after the established time for the return of his money, and when he requested it, he was given only words in repayment. Whereupon Salabaetto recognized the cunning of the wicked woman, as well as his own lack of intelligence, and realizing that he could say whatever he liked to her but unless she was willing, he could do nothing, for he had neither a written receipt of the loan nor a witness to the transaction; and since he was ashamed to complain about it to anyone, both because he had been forewarned and also because of the well-earned ridicule awaiting him for his stupidity, sorrowful beyond all measure, he wept in silence over his folly. And after he received a number of letters from his superiors requesting that he change the money and forward it to them, fearing that his error would be discovered by remaining there and not doing what they asked, he decided to leave; so, boarding a small ship, he went not to Pisa, where he should have gone, but to Naples.

Now at that time there lived in Naples a fellow citizen of ours, Pietro dello Canigiano, a man of outstanding intellect and subtle wit, who was treasurer of Her Highness the Empress of Constantinople and a great friend of Salabaetto and his family. Since he was a most discreet gentleman, a few days after his arrival there, Salabaetto sorrowfully told him what he had done and all about his wretched misfortune, asking him for assistance and advice in finding a means of livelihood there in Naples, declaring that he intended never to return to Florence.

Distressed by what he heard, Canigiano said:

"You have acted badly, behaved badly, obeyed your employers badly, and spent too much money too quickly in easy living; but what's done is done and now we must find a remedy." And clever man as he was, he quickly saw what had to be done, and he explained it to Salabaetto, who was delighted with the plan and set out to follow it.

With the money he still had of his own and with what Canigiano lent him, he ordered a number of well-tied and well-packed bales of cargo, and having bought and filled about twenty oil casks, he had the whole thing loaded on board and returned to Palermo. Having given the invoice for the bales to the customs officials, as well as the value of the casks, and having registered everything under his own name, he had his goods stored, declaring that until the other merchandise which he was expecting had arrived, he wished to leave them there. When Jancofiore heard about this and discovered that the goods he had brought were worth at least two thousand gold florins or more, not to mention that he was expecting even more merchandise valued at more than three thousand, she felt she had aimed her sights too low and decided she would return his five hundred florins to him in order to get hold of the better part of five thousand; so she sent for him.

Having become more shrewd by now, Salabaetto went to see her; pretending to know nothing about the goods he had brought, she welcomed him enthusiastically and said: "Now look, if you are angry with me because I failed to return your money on time . . . ?"

Salabaetto began to laugh, saying:

"Madonna, to tell the truth, I was a little annoyed, considering that I was ready to pluck out my own heart and give it to you, if I thought it would please you; but I want you to hear how angry I am with you. The love I bear for you is so great and so deep that I have sold nearly all of my possessions, and now I have brought here with me a quantity of merchandise worth more than two thousand florins, and I am expecting another shipment from the West worth more than three thousand; I intend to establish a business in this city and to remain here in order to be near you, for I am happier in loving you than any other lover could possibly be."

To this, the lady said:

"You see, Salabaetto, anything profitable you do makes me very happy, for I love you more than my very life, and I am delighted that you have returned with the intention of remaining, for I am hoping that we can still have some good times together, but I do want to apologize a little for those times before you left when you wanted to visit with me but were unable to do so, and those times when you did come but were not as cheerfully received as you used to be, and also, you must forgive me for not returning your money to you at the promised time. But you must realize that I was deeply distressed and afflicted at that time, and no matter how much a person loves another, no one in such a condition can be as cheerful and attentive toward the other as she might, nonetheless, like to be. Furthermore, you must know how very difficult it is for a woman to get her hands on a thousand gold florins, for all we get day in and day out are lies and broken promises, and as a result, we, too, are forced to lie to others; it was for this reason alone, and for no other fault of my own, that I did not return your money to you. But I did get the money shortly after your departure, and had I known where to forward it to you, you can be certain I would have sent it to you, but since I didn't know, I kept it safe for you." And having sent for the purse containing the very florins Salabaetto had brought to her, she put it into his hands and said: "Count them to see if there are five hundred."

Salabaetto had never been so happy, and after counting the money and finding that there were indeed five hundred, he answered her, saying:

"Madonna, I know you are telling the truth, but you have done more than enough, and let me tell you that because of what you have done, as well as for the love I bear you, you have but to request of me any sum of money for any of your needs and if I can do so, it is yours; and as soon as I have established my business here, you may put me to the test."

Having thus renewed, at least in words, his love for her, Salabaetto began once again to enjoy her intimacy, while she pleased him and entertained him with all she had, pretending to feel for him the deepest love.

But since Salabaetto wished to punish her deception with a trick of his own, one day, having been invited to come to her home for supper and to spend the night with her, he arrived there looking distraught and sad, as though all he wanted was to die. Jancofiore kissed and embraced him and began to ask him why he was so unhappy. Having encouraged her to question him for some time, Salabaetto said:

"I am ruined, for the ship carrying the merchandise I was expecting has been seized by pirates from Monaco and they are holding it for a ransom of ten thousand gold florins, of which I must pay my share of a thousand florins, and I don't even have a florin to my name, since the five hundred you gave me I immediately sent to Naples to invest in more cloth to be shipped to me here. And if I were to sell off right now the merchandise I have here in storage, I would only get half price for it, as it is out of season; and nobody knows me well enough around here to lend me the money, and so I don't know what to do or say; but if I don't send the money soon, my goods will be taken to Monaco, and I'll never see any of them again."

The lady, who was most distressed by this news, because she thought she was going to lose all this money, began thinking of some means to prevent the merchandise from being taken to Monaco, and said:

"God knows how sorry I am for your sake, but what good is it to get upset over it? If I had the money, God knows I would lend it to you immediately, but I do not have it. It is true that there is that certain person who lent me the other five hundred florins when I needed them a while back, but he gets usurious interest rates for money—he wants no less than thirty percent; if you turn to this kind of a person, you will have to guarantee the loan with substantial security, and as for me, in order to help you, I am prepared to pawn all my belongings and myself included, for whatever sum he is willing to lend us; but how will you guarantee the rest of the loan?"

Salabaetto knew what motives prompted the woman to offer him this favor, and he realized that she was that person who would be lending him the money, and all this delighted him, so first he thanked her, and stated that his need was too pressing to allow him to pass up the loan because of the exorbitant interest rates; then he added that he would guarantee the loan with the goods he held in deposit at the customshouse, registering them in the name of the person who lent him the money, but that he wished to keep possession of the key to the warehouse so that in case someone asked to see the merchandise, he would be able to show it to them, and also so that none of it could be tampered with, moved, or exchanged. The lady said she thought this was a good idea and that his guarantee was a very suitable one; and so at daybreak, she sent for a broker whom she knew she could trust, and after discussing the affair with him, she gave him a thousand gold florins, which the broker then lent to Salabaetto after having everything Salabaetto possessed at the customshouse put under his own name; after signing and countersigning a number of receipts for each other, the two men, all in agreement, now went their separate ways to tend to other business.

As soon as he could, Salabaetto boarded a ship, and with the one thousand five hundred gold florins, he returned to Pietro dello Canigiano in Naples, from where he made just and full remittance to his employers in Florence for the cloth they had shipped to him. And once he had paid Pietro, as well as everyone else to whom he owed something, for several days he rejoiced with Canigiano over the trick he had played on the Sicilian woman; then, no longer wishing to be a merchant, he left Naples and went to Ferrara.

When Jancofiore discovered that Salabaetto was nowhere to be found in Palermo, she began to wonder and to become suspicious; and after waiting for him for a good two months and realizing that he was not going to return, she had the broker force his way into the warehouse. First of all, they sounded the casks which she thought were full of oil, only to discover they were filled with seawater, except for a small amount of oil floating over the water near the spout; then, undoing the bales, she found that all except two, which did contain cloth, were full of hemp; in short, all together it was not worth more than two hundred florins. For quite some time, Jancofiore, who realized she had been outwitted, wept over the five hundred florins she had given back and even longer over the thousand she had lent out, often saying as she did: "If with a Tuscan you would deal, be sure to keep your eyes well peeled!" And so, left with her loss and her ridicule, Jancofiore made the discovery that some people can be just as clever as others.

[Eighth Day, Conclusion]

✤

WHEN Dioneo had completed his story, Lauretta, realizing that the end of her reign had come, praised the advice of Pietro Canigiano, which appeared to have been excellent judging from the results, as well as Salabaetto's wisdom, which was no less praiseworthy for having put the advice into practice, and then removing the laurel crown from her head, she placed it on Emilia's, saying in a charmingly feminine way: "Madam, I do not know how good a Queen we shall have in you, but we shall certainly have a beautiful one. Act in such a way, then, that your deeds match your beauty." Then she sat down again.

Emilia was somewhat embarrassed, not so much from the fact she had been made queen, but, rather because she found herself being praised in public for something which ladies desire most, and her face looked like a fresh rose at the break of dawn; then, keeping her eyes lowered long enough for the blush to vanish, she made arrangements with her steward for all the necessities the company required, and then she said:

"Delightful ladies, we have often observed that oxen, after they have labored under the yoke for part of the day, are relieved of their yokes, set loose, and allowed to roam freely wherever they wish through the woods to pasture; and we also observe that woods filled with a number of different trees are not less, but rather much more, beautiful than woods where we see only oak trees; because of this, I feel that since for many days

now we have been telling stories under the restraint of a set
theme, it would not only be useful but fitting that we, no less
than others who have labored under restraint, wander about for
a time and in so doing, renew our strength to return to the yoke.
And so, tomorrow, when you continue your delightful storytell-
ing. I do not intend to restrict what you say to any particular
topic but, rather, I wish for each of you to tell a story about
whatever you please, for I am thoroughly convinced that you
will find it no less entertaining to discuss a variety of things
than if we had limited ourselves to just one subject alone; hav-
ing done this, the person who succeeds me in this kingdom will
find us more refreshed, and thus be able with greater confidence
to restrict us to the customary rules." And having said this, she
granted each one of them leave until suppertime.

Each of them praised the Queen for what she had said in her
wisdom, and rising to their feet, they turned to entertaining
themselves in one way or another: the ladies in making garlands
or amusing themselves. the young men playing games and sing-
ing; and in this fashion, they passed the time until the supper
hour. When it was time, they gathered around the beautiful
fountain and dined in merriment and delight, and as was their
custom, after dinner they amused themselves by singing and
dancing. Finally, in the style of her predecessors, notwithstand-
ing the fact that others in the group had already sung a number
of their own songs without being asked, the Queen ordered Pan-
filo to sing a song of his own. Without hesitation he began as fol-
lows:

> So great, oh Love, the good,
> the joy, and the delight I feel through you,
> that happily I burn within your fire.
>
> The overflowing happiness within my heart,
> born of the lofty and beloved joy
> which you have given me,
> cannot remain contained, but issues forth
> to shine upon my glowing face,
> revealing my true happiness:
> for just to be in love
> with someone of so high and noble state
> makes all the burden of my burning easy.
>
> I cannot sing you in a song
> nor sketch with my own hand

the good, Love, that I feel;
and even if I could, I'd have to hide it,
for were it known,
my joy would change to grief,
but I'm so happy now
that words would be too weak and insufficient
to give the slightest sense of how I feel.

Who would have ever thought my arms
could stretch so high
so as to ever reach her there,
or that I could ever touch my face
there where I did and where
I found grace and salvation?
None would believe
my good fortune; and so I burn, concealing
the thing which gives me happiness and joy.

Panfilo's song came to an end, and while everyone had sung its refrain in a chorus, there was no one present among them who did not pay the strictest attention to its words, trying to guess what it was Panfilo sang that he was obliged to keep concealed; and although a number of them came up with a variety of explanations, none of them managed to hit upon the truth of the matter. But when the Queen heard Panfilo's song come to an end and saw that the young ladies and men were anxious to retire, she ordered everyone to go to bed.

[Ninth Day, Title Page]

✦

Here ends the eighth day of The Decameron: *and the ninth day begins, during which, under the reign of Emilia, everyone tells whatever story he pleases on the topic he likes the most.*

[Ninth Day, Introduction]

✦

THE light, from whose splendor the darkness flees, had already changed all the deep blue of the eighth heaven* to pale celestial hues, and the little flowers scattered throughout the meadows had already begun to raise their blossoms, when Emilia arose and had her companions and the young men summoned. In answer to her call, they set out following the Queen's leisurely steps in the direction of a little wood not far from the palace, and entering the wood, they saw animals, such as roebucks, deer, and other species, which, almost sensing that they were safe from hunters because of the existing plague, let them come close to them, much the same way a tame and friendly animal might do. And drawing near now to one of them and now to another, as if about to touch them, they made them run and leap about, and in this way they amused themselves for some time. But since the sun had risen high by now, it seemed to them all a good time to return.

*According to the Ptolemaic system of the universe (in which the earth rather than the sun, was located at the center,) the eighth heaven was the sphere of the fixed stars.

They were all wearing garlands of oak leaves, their hands full of sweet-smelling herbs or flowers, and anyone meeting them on the way could only have said: "Either these people will not be vanquished by death, or should they be, they will certainly die happy." So then, step by step, jokingly singing and exchanging witty remarks, they made their way back to the palace, where they found everything prepared to the last detail and their servants joyful and festive. They rested there for a while, but none of them sat down at the table before six canzonets, each more beautiful than the one before it, were sung by the young men and ladies. After this, when they had washed their hands, the steward, following the Queen's wishes, sat them all at the table where, once the food was served, they ate happily. And after rising from the meal, they gave themselves over to dancing and making music for some time, and then the Queen gave her permission for anyone who wished to do so to take a nap. But at the usual hour, each of them went to the usual place where they gathered to tell stories; whereupon the Queen, glancing at Filomena, ordered her to begin the day's storytelling; smiling, Filomena began in this fashion:

[Ninth Day, First Story]

Madonna Francesca, loved by a certain Rinuccio and a certain Alessandro, but loving neither of them in return, makes one of them play dead in a tomb and gets the other one to go in to carry out what he thinks is a dead body; and when they are unable to complete their task, she discreetly manages to rid herself of the both of them.

My lady, since it is your wish, I am delighted to be the first to joust in this open and free field of storytelling, into which your generosity has brought us all; and if I do well, I have no doubt that those who come after me will do as well and even better. Charming ladies, many is the time in our discussions that we have demonstrated the greatness and diversity of Love's powers; however, I do not believe we have exhausted the subject, nor could we ever, even if we were to speak of nothing else for an entire year. And since Love not only leads lovers to run certain deadly risks, but also persuades them to enter into the home of the dead pretending to be dead, there is a tale I would like to tell you concerning this subject, in spite of the many already told, whereby you will be able to appreciate not only Love's power but also the ingenious way in which a worthy lady manages to rid herself of two men, both of whom were unwanted suitors.

Let me say, then, that in the city of Pistoia, there once lived a very beautiful widow, with whom two of our fellow Florentines, living there after being banished from Florence, by chance happened to fall in love, neither one of them knowing about the other's love. One was called Rinuccio Palermini and the other Alessandro Chiarmontesi, and being most passionately in love, each of them was secretly doing his utmost to win the love of this lady. And since this noble lady, whose name was Madonna Francesa de' Lazzari, was constantly being pestered by messages and entreaties from both of these men, to which she had on occasion rather unwisely lent an ear, and being unable to get out of this situation, as she was prudent enough to wish, at last there came to her a plan by which she might rid herself of their worrisome attention: that is, she would request of them a service which she felt neither of them could perform (even though it would be something quite possible to do), so that when they found themselves unable to carry out her request, she would have a plausible and apparently justifiable cause for refusing to receive their messages any longer; and the plan was this.

On the day this idea came to her, a man died in Pistoia who, in spite of his noble lineage, was reputed to be not only the worst person in Pistoia but in the whole world, and moreover, he had such an ugly and deformed face that anyone who had not known him, on seeing him for the first time when he was alive, would have been scared stiff of him. And he was buried in a tomb outside the church of the Franciscans; the lady thought this offered an excellent opportunity for her to put her plan into action.

And so she said to one of her maidservants:

"You know how annoying and vexing I find the messages those two Florentines, Rinuccio and Alessandro, pester me with every day. Well, now, I am not at all disposed to requite them with my love, and in order to rid myself of them, I have decided, because of the grand promises they are always making, to put them to a test, to which I am certain they will not prove equal, and this way I shall rid myself of the nuisance: let me tell you how. You know that Scannadio"—this was the name of the wicked man we mentioned earlier—"was buried at the convent of the Franciscans this morning, the sight of whom when he was still alive, not to mention now that he is dead, would terrify the most courageous men in the land; now first you are to go in secret to Alessandro and tell him: 'Madonna Francesca sends this message to you, that the time has now come for you to enjoy her love, which you have desired so very much, and that you may be with her, whenever you like, under the following conditions: for reasons you will learn about later, this evening a relative of hers must bring to her home the body of Scannadio, who was buried this morning; and being afraid of the body, dead as it is, she does not want the corpse in her house. Therefore, she begs you to do her a special favor, that is, around bedtime you are to go to the tomb where Scannadio has been buried, go inside, put on his clothes, and remain there as if you were the dead man until someone comes to get you; then, without saying a word or making a sound, allow yourself to be removed from the tomb and brought to her house, where she will welcome you, then you shall stay with her as long as you like, leaving the rest for her to worry about.' And if he says he is willing to do this, all fine and good, but if he says he is unwilling, then tell him for me that he had better not show his face in my presence ever again, and if he values his life, he will be careful never to send another messenger or entreaty. After this, you are to go to Rinuccio Palermini and tell him the following: 'Madonna Francesca says she is ready to fulfill your every wish as soon as you do her a great favor, which is that tonight around midnight you are to go to the tomb where Scannadio was buried this morning and, without uttering a word about whatever you see or hear, you are carefully to remove his corpse and bring it home to her house. There, you will discover why she asks this favor of you, and you will have your pleasure of her; and if you are not willing to do this, from this moment on, she orders you nevermore to send her another messenger or entreaty.'"

The maidservant went to both men and said exactly what she had been instructed to say to each one, and both of them answered that they would go to Hell itself, no less a tomb, if it pleased her. The maidservant delivered their reply to the lady, who then waited to see if they were crazy enough to carry out her wishes.

Then, when night came, and around the hour most people fall asleep, dressed in nothing but his doublet, Alessandro Chiarmontesi left his home in order to take the place of Scannadio inside the tomb, and as he was on his way he had a terrifying thought which made him say to himself: "Hey, what kind of a fool am

I? Where am I going? How do I know that this lady's relatives, perhaps having discovered I love her, and thinking who knows what I might have done to her, are forcing her to arrange all this in order to murder me in that tomb? If that happens, I'd get the worst of it, and no one in the world would be the wiser, and they'd get away with it. Or, how do I know that some enemy of mine, with whom she might well be in love, wants to do her the favor of murdering me?" And then he said: "But let's suppose that none of these things is true and that her relatives really do want to carry me to her home; how am I supposed to believe that all they want is to take Scannadio's corpse in their arms and deliver it to her? On the contrary, I'm forced to believe that they want it to tear it to pieces perhaps because of some harm he did them in the past. This lady says no matter what I hear I mustn't breathe a word of it, but if they gouge out my eyes, or pull out my teeth, or cut off my hands, or play some other horrible trick on me, what would I do then? How could I remain silent? And if I talk and they recognize me, they might hurt me; but if they don't do anything to me, I shall have gained nothing, for they will not leave me with the lady in any case; and then the lady will claim that I disobeyed her orders and will never do anything I want."

At this point he was ready to return home, but yet his great love pushed him forward with arguments countering his fears with such force that they brought him to the tomb. Having opened the tomb, he went inside, stripped Scannadio's corpse, and put on his clothes, and then, closing the tomb above him, he lay down in Scannadio's place and began to think about the kind of man the corpse had been as well as the stories he had heard concerning things that happen in the night, not only in the tombs of the dead but in other places as well. Every hair on his body stood on end, and he began to think that Scannadio at any moment would stand straight up and cut his throat right there on the spot. But his fervent love came to the rescue, and he overcame these and his other terrifying thoughts, and lying there as if he were dead, he waited to see what was going to happen to him.

Around midnight, Rinuccio left his house to do what his lady had sent word for him to do; and on his way, he began mulling over in his mind all the possible things that could happen to him, such as falling into the hands of the authorities with Scannadio's corpse on his shoulders and being condemned to burn at the stake for witchcraft, or incurring the wrath of Scannadio's relatives if he was discovered, and other similar possibilities—all of which almost stopped him from going on. But then he changed his mind and said:

"Well, am I to say no to the first thing asked of me by this noble lady, whom I have loved so much and still love, especially since I shall gain her favor by doing this? Even if it meant certain death because of this, I must set myself to doing what I promised her I would do." Continuing on his way, he reached the tomb and opened it quite easily.

When Alessandro heard the tomb open, he was filled with terror but managed, nevertheless, to remain still. Rinuccio went inside, and thinking that he was picking up the body of Scannadio, he grabbed Alessandro by his feet and dragged him out, and hoisting him up onto his shoulders, he started off in the direction of the noble lady's house; and since it was pitch-dark outside, he was unable to see where he was going, and not paying too much attention to what he was carrying, from time to time he would bump into one edge or another of the benches which were lining the street. Rinuccio was nearly at the doorstep of his noble lady, who had been watching with her maidservant at the window waiting to see if Rinuccio would bring Alessandro back, already prepared with some excuse to send them both away, when the city guards, who had been lying in ambush in that neighborhood secretly waiting to capture a bandit, happened to hear the trampling noise Rinuccio made with his feet and quickly produced a lantern to see what was happening and what to do about it, shouldering their shields and lances, as they cried: "Who goes there?" Rinuccio knew who they were, and with no time to compose his thoughts, he let Alessandro drop and ran off as fast as his legs could carry him. Alessandro quickly jumped to his feet, and in spite of the dead man's shroud on his back, which happened to be very long, he, too, took off running.

With the aid of the light the guards had produced, the lady could clearly see Rinuccio carrying Alessandro on his back, and she also saw Alessandro dressed in Scannadio's clothes, and she was rather amazed to see how daring both of them were, but for all her amazement, she had a good laugh when she saw Alessandro being dumped on the ground and then when she saw the two of them running off. Overjoyed by this unexpected turn of events and praising God for rescuing her from the nuisance they caused her, she turned from her window and went to her room, agreeing with her maidservant that both men must certainly have loved her very much to have done, as it appeared, what she ordered them to do.

Upset and cursing his bad luck, Rinuccio did not return home in spite of it all, but waiting until after the guards had left the neighborhood, he went back to where he had dropped Alessandro and groping around, he tried to find the body and complete his task; but when he did not find it, thinking that the guards had taken it away, he went home feeling miserable. Alessandro, in like manner, not knowing what else to do, went home, without learning who it was that had carried his body off, and he was grief-stricken over his disastrous luck.

The next morning, when Scannadio's tomb was discovered open and his corpse was nowhere to be seen—for Alessandro had rolled it down into the back of the tomb—all of Pistoia was full of different explanations for what had happened, the more simpleminded people believing his body had been spirited off by devils. Nevertheless, each of the two lovers, having informed the lady of what he had done and what had happened, using this as an excuse for not having completely fulfilled her orders, asked for her forgiveness and her love. Pretending that she believed neither of the two and sharply replying that she wanted nothing to do with either of them, since they had not done what she had asked of them, she managed to get rid of them both.

[Ninth Day, Second Story]

❊

An Abbess quickly gets up from her bed in the dark in order to catch one of her nuns who was reported to be in bed with her lover; the Abbess herself is in bed with a priest, and she puts his pants on her head, thinking that she is putting on her veil; when the accused nun sees the pants and points them out to the Abbess, she is set free and is allowed to be with her lover.

WHEN Filomena was silent, and the wisdom the lady showed in ridding herself of the men whose love she did not want had been praised by everyone, while on the other hand they all considered the daring presumption of the lovers to be madness rather than love, the Queen then graciously said to Elissa: "Elissa, continue," and she immediately began:

Dearest ladies, as was explained, Madonna Francesca knew how to rid herself of a nuisance most wisely, but there is also the case of a young nun who, with the assistance of Fortune, freed herself from an impending danger by speaking cleverly.

And as you know, there are many people who, in their great foolishness, set themselves up as teachers and judges over others, and as you will learn from my story, Fortune, on occasion, puts them deservedly to shame, as happened to an Abbess under whose rule there lived a nun about whom I shall tell you.

I would have you know that in Lombardy there is a convent very famous for its sanctity and religious spirit. Among the nuns there lived a young lady of noble blood endowed with marvelous beauty, whose name was Isabetta. One day she came to the convent's grating to speak to a relative, and she fell in love with a handsome young man who was with him; and the young man, seeing how beautiful she was and understanding how she felt about him from her eyes, also fell in love with her; and much to the discomfort of them both, they bore this fruitless love for some time.

Finally, since each desired the other, the young man devised a means of seeing his nun secretly; this was agreeable to her, and he visited her not once, but many times, to their mutual delight. But as this went on for some time, it happened one night that he was seen by one of the nuns as he was leaving Isabetta's cell, without either of them knowing it. The nun told the news to several others, and at first they wanted to denounce her to the Abbess, Madonna Usimbalda, a good and holy woman in the opinion of her nuns and all those who knew her. But after they thought it over, they decided to have the Abbess catch her with her young lover so that there would be no way of denying the fact; and so they remained silent and secretly kept watch over her in turns in order to catch the lovers.

Now Isabetta knew nothing about any of this, and one night, when she had her lover come to her, it was immediately noted by the nuns who were keeping watch; then when the time seemed right, a goodly part of the night already having passed, they divided themselves into two groups: one stood guard outside the entrance to Isabetta's cell, while the other ran to the bedroom of the Abbess, who, as soon as she acknowledged their knocking at her door, was told:

"Get up, Mother Superior, get up quickly! We've discovered that Isabetta has a young man in her cell!"

That night the Abbess was in the company of a priest whom she often had brought to her bedroom in a chest, and when she heard the noise, fearing that the nuns in their excessive haste and zeal might beat down the door, she got up quickly and dressed in the dark as best she could; and thinking that she had picked up her folded nun's veil of the sort which is called "psal-

ters," she picked up the priest's pants instead; and she was in
such a hurry that, without realizing it, she threw his pants over
her head in place of her "psalters," left her bedroom, and
quickly locked the door behind her, saying:

"Where is this cursed woman?"

The other nuns were so anxious and eager to catch Isabetta in
the act that they did not notice what the Abbess had on her
head; she reached the door of the cell and, with the help of the
other nuns, forced it open. They rushed in and found the two
lovers in each other's arms, and they, taken so suddenly by sur-
prise, not knowing what to do, lay there motionless.

The young girl was immediately led off by the other nuns to
the convent's meeting hall. The young man remained there; he
dressed, and then waited to see how the affair was going to end,
intending to harm as many of them as he could if anything
should happen to his young novice, and to take her away with
him.

Having taken her seat in the meeting hall in the presence of
all the nuns, who were looking only at the guilty girl, the Abbess
began to vilify the young nun in terms never before used to a
woman, telling her how her indecent, her depraved actions, had
they ever become known outside the convent, would ruin its
sanctity, honesty, and its good name; and to her verbal abuse,
she added the most serious of threats.

The young girl, in her timidity and shame, knowing she was
guilty, did not know how to reply, hoping with her silence to
arouse a feeling of compassion in the others. And as the scolding
of the Abbess continued, the young girl happened to look up and
see what the Abbess was wearing on her head, with suspenders
dangling on either side. Realizing what the Abbess had been up
to, she regained her self-confidence and said:

"Mother, God help you, but tie up your wimple and then tell
me what you will."

The Abbess, who did not understand what she meant, replied:

"What wimple, you wicked woman? Even now you have the
nerve to be clever? Do you think what you have done is a joking
matter?"

Then, a second time, the young girl said:

"Mother, I beg you to tie up your wimple; then say anything
you please to me."

At this, several nuns glanced up at the Abbess's head, and she,
too, put her hands there, and then they all understood why Isa-
betta had spoken as she had. When she realized that she was
equally guilty and that there was no way to cover up her sin

from the others, the Abbess changed her tone and began to speak in a completely different manner, concluding that it was impossible for people to defend themselves from the desires of the flesh, and she said that everyone there should enjoy herself whenever possible, provided that it be done as discreetly as it had been until that day.

And after Isabetta was set free, the Abbess went back to sleep with her priest, and Isabetta with her lover; and in spite of all the other nuns that envied her, Isabetta had him come to her many times; the other nuns, without lovers, sought their solace secretly in the best way they knew how.

[Ninth Day, Third Story]

*

Urged on by Bruno, Buffalmacco, and Nello, Master Simone gives Calandrino to believe that he is pregnant; Calandrino gives them capons and money in return for medicine, and he is cured without giving birth.

AFTER Elissa had finished her story, and all the ladies had given thanks to God for such a felicitous rescue of the young nun from the fangs of her envious sisters, the Queen ordered Filostrato to continue; without waiting for further instructions, he began:

Most beautiful ladies, the ill-bred judge from the Marches, about whom I spoke to you yesterday, took from the tip of my tongue a story which I was going to tell you about Calandrino; and although we have heard a lot about him and his companions, since anything we say about him can only add to our fun, I shall now tell you the story I meant to tell you yesterday.

From previous discussions you have a clear picture of Calandrino and the others I shall be referring to in this story; and so, without saying any more about them, let me begin by telling you that one day an aunt of Calandrino's happened to die and leave him two hundred lire in silver coins of small value: because of this, Calandrino began saying that he wanted to buy a farm, and he started bargaining with as many brokers as there were in Florence, as if he had ten thousand gold florins to spend, but when it finally came down to the actual asking price of the farm, the deal always fell through. Bruno and Buffalmacco, who knew about these negotiations, told him more than once that he would be better off enjoying his money with them, rather than going off to buy land—which, in any case, would not be enough to make a couple of mud balls; but far from convincing him, they couldn't even manage to squeeze a single dinner out of him.

One day, as they were complaining about this with each other, they were joined by a companion of theirs, a painter whose name was Nello, and all three of them decided that they were going to find a way to grease their snouts at Calandrino's expense. After arranging what they would do among themselves, without further delay, the following morning they waited for Calandrino to leave his house, and before he had gone very far, Nello went up to him and said: "Good morning, Calandrino."

Calandrino answered by saying that he hoped God would grant him a good morning and a good year too. Then, Nello, hesitating a moment or two, began to stare at his face, which made Calandrin ask: "What are you staring at?"

And Nello said to him: "Did something happen to you last night? You don't look your usual self."

Calandrino at once began to wonder, and he said: "Oh my! Not myself! What do you think could be wrong with me?"

Nello replied: "Well, I'm not saying you're sick or anything, it's just like you're all changed or something, but it's probably nothing." And then he left him.

All worried but not feeling that anything in the world was the matter with him, Calandrino went on his way; but Buffalmacco, who was not too far away, on seeing him leaving Nello, walked up to him, and after greeting him, he asked if he was feeling all right. Calandrino answered: "I don't know, but just a moment ago Nello was telling me I looked all different to him; could it be I've come down with something?"

Buffalmacco said: "Well, you might have caught a little something, but it's probably nothing; you just look a little dead, that's all!"

Calandrino already felt he had a fever; and then Bruno arrived, and, before saying anything else, he said: "Calandrino, what's wrong with your face? You look like you died: how are you feeling?"

Calandrino, having heard them all say what they did, was absolutely convinced that he was a very sick man, and full of worry, he asked them: "What should I do?"

Bruno said:

"I think you ought to go home and go to bed, cover yourself up very well, and then send a urine specimen to Doctor Simone, who is a very close friend of ours, as you know. He'll tell you right away what you have to do: we'll go with you, and in case you need anything, we'll get it for you."

And after Nello joined them, they all went home with Calandrino, who, completely exhausted, dragged himself to his bedroom, saying to his wife: "Come and cover me up good, I feel awfully sick."

So he was put to bed and a servant girl was sent with his urine specimen to Doctor Simone, who was then located in the Old Market under the sign of the melon; and Bruno said to his companions: "You stay here with him, and I'll go and see what the doctor says, and if necessary, I'll bring him back here with me."

Calandrino then exclaimed: "Ah, yes, my friend, go and let me know how things stand, I feel I don't know what's inside me."

Bruno left for Doctor Simone's and arrived there before the servant girl who was carrying the specimen, and he informed Doctor Simone of the plan; and so, when the girl arrived, the doctor, after examining the specimen, said to her:

"Go back to Calandrino and tell him to keep good and warm, and I'll be over to see him right away and tell him what he has and how to take care of it."

The girl delivered the message, and it was not long before the doctor and Bruno arrived; the doctor sat down beside Calandrino and began to take his pulse, then after a while in the presence of Calandrino's wife, he said: "Look, Calandrino, let me tell you friend to friend, there's nothing wrong with you except for the fact that you're pregnant."

When Calandrino heard this, he began howling with despair and saying: "Ah, Tessa, you did this to me, you're the one that always wanted to be on top; I told you it would happen."

When the woman, who was a very modest sort of person, heard her husband speak in this fashion, she blushed all over with shame, and lowering her head, she left the bedroom without uttering a word. Continuing his complaint, Calandrino continued to wail, saying: "Ah, poor me, what can I do? How will I give birth to this child? Where will it come out? It's clear, this is the end of me, all because of the lust of this wife of mine, may God make her as miserable as I wish I were happy; but if I were well, which I'm not, I'd get up and give her such a beating I'd break every bone in her body—though it serves me right, I should never have let her get on top. But if I get out of this mess, she'll die from frustration, she can bet on that, before I let her have it again!"

Bruno, Buffalmacco, and Nello were bursting with the desire to laugh out loud as they listened to Calandrino's comments, but they managed to control themselves, although Doctor Simonkey* guffawed so uproariously that you could have pulled every tooth out of his mouth, one after the other. But then, finally, Calandrino, throwing himself at the mercy of the doctor, begged him to advise and assist him in all this, and the doctor said to him:

"Calandrino, I don't want you to be frightened, for, praise be to God, we have diagnosed your case early enough to cure you of it with little trouble and in only a few days; but it will take a bit of money to do it."

Calandrino replied:

"Oh, doctor, of course, for the love of God. I've got two hundred lire here that I wanted to buy a farm with, and if you need them all, take them, just so long as I don't have to give birth, because I don't know how to! When women are about to give birth, I've heard them make such a racket, and even with the large thing they have to do it with, that if I had to put up with that pain, I'm sure I would die before I gave birth."

The doctor said:

"Don't worry about it. I'll make you a special distilled potion which is very good and very pleasant to drink, and in three days everything will be taken care of, and you'll be healthier than a fish; but see to it that you are wiser afterward, and do not get yourself into such a foolish position again. Now, for this liquid we need three brace of good, fat capons, and for the other items you'll be needing, you can give these men five lire in small silver coins with which to buy them, and have everything brought to my shop; tomorrow morning, in God's name, I shall send you that distilled beverage, and you can start drinking a nice big glass of it at a time."

When Calandrino heard this, he said: "Doctor, I'm in your hands"; and after giving five lire to Bruno as well as the money to buy three brace of capons, Calandrino begged him to do everything possible to help him out in this regard.

The doctor left and prepared a quantity of some liquid concoction for Calandrino and sent it to him. Bruno bought the capons and other essential delicacies for a good meal and polished them off in the company of the doctor and his friends. Calandrino drank the liquid for three mornings, and then the

---

*Here the narrator pokes fun at Simone, elsewhere the butt of practical jokes (VIII, 9), by twisting his name to *Scimmione*, implying that he is no smarter than a monkey.

doctor came to visit him, along with his companions, and having
taken his pulse, he announced:

"Calandrino, there is no doubt about it, you're cured; so, from
now on, you can safely go about your business, and there's no
need to stay at home any longer."

Delighted, Calandrino got up and started going about his
business, and wherever he happened to meet somebody he would
speak in glowing terms about Doctor Simone and the wonderful
cure he had given him, which in a matter of just three days
unimpregnated him with absolutely no pain at all; and Bruno,
Buffalmacco, and Nello were pleased with the clever way they
managed to get around Calandrino's stinginess—though Monna
Tessa, discovering all this, never stopped grumbling about it with
her husband.

[Ninth Day, Fourth Story]

*Cecco, the son of Messer Fortarrigo, gambles away all his pos-
sessions at Bonconvento as well as the money belonging to
Cecco, son of Messer Angiolieri; he then runs after Cecco in his
shirt and, claiming that he had been robbed by him, he has him
seized by peasants; he puts on his clothes, mounts his palfrey,
and rides away, leaving Cecco in his shirtsleeves.*

THE whole group reacted to the words Calandrino said about his
wife with the heartiest of laughter; but when Filostrato fell
silent, Neifile began, just as the Queen wished her to.

Worthy ladies, if it were not more difficult for people to show
their wisdom and virtue to others rather than their folly and
their vice, many a man would work hard, but in vain, to curb
his tongue: the foolishness of Calandrino has made this very
clear, for there was no need for him, in curing the sickness his
simplemindedness made him believe he had, to reveal in public
his wife's secret pleasures. This story brings to mind a tale of a
different sort, one which tells how the cunning of one man de-
feats the wisdom of another to the serious harm and shame of
the one defeated, and I would like to tell it to you.

Not many years ago, there lived in Siena two young men in
their manhood, each of whom was named Cecco, but one was the
son of Messer Angiulieri, and the other was the son of Messer

Fortearrigo. And while these two men did not see eye to eye in many things, there was one thing—namely, that both of them hated their fathers—in which they so thoroughly agreed that they became good friends and often they could be found in each other's company. But when Angiulieri, who was a handsome and well-bred man, but living rather poorly in Siena on the allowance his father was giving him, heard that a certain Cardinal who was a great patron of his had gone as papal legate to the Marches of Ancona, he decided to go there to see him, hoping in this way to better his condition. And having informed his father of this, he made an agreement with him to receive in a single payment what his allowance would be for a six-month period, so that he could buy clothes, furnish himself with a mount, and travel there in style.

And while he was looking for someone to take with him as his servant, Fortarrigo happened to hear about his intentions, and he immediately went to Angiulieri and, as best he knew how, he begged Angiulieri to take him along, telling him that he wanted to be his servant, his retainer, and to do everything for him, with no wages at all, just his living expenses. To this offer, Angiulieri replied that he did not wish to take him along, not because he felt he could not do everything as well as a good servant would but rather because he gambled and sometimes he got drunk as well; to this Fortarrigo answered that he would absolutely give up both the one and the other vice, and he swore he would keep his promise, and to it he added so many entreaties that Angiulieri finally gave in and agreed to it.

And so one morning, the two of them set out together and reached Bonconvento in time for lunch, after which Angiulieri, since the heat of the day was intense, had a bed prepared in the inn, and with Fortarrigo's help, he undressed and went to bed, telling his servant to call him when the hour of nones struck. While Angiulieri was sleeping, Fortarrigo went down to the tavern and there, after drinking quite a bit, he started gambling with some people who, in not much time at all, won whatever money he had on him, as well as all the clothes he was wearing. Anxious to win back his losses, he went, wearing nothing but his shirt, back up to the room where Angiulieri slept, and seeing him fast asleep, took all the money from his purse, and returning to the game, managed to lose it all, just as he had the other money.

Angiulieri awakened, got up, dressed himself, and asked for Fortarrigo, and when he did not find him, Angiulieri assumed that he was asleep somewhere drunk, as he was often in the habit of being; and so, deciding to abandon him where he was,

Angiulieri had his palfrey saddled and packed with the intention of finding himself another servant at Corsignano, but when he went to pay the innkeeper before leaving, he found he had no money, and the uproar that followed was enormous: the whole place was in turmoil, with Angiulieri claiming he had been robbed at the inn and threatening to go to Siena and have them all arrested. Just then Fortarrigo, who had come back to take Angiulieri's clothes just as he had stolen his money, arrived in his shirtsleeves, and when he saw Angiulieri about to ride off, he said:

"What's this, Angiulieri? Are we leaving already? Hey, wait a while. The man who lent me thirty-eight shillings for my doublet should be here any moment now, and I'm sure he'll let us have it back for thirty-five if we pay him immediately."

And during this exchange of words, a man appeared on the scene who made it clear to Angiulieri that Fortarrigo was the one who had stolen his money by showing him the amount of money he had lost. And so Angiulieri, outraged by it all, gave Fortarrigo the soundest of tongue-lashings, and he would have done him in, had he not feared the laws of man more than those of God; and so, threatening to have him hanged by the neck or to make sure he was banished upon pain of death from Siena, Angiulieri mounted his horse.

As if Angiulieri had been speaking not to him but to someone else, Fortarrigo said:

"Come on now, Angiulieri, enough of this kind of talk which doesn't lead anywhere. Let's discuss the problem at hand: we can have the doublet for thirty-five shillings if we pay him back immediately, but if we delay for as much as a day, he won't take less than the thirty-eight he lent me for it; and he's doing me this favor only because I bet the money on his advice. Now, why don't we just save ourselves these three shillings?"

Angiulieri, as he listened to him speak this way, was getting frantic, especially since he saw the people who were standing around were staring at him and seemed to be under the impression that Fortarrigo had not gambled away Angiulieri's money but, rather, that Angiulieri still had some of Fortarrigo's: and he said to him:

"What do I have to do with your doublet? May you be hanged by the neck! Not only have you robbed me and gambled away my money, but on top of it all, you now keep me from leaving and even make fun of me."

Fortarrigo nevertheless continued to act as if what Angiulieri was saying was not directed at him, and he replied:

"Say, why don't you want me to save these three shillings? Don't you think I'll give them back to you again? Come on, do it for the sake of our friendship! Why are you in such a hurry? We can still easily get to Torrenieri by early evening. Go find your purse; I tell you, not if I were to look all over Siena could I find a doublet which suited me as well as that one—and to think that I let that fellow have it for thirty-eight shillings! It's worth at least forty, or even more, so you're making me a loser twice over!"

Angiulieri, distraught beyond patience at first being robbed by Fortarrigo and now delayed with this prattle of his, made no reply but turned his mount's head and took the road for Torrenieri. But Fortarrigo suddenly thought of a cunning plan and began, in his shirtsleeves just as he was, to jog behind him; he had been running for a good two miles, begging Angiulieri all the way for his doublet, when just as Angiulieri began to quicken his pace in order to remove this nuisance from his ears, Fortarrigo spotted some workers in a field near the road ahead of Angiulieri; Fortarrigo began shouting to them at the top of his voice:

"Grab him, grab him!" And so, some armed with shovels and others with hoes, blocking the road in front of Angiulieri, whom they thought had robbed the man running behind him screaming in his shirtsleeves, they stopped and seized Angiulieri, and little good it did to Angiulieri to explain to them who he was and how things really stood.

But Fortarrigo arrived on the spot and with a look of rage, he declared: "I don't know what's stopping me from killing you, you treacherous thief, running off with my belongings the way you did!" Then, turning to the peasants, he announced:

"Gentlemen, you can see for yourselves the sorry state he left me in at the inn, after gambling away everything he owned! But I can say that thanks to God and to yourselves, I have at least salvaged this much, for which I shall always be grateful to you."

Angiulieri told them a different story, but his words were ignored. With the help of the peasants, Fortarrigo pulled him from his horse to the ground, stripped him of his clothes, and put them on himself; then he mounted the horse, and leaving Angiulieri there in his shirtsleeves and bare feet, he returned to Siena and told everyone he had won the palfrey and the clothes from Angiulieri. So Angiulieri, who intended to present himself to the Cardinal in the Marches as a wealthy man, instead returned to Bonconvento impoverished and in his shirtsleeves, not daring for the time being to return to Siena out of shame, but, rather, after borrowing some clothes, he got on the nag which Fortarrigo had been riding and went back to his relatives in Corsignano until his father once again came to his rescue. And while Fortarrigo's cunning did upset Angiulieri's good intentions, he did not go unpunished when the proper place and time presented themselves.

[Ninth Day, Fifth Story]

❋

Calandrino falls in love with a young woman, and Bruno writes down a magic formula for him with which, as soon as he touches her, she goes off with him; but when he is discovered by his wife, he finds himself in a serious and painful predicament.

WHEN Neifile's not-so-lengthy story came to an end, the group disposed of it without much laughter or comment, and the Queen, turning to Fiammetta, ordered her to continue; delighted, she answered that she was most willing, and she began:

Most gracious ladies, as I believe you know, there is no subject, no matter how much it is discussed, that ever fails to give even more pleasure when the person who chooses to discuss it picks the proper time and place. And because of this, considering our reason for being here, which is to make merry and have a good time and for no other purpose, I deem this is the proper place and time for whatever gives us pleasure and amusement; and even if such a topic were to be discussed a thousand times, we could return to it over and over again, and it would give us nothing but joy. Therefore, even though we have talked about Calandrino's behavior many times before, since, just as Filostrato pointed out a little earlier, it is always an amusing topic, I shall venture to add an additional tale to those already told. If I had wished or wanted now to depart from the truth of the matter, I could have easily or could even now conceal the truth under fictitious names, but since to depart from the truth of how things really happened in storytelling greatly diminishes the pleasure of the listeners, I shall tell it to you as it actually happened for the reason mentioned above.

Niccoló Cornacchini was a fellow townsman of ours and a rich man, and among the various properties he owned, there was a beautiful one at Camerata, upon which he had built a fine and handsome mansion, and he arranged for Bruno and Buffalmacco to paint it with frescoes throughout; since the job was a big one, Bruno and Buffalmacco took Nello and Calandrino along with them and began the work. Now, although some of the rooms were furnished with beds and other essential pieces of furniture, none of the family lived there except for an old woman servant who was the caretaker of the place, and accordingly one of the sons of the said Niccolò, whose name was Filippo, being young and wifeless, was sometimes in the habit of bringing some woman or other there for his amusement, keeping them there for a day or two, and then sending them away.

Now on one of these occasions it happened that he brought with him a woman whose name was Niccolosa, who was kept in a house in Camaldoli by a scoundrel named Mangione, who hired her out. This woman had a beautiful body and dressed rather well, and for a woman of her kind, she was very well-mannered and well-spoken; one day around noon, having left her room dressed in a white shift, her hair tied up in a bun, she happened to be at the well in the courtyard of the building washing her hands and face, while Calandrino was there getting some water, and he greeted her in a friendly manner. She responded and then began to stare at him, more because Calandrino seemed to her to be an odd individual rather than for any flirtatious reason. Calandrino began to stare at her, and finding her to be beautiful, he came up with various excuses for staying with her and not returning to his companions with the water; but since he did not know her, he dared say nothing to her. When she noticed he was staring at her, in order to make fun of him, she would look at him from time to time and heave a sigh or two; because of this, Calandrino immediately fell in love with her, and he did not leave the courtyard until Filippo called her into his room.

When Calandrino returned to his work, he did nothing but sigh; when Bruno, who always observed whatever he was doing because he took great delight in Calandrino's behavior, noticed this, he said: "What the devil is wrong with you, Calandrino, my friend? You do nothing but sigh."

To this, Calandrino replied: "My friend, if I had someone to help me, I'd be fine."

"What do you mean?" asked Bruno.

To this, Calandrino answered:

"Don't tell anyone; but there is a young woman downstairs who is more gorgeous than a nymph, and she is so passionately in love with me you'd be amazed; I just noticed it a moment ago when I went to get the water."

"Ah," exclaimed Bruno, "be careful that she isn't Filippo's wife."

Calandrino said:

"I think she is, because when he called her she went into his bedroom, but what do I care anyway? I'd steal her from Christ himself, let alone from Filippo. The truth is, my friend, I like her so much, I can't begin to tell you."

Then Bruno said:

"I'll find out who she is for you, and if she's Filippo's wife, I'll fix things up for you in no time, because she's a good friend of mine. But how can we arrange things without Buffalmacco's finding out about it? I never get a chance to speak to her without his being around."

Calandrino said:

"I don't care about Buffalmacco, but we've got to be careful of Nello, since he's related to Tessa and could spoil everything."

Bruno said: "You're right."

Now Bruno knew who the woman was, for he had seen her arrive at the house, and besides, Filippo had told him all about her; and so when Calandrino left his work for a moment and went to see her, Bruno told everything to Nello and Buffalmacco, and together they secretly agreed on what they were going to do about this love affair of Calandrino's.

And when Calandrino came back, Bruno whispered to him: "Did you see her?"

Calandrino replied: "Ah, that I did, and she slays me!"

Bruno declared: "I want to see if she's the one I think she is, and if that's the case, then leave everything to me."

Then Bruno went downstairs, and finding Filippo and the woman, he carefully explained to them the kind of person Calandrino was and what he had said about them, and then he arranged what each of them would do and say in order to get some fun out of Calandrino's love affair; returning to Calandrino, he said:

"It sure is her, so this affair has to be handled very wisely, for if Filippo found out about it, all the water in the Arno couldn't wash our hands of it. But what do you want me to tell her for you, if I get a chance to speak to her?"

Calandrino replied:

"Christ's sake! First of all, you tell her that I wish her a thousand bushels of that stuff good to fatten up a girl, and that I am her servant, and if there's anything she wants . . . do you get my meaning?"

Bruno said: "Sure, leave everything to me."

When suppertime came, they left their work and went downstairs into the courtyard, where Filippo and Niccolosa were standing around for Calandrino's benefit; and Calandrino began to stare at Niccolosa and perform the world's weirdest antics, the likes of which even a blind man would have noticed. As for Niccolosa, she did everything she thought would excite him, according to the information she had received from Bruno, and took the greatest delight in the world in Calandrino's antics. Filippo, as well as Buffalmacco and the others, pretended to be talking and not to notice what was going on.

But after a while, however, to Calandrino's greatest displeasure, they left; and as they were traveling toward Florence, Bruno said to Calandrino:

"You sure do make her melt like ice in the sun; for Christ's sake, I'll bet if you bring your rebec here and sing her some of your love songs, she'd jump right out of the window to the ground to get to you."

Calandrino said: "Do you think so, my friend? Do you think I should go and get it?"

"Yes, I do," replied Bruno.

Calandrino said to him:

"You didn't believe me today when I told you, my friend: there's no doubt about it, I know better than any man how to get what I want. Who, besides me, would have known how to make a lady like her fall in love so quickly? Well now, do you think it could have been done by any of those young men so full of hot air who parade up and down all day long, and who are not even capable of picking up three handfuls of nuts in a thousand years? Now, just wait till you see what I can do with my rebec. Some playing you'll see! And I'll have you know I'm not as old as I look, and she sure noticed that, she did; but I'll make her notice it in some other way, if I get my paws on her, I swear to God, I'll play such a game with her that she'll chase me like crazy!"*

"Oh," exclaimed Bruno, "you'll stick your snout right in her. I can just see you now, with those lute-peg teeth of yours biting into that ruby-red mouth of hers and those two cheeks which look like roses, and then eating her all up."

When Calandrino heard these words, he imagined he was actually into the act itself, and he went around singing and skipping

---

*The original reads "like the madwoman after her son" (*come va la pazza al figliuolo*).

about, so happy that he almost jumped out of his skin. On the following day, he brought his rebec, and with it he sang a number of songs to the great amusement of everyone in the group; and to be brief about it, he became so eager to see her, and as often as he could, that he did no work at all, for a thousand times a day he would dash about to catch a glimpse of her, now at the window, now at the door, and now in the courtyard, while she, cunningly following Bruno's instructions, gave him every opportunity to do so. Bruno also took charge of Calandrino's messages, and on occasion he would even write an answer on her behalf: when she was not around, which was most of the time, Bruno would supply him with letters from her in which she gave him great hopes for fulfilling his desires but explained that since she was presently staying at some relatives' home, he could not see her. And in this manner, Bruno and Buffalmacco, who manipulated the affair, derived the greatest delight in the world from Calandrino's antics, and every so often they made Calandrino give them, as if at the lady's request, such things as an ivory comb, or a purse, or a little knife, and other such trifles, bringing him back in return some fake rings of no value whatsoever, which Calandrino accepted with the greatest of joy; and besides this, they got some good meals and other little favors out of him, which he offered them as encouragement to work on his behalf.

Now, after they had kept him on tenterhooks this way for a good two months without doing anything more, Calandrino, realizing that the job was coming to an end and that if he did not reap the fruits of his love before the work was completed he would never have another chance, began to press and solicit Bruno insistently; and so when the girl came there the next time, Bruno, after first making arrangements with Filippo and the girl as to what they had to do, said to Calandrino:

"Look here, my friend, this lady has promised me at least a thousand times that she is ready to do whatever you wish her to, and then she does nothing about it, and it seems to me she is leading you around by the nose. So, since she's not doing what she promised, we shall have to make her do it whether she wishes or not, if you agree to it."

Calandrino answered: "Ah, yes, for the love of God, let's do it and quick!"

Bruno said: "Do you have the courage to touch her with a magic formula I'll give you?"

"Of course," Calandrino said.

"Well, then," said Bruno, "get me some unborn-lamb parchment, a live bat, three grains of incense, and a candle that has been blessed, and leave it to me."

Calandrino spent that entire evening with his snares trying to catch a bat, and after he finally caught it, he took it, along with the other items, to Bruno. Bruno, withdrawing into a room, wrote on the parchment some nonsense phrases of his in magic-looking letters and then took it back to Calandrino, saying:

"Calandrino, you can be sure that if you touch her with this writing, she will come with you immediately and do anything you like. So if Filippo goes anywhere today, get near her somehow, touch her, and go to the hayloft at the side of the house, which is the best spot in the world, because nobody ever goes there, and you'll see that she'll come; and when she does, you know exactly what you have to do."

Calandrino was the happiest man in the world, and taking the writing, he said: "My friend, leave everything to me."

Nello, of whom Calandrino had to be very careful, was enjoying this affair just as much as the others, and with the rest of them, he had a hand in the trick; and so, just as Bruno had ordered him, he sent to Florence to Calandrino's wife and said to her:

"Tessa, you know how badly Calandrino beat you up without any reason the day he came home with the stones from the Mugnone; well, now I want you to get even with him, and if you don't, don't ever consider me a relative or a friend of yours again. Calandrino has fallen in love with a woman back there, some tramp who is always locking herself up with him in a room, and just a little while ago they agreed to get together very soon; so I want you to come up there and see for yourself, catch him, and fix him good."

When the woman heard this, she took it as no joke, and rising to her feet, she started saying:

"Ah, you common thief, so you're trying to put one over on me, are you? By the cross of God, you're not going to get away without paying for it!"

She grabbed her cloak, and taking a serving girl along to accompany her, she went racing off with Nello up to that place. When Bruno saw her coming from a distance, he said to Filippo: "Here comes our friend."

So Filippo went to where Calandrino and the others were working and said:

"Men, I must go to Florence immediately. Work hard." And

leaving them, he went to hide in a place where, without being seen, he could observe what Calandrino would be doing.

When Calandrino thought Filippo was far enough away, he went down into the courtyard, where he found Niccolosa by herself; he began talking with her, and she drew closer to him, and knowing very well what she was supposed to do, she employed a bit more familiarity with him than she usually did, whereupon Calandrino touched her with the writing. And as soon as he touched her, without saying a word he turned his steps toward the hayloft, and Niccolosa followed behind him; and once inside, she shut the door, embraced Calandrino, and threw him down on the ground covered with straw, and then she climbed on top of him, and straddling him, she pinned his shoulders to the ground with her hands so that he could not get close to her face, and then, as if gazing upon her greatest desire, she said:

"Oh, my sweet Calandrino, heart of my body, my soul, my salvation, my repose, how long I have waited to have you and to hold you to my breast! Your charm has pulled the legs right out from under me; you have enchanted my heart with your rebec; can it be true that I am holding you in my arms?"

Hardly able to move, Calandrino replied: "Ah, my sweet soul, let me kiss you."

Niccolosa said:

"Oh, you're in such a hurry! First, let me have a long look at you: let me fill my eyes with this sweet face of yours!"

Bruno and Buffalmacco had joined Filippo, and all three of them were watching and listening to this spectacle, and just when Calandrino was about to kiss Niccolosa, Nello arrived on the scene with Monna Tessa; as he arrived, Nello remarked: "I swear to God they're together"; when they reached the entrance to the hayloft, the woman, burning with anger, banged the door open with her hands, and once inside, she saw Niccolosa on top of Calandrino; when Niccolosa saw her, she quickly got up and ran off to where Filippo was hiding.

Before Calandrino could get up, Monna Tessa rushed at his face with her nails, and clawed him all over; and grabbing him by the hair, she pulled him all over the place as she said:

"You lousy, rotten dog, so this is what you do to me? Damn all the love I've given you, you old fool! So you don't think you have enough to do at home, and you've fallen in love with someone else? Here's a fine lover for you! Do you have any idea what you are, you villain? Do you know what you are, you sorry husband? Why, if you were squeezed dry, enough juice wouldn't come out to make a sauce. By God's faith, that woman making you pregnant just then* wasn't your wife Tessa, and may God punish whoever she was, for she must really be a poor creature to ever want a jewel like you!"

When Calandrino saw his wife coming in, he was so startled he did not know if he was dead or alive and lacked the courage to put up any defense against her; so, all scratched up, hair pulled out, and roughed up, he picked up his hat, got to his feet, and started begging humbly for his wife not to scream, unless she wanted to see him cut up into little pieces, since the woman who had been with him was the wife of the master of the house.

The woman answered: "Whoever she is, I hope God gives her a bad time!"

Bruno and Buffalmacco, who with Filippo and Niccolosa had laughed to their hearts' content over this spectacle, came in, pretending to have been attracted by all the noise; and after much discussion, they calmed down the woman, and advised Calandrino to go back to Florence and never come back there again, lest Filippo catch wind of the matter and do him some harm. And so then, Calandrino, forlorn and in a sorry state, all torn and scratched to pieces, returned to Florence, never daring to go back up there again, and resigned to being nagged and tormented day and night by the reproaches of his wife, he thus ended his passionate love affair, having provided a good deal of laughter for his companions, as well as for Niccolosa and Filippo.

[Ninth Day, Sixth Story]

❊

Two young men take lodgings at someone's home, where one of them lies with the host's daughter, while his wife inadvertently lies with the other; the man who was with the daughter gets into bed with her father and tells him everything, thinking he is speaking to his companion; they start quarreling; when the wife realizes what has happened, she gets into her daughter's bed and then, with certain remarks, she reconciles everyone.

CALANDRINO, who had made the company laugh on previous occasions, did so this time as well; and no sooner had the ladies

*See IX, 3.

ceased discussing his antics than the Queen commanded Panfilo to tell a story, and he said:

Praiseworthy ladies, the name of Niccolosa, who was loved by Calandrino, calls to mind a tale about another Niccolosa, which I should like to tell you, for in it you will see how a good woman's quick presence of mind prevented a serious scandal.

In the valley of the Mugnone, not long ago, there lived a worthy man who for a charge provided food and drink to travelers; and though he was a poor man and his house was small, he would, from time to time, in cases of extreme emergency, provide lodgings not for strangers but for someone he knew. Now this man had a wife who was a beautiful woman, and by her he had two children: one was a lovely and sprightly girl of about fifteen or sixteen years old, who still had no husband; the other was a small boy who was less than a year old and still nursing at his mother's breasts.

The young girl had caught the eye of a handsome and charming young gentleman from our city, who spent much time in the country, and he fell passionately in love with her; and she, who was very proud of being loved so passionately by such a young man, striving to retain his affection with pleasing glances, fell as much in love with him; and on numerous occasions such a love could have been consummated to the delight of both parties, if Pinuccio (this was the young man's name) had not feared disgracing the young lady and himself. But then, as their ardor increased from day to day, Pinuccio felt that he had to be with the girl and that he had to find a way to take lodgings with her father, for if he could do that, knowing the layout of the girl's house, he might be able to get together with her without anyone's seeing them; and no sooner did this idea come into his head than he immediately put it into effect.

Late one afternoon, Pinuccio, together with a trusted companion of his named Adriano, who knew all about his love, hired two packhorses, and having loaded them with a couple of saddlebags stuffed probably with straw, they left Florence, and after riding around in a circle, they came to the Mugnone river valley when it was already dark. And from there they turned their horses around to make it seem as though they were returning from Romagna, and rode toward the house of that worthy man and knocked at his door; since the man was a friend of theirs, he immediately opened the door, and Pinuccio said to him:

"Look, you'll have to put us up for the night. We thought we would make it to Florence, but as you can see, we only made it as far as here at this late hour."

To this, the innkeeper replied:

"Pinuccio, you are well aware how poorly equipped I am to lodge such gentlemen as yourselves; however, since this late hour has caught you here and there is not time to go elsewhere, I shall gladly put you up for the night as best I can."

So the two young men, after dismounting and stabling their nags, went into the small house, and since they had brought plenty to eat for supper, they ate supper with their host. Now the host had only one very tiny bedroom, into which he had squeezed three small beds as best he could; nor was there much space left over, what with two of them along one wall of the bedroom and the third on the opposite side against the other wall, and only with great difficulty could you pass between them. The host had the least uncomfortable of the three beds made up for his two friends and then invited them to lie down; then, after a while, when the two of them appeared to be asleep, but neither of them was really asleep, the host had his daughter go to bed in one of the two remaining beds, and he and his wife got into the other bed, by the side of which she placed the cradle in which she kept her infant son.

After things had been arranged in this manner and Pinuccio had observed everything, a little later, when he thought everyone was asleep, he quietly got up and went over to the little bed where his lady love was lying and he lay down beside her; although she was frightened by his appearance she welcomed him joyously, and together they enjoyed that pleasure which they had so much desired. And while Pinuccio was with the girl a cat happened to knock some things over, and the noise woke up the wife, who, fearing it was something else, got out of bed, and in the dark, naked as she was, she went over to where she had heard the noise. Adriano, who had not heard the noise, happened to get up because of a physical need, and as he was going to satisfy it, he discovered the cradle the lady had placed by her bed, and unable to get by it without moving it, he took it, lifted it up from the spot where it was standing, and placed it beside the bed in which he slept; after satisfying the need which had gotten him up, he returned to his bed, and without paying any attention to the cradle, climbed back into it.

After investigating and discovering that what had fallen down was of no importance, the wife yelled at the cat, and without bothering to light a lamp in order to look around, she returned to the bedroom and groped her way straight to the bed where her husband was sleeping; but finding no cradle there, she said to herself: "Oh, how stupid of me. Look what I was about to do!

Good God, I was heading straight for the bed of my guests!"
Going on a bit farther and finding the cradle, she got into bed
with Adriano, thinking she was in bed with her husband. Adri-
ano, who had not yet fallen back to sleep, gave her a happy wel-
come when he felt her there, and without saying a word, he
came hard about on her, to the great delight of the lady.

And while they were thus engaged, Pinuccio, having had the
pleasure he desired and now fearing that he might fall asleep
with his young lady, arose from her side in order to return to his
own bed; when he reached it, discovering the cradle there, he
thought it was the bed of his host, and so, going a bit farther
ahead, he got into bed with the host, who awakened on Pinuc-
cio's arrival. Believing that he was next to Adriano, Pinuccio
said:

"I swear there was nothing sweeter than being in bed with
Niccolosa. Jesus, I had the greatest time with her a man could
ever have with a woman, and I can tell you, I stopped up her
front door at least six times before leaving her."

When the innkeeper heard this bit of news, he was not overly
pleased by it, and at first said to himself: "What the hell is he
doing here?" Then, more angry than well-advised, he said:
"Pinuccio, what you have done is truly foul, and I don't know
why you did it to me: but, by the body of Christ, I shall make
you pay for it."

Pinuccio, who was not the most intelligent young man in the
world, realizing his mistake, did not try to make amends as best
he might have, but replied: "How will you pay me back? What
could you do to me?"

The innkeeper's wife, who thought she was with her husband,
said to Adriano: "Oh, my, listen to our guests, they're quarreling
with each other."

Laughing, Adriano said: "Let them alone, and to hell with
them—they drank too much last night."

Thinking she heard her husband grumbling over there and now
hearing Adriano, the lady immediately realized where she was
and whom she was with; so, being a woman of some intelligence,
without saying another word, she got out of bed and, picking up
her son's cradle, she groped her way across the room, for there
was no light at all, and put it beside the bed in which she
thought her daughter was sleeping and got in beside her; and
pretending she had just been awakened by the racket her hus-
band was making, she called out to him asking him why he was
arguing with Pinuccio, and her husband replied: "Didn't you
hear what he says he did to Niccolosa tonight?"

His wife said:

"He's lying through his teeth, he never slept with Niccolosa; why, I've been lying here and haven't closed my eyes once, and you're a fool if you believe him. You drink so much in the evening that you dream all night and wander about without knowing it, and you think you've performed all sorts of miracles; it's a great pity you don't all break your necks! But what's Pinuccio doing over there? Why isn't he in his own bed?"

At this point, seeing how cleverly the lady was covering up her own shame and that of her daughter, Adriano said:

"Pinuccio, I've told you a hundred times that you shouldn't wander about at night and that this bad habit of yours of getting up in your sleep and then telling stories that you've dreamed up would get you in trouble one day. Now come back here, damn you!"

When the host heard what his wife and Adriano were saying, he began to believe that Pinuccio was really dreaming; so, taking him by the shoulders, he began shaking him and calling him; he said: "Pinuccio, wake up, go back to your bed."

Having understood everything that they said, Pinuccio, pretending that he was still dreaming, began uttering nonsense, as the host roared with laughter over this. Finally, as he felt himself being shaken, he pretended to awaken, and calling Adriano, he said: "Is it morning already? Why are you calling me?"

Adriano replied: "Yes, it is, come over here."

Continuing his act, and pretending to be very sleepy, Pinuccio finally got up from the host's side and went back to bed with Adriano, and when day came and they got out of bed, the host began to laugh and to make fun of Pinuccio and his dreams. And in this manner, between one joke and another, the two young men got ready, saddled their nags, packed their saddlebags, and after having a drink with the host, they got on their horses and went on to Florence, no less delighted with the adventure than with the way things turned out. And then afterward, Pinuccio found other ways of meeting with Niccolosa, who kept insisting to her mother that Pinuccio really had been dreaming; and thus, remembering Adriano's embraces, the woman was convinced that she alone had been the only one awake.

[Ninth Day, Seventh Story]

✳

Talano d'Imole dreams that a wolf rips apart his wife's throat and face; he tells her to be wary of this; she does not do so, and it happens to her.

WHEN Panfilo's story came to an end and the lady's resourcefulness was praised by everyone, the Queen told Pampinea to tell her story, and so she began:

Delightful ladies, we have discussed on previous occasions how truth may be revealed by dreams, which many of us are wont to scoff at; and even though this topic has been treated before, I cannot leave it without telling you a rather brief little tale about what happened, not so long ago, to a neighbor of mine who did not believe a dream her husband had in which she appeared.

I do not know whether or not you are acquainted with Talano d'Imolese, a very honorable man. This man had taken as his wife a young lady named Margherita, more beautiful than all other women, but also more ill-tempered, unpleasant, and cantankerous than any other, and to such a degree that she would never follow anyone's advice, nor was anyone ever able to please her. Though Talano found this difficult to bear, since he could do nothing about it, he had to put up with it.

Now it happened one night while Talano was asleep with this Margherita of his in their country house that he dreamed he saw his wife walking around in a very beautiful forest, which was not far away from the house they owned; and while he watched her wandering about in this manner, he imagined that a large and ferocious wolf came out from a certain part of the woods and suddenly leaped at her throat, dragging her to the ground as she screamed for help and tried to free herself. When she escaped from its jaws, her entire face and throat appeared to be torn to pieces.

When the man got up the next morning, he said to his wife: "Madam, although your ill temper has never allowed me to enjoy a single pleasant day with you, I should nevertheless be unhappy if any harm came to you; and so, if you take my advice, you will not leave the house today." When she asked him why, he recounted his dream in detail to her.

Tossing her head, the lady declared:

"Evil wishes beget evil dreams. You are pretending to be very considerate of me, but you are dreaming about me what you would like to see happen to me, and you can be sure that I shall be most careful, today and always, never to make you happy with this or any other misfortune of mine."

Then Talano replied:

"I was certain that you were going to say this, for that's the thanks you get when you waste favors on an ungrateful person; but believe what you like; for my part, I am speaking for your own good, and once more, I advise you to stay inside the house today, or at least to keep away from our woods."

The lady said: "All right, I'll do that," but later, she began to think to herself: "You see what a crafty fellow he is, thinking he could scare me away from going into our woods today? I'm sure he's made an appointment with some wretch of a woman, and he doesn't want me to find him there. Ah! He'd certainly eat well at a dinner for the blind,* and I'd be a real fool to believe him and not see through his plan! He's certainly not going to get away with this; even if I have to stay there the whole day, I'm going to see what business it is he's up to now."

No sooner had she reached this conclusion than her husband left the house by one exit and she by another; and as quickly as she could, she secretly made for the woods, and there, in the thickest place she could find, she hid herself, and kept a close lookout on all sides to see if anyone was coming. And while she waited this way, without the slightest fear of there being a wolf in the area, suddenly, from a dense thicket near her, there emerged a large and ferocious wolf. She scarcely had time to cry "God, help me!" before the wolf had leaped at her throat, and seizing her tightly, began to carry her off as if she were a baby lamb. The wolf held her throat so tightly that she was unable to scream or to help herself in any way; and the wolf, as it carried her off, would have strangled her without any doubt if it had not run into some shepherds, who by yelling at it forced the beast to drop her. The poor and unfortunate woman, having been recognized by the shepherds, was carried to her home by them, and after being treated for a long while by doctors she was cured, but not so completely that her entire throat and a part of her face were not disfigured in the process, and whereas earlier she had been beautiful, she was from then on hideous and disfigured.

*That is, he would eat there so that unseen by the blind he could steal their food.

Thus being ashamed to show herself in public, she often wept miserably over her ill temper and her refusal to believe, though it would have cost her nothing, in the truth of her husband's dream.

[Ninth Day, Eighth Story]

✦

Biondello plays a trick on Ciacco in regard to a dinner, for which Ciacco carefully takes his revenge by having Biondello soundly thrashed.

EVERYONE in the merry company declared that what Talano had seen while he was asleep was not a dream but rather a vision, since it happened exactly as he dreamed it. But when they all fell silent, the Queen ordered Lauretta to continue, and she said:

Most wise ladies, just as almost all those who have spoken before me today were moved to discuss something previously talked about, in like manner, the inflexible vendetta carried out by the scholar, recounted yesterday by Pampinea, prompts me to tell you of another vendetta which had very serious consequences for the man who suffered its effects, although it was not as harsh as that one.

Let me tell you, then, that in Florence there once lived a man everyone called Ciacco, who was the greatest glutton who ever lived, and since his means could not sustain the expenses his gluttony required, being the extremely well-mannered man that he was, full of clever and delightful witticisms, he devoted himself to being not precisely a courtier but rather a sharp conversationalist, and to frequenting the company of wealthy people who delighted in eating good food; and with such people he would very often dine or take supper, even when he was not always invited. There also lived in those days in Florence a person who was called Biondello, a little fellow, always extremely well dressed and neater than a fly, with a cap on his head of long, blond hair, done up in such a way that not a strand of hair was out of place, and this fellow exercised the same trade as Ciacco.

One morning during Lent, when Biondello happened to be at the fish market buying two huge lampreys for Messer Vieri de' Cerchi, he was observed by Ciacco; approaching Biondello, Ciacco said: "What's going on here?"

To this question, Biondello replied:

"Last night, three other lampreys, even more beautiful than these, and a sturgeon were sent to Messer Corso Donati, but since they were not sufficient to feed a number of gentlemen he invited, he had me buy these other two. Won't you be coming?"

Ciacco answered: "You can be sure I'll be there."

And so, at what seemed to him the proper time, Ciacco went to Messer Corso's home and found him there with some of his neighbors, who were waiting to go to dine; when he was asked by them what he was doing there, Ciacco answered: "Sir, I am here to dine with you and your company."

To this, Messer Corso said: "You are most welcome, and since it is time, let us go."

Then, after sitting down to the table, they were first served some chickpeas and tuna bellies, then some fried fish from the Arno River, and nothing else. Ciacco, who realized the trick Biondello had played on him, was more than just slightly upset by it, and decided to pay him back for it; not many days passed before he bumped into Biondello, who had already made a great many people laugh over this trick of his. When Biondello saw Ciacco coming, he greeted him, and with a smile asked him how Messer Corso's lampreys had tasted; to this question, Ciacco replied: "Before the end of the week, you'll know much better than I."

After leaving Biondello, Ciacco set to work without delay, and having agreed on a price with a clever marketman, he gave him a big glass flask, led him to a place in the Loggia de' Cavicciuli, and pointing out to him a gentleman named Messer Filippo Argenti—an enormous, muscular, powerful man, who was more haughty, irascible, and touchy than any other man alive—he said to him: "You will go to him with this flask in your hand and say the following: 'Sir, Biondello sends me to you, and he begs you to be so kind as to rubify this flask with your good red wine, for he wishes to have some fun with his drinking buddies'; and be careful that he doesn't get his hands on you, or he's sure to give you a bad time of it, and you would spoil my plans."

The marketman said: "Do I have to say anything else?"

Ciacco replied: "No, go on now, and as soon as you have said this, come back here to me with the flask, and I'll pay you."

And so the marketman went and delivered the message to Messer Filippo. When Messer Filippo heard what the man had to say, he turned red in the face with anger, for he was a short-tempered man, and realizing that Biondello, whom he knew, was playing a trick on him, he said:

"What is all this 'rubify' and 'drinking buddies'? God damn both you and him!" He got to his feet and stretched out his arm to grab the marketman with his hand, but the marketman, who was on his guard, quickly ran off and then returned by another route to Ciacco, who had watched the whole thing, and he told Ciacco what Messer Filippo had said.

Satisfied, Ciacco paid the marketman, but from then on he had no rest until he found Biondello, to whom he said:

"Has it been a long time since you've been to the Loggia de' Cavicciuli?"

Biondello answered: "Not long: why do you ask?"

Ciacco said: "Because I know that Messer Filippo was looking for you, but I don't know what he wants."

Then Biondello said: "Thanks, I'm going in that direction, so I'll have a word with him."

When Biondello left, Ciacco followed behind to see how the affair was going to turn out. Messer Filippo, unable to catch up with the marketman, was left terribly upset and consumed with anger, for he could make no sense at all out of the words spoken by the marketman except that Biondello, prompted by some other person, was probably making fun of him; and it was just as he was seething with anger this way that Biondello arrived. When Filippo spotted him, he ran to meet him and gave him a terrific punch in the face.

"Ouch! Sir," exclaimed Biondello, "what's the meaning of this?"

Grabbing him by the hair, ripping the cap off the top of his head, throwing his cloak on the ground, and punching him hard in the meantime, Messer Filippo exclaimed:

"Scoundrel, you're certainly going to find out what it means now! So you send me people with all this talk of 'rubifying' and 'drinking buddies'? Do you think I'm some kind of child you can make fun of?"

As he said all this, Filippo was pounding Biondello all over his face with his fists, which were like iron, and he left not a hair on his head in place; rolling him about in the mud, he tore the clothes off his back; and Filippo so enthusiastically performed his task that from the moment he began, Biondello was unable to get even a single word out or even to ask why Filippo was doing all this to him. What he heard, of course, was Filippo say something about 'rubifying' and 'drinking buddies,' but he had no idea what all this meant. Finally, after Messer Filippo had given him a sound thrashing and a big crowd had gathered around them, with the greatest difficulty in the world, they managed to pull Biondello out of his clutches, all messed up and disheveled as he was; then they explained to him why Messer Filippo had done this, reproaching Biondello for having sent Filippo the message and telling him that from now on, he should keep in mind what kind of fellow Messer Filippo was and that he was not a man to be dealt with lightly. Weeping, Biondello made excuses, stating that he had never sent anyone to Messer Filippo for wine; but later, after he had fixed himself up a bit, forlorn and sorrowful, he returned home, knowing that this affair must have been the work of Ciacco.

Then, after a number of days had passed, when the bruises had faded from his face, Biondello began going out again, and he happened to run into Ciacco, who asked him with a smile: "Biondello, how did Messer Filippo's wine taste to you?"

Biondello replied: "Just about the same as Messer Corso's lampreys tasted to you!"

Then Ciacco said:

"From now on, it's up to you: whenever you wish to treat me to the kind of meal you did, I'll treat you to the kind of drink you got."

Knowing he was better able to wish Ciacco ill than to do him any real harm, Biondello bid him good day, and from that time on, he was always careful never to play any more tricks on Ciacco.

[Ninth Day, Ninth Story]

✤

Two young men ask advice from Solomon, one of them as to what he must do to be loved, the other as to how he should punish his stubborn wife: Solomon tells the first man to love and the other to go to the Goose Bridge.

IF Dioneo's privilege was to be respected, no one remained to tell a story other than the Queen; and after the ladies had laughed heartily over the unfortunate Biondello, she cheerfully began to speak in this manner:

Lovable ladies, if the order of things is considered with a sound mind, it is very easy to see that women in general are subservient by nature, custom, and laws to men by whose judgment they ought to be ruled and governed; and therefore, if any woman wishes to have tranquillity, comfort, and rest, she must be humble, patient, and obedient to the man to whom she belongs, as well as being chaste, which is the crowning and special treasure of every wise woman. And even if this were not taught us by the law, which concerns the common good in all matters, and usage (or custom, as we may wish to say), whose force is very powerful and revered, Nature very clearly demonstrates it to us, for she has made us delicate and soft in our bodies, timid and easily frightened in our hearts, kindly and compassionate in our minds, and she has bestowed upon us weaker physical strength, pleasing voices, and soft bodily movements: all these things testify to our need for the guidance of another. And there is every reason that anyone who requires assistance and guidance should be obedient, submissive, and respectful to his ruler. And whom do we have as our rulers and protectors if not men? Therefore, we should subject ourselves to men, paying them the highest of honors, and I believe that anyone who does otherwise deserves not only harsh criticism but also severe punishment. I have on other occasions expressed such a view, and just a while ago my opinions were confirmed by what Pampinea told us concerning Talano's stubborn wife, upon whom God visited that punishment which her husband did not know how to give her; and therefore, as I have already said before, in my judgment, all those women deserve firm and harsh punishment who are not pleasant, kindly, and compliant, as Nature, usage, and the laws require. And so it is a pleasure for me to tell you about the piece of advice Solomon once gave, since it is a useful medicine for curing those women who suffer from such a disease; and let no woman who considers herself undeserving of such a medicine feel that this is intended for her, though men do have a proverb which says: "Both good and bad horses require the spur, just as both good and bad women require the stick." Anyone who sees the humor in these words will readily agree that they are true; but I say that they are also admissible if they are considered in their moral sense. All women by nature are pliant and yielding, and therefore, for those women who allow themselves to go far beyond the bounds imposed upon them, the stick is required to correct their transgressions; and in order to sustain the virtue of those other women, so that they will not allow themselves to overstep these limits, the stick is required to encourage and frighten them. But now, let us set aside this preaching, and coming to what I have in mind to tell you, let me say that when the lofty fame of Solomon's miraculous wisdom, as well as his reputation for generously demonstrating this wisdom to anyone who wished to verify it in person, had spread over the entire world, many people from different parts of the globe, moved by their most pressing and perplexing problems, flocked to him for advice; and among those who came there for that reason was a young and very wealthy nobleman named Melisso from the city of Laiazzo where he was born and bred. And as he rode in the direction of Jerusalem, after leaving Antioch he happened to find himself in the company of another young man named Giosefo, who was taking the same road as he, and with whom he rode for some time. As is the custom of travelers, Melisso began to converse with him. Having learned Giosefo's station in life and from where he came, Melisso asked him where he was going and why. Giosefo replied that he was going to Solomon to seek his counsel as to how he should deal with his wife, who was the most stubborn and perverse woman in the world and whom, in spite of all his entreaties, praises, and everything else, he was unable to dissuade from her pigheadedness, and then Giosefo, in like manner, asked where Melisso was from and where he was going and why.

To this, Melisso replied:

"I am from Laiazzo, and just as you suffer a misfortune, so, too, do I suffer from one; I am a rich young man and spend my money giving banquets and entertaining my fellow citizens, and the strange and unusual thing about it is that for all this, I am unable to find someone who loves me, and so I am going where you are going to seek advice about what to do in order that I may be loved."

So the two companions traveled along together, and once they reached Jerusalem and were ushered into the presence of Solomon by one of his lords, Melisso briefly explained his problem to him, to which Solomon replied: "Love."

After Solomon had said this, Melisso was immediately ushered out, and Giosefo explained his reason for being there; to him, Solomon gave no other reply but "Go to the Goose Bridge." And as soon as Solomon said this, without any delay, Giosefo was removed from the King's presence; and finding Melisso waiting for him there, he told him the response he had received.

The two men, thinking about Solomon's words but unable to see any meaning in them or remedy for their problems, feeling they had been made fools of, set out for home. And having traveled for a number of days, they came to a river over which there was a beautiful bridge; and since a long caravan of mules and packhorses loaded with merchandise was crossing, they had to wait until all of them had passed over. And when almost all of them had crossed over, there happened to be one mule there

that was balking, as we often see mules do, and that would, un-
der no conditions, move ahead: because of this, a muleteer
picked up a stick and began, at first rather gently, to beat the
mule in order to make it cross. But the mule, turning sideways
now to one side of the bridge and now to the other, and some-
times turning right around, was in no way willing to cross; and
so the muleteer, angered beyond all measure, began to beat the
daylights out of the mule with the stick, now on its head, now on
its flanks, and now on its rump, but all was in vain.

And so Melisso and Giosefo, who were standing by watching
the spectacle, would say to the muleteer from time to time: "Ah,
you wicked man, what are you doing? Do you want to kill it?
Why don't you try leading it off kindly and quietly? He'll come
more readily than by beating him, the way you're doing."

To this the muleteer replied: "You know your horses, and I
know my mule! Let me handle it." And having said this, he be-
gan once more to beat the mule, and he gave it so many blows
on one side and on another that the mule moved on, and the mu-
leteer won the contest.

As the two young men were then about to leave, Giosefo
asked a kindly man, who was seated at the head of the bridge,
what this place was called; to this, the kindly man replied: "Sir,
this is called the Goose Bridge."

When Giosefo heard this, he quickly remembered Solomon's
words and said to Melisso:

"Now let me tell you this, my friend, the advice Solomon gave
me may yet prove to be good and sound, for now it is very clear
to me that I never knew how to beat my wife, and this muleteer
has shown me what I must do."

Then, after a few days, they reached Antioch, and Giosefo in-
vited Melisso to stay with him for several days to rest. After re-
ceiving a rather cool greeting from his wife, Giosefo told her
that she was to fix whatever Melisso ordered for supper; since
Melisso saw that this would please Giosefo, he hastened to ex-
plain what he wanted in a few words. Just as she was accus-
tomed to doing in the past, the woman did not do as Melisso
requested but, rather, she did the exact opposite.

When Giosefo saw this, he said angrily: "Didn't he tell you
how you were to fix his supper?"

Turning arrogantly to Melisso, his wife replied: "What are you
talking about? Hey! If you're going to eat supper, eat it! If I
was told otherwise, I preferred to do it this way; if you like it,
you like it; if not, that's the way you get it!"

Melisso was astonished at the woman's reply and criticized her harshly: when Giosefo heard this, he said:

"Lady, you're just the same as ever, but believe me, I shall make you change your ways." Turning to Melisso, he said: "My friend, we shall soon see what kind of advice it was that Solomon gave us, and please be good enough to remain here and observe and consider what I am about to do as merely a game. And to keep yourself from interfering with what I do, bear in mind the answer that the muleteer gave us when we took pity on his mule."

To this request, Melisso said: "I am a guest in your home, and I have no intention of departing from your wishes."

Giosefo found a stout stick from a young oak tree and went into his wife's bedroom, to which she had gone grumbling and in an angry mood after leaving the table; and seizing her by the hair, he threw her to the floor at his feet and began to whip her fiercely with the stick. First the woman began to scream and then to threaten him, but when she saw that in spite of all her efforts, Giosefo would not stop, battered all over as she was, she began to beg for God's mercy not to kill her, declaring, moreover, that she would never do another thing to displease him. In spite of all this, Giosefo did not cease; on the contrary, he beat her all the more, one blow more fierce than the next, now on her ribs, now on her thighs, and now on her shoulders, as he went looking for all her joints, and he did not stop until he was exhausted—in short, there was not a bone or any place on the good woman's back which was not bruised. And after he had done all this, he went up to Melisso and said to him:

"Tomorrow we'll see how the advice 'Go to Goose Bridge' has fared." He rested awhile and then washed his hands and ate supper with Melisso, and when it was time, they went to bed.

The wretched woman got up from the floor with great difficulty and threw herself on the bed, where, as best she could, she rested, and on the following morning, after getting up very early, she asked Giosefo what he wanted her to fix for dinner. Laughing over this with Melisso, he gave his orders; and then, when it was time, they came home and discovered that everything had been prepared extremely well and according to the orders he had given; and so they highly praised the advice which they had at first badly understood.

After a few days, Melisso left Giosefo and returned to his home, and he explained to someone who was a wise man what he had learned from Solomon and this man said to him:

"He could not have given you sounder or better advice. You

know you really do not love anyone and that the banquets you give and the favors you perform do not stem from any love you bear for someone else but rather from your own vainglory. Love, therefore, just as Solomon has told you, and you will be loved."

And so in such fashion was the shrew punished, and the young man by loving was loved in return.

[Ninth Day, Tenth Story]

✦

At Compare *Pietro's request, Father Gianni casts a spell in order to turn his wife into a mare; but when it comes time to stick the tail on, Pietro, by saying that he doesn't want a tail, ruins the whole spell.*

THIS tale told by the Queen caused some murmuring among the ladies and some laughter from the young men. Then, as soon as they had quieted down, Dioneo began to speak in this fashion:

Charming ladies, the beauty of a flock of white doves is enhanced more by a black crow than by a pure white swan; and in like manner, one less intelligent person among many who are wise will sometimes add not only splendor and beauty to their wisdom but delight and amusement as well. Accordingly, since you are all ladies of the utmost discretion and restraint, whereas I am more or less of a simpleton who makes your virtue more resplendent with my own deficiencies, you should hold me more dear than if I were to diminish your virtue with my own superior worth; and hence, in telling you the story I am about to relate I must have greater license, in order to show myself for what I truly am, and I must be more patiently tolerated by you than if I were a wiser man. I shall tell you a story, then, which is not very long, in which you will learn how carefully the instructions of those who do things under the power of a spell should be followed, and how the slightest deviation from the rules can spoil all the magician's work.

A year or so ago at Barletta there was a priest called Father Gianni di Barolo who, because his church was a poor one, was obliged to earn his living by transporting goods with his mare here and there to the various fairs of Puglia, and by buying and selling. As he went about his business, he became very friendly with a man who was called Pietro da Tresanti, who practiced the same trade with a donkey, and as a sign of his love and friendship, he always addressed him in the fashion of Puglia as *Compare* Pietro. And whenever Pietro came to Barletta, he always invited him to his church, where he gave him lodgings and entertained him as best he could.

Compare Pietro was a very poor man who owned a small house in Tresanti, barely large enough for him, his young and beautiful wife, and his donkey. But whenever Father Gianni happened to be in Tresanti, he always took him to his home and tried to entertain him as best he knew how in gratitude for the hospitality his friend had shown him in Barletta. But there was the problem of lodgings: since *Compare* Pietro had only one small bed, in which he and his beautiful wife slept, he could not entertain Father Gianni as he wished. Father Gianni, therefore, was forced to sleep on a pile of straw in the stable with Pietro's donkey and his own mare for company.

Pietro's wife knew how well the priest entertained her husband at Barletta, and often, when the priest came, she would suggest that she go sleep with a neighbor of theirs named Zita Carapresa di Giudice Leo, so that the priest could sleep with her husband in their bed. And she suggested this many times to the priest, but he would never agree to it; in fact, on one occasion he said to her:

"*Comare* Gemmata, don't bother about me. I'm fine. You see, whenever I want to, I can change this mare of mine into a beautiful young girl and lie with her. Then, whenever I wish, I can turn her back into a mare. And so I'd never want to be separated from her."

This story amazed the young woman, who believed it. She told the story to her husband, and then added: "If he is such a good friend of yours, why don't you have him teach you this magic spell so that you can turn me into a mare and go about your business with both a donkey and a mare? That way, we'll make twice as much money. And once we're home, you can turn me back into a woman, the way I am now."

Compare Pietro, who was more or less a simpleton, believed this story and took his wife's advice. As best he knew how, he began urging Father Gianni to teach him the magic spell. Father Gianni tried his best to dissuade him from this foolishness, but was unable to, and he said:

"Very well, since you will have it no other way, we shall get up early tomorrow morning as usual, before dawn, and I shall show you how it is done. The most difficult part of this task, as you shall soon see, is sticking the tail on."

Compare Pietro and *Comare* Gemmata, who hardly slept a wink that night, so eagerly were they looking forward to the coming event, got out of bed before day was about to break and woke up Father Gianni, who, still in his nightshirt, came into *Compare* Pietro's little bedroom and said:

"There is no person in the world other than you for whom I would do this favor, and since it pleases you, I shall do it; but you must do what I tell you to do if you want it to succeed."

The two said that they would do whatever he told them to do, and so Father Gianni picked up a candle, put it in *Compare* Pietro's hand, and said to him:

"Watch carefully everything I do and memorize what I say, and no matter what you hear me say or see me do, be sure you do not utter a word; otherwise you will ruin everything. And pray to God that the tail sticks on firmly!"

Compare Pietro took the candle and said that he would do as he was told. Then Father Gianni made *Comare* Gemmata take off all her clothes and stand with her hands and feet on the ground as if she were a mare, warning her as well that no matter what happened she was not to utter a word; and as his hands caressed her face and her head, he began to say:

"Let this be the beautiful head of a mare."

Then, stroking her hair, he said:

"Let this be the beautiful mane of a mare."

And then, fondling her arms, he said:

"And let these be the beautiful front legs and hooves of a mare."

Then, as he fondled her breasts, finding them to be round and firm, a certain something-or-other was aroused, and it stood straight up, and he said:

"And let this be the beautiful chest of a mare."

And he did the same thing to her back, her stomach, her buttocks, her thighs, and her legs; and finally, with nothing left to do but the tail, he lifted his nightshirt and took out his tool for planting men, and quickly sticking it into the furrow for which it was made, he said:

"And let this be the beautiful tail of a mare."

When *Compare* Pietro, who had carefully observed everything up to that point, saw this last maneuver, he said disapprovingly:

"Oh, Father Gianni, no tail! I really don't want a tail there!"

The vital liquid which all plants need to take root had already come when Father Gianni, having pulled it out, replied:

"Alas! *Compare* Pietro! What have you done? Didn't I warn you not to say a word about what you saw? The mare was just about to be made, but now your babbling has ruined everything, and there's no way of ever making another one."

Compare Pietro said:

"That's fine with me—I didn't want that kind of tail anyway! Why didn't you ask me to do it? Besides, you stuck it on too low."

Father Gianni replied:

"Because it was your first time, and you wouldn't have known how to stick it on as well as I can."

The girl, hearing these words, rose to her feet, and in all seriousness she said to her husband:

"You're an idiot! Why did you ruin both your business and mine? Have you ever seen a mare that didn't have a tail? So help me God, poor man that you are, you deserve to be even poorer!"

Now that there was no longer any way to change the girl into a mare because *Compare* Pietro had spoken when he had, she, sad and forlorn, put on her clothes again, and *Compare* Pietro prepared to take up his old trade again with just one donkey as he was used to; and with Father Gianni he went off to the fair at Bitonto, but never again did he ask his friend for the same favor.

[Ninth Day, Conclusion]

How much the ladies laughed over this story, whose meaning was better grasped than Dioneo had intended, may be left to the imagination of that fair reader of mine who is still laughing over it. But now the stories had come to an end, the sun's heat had already begun to grow cooler, and the Queen, knowing that her reign was coming to an end, rose to her feet and, removing her crown, placed it on the head of Panfilo, who alone remained to be honored with such favor, and, smiling, she said:

"My lord, you are left with a difficult task, for you, being the last, must make amends for my shortcomings and those of the others who have held the position you now hold. May God grant you His grace, just as He has granted it to me in proclaiming you King."

Happy to accept the honor, Panfilo replied:

"Your excellence and that of my other subjects will ensure that my reign will be as worthy of praise as the others before it have been." And following the custom of his predecessors, having made the necessary arrangements with the steward, he turned to the waiting ladies and declared: "Enamored ladies, Emilia, who has been our Queen today, in her wisdom gave you the freedom to tell whatever story pleased you most, so that you might give your talents a rest, but now that we have rested, I think it better that we return to our normal rule, and therefore tomorrow I want each of you to be ready to tell a story on a subject concerning those who have acted generously or magnificently in affairs of the heart or other matters. Telling these stories and hearing them will, without a doubt, kindle your spirits to follow a lofty course of action (your spirits, in fact, are already well disposed in that direction), and in so doing, our lives, which cannot be anything but brief within our mortal bodies, will be perpetuated through fame of our praiseworthy achievements, which anyone who thinks beyond his belly should not only desire but strive for with every bit of his strength."

The topic pleased the happy group, and with the new King's permission they all arose from where they were sitting and turned to their usual pastimes, each doing whatever pleased him most; and this they did until it was time for supper, to which they came in a festive mood, and at the end of the meal, having been served meticulously and with decorum, they arose and started their usual dances, and after singing nearly a thousand songs, all more amusing in their lyrics than masterful in their melodies, the King ordered Neifile to sing a song of her own; in a clear and happy voice, she immediately began to sing most charmingly:

I'm young and how I love to sing
and take delight in early spring,
all thanks to Love and the sweet thoughts it brings.

I wander through green fields and see
golden and white and red blooms grow,
roses upon their thorns, and whitest lilies,
and I compare all these to him
whose face that capturing my love,
holds on to me and always will,
as one who wishes naught but his delight.

When I find one among these blooms,
a flower, I feel, most like him,
I pluck it, kiss it, speak to it,
and so, in my own way, I open up
my soul to it and to my heart's desire;
then with the rest, I weave it in a crown
of flowers for my fine and golden hair.

And the delight a flower gives the eyes
through nature's power I receive, but more,
as though I saw in person he
who has inflamed me with his gentle love;
and what its perfume does to me
could never be expressed in words alone;
my sighs, though, bear true witness of its power.

The sighs that issue from my breast are never
harsh and troubled, as other women's are,
but, rather, soft and warm they come from me
and rush into the presence of my love,
and when he feels them, straightaway he moves
to give me pleasure, and he comes just when
I am about to say: "Ah, come, lest I despair."

Neifile's song was highly praised by the King and all the
ladies; then, since much of the evening had already passed, the
King ordered that all of them should go and rest until morning.

[Tenth Day, Title Page]

❧

Here ends the ninth day of The Decameron: *and the tenth and last day begins, in which, under the rule of Panfilo, stories are told concerning those who have acted generously or magnificently in affairs of the heart or other matters.*

[Tenth Day, Introduction]

❧

SOME of the small clouds in the west were still a rosy color while those in the east, caught by the rays of the approaching sun, were shining gold around their edges when Panfilo got up and had the ladies and his companions roused. And once they were all there, he discussed with them the place they should go to amuse themselves, and accompanied by Filomena and Fiammetta, he set out at a slow pace with all the others following them. They walked along for quite some time amusing themselves by discussing a number of things concerning their plans for the future, and answering each other's questions, until, after having walked a good distance, they found the sun had become too hot, and they returned to the palace. And there, having gathered around the clear fountain and rinsed some glasses, whoever wished to do so drank, and then, in the pleasant shade of the garden, they wandered about amusing themselves until it was time to eat. And after they had eaten and slept, as was their custom they all gathered at the place chosen by the King, and there the King ordered Neifile to tell the first tale; and she began cheerfully in this fashion.

[Tenth Day, First Story]

❧

*A knight is in the service of the King of Spain; he feels he has
been poorly rewarded, and so the King first provides him with
clear proof that this is not his fault but, rather, that of his own
wretched Fortune, and then handsomely rewards him.*

HONORABLE ladies, I must consider it a great favor indeed for our
King to have charged me with speaking first on such a topic as
munificence. Even as the sun is the beauty and ornament of the
whole of the heavens, so, too, munificence is the splendor and
light of every other virtue. So I shall tell you a rather charming
little tale, which in my opinion can surely be nothing but
profitable to recall to mind.

I want you to know, then, that among the many valorous
knights that have lived in our city as far back as I can recall,
there was one Messer Ruggieri de' Figiovanni, who was perhaps
the finest; being both a rich and courageous man and realizing
that because of the quality of life and customs in Tuscany there
would be little or no opportunity for him to demonstrate his
worth by continuing to live there, he decided to go for a time
into the service of Anfonso, the King of Spain, whose reputation
for valor surpassed that of any other ruler of his times. And so,
most honorably equipped with arms, horses, and servants, he
went to Anfonso in Spain, and he was graciously received by the
King.

And so, Messer Ruggieri settled there, living in splendor and
performing amazing feats of arms, and in a short time he be-
came known as a valiant man. But after living there for a good
long while and observing the King's ways very closely, it seemed
to Ruggieri that the King was giving away castles, cities, and
baronies to one knight after another without showing much dis-
cernment, for he was rewarding those who did not deserve it;
and since Messer Ruggieri, who knew his own merits, was given
nothing, he felt that this had greatly diminished his reputation.
So he decided to leave, and asked the King for his permission to
do so. The King granted it and gave him one of the best and
most handsome mules that had ever been ridden, which Messer
Ruggieri greatly appreciated since he had a long journey before

him. And then the King ordered one of his own trusted servants to arrange, in whatever way he thought best, to ride along with Messer Ruggieri without appearing to have been sent by the King, and to pay close attention to everything Messer Ruggieri said, in such a manner that he would be able to repeat every word to him; and the King also told the servant to order the knight to return to him on the second morning. The servant kept watch, and when Messer Ruggieri left the city, he very skillfully joined his company, giving him to believe that he, too, was traveling to Italy.

And so, as Messer Ruggieri rode the mule given him by the King, discussing one thing and another with the servant, around the hour of tierce, he said: "I think it would be a good idea to relieve these animals."

So they stopped at a stable, and all the animals except the mule relieved themselves; then they rode on, with the servant continuing to listen to the knight's remarks, and they came to a river, where, as they were watering their animals, the mule relieved itself in the stream; when Messer Ruggieri observed this, he declared: "Ah, God curse you, you beast, for you're just like the man who gave you to me."

The servant overheard this remark, and while he heard many other remarks all during the day as he traveled with the knight, he never heard another which was not spoken in the highest praise of the King; and so on the following morning, after they mounted their horses and were about to ride off to Tuscany, the servant delivered the King's order to the knight, and Messer Ruggieri returned immediately. And as soon as the King learned what he had said about the mule, he had Ruggieri summoned, and welcoming him with a smile, he asked him why he had likened him to his mule or, rather, why he had likened the mule to him.

With great candor, Messer Ruggieri told him:

"My lord, I likened it to you because just as you give gifts when you should not and then don't give them when you should, in like manner, the mule did not relieve itself where it should have but did so where it was not supposed to."

Then the King declared:

"Messer Ruggieri, the fact that I did not give you gifts as I did to many others who, compared to you, were worth nothing did not occur because I failed to recognize that you are a most worthy knight, deserving of every great gift. Instead, it was your Fortune, which did not provide me with the proper occasion, that was to blame—not I. And I shall show you very clearly that I am speaking the truth."

To this, Messer Ruggieri replied:

"My lord, I am not angry over failing to receive gifts from you, for I did not wish to become wealthier, but, rather, because I did not receive from you any kind of recognition of my valor. Nevertheless, I accept your excuse as a valid and honest one, and though I am ready to witness whatever you wish to show me, I accept what you say without any proof."

The King then led him into a great hall where, just as he had arranged previously, there were two huge locked chests, and in the presence of many people, he said to Ruggieri:

"Messer Ruggieri, in one of these chests there are my crown, royal scepter, orb, and many of my beautiful belts, broaches, rings, and every other precious jewel that I possess; the other chest is filled with earth. Choose one of them, and whichever you choose is yours to keep, and then you will see who has been unappreciative of your valor, I or your Fortune."

Seeing that it would please the King, Messer Ruggieri chose one of them, which the King ordered to be opened, and it was found to be the one filled with earth; whereupon the King declared, laughing:

"You can see for yourself, Messer Ruggieri, that what I have said about your Fortune is true; but your valor surely deserves my opposition to Fortune's powers. I realize you have no wish to become a Spaniard, and for this reason, I do not wish to give you a castle or a town here, but I wish to give you the chest of which Fortune has deprived you so that you may take it with you to your own country, and with your neighbors you may deservedly glory in your valor to which my gifts bear witness."

Messer Ruggieri accepted the chest and after rendering to the King the thanks appropriate for such a gift, he returned with it, most happily, to Tuscany.

[Tenth Day, Second Story]

❀

Ghino di Tacco captures the Abbot of Clignì, treats him for a stomachache, and then releases him; when the Abbot returns to the Court of Rome, he reconciles Ghino with Pope Boniface and makes him a member of the Order of the Hospitalers.

AFTER the generosity displayed by King Anfonso for the Florentine knight was praised by all, the King, who had liked the tale very much, ordered Elissa to continue; and she immediately began:

Delicate ladies, no one can say that for a king to have been generous and to have displayed his generosity to a man who has served him is not praiseworthy and a great thing, but then what are we to say when we are told about a cleric who displayed amazing generosity toward a person, when no one would have blamed him if he had treated him as an enemy? Certainly, one can only say that what was a virtue in the King was a miracle in the cleric considering that all clerics are avaricious, even more so than women, and are at daggers drawn with any charitable instinct; and whereas every man naturally hungers to take revenge for the offenses he has received, the members of the clergy, as we may observe, for all their preaching of patience and their recommending above all the forgiveness of offenses, surpass all other men in their zeal for seeking revenge. But in the tale you are about to hear, you will clearly see just how generous a cleric can be.

Ghino di Tacco, notorious for his fierceness and acts of robbery, having been banished from Siena and declared an enemy of the Counts of Santafiore, staged a rebellion in Radiofani against the Church of Rome. Living in that town, he saw to it that anyone passing through the surrounding countryside was set upon and robbed by his marauders. Now, during the time Pope Boniface VIII reigned in Rome, the Abbot of Clignì, reputed to be one of the richest prelates in the world, came to the papal court, and there, falling sick with a stomachache, the Abbot was advised by his physicians to go to the baths of Siena, where without fail he would be cured. So, as soon as the Pope gave him leave to depart, without the slightest concern over Ghino's notoriety, he set out, taking with him a great entourage of servants, mules, horses, and other trappings.

Ghino di Tacco, when he heard of his coming, spread his nets, and without allowing as much as a single stableboy to slip through, he trapped the Abbot with all his servants and possessions in a narrow pass. This done, he had one of the ablest of his men go with a strong escort to the Abbot, and courteously request on his behalf that the Abbot agree to dismount at Ghino's castle. When the Abbot heard this request, all enraged, he replied that he would do nothing of the kind, that he had nothing to do with Ghino, and that he intended to go on and would like to see who was going to stop him from doing so.

To this remark, the ambassador, speaking humbly, replied:

"Sir, you are in a place where, except for God's power, we fear nothing, and where excommunications and interdicts are themselves excommunicated; therefore, for your own good, be kind enough to favor Ghino in this regard."

By the time these words were spoken, the whole place had been surrounded by highwaymen, and so the Abbot, seeing himself and his men trapped, set out, greatly annoyed, with the messenger along the road to the castle together with his retinue and all his goods. After he dismounted, just as Ghino instructed, he was lodged all by himself in a very dark and uncomfortable little room of a large house, while all the other men were given good accommodations in the castle according to their rank, and the horses and all the baggage were placed in a safe place, and not a thing was touched.

Once this was done, Ghino went to the Abbot and said to him:

"Sir, Ghino, whose guest you are, sends me here to request that you be good enough to inform him where you were going and for what reason."

The Abbot, like a wise man, had already put aside his haughtiness, and he explained where he was going and why. Ghino listened to him and then took his leave, having decided to try to cure the Abbot without recourse to the baths. Having ordered that a large fire be kept burning in the little room and that it be well guarded, Ghino did not go back to the Abbot until the following morning, when he returned bringing him two slices of toasted bread wrapped in the whitest of napkins, and a large glass of Vernaccia wine from Corniglia, which was from the Abbot's own stores, and he said to the Abbot:

"Sir, when Ghino was younger, he studied medicine, and he says he learned that there is no better medicine for a stomachache than the medicine he is preparing to give you, which begins with these things I bring you; take them, therefore, and be of good cheer."

The Abbot, whose hunger was greater than his desire to exchange witty remarks, ate the bread and drank the Vernaccia wine, although he was still outraged. Then he uttered a number of haughty remarks, asked a lot of questions, gave a good deal of advice, and, above all, he asked to be allowed to see Ghino. Listening to all this, Ghino let a good deal of what he said pass by, for much of it was pointless, while he very politely answered some of the other questions, affirming that as soon as Ghino was able, he would come to visit the Abbot; and having said this, he left him and did not return until the following day, when he brought the same quantity of toasted bread and Vernaccia wine. And Ghino kept the Abbot on this diet for a number of days, until he noticed that the Abbot had eaten some dried beans which he had secretly and deliberately brought to his room.

And then he asked the Abbot on Ghino's behalf how his stomach was feeling, to which the Abbot replied:

"It seems fine to me; now if I were only out of his clutches—other than that, I have the greatest urge to eat, now that his medicines have completely cured me."

Then Ghino had the Abbot's own servants decorate a handsome room for him with all his own effects and made arrangements for a grand banquet to which the Abbot's entire retinue, as well as many of the men at the castle, were invited. On the next morning he went to the Abbot and said:

"Sir, since you feel so well, it is time to leave your sickroom." Taking him by the hand, he led him into the room which had been decorated for him and left him there with his own servants, while he himself went off to see that the banquet was being magnificently prepared.

The Abbot passed some time with his attendants, telling them about the kind of life he had been leading, whereas they, on the other hand, all agreed that they had been marvelously treated by Ghino. But it was time to eat, and the Abbot with all the others were served a succession of fine foods and wines, though Ghino still did not reveal his identity to the Abbot. And then, after the Abbot had passed several days there in this fashion, Ghino had all his effects put into a great hall, while in a courtyard below the hall he had assembled every one of his horses right down to the most flea-bitten nag. Then Ghino went to the Abbot and asked him how he felt and if he thought he was strong enough to ride his horse; to the question, the Abbot replied that he was very strong, his stomach was fully cured, and he would be fine the moment he was out of Ghino's clutches.

Then Ghino led the Abbot to the hall where all of his effects and servants were, and afterward he had him go to the window from where he could see all his horses, and said:

"Lord Abbot, I want you to know that it was not a wicked soul but rather the fact of being a nobleman driven from his home in poverty with many a powerful enemy that drove Ghino di Tacco, who I am, to become a highway robber and an enemy of the Court of Rome in order to defend his life and his nobility. But because you appear to be a valiant gentleman, and because I have cured you of your stomach ailment, I do not intend to treat you as I would anyone else, from whom, were he to fall into my hands as you have, I would take whatever portion of his possessions I wished. Instead I mean for you, bearing in mind my needs, to give me that portion of your possessions which you yourself desire. All your property is spread out before you here, and you can see your horses for yourself from this window; therefore, take a portion or all of it as you wish, and from this time on, you are free to stay or leave, as you please."

The Abbot was amazed to hear a highwayman speak such generous words, and since they pleased him very much, his anger and indignation immediately disappeared, or rather, they were transformed into goodwill, and with all his heart he became Ghino's friend, and he ran to embrace him, saying:

"I swear to God that to win the friendship of the kind of man I now believe you to be, I would be willing to put up with far greater injury than that I thought I was suffering until now. Cursed be the Fortune which has forced you into such an infamous profession!" And after he had said this, choosing from among his many possessions only those few which were essential, and doing likewise with his horses, the Abbot left all the rest to Ghino and returned to Rome.

The Pope had learned about the capture of the Abbot, and it upset him greatly. But when he saw the Abbot, he asked him if the baths had done him any good; and to the question, the Abbot replied with a smile: "Holy Father, I discovered an excellent physician much closer than the baths, who has completely cured me." And he explained the doctor's methods, which made the Pope laugh; and then, continuing with his explanation, the Abbot, moved by a generous impulse, asked a favor of the Pope.

The Pope, thinking that he would ask for something quite different, freely agreed to do whatever he requested and then the Abbot said:

"Holy Father, what I intend to ask of you is that you restore Ghino di Tacco, my physician, to your good graces, for among all the valiant and noteworthy men I have ever met, he is certainly one of the greatest, and the evil he has done I feel is far more the fault of Fortune than his own. If you will provide him with just enough to live according to his station which will allow him to change his Fortune, I have no doubt whatsoever that in a very short time, you will find him to be the kind of man he appears to me to be."

When the Pope heard this, being a man with a generous heart and well disposed to men of worth, he said that if Ghino was the kind of man the Abbot said he was, he would gladly agree to do so and that he should make arrangements for Ghino to come with full assurance to Rome. And so Ghino arrived at the court under safe conduct in accordance with the Abbot's wishes; nor was he there for very long before he was acknowledged by the Pope to be a worthy man, and once he was reconciled with him, the Pope bestowed upon him a large priory belonging to the Order of the Hospitalers,* having first appointed him a knight of that order. And this post, as a friend and a servant of Holy Mother Church and the Abbot of Cligni, Ghino held for as long as he lived.

[Tenth Day, Third Story]

Mithridanes, envious of Nathan's reputation for courtesy, sets out to murder him, and after accidentally coming across Nathan without recognizing him, and learning from Nathan himself how he might carry out his intentions, Mithridanes comes upon Nathan in a wood, as Nathan had arranged. Recognizing Nathan, Mithridanes is ashamed and becomes his friend.

EVERYONE felt what they had heard—that is, that a clergyman actually performed an act of generosity—was certainly something close to a miracle. Then, as soon as the ladies stopped discussing the story, the King ordered Filostrato to proceed, and he began immediately:

Noble ladies, the King of Spain's generosity was great and that of the Abbot of Cligni probably a thing unheard of until that day. But I think you will find it no less marvelous to hear of a man who, in order to show his generosity toward another man who was out for his blood as well as his very life, prudently arranged to give him what he wished; and this same man would have given him his very life if the other man had wished to take it, as I intend to show you in this little story of mine.

It seems quite certain, if we believe what is said by certain Genoese and others who lived in those parts, that in the region of Cathay there once lived a man of noble lineage, wealthy beyond all measure, whose name was Nathan. Since this man lived by a road along which, almost of necessity, everyone who wished to go from west to east or from east to west had to pass, and

*A religious military order first established in Jerusalem in the twelfth century.

since he possessed a great and generous spirit and wished to be known for his good deeds, he gathered together there a number of master builders, and in a brief space of time he had built one of the largest, most beautiful, and most richly decorated palaces that had ever been seen, and he had it excellently equipped with all those things that were suitable for the reception and the entertainment of gentlemen. And as he had a large and splendid retinue of servants, he would welcome and entertain in a delightful and festive manner all who came there. He persevered so in this laudable custom that his fame spread not only throughout the East but also through most parts of the West.

And when he was already old in years but not yet weary of dispensing his generosity, his fame happened to reach the ears of a young man named Mithridanes, who came from a part of the country not far from where he lived and who, feeling that he was no less rich than Nathan, became envious of Nathan's fame and his virtue and made up his mind that, with even greater generosity, he would either nullify Nathan's reputation or eclipse it. And so he had a palace built similar to Nathan's and began to entertain anyone who came there in the most extravagant way ever heard of; and there is no doubt that in just a short time he became very famous.

Now one day while the young man was all alone in the courtyard of his palace, a woman happened to come in through one of the palace gates to ask him for alms, and she received them. She then returned through a second gate, went to him again and received more, and this she did through twelve gates in succession; and when she returned for the thirteenth time, Mithridanes declared: "My good woman, you are quite insistent in this begging of yours," but, nonetheless, he gave her the alms.

When the old lady heard his remark, she said:

"Oh, how wonderful is the generosity of Nathan! For when I entered the thirty-two gates of his palace, even as this one has, and asked him for alms, never did he show that he recognized me, and I always received them from him; but here, I have only to come through thirteen gates and I am recognized and scolded." And so saying, she left, never to return there again.

Mithridanes, hearing the old woman's words, took them as a slight to his own reputation, and he went into a violent rage and said:

"Ah, how shall I ever equal the greatness of Nathan's generosity, not to mention outdoing it as I am trying to do, when I am unable to approach him in even the most insignificant of matters? I shall truly be laboring in vain, unless I do something to

remove him from the face of the earth; since old age has not re-
moved him, I shall have to do it with my own hands and with-
out delay."

So, rising impulsively to his feet without telling anyone about
his decision, he set out on horseback with a small escort and af-
ter three days reached the place where Nathan lived. After or-
dering his companions to pretend that they were not with him or
that they did not know who he was and to find lodgings for
themselves until they received further orders from him, he went
off by himself, and around dusk, while in the vicinity of the beau-
tiful palace, he came across Nathan, who was all alone and sim-
ply dressed, taking a walk for his pleasure. Not knowing who he
was, he asked him if he might be able to tell him where Nathan
lived.

Nathan cheerfully replied:

"My son, no one in these parts would know how to show you
the way better than I, and so whenever you like, I'll take you
there."

The young man said that he would like that very much but
that if it was possible, he would not like to be seen or known by
Nathan; to this request, Nathan replied: "I shall see to that as
well, since it is your wish."

Mithridanes, then, dismounted and walked with Nathan, who
before long engaged him in delighted conversation until they
reached his beautiful palace. There, Nathan had one of his ser-
vants take the young man's horse, and then he whispered into
his ear an order to quickly instruct everyone in the household
not to tell the young man that he was Nathan. And this was
done. Then, once inside the palace, Nathan saw to it that
Mithridanes was lodged in a very handsome room where no one
had access to him, except those he had selected to serve him and
where he himself kept him company, seeing to it that he was
royally entertained.

Having been together awhile, though he revered the man as if
he were his father, Mithridanes could not refrain from asking
him who he was, and to this Nathan replied:

"I am a humble servant of Nathan's, and although I have
grown old in his service since my childhood, he has never raised
me any higher than the rank you see me in now, and so while
everyone else may praise him most highly, I have very little to
praise him for."

These remarks gave Mithridanes some hope of carrying out
his wicked plan with more safety and assurance; then Nathan
very politely asked Mithridanes who he was and what had

brought him to those parts, offering his advice and assistance in whatever way possible. Mithridanes paused awhile before answering, and then, finally deciding to take Nathan into his confidence, after much circumlocution, and after pledging him to secrecy, asking his advice and assistance, he revealed everything to him: his identity, why he had come, and what had moved him to do so.

When Nathan heard Mithridanes' explanation and his cruel proposal, he was very much disturbed, but without much hesitation, with stout heart and courageous face, he answered him:

"Mithridanes, your father was a noble man, and you show that you do not wish to stray from following his example by the fact that you have undertaken the lofty enterprise that you have, wherein you show generosity to every man. I commend most highly the envy that you bear for Nathan's virtue, for if there were much more of such envy, the world, which is indeed wretched, would soon become good. I shall without question keep the plan you have revealed to me a secret, in support of which I can offer you useful advice more easily than great assistance; and my advice is this: approximately a half mile away from here, you can see a wood, in which almost every morning Nathan enjoys himself by taking a long walk all by himself. There it will be an easy matter to find him and to do to him what you wish. But if you kill him, in order for you to escape safely to your home, you should leave the wood not by the road you entered here but, rather, by the road you see on the left, for, though it is a bit rougher, you will find it closer to your home and a more secure route."

As soon as Mithridanes received this information and Nathan had left him, he secretly informed his companions, who were also staying in the palace, where they were to wait for him on the following day. And when the new day dawned, Nathan, who had no misgivings about the advice he had given Mithridanes nor any intention of changing his mind in the slightest, went into the wood all alone to meet his death.

Mithridanes arose, took his bow and sword, which were the only weapons he had, mounted his horse, and rode off to the wood, where from a distance he observed Nathan walking around all alone; but having decided that he wanted to see and to hear Nathan speak before attacking him, he galloped toward him, and seizing him by the turban he was wearing, Mithridanes declared; "Old man, you are as good as dead!"

In answer to this remark Nathan said only: "Then I must deserve it."

When Mithridanes heard his voice and looked into his face, he immediately recognized him as the man who had received him so kindly, kept him company affectionately, and advised him faithfully. His furor immediately subsided and his anger changed to shame. Throwing away the sword he had drawn in order to strike Nathan, he got off his horse and, weeping, threw himself at Nathan's feet, saying:

"Dearest father, how clearly I see your generosity, when I consider the precautions you took to come here secretly and give me your life which I, with no good reason, told you yourself I wanted. But God, who was more concerned with my duty than I myself, at precisely the moment when the need was the greatest, opened the eyes of my intellect, which wretched envy had sealed for me. And so, as much as you were ready to please me, I am all the more conscious of the need to repent of my error; therefore, take whatever vengeance you deem is fitting to my sin."

Nathan made Mithridanes rise to his feet, tenderly embraced and kissed him, and said to him:

"My son, as for your undertaking, whether you call it wicked or otherwise, there is no need to ask or to grant forgiveness, for you pursued it not out of hatred but, rather, in order to be held in greater esteem. So live, then, and have no fear of me, and rest assured that no other man alive loves you as I do, considering the nobility of your spirit, which gave itself over not to amassing wealth, as the miserly do, but, rather, to spending the wealth you have amassed. Do not be ashamed for having wished to kill me in order to become famous, nor should you think that it surprises me that you did. The most powerful of emperors and the greatest of kings practice practically no other art but killing—not just a single man as you wished to do but, rather, countless numbers—as well as burning towns and destroying cities, in order to increase their kingdoms and, as a result, their fame; and so, if you wished to kill only me to become more famous, you were doing nothing amazing or unusual but rather something which is very commonplace."

Mithridanes, while refusing to excuse his own perverse desire, nevertheless commended the honorable explanation Nathan had found to excuse it, and he concluded by saying that he was amazed beyond measure how Nathan could have been prepared to supply him with both the means and the advice for accomplishing his purpose; to this, Nathan said:

"Mithridanes, you should not marvel at my advice and my readiness, for ever since I became my own master and have been disposed to pursue the very same goals you have pursued, no one has ever happened by my home whom I did not satisfy to the limits of my power in anything he requested of me. You came here seeking my life, and when I heard you ask for it, so that you would not be the only man to leave here without having obtained his request, I immediately decided to give my life to you, and in order that you might take it, I gave you the advice I felt best suited for allowing you to take my life without losing your own. Therefore, I say to you once again: I beg you that if this is what you wish, take it and satisfy yourself. I know no other way of using it more worthily. I have already used my life for eighty years, spending it for my own pleasures and comforts, and I realize that, being subject to the laws of Nature, just as it happens to all men and to things in general, my life is left to me for only a little while longer; and so I think it much better to give it away, as I have always given away and spent my treasures, than to try to preserve it until it is taken away from me against my will by Nature. To give away a hundred years would be a small gift; how much smaller a gift, then, is it for me to give away the six or eight years that I have left? Take my life, therefore, if that pleases you, I beg you; for as long as I have lived here, I have never found anyone else who ever wanted it. And if you, who ask for it now, do not take it, I doubt that I shall ever find anyone else. But even if I happened to find someone else, I realize that the longer I hold on to it, the less value it has; and so, before it becomes more worthless, take it, I beg of you."

Mithridanes, being most ashamed of himself, said:

"God forbid that I should take such a precious thing as your life, much less wish to do so, as I did a while ago; rather than diminish the years of your life, I should gladly add to them with my own."

To this, Nathan promptly said:

"And if you could, would you really add them to mine? Would you make me do something which I have never done for anyone else—that is, to take something belonging to you, when I have never ever taken anything from anyone?"

"Yes," Mithridanes replied quickly.

"Then," declared Nathan, "do just as I tell you. Remain here, young as you are, in my home, and you shall bear the name of Nathan, while I shall go to your home and always be called Mithridanes."

Then Mithridanes answered:

"If I had known how to act as well as you know and have known, I would accept the proposal which you offer me without much reflection, but since I am quite certain that my actions would only diminish Nathan's fame, I do not intend to spoil in another man that which I did not know how to bring to completion in myself, and I shall not accept."

After this and many other delightful topics had been discussed by Nathan and Mithridanes, together they returned, at Nathan's request, to the palace, where for several days Nathan entertained Mithridanes in magnificent fashion, encouraging him with all his skill and wisdom to persevere in his grand and lofty enterprise. And when Mithridanes wished to return home with his companions, Nathan, having made him see all too clearly that he could never surpass him in generosity, allowed him to depart.

[Tenth Day, Fourth Story]

✦

Messer Gentil de' Carisendi, having arrived from Modena, takes from her tomb a lady he has loved who has been buried for dead; after she has been revived, she gives birth to a male child, and Messer Gentile restores her and her son to Niccoluccio Caccianimico, her husband.

EVERYONE thought it marvelous that a man should be generous with his own blood, and they affirmed that Nathan had certainly surpassed the generosity of the King of Spain and the Abbot of Clignì. But then, after one thing and another was said about all this, the King, glancing at Lauretta, motioned to her that he wished for her to speak. And so, Lauretta began immediately:

Young ladies, we have heard told of such magnificent and beautiful things, it seems to me that there is nothing left for us to say as we tell our stories, since they have all been so full of the highest possible feats of generosity as could be recounted, unless we turn our hand to matters concerning love, which always provide an abundant supply of tales on every topic. And so, for this reason and also because our age especially inclines us in that direction, it is my pleasure to tell you about a generous act performed by a man in love. All things being considered, it will not seem to you any less of an accomplishment than some of the others already related, if it is true that treasures are given away, enmities forgotten, and one's very life, honor, and, what is even more important, one's reputation placed in a thousand dangers in order to possess the thing beloved.

There was once, then, in Bologna, that most noble city in Lombardy, a gentleman named Messer Gentil Carisendi, whose virtue and nobility of blood was very considerable indeed, and who as a young man fell in love with a gentlewoman named Madonna Catalina, the wife of one Niccoluccio Caccianimico. Because he was not loved in return by the lady, in desperation, he left Bologna for Modena, where he had been appointed *podestà*.

At that time, Niccoluccio was not in Bologna, and his wife, because she was pregnant, had gone to stay at one of his estates about three miles outside the city, and there she happened to be stricken with a serious illness, which was so fierce and so strong that it took all signs of life from her and, as a result, she was pronounced by several different doctors to be dead. Since even her closest relatives stated they had heard from her own lips that she had not been pregnant long enough for the creature to have been perfectly formed, without giving it a second thought and with much weeping, they buried her just as she was, within a tomb in a church nearby.

This event was immediately reported to Messer Gentile by a friend of his, and in spite of the fact he had in no way received her favors, he deeply grieved and at length said to himself:

"There you are, Madonna Catalina, dead. While you were alive, I never received even as much as a single glance from you, and now that you are unable to defend yourself, dead as you are, I am determined to take a kiss or two from you."

Night had already fallen, and having said this, he made arrangements to depart in secret, took to his horse accompanied by a servant of his, and without stopping, he rode until he reached the place where the lady was buried. After opening the tomb, he cautiously entered it, and lying down beside her, he put his face next to the lady's and kissed it many times, weeping copious tears. But as we know, man's appetite is satisfied with no limits but always desires more, especially the appetite of lovers, and so, after Messer Gentile had first made up his mind to tarry there no longer, he then said:

"Ah! Why should I not just touch her on the breast a little, since I am here? I shall never be able to touch her again, nor have I ever touched her before."

Overcome, then, by his appetite, he placed his hand upon her breast; and having held it there for a while, he thought he felt a faint beating of her heart. When he recovered from his fear, he examined her more carefully and discovered that she was clearly not dead, though he thought the life left in her was weak and fading away. So, as gently as he could, assisted by his servant, he carried her from the tomb, and having placed her on his horse, he took her in secret to his home in Bologna.

His mother, a wise and worthy woman, was there, and after listening at length to everything her son told her, moved by compassion, she skillfully brought the lady back to her senses by means of hot baths and the warmth of the fire; and when the lady came to her senses, she heaved an enormous sigh and exclaimed: "Oh, where am I now?"

To this, the worthy woman replied: "Be of good cheer, for you are in a safe place."

Having recovered, she began looking around her, but she did not know exactly where she was; then, seeing Messer Gentile in front of her, full of amazement, she begged his mother to explain to her how she happened to be there. Messer Gentile then told her everything in great detail. She grieved over this, but then after a while she thanked him as best she knew how and begged him, in the name of the love he had borne her, and of his sense of honor, not to do anything to her in his home which would be detrimental to her honor or that of her husband, and to allow her to return to her own home at daybreak.

To this request, Messer Gentile replied:

"My lady, whatever my desire for you may have been in the past, I do not intend now, or in the future (since God has granted me the grace of restoring you to life from the brink of death, because of the love I once bore for you), to treat you here or elsewhere as anything but a dear sister. Still the good turn I did you last night deserves some sort of reward, and so I wish you would not deny me the favor I am about to ask of you."

To this request, the lady kindly answered that she was willing to do so, provided she was able and that it was the proper thing to do. Then Messer Gentile declared:

"My lady, all of your relatives and every citizen of Bologna are absolutely convinced you are dead, and so there is no one waiting for you at home any longer; therefore, I ask you as a favor to be good enough to stay here in secret with my mother until I return from Modena, which will be soon. And the reason I am asking this of you is that I intend to make of you, in the presence of the city's leading citizens, a precious and solemn gift to your husband."

Realizing that she was obligated to the gentleman and that his request was a proper one, no matter how much she wished to make her relatives happy with the news that she was alive, the lady decided to do what Messer Gentile asked. And so, on her word of honor she agreed to his request. And no sooner had the words of her promise been spoken then she felt that the time for her childbirth had arrived; and so, assisted tenderly by Messer Gentile's mother, not long afterward she gave birth to a handsome male child, which increased enormously the happiness of Messer Gentile as well as her own. Messer Gentile ordered that she be given everything that she needed and for her to be treated as if she were his own wife. Then he returned secretly to Modena.

When he had completed his term of office and was able to return to Bologna, he made certain arrangements for the morning he was supposed to return to the city. He had a great and sumptuous banquet prepared at his home, to which a number of Bolognese noblemen were invited, among whom was Niccoluccio Caccianimico, and upon his return, having dismounted and gone in to be with his guests, after first looking in on the lady and finding her more beautiful and healthier than ever and her son doing well, he, unbelievably happy, showed his guests to the table and saw to it that they were magnificently served a number of dishes.

As the end of the banquet was drawing near, having told the lady what he intended to do beforehand and arranged with her the manner in which she was to behave, he began to speak in this fashion:

"Gentlemen, I remember having heard at some time that in Persia there once existed what I consider to be a delightful practice, whereby whenever a person wishes to highly honor a friend, he would invite him to his home, and there he would show him the thing, be it his wife or mistress or daughter, or what you will, which he holds most dear, and asserting at the same time that if it were possible, just as he has shown him this thing, he would even more gladly show him his heart; I intend to observe this custom in Bologna. You have most kindly honored my banquet, and I should like to pay honor to you in the Persian fashion, revealing to you the most precious thing that I have or ever will have in the world. But before I do this, I beg you to give your opinion on the problem I am about to put before you. A certain person has in his home a good and most faithful servant who falls seriously ill; this person, without waiting for his sick servant to die, has him carried out to the middle of the street and is concerned with him no longer; a stranger comes along and, moved by compassion for the sick man, takes him home with him, and with much care and expense, restores the servant to his previous health. Now, I should like to know whether, if the second man retains this servant and employs his services, the servant's first master has the right to complain or to blame the second master. Should he refuse to give back the servant when he is requested to do so?"

After the gentlemen had discussed the various points of view among themselves and all had agreed on a response, they charged Niccoluccio Caccianimico with making the reply, because he was an eloquent speaker. After first praising the Persian custom, Niccoluccio then declared that he and the others were all of one opinion: that the first master had no further claims on his servant, since not only had he abandoned him in such unfortunate circumstances but had thrown him out, and that as a result of the good works performed by the second master, it would seem that he had justly become his servant, because in keeping him, no harm, violence, or injury was done to the first master. All the others seated at the table (and there was many a worthy gentleman among them) unanimously agreed with Niccoluccio's reply.

Delighted with such a reply and with the fact that Niccoluccio had been the one to make it, Messer Gentile declared that he was of the same opinion, and then he said: "The time has arrived for me to honor you according to my promise." After calling two of his servants, he sent them to the lady, who, he had seen to it, was magnificently dressed and adorned, and he had them request that she be good enough to come and grace the noblemen with her presence.

Taking her lovely son in her arms, the lady entered the hall, accompanied by the two servants, and at Messer Gentile's request, she sat down beside one of the worthy gentlemen, and then he said:

"Gentlemen, this is the most precious thing I have or ever hope to have. Look and see if you think I am right."

The gentlemen welcomed her and praised her highly and having told the knight that he should, indeed, consider her most precious, they began to gaze at her. And there were a good many of them who would have said who she actually was if they had not thought she was dead. But Niccoluccio, who had moved a few steps away from the knight, stared at her more than all the others, burning with desire to know who she was; and no longer able to contain himself, he asked her if she was from Bologna or a foreigner. When she heard her husband ask this question, only with great difficulty did the lady refrain from answering; but in order to remain true to the agreement she had made, she remained silent. Some other person asked her if that was her young son, and another inquired if she was Messer Gentile's wife or a relative of his in some way; to these questions, she made no reply whatsoever.

But when Messer Gentile joined his guests again, some of them said:

"Sir, this thing of yours is a beauty, but it appears that she is mute. Is this the case?"

"Gentlemen," said Messer Gentile, "the fact that she has not spoken for the moment is no small proof of her virtue."

"Tell us, then," continued one of the guests, "who she is."

The knight declared:

"That I shall gladly do, provided you promise me, no matter what I may say, not to move from your place until I have finished my story."

When everyone had agreed to this and the tables had been cleared, Messer Gentile, now seated beside the lady, said:

"Gentlemen, this lady is that loyal and faithful servant about whom I posed my question to you a while ago. When her own relatives, who considered her of little value, cast her out into the middle of the street as one would a vile and worthless object, she was rescued by me, and with my care and my own two hands, I saved her from death; and God, favoring me for my pure affection for her, has, through me, transformed her from a frightening corpse into so beautiful a thing. But so that you may more easily understand how this all happened to me, I shall make it clear to you in a few words." Beginning from the time he first fell in love with her up until the present, to the great amazement of his listeners, he told them everything that had happened, and then he added: "And so, unless all of you, and especially Niccoluccio, have changed your opinion from a moment ago, this lady is rightfully mine, nor could anyone legitimately ask me for her."

No one replied to this statement, and on the contrary, everyone waited to see what he was going to say next. Niccoluccio, the others who were present there, and the lady all wept with compassion; then Messer Gentile stood up, and taking the small child in his arms and the lady by her hand, he walked toward Niccoluccio and said:

"Stand up, *compare*; I shall not return your wife to you, whom you and her relatives cast aside, but I wish to give you this lady, my *comare*, together with this little son of hers, whom

I am certain was begotten by you and whom I held at the baptismal font and christened with the name Gentile. And I beg you that she not be held less precious because of the fact that she stayed in my home for nearly three months, for I swear to you in the name of God, who perhaps caused me to fall in love with her so that my love might be, as it has been, the cause of her salvation, that she never lived more virtuously with her father or mother or with you than she lived with my mother in my home." And when he had said this, he turned to the lady and said: "My lady, from now on, I release you from every promise you made me, and I leave you free to return to Niccoluccio." And with that he placed the lady and her child in Niccoluccio's arms and returned to his seat.

Niccoluccio eagerly received his wife and child, his joy being all the greater, having been far removed from any such hopes, and as best he could and knew how, he thanked the knight. The other guests, all weeping from emotion, praised Messer Gentile most highly, and he was commended by anyone who heard the story. The lady was welcomed back to her home with the greatest rejoicing, and she was regarded with awe by the people of Bologna for some time to come as if she were someone returned from the dead. And Messer Gentile remained forever a friend of Niccoluccio, his relatives, and the lady's family.

What, then, do you say about this story, gracious ladies? Do you think that a king's gift of his scepter and crown, or an abbot's act of reconciling an outlaw to the Pope at no cost to himself, or an old man's exposing his throat to his enemy's sword was equal to the gesture of Messer Gentile? For here we have a young and amorous man, who felt he had the just right to possess that which the negligence of others had cast aside and which he, because of his good fortune, had taken in. Yet he not only virtuously tempered his passion, but he also generously returned, as soon as he possessed it, the thing he had always wanted and sought to steal with all his heart. Certainly, none of the stories told so far seems to me equal to this one.

[Tenth Day, Fifth Story]

❧

Madonna Dianora asks Messer Ansaldo to give her a garden that would be as beautiful in January as in May; by hiring a magician, Messer Ansaldo manages to grant her wish; her husband agrees that she must fulfill Messer Ansaldo's desires, but when Messer Ansaldo hears of her husband's generosity, he frees her from her promise, and the magician, refusing to accept anything from him, also frees Messer Ansaldo from his.

EVERY member of the merry company had already praised Messer Gentile to the skies, when the King ordered Emilia to continue, and she, longing to speak, self-confidently began as follows:

Tender ladies, no one can reasonably say that Messer Gentile did not act generously, but if anyone were to claim that it would be impossible to act more generously, it would not be hard to show the contrary, as I mean to show you in this little tale of mine.

In Friuli, a rather cold province but one which boasts of beautiful mountains, many rivers, and clear springs, there is a town called Udine, in which there once lived a beautiful and noble lady named Madonna Dianora, the wife of a very wealthy man named Gilberto, a very pleasant and amiable person. Such was this lady's worth that she was greatly loved by a famous and noble baron of high rank, whose name was Messer Ansaldo Gradense and who was known everywhere for his feats of arms and chivalry. And while Messer Ansaldo loved Madonna Dianora passionately and did everything he could to be loved in return by her, often sending her numerous messages with this end in mind, he labored in vain. And when the lady, having become weary of the knight's entreaties, realized that no matter how much she denied him everything he requested, he nevertheless continued to love her and to implore her, she decided to rid herself of him by making a strange and, in her judgment, impossible request.

And so she said the following to a woman who often came to her on his behalf:

"Good woman, you have assured me many times that Messer

Ansaldo loves me above all other things, and you have, on his behalf, offered me marvelous gifts; he may keep these gifts, for they could never bring me to love him or to fulfill his pleasure. But if I could be certain he loved me as much as you say he does, I would be moved without a doubt to love him and to do whatever he wished. And so, whenever he is willing to provide me with proof by doing what I request, I shall be ready to do whatever he wants."

The good woman said: "What is it, my lady, that you wish him to do?"

The lady replied:

"What I desire is this: in the month of January which is soon to come, I want there to be on the outskirts of town a garden full of green grass, flowers, and leafy trees no different from one in the month of May; if he is unable to do this, he should never again send you or anyone else to me, for if he continues to bother me, just as until now I have completely concealed everything from my husband and my relatives, I shall, by complaining to them about him, seek to get rid of him."

When the knight heard his lady's request and offer, no matter how difficult or rather impossible a task he felt it was to fulfill, and in spite of the fact that he realized the lady had made this request for no other reason than to destroy his hope, nevertheless, he made up his mind to try to do what he could. He sent word to all parts of the world to find out if there was someone who might provide him with assistance or advice, and a certain man came to him who offered to do it by means of magic, provided he was well paid. Messer Ansaldo came to an agreement with him for an enormous sum of money and then happily awaited the time the lady had set for him. When it arrived and the weather was bitter cold and everything was covered with snow and ice, in a most beautiful meadow near the town, the worthy man, on the night before the first day of January, employed his magic to such effect that on the following morning there appeared, according to the testimony of those who saw it for themselves, one of the most beautiful gardens that had ever been seen, with grass, trees, and fruit of every kind. As soon as Messer Ansaldo saw the garden, with great joy he had gathered some of the most beautiful fruits and flowers growing there and then secretly had them presented to the lady, inviting her to come and see the garden she had requested so that she would not only realize how much he loved her but would also recall the promise she had made to him, sealed with her oath, and in so doing would seek, as a woman of good faith, to keep her promise.

The lady had heard much talk about the marvelous garden, and when she saw the flowers and fruit, she began to regret her promise. In spite of her regret, curious as she was to see so unusual a thing, she went with many other ladies of the town to have a look at the garden; after praising it very highly, and not without amazement, she returned home the most sorrowful of women, thinking about what she was obliged to do because of it. So intense was her grief that she was unable to conceal it, and her husband, who could not help noticing it, insisted on knowing the cause of it. Out of shame, the lady kept silent for a long time; then, finally compelled to speak, she revealed everything to him.

When Gilberto heard all this, at first he was very much disturbed; but then, when he considered his wife's pure intentions, he put aside his anger and said:

"Dianora, it is not proper for a wise or virtuous woman to pay attention to messages of that sort or to fix a price on her chastity with anyone, under any circumstances. Words received by the heart through the ears have more power than many would believe, and almost everything becomes possible for lovers. Hence, you did wrong first by listening and then by bargaining, but since I know the purity of your heart, I shall allow you, in order to absolve you of the obligation of your promise, to do something which perhaps no other man would allow, being also moved by my fear of the magician, whom Messer Ansaldo, if we were to disappoint him, would perhaps have do us harm. I want you to go to him, and by any means possible, short of your chastity, seek to be released from this promise, and if that is impossible, then this one time you must give him your body, but not your heart."

When the lady heard her husband, she wept and refused to accept such a favor from him. But no matter how much the lady objected, Gilberto insisted that she do it, and so, the following morning, around daybreak, without dressing up too much, the lady, preceded by two of her retainers and followed by one of her maidservants, went to Messer Ansaldo's home.

When he heard that the lady had come to him, he was quite amazed, and so, rising, he sent for the magician, and said to him: "I want you to see how much good your art has procured me." And then he went to greet her, and with no display of unbridled passion, with reverence he received her courteously, after which he had everyone go into a beautiful room where a big fire was burning, and after arranging for her to be seated, he said:

"My lady, I beg you, if the long love which I have borne you deserves any reward, be good enough to tell me the real reason why you have come here at such an hour and with such an escort."

Ashamed and with tears welling in her eyes, the lady replied:

"Sir, neither because I love you, nor because of my promise do I come here, but, rather, because of my husband's orders. Having more consideration for the labors of your unbridled passion than for his or my honor, he has made me come here; and it is at his command that I am disposed, this one time, to fulfill your every desire."

If Messer Ansaldo was astonished when she began speaking, he was even more so after she finished. Moved by Gilberto's generosity, his passion began to change into compassion, and he said:

"My lady, since things are as you say, God forbid that I should soil the honor of a man who has taken pity on my love, and so, as long as you wish to stay here, you will be treated just as if you were my sister, and whenever you like, you are free to leave, provided that you give your husband such thanks as you deem befitting such courtesy as his, and that henceforth you always consider me as a brother and your servant."

When the lady heard these words, happier than ever before, she said:

"Nothing could ever make me believe, considering your manners, that anything else could have resulted from my coming here than what I see you have made of it, and I shall always be obliged to you for this."

And having taken her leave, honorably escorted, she returned to Gilberto and reported to him what had happened; and as a result, a very close and loyal friendship grew up between Gilberto and Messer Ansaldo.

When Messer Ansaldo was ready to give the magician his promised fee, the magician, having witnessed the generosity of Gilberto toward Messer Ansaldo and that of Messer Ansaldo toward the lady, said:

"God forbid that having seen Gilberto so generous with his honor and you with your love, I should not be just as generous with my reward; and so, recognizing the justice of leaving the reward with you, it is my intention that you keep it."

The knight was embarrassed and tried to make him take if not all of the money, at least a part of it; but he labored in vain, and after the third day, when the magician had removed his garden and wanted to depart, Messer Ansaldo bid him Godspeed. And with his sensual passion for the lady extinguished in his heart, there remained the honest flame of affection.

What shall we say of this, loving ladies? Shall we place the lady who was almost dead and the love already grown lukewarm through lost hope above the generosity of Messer Ansaldo, who was more warmed with love than ever and kindled with even more hope, who held in his very hands the catch he had pursued for so long a time? It seems foolish to me to believe that his kind of generosity could ever be compared to the other.

[Tenth Day, Sixth Story]

❦

The old and victorious King Charles, having fallen in love with a young girl, then regrets his foolish fancy and arranges honorable marriages for both the girl and one of her sisters.

WHO could possibly recount in full the various discussions taking place among the ladies as to which man, Gilberto, Messer Ansaldo, or the magician, had shown the greatest generosity in Madonna Dianora's regard? It would take too long. But after the King had allowed them to debate for a while, looking at Fiammetta, he ordered her to end their discussions by telling a story. Without further delay, she began:

Splendid ladies, I have always been of the opinion that in companies such as our own, one should speak in such general terms that the meaning of what we say may never give rise to argument because of something too narrowly defined; such discussions are better kept among scholars in schools than among us, who have all we can do to manage our distaffs and spindles. And since I had a somewhat ambiguous story in mind, and observing your disagreement over the stories already told, I shall set that tale aside and tell you another one, concerning not a man of little importance but rather a valiant king, and how he acted chivalrously without in the slightest way diminishing his reputation.

You have all heard mentioned on many occasions King Charles the Old, or rather the First, through whose magnificent enterprise, and later through whose glorious victory over King

Manfredi,* the Ghibellines were driven out of Florence and the Guelphs were returned to the city. Because of this a knight named Messer Neri degli Uberti left Florence with his entire household and a great deal of money, having decided that he would not settle anywhere else except under King Charles' protection. And so he went to Castello da mare di Stabia, where he could live in a solitary place and spend the rest of his days in peace. And there perhaps a stone's throw away from the other houses in the district among the olive, hazel, and chestnut trees which abound in that area, he bought a piece of property, on which he built a handsome and comfortable home with a delightful garden to the side of it, in the middle of which, since it had an ample supply of fresh water, in good Florentine fashion, he constructed a fine, clear fishpond, which he had no trouble stocking with all kinds of fish.

And while he dedicated all his time to making his garden even more beautiful, it happened that King Charles, during the hot weather, came to Castello a mar to rest for a while, and when he heard of the beauty of Messer Neri's garden, he wished to see it. But having learned to whom the garden belonged, he decided that since the knight was a member of a faction hostile to his own he would make his visit a more informal one, and he sent word to the knight saying that he and four of his companions would like to dine privately with him in his garden. This pleased Messer Neri very much, and after making splendid preparations, arranging with his servants everything that had to be done, as cordially as he could, he received the King in his beautiful garden. When the King had seen and praised all of Messer Neri's garden and house, he washed his hands and sat down at one of the tables set along the fishpond, and ordered one of his companions, Count Guido di Monforte, to sit down on one side of him and Messer Neri on the other; and then he commanded the other three men who had come with him to wait upon them according to Messer Neri's instructions. The food served was exquisite, the wines were the best and most precious, the service fine and most admirable indeed, without the slightest noise or disturbance—all of which the King commended very highly.

And while he was happily eating his meal and enjoying the solitude of the place, there entered the garden two young girls, each about fifteen years of age, their hair as blond as strands of gold, all in curls surmounted by a delicate garland of periwinkle blossoms, and they looked more like angels than anything else, so

*Manfredi was killed at the battle of Benevento in 1266.

lovely and delicate were their faces. They were dressed in garments of the thinnest linen, as white as snow upon their skin, fitting tightly at the waist and extending from there in bell-shaped fashion, all the way down to their feet. The girl who came first carried two fishnets over her left shoulder and held a long pole in her right hand; the other girl who came after her carried a frying pan over her left shoulder and a bundle of kindling wood under the same arm, with a tripod in one hand and a terra-cotta oil container and a small, lighted torch in the other; the King was surprised to see them, and he waited in suspense to see what this meant.

The young girls came forward, chaste and modest in their bearing, and paid homage to the King; then they went to the edge of the fishpond, where the girl holding the pan laid it down, together with the other things she was carrying, and took the pole which the other girl had in her hand, and they both waded into the fishpond until the water was up to their breasts. One of Messer Neri's servants quickly lit a fire near the edge of the pool, and placing the pan on the tripod and pouring oil into it, he began waiting for the young girls to throw him some fish. While one of them felt around in those places where she knew fish would be hiding, and the other tossed the nets, to the great delight of the King, who was closely watching all of this, in no time at all they had caught a sizable quantity of fish; and they threw some of their catch to the servant, who put them into the pan while they were still half alive, and then as they had been instructed to do, they selected the most beautiful fish and began tossing them onto the table before the King, Count Guido, and their father. These fish flopped about upon the tabletop, a sight from which the King took the greatest of pleasure; and in like manner, picking up some of the fish, he politely tossed them back to the young girls, and in this fashion they played about for as long as it took the servant to cook the fish he had been given; and at Messer Neri's orders, this fish, intended more as an appetizer than as a choice and delicate dish, was placed before the King.

When they saw that the fish had been cooked and they had now caught enough of them, the young maidens—their white, thin garments clinging to their skin concealing hardly any part of their delicate bodies—emerged from the fishpond; and after picking up all the things they had brought with them, they shyly passed before the King and returned to the house. The King, the Count, and the other men who were serving had examined these young girls very closely, and each of the men had secretly admired the girls greatly for their lovely faces and shapely bodies, as well as for their delightful and pleasing manners. But the King had been charmed more than anyone else, and so attentively had he been watching every part of their bodies as they emerged from the water that if someone were to have pinched him at that moment, he would not have felt it. And as he thought more about them, not knowing who they were or how they happened to be there, the King felt rising in his heart such a burning desire to please them that he realized full well he might fall in love if he was not on his guard; nor did he even know which of the two pleased him the most, so much did one resemble the other in every respect.

But after dwelling on this question for some time, he turned to Messer Neri and asked him who the two maidens were; to this, Messer Neri replied: "My lord, these are my daughters, born in the same childbirth, one of whom is called the beautiful Ginevra, the other the fair Isotta." The King praised them highly and urged him to bestow them in marriage, to which Messer Neri replied apologetically that he no longer had the means to do so.

And by the time supper was almost over, with only the fruit remaining to be served, the two young girls appeared again dressed in two very beautiful silk robes, bearing two enormous silver trays filled with all kinds of fruits that were in season, and they set these trays upon the table before the King. And having done this, they stepped back a bit and began to sing a song whose words began:

> The point that I have reached, O Love,
> could not be told in many words,

singing with such sweetness and delight that the King, who was looking on and listening with pleasure, thought that all the hierarchies of the angels had descended there to sing. And when their song was finished, they knelt down and respectfully asked the King for his permission to leave, and though he was sorry to see them go, he nonetheless granted their request with apparent cheerfulness. And so the supper was over, and the King with his companions, having mounted their horses, left Messer Neri, and returned to the royal palace, discussing one thing and another on their way.

There the King kept his passion a secret, and in spite of all the affairs of state that occupied him, he could not forget the beauty and charm of the beautiful Ginevra, for love of whom he also loved the sister who resembled her; and so he got caught up in the snares of Love and could scarcely think of anything else; and feigning other motives, he struck up a close friendship with Messer Neri, and very often he would visit his beautiful garden in order to see Ginevra. And when he could no longer bear it, seeing no other alternative, he decided to take away not only one but both of the young girls from their father, and he revealed his love and intention to Count Guido, who since he was a valiant man, replied:

"My lord, I am very surprised at what you tell me, more so than anyone else might be, for I think I am more familiar with your ways than anyone else, since I have known you from your youth to this very day. And I cannot remember your having such a passion even in your youth, when Love could more easily have gotten his claws into you. To hear now, when you are nearing old age, that you have fallen in love, seems so curious and so strange to me that it is almost like a miracle. And if it were my duty to reproach you for this, I know very well what I would say to you about it, considering that you are still shouldering arms in a kingdom recently acquired, and among a people you do not know who are full of deceptions and treacheries, and totally preoccupied as you are with very serious problems and affairs of state, to the extent that you are yet unable to rest upon your throne—and in the midst of all this, you have made room for the temptations of love. This is not the action of a magnanimous king but rather a faint-hearted young man. Furthermore, what is worse is that you say you have decided to take away both daughters from the poor knight who honored you, in his own home, beyond his means, and who, in order to honor you even more, presented his daughters to you almost naked, demonstrating by this gesture how much faith he has in you, and how he firmly believes you to be a king and not a rapacious wolf. Now, have you forgotten so quickly that it was the violence which Manfredi committed against women that opened up to you the road to this kingdom? Was ever an act of betrayal committed more worthy of eternal punishment that this one would be, where you deprive a man who has honored you of his own honor, his hope, and his consolation? What would be said of you if you did this? Perhaps you think it would be sufficient excuse to say: 'I did it because he is a Ghibelline.' Now is this a king's justice, that those who run to him for protection, whoever they may be, are treated in this manner? I call to your attention, my King, that it was most glorious indeed to have conquered Manfredi, but it is much more glorious to conquer yourself; and since you have others to rule over, conquer yourself and restrain this passion of yours, and do not mar with such a stain all that you have so gloriously achieved."

These words bitterly pierced the King's heart, all the more so because he realized they were true; and so, after a few fervent sighs, he declared:

"Count, I truly believe that for the well-trained warrior, any enemy, no matter how powerful, is far weaker and easier to conquer in comparison to his own appetite; but although the effort required will be great and the strength necessary incalculable, your words have spurred me on to such an extent that, before too many days pass by, I shall demonstrate to you by my actions that just as I know how to conquer others, in like manner I know how to master myself."

Nor did many days elapse after these words were spoken before the King, having returned to Naples, in order to deprive himself of the opportunity to commit an unworthy act, as well as to repay the knight for the honor he had bestowed on him, resolved to marry off the two young girls, not as the daughters of Messer Neri but as if they were his very own—even though it was difficult for him to make someone else the possessor of the thing he most desired for himself. And with Messer Neri's consent, after bestowing magnificent dowries on each of them, he gave the beautiful Ginevra to Messer Maffeo da Palizzi and the fair Isotta to Messer Guiglielmo della Magna, both of whom were noble knights and grand barons. And after consigning the girls to them, with incalculable grief, he went off to Puglia, where with continuous effort he so mortified his burning desire that, having broken and shattered his amorous chains, for as long as he lived he remained freed of such a passion.

There will probably be some people who will claim that it was a small matter for a king to have given two young girls in marriage, and I would agree with them; but I would say that it is great, very great indeed, if we consider that it was a king in love who did this, giving in marriage, as he did, the girl whom he loved, never having taken or plucked a leaf, flower, or fruit from his love. And there you have the actions of a magnificent king: richly rewarding a noble knight, honoring in praiseworthy fashion the young girls he loved, and firmly overcoming his own feelings.

[Tenth Day, Seventh Story]

❋

On learning about the fervent love borne for him by Lisa, who has fallen ill because of it, King Peter comforts her and then gives her in marriage to a young nobleman; and after kissing her on the brow, he declares himself to be her knight forevermore.

WHEN Fiammetta had come to the end of her story, and the stalwart generosity of King Charles had been highly praised (although one of the ladies present, who was a Ghibelline, would have nothing to do with praising him), Pampinea, having received the King's command, began:

No discerning person, illustrious ladies, would disagree with what you have said about good King Charles, unless she had other reasons for disliking him; but since this reminds me of a deed perhaps no less commendable that was performed by an adversary of his for the sake of a young girl from our city, I should like to tell you about it.

During the time when the French were driven from Sicily*, there lived in Palermo an apothecary and fellow citizen of ours named Bernardo Puccini, an extremely wealthy man who had by his wife only one daughter, who was very beautiful and at that time of marriageable age. And when King Peter of Aragon became lord of the island, he held a marvelous celebration with his barons in Palermo. During the celebration, while he was jousting in the Catalan fashion, the daughter of Bernardo, whose name was Lisa, happened to catch sight of him riding by on horseback from a window where she was standing with some other women. She found him so wondrously pleasing that after watching him go by a time or two again, she fell passionately in love with him.

When the festivities were over and she was at home with her father, she could think of nothing else but this magnificent and lofty love of hers; and the thing which troubled her the most was the knowledge of her lowly birth, which left her hardly any hope for a happy ending. But this did not make her love the King any less, though out of fear of making things worse for herself, she did not dare to reveal her love. The King was nei-

*A reference to the Sicilian Vespers (March 31, 1282).

ther aware of this nor did he care about it, and this caused her intolerable sorrow, beyond all measure. Because of this, as her love kept growing, it was joined by melancholy, and unable to endure it any longer, the beautiful young girl fell ill, and from day to day, she visibly began to waste away as snow melts in the sun. Her father and mother, sorrowful over this misfortune, did all they could to help her with their continuous attention and with physicians and medicines. But nothing helped, because having despaired of her love, the girl had decided she no longer wished to live.

Now since her father had offered to do anything she wished, the idea came to her that before she died she might let the King know about her love and her decision to live no longer, if she could find some proper means of doing so; and so one day she requested that Minuccio d'Arezzo come to her. Minuccio was, in those days, considered a very fine singer and musician and was well liked by King Peter, and Bernardo, thinking that Lisa wished to hear him play and sing some music, had Minuccio sent for. Like the obliging man that he was, he immediately came to her, and after comforting her somewhat with soothing words, he played some dance songs sweetly on his viol and then sang her some songs, all of which only provided more fire and flame to the young girl's love, rather than the intended consolation.

The young girl then told him that she wished to say a few words to him in private, and when everyone else had left, she said to him:

"Minuccio, I have chosen you as the most trusted custodian of a secret of mine, hoping first of all that you will never reveal it to anyone, except to the man whose name I shall tell you, and second, that you will help me in this matter to the best of your ability. This I beg you to do. Now I want you to know, my dear Minuccio, that on the day when our lord King Peter held the grand feast celebrating his accession to the throne, as fate would have it, I happened to see him jousting, and such was the flame lit in my heart for love of him that it has brought me to the condition in which you see me now. And since I realized how inappropriate for a King my love was, and unable either to cast it out or to lessen it, all of which is too much for me to bear, I have chosen, since it entails less pain, to die; and die I shall. The truth is that I would depart this life in profound desperation were he not first to learn of my love, and since I know of no one who might better relay this intention of mine to him than you, I wish to entrust you with this task, and I beg you not to refuse to do it for me. And when you have done this, inform me of the

fact, so that I may die in peace, unburdened of these pains."
Having said this, in tears, she fell silent.

Minuccio, amazed both at the nobility of her spirit as well as
the harshness of her resolution, was greatly troubled by it all,
and then suddenly he thought of how he could virtuously be of
service to her, and he said:

"Lisa, I give you my word of honor, by which you may rest
assured you will never find yourself deceived; furthermore, I
praise you for such a lofty enterprise as that of setting your
heart on so great a king, and I offer you my assistance, with
which, if you be of good cheer, I hope to do what will enable
me, before three days have passed, to bring you news that will
prove very dear to you; and so as not to lose time, I should like
to go and begin." And after Lisa had begged his assistance once
more and had promised him to take heart, she bid him go with
God's blessing.

Minuccio left and went in search of one Mico da Siena, who
in those days was considered quite a good rhymester, and with
entreaties, he convinced him to compose the following little song:

Arise, my Love, and go to see my lord,
and tell him of the torments I am suffering,
and tell him I am close to death,
for I must hide my yearning out of fear.

With clasped hands, Love, I beg of you,
go to the place where my lord dwells.
Tell him how much I want him, how I love him,
so sweetly is my heart in love;
and that I fear to die from all the fire
enflaming me, and that I cannot wait
to free myself from pain as sharp as this,
which I endure for his sake as I yearn,
fearing, feeling all my shame.
Ah! for God's sake, make it known to him.

Love, ever since I fell in love with him,
you failed to match my courage with my fear
of making clear to him just once
my feelings for this man
who keeps me in such pain,
and death is hard to die this way!
Perhaps he would not be displeased
to learn of all the pain I feel

if only you had given me
courage to reveal my state to him.

But since it did not please you, Love,
to grant me so much boldness, enough
to make my heart known to my lord,
O grief, by semblance or by sign,
I beg you then, O my sweet lord,
to go to him, remind him of that day
when I first saw him with his shield and lance,
bearing arms with other knights,
and took to gazing at him,
so much in love now that my heart is dying.

Minuccio immediately set these words to music with a soft and
sorrowful melody, just as their subject required, and on the third
day he went to the court, where King Peter, who was still at the
table eating, asked him if he would sing something to the tune of
his viol. Whereupon he began to play his song, singing so sweetly
that everyone in the royal hall seemed enchanted by it, so much
so that they all fell silent and were enraptured in listening to it,
the King perhaps more than anyone else. And after Minuccio had
presented his song, the King asked him from where it had come,
for he could not recall having heard it before.

"My lord," replied Minuccio, "not even three days have
passed since the words and the melody were composed." And
when the King asked him for whom it had been written,
Minuccio answered: "I dare not reveal this to anyone but you."

Eager to be told, the King, after having the tables cleared,
took Minuccio with him to his chambers, where Minuccio told
him everything he had heard in great detail. The King was de-
lighted with the story, praised the young girl most highly, and
declared that such a worthy young lady deserved his compassion;
and so he instructed Minuccio to go to her on his behalf and to
comfort her, telling her that without fail he would come to visit
her that day around vespers.

Minuccio, most delighted to be the bearer of such good news,
took his viol and quickly went to the young girl, and speaking to
her in private, he told her everything that had occurred, after
which he sang her the song to the tune of his viol. The young girl
was so happy and contented by this that her health immediately
began to show marked signs of improvement, and without anyone
in the house knowing or suspecting the reason for it, she began
eagerly to wait for vespers, at which time she would see her

lord. The King, being a generous and kind ruler, having thought at length about what he had heard from Municcio, and remembering quite clearly the young girl and her beauty, felt even more compassionate than he had before; and around the hour of vespers, he mounted his horse, and as if riding just for fun, he rode to the place where the house of the apothecary stood. And there, having asked that the very beautiful garden which belonged to the apothecary be opened to him, once inside, he dismounted, and after a while he asked Bernardo about his daughter and whether he had given her in marriage yet.

To this Bernardo replied:

"My lord, she is not married; as a matter of fact, she has been and is still now very ill, though it is true that since the hour of nones today she has miraculously improved."

The King immediately understood what this improvement meant, and he said:

"In good truth, it would be a great shame if so beautiful a creature were taken from the world so soon; let us pay her a visit."

Shortly thereafter, in the company of Bernardo and only two companions, he went to her bedroom, and having entered, he approached the bed, where he found the young girl sitting up a bit, waiting eagerly to see him; and he, taking her by the hand, said:

"My lady, what does this mean? You are young, and you should be providing comfort for others, yet you have allowed yourself to be ill! We pray you be good enough, for our sake, to cheer up so that you will soon be well."

When she felt her hands touched by the man whom she loved above all else, the young girl, although she was somewhat embarrassed, felt, nonetheless, as much joy in her heart as if she had been up in Paradise itself; and as best she could, she answered him:

"My lord, only my wish to bear the most weighty burdens with my feeble strength was the cause of my illness, from which, thanks to your assistance, you will soon see me freed."

Only the King understood the hidden meaning of the young girl's words, and he held her in even higher regard, and to himself, time and again, he cursed Fortune for having made her the daughter of such a man; and then, having stayed awhile with her and comforted her still more, he departed. This courtly gesture of the King was much praised and was considered to be a great honor for the apothecary and his daughter; and she was as happy as any woman ever was with her lover. Assisted by her renewed hopes, in a few days she was well again and more lovely than ever before.

But then, once she was well again, the King, having discussed with the Queen how he should reward such a love as hers, mounted his horse one day and in the company of many of his barons he went to the apothecary's home, and having entered the garden he had the apothecary and his daughter summoned; and then the Queen arrived there with many of her ladies-in-waiting, and taking the young girl into their midst, they began a marvelous celebration. And after a while, the King, together with the Queen, called Lisa, and the King said to her:

"Worthy young lady, the great love you have borne for us has earned for you a great honor, which, for the sake of our love, we trust will please you. And the honor is this: since you have as yet to marry, we wish for you to accept as your husband the man we shall give you, but this notwithstanding, it is our intention to remain forever your knight, while asking no more of your great love than a single kiss."

The young girl, whose entire face had turned red from embarrassment, making the King's pleasure her own, in a low voice replied in this manner:

"My lord, I am quite convinced that if it were known I was in love with you, most people would think I was mad, and perhaps they would even think that I had lost my senses and that I did not understand the difference between my rank and your own. But God, who alone sees into mortal hearts, knows that from the very first moment I found you pleasing, I have known you to be a king and myself the daughter of Bernardo the apothecary, and that it was unseemly for me to direct the ardor of my affection toward such lofty heights. But as you realize better than I, no one on earth falls in love by deliberate choice but, rather, by impulse and desire. Often I would force myself to resist this law, and when I could resist no longer, I fell in love with you, and I love you and shall always love you. And the truth is that the moment I fell in love with you, I decided that I would make your will my own; and therefore, not only would I willingly take as husband and hold dear any man it pleased you to give me, who will bestow upon me honor and dignity, but I would, were you to tell me to, walk through fire, and if I thought it would give you pleasure, be delighted to do so. And as for having you, the King, as my knight, you know how well it would suit someone of my condition, so I shall say no more about this matter; nor shall I grant the single kiss you require of my love without the permission of my lady the Queen. Nevertheless, for all the kindness which you and my lady the Queen, who is here present, have displayed toward me, may God on my behalf render both thanks and reward to you, since I, alone, could never repay you." And then she was silent.

The Queen was very much pleased with the young girl's reply and thought her to be as wise as the King had said. The King had the father and mother of the young girl summoned, and upon hearing that they were happy with what he intended to do, he sent for a young man named Perdicone, who was poor but of noble birth, and placing some rings in his hand, he induced the young man, who was not unwilling, to take Lisa in marriage.

In addition to the many and precious jewels which the King and Queen bestowed upon the young girl, the King forthwith bestowed upon him Cefalù and Calatabellotta, two very fine and fruitful estates, declaring:

"These we give you as your lady's dowry: what we intend to do for you, you will see in due course." Having said this, the King turned toward the girl and said: "Now we wish to take the fruit of your love which is due us," and holding her head with both his hands, he kissed her on the brow.

Perdicone, Lisa's father and mother, and Lisa herself, all of whom were delighted, celebrated the happy marriage with a magnificent feast; and as many people will affirm, the King held closely to the pact he made with the girl, and for as long as he lived, he always considered himself her knight and never did he engage in any feat of arms without displaying exclusively the favor the girl sent him.*

And it is precisely in acting this way that one wins the hearts of one's subjects, provides for others the example of good deeds, and acquires eternal fame; but today few, if any, rulers manage to aim the bows of their intellects in that direction, having become for the most part cruel and tyrannical.

---

*Knights, according to courtly tradition, carried a symbolic token from their ladies (usually a kerchief or ribbon) into tournaments or battle.

[Tenth Day, Eighth Story]

❧

Sophronia, believing that she is the wife of Gisippus, is actually married to Titus Quintus Fulvius, with whom she goes to Rome, where Gisippus arrives in an impoverished state. Believing that he has been scorned by Titus, he claims, in order to be put to death, that he has murdered a man; when Titus recognizes him, in order to save Gisippus he declares that he himself committed the murder. When the actual murderer perceives this, he confesses; as a result, they are all freed by Octavianus, and then Titus gives Gisippus his sister in marriage and shares all his possessions with him.

AFTER Pampinea had finished speaking and each of the ladies, but most of all the one who was a Ghibelline, had praised King Peter, Filomena, at the King's command began:

Magnificent ladies, who does not know that kings can do, whenever they wish, all sorts of wonderful things, and that they are, consequently, above all others called upon to display generosity? Therefore, whoever has the power and does what is befitting him, does well; but we must not be too amazed, nor should we praise him so highly, as we ought to another who accomplishes the same thing when, his means being less, less is expected of him. And so, if you exalt the deeds of kings so much and they seem illustrious to you, I do not doubt in the slightest that you will delight in and praise even more those of our equals whenever their deeds resemble or are even greater than those of kings. Hence, I have decided to tell you a story about the praiseworthy and magnificent way in which two ordinary citizens acted toward each other.

Now, in the time when Octavianus Caesar, before he was called Augustus, was ruling the Roman Empire in the office known as the Triumvirate, there was in Rome a gentleman named Publius Quintus Fulvius; this man had a son of amazing intelligence named Titus Quintus Fulvius, whom he sent to study philosophy in Athens, doing all he could to commend him to a very old friend of his, a noble Athenian named Chremes. Titus was lodged by him in his own home in the company of one of his sons named Gisippus, and both Titus and Gissippus were put under the guidance of a philosopher named Aristippus.

And as the two young men spent much time in each other's company, they discovered they had so much in common that there sprang up between them a sense of brotherhood and friendship so strong that nothing but death itself might separate them: neither of them ever felt happy or at ease except when with the other. Having begun their studies, since both were endowed with the highest intelligence, they rose to the glorious heights of philosophy side by side and with marvelous acclaim. And living this way, they spent a good three years to the greatest delight of Chremes, who looked upon them both alike as his sons. At the end of that time, Chremes, already an old man, passed from this life as all living things must eventually do. Both of them felt equal grief, as if they had lost a common father, nor were the friends or relatives of Chremes able to discern which of the two was in more need of consolation because of their unfortunate loss.

A few months later, some friends and relatives of Gisippus met with him, along with Titus, and urged him to take a wife; and they found him an Athenian girl of astonishing beauty and noble breeding, whose name was Sophronia and who was about fifteen years of age. And as the appointed time of their nuptials was drawing near, one day Gissippus asked Titus, who had not yet seen the girl, to go with him to see her. They went to her house and with the girl sitting between them, interested in the beauty of his friend's bride, Titus began to scrutinize her very closely, and finding every part of her most pleasing indeed and silently extolling her beauties to himself, he began to burn with love for her, more so than any lover had ever burned for any lady, but he showed no sign of it. Then, after spending some time with her, they left and returned home.

There Titus, after entering his bedroom alone, began to think about the pleasing young girl, and the more he thought about her, the more enamored he became. When he realized this, after a number of passionate sighs, he began thinking to himself:

"Ah, how miserable your life is, Titus! Where and upon whom have you fixed your heart, your love, and your hope? Do you not realize that the favors you have received from Chremes and his family, as well as the perfect friendship which exists between you and Gisippus, whose bride she is, requires that you treat this girl with the same respect you would a sister? Whom, then, do you love? Will you allow yourself to be carried away by deceitful love, by flattering hope? Open the eyes of your mind, you miserable creature, and know yourself for what you are. Give way to reason, restrain your lustful appetite, temper your unhealthy desires, and direct your thoughts to something else; oppose your lust from the outset and conquer yourself while you still have time. It is not fitting for you to want this, it is not honest; and even if you were certain (which you are not) of obtaining the thing you wish to pursue, you should flee from it, if you have any concern for what true friendship requires and for what you owe to it. What, then, should you do, Titus? You should abandon this unseemly love if you wish to do what is proper."

But then, remembering Sophronia, and completely changing his mind, he condemned everything he had thought and he said:

"The laws of love are more powerful than all the others: they break not only those of friendship but divine laws as well. How often in the past have fathers loved their daughters, brothers their sisters, and stepmothers their stepsons? Things more monstrous than one friend loving the wife of another have happened thousands of times in the past. Besides this, I am a young man, and youth is completely controlled by the laws of love; so, whatever pleases Love should also please me. Virtuous deeds suit older men; I can only wish what Love wishes for me. The beauty of this lady deserves to be loved by everyone, and if I who am a young man, love her, who can rightly reproach me for it? I do not love her because she belongs to Gisippus; on the contrary, I love her because I would love her no matter to whom she belonged. Here Fortune is at fault, for it is she who gave her to my friend Gisippus rather than to another man; and if anyone has to love her (as she rightly deserves to be for her beauty), then Gisippus should be all the more happy when he discovers that is I who love her rather than someone else." And from this argument he began reproaching himself and returned to its contrary argument, and from that to this and from this to that, spending not only that day and the following night, but many others as well, until finally, from loss of food and lack of sleep over it all, he was forced out of weakness to take to his bed.

Gisippus, who had seen him full of thought for many days and who now saw him ill, was very distressed, and with all possible skill and care, never leaving his side, he sought to comfort him and often with insistence he would ask him the reason for his pensiveness and his illness. But after having given him a number of meaningless answers on more than one occasion, all of which Gisippus had recognized as such, Titus found himself constrained to answer, and with sobs and sighs, he answered Gisippus in this manner:

"Gisippus, if only the gods had so willed it, I would have preferred to die rather than to live any longer, considering how Fortune has brought me to the point where my virtue had to be put to the test and where, to my greatest shame, you have found it wanting; but I am certain that before long I shall receive the reward I deserve, that is, death, which would be dearer to me than living with the memory of my baseness, the cause of which—since there is nothing I should or could conceal from you—I shall reveal to you, but not without great embarrassment."

And starting from the beginning, Titus explained to Gisippus the reason for his brooding and his struggle between these contrasting thoughts, and finally, which of his thoughts had been victorious, and how he was dying for love of Sophronia, affirming that since he realized how very unbecoming this was for him, as penance he had made up his mind to die, which he believed would soon come to pass.

Upon hearing this and seeing his weeping, Gisippus at first remained silent, for he, too, although more temperately, was taken by the charm of the beautiful young woman. But without hesitation, he decided that the life of his friend was more dear to him than Sophronia, and so, his own tears encouraged by the other's tears, he answered him:

"Titus, if you were not in need of comfort as you are, I would lament the fact that you are a man who has violated our friendship by keeping your very serious passion concealed for so long a time from me. And even if your thoughts did not seem proper to you, there was no reason to hide them from your friend any more than if they were proper, for just as anyone who is a friend will take delight in sharing the proper thoughts of a friend, so, too, will he try to remove the improper ones from his friend's heart; but putting that aside for now, let me come to what I know is a problem I realize to be of greater urgency. That you are passionately in love with Sophronia, who is betrothed to me, does not amaze me in the least. In fact, I would be amazed if this were not the case, considering her beauty and your own nobility of heart, which makes you all the more susceptible to passion the greater the excellence of the object that rouses your delight. And as much as you are right in loving Sophronia, you are wrong in complaining that Fortune (although you do not say as much) has conceded her to me, since you think your love would be more proper if she had been anyone

else's but mine. But if you are as wise as you usually are, think
how lucky you are: could Fortune have given her to a better
person than I? If any other man possessed her, no matter how
proper your love might have been, he would have loved her more
for himself than for you, a thing of which, if you consider me
your friend, as I am, you need have no fear. And the reason is
this: I cannot remember, from the time we first became friends,
ever owning something that was not as much yours as it was
mine. And even if things had progressed to the point that I
could not do otherwise, I would still do with her what I did with
my other possessions before, but as things stand now, I can do
otherwise and make her yours alone, and this I will do, for I do
not know how you could hold my friendship dear if I were un-
able to do your will rather than my own when the matter can be
so properly arranged. It is true that Sophronia is my betrothed,
and that I love her very much and was anxiously awaiting our
marriage, but since you, who are much more in love than I,
desire more ardently so precious a thing as she, rest assured that
she shall enter my bedroom not as my wife but as yours. And so
put aside your brooding, dismiss your melancholy, call back your
lost health, your comfort, and your happiness, and from this mo-
ment on, joyfully await the rewards of your love, one much
more worthy than mine ever was."

When Titus heard Gisippus speak this way, he was as much
pleased by the flattering hope offered him by Gisippus as he was
ashamed by the knowledge of his duty, which showed him that
the greater Gisippus's generosity was, the more improper was it
for him to take advantage of it; and so, still in tears, he an-
swered with difficulty as follows:

"Gisippus, your generous and true friendship clearly tells me
what it is up to me to do. God forbid that I shall ever take from
you for my own the one whom He has given to you, as the more
worthy. If He had seen that she was more suitable for me, nei-
ther you nor anyone else could possibly believe that He would
have given her to you. Rejoice, then, in His choice, in His
discreet counsel and His gift, and let me waste away in tears, a
fate He has prepared for one who is unworthy of so great a
blessing; for I shall either conquer my tears and thus make you
happy, or they shall conquer me and I shall be put out of my
misery."

To this Gisippus replied:

"Titus, if our friendship allows me sufficient license to compel
you to follow my wishes and can induce you to follow them, this
is the time I most certainly plan to employ it; and if you do not

onsent willingly to my entreaties, with whatever force one must
mploy in the interests of a friend, I shall make Sophronia
ours. I know what the powers of Love can do, and I know that
ot only once but many times, they have led lovers to an un-
appy death; and I see you so close to death that you can no
onger turn back nor vanquish your tears, but if you go on like
his, you will destroy yourself and because of this, without a
loubt, I would soon follow after you. Therefore, even if I loved
ou for no other reason, your life is dear to me because by own
lepends on it. Sophronia, then, will be yours, for you would not
asily find another woman who pleases you as much; and I can
asily turn my love toward another, and thus make both you and
ne happy. I should perhaps not be so generous in this matter, if
vives were as rare and to be found with as much difficulty as
ne is able to find friends. And so, since I can very easily find
nother wife but not another friend, I prefer to transfer her to
ou rather than to lose you—I do not say lose her, for I would
tot be losing her in giving her to you but rather I would be
ransferring her to another me, that is, from good to better. So,
f my entreaties mean anything to you in any way, I beg you to
ast aside your sorrow and at one and the same time bring com-
ort to both yourself and me, and with good hope prepare to
eize the happiness for which your ardent passion yearns."

Titus was ashamed to agree to the idea that Sophronia should
ecome his wife and would have nothing to do with it at first,
out pulled on the one side by his love and encouraged on the
other by the pleas of Gisippus, he said:

"Look here, Gisippus, I cannot say whether I would be pleas-
ng you or myself more in doing what you tell me would please
you so much; but since your generosity is so great that it van-
quishes my rightful shame, I shall do it. But you may be sure of
this, that I am not doing this as a man who fails to realize he is
receiving from you not only the woman he loves but with her his
very life as well. May the gods allow me to be able to prove to
you yet with honor and with benefit to yourself how grateful I
am for what you are doing for me, you who have more compas-
sion for me than I do for myself."

Following these words, Gisippus said:

"Titus, if we want to succeed in this affair, this is what I
think we should do: as you know, after lengthy negotiations be-
tween my relatives and those of Sophronia, she has become my
promised bride; and so if I were now to announce that I no
longer wish to have her as my wife, the greatest scandal would
result and both her relatives and my own would be upset. This

would not bother me at all, if I could be sure that she would b
come your wife, but I am afraid, if I abandon her in this ma
ner, her parents will immediately give her to somebody else, ar
that somebody will not necessarily be you, and thus you w
have lost that which I shall not have gained. Therefore, it seen
to me, if you agree, that I should continue with what I have a
ready started, and that I should take her to my home as n
wife and celebrate the marriage; and then we shall arrange f
you to sleep with her as if she were your wife. Then, at the rigl
time and place, we shall make the matter public; and if everyor
is pleased, that will be fine, and if they are not pleased, the dee
in any case will have been done, and since there can be no tun
ing back, they will, of necessity, have to be satisfied."

Titus liked this suggestion, and so when Titus was healthy an
strong again Gissippus welcomed Sophronia into his home as h
wife, and after a great celebration, when night came all th
ladies left the new bride in the bed of her husband and departed

The bedroom of Titus was connected to that of Gisippus, an
one could pass directly from one into the other; so when Gisip
pus went to his bedroom, after all the lights had been exti
guished, he went quietly into Titus's room and told him that h
should go to bed with his lady. When Titus heard this, he was s
overcome with shame that he wanted to change his mind and r
fuse to go, but Gisippus, whose intentions to do Titus's pleasur
were as sincere as his words, after a lengthy argument, manage
nevertheless, to send him in to her. And as soon as Titus got int
her bed, he took her in his arms and almost as if in jest, h
softly asked her if she wished to be his wife. And she, believin
him to be Gisippus, replied that she did; whereupon, he said, a
he slipped a beautiful and precious ring on her finger: "And
wish to be your husband." And then the marriage was consum
mated, as Titus took long and amorous pleasure of her, withou
her or anyone else perceiving that it was not Gisippus who wa
sleeping with her.

This was the way the marriage of Sophronia and Titus stoo
then, when Publius, Titus's father, passed from this life; and a
a result, Titus received written word to return to Rome withou
delay in order to attend to his interests; and so after consultin
with Gisippus, he decided to go to Rome and to take Sophroni
with him, something which he should not nor could not easily d
without revealing to Sophronia how things actually stood. An
so, one day, they called her into the room, and they explained t
her in great detail how things stood, proving it to her by men
tioning a number of things which had happened between Titu

nd herself. Having cast a rather indignant glance first at one
nd then at the other, she immediately broke into tears, com-
plaining bitterly about the trick Gisippus had played on her, and
before a word of this was mentioned in Gisippus's house, she
went to her father's home and told him and her mother about
the deception which she and they had suffered at the hands of
Gisippus, adding that she was the wife of Titus and not of
Gisippus, as they believed. Sophronia's father considered it a
grave matter and complained long and loudly to his own rela-
tives as well as those of Gisippus, and the local talk and discus-
sion about it was extensive and intense. Gisippus was hated by
his relatives and those of Sophronia, and everyone said that he
deserved not only to be reproached but also to be severely pun-
ished. But he maintained that he had done an honest deed and
that the relatives of Sophronia should thank him, for he had
married her to a man better than himself.

On the other hand, Titus, who heard everything that was going
on, managed to bear up under his great pain; and since he knew
that the Greeks were accustomed to making a lot of noise and
threats over things until the moment they found someone to an-
swer them back, at which time they would become not only
humble but extremely servile, Titus decided he could no longer
stand all their talking and that it deserved an answer. With the
heart of a Roman and the wit of an Athenian he managed, after
careful preparation, to have the relatives of Gisippus and So-
phronia gather in a temple. Then, walking in accompanied only
by Gisippus, he spoke to the people waiting there in this man-
ner:

"Many philosophers believe that mankind's actions conform to
the will and decree of the immortal gods, and hence, there are
some who assert that all which is done or that will be done here
on earth is the result of necessity, while still others maintain
that this necessity impinges only upon what has already hap-
pened in the past. If these opinions are examined carefully, it
will immediately become apparent that to criticize something
which cannot be changed amounts to nothing less than an at-
tempt to show that you are wiser than the gods, who, we are
obliged to believe, control and govern us, as well as our affairs,
with eternal and infallible logic. And so, just as you may readily
see that to take issue with their actions is an act of insane and
senseless presumption, in like manner, you may appreciate with
what chains those people who allow themselves to be carried
away by such daring deserve to be bound. In my opinion, you
are all to be included among such people, if it is true what I

have been told you have said and still are saying about So
phronia's becoming my wife after you had given her to Gisippus
for you do not consider the fact that *ab eterno** it had been de
cided that she was to become my wife and not that of Gisippus
as is now plain from the actual outcome. But since a discussion
of the secret providence and intention of the gods is for man
people a difficult and weighty subject to comprehend, let us sup
pose that the gods play no role in any of our affairs, and I shal
be happy to pass to an argument based upon purely human con
siderations; and in appealing to them, I shall be obliged to d
two things very contrary to my nature. First, I shall have t
praise myself a little; and second, I shall have to criticize an
condemn to a certain degree someone else. But since I do not in
tend to stray from the truth in either one or the other case, an
since this is what the present occasion demands, I shall never
theless proceed. Aroused more by anger than by reason, wit
your complaints and your continuous muttering—no, rather, lou
outcries—you castigate, attack, and condemn Gisippus for hav
ing given me by his own decision the wife you had arranged t
give to him; and in so doing I consider him worthy of the highes
praise, and the reasons are these: first, because he did what
true friend should do; and second, because he acted more wisel
than you have. It is not my intention to explain at the momen
what the holy laws of friendship require one friend to do for an
other, being content simply to have reminded you of these law
here and that the bond of friendship is more binding than tha
of blood or kinship, for the friends we have we choose for our
selves, but Fortune provides us with our relatives. And so, then
the fact the Gisippus held my life more dear than he did you
goodwill should surprise none of you, for I am his friend or con
sider myself as such. But let us come now to the second reason
which is that he has been much wiser than you have been, an
one which I shall have to demonstrate with greater insistence
for it seems to me you understand nothing about the providenc
of the gods, and know even less about the consequences o
friendship. Let me say then that it was your foresight, you
counsel, and your deliberation that gave Sophronia to Gisippus
young man and a philosopher, and that it was his decision tha
bestowed her upon a young man and a philosopher; your deci
sion gave her to an Athenian, whereas the decision of Gisippu

---

*"From eternity" or "from the beginning": here Titus seems to b
guilty in this specious argument of the same presumption he criticize
in his audience.

gave her to a Roman; yours gave her to a noble young man, that of Gisippus gave her to an even nobler young man; you gave her to a rich young man, Gisippus gave her to an even richer young man; your decision gave her to a young man who not only did not love her but who hardly knew her, while Gisippus gave her to a young man who loved her more than his every happiness and his very life itself. And that what I say is the truth and that what he has done is more worthy of praise than what you have done, let us examine the matter in more detail. That I am a young man and a philosopher just as Gisippus is, my face and my studies make clear, without having to pursue the matter further; we are both the same age, and we have always advanced on equal footing in our studies. It is true that he is an Athenian while I am a Roman. But if the fame of these cities is to be discussed, let me say that I come from a city which is free, while his pays tribute; I would also add that I come from a city that is the mistress of the entire world, while his city is obedient to my own; I would remind you that mine is a city flourishing in arms, imperial power, and the arts, while his can boast only of the arts. Besides this, in spite of the fact that you see me here as a rather humble scholar, I was not born from the dregs of the Roman populace; my houses and the public places of Rome are filled with ancient statues of my ancestors, and the annals of Rome are filled with the many triumphs celebrated on the Capitoline Hill of Rome by the Quintii: nor has our family fallen into decay because of its antiquity; on the contrary, the glory of our name flourishes today as never before. Out of modesty, I shall be silent about my wealth, remembering that honorable poverty has always been the ancient and best legacy of the noble citizens of Rome; but if poverty is to be condemned by the vulgar and riches praised, with these I am well provided, not as one who is greedy but rather as one who is favored by Fortune. And I know full well how happy you were and would still be to have Gisippus here as your kinsman, but there is no reason why I should be any less dear to you in Rome, considering that with me there, you will have an excellent host, as well as a useful, solicitous and powerful patron, both in your public as well as in your private needs. Who, therefore, setting aside his blind passion and looking at the matter reasonably, would praise your advice higher than that of my friend Gisippus? Surely no one. And thus Sophronia is well married to Titus Quintius Fulvius, the noble, wealthy citizen of Rome, born of an ancient family and friend of Gisippus; and therefore, anyone who is disturbed by this or who complains about it does not do what he should nor does he know what he is doing. There will perhaps be some who say that they do not complain about Sophronia's being the wife of Titus but that they complain, instead, about the manner in which she became his wife, secretly, on the sly, without telling friends or relatives anything about it. But there is nothing miraculous about this, nor is it the first time that such a thing has happened. I shall gladly leave aside those women who have taken a husband against the wishes of their father, and those who have eloped with their lovers, those who were mistresses before they were wives, and those who announced their marriages with their pregnancies and childbirths rather than with their words, thereby forcing their fathers to consent. This did not happen in Sophronia's case; on the contrary, she was carefully, discreetly, and honorably given by Gisippus to Titus. There will be those who will claim that Gisippus had no right to give her in marriage; these are foolish and womanly complaints, the result of shallow reasoning. Is it not Fortune once again employing here her different ways and strange means to bring things to their determined ends? What do I care if a shoemaker or even a philosopher tends to one of my affairs according to his own judgment, either in secret or in the open, if the end result is good? I should be careful, if the shoemaker has been indiscreet, to make sure he does nothing else for me in the future and to thank him for what he has done. If Gisippus has married Sophronia well, going around complaining about him and his methods is unnecessarily stupid; if you have no confidence in his judgment, see to it that he never marries again, and thank him for doing it this time. Nevertheless, I would have you know that never did I seek, either by guile or fraud, to impose any stain upon the honesty and the purity of your blood in the person of Sophronia; and regardless of the fact that I secretly took her as my wife, I did not come here as a thief to steal her virginity away from her, nor did I wish to possess her in any way that was not honorable like someone who was an enemy or rejected your kinship; but passionately inflamed by her charming beauty and her virtue, I realized that if I had sought her hand in the manner you might have wished, I would never have had her, since loving her as much as you do, you would have feared that I might take her away to Rome. And so I used the secret means which now are revealed to you, and I made Gisippus agree to do, in my name, what he was not disposed to do; and then, though I was passionately in love with her, I sought her embraces not as a lover but rather as a husband, for, as she herself can truthfully testify, I never came close to her before I had married her with the proper words and ring and had asked her whether she wanted me as her husband—to which she answered that she did. If she feels she was deceived she should not blame me but rather herself for not asking me who I was. So, then, this is the great crime, the great sin, the great wrong committed by Gisippus, my friend, and by me, her lover, that Sophronia secretly became the wife of Titus Quintius; for this reason you tear him apart, and menace and plot against him. What more would you have done if he had given her to a peasant, some scoundrel, or a servant? What chains, what prison, what cross would be sufficient punishment for this? But let us put this matter aside for now; for something I was not expecting has now happened: that is, my father has died and I must return to Rome, and since I wish to take Sophronia with me, I have revealed to you what perhaps I should otherwise have kept secret; and, if you are wise, you will cheerfully accept this, for if I had wished to deceive or insult you, I could have left her scorned—but God forbid that such cowardice could ever dwell in a Roman heart! Therefore, she, Sophronia, by the consent of the gods, the power of the laws of men, the praiseworthy good sense of my friend Gisippus, and my own lover's wit, is mine. But it seems that you, perhaps because you consider yourselves to be wiser than the gods or other men, disapprove of this, and you foolishly persist in doing two things that I find most disturbing: first, you hold on to Sophronia, which you have no right to do without my consent; second, you treat Gisippus, to whom you are rightly under great obligation, as an enemy. I do not intend at the moment to explain to you further how foolishly you act in these matters, but as my friends, I would advise you to set aside your indignation, to abandon all your resentments, and to return Sophronia to me, so that I may cheerfully depart as your kinsman and continue to live as such. Rest assured of this, that whether or not what has happened pleases you, if you mean to do otherwise, I shall take Gisippus away and without fail, when I reach Rome, I shall take back the woman who is rightfully mine, in spite of all your objections; and I shall teach you from experience just how much the anger in a Roman heart can achieve once made a lifelong enemy."

After Titus had spoken in this manner, he rose to his feet, his face flushed with anger, and taking Gisippus by the hand, he led him out of the temple as he shook his head from side to side and cast menacing looks at all those present, showing how little they all meant to him.

The people he had left behind in the temple, some persuaded

by Titus's arguments concerning his kinship and friendship, and others terrified by his parting words, unanimously agreed that it was better to have Titus as their kinsman, since Gisippus had no wish to be, than to have lost a kinsman in Gisippus and to have acquired an enemy in Titus. And so they went and found Titus and told him that they were delighted that Sophronia was his and to have him as a cherished relative and Gisippus as a good friend; then, following a friendly and familylike celebration all together, they went their separate ways and sent Sophronia back to Titus. Like the wise woman that she was, she made a virtue of necessity and soon directed the love she had felt for Gisippus toward Titus, and with him she left for Rome, where she was received with great honor.

Gisippus, who had remained in Athens, was now held in low esteem by everyone. After a short time, as a result of certain factional disputes within the city, he was driven out of Athens along with everyone in his household, and impoverished and miserable, he was condemned to perpetual exile. In this condition, Gisippus had not only become poor but a beggar as well, and as best he could he made his way to Rome to see if Titus still remembered him. On learning that Titus was still alive and that he was admired by all Romans, he found where his house was and he went to wait there for Titus to appear. And because of the miserable state he was in, Gisippus did not dare to say a word but rather endeavored to make himself seen so that Titus might recognize him and have him sent for; but Titus passed by, and Gisippus thought that Titus had seen him but that he pretended not to recognize him, and recalling all that he had done for Titus, indignant and desperate, he departed.

It was already dark, and Gisippus was hungry and without any money; not knowing where he would go and wanting more than anything else to die, he came to a very deserted place in the city where he saw a large cave, into which he crept with the intention of spending the night, and there upon the bare ground, ill-clad and overcome by much weeping, he fell asleep. Into this cave two thieves, who had gone out together during the night to commit a robbery, returned at daybreak after carrying out the crime, and when an argument ensued, one of them, the stronger of the two, killed the other and ran away. Gisippus had overheard and witnessed all this, and it seemed to him that he had now discovered a way to obtain the death he so much desired without resorting to suicide; and so he stayed there until the officers of the guard, who had heard about the crime, arrived there and angrily carried Gisippus off as their prisoner. When Gisippus was questioned, he confessed that he had murdered the man and that then he was unable to find his way out of the cave; as a result, the praetor, who was called Marcus Varro, ordered that he be put to death on the cross, as was the custom in those days.

By chance Titus just happened to turn up at the praetor's court at that hour; and staring into the condemned man's wretched face as he listened to the reason for his arrest, he immediately recognized him to be Gisippus and he marveled at his miserable fortune and at how he ever happened to be there. And most fervently desiring to help him, but seeing no other way to save him other than by accusing himself in order to clear Gisippus, he quickly stepped forward and shouted:

"Marcus Varro, recall the poor man you have just condemned, for he is innocent. I have offended the gods enough with one crime, by killing the man your guards discovered dead this morning, without wishing to offend them now with the death of another innocent man."

Varro was astonished and regretted that the entire court had also heard Titus; but since he was unable to do honorably but what the laws commanded, he had Gisippus brought back, and in the presence of Titus, he said to Gisippus:

"How could you be so foolish as to confess, without being tortured to do so, to a crime you never committed, when in so doing you would lose your life? You stated that you were the one who last night had murdered a man, and now this other person appears and states that not you but he has killed him."

Gisippus looked and saw that the man was Titus, and he clearly understood that he was doing this to save him out of gratitude for the favor he had at one time received from Gisippus; and so, weeping out of compassion, Gisippus replied:

"Varro, the truth is I killed him, and the pity of Titus is too late to save me now."

Then Titus, for his part, said:

"Praetor, as you can see, this man is a foreigner and was found unarmed beside the dead man, and you can tell it is his poverty that is the reason he wants to die; therefore, free him, and punish me, for I deserve it."

Varro was astonished at the insistence of these two men and had by now assumed that neither of the two was guilty; and as he was thinking about how he could manage to set them free, all of a sudden there came forward a young man named Publius Ambustus, a hardened criminal and a man well known as a thief to all the Romans, and the person who had actually committed the murder. Knowing that neither of the two men was guilty of the crime of which they were both accusing themselves, he was moved by the greatest compassion, and so overwhelmed was his heart with the innocence of the two friends, that moved by great pity, he stepped up to Varro and said:

"Praetor, fate compels me to resolve the difficult problem of these two men, and I do not know what god within me it is who presses and torments me into revealing to you my sin; therefore, be advised that neither is guilty of the crime to which each one confesses. The truth is that I am the one who killed that man this morning around daybreak; and that poor fellow standing there I saw sleeping while I was dividing the loot with the man I killed. There is no need for me to clear Titus; everyone knows that he is not a man of such sorts. Free him, then, and punish me according to the law."

Octavianus, who by this time had heard about the affair, had the three men brought before him and demanded to know the reason why each of them wished to be convicted; and each man told his story. Octavianus freed the two friends because they were innocent and the third man for the sake of the other two.

The first thing Titus did was take his friend Gisippus aside and scold him severely for his lukewarm trust and diffidence, after which he made a great fuss over him before taking him to his home, where Sophronia, with tears of compassion, received him as a brother. And having restored his spirits somewhat, and having clothed him once again in a way befitting his worth and station, Titus first made Gisippus the joint owner of all his money and possessions, and then he gave him as his wife one of his young sisters, who was named Fulvia; then he said to him:

"Gisippus, now you must decide whether to live here close to me or to return with everything I have given you to Greece."

Prompted on one hand by the exile he had suffered from his native city, and on the other by the love which he rightly owed to the welcome friendship of Titus, Gisippus decided to become a Roman; and there in Rome with his Fulvia, and Titus with his Sophronia, they all lived together in the same house happily and for a long time to come, and with each passing day they became, if such a thing was possible, even better friends.

Friendship, therefore, is a most holy thing, not only worthy of singular reverence but to be commended forevermore as the most discreet mother of generosity and good conduct, the sister of gratitude and of charity, the enemy of hatred and avarice, always prepared, without waiting to be begged, to do virtuously for others that which it would have done for itself; today only on the rarest of occasions do we see its most sacred results in any two people, for to the fault and the shame of man's wretched cupidity, which cares only for its own interests, friendship has been banished to the extreme corners of the earth and left in perpetual exile. What love, what riches, what kinship could have made Gisippus feel so deeply in his heart the ardor, the tears, and the sighs of Titus so that he gave to Titus his own lovely and gracious bride whom he loved—if not for friendship? What laws, what threats, what fear could have moved the youthful arms of Gisippus to abstain from the embraces of the beautiful young lady in lonely and half-lit places or even in his own bed, perhaps at times despite her own invitation—if not for friendship? What rewards, what recompenses, and what gains could have caused Gisippus not to care about losing his relatives and those of Sophronia, not to concern himself with the coarse jibes of the multitude, not to worry about the jokes and the sneers in order to content his friend—if not for friendship?

Moreover, what could have moved Titus, who, though he might blamelessly have pretended not to see Gisippus, unhesitatingly sought his own death in order to spare Gisippus from the crucifixion which he himself was seeking—if not for friendship? What could have made Titus be so readily generous as to share his great patrimony with Gisippus, whose own possessions had been seized from him by Fortune—if not for friendship? Who could have made Titus so zealously and without hesitation concede his own sister to Gisippus, when he could see him in extreme poverty and utter misery—if not for friendship?

So let men go on wishing for a multitude of relatives, hosts of brothers and of children, and to increase the number of their servants with their wealth. But what they do not realize is that every one of them, no matter who he may be, is more concerned over the smallest danger to himself than he is eager to protect his father, or his brother, or his master from great peril—whereas between friends exactly the opposite happens.

[Tenth Day, Ninth Story]

❖

Saladin, disguised as a merchant, is entertained by Messer Torello; a crusade is launched; Messer Torello gives his wife a date before which she is not to remarry. He is captured, but because of his skill in training hunting birds, he comes to the at-

tention of the Sultan, who recognizes him and reminds him of their first meeting, entertaining him most lavishly. Messer Torello falls ill, and by magic he is taken back overnight to Pavia; and at the celebration of his wife's remarriage, he makes himself known to her, and then returns with her to his home.

FILOMENA's words had already drawn to a close, and the generous gratitude of Titus had been praised highly by everyone, when the King, reserving for Dioneo the last turn to speak, began in this manner:

Charming ladies, without a doubt Filomena is right in what she says about friendship, and with good reason at the end of her remarks she complains of how friendship is so little esteemed by men today. And if we were gathered here to correct the defects of the world or even to criticize them, I would follow her words with a long sermon. But since our goal lies somewhere else it has occurred to me to tell you by means of a story, one which is perhaps rather long but nonetheless entirely entertaining, about one of Saladin's generous deeds; and from the things you hear in my tale, you will see that although our vices may prevent us from winning completely the friendship of another, we may at least take delight in acts of courtesy with the hope that sooner or later our actions will be rewarded.

Let me say, then, that according to what some people claim, in the time of Emperor Frederick I, the Christians launched a great crusade to regain the Holy Land.* Saladin, a most worthy lord and then Sultan of Babylon, having heard about it sometime in advance, decided to see for himself what preparations the Christian leaders were making for this crusade so that he might better prepare to defend himself. First he settled all his affairs in Egypt, and then, disguised as a merchant going on a pilgrimage, accompanied solely by three servants and two of his senior and most judicious men, he set out on his way. After inspecting a number of Christian provinces, one evening, while they were riding through Lombardy on their way to crossing the mountains, on the road from Milan to Pavia around the time of vespers, they happened to encounter a nobleman whose name was Messer Torello from Stra in the province of Pavia and who with all his servants, dogs, and falcons was on his way to spend some time at one of the beautiful estates he owned on the banks of the Ticino River.

---

*The Third Crusade, began in 1189, in which Frederick died (1190).

When Messer Torel caught sight of these men, he decided that they were foreigners and of noble birth, and he wished to do them honor. So, as soon as Saladin asked one of Messer Torello's servants how much farther it was from there to Pavia and whether they would be able to enter the city at that hour, Torello, not giving his servant a chance to reply, answered himself: "My lords, you cannot reach Pavia in time to enter the city."

"Well, then," said Saladin, "would you be so kind as to show us, since we are foreigners, where we can best spend the night?"

Messer Torello said:

"I shall gladly do so; I was just about to send one of these servants of mine on an errand to a place not far from Pavia: I shall send him with you, and he will take you to a place where you will find very comfortable lodgings."

Then, going up to one of his most intelligent servants, he told him what he was to do and sent him off with the group, while he himself rode quickly off to his home, where he arranged for the best possible supper to be prepared and the tables to be set up in one of his gardens. And when this was done, he went to the entrance of his house to await his guests. The servant, while discussing a number of topics with the noblemen, managed to lead the group down certain roads, which without their realizing it, brought them to the home of his master.

When Messer Torel saw them, he went on foot to meet them, and laughing he declared:

"My lords, you are most very welcome."

Saladin, who was very astute, realized that this knight had been afraid they would not have accepted his invitation if he had invited them the first time they met. So in order to make it impossible for them to refuse to spend the evening with him, he cleverly had them brought to his home; and then, Saladin, having returned the greeting, said:

"Sir, if it were possible to complain of courtly men, we should have cause to complain of you, for to say nothing of the fact that you have taken us somewhat out of our way, you have in a way constrained us to accept this extraordinary gesture of yours, when all we did to merit your hospitality was to exchange a single greeting."

The knight, who was wise and well-spoken, said:

"My lords, what you shall receive from me, judging from your appearance, will be but poor hospitality by comparison to what you deserve; but the truth is that outside Pavia, you could not have found a decent place to stay, and so do not be upset if you have journeyed a bit farther in order to enjoy a little less discomfort."

And when he said this, his servants encircled the visitors, and as soon as they had dismounted, the servants led their horses to the stables; and Messer Torello took the three noblemen to the rooms that had been prepared, where he had their boots removed for them. After this, for their refreshment, he offered the coolest of wines, detaining them with delightful conversation until it was time for supper.

Saladin, both of his companions, and his servants all knew Italian and so they had no difficulty understanding or making themselves understood, and all of them agreed that this knight was the nicest, most well-bred gentleman, as well as the best talker, that they had ever encountered. For his part, Messer Torello thought that these three men were magnificent gentlemen, much more so than he had thought earlier, which made him all the more sorry he could not entertain them that evening in company and with a more sumptuous feast. Therefore, he decided he would make amends for this the following morning, and after he told one of his servants what he had in mind to do, he sent him off to Pavia, which was rather close by and always left some of its gates open, with a message for his wife, who was a very intelligent and high-minded lady.

After that, he led the noblemen into the garden and politely asked them who they were; to this Saladin replied:

"We are Cypriot merchants, and we are on our way from Cyprus to Paris to conduct some business of ours."

Then Messer Torello said:

"Would to God that this country of ours produced the kind of gentlemen that I see merchants of Cyprus are!"

And after they had discussed these and other matters for a while, it was time for supper. Messer Torello invited them to do him the honor of sitting at his table, and considering the fact that it was an impromptu meal, they were most elegantly and well served. Nor had it been long since the tables had been cleared when Messer Torello, realizing that they were tired, had them shown to the luxurious beds where they would sleep, and soon afterward he too retired to bed.

The servant, who had been sent to Pavia, delivered the message to his wife, who, in a spirit more regal than womanly, immediately called together a good number of Messer Torello's friends and servants, made all the necessary arrangements for a great banquet, and besides seeing to it that invitations to the feast were delivered by torchlight to the noblest citizens, also saw to it that there were enough clothes and silks and furs on hand, and down to the last detail, she carried out the orders that her husband had sent her.

At daybreak when the gentlemen had arisen, Messer Torello invited them to mount their horses, and having his falcons brought to him, he led them to a nearby marsh, and there showed them how well his birds could fly; but when Saladin asked if there was someone who could take them to the best inn in Pavia, Messer Torello said: "I'll do it myself, since I have to go there in any case." They believed him and were glad, and together they started on their way; and reaching the city when it was already past tierce, believing that they were heading for the best inn, they arrived with Messer Torello at his own home, where a good fifty of the most important townspeople had already assembled to greet the gentlemen and were quickly at their service holding their bridles and stirrups.

When Saladin and his companions saw this, they realized only too well what this meant, and they said:

"Messer Torello, this is not what we requested of you. Last night you did so much for us, much more than we deserved, and so now you could quite properly have allowed us to be on our way."

To this Messer Torello replied:

"My lords, for what was done to you last night, I owe a debt of gratitude more to Fortune than to yourselves, for she overtook you on the road at an hour when you were forced to enter my humble home, but for what I shall do for you this morning, I, together with all these noblemen who surround you here, are beholden to you, but if it seems courteous to you to refuse to dine with all of them, you are at liberty to do so, if you wish."

Overcome by all this, Saladin and his companions dismounted, and they were welcomed by the noblemen and then cheerfully led off to the rooms which had been most lavishly prepared for them; and after removing their riding apparel and refreshing themselves a bit, they made their way into the dining hall, which had been splendidly decorated. Then, having washed their hands, with much pomp and ceremony they were seated at the table and served a series of dishes in such magnificent fashion that had the Emperor himself been present, it would have been impossible to pay him greater honor. And even though Saladin and his companions were great lords and accustomed to witnessing the most splendid of things, they were, nevertheless, most astonished by this meal, and it seemed to them to be one of the finest they had ever seen, considering the position of the knight, whom they knew to be a private citizen and not a lord.

Once the meal was over and the tables cleared away, and they had discussed a number of learned things for a time, since it was very hot, at Messer Torel's suggestion, all the gentlemen of Pavia went to rest, and he remained alone with his three guests. And so that none of his cherished possessions should go unseen by his guests, he took them to a room, and there he sent for his fine wife. She was a very beautiful and tall woman, dressed in rich garments, and with her two little children on either side of her, looking like two angels, she came before them and cheerfully greeted them. When the guests saw her, they rose to their feet and received her with deference, and inviting her to sit in their midst, they made a great fuss over her and her two beautiful children. And then, having entered in pleasant conversation with them and after Messer Torello had left the room, she graciously asked them where they were from and where they were going; to this question, the gentlemen gave the same reply they had given to Messer Torello.

Then, the lady, with a smile on her face, said:

"Then I see that my womanly intuition will be useful, and so I beg you as a special favor to neither refuse nor disparage this trifling little gift which I shall have brought to you, but keeping in mind that women give smaller gifts in accordance with their smaller hearts, I trust you will pay more attention to the good will of the donor than to the quality of the gift."

And she had two pairs of robes brought forth for each of the guests—one lined with silk and the other with fur, both of which were better suited to a prince than to a private citizen or merchant—and she presented them together with three silken jackets and undergarments, saying:

"Take these; I have dressed you in clothes like my husband's, and as far as the other things are concerned they are of little value, but you might find them useful, considering how far away you are from your womenfolk, the length of the journey you have made, and the distance you still have to travel, and since I know that merchants are neat and fastidious people."

The gentlemen were amazed, and they clearly saw that Messer Torello meant to omit no aspect of courtesy in their regard, and they began to suspect, upon observing the luxurious quality of the robes, which were unlike those of any merchant that Messer Torel had recognized them; nonetheless one of them replied to the lady:

"My lady, these are magnificent things not to be taken lightly

ere it not for your entreaties which make it impossible for us
o refuse."

When this was done, and Messer Torel had already returned,
he lady, after bidding them farewell, left the room and saw to
: that similar gifts were provided for their servants, according
o their rank. After much insistence, Messer Torello managed to
ersuade them to spend that entire day with him; and so, after
hey had rested, they donned their robes, and with Messer
Torello they rode around the city for some time; and when it
vas time for supper, they sat down to a magnificent dinner in
he company of many distinguished guests.

And when it was time, they went to bed, and when they arose
t daybreak, they discovered that their tired nags had been re-
·laced by three fine and sturdy palfreys, and that strong, fresh
torses had also been provided for their servants; on seeing this,
Saladin turned to his companions and said:

"I swear to God that there never was a more perfect, court-
·ous, and considerate man than this one; and if the Christian
tings are kings the way this man is a knight, the Sultan of Bab-
·lon will find it difficult to resist a single one of them, let alone
he number who are preparing to march against him!"

But realizing that it was impossible to refuse Messer Torello,
fter thanking him most graciously for his gifts, they mounted
heir horses.

Messer Torello, with many of his companions, accompanied
he gentlemen for a long stretch of the road leading away from
he city; although Saladin was reluctant to depart from Messer
Torello, having become so fond of him, yet, knowing that he had
o make haste, he begged Messer Torello to turn back; and
Messer Torello, who was no less displeased at having to leave
hem, said:

"My lords, I shall do so, since that is your wish; but I should
ike to tell you this: I do not know who you are, nor do I wish
o know more than you are willing to tell me; but whoever you
.re, you shall never make me believe that you are merchants. I
·id you Godspeed."

Saladin, who had already taken his leave of Messer Torello's
·ompanions, answered by saying:

"Sir, someday we might have the opportunity to show you
·ome of our merchandise, and in so doing convince you of it.
And now, God be with you."

Then Saladin rode off with his companions, determined that if
·e lived long enough and the war which was coming did not do
·im in, he would show Messer Torello no less honor than Messer

Torello had shown him; and for some time he spoke with h̶
companions about Messer Torello, his wife, and all his gifts, f̶
vors, and kindnesses, praising one more than the other. B̶
when, not without great fatigue, he had visited the entire Wes̶
he returned by sea with his companions to Alexandria, wher̶
now fully informed, he drew up his plan of defense. Mess̶
Torello returned to Pavia, and although he wondered for a lo̶
while who these three men might have been, he never arrived ̶
the truth or even came close to it.

When the time for the crusade arrived, and great preparation̶
were being made everywhere, Messer Torello, in spite of h̶
wife's entreaties and tears, was fully determined to go wit̶
them. Then once he had made all the necessary preparations an̶
was about to ride off, he said to his wife, whom he dearly loved:

"As you see, my lady, I am going on this crusade as much f̶
the honor of my body as for the salvation of my soul; I com̶
mend to your care our possessions and our honor. And since ̶
am as certain of my departure as I am uncertain of my retur̶
because of a thousand misfortunes that could befall me, I wa̶
you to do me a favor: whatever happens to me, as long as yo̶
have no positive news that I am alive, wait for me one year, on̶
month, and one day before remarrying, beginning from this, th̶
day of my departure."

The lady, who was weeping profusely, replied:

"Messer Torello, I do not know how I shall be able to endur̶
the sorrow with which your departure leaves me; but if my li̶
be stronger than my sorrow and if anything should happen ̶
you, you may live and die in the knowledge that I shall live an̶
die as the wife of Messer Torello and of his memory."

To this Messer Torel said:

"Lady, I am convinced that if it were up to you, what you ar̶
promising me would come to pass, but you are a young woma̶
you are beautiful, and you come from a famous family, an̶
your great virtues are known to everyone. Because of this, ̶
have no doubt whatsoever that as soon as they suspect I ar̶
dead, many a fine gentleman will ask your hand from you̶
brothers and relatives, and whether or not you like it, you wi̶
be unable to defend yourself from their demands and of neces̶
sity you will have to comply with their wishes. Ard this is why ̶
ask you to wait no longer than the period I have mentioned."

The lady said:

"I shall do whatever I can to keep my promise; and though ̶
may be compelled to do otherwise, I shall certainly obey you i̶

the deadline you impose upon me. But I pray to God that neither you nor I shall now be reduced to such extremes!"

When she had finished speaking, the lady burst into tears and embraced Messer Torello, after which she took a ring from her finger and gave it to him, saying:

"If I should happen to die before I see you again, remember me whenever you look upon this."

After taking the ring, Messer Torello mounted his horse and, having bid everyone farewell, he set out on his journey. He reached Genoa with his followers, boarded a galley, and sailed away. In a short time he reached Acre, where he joined the rest of the Christian army. But in no time at all the army was afflicted by a great and deadly plague, in the course of which, whether because of the skill or the good fortune of Saladin, almost all of the Christian troops that survived were captured alive by Saladin and then divided up and imprisoned in a number of different cities. Among those taken prisoner was Messer Torello, and he was taken in captivity to Alexandria, where, since no one knew who he was, and he was afraid to reveal his identity, he was of necessity compelled to train hunting birds, an art in which he was a great expert. And because of such talent, news of him reached Saladin, who had him removed from prison and appointed him his falconer. Messer Torello, who was called simply "Saladin's Christian" and who had failed to recognize Saladin, nor did Saladin recognize him, thought only of Pavia and had tried to escape on numerous occasions but always unsuccessfully. And so when a group of men from Genoa arrived as ambassadors to Saladin in order to arrange for the ransom of certain of their fellow citizens, Messer Torello, just as these men were about to depart, decided he would write to his wife telling her that he was alive, that he would return to her as soon as he could, and that she should wait for him, and this he did; and then he earnestly begged one of the ambassadors, whom he knew, to see that his letter reached the hands of the Abbot of San Piero in Ciel d'Oro, who was his uncle.

And leading this kind of life, one day Messer Torello, while Saladin was discussing his hunting birds with him, happened to smile and by so doing he made an expression with his mouth which Saladin had especially noted when he was at his home in Pavia.. This expression made Saladin remember Messer Torello, and he began to stare closely at him, and it seemed to Saladin that this really was Messer Torello and so, abandoning their first topic of discussion, Saladin said:

"Tell me, Christian, what country do you come from in the West?"

"My lord," replied Messer Torello, "I am a Lombard, from a city called Pavia, a poor man of low birth."

When Saladin heard this, he was almost certain that his guess was correct, and happily he said to himself: "God has granted me the opportunity to show this man how much his hospitality pleased me." And without saying another word, he had all of his robes laid out in display in a room, and taking Messer Torello inside, he said: "Look, Christian, and see if among these robes there are any you have ever seen before."

Messer Torello began to look around and he saw the robes his wife had given to Saladin, but he could not believe that they could possibly be the ones they were. Nevertheless, he replied:

"My lord, I do not recognize any of them, though it is certainly true that these two look like the robes I myself once wore and with which I once dressed three merchants, who happened upon my house."

Then Saladin, no longer able to restrain himself, embraced Messer Torello tenderly and exclaimed:

"You are Messer Torel from Stra, and I am one of the three merchants to whom your wife gave these garments; and now the time has come to assure you of the quality of my merchandise, which, when I left you, I said might eventually come to pass."

When Messer Torello heard this, he began to feel delighted and ashamed at the same time: delighted at having been able to entertain such a distinguished guest, ashamed at how poorly he thought he had done so. But Saladin said to him:

"Messer Torello, since God has sent you here to me, from now on you must consider yourself, and not me, the master here."

After much rejoicing in each other's company, Saladin had Messer Torello dressed in regal garments, and having presented him to the company of all his greatest barons, to whom he spoke at great length in praise of Messer Torello's excellence, Saladin ordered each of them, if they valued his favor, to honor Messer Torello as if it were he they were honoring. And from that time forth, this is what each one of them did, but the two lords who had been with Saladin in his house did so even more than the others. The heights of this sudden glory in which Messer Torel found himself to some extent took his mind away from the affairs of Lombardy, especially since he fervently believed that his letters must have reached his uncle.

On the day when Saladin took the Christians prisoner, a Provençal knight of little repute named Messer Torel from

Dignes had been killed and buried on the battlefields or, rather, in the Christian army camp. And because of this, since Messer Torel from Stra was known throughout the army for his nobility, anyone who heard that "Messer Torello is dead" thought that this referred to Messer Torel from Stra and not to the one from Dignes. By the time those who had been deceived might have been undeceived, Messer Torello had been taken prisoner, and so, many Italians returned home with this news of his death, and among them there were even some who were presumptuous enough to dare to claim they had seen Messer Torello's dead body and had been present at his burial. When this was learned by his wife and relatives, it was the cause of deep and immeasurable grief not only for them, but for anyone who had known him.

It would be difficult to describe the extent and depth of the sorrow, the unhappiness, and the woe of his wife; but after several months of continuous mourning, when her grief began to subside somewhat, and she was being courted by some of the greatest men in Lombardy, her brothers and her other relatives began urging her to remarry. Although she refused many times and with great lamentation, she was finally forced to do as her relatives wished, but on the condition that she be allowed to remain without a husband for as long a time as she had promised Messer Torello.

With things being such for his lady in Pavia and with only about eight days left before she would be forced to take a husband, it happened that in Alexandria one day Messer Torello caught sight of one of the men he had seen board the ship with the Genoese ambassadors that had been bound for Genoa. He had him summoned, and asked him what kind of a journey they had had and when they had reached Genoa. To this question, the man replied: .

"My lord, the galley made an unlucky voyage, as I heard in Crete, where I left it; for when it was nearing Sicily, a treacherous north wind arose and drove her into the Barbary reefs, and no one survived, and among those who perished were two of my own brothers."

Messer Torello believed the man's words, which were indeed true, and remembering that the period of time he had asked his wife to give him would expire in a few more days, and realizing that no news of his whereabouts could have reached Pavia, he felt certain that by now his wife was about to be remarried. He fell into such a state of despair over this that he lost his appetite, took to his bed, and resolved to die. When Saladin, who loved him greatly, heard about this, he came to see him. Having learned, after numerous and repeated entreaties, the reason for his grief and his illness, he reproached Messer Torello severely for not having told him about the problem earlier, and then he begged him to take heart, telling him that if he did so, he would see to it that he would be in Pavia by the prescribed date; and he told him how it would occur. Messer Torello, trusting in Saladin's words and having heard on many occasions that such a thing was possible and had been done many times before, began to take heart and to urge Saladin to see to this immediately. Saladin ordered one of his magicians, whose magic craft he had already had occasion to test, to find a way to transport Messer Torello overnight upon a bed to Pavia; the magician replied that this could be done, but for Messer Torello's own good, it would be better if he put him to sleep.

This arranged, Saladin returned to Messer Torello, and discovering that he was still fully determined to be in Pavia on the prescribed date, if he could, or to die if he could not, Saladin said this to him:

"Messer Torello, God knows I cannot blame you in the slightest if you love your wife so dearly and are afraid of losing her to someone else, for among all of the many women I have ever met, she is the one whose behavior, manners, and demeanor —to say nothing of her beauty, which is but a flower that will fade—seem most worthy of praise and to be cherished. Since Fortune has brought you here, I should have liked nothing more than for the two of us to spend the rest of our lives here together, ruling as equals over the kingdom I possess. But God has willed that this wish of mine not be granted, and now that you have decided either to die or to return to Pavia by the prescribed time, I truly wish I had known in time about this so that I might have been able to return you to your home with the honor, the magnificence, and the company which your excellence deserves; but since this has not been allowed to me, and you, moreover, desire to be there at once, I will do my best to get you there in the manner I described to you."

To this Messer Torello replied:

"My lord, apart from your words, your deeds have clearly demonstrated your goodwill toward me, which I do not deserve to such a high degree, and even if you had said nothing, I live and shall die completely convinced that what you say is true. But since I have made my decision, I beg you to do at once what you said you would, for tomorrow is the last day that she will wait for me."

Saladin said that it would be done without fail, and on the following day, since he intended to send him on his way the same evening, he had set up in a large room a most beautiful and luxurious bed, all made of mattresses which, according to their custom, were covered in velvets and cloth of gold. Saladin had spread over the bed a quilt embroidered in oval patterns with the largest of pearls and the most expensive of precious stones, which later on were considered in these parts to be a priceless treasure, as well as two pillows such as a bed of this opulence called for. When this was done, he ordered that Messer Torello, who had by now regained his strength, be dressed in a robe after the Saracen fashion, the richest and the most beautiful thing ever seen by anyone, and upon his head, after their fashion, he had one of his longest turbans wound. And since the hour was late, accompanied by many of his barons, Saladin went into the room where Messer Torello was, and sitting down beside him, almost in tears, he began to say:

"Messer Torello, the hour which must separate me from you is drawing near, and since I can neither accompany you myself nor have you accompanied, because the kind of journey you have to undertake does not permit this, here in this room I must take my leave of you, and this I have come to do. And so before I bid you Godspeed, I beg you in the name of the love and the friendship which exists between us to remember me; and if it is possible, before our lives come to an end, I beg you, once you have put your affairs in order in Lombardy, to come at least once to visit me so that, just as I shall rejoice upon seeing you again, I shall also be able to make up for the loss of pleasure which now your haste to be gone imposes on me. Until this comes to pass, I beg you not to be weary of visiting me with your letters and to make any request of me you please, for there certainly is no man alive for whom I would fulfill a request more gladly than for you."

Messer Torello could not hold back his tears, and hindered by them, he managed to say only a few words declaring that it would be impossible for him to forget Saladin's kind deeds and excellence, and that without fail he would do as Saladin requested, if he was given the chance. And so, embracing him tenderly and kissing him, with many tears Saladin bid him Godspeed and left the room; then all of the other barons took their leave of him and accompanied Saladin to the room where the bed had been prepared.

But it was already late, and the magician was anxious to conclude his work. A physician arrived with a certain drink, and after telling Messer Torello that he was to drink it in order to keep up his strength, he gave it to him and made him drink it. It was not long before he fell asleep. As he slept, he was carried at Saladin's command to the luxurious bed, upon which Saladin had placed a large and beautiful crown of great value, which he had marked in such a way so that later on, it would be clear that he had sent it to Messer Torello's wife. And then he slipped onto Messer Torello's finger a ring set with a ruby that looked like a glowing torch, it sparkled so, and whose value could hardly be assessed. Then he had Messer Torello girded with a sword, the ornamentation of which would also be difficult to appraise; and besides this, he pinned upon his chest a broach containing pearls the like of which were never seen, as well as many other precious stones. Then on both sides of Messer Torello, he had placed two of the largest gold bowls filled with doubloons, and all around him he had strewn many pearl necklaces, rings, belts, and other things, which would take too long to describe. And after this was done, Saladin kissed Messer Torello once again, and told the magician to make haste; and so in Saladin's presence the bed and Messer Torello suddenly disappeared, while Saladin remained there speaking with his barons about Messer Torello.

Just as he had requested, Messer Torello was deposited with all the aforementioned gems and finery in the Church of San Piero in Ciel d'Oro in Pavia, where he was still sleeping when matins were rung and the sacristan entered the church with a light in his hand and suddenly caught sight of the bed. Not only was he astonished, but he was so terrified that he turned on his heels and fled. When the Abbot and the monks saw him running off, they were amazed and asked him why. The monk told them.

"Oh," declared the Abbot, "you're not a child anymore, nor are you a newcomer to this church to be so easily frightened. Now let's all go and see what scared you so."

So they lit more torches, and when the Abbot with all his monks entered the church, they saw this bed which was so marvelous and sumptuous, and upon it they saw the knight who was sleeping; and just as they were casting a wary and timorous eye over the fine jewels, never daring to get near the bed, the power of the drink began wearing off, and Messer Torel, while he was awakening, happened to utter a deep sigh. The monks, on seeing this, and the Abbot too, were terrified, and screaming "God, help us!" they all fled. When Messer Torello opened his eyes and looked all around him, he realized to his great joy that he was in the very place where he had asked Saladin to be left. Although he had known of Saladin's generosity in the past, when he sat up and looked closely at all the things surrounding him, he was all the more conscious of it and considered it to be even greater. Meanwhile he could hear the monks running off, and imagining why, without making any movements, he began calling the Abbot by name, begging him not to be afraid, for he was Torel, his nephew. The Abbot, upon hearing this, became even more frightened, for he believed that Messer Torello had been dead for many months now; but after a while, reassured by sound reasoning, and hearing his name still being called, the Abbot made the sign of the cross and went to Messer Torello.

Messer Torel said to him:

"Oh, father, what are you afraid of? I am alive, thanks be to God, and I have returned here from across the sea."

Although Messer Torello had a long beard and was dressed in Arab clothes, the Abbot, after a while, still managed to recognize him; and being completely reassured, he took him by the hand and said: "My son, you are most welcome," and then he continued:

"You should not be astonished at our fear, for in this city there is not a man who does not firmly believe you are dead, so much so that I can tell you Madonna Adalieta, your wife, overcome by the entreaties and the threats of her relatives, and quite against her will, has been forced to remarry. This morning she must go to her new husband, and the wedding celebration as well as all the preparations for the banquet have all been arranged."

He arose from the luxurious bed, and happily greeting the Abbot and the monks, Messer Torello begged each one of them not to speak of his return until he had attended to a certain bit of business. Then, after storing the precious jewels in a safe place, he told the Abbot what had happened to him up to that time. Delighted by his good fortune, the Abbot, together with Messer Torello, gave thanks to God. Then Messer Torel asked the Abbot who the new husband of his wife was. The Abbot told him.

Then Messer Torel said to him:

"Before anyone learns of my return, I intend to see how my wife behaves at these nuptials; and although I know it is not customary for churchmen to attend such banquets, out of your love for me, I would like you to arrange for the two of us to attend."

The Abbot replied that he would gladly do this; and at daybreak, the Abbot sent a message to the bridegroom saying that he wished to come to the wedding feast with a companion, to which the gentleman answered that he would be delighted to have them. When it was time for the banquet, Messer Torello, still dressed in the same clothes he had arrived in, went with the

Abbot to the home of the bridegroom, and he was stared at in amazement by everyone who saw him, but recognized by no one. The Abbot told everyone that he was a Saracen sent by the Sultan to the King of France as his ambassador. And so Messer Torello was seated at a table directly in front of his wife, whom he stared at with the greatest of delight, and it seemed to him from the look on her face that she was upset by these nuptials. She, too, would look at him from time to time, not because she in any way recognized him, for her firm conviction he was dead had removed that possibility, but, rather, because of his long beard and strange garb.

But then, when Messer Torello felt it was time to find out whether she would recognize him, taking the ring that he had been given by his wife upon his departure, he called to the young boy who was serving her and said to him:

"Tell the new bride for me that in my country, whenever any stranger, such as myself, attends the wedding feast of a new bride, such as she, it is the custom for the bride to send him the cup from which she is drinking full of wine as a sign that she is pleased to have him there; and then, when the stranger has drunk his fill, the cup is recovered and the bride drinks what is left."

The young boy delivered the message to the lady, who, being the well-mannered and wise woman that she was and believing him to be an important dignitary, in order to demonstrate that she was pleased by his visit, gave orders for the large golden goblet which stood before her to be washed and filled with wine and taken to the gentleman; and this was done. Messer Torello, having placed her ring in his mouth, drank in such a way as to let the ring slip into the goblet without anyone's noticing it, and then leaving only a little bit of wine in the goblet, he recovered it and sent it back to the lady. As the custom required, the lady took the goblet, and as she uncovered it and put it to her lips and saw the ring, without saying anything, she stared at it for a while; and realizing that the ring was the one she had given to Messer Torello upon his departure, she took it and stared directly at the man she thought was a stranger, and having recognized him by now, as if she had gone insane, she pushed over the table in front of her and shouted: "This man is my lord, this is truly Messer Torello!" Running over to the table at which he was seated, without any regard for her own clothes or anything that was on the table she threw herself across it as far as she could and embraced Messer Torello tightly, nor could she be pulled away from his neck no matter what anyone there said or did until Messer Torello himself told her to take hold of herself a bit, for there would be ample time to embrace him later.

Whereupon she stood up; and with the wedding feast by now in total confusion, but also happier than ever at the return of such a knight, Messer Torello requested everyone to remain silent. Then he recounted to everyone what had happened to him from the day of his departure until the time he had arrived there, concluding by saying that the gentleman who, believing him to be dead, had taken his lady as his wife should not take it badly if he, being alive, had now reclaimed her. The bridegroom, although somewhat embarrassed, in an amicable fashion replied that Messer Torello should dispose freely of what belonged to him as best he pleased. The lady then took off the ring and the crown she had received from the bridegroom and put on the ring she had taken from the goblet as well as the crown the Sultan had sent to her. Then, leaving the house they were in, with the entire wedding party, they went to the home of Messer Torello, and there his grieving friends and relatives and all the town's citizens, who looked upon him as if at a miracle, rejoiced with him in long and happy celebration.

After giving some of his precious jewels to the man who had borne the expenses of the wedding feast, as well as to the Abbot and to numerous others, Messer Torello, having sent more than one messenger to Saladin informing him of his happy return home and declaring himself to be Saladin's friend and servant, lived many more years with his worthy wife, performing more courteous deeds than ever before.

Such then was how the troubles of Messer Torello and those of his dear wife came to an end and how they were rewarded for their prompt and cheerful acts of courtesy. Many try to do the same, and although they possess the means to do so, they perform such deeds so badly that before they are finished, they cost more than they are worth. Thus, if no reward accrues to them, neither they nor others should be surprised.

[Tenth Day, Tenth Story]

❈

The Marquis of Sanluzzo is urged by the requests of his vassals to take a wife, and in order to have his own way in the matter, he chooses the daughter of a peasant and by her he has two children, whom he pretends to have put to death. Then, under the pretense that she has displeased him, he pretends to have taken another wife, and has their own daughter brought into the house as if she were his new wife, having driven out his real wife in nothing more than her shift. Having found that she has patiently endured all this, he brings her back home, more beloved than ever, shows their grown children to her, honors her, and has others honor her, as the Marchioness.

THE lengthy tale of the King, which, judging by the expression on everyone's face seemed to have pleased them all, came to an end, and laughing, Dioneo said:

"The good fellow who was looking forward to lowering the ghost's stiff tail the following night wouldn't have given you two cents for all the praises you are lavishing upon Messer Torello."* And then, realizing that he alone remained to speak, Dioneo began:

Gentle ladies of mine, it seems to me this day has been devoted to kings, sultans, and people like that; therefore, in order not to stray too far from your path, I should like to tell you about a marquis and not about a generous act of his but, rather, about his insane cruelty, which, while good did result from it in the end, I would never advise anyone to follow as an example, for I consider it a great shame that he derived any benefit from it at all.

A long time ago, there succeeded to the Marquisate of Sanluzzo the firstborn son of the family, a young man named Gualtieri, who, having no wife or children, spent his time doing nothing but hawking and hunting, never thinking of taking a wife or of having children—a very wise thing to do on his part.

---

*A reference to the story of Gianni Lotteringhi (VII, 1), told by Emilia.

This did not please his vassals, and they begged him on many an occasion to take a wife so that he would not be without an heir and they without a master; they offered to find him a wife born of the kind of mother and father that might give him good expectations of her and make him happy. To this Gualtieri answered:

"My friends, you are urging me to do something that I was determined never to do, for you know how difficult it is to find a woman with a suitable character, and how plentiful is the opposite kind of woman, and what a wretched life a man would lead married to a wife that was not suitable to him. And to say that you can judge daughters by examining the characters of their fathers and mothers (which is the basis of your argument that you can find a wife to please me) is ridiculous, for I do not believe that you can come to know all the secrets of the father or mother; and even if you did, a daughter is often unlike her father and mother. But since it is your wish to tie me up with these chains, I shall do as you request; and so that I shall have only myself to blame if things turn out badly, I want to be the one who chooses her, and I tell you now that if she is not honored by you as your lady—no matter whom I choose—you will learn to your great displeasure how serious a matter it was to compel me with your requests to take a wife against my will." His worthy men replied that they would be happy if only he would choose a wife.

For some time Gualtieri had been impressed by the manners of a poor young girl who lived in a village near his home, and since she seemed very beautiful to him, he thought that life with her could be quite pleasant; so, without looking any further, he decided to marry her, and he sent for her father, who was extremely poor, and made arrangements with him to take her as his wife. After this was done, Gualtieri called all his friends in the area together and said to them:

"My friends, you wished and continue to wish for me to take a wife, and I am ready to do this, but I do so more to please you than to satisfy any desire of mine to have a wife. You know what you promised me: to honor happily anyone I chose for your lady; therefore, the time has come for me to keep my promise to you, and for you to do the same for me. I have found a young girl after my own heart, very near here, whom I intend to take as my wife and bring home in a few days. So, make sure that the wedding celebrations are splendid and that you receive her honorably, so that I may consider myself as happy with your promise as you are with mine."

The good men all happily replied that this pleased them very much and that, whoever she was, they would treat her as their lady and honor her in every way they could; and soon after this, they all set about preparing for a big, beautiful, and happy celebration, and Gualtieri did the same. He had an enormous and sumptuous wedding feast prepared, and he invited his friends and relatives and the great lords and many others from the surrounding countryside. And besides this, he had beautiful and expensive dresses cut out and tailored to fit a young girl whom he felt was about the same size as the young girl he had decided to marry; he also saw to it that girdles and rings were purchased and a rich and beautiful crown and everything else a new bride might require. When the day set for the wedding arrived, Gualtieri mounted his horse at about the middle of tierce, and all those who had come to honor him did the same; when all was arranged, he said:

"My lords, it is time to fetch the new bride."

Then he with his entire company set out, and eventually they arrived at the little village; they came to the house of the girl's father and found her returning from the well in great haste in order to be in time to go and see the arrival of Gualtieri's bride with the other women; when Gualtier saw her, he called her by name—that is, Griselda—and asked her where her father was; to this she replied bashfully:

"My lord, he is in the house."

Then Gualtieri dismounted and ordered all his men to wait for him; alone, he entered that poor, little house, and there he found Griselda's father, who was called Giannucole, and he said to him:

"I have come to marry Griselda, but before I do, I should like to ask her some things in your presence."

And he asked her, if he were to marry her, would she always try to please him, and would she never become angry over anything he said or did, and if she would always be obedient, and many other similar questions—to all of these she replied that she would. Then Gualtieri took her by the hand, led her outside, and in the presence of his entire company and all others present, he had her stripped naked and the garments he had prepared for her brought forward; then he immediately had her dress and put on her shoes, and upon her hair, disheveled as it was, he had a crown placed; then, while everyone was marveling at the sight, he announced:

"My lords, this is the lady I intend to be my wife, if she will have me as her husband."

And then, turning to Griselda, who was standing there blushing and perplexed, he asked her:

"Griselda, do you take me for your husband?"

To this she answered: "Yes, my lord."

And he replied: "And I take you for my wife."

In the presence of them all he married her; then he had her set upon a palfrey and he led her with an honorable company to his home. The wedding feast was great and sumptuous, and the celebration was no different from what it might have been if he had married the daughter of the King of France. The young bride seemed to have changed her soul and manners along with her clothes: she was, as we have already said, beautiful in body and face, and as she was beautiful before, she became even more pleasing, attractive, and well mannered, so that she seemed to be not the shepherdess daughter of Giannucole but, rather, the daughter of some noble lord, a fact that amazed everyone who had known her before. Moreover, she was so obedient and indulgent to her husband that he considered himself the happiest and the most satisfied man on earth. And she was also so gracious and kind toward her husband's subjects that there was no one who was more beloved or gladly honored than she was; in fact, everyone prayed for her welfare, her prosperity, and her further success. Whereas everyone used to say that Gualtieri had acted unwisely in taking her as his wife, they now declared that he was the wisest and the cleverest man in the world, for none other than he could have ever recognized the noble character hidden under her poor clothes and peasant dress.

In short, she knew how to comport herself in such a manner that before long, not only in her husband's marquisate but everywhere else, her virtue and her good deeds became the topic of discussion, and for anything that had been said against her husband when he married her, she now caused the opposite to be said. Not long after she had come to live with Gualtieri, she became pregnant, and in the course of time she gave birth to a daughter, which gave Gualtieri much cause for rejoicing. But shortly afterward, a new thought entered his mind: he wished to test her patience with a long trial and intolerable proofs. First, he offended her with harsh words, pretending to be angry and saying that his vassals were very unhappy with her because of her low birth and especially now that they saw her bear children; they were most unhappy about the daughter that had been born, and they did nothing but mutter about it. When the lady heard these words, without changing her expression or intentions in any way, she answered:

"My lord, do with me what you think best for your honor an·
your happiness, and no matter what, I shall be happy, for I real·
ize that I am of lower birth than they and am not worthy of thi·
honor which your courtesy has bestowed upon me."

This reply was very gratifying to Gualtieri, for he realize·
that she had not become in any way haughty because of the re·
spect which he or others had paid her. A short time later, havin·
told his wife in vague terms that his subjects could not tolerat·
the daughter to whom she had given birth, he spoke to one o·
her servants and then sent him to her, and he, with a very sa·
look on his face, said to her:

"My lady, since I do not wish to die, I must do what my lor·
commands. He had commanded me to take this daughter o·
yours and to . . ." And he could say no more.

When the lady heard these words and saw her servant's face
she remembered what her husband had said to her and under-
stood that her servant had been ordered to murder the child; so
she quickly took the girl from the cradle, kissed her and blessed
her, and although she felt great pain in her heart, showing no
emotion, she placed her in her servant's arms and said to him:

"There, do exactly what your lord and mine has ordered you
to do, but do not leave her body to be devoured by the beasts
and birds unless he has ordered you to do so."

The servant took the child and told Gualtieri what the lady
had said, and he was amazed at her perseverance; then he sent
the servant with his daughter to one of his relatives in Bologna,
requesting that she raise and educate the girl carefully but with-
out ever telling whose daughter she was. Shortly after this, the
lady became pregnant again, and in time she gave birth to a
male child, which pleased Gualtieri very much; but what he had
already done to his lady was not enough to satisfy him, and he
wounded the lady with even a greater blow by telling her one
day in a fit of feigned anger:

"Lady, since you bore me this male child, I have not been
able to live with my vassals, for they bitterly complain about a
grandson of Giannucolo's having to be their lord after I am
gone. Because of this, I am very much afraid that unless I want
to be driven out, I must do what I did the other time, and then,
finally, I shall have to leave you and take another wife."

The lady listened to him patiently and made no other reply
than this:

"My lord, think only of making yourself happy and of satisfy-
ing your desires and do not worry about me at all, for nothing
pleases me more than to see you happy."

After a few days, Gualtieri sent for his son in the same way he had sent for his daughter, and, again pretending to have the child killed, he sent him to be raised in Bologna as he had his daughter; and the lady's face and words were no different from what they were when her daughter had been taken, and Gualtieri was greatly amazed at this and remarked to himself that no other woman could do what she had done. If he had not seen for himself how extremely fond she was of her children as long as they found favor in his sight, he might have thought that she acted as she did in order to get rid of them, but he realized that she was doing it out of obedience.

His subjects, believing he had killed his children, criticized him bitterly and regarded him as a cruel man, and they had the greatest compassion for the lady; but she never said anything to the women with whom she mourned the deaths of her children. Then, not many years after the birth of their daughter, Gualtieri felt it was time to put his wife's patience to the ultimate test: he told many of his vassals that he could no longer bear having married Griselda and that he realized he had acted badly and impetuously when he took her for his wife, and that he was going to do everything possible to procure a dispensation from the Pope so that he could marry another woman and abandon Griselda; he was reprimanded for this by many of his good men, but the only answer he gave them was that this was the way it ~~ to be.

When the lady heard about these matters and it appeared to her that she would be returning to her father's house (perhaps even to guard the sheep as she had previously done) and that she would have to bear witness to another woman possessing the man she loved, she grieved most bitterly; but yet, as with the other injuries of Fortune which she had suffered, she was determined to bear this one, too, with firm countenance. Not long afterward, Gualtieri had forged letters sent from Rome, and he showed them to his subjects, pretending that in these letters the Pope had granted him the dispensation to take another wife and to abandon Griselda; and so, having his wife brought before him, in the presence of many people he said to her:

"Lady, because of a dispensation which I have received from the Pope, I am able to take another wife and to abandon you; and because my ancestors were great noblemen and lords of these regions while yours have always been peasants, I wish you to be my wife no longer and to return to Giannucolo's home with the dowry that you brought me, and I shall then bring home another more suitable wife, whom I have already found."

When the lady heard these words, she managed to hold back her tears only with the greatest of effort (something quite unnatural for a woman), and she replied:

"My lord, I have always known that my lowly origins were in no way suitable to your nobility, and the position I have held with you I always recognized as having come from God and yourself; I never made it mine or considered it given to me—I always kept it as if it were a loan. If you wish to have it back again, it must please me, which it does, to return it to you: here is your ring with which you married me; take it. You order me to take back with me the dowry I brought you, and to do this no accounting on your part, nor any purse or beast of burden, will be necessary, for I have not forgotten that you received me naked; and if you judge it proper that this body which bore your children should be seen by everyone, I shall leave naked; but I beg you, in the name of my virginity which I brought here and which I cannot take with me, that you at least allow me to take away with me just one shift in addition to my dowry."

Gualtieri, who felt closer to tears than anyone else there, stood, nevertheless, with a stern face and said:

"You may take a shift."

Many of those present begged him to give her a dress, so that this woman who had been his wife for more than thirteen years would not be seen leaving his home so impoverished and in such disgrace as to leave clad only in a shift; but their entreaties were in vain, and in her shift, without shoes or anything on her head, the lady commended him to God, left his house, and returned to her father, accompanied by the tears and the weeping of all those who witnessed her departure.

Giannucolo, who had never believed that Gualtieri would keep his daughter as his wife, and who had been expecting this to happen any day, had kept the clothes that she had taken off that morning when Gualtier married her; he gave them back to her, and she put them on and began doing the menial tasks in her father's house as she had once been accustomed to doing, suffering with brave spirit the savage assaults of a hostile Fortune.

Once Gualtieri had done this, he then led his vassals to believe that he had chosen a daughter of one of the Count's of Panago for his new wife; and while great preparations were being made for the wedding, he sent for Griselda to come to him, and when she arrived he said to her:

"I am bringing home the lady I have recently chosen as my wife, and I want to give her an honorable welcome when she first arrives; you know that I have no women in my home who know how to prepare the bedrooms or do the many chores that are required by such a grand celebration, and since you understand these matters better than anyone else in the house, I want you to make all the arrangements: invite those ladies whom you think should be invited, and receive them as if you were the lady of the house; then when the wedding is over, you can return to your home."

These words were like a dagger in Griselda's heart, for she had not yet been able to put aside the love she felt for him as she had learned to live without her good fortune, and she answered:

"My lord, I am ready and prepared."

And so in a coarse peasant dress she entered that house which she had left a short time before dressed only in a shift, and she began to clean and arrange the bedrooms, to put out hangings and ornamental tapestries on the walls, to make ready the kitchen, and to put her hands to everything, just as if she were a little servant girl in the house; and she never rested until she had organized and arranged everything as it should be. After this, she had invitations sent in Gualtieri's name to all the ladies of the region and then waited for the celebration; when the day of the wedding came, though the clothes she wore were poor, with the courtesy and graciousness of a lady, she cheerfully welcomed all the women who arrived for the celebration.

Gualtieri had seen to it that his children were raised with care in Bologna by one of his relatives who had married into the family of the Counts of Panago. His daughter was already twelve years old and the most beautiful thing ever seen; the boy was six. He sent a message to his relative in Bologna, requesting him to be so kind as to come to Sanluzzo with his daughter and his son, and to see to it that a fine and honorable retinue accompany them, and not to reveal her identity to anyone but to tell them only that he was bringing the girl as Gualtieri's bride.

The nobleman did what the Marquis had asked him: he set out, and after several days he arrived at Sanluzzo at about suppertime with the young girl, her brother, and a noble following, and there he found all the peasants and many other people from the surrounding area waiting to see Gualtieri's new bride. She was received by the ladies and then taken to the hall where the tables were set, and there Griselda, dressed as she was, cheerfully met her and said to her:

"Welcome, my lady!"

The ladies, many of whom had begged Gualtieri (but in vain) either to allow Griselda to stay in another room or that some of the clothing that had once been hers be lent to her so that she would not have to meet his guests in such condition, sat down at the table and were served. Everyone looked at the young girl and agreed that Gualtieri had made a good exchange; but it was Griselda above all who praised her as well as her little brother.

Gualtieri, who felt that he now had enough evidence of his wife's patience, having seen that these unusual circumstances had not changed Griselda one bit. and certain that her attitude was not due to stupidity, for he knew her to be very wise, felt that it was time to remove her from the bitterness he knew to be hidden behind her impassive face, and so he had her brought to him, and in the presence of everyone, he said to her with a smile:

"What do you think of my new bride?"

"My lord," replied Griselda, "she seems very beautiful to me, and if she is as wise as she is beautiful, which I believe she is, I have no doubt that living with her will make you the happiest man in the world. But I beg you with all my heart not to inflict those wounds upon her which you inflicted upon that other woman who was once your wife, for I believe that she could scarcely endure them, not only because she is younger but also because she was reared in a more refined way, whereas that other woman lived in continuous hardship from the time she was a little girl."

When Gualtieri saw that she firmly believed the girl was to be his wife, and in spite of this said nothing but good about her, he made her sit beside him, and he said:

"Griselda, it is time now for you to reap the fruit of your long patience, and it is time for those who have considered me cruel, unjust, and bestial to realize that what I have done was directed toward a preestablished goal, for I wanted to teach you how to be a wife, to show these people how to know such a wife and how to choose and keep one, and to acquire for myself lasting tranquillity for as long as I lived with you. When I decided to marry, I greatly feared that the tranquillity I cherished would be lost, and so, to test you, I submitted you to the pains and trials you have known. But since I have never known you to depart from my wishes in either word or deed, and since I now believe I shall receive from you that happiness which I always desired, I intend to return to you now what I took from you for a long time and with the greatest of delight to soothe the wounds that I inflicted upon you. And so, with a happy heart receive this girl whom you suppose to be my bride, and her brother as your very own children and mine; they are the ones you and many others have long thought I had brutally murdered; and I am your husband, who loves you more than all else, for I believe I can boast that no other man exists who could be as happy with his wife as I am."

After he said this, he embraced and kissed her, and she was weeping for joy; they arose and together went over to their daughter, who was listening in amazement to these new developments; both of them tenderly embraced first the girl and then her brother, thus dispelling their confusion as well as that of many others who were present. The ladies, who were most delighted, arose from the tables, and they went with Griselda to her room, and with a more auspicious view of her future, they took off her old clothes and dressed her in one of her noble garments, and then they led her back into the hall as the lady of the house, which she, nonetheless, appeared to be even when she wore rags.

Everyone was very happy with the way everything had turned out, and Griselda with her husband and children celebrated in great style, with the joy and feasting increasing over a period of several days; and Gualtieri was judged to be the wisest of men (although the tests to which he had subjected his wife were regarded as harsh and intolerable), and Griselda the wisest of them all.

The Count of Panago returned to Bologna several days later, and Gualtieri took Giannucolo from his labor, setting him up in a way befitting his father-in-law so that he lived the rest of his days with honor and great comfort. After giving their daughter in marriage to a nobleman, Gualtieri lived a long and happy life with Griselda, always honoring her to the best of his ability.

What more can be said here, except that godlike spirits do sometimes rain down from heaven into poor homes, just as those more suited to governing pigs than to ruling over men make their appearances in royal palaces. Who besides Griselda could have endured the severe and unheard-of trials that Gualtieri imposed upon her and remain with a not only tearless but a happy face? It might have served Gualtieri right if he had run into the kind of woman who, once driven out of her home in nothing but a shift, would have allowed another man to warm her wool in order to get herself a nice-looking dress out of the affair!

[Tenth Day, Conclusion]

❦

DIONEO's tale had ended, and the ladies, some taking one side and some taking the other, some criticizing one thing about it and some praising another, had discussed the story at great length when the King, looking up at the sky and seeing that the sun had already sunk low toward the hour of vespers, began, without getting up, to speak in this fashion:

"Lovely ladies, as I believe you know, human wisdom does not consist only in remembering past events or in knowing about present ones, but rather in being able, with a knowledge of both one and the other, to predict future events, which wise men consider the highest form of intelligence. As you know, it will be fifteen days tomorrow that we left Florence in order to find some means of amusement, to preserve our health and our lives, and to escape from the melancholy, suffering, and anguish which has existed continuously in our city since the beginning of the plague. This goal, in my opinion, we have virtuously achieved; for, as far as I have been able to observe, even if the stories we have told were amusing, and possibly of the sort conducive to arousing our carnal appetites, and though we have continually eaten and drunk well, played and sung (all things which may well incite weaker minds to less proper behavior), neither in word nor in deed nor in any other way do I feel that either you or ourselves are worthy of criticism. Constant decorum, constant harmony, and constant fraternal friendship are, in fact, what I have seen and felt here—something which, of course, pleases me, for it redounds to both your honor and merit and mine. And therefore, to prevent an overly practiced custom from turning into boredom as well as to prevent anyone from criticizing our having stayed here too long, I now think it proper, since each of us has, with his own day of storytelling, enjoyed his share of the honor that still resides in me, that, with your approval, we return to the place from where we came. Not to mention the fact that, if you consider the matter carefully, since our company is already known to many others in these parts, our numbers could increase in such a way as to destroy all our pleasure. Therefore, if you approve of my suggestion, I shall retain the crown given me until our departure, which I propose should be tomorrow morning; if you decide otherwise, I am already prepared to crown someone else for the next day."

The discussion between the ladies and the young men was long, but finally, having decided that the King's advice was sensible and proper, they all decided to do as he had said; and so, having sent for the steward, the King discussed with him the arrangements that had to be made for the following morning and then, having given the group their leave until suppertime, he rose to his feet.

The ladies and the other young men got up too, and as they usually did, some turned their attention to one amusement and others to another; and when it was time for supper, with the greatest of delight they went to the table; and after supper they began to sing and play and dance; and while Lauretta was leading a dance, the King ordered Fiammetta to sing a song, which she began to sing, most delightfully, in this fashion:

If there could be Love without jealousy,
then I know that no woman born,
no matter who, could have more joy than I.

If it be carefree youth
that please a lady in her handsome lover,
or the height of virtuousness,
or daring prowess, courage,
intelligence, good manners, eloquence,
or perfect elegance,
then I'm the one who's pleased, whose happiness
in love the way I am,
rests all within the man who is my hope.

But since I'm well aware
that other ladies are as wise as I,
I tremble with my fear
and dread the worst will happen:
that others will attempt to take
the man who took my heart from me.
And so, the thing that is my greatest fortune
makes me, in misery,
sigh deep and lead a wretched life.

If I felt that my lord
could be as faithful as he's valiant,

never would I be jealous;
so many men like this there are—
who need but one inviting glance—
I think all men are horrible!
This grieves my heart, and makes me want to die;
because whenever women look his way,
I dread and fear that I'll be robbed of him.

For God's sake, then, let every single
woman be warned that she dare not
practice such an outrage;
because should any one of them,
with words, or signs, or blandishments
attempt to harm me in this way,
and I should learn of it,
then may I be deformed
if I don't make her weep her bitter folly!

When Fiammetta had finished her song, Dioneo, who was sitting beside her, said with a laugh:

"Madam, you would be doing all the other ladies a great kindness if you would reveal your lover's name to them, so that out of ignorance they would not take from you what is yours, since this would make you so angry!"

After this song, they sang many others; and when it was nearly midnight, they all, at the King's request, went to bed.

By the time they arose at dawn of the new day, the steward had already sent all of their possessions on ahead, and so, under the guidance of their prudent King, they returned to Florence; and having taken their leave of the seven ladies at Santa Maria Novella, from where they had all set out together, the three young men went off to see to their other pleasures, while the ladies, when they felt it was time, returned to their homes.

[The Author's Conclusion]

❧

Most noble ladies, for whose happiness I have set myself to this lengthy task, I believe that with the assistance of divine grace and your pious prayers, rather than my own merits, I have com-

●letely fulfilled what I promised to do at the beginning of the present work; now, after rendering thanks first of all to God and then to you, it is time for me to rest my pen and my weary hand. But before I rest, since it is very clear to me that these tales of mine can expect no more special immunity than anything else can (and, indeed, I recall having demonstrated this in the Prologue of the Fourth Day*), I intend to reply briefly to several objections that perhaps some of you, as well as others, might have wished to voice. There will, perhaps, be some among you who will say that I have taken too much license in writing these tales; that is, I have sometimes made ladies say things, and more often listen to things, which are not very proper for virtuous ladies to say or hear. I deny this, for nothing is so indecent that it cannot be said to another person if the proper words are used to convey it; and this, I believe, I have done very well.

But let us suppose that you are right (I do not intend to argue with you, for you are certain to win); then, let me say that I have a number of reasons ready to explain why I have done as I did. First of all, if there are some liberties taken in any of the tales, the nature of the stories themselves required it, as will be clearly understood by any sensitive person who examines them with a reasonable eye, for I could not have told them otherwise without totally distorting their form. And if they do contain a few expressions or little words here and there that are somewhat freer than a prude might find proper (ladies of the type who weigh words more than deeds and who strive more to seem good than to be so), let me say that it is no more improper for me to have written these words than for men and women at large to fill their everyday speech with such words as "hole," "peg," "mortar," "pestle," "wiener," and "fat sausage," and other similar expressions.† Moreover, my pen should be granted no less freedom than the brush of a painter who, without incurring censure or, at least, any which is justified, depicts Saint Michael wounding the serpent with a sword or a lance and Saint George slaying the dragon wherever he pleases, not to mention the fact that he shows Christ as a man and Eve as a woman, and nails to the cross, sometimes with one nail, sometimes with two, the feet of Him who wished to die there for the salvation of mankind.

---

*The reader will recall the narrator stated that "only misery is without envy in this world."

†These terms, of course, all have sexual connotations.

What is more, one can see quite clearly that these tales were not told in a church, where things must be spoken of with the proper frame of mind and suitable words (despite the fact that even more outrageous stories are to be found in the church's annals than in my own writings). Nor were they held in the schools of the philosophers, where a sense of propriety is required no less than anywhere else, nor in any place among churchmen or philosophers. But they were told in gardens, in a place suited for pleasure, in the presence of young people who were, nevertheless, mature and not easily misled by stories, and at a time when going about with your trousers over your head was not considered improper if it helped to save your life.

But as they stand, these tales, like all other things, may be harmful or useful depending on who the listener is. Who doesn't know that wine is good for the healthy, as Cinciglione, Scolaio,* and many others will tell you, but harmful to anyone suffering with a fever? Shall we say, then, because wine is harmful to those with a fever that it is wicked? Who does not know that fire is most useful, not to say necessary, to mankind? Because it destroys homes, villages, and cities, shall we say that it is wicked? In like manner, weapons defend the lives of those who wish to live peacefully, and they also, on many occasions, kill men, not because of any wickedness inherent in them but because those who wield them do so in an evil way.

A corrupt mind never understands a word in a healthy way. And just as fitting words are of no use to a corrupt mind, so a healthy mind cannot be contaminated by words which are not so proper, any more than mud can dirty the rays of the sun or earthly filth can mar the beauties of the skies. What books, what words, what letters are more holy, more worthy, and more revered than those of the Holy Scriptures? And yet there are many who have perversely interpreted them and have dragged themselves and others down to eternal damnation because of this. Everything is, in itself, good for some determined goal, but badly used it can cause a good deal of harm; and I can say the same of my stories.

Whoever wishes to derive evil counsel from them or use them for wicked ends will not be prohibited from doing so by the tales themselves if, by chance, they contain such things and are twisted and distorted in order to achieve this end; and whoever wishes to derive useful advice and profit from them will not be

---

*Proverbial drunkards.

prevented from doing so, nor will these stories ever be described or regarded as anything but useful and proper if they are read at those times and to those people for whom they have been written. The lady who is forever saying her prayers or baking up cookies or other goodies for her confessor should leave my tales alone. My stories run after no one asking to be read, though there is many a bigot out there who whenever the occasion arises will say and even do the kinds of things found in my stories!

There will also be those who will say that some stories here might well have been omitted. This may be true, but I could do nothing but write down the tales as they were told, which is to say that had those ladies telling them told them better, I would have written them better. But let us suppose that I was the one who created these stories as well as the one who wrote them down (which I was not). Then, let me tell you that I would not be ashamed if they were not all good, since no artisan, save God Himself, can create everything perfect and complete; even Charlemagne, who first created the Paladins, did not know how to make enough of them to form an army.

One must be ready to find different characteristics in a multitude of things. No field was ever so well cultivated that it did not contain nettles, brambles, or some other kind of thorny shrub mixed among the better plants; moreover, in speaking to unassuming young ladies, as most of you are, it would have been foolish to go about trying to find fancy stories and to take great pains speaking in an extremely formal manner. However, whoever reads through these stories can leave aside those he finds offensive and read those he finds pleasing; and in order not to deceive anyone, every story has inscribed upon its brow a summary of what is hidden in its bosom.

Also, I suppose there will be people who will say that some of the stories are too long; to them I say once more that for those people who have something better to do with their time, it would be foolish to read any of these tales, no matter how short they might be. And even though much time has passed since I began to write these stories until this moment when my labor is drawing to a close, I have not forgotten that I said I was offering this work of mine to idle ladies and to no others; and for those who read to pass the time of day, no tale can be too long if it serves its purpose. Brevity is much more fitting for the studious, who toil not just to pass the time away, but to employ their time to the greatest advantage, but not so for you ladies, who have all that time free which you do not spend on amorous pleasures. Besides this, since none of you has been to Athens, Bologna, or Paris to study, one must speak to you in a more extended fashion than to those who have sharpened their wits with their studies.

There are, without a doubt, some others among you who will say that the stories told are too full of nonsense and jokes and that it is not proper for a man of weight and gravity to have written this way. To them I am obliged to render thanks, and I do so for their zeal and concern for my reputation, but I wish to answer their objections in this way: I confess that I do have weight and to have been weighed many a time in my day. And so, speaking to those ladies who have not weighed me, let me assure them that I am not heavy at all—on the contrary, I am so light that I float on water; when you consider that the sermons delivered by friars to reproach men for their sins are, for the most part, full of nonsense, jokes, and foolishness, I felt that these same things would not be out of place in my stories, which are, after all, written to drive away a lady's melancholy. However, should they find themselves laughing too much, they can easily remedy this by reading the Lament of Jeremiah, the Passion of Our Savior, or the Lament of Mary Magdalene.

And who would doubt that there are still others who would say that I have an evil and poisonous tongue, because in some places I write the truth about the friars? I plan to forgive those who say this, for it is hard to believe that anything but a good motive moves them, since friars are good fellows who forsake the discomforts of life for the love of God, and do their grinding when the pickings are good, and say no more about it; and if it were not for the fact that they all smell a little like goats, it would be most pleasant, indeed, to deal with them.

I must confess, however, that the things of this world have no stability whatsoever—they are constantly changing, and this might have happened with my tongue. I do not trust my own judgment (which in matters concerning myself I avoid as best I can), but a short time ago, a neighbor lady of mine told me that I had the best and the sweetest tongue in the world—and to tell the truth, when she said this, only a few of the above stories remained to be written. But now let what I have just said suffice as a reply to those ladies who have argued so spitefully.

I shall leave it to every lady to say and believe as she pleases, for the time has come to end my words and to humbly thank Him who with His assistance has brought me after so much labor to my desired goal, and may His grace and peace be with

ou always, lovely ladies, and if, perhaps, reading some of these
tories has given any of you some little pleasure, please do
emember me.

Here ends the tenth and last day of the book called *The
Decameron*, also known as *Prince Galeotto*.

[Selected Bibliography]

❖

ENGLISH TRANSLATIONS OF BOCCACCIO'S WORKS

Amorous Fiammetta. Translated by Bartolomew Young. Westport, Conn.: The Greenwood Press, 1970.

Boccaccio on Poetry, Being the Preface and the Fourteenth and Fifteenth Books of Boccaccio's Genealogia Deorum Gentilium. Edited and translated by Charles G. Osgood. Indianapolis: Bobbs-Merrill, 1956.

The Book of Theseus: Teseida delle Nozze d'Emilia. Translated by Bernadette Marie McCoy. New York: Medieval Text Association, 1974.

Concerning Famous Women. Translated by Guido Guarino. New Brunswick, N.J.: Rutgers University Press, 1963.

The Corbaccio. Translated by Anthony Cassell. Urbana: Illinois University Press, 1975.

The Decameron: A Norton Critical Edition. Edited and translated by Mark Musa and Peter Bondanella. New York: Norton, 1977. (Includes critical essays.)

The Fates of Illustrious Men. Translated by Louis Brewster Hall. New York: Ungar, 1965.

The Filostrato of Giovanni Boccaccio: A Translation with Parallel Text. Translated by N.E. Griffin and A.B. Myrick. New York: Biblo and Tannen, 1967.

The Nymph of Fiesole. Translated by Daniel J. Donno. New York: Columbia University Press, 1960.

Nymphs of Fiesole. Translated by Joseph Tusiani. Rutherford, N.J.: Fairleigh Dickinson University Press, 1971.

The Story of Troilus. Translated by R.K. Gordon. New York: Dutton, 1964, (Contains a translation of *Il Filostrato*.)

CRITICAL STUDIES OF BOCCACCIO AND
THE DECAMERON

Almansi, Guido. *The Writer as Liar: Narrative Technique in th Decameron.* London: Routledge and Kegan Paul, 1975.

Baratto, Mario. *Realtà e stile nel Decameron.* Vincenza: Ne Pozza, 1974.

Bergin, Thomas G. *Boccaccio.* New York: Viking, 1981.

Branca, Vittore. *Boccaccio: The Man and His Works.* Trans lated by Richard Monges. New York: New York Universit Press, 1976.

Clements, Robert J., and Joseph Gibaldi. *Anatomy of the No vella.* New York: New York University Press, 1977.

Cottino-Jones, Marga, and E.F. Tuttle, eds. *Boccaccio: Secoli vita.* Ravenna: Longo, 1977. (Many articles in English.)

Corrigan, Beatrice, ed. *Italian Poets and English Critics, 1775 1859: A Collection of Critical Essays.* Chicago: University o Chicago Press, 1969.

Deligiorgis, Stavros. *Narrative Intellection in the Decamero* Iowa City: University of Iowa Press, 1975.

Dombroski, Robert S., ed. *Critical Perspectives on the De cameron.* New York: Barnes & Noble, 1976.

Esposito, Enzo (with Christopher Kleinhenz). *Boccacciana: A Essay in Bibliography (1933–1974).* Ravenna: Longo, 1977.

Getto, Giovanni. *Vita di forme e forme di vita nel Decamero* Turin: Petrini, 1958.

Hollander, Robert. *Boccaccio's Two Venuses.* New York: Colum bia University Press, 1977.

Lee, A.C. *The Decameron: Its Sources and Analogues.* Ne York: Haskell House, 1972.

Marcus, Millicent. *An Allegory of Form: Literary Self-Co sciousness in the Decameron.* Saratoga: Anma Libri, 1979.

Potter, Joy H. *Five Frames for the Decameron: Communicatio and Social Systems in the Cornice.* Princeton: Princeton Un versity Press, 1982.

Russo, Luigi. *Letture critiche del Decameron.* Bari: Laterz 1977.

Scaglione, Aldo. *Nature and Love in the Late Middle Age* Berkeley: University of California Press, 1963.

Sklovsky, Viktor. *Lettura del Decameron.* Bologna: Il Mulin 1969.

Todorov, Tzvetan. *Grammaire du Décameron.* The Hague Mouton, 1969.

Wright, Herbert G. *Boccaccio in England from Chaucer to Tennyson.* London: Athlone Press, 1957.

The list above includes only relatively recent books. For the many, many critical articles on Boccaccio and his works, consult Esposito's bibliographical study above, as well as the yearly bibliography contained in a periodical devoted to Boccaccio studies, *Studi sul Boccaccio,* which often includes essays in English.

MENTOR Books of Special Interest

MENTOR Books of Plays

**Buy them at your local
bookstore or use coupon
on next page for ordering.**

World Drama from SIGNET CLASSIC